Chris

CW0045622З

THE EMPEROR'S
ARMIES

Chris Wraight

BLACK LIBRARY

A BLACK LIBRARY PUBLICATION

Sword of Justice first published in 2010.
Sword of Vengeance first published in 2011.
Feast of Horrors first published in 2010.
Duty and Honour first published in 2012.
This edition published in Great Britain in 2016 by
Black Library,
Games Workshop Ltd.,
Willow Road,
Nottingham,
NG7 2WS, UK.

10 9 8 7 6 5 4 3 2 1

Produced by Games Workshop in Nottingham.

A CIP record for this book is available from the British Library.

UK ISBN 13: 978 1 78496 406 1
US ISBN 13: 978 1 78496 407 8

See Black Library on the internet at

blacklibrary.com

Find out more about Games Workshop
and the world of Warhammer 40,000 at

games-workshop.com

Printed and bound by CPI Group (UK) Ltd, Croydon, CR0 4YY

This is a dark age, a bloody age, an age of daemons
and of sorcery. It is an age of battle and death, and of the
world's ending. Amidst all of the fire, flame and fury
it is a time, too, of mighty heroes, of bold deeds
and great courage.

At the heart of the Old World sprawls the Empire, the
largest and most powerful of the human realms. Known for
its engineers, sorcerers, traders and soldiers, it is
a land of great mountains, mighty rivers, dark forests
and vast cities. And from his throne in Altdorf reigns
the Emperor Karl Franz, sacred descendant of the
founder of these lands, Sigmar, and wielder
of his magical warhammer.

But these are far from civilised times. Across the length
and breadth of the Old World, from the knightly palaces
of Bretonnia to ice-bound Kislev in the far north, come
rumblings of war. In the towering Worlds Edge Mountains,
the orc tribes are gathering for another assault. Bandits and
renegades harry the wild southern lands of
the Border Princes. There are rumours of rat-things, the
skaven, emerging from the sewers and swamps across the
land. And from the northern wildernesses there is the
ever-present threat of Chaos, of daemons and beastmen
corrupted by the foul powers of the Dark Gods.
As the time of battle draws ever near,
the Empire needs heroes
like never before.

TOTAL WAR
WARHAMMER

The Old World echoes to the clamour of ceaseless battle. The only constant is WAR!

A fantasy strategy game of legendary proportions, Total War: WARHAMMER combines an addictive turn-based campaign of epic empire-building with explosive, colossal, real-time battles, set in the brooding and bloody world of Warhammer Fantasy Battles.

Command one of four wholly different Races: The Empire of Men, the stoic Dwarfs, the bloodthirsty Greenskin hordes and the dark and elegant lords of the undead, the Vampire Counts. In Total War: WARHAMMER, it is up to you to consolidate and expand your territory, marshalling powerful armies and using them to carve a path of conquest across the Old World, shaping it to your liking as you go.

Train mighty wizards and shamans to heal the wounded, raise the dead or consume your enemies in maelstroms of magic. Take to the skies for the first time in a Total War game as you field a host of flying creatures and monsters, from majestic griffons to mighty dragons. Lead you forces into battle with Legendary Lords from the Warhammer Fantasy Battles world, arming them with epic weapons, armour and deadly battle-magic. Unlock narrative quest-chains for your Legendary Lords and engage in hand-crafted spectacular quest-battles.

As you spread your influence throughout the Old World, you'll form strong alliances and bitter rivalries, tallied in blood and gold. Will you become a magnanimous and diplomatic leader, protected by treaties and agreements between friends? Or will you make a name for yourself as a ruthless warlord, mercilessly slaughtering any and all who stand in your way as you sculpt a sanguine path to total domination.

Whether you lead by sword or silver, the enemies you make on the campaign map, the mighty foes that render your troops asunder and plague your general's nightmares will in time be overshadowed by a far more terrible threat.

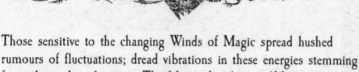

Those sensitive to the changing Winds of Magic spread hushed rumours of fluctuations; dread vibrations in these energies stemming from their ethereal source. The fabric of reality itself begins to buckle and bend, threatening to come undone altogether. The Realm of Chaos swells.

Unspeakable things gather in the northernmost parts of the Old World. Here, the physical world and the realm of Chaos overlap, and the nefarious energies from beyond ebb and flow. The Ruinous Powers that have, for time immemorial, presided over this seething place of unnatural darkness grow restless. Talons, claws, tentacles, shapes without form, name or number itch for new territories to torment and new flesh to tear.

The true power of Chaos comes from an immaterial reality, parallel to the mortal realm of the Old World. Here, the formless flux has coagulated to form many abominations, four of which have grown to be creatures of unimaginable power, the Four Chaos Gods. Nurgle is the god of decay, despair and disease. Slaanesh represents decadence, excess, pleasure and self-indulgence. Tzeentch is the god of change and magic. Khorne is associated with hatred, rage, bloodshed and war. Chaos is a seductive force. Those who embrace it and devote themselves to the Ruinous Powers become increasingly corrupted by its influence. Some develop physical mutations to better serve their dark lords' nefarious purposes whilst some are affected in more subtle ways.

To these Dark Gods, the squabbles of the mortal realms are as two rats fighting over scraps. Whatever differences they possess are meaningless. All are mere vermin to be exterminated. As ill winds howl southwards, they set in motion the wheels of a prophecy conceived to eclipse all light and plunge the Old World into the pitch darkness of pure Chaos.

Chaos energy is the source of all magic in the world. It first entered the Old World long ago. This event, known as the Coming of Chaos, engulfed the polar areas of the world in dark energy, creating uncontrollable gateways from which the forces of Chaos spill forth.

As these energies interact with those of the physical world, they are transmuted into the Winds of Magic. Sorcerers and shamans are able to harness and refine this energy in its various forms to serve their own purposes. The risks of commanding such powers should not be underestimated however, and the arrogance and lust for power of mortal spellcasters has often seen

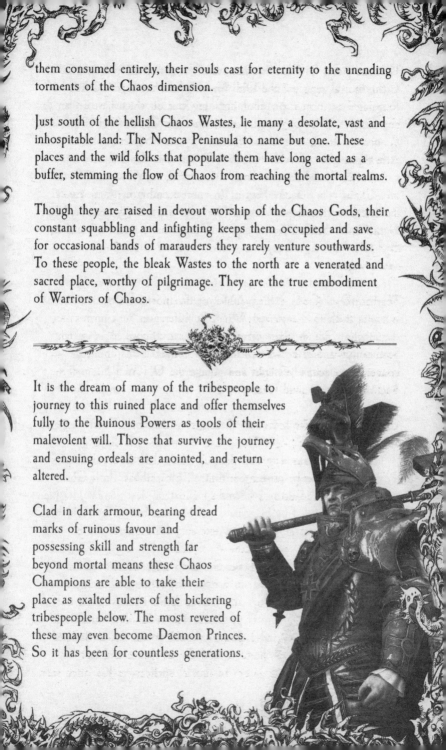

them consumed entirely, their souls cast for eternity to the unending torments of the Chaos dimension.

Just south of the hellish Chaos Wastes, lie many a desolate, vast and inhospitable land: The Norsca Peninsula to name but one. These places and the wild folks that populate them have long acted as a buffer, stemming the flow of Chaos from reaching the mortal realms.

Though they are raised in devout worship of the Chaos Gods, their constant squabbling and infighting keeps them occupied and save for occasional bands of marauders they rarely venture southwards. To these people, the bleak Wastes to the north are a venerated and sacred place, worthy of pilgrimage. They are the true embodiment of Warriors of Chaos.

It is the dream of many of the tribespeople to journey to this ruined place and offer themselves fully to the Ruinous Powers as tools of their malevolent will. Those that survive the journey and ensuing ordeals are anointed, and return altered.

Clad in dark armour, bearing dread marks of ruinous favour and possessing skill and strength far beyond mortal means these Chaos Champions are able to take their place as exalted rulers of the bickering tribespeople below. The most revered of these may even become Daemon Princes. So it has been for countless generations.

In recent times however, the clamour of infighting that has kept Chaos-worshipping tribes divided for millennia has begun to fade. Rumours have begun to spread, speaking of a far greater force than any Chaos Champion bringing these unruly lands to heel and uniting them under the banner of the one true favoured Son of Chaos. A being of pure malevolence and sheer will, this figure represents the culmination of the Ruinous Powers' machinations. A warlord to end all wars, he stands at the head of an unbreakable army whose ranks swell with horrors beyond count. He is the supreme champion of the Dark Gods, the Everchosen, and the Three-Eyed King. His name is Archaon.

One of the most infamous and iconic characters in the world of Warhammer Fantasy Battles, Archaon's story is one written in blood coursing with loss, rage and hatred. Rumoured to be a former Templar of Sigmar, Archaon is said to have discovered an ancient manuscript. Contained within this were certain truths about the nature of Chaos. His perceptions shattered, he cursed the gods he had lived to serve and then took great lengths to sever all mortal tethers before setting out on a path towards his inevitable destiny: to become the Everchosen, the harbinger of the End Times.

When he finally stood in that perilous place that the Ruinous Powers call home he prostrated himself before those Dark Gods, offering himself to them as a tool of unilateral destruction. His life unnaturally extended by his Chaos patrons, his next task would be to gather the Artefacts of Chaos necessary for his coronation.

With this done, his quest to become the Everchosen would be completed, but his true mission would only have just begun. It is at his behest that the followers of Chaos will bend the knee. It is under his banner that the Warriors of Chaos will unite. The world shall quake at his footsteps and at his command, it will fall to darkness.

In Total War: WARHAMMER, the threat of the expanding Chaos realm may not seem too pressing at the outset of your campaign. As your dominion grows and you conquer new lands and foes however, it will develop into a palpable danger that will require all your wisdom and guile to deal with effectively. The armies of Chaos are gathering, with Archaon the Everchosen leading the march.

Whether you build your empire on diplomacy or subjugation, the alliances and conflicts of the Old World will be but shadows in the light of what is to come. Nations, borders, races. All are meaningless to the encroaching forces of Ruin. As leader, will you remain distracted with the enemies that plague your borders and ignore the encroaching northern hordes until it's too late? Or, will you rally your populace, call in all favours and galvanise your forces, riding to meet the Chaos onslaught with sword in hand?

Chaos is an insidious force indeed, one that poses just as much of a threat from within as it does from without. Even with the strongest fortifications to defend from the northerly Chaos hordes, if you neglect your own lands you may find that the seeds of Chaos begin to sprout within your own walls.

Desperate people will often look to dark places for salvation, and if you cannot keep yours happy, you may find them abandoning their native faith to devote themselves to the Ruinous Powers. Should this occur, you may find pockets of dissent blooming into fully-fledged religious uprisings. Deal with these cultists quickly or else watch helplessly as your hard-won provinces fall to the Dark Gods' will.

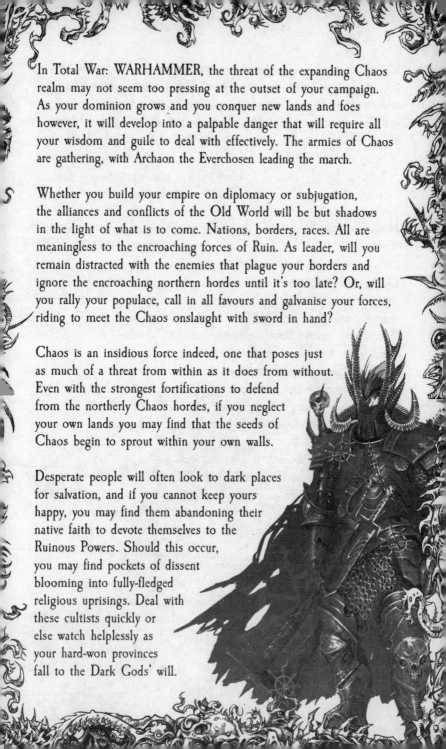

Regardless of what race you choose to play as, the threat of Chaos is something you will have to address. Whether you occupy yourself with matters at home, dissolving conflicts within your own borders, or ride to face the wrath of the Dark Gods head on, your actions will dictate the fate of your people and indeed the entire Old World.

Now, delve further into the lore of Warhammer Fantasy Battles with these selected stories which helped inspire Total War: WARHAMMER and may help inspire you on your campaigns within it...

CONTENTS

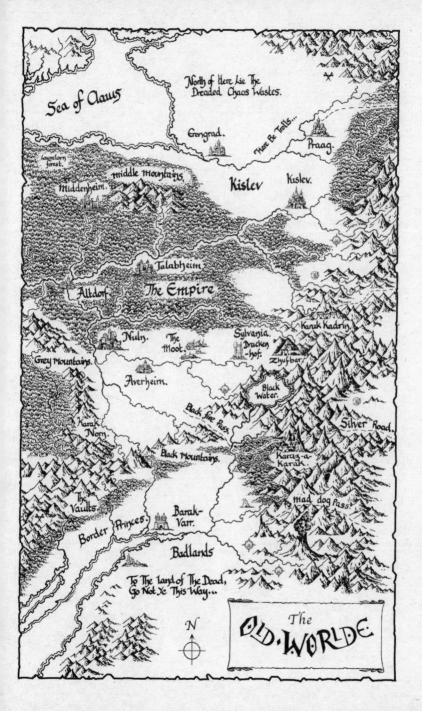

SWORD OF JUSTICE

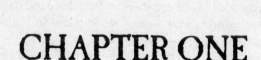

CHAPTER ONE

Andreas Grunwald scrambled backwards up the ridge. The beast was on him. Its musk was sharp in his nostrils. It sensed a kill.

Grunwald gripped his sword more tightly. He could feel his muscles protest. He was tired to the bone. His thick clothes hung from his body, heavy with rain. The water streamed across his face, nearly blinding him.

The beast bellowed, and charged up the slope.

'Sigmar,' whispered Grunwald. It was twice his height. Powerful muscles bunched under matted fur. Massive hands swung a crude, notched cleaver. A trooper's sword still stuck out from its back, right where the man had plunged it, seconds before his death under the hooves.

Grunwald steadied himself, testing the uncertain ground beneath him. A heartbeat too soon, and he'd be lost. Timing was everything.

The beast was on him. Grunwald swung his broadsword. The blade sliced through the air, gore flying from the steel. The cleaver rose to parry. At the last moment, Grunwald shifted his balance, falling to one side, twisting the sword around the cleaver. He dropped to one knee, slipping under the beast's guard. With all the strength that remained, he plunged his sword-tip upwards. The point was still keen. It punctured flesh, running deep into the beast's innards.

The creature roared in pain. Its weight was thrown forward. The cleaver fell heavily, but Grunwald stayed firm, both hands on the blade, twisting it further. Thick entrails slipped down the edge, hot against his flesh. For a moment, the beast's head lolled a few inches from his own. Grunwald could see agony on the horse-like features. So human. So utterly inhuman.

The light extinguished in its whiteless eyes. The beast's bellows drained to a low growl, and it toppled. Grunwald pulled the sword free as the massive body rolled onto the sodden grass. Panting, his arms throbbing, he stood up and stole a look along the ranks of men on either side.

The line was still intact. All along the ridge, the other Imperial troops held their positions. Eight hundred men, Reikland state troopers, battled to hold the high ground. They were arranged in long ranks, three deep. The halberdiers and pikemen were in the forefront, desperately trying to repel the beastmen advance from the forest cover at the base of the rise. Behind them, archers and handgunners struggled to maintain a protective barrage. The foul beasts were still trying to force the ascent. There were hundreds of them, surging up the slope. More emerged from the forest canopy every moment. Even though it was the middle of the day, the lowering sky made it look much later.

'Use the damn Helblasters!' Grunwald shouted, staggering back up the bank.

As he went, he felt fingers close over his ankle. A grasp like a steel trap. The beast wasn't dead.

With a cry of exhausted frustration, Grunwald arced the sword back round. He stabbed down again and again, hacking at the stinking flesh. The monster's blood, hot and black, coated him. Still he plunged, working the blade like a blacksmith's hammer. Only when he felt dizzy from the effort did he stop. By the time he was done, the carcass at his feet was little more than a puddle of meat and hair.

Finally, the Helblasters blazed out. From higher up the ridge, a volley of shot flew through the air. There weren't many of the precious guns left, but their cargo was still deadly. The front ranks of the beastmen stumbled, their fury broken. The creatures were deadly up close, but they had no answer to the artillery.

A second volley rang out, close-packed and lethal. More beasts fell. For a moment, the ragged lines wavered. They were driven by bloodlust, but they could still taste fear. The pikemen on the front lines sensed a change. Some began to creep forward.

'Hold your positions, you dogs!' Grunwald bellowed. All down the line, sergeants shouted the same thing. Staying tight against the ridge-top was their only chance. The guns bought them time, nothing more.

From over the heads of the defending lines, arrows span into the faltering ranks of beasts. Only a few found their mark, and the cattle-like roar of attack started up again. But the Helblasters had a third load to deploy. The barrels were rotated, and the shot rang out again.

That was enough. The beasts disengaged. Huge, shaggy creatures lumbered back to the cover of the trees below. Between them, smaller horrors scampered for cover. They didn't go far. A few hundred yards away, the open ground was swallowed by the forest. They were safe in there. Safe to lick their wounds, regroup, and come back stronger. It wouldn't be long.

Grunwald limped back up along the ridge. All around him, detachments were re-forming. The harsh cries of the sergeants rang out amid the shuffling lines. Discipline was everything. As soon as the perimeter broke, it was over. For all of them. On the far side of the ridge lay the road, the vital artery they were protecting. The surface was churned and shiny with mud, but it was still more passable than the tangled forest around. It had to stay open. The Cauldron was only a few miles to the north, but every yard of it counted.

As Grunwald gained the higher ground, he saw Ackermann heading towards him. The captain was as covered in blood, sweat and grime as he was. His chainmail was caked in red filth and his beard was twisted and matted. Despite everything, Grunwald let slip a grim smile. The two of them looked like carnival grotesques.

'What d'you think?' growled Ackermann. He was breathing heavily, and he cradled his shield-arm gingerly.

Grunwald took a long look along the lines. The whole regiment was arranged near the summit of the snaking ridge. High up the slope, the pikemen had dug in. Inbetween the extended pikes crouched the halberdiers, supported by a secondary row of state troopers. Further up the ridge, archers and handgunners had been placed, high enough up to have a line of sight over the halberdiers' heads, but close enough to give the troops cover. Dotted amongst the pistoliers were the few artillery pieces they had left. They'd proved their worth already, and steamed ominously in the rain.

'We can't take too much more of this,' said Grunwald. 'They'll come again soon.'

Ackermann nodded.

'That they will. We're losing men, sir. We'll have to pull back.'

'Where to? There's nothing behind us but trees all the way back to the Cauldron.'

Ackermann muttered into his beard.

'He's not coming. This is a damn fool errand. This ridge'll be our grave.'

Grunwald lost his smile.

'Orders are orders,' he snapped. 'Until we get the signal, we hold the position.'

Grunwald's voice was iron-hard. Ackermann hesitated, then nodded. He looked resigned.

'Yes, sir.'

He headed back towards the front lines. Grunwald watched

him go. The man was right. Ackermann was a veteran of twenty years. Few in the ranks lasted that long in the Emperor's armies. He knew what he was doing. So did Grunwald. The longer they stayed on the ridge, the more beasts would come. The hordes were massing. Sooner or later, their position would become impossible.

Grunwald turned from the ridge and looked back to the empty road.

'Where is he?' Grunwald hissed impatiently.

His thoughts were interrupted. Back down at the foot of the ridge, the bellowing had begun again. The trees shook, and the first beasts burst from cover once more.

Wearily, Grunwald took up his broadsword and headed back to the ranks. The answer would have to wait.

North of the ridge, above the mighty Turgitz Cauldron, the sky was black with piled cloud. Squalls were being driven east by a powerful gale and the western horizon was dark with more. There would be no let-up.

Captain Markus Bloch strode up the steep sides of the bastion, his halberd light in his hands. The streaming rain did nothing to dampen his spirits. He'd been on campaign in Nordland and was used to the ice-cold blasts from the Sea of Claws. There was little the Drakwald could offer in comparison. He let the rivulets run down his grizzled face and under the collar of his jerkin.

He paused for a moment to survey the scene. The Cauldron was a vast, natural depression in the otherwise seamless forest. It was several miles across, huge and stark. Few trees grew within its limits. The earth enclosed by it was dark and choked with stone. The rain had turned it into a thick slurry of mud, but it was still more easily negotiated than the endless twisted leagues of woodland beyond.

The army had chosen to make its stand in the time-honoured place. The bastion was the name given to the vast outcrop of dark rock that rose up in the very centre of the ancient bowl. It rose in a smooth hump from the floor of the Cauldron, half a mile wide and three hundred yards high at the summit. It was like a huge, natural fortress, capable of housing thousands of men and beasts on its back. The incline was shallow enough to ride a horse up on the lower flanks, but soon got steeper. All the way up the flanks of the mighty rock formation, terraces and clefts offered protection from the elements. Centuries of use had worn pathways between them into the hard stone. At the pinnacle, high above the Cauldron, great spikes of rock twisted up into the air like a crown.

The terraces carved into its flanks had been the redoubt of choice for commanders since before the annals of the Empire had been started. The local people, such as there were, said that Sigmar had created it with a celestial plough taken from Ulric while the god of war slept. Bloch was a devout man, but he wasn't stupid enough to believe stories like that. The Cauldron was just what it was – a place where armies had come to fight for thousands of years. Maybe the blood in the soil was why the trees never grew back.

All around him, the host was preparing for battle. Companies were being marched into position by their captains. They looked like drowned rats, shuffling miserably in the downpour. As always, there was confusion. This was a large army. It took a lot of organising, crammed along the narrow pathways scored into the natural citadel of stone. There were baggage trains and artillery wains, all of which could be accommodated comfortably in the natural gorges of the huge edifice. Several thousand foot soldiers, three companies of cavalry, artillery barrages, irregulars, and mercenaries all crouched in their positions. The bulk of the army were halberdiers and spearmen, augmented with smaller detachments of handgunners and archers. There were more elite soldiers too, such as Baron Ostmer's own greatswords and a whole company of Knights Panther. Almost all the forces were now deployed on the bastion, leaving the wide floor of the Cauldron empty. The only exceptions were those who had ridden off to hold the southern approaches in the hope that Helborg would still come. Much as he liked a fight, Bloch didn't envy them at all.

He absently ran his finger along the blade of his halberd. It probably needed sharpening. Too late now. He'd have to test the edge on the necks of beastmen instead, and they'd be here soon enough. They'd been massing for months, raiding and pillaging. The decision had been taken to quash their menace in one massive, orchestrated campaign. As Bloch gazed across the hurriedly organising ranks, that decision didn't look as good as it had done in Altdorf.

He turned away from the vista and resumed his walk up the slope of the bastion. Ahead of him, a familiar figure waited.

'Herr Bloch,' said Verstohlen. 'You're getting wet.'

Bloch never knew when Pieter Verstohlen was mocking him. It was always the same with the damned aristos. Their cut-glass accents were designed to make you feel inferior. Not that Verstohlen had ever explicitly said anything to slight his honour. He'd always been the soul of politeness. But Bloch didn't like it. There was a place for smooth manners and cleverness, and it wasn't on the battlefield.

'That I am,' replied Bloch. 'I see you've come prepared.'

Verstohlen wore a wide-brimmed leather hat and a long coat. At his belt were two exquisite flintlocks. He wore a finely-tailored jacket and hard-wearing boots. It was all plain, understated and utilitarian, but Bloch was enough of a man of the world to know how expensive it was. Unlike most of the men of the army, Verstohlen wore clothes that fitted him. They'd been tailored. It was unnerving. Unnatural.

Verstohlen nodded, and the rainwater slewed from the brim of his hat.

'As always,' he said. 'No word of Commander Grunwald?'

Bloch shook his head.

'We got a message at dawn. He's engaged them to the south. Nothing since then.'

'Is it wise, to wait so long? I'm not a commander, but...'

Bloch scowled. What *was* Verstohlen, exactly? He could almost have passed for a witch hunter, but the man was no Templar of Sigmar. He had the trust of the big man, that was certain, but why? It wasn't like him to listen to a civilian.

'He'll hold the line,' snapped Bloch, unwilling to debate tactics with the man. 'He knows what he has to do.'

'I'm sure you're right, Herr Bloch. But, as I understand it, the support from Marshal Helborg was due to arrive last night. If he's not here now, and there is no prospect of his appearance from the dispatches, then perhaps keeping the road open is an unnecessary risk. The beastmen are already massing. Herr Grunwald is exposed.'

Bloch didn't want to agree with him, but there was something in what he said. The big man was waiting too long. Helborg wouldn't arrive. They all knew it. There was no point in pretending otherwise.

'So what d'you want to do?' he asked, affecting a casual disdain. 'Try to persuade the chief? Good luck.'

Verstohlen remained impassive. He never seemed to react to anything. He had ice running through his veins. That was another thing Bloch didn't like. A soldier should have some passion. Some *spirit*.

'Where are you assigned?' asked Verstohlen.

'On the west front of the bastion with the Fourth and Ninth halberdiers. Why?'

'Keep an eye on the southern approaches, will you? I will try to remedy this myself, but I may run out of time. Keep some good men about you. There may be a need to make adjustments. Grunwald is a good fighter. We can't afford to lose him.'

Bloch felt one of his fists balling, and unclenched it. Why did Verstohlen's speech irritate him so much? It wasn't even that the man was weak. Bloch knew that Verstohlen had killed plenty in his time. Those pistols weren't for show, but there was something strange about him. He didn't fit. And in an army, where you had to trust the man at your shoulder like no other, that was a problem.

'I'll see what I can do,' said Bloch, turning away. He could hear Verstohlen start to say something else, but he pretended not to hear, and the rain drowned it out.

Bloch stalked over to his regiment. In the north, a low

rumble of thunder echoed. The troops looked up nervously. At the edge of his vision, he was dimly aware of Verstohlen shrugging and walking off towards the command post. He took up his place beside the halberdiers.

'All right, lads,' he said. 'The waiting's almost over.'

There were a few murmured responses, but no fancy words. These were his kind of men. Grim, stoic, simple. Good to have at your shoulder.

He stared out westwards. The rain continued to drum on the rock. Far below the bastion, at the edge of the Cauldron's sheer sides, the trees were tossed about by the wind. In the far distance, right on the edge of hearing, there was a faint howling. The storm was coming. When it broke, the creatures of the forest would be hard on its heels.

Back on the ridge, the beastmen had come again. This time there were more. They piled out from under the tree line, bellowing with a fresh fury. Huge creatures strode amongst them, towering over the scampering horrors at their feet. One had the shoulders of a giant bull, the colour of dried blood and scored with tattoos. When it roared, the earth shook.

Grunwald hefted his broadsword with foreboding.

So many.

'Hold your fire,' he cried. 'Wait for the signal!'

All along the line, archers fitted their arrows to the string. They looked pale with fear. The constant attacks had got to them. Handgunners took aim, squatting amongst them, sheltering the match cord against the rain. Pikemen fingered the poles of their weapons agitatedly, waiting for the horrendous clash of arms.

The gap closed. The eyes of the beasts became visible. They were like burning coals. They tore up the ridge towards the defenders.

'Helblasters!' shouted Grunwald.

With a crack, the cannons ignited. Grape and shot spun into the oncoming tide, punching holes in the first rank. Squeals of agony mingled with the guttural baying.

Still the beasts came.

'Gunners!'

The handgunners released their first volley. In the wake of their lead shot, arrows whined into the fray. More beasts fell, clutching at their sides in pain. They were trampled by their fellows.

Still the beasts came.

'Blades!'

The pikemen lowered their poles and thrust them forward. The front row of creatures slammed into them. Some were impaled, seemingly heedless of the pain. Others leapt over the steel tips, just as far as the waiting line of halberds. The blades whirled, and the beastmen were thrown back. As long as the ranks held, there was no way through.

Grunwald sprang from his vantage point and entered the fray. There was no point standing back once battle had been joined. Now the assault was on them, and every sword was needed. With his last glance towards the forest edge, he saw the scale of the task. There were more beastmen then ever. The ground beneath the ridge boiled with grotesque bodies. They were clambering over one another to get at them. They only sensed one thing, only smelled one thing, only lusted for one thing. Blood. Their blood.

'For Sigmar!' he shouted, and hurled himself into the assault.

If they wanted his, they'd have to earn it.

Verstohlen hurried through the ranks towards the command enclosure near the summit of the bastion. On either side of him, close-knit detachments of troopers waited nervously. They had the advantage of high ground, but little else. The beastmen could scale the slopes with ease, and there would soon be scores of them. The Imperial advance into the forest had roused the whole Drakwald. Verstohlen was as versed in the lore of the wilderness as any seasoned general. When there was blood to be spilled, they would come.

Ahead of him, the massed flags and standards marked

out the general's vantage point. Functionaries were scurrying around it, desperately conveying last-minute orders to the field captains. The ornate battle standards flapped wildly, driven by the wind. There was no sign of the commander. Verstohlen looked around in vain, before catching sight of Tierhof, the Master of Ordnance.

'Where's the general?' asked Verstohlen. Tierhof looked at him coldly. They all did, these soldiers. For some reason, he seemed to repel them. One day he would have to work out why and do something about it.

'With the Knights Panther,' said Tierhof. 'What do you want him for? He'll be riding to the front in moments.'

Verstohlen sucked his teeth irritably.

'Then I'm too late,' he said. 'Have you had word from Herr Grunwald?'

'Not since the morning.'

'And from the Marshal?'

Tierhof laughed. It was not a merry sound.

'You're still expecting him? We're alone here, Verstohlen. You'd better get used to it.'

The Master made to leave, but Verstohlen was insistent.

'If we no longer expect Helborg, then we must send word for Grunwald to withdraw. The forest is alive with beastmen. He cannot hold his position.'

Tierhof gave him a disdainful look.

'The plans have been drawn up. The southern flank is held by Grunwald. Whether or not Helborg arrives, he must hold the line until the deployment is complete. There's no time to give you a lecture on tactics, Verstohlen, I'm needed with the gunnery crews.'

Tierhof gave a brief nod, and was gone. Verstohlen stood alone, forgotten amongst the bustle of the senior officers. From far down below, cries of alarm rose into the air. The scouts had sighted something. Trumpets rang out across the bastion, and the clash and scrape of steel blades being raised echoed around the defensive lines.

'So this is it,' said Verstohlen to himself, taking a flintlock from his holster and checking it over. 'Too late for Helborg now. And maybe for all of us.'

'Fall back! Fall back!'

The beastmen had broken through the defenders and on to the ridge. The huge bull-like monsters, blood-red and rearing furiously, shattered the fragile defensive lines. Even as Grunwald raced towards it, he could see the defences around him disintegrate. As long as they maintained a solid line, backed up with artillery and archery, they could hold out. Once a melee had formed, there were too few of them. The beasts numbered in their thousands.

The breach became a rout. Pikemen and halberdiers, hurrying to escape the swelling tide of beastmen, were trampled in their wake. The Helblasters roared a final time, and then the monsters were among them. Tusks gored with a blind fury. They hated the machines more than anything.

'To me!' cried Grunwald, swinging his broadsword wildly over his head. They had to stay together. An orderly retreat could still be salvaged, but the moment was slipping.

He stood at the summit of the ridge, eyes flickering as he assessed the situation. The regiment standard-bearer was soon beside him, sliding in the mud. All around, men toiled to escape the frenzy behind them. Some still fought. Ackermann was right in the thick of it, hammering away at the advancing beastmen with a fury nearly as savage as their own.

'Retreat, Morr damn you!' bellowed Grunwald.

The disengaged Imperial forces began to run down the far side of the ridge, down past the road and into the waiting maw of the forest below. There was no mad dash. Companies kept close together, their halberds and pikes in formation. They knew they'd have to cut their way out. Panic would finish them for good.

Cursing, Grunwald ran over to Ackermann. The man was holding his ground, trying to give the breaking ranks behind him more time. A goat-faced monster towered over him, raining down blows with a cudgel. Ackermann raised his shield to parry, but it was knocked from his grasp. The goat-creature bared its yellow teeth and swooped for the kill.

Grunwald barrelled into it, knocking it sideways. He felt his bones jar as the beastman reeled. It recovered quickly, whirling around. But Ackermann had recovered too. With a vicious slice, his blade took the creature's distorted head clean off its shoulders. For a moment, that opened a gap. Grunwald grabbed Ackermann and pulled him from the fighting. The beasts were trampling the Helblasters in an orgy of rage. This was their opportunity. They had to withdraw.

'I can hold them!' spat Ackermann, regaining his balance and running alongside Grunwald.

'Use your eyes!' snapped Grunwald. There was no time to argue. As he ran, one of the swifter creatures, skinny with legs like a dog's, tried to drag him down. He smashed his pommel into its face, barely breaking stride.

Ahead of him, the bulk of the regiment was streaming down the far side of the ridge. The foremost were already in the trees beyond. Those too slow or unlucky were caught by the beastmen, now swarming over the defences. The sound of their flesh ripping was like a stab in Grunwald's stomach. The vantage point had been lost. Their only hope was to keep ahead of the pursuing beasts. If they were surrounded in the deep forest, there was no hope.

He and Ackermann reached the base of the ridge and plunged into the shadows of the trees. Grunwald's earlier fatigue had left him. Now all that was left was the sharp fear that came from being hunted. They were at his heels. Even as he sped through the forest, leaping over fallen trunks in the semi-dark, he could hear them crashing through the undergrowth. The bellows had risen in ferocity. The Helblasters were forgotten. Now they were after human prey.

At his side, Ackermann laboured. He was a thick-set man clad in chainmail. Already his face was red and streaming with sweat. Ahead of him, he could see the rearmost ranks of the halberdiers. To their credit, they were still holding together. Maybe half of them had made it down, perhaps more.

'How far?' gasped Ackermann.

'A mile to the Cauldron's edge, then more to the bastion. But we'll be seen by the sentries.'

Ackermann spat as he ran.

'If they're still there.'

Grunwald felt the creepers snag at his feet. His heart hammered. One false step, and he'd be down amongst the briars. The light was poor. Little rain penetrated the thick canopy above, but the ground was a treacherous mire. He could hear his own breathing, heavy and thick. His muscles protested. His legs felt as heavy as lead. But he had to keep going.

'Commander!'

The voice rang out through the trees. Grunwald spun round. A detachment of troopers had lagged behind. They were in the very jaws of the pursuit. Even as he watched, two of them were cut down by the lumbering beasts behind. They would never make it.

Ackermann responded instantly. He abandoned the flight, and ran back to their aid.

'Morr *damn* his eyes,' muttered Grunwald, struggling to stay with him. He knew he should keep going, marshal the retreat. But he couldn't leave a man behind. Ackermann would be the death of him.

Then he fell. Something twisted round his feet in the murk, and he staggered forward. He landed heavily in the stinking gunge, his sword spinning into the gloom. He rolled over quickly, only to see the towering shape of a beastman above him. It whinnied with triumph, and raised its blade.

'Merciful Sigmar…' whispered Grunwald, scrabbling backwards. Too slow. He'd never make it.

The blade fell.

The full force of the storm hit the Cauldron. All across the northern horizon, thunder rumbled. Forks of lightning lit up the trees in savage relief and insubstantial, bestial shapes seemed to march across the heavens. It was barely after noon, but already as dark as dusk. The sun, ever the friend of man, was hidden. In its absence, the horrors of the forest would come out to play.

Bloch peered down from the bastion. The beasts had not made themselves known yet. The expanse below them was still empty and howling with wind, but he knew they were there, just on the edge of sight, sheltering in the eaves. As he watched, the last of the scouts rode hard across the Cauldron's base, anxious to get back to the safety of the rock before the beasts came after them.

One of them made it to safety and rode up towards Bloch's position. As the incline became too steep, he dismounted and walked the horse up through the defensive lines.

'How many?' demanded Bloch as the man passed him.

The scout looked back blankly for a moment before answering. His steed's flanks were coated with sweat and rainwater, and it shivered as it stood. The man's cloak was sodden, and his face was grey. Bloch noticed that his hands shook too as they held the reins.

'More than I've ever seen,' he said weakly. He looked resigned. 'Thousands. *Thousands.*'

Bloch looked uneasily over at his men. He didn't want to get them more scared than they were already. He laughed casually, hoping it sounded convincing.

'Lots of them, eh?' he said, and gave his halberdiers a knowing look. 'Just like at Kreigschelff, I'll warrant. And they ran back into the woods with their tails between their legs, then. It won't be any different this time.'

The scout didn't respond to the bravado. His long dark hair hung slick against his face. He was still shaking, and it wasn't from the cold.

'The whole forest's alive,' the scout murmured, not really looking at anything in particular, lost in his own private horror. 'D'you hear me? They're coming for us. They're numberless. The forest is alive.'

Bloch wanted to respond, but something in the scout's expression stopped him dead. The man had lost it. He'd stared into the abyss, and it had got to him.

'Go on,' he snapped. 'Get up to the command post. They'll want your report, if you've the stomach to deliver it.'

The man didn't reply, but turned back to his horse and trudged up the slope towards the limp row of standards at the summit.

Bloch felt disgust well up within him. Giving in before a blow had even been struck was spineless. That was the problem with the Empire of his time. If Magnus the Pious had had to work with such weaklings, Praag would never had been recovered.

He turned to his men. They looked up at him expectantly, like children to their father. Some of them were barely more than boys. A few clasped their halberds in fear, their knuckles white. The scout's mood was contagious.

'Don't listen to that filth, lads,' said Bloch, sweeping his gaze across them, daring any not to meet it. 'He's been out on his own for too long. We're all in this together. Remember, no backward step. No surrender.'

He lifted up his halberd and planted it firmly against the stone.

'There are thousands of us here, all good men of the Reikland. They've no answer to honest courage, these beasts. And you know who's leading us. The big man. He'll see us–'

His speech broke off. All around the Cauldron, a low drumming had started. Long, deep rolls began to thud out from the trees. It grew in volume. Across the bastion, men halted their chatter, and fell silent. The drums were coming from everywhere. North, east, west. The bastion was almost entirely encircled. The floor of the Cauldron seemed to resonate with the rhythm. Only from the south was there no noise. Where Grunwald had been stationed. The beastmen still hadn't closed off those approaches. Perhaps the commander still held his position. He should have been called back. He was doomed.

Despite himself, Bloch felt his nerve begin to go. How many must there be, to make that much noise? He remembered the ashen face of the scout.

The forest is alive.

He took a deep breath and clutched the shaft of his halberd.

'Come and get it then, you bastards,' he hissed, flexing his arms in readiness. 'Just come and get it.'

Grunwald couldn't even scream. He saw the blade descend, powerless to resist. Then there was a dark shape, tearing in from his left. A man slammed into the beast, knocking them both to the floor.

Ackermann.

Grunwald scrambled to his feet. All around him, there were cries of combat from the trees. His men were being slaughtered. He retrieved his blade from the undergrowth, hands slipping as he fumbled for it. The creature and Ackermann rolled through the bracken, each trying to gouge and throttle the other. Grunwald raced over to them. The shadows were heavy. It was hard to make out which was which. But then, from the north, a flicker of lightning penetrated the gloom. A twisted, tooth-filled face leered up at him from the forest floor, streaked with blood and rain.

Grunwald plunged his sword down. There was a scream, a twisted mockery of a man's pain. Then a gurgling. Then limpness. Grunwald withdrew the blade and grabbed Ackermann's shoulder.

'Come on.' he hissed. 'They're all around us!'

Ackermann rolled over. Where his face had been, there was nothing but a pulpy mass. One of the creature's teeth had broken off and gleamed within the exposed slick of muscle and sinew.

Filled with horror, Grunwald let Ackermann's body drop. He could hear more beasts coming up fast.

He ran.

On either side, the trees flitted passed him like shades of death. Grunwald didn't dare look back, though he could hear the heavy panting of the creatures close by. They were on his heels, loping like wolves. He gritted his teeth, willing his legs to keep working. They were all around him. They'd got Ackermann, and now they were coming for him.

He kept running. Ahead, there was nothing but shadow, nothing but more trees. He'd lost sight of his men. All those behind him were dead or scattered. He was prey, alone in the woods.

Then, against all hope, he saw the break. It wasn't over yet. He'd come further than he'd thought. There were only two places for miles around where the tree cover broke. One was the road. The other was the Cauldron.

From behind him, he could hear howls of frustration rise. They knew he was close to evading them. With a final, agonising spurt, Grunwald picked up speed. He leapt over fallen branches, barged through whipping thickets. There was no point in being cautious. If he tripped or slowed again, he was dead.

The light grew. All of a sudden, he broke out into the open.

The trees fell back. The vast plain of the Cauldron yawned away. It looked like a vision of some daemonic nightmare. Lightning licked the northern rim. Echoing drums rolled and boomed from all directions. The rain fell in sheets. In the centre of the depression, the dark form of the bastion soared upwards. As he ran, Grunwald could see the detachments of men arrayed on its flanks, deployed just as his own regiment had been on the ridge. The entire army had been placed on the stone walls. There were rows and rows of halberdier companies arranged across the terraced flanks of the rock, all facing out across the plain. He could see artillery emplacements further up, dozens of them. He knew there were knightly companies among them too, as well as greatswords, handgunners, and all the troops that the Reikland could afford.

But it was a time of war across the Empire. In years past, the army would have been even greater. There would have been battle wizards, great cannons and engines of war. Many of these were detained north of Middenheim or on the blasted fields of Ostland. In desperate times, the general made do with what he had to hand, even for a campaign as prestigious as this one.

Ahead of him, out on the Cauldron floor, he caught sight of the broken remnants of his own forces. They were running, just like him. Like storm-tossed birds, they were fleeing before the deluge hit.

Grunwald felt his vision begin to waver. He was exhausted. He could feel his final strength giving out. The hours of fighting had taken their toll.

He risked a look backwards, expecting to see a few dozen beastmen pursuing him. But there were more. Many more. He was flying ahead of the horde itself. From left to right, his vision was filled with hollering, baying, snarling creatures. They had chosen their moment, and the woods were emptying. On all sides of the Cauldron, they poured towards the Imperial bulwark.

Grunwald kept going. His fear was giving way to despair. He'd never reach the bastion. Neither would his men. At the last, they'd be overtaken. So close.

His features twisted in pain. His lungs felt fit to rupture, his legs ready to give out.

So close.

'Sir, there's movement on the plain.'

Bloch pushed the halberdier away irritably.

'I can see that, lad. Stop waving that blade in my face.'

He peered forward, shading his eyes from the rain. There were men running across the base of the Cauldron towards the bastion. They looked like insects.

'Grunwald,' he breathed. 'Has to be.'

Above them, a trumpet sounded. There was the clatter of arms. All the men on the south-facing flanks had seen it. A few hundred survivors. Half of Grunwald's command, no more.

Behind the running figures, towards the edge of the Cauldron, the beasts had broken cover. They poured from the trees in all directions. Tattered banners lurched along with them, daubed with crude figures. The eight-pointed star was on many of them. From others, mutilated human corpses hung. The drummers came out into the open. The noise rose even further. The bastion felt like an island in a sea of madness. Soon the tide would be lapping at their feet.

Bloch glanced back down at the fleeing men. His mind working quickly, he gauged the distance. They'd be overtaken. Unless something was done, he'd have to watch as his comrades were butchered before his eyes.

Not on his command.

'Fourth Company!' he cried, striding from his vantage point. 'Form a detachment. We're going down. Ninth Company, remain in reserve.'

To their credit, the halberdiers of the Fourth got into position quickly. They could all see the beastman horde approach. Some, the less experienced, looked ready to vomit. Even the old dogs of war said nothing. This was dangerous. But Bloch didn't ask the men to do anything he wouldn't, and they knew it. At heart, he was one of them. The trappings of command would never change that.

'Let's go,' he said.

The company filed along their defensive terrace and down the slope towards the Cauldron's floor. As they descended, the noise grew. At the base of the bastion, it was deafening.

'Keep tight,' warned Bloch. In the distance, he could see the first ranks of the beastmen. They weren't far away. The remnants of Grunwald's regiment were closer. They looked at the end of their strength. 'Let's get them home.'

He broke into a run. Behind him, his men did the same. Halberds were lowered. Even in the driving rain, the sharpened steel glinted menacingly. Bloch trusted his men. He'd drilled them hard. They stayed together, running in close formation. The distance closed.

Bloch felt his heart begin to thump harder. This was it. The first action. He gripped his halberd tightly, lowered the blade, and sought out his target. The rest was up to fate.

Verstohlen ran along the southern terrace. They could all see what was happening. Grunwald's men would be slaughtered.

The halberdiers moving to intercept them were too few. No other commanders would leave their defensive positions. He had to find the general. Losing Grunwald would be a disaster. Losing Bloch would be, if anything, worse. He began to regret his intervention with the halberdier captain.

He caught sight of Morgart, the captain of the Fifth Company of handgunners. He was standing with his men, watching. It was like some grim kind of spectator sport.

'Where's the general?' Verstohlen snapped.

Morgart shrugged.

'You tell me,' he said. 'If he's got any sense, on the road back to Altdorf.'

Verstohlen shot him a contemptuous look.

'Watch your tongue,' he said. 'If you knew him, you'd never say such a thing.'

Morgart was about to reply, but there was a commotion on the terraces above. Men were moving down to the lower slopes. Hooves clattered on the rock. Horses were being led down the winding paths from the summit. The Knights Panther. In the incessant rain their elaborate heraldry was soaked and sodden, but they still looked formidable in their plate armour and exotic hides. Their massive horses, enclosed in heavy barding, trod proudly. There was a whole company, nearly a hundred knights.

Verstohlen felt his heart leap. He rushed over to the preceptor, a tall, grim man with a hooked nose and scarred cheek. He knew him by reputation only. Leonidas Gruppen, scourge of the lower Drakwald.

'Preceptor, you're riding out?' he asked.

Gruppen looked down at Verstohlen warily. They all did, these soldiers.

'Those are my orders,' he said. His voice was as hard as the rain-beaten rock beneath them.

'Wait for me to join you,' urged Verstohlen. 'You could use a good shot.'

Gruppen kept walking.

'This is a time for warriors, counsellor,' he said. All around him, his knights were preparing to mount up. Squires hurried to their sides with lances. Helmets were donned, and the visors snapped shut. They were calm. Icy, even. The soldiers clustered around gazed at them in awe.

'You dare to speak to me thus?' said Verstohlen, his impatience rising. 'I have the ear of the general. Has he ordered this? Where is he?'

Then, from the midst of the knights, a new figure emerged. He was clad in full plate armour, heavy and ornate. His horse was a sable charger, a hand taller than the others, led by a squire in the livery of the Emperor. Imperial emblems had been draped across its flanks. Foremost among them was the Imperial seal, flanked by griffons rampant, the personal device of the Emperor. A laurel wreath crowned with an iron skull encircled his helm, and a pendant in the form of Ghal Maraz hung from his neck. His visor was raised, exposing his war-battered face. A voluminous beard hung from the close helm. Under the raised visor, his eyes glittered darkly. He carried himself with the utter assurance of command. Old scars covered the little skin that was exposed. Beside him, the formidable warrior Gruppen looked as callow as a milkmaid.

As he approached, the knights withdrew respectfully. Even against the towering pinnacle of the bastion, wreathed in wind and lashed by rain, he seemed the most immovable object in the whole landscape.

'He is here,' said Ludwig Schwarzhelm, the Emperor's Champion. At his side the Rechtstahl, the famed Sword of Justice, glinted. The blade was naked and rainwater ran down the steel. 'Give Verstohlen a horse. Then we ride.'

CHAPTER TWO

Bloch felt a lurch in his guts. Out on the Cauldron floor, mere yards ahead of his position, the beastmen had caught up with Grunwald's men. He saw some of them get taken down, dragged to the rock floor. It looked like there were less than three hundred of them, a poor return for those who had set off towards the ridge.

'Faster!' he bellowed to his own men, and squeezed a dram more effort from his labouring thighs. All around him, the halberdiers responded. They were closing in on the slaughter, coming closer with every footfall.

A few heartbeats more and they were in amongst them. Some of Grunwald's men, seeing the halberdiers arrive, tried to turn and fight. They looked near death from exhaustion.

'Get to the bastion!' roared Bloch, pushing them back towards the pinnacle. 'You're no good here.'

The beastman vanguard was made up of their faster creatures, not the heavy gors. They were slim-limbed and flighty, bizarre amalgams of deer, dog and man. Already Bloch's troops were in the thick of them. They'd kept close formation on the run. Now they sliced through the beast attack, forming a cordon around Grunwald's stumbling troops, giving them the time to get back to the bastion.

Bloch ploughed on. A fawn-coloured monstrosity, more whippet than man, leapt up at him. Three rows of teeth snapped at his face. Bloch's halberd flashed, and the creature span into the mud, whimpering. A sharp downward blow and it was silenced. These front runners were easy to dispatch. When the gors caught up, then things would get interesting.

'Captain!' came a weary voice. Grunwald.

The commander limped towards him. His face was grey, his uniform caked in blood and grime. Beyond him, Bloch's halberdiers rushed to hold the oncoming beasts back. Cries of battle, human and inhuman, rose into the gathering dark.

Bloch rushed over to him, catching him just as he stumbled to the ground.

'Are you the last?'

Grunwald nodded breathlessly.

'Anyone behind has been taken,' he panted. 'The forest is alive.'

'So I've heard.'

Grunwald looked up at him, his breath gradually equalising.

'You must pull back! They're all over the Cauldron.'

'Tell me something I don't know,' muttered Bloch, looking up to appraise the situation. It was getting difficult. The greater mass of beastmen had caught up with the outrunners. The line of halberdiers held against them, but they'd soon be overwhelmed.

'Get back to the rock,' said Bloch, pushing Grunwald roughly to his feet. 'We'll manage the retreat.'

Grunwald, his face drawn with fatigue, began to run again, limping after the straggling remnants of his command as they staggered towards the rock. Bloch turned away from him. Now his own detachment was the priority.

'Fall back!' he shouted, joining them at the front line. 'Keep your face to the enemy. Run, and you'll never see home again.'

He hefted his halberd, pushed his way past one of his own men, and brought it tearing downwards. With a satisfying crunch, it pierced the skull of a roaring horror on the beasts' front line. On either side of him, his troops worked their own blades skilfully. They struck in sequence, guarding each others' flanks, maintaining the curtain of steel. After each offensive stroke, every successful rebuttal, they fell back in unison, letting the beasts come after them.

Bloch began to work up a sweat. He felt his muscles bunch in his arms. The stench of the beasts was everywhere, and their dark blood splattered against his face and chest. As his blade worked, he began to sense the strange, feral enjoyment that always accompanied the thick of battle. The line was holding, his company was maintaining its shape, and the Sigmar-forsaken beasts were falling under the blade. This was battle as he liked it.

Then the gors arrived.

With a horrifying roar, two massive beasts powered their way through the ranks, pushing their squealing kin aside. Their skin was black and their squat bull-faces burned with feral malice. The eight-pointed star had been scored into their chests and old blood laced their thick hides. When they bellowed, the pools of rainwater shivered. Heedless of anything but their battle-lust, they hurled themselves at the fragile halberdier lines.

Bloch manoeuvred himself into the path of the biggest, holding his halberd tightly in both hands. The angle would have to be just right. He felt his mouth go dry.

The bull lurched towards him, roaring some obscene mockery of language. One of Bloch's men, knocked off-balance by an unlucky stroke, blundered into its path. The bull swatted him aside casually with a vast clenched fist. Bloch heard the spine snap cleanly. The monster launched itself at Bloch. Spittle flew into his face, thick and stinking.

Bloch roared his defiance in turn. He thrust his blade at the creature's chest. The aim was good, angled upwards and left. The bull leapt to one side, evading the tip. Bloch had been expecting the feint, and twisted the shaft to match. The blade struck the creature's flank below its enormous ribcage.

The bull bellowed. Ignoring the wound, it ground onwards, churning the earth with its cloven hooves. Bloch was pushed back, his halberd still in his hands. It was wrenched free. He grasped for the sword at his belt. Too late. The hammer-fist struck him on the shoulder.

Bloch flew back, landing heavily a yard distant. His vision swam. He could feel hot blood trickle down his stomach. The earth under him swayed. The bull, now just a blurred mass, charged him again. He tried to rise to his feet, but his legs felt like congealed fat. The ground drummed, as if a whole herd of horses was thundering across it. His shaking fingers found the pommel of his sword and he drew it from the scabbard. The bull came on.

Bloch raised the blade, trying to clear his vision. He saw his own halberd protrude from the monster's flank like a mockery of his weakness. But there was no giving ground now, no escape.

Feet apart, heart thudding, head low, he waited for the collision.

The afternoon was waxing, and the last of the meagre light was fading. Heavier clouds rolled across the Cauldron from the north. Verstohlen stood with the company of knights at the very base of the bastion where the rock surface gave way to the level surface of the Cauldron. Out on the plain he could see the hordes of beastmen charging from the tree cover. Closer to hand, he could also see the knot of fighting around the halberdiers. In moments they would be overwhelmed. Time was running out to effect any kind of rescue.

As the knights did around him, he mounted expertly. His steed, a chestnut rider's horse as opposed to the massive chargers of the Knights Panther, was agitated. They always were when the beastmen were present. The steeds seemed to recognise the unholy spoor of the twisted creatures. His mount whinnied nervously, shaking the bridle.

'Easy,' whispered Verstohlen, bringing the nervous creature under control quickly. It was important the knights saw he could be relied on to master his steed. Schwarzhelm knew his quality, but the others didn't. Anonymity had its price.

The Emperor's Champion said no more, snapped his visor shut and kicked his horse into a trot. The knights fell in behind him, a glittering column of dark metal in the rain. Verstohlen joined them at the rear, keeping one hand on the reins and one on his pistol. If he was lucky, he'd get two shots away before switching to a blade.

The knights picked up speed. They left the defensive terraces behind. The hooves rang out against the stone. Verstohlen began to feel his pulse quicken. Out in the gathering darkness, the howling and drumming was getting wilder. Beasts were pouring into the Cauldron, drawn by the aroma of human fear. Soon the knights would be right in among them.

'Merciful Verena, ward all harm,' he whispered devoutly.

At the head of the column, Schwarzhelm reached the floor of the Cauldron and the pace rose again. Trots turned into a canter, and the canter into a thundering gallop. They headed straight for Bloch's embattled halberdiers. Ahead of Verstohlen, the knights lowered their lances and adjusted their formation. With complete precision, moving at increasing speed, the charging formation extended into a line. Verstohlen manoeuvred himself behind the left flank. He'd be no good in the first clash, but his pistol would come into its own when the ranks were broken.

Hooves hammering, Gruppen's company flew towards the oncoming horde, the rain-driven wind rushing past their ears. The lance-tips lowered further, each knight picking his target. The seething mass of approaching beastmen neared. With every thrust of the horses' powerful muscles, the enemy came into sharper relief.

Verstohlen crouched in the saddle, peering out into the gloom. His heart raced. There they were, the halberdiers. Surrounded, overrun. He glanced down at his flintlock. The cool weight was reassuring.

The knights needed no orders to engage. Gruppen was as silent as the rest of them. Like the dread wings of Morr, the mounted formation swept past the knot of beleaguered troops and into the horde of beasts beyond.

The clash was sickening. Lances ran the creatures clean through, lifting them from the ground or shattering into wickedly sharp shards. The force of the charge knocked even the heavier gors backwards. Some were ridden down, others cut apart where they stood. The knights surged on, discarding their broken lances and pulling long broadswords from their scabbards for the return sweep.

One of the monsters, a massive bull-creature with a halberd protruding from its flanks, stood its ground. Denied its prey by the sudden charge, it roared defiance at the charging knights. The halberdier captain, looking shaky on his feet, staggered out of harm's way. Schwarzhelm, right at the apex of the charge, kicked his charger towards the gor. At the last moment, in a move of superlative horsemanship, he drew the head of his steed aside. The bull-creature lunged and missed. Schwarzhelm's sword flashed, and the gor's head slipped down its chest, severed clean from its shoulders. The mighty body toppled, crashing into the mud.

Verstohlen galloped along in Schwarzhelm's wake. A second huge beast rose from the wreckage and made to leap on to the back of a passing knight. He took aim and sent a piece of shot between its eyes. The creature snapped back, rolling its death-throes across the mire. Verstohlen kicked his horse's flanks, and it leapt smoothly over the writhing horror. He flicked the mechanism on the flintlock, bringing the second barrel into play. An ingenious device and one which had never let him down.

He raised the pistol to fire again, but the beasts were fleeing, loping back the way they'd come, waiting for more of their kin to reach them. For the moment, the charge of the knights had broken them. Despite losses, the halberdier company had survived.

Verstohlen looked about him. The halberdiers were taking

their chance and were staggering back to the bastion as fast as they could. Below him, the one Schwarzhelm had rescued was struggling to keep up. The face was familiar.

'Herr Bloch!' Verstohlen yelled, pulling his steed around and shifting forward in the saddle. 'Mount up behind me!'

Bloch, looking up blearily, took a moment to recognise what was happening. He was wounded, and his eyes weren't focussing properly.

'What in the name of damnation are *you* doing here?' he said, his speech slurring.

Verstohlen laughed, extended a hand and helped pull him up. The man was heavy, and the horse protested, but they managed it.

'Don't expect much respite when we get back to the rock,' said Ver-stohlen, following the knights as they regrouped and began to ride hard back to the bastion. Already the gap they had cut was filling with beasts. 'We've got you out of this mess, but the fighting has only just started.'

With the retreat of the knights, the Cauldron was left to the beasts. Uncontested, the hordes swept across the open space. Viewed from the temporary safety of the bastion, it seemed as if the entire bowl was filled with howling shapes. More and more emerged from the woods. Capering dog-faced creatures were pushed aside by heavy gors from the heart of the forest. They strode to the front of the crowd, lowing and growling as they came. More tattered standards were brought forth from the trees, each decorated with some rough image of Chaos. Some of the men unlucky enough to be caught out in the open now hung from the wooden frames, carried aloft by massive, hulking bearers. Even from the vantage point of the rock, it was clear that they were still alive.

Back at the summit of the bastion, still breathing heavily from his exertions, Ludwig Schwarzhelm stood on a slender outcrop, watching the enemy massing. The light was still bad, but he could see the thousands of beastman warriors clearly enough. Many more than he'd been told would be there. The reports had been inaccurate. The campaign was in danger of becoming a massacre.

Gruppen stood at his side, looking at the gathering horde through his eyeglass.

'Even with the Reiksguard, we'd be pressed.'

Schwarzhelm didn't reply. He let his heart rate return to normal. Helborg's absence had left them dangerously exposed. His forces were half as strong as they should have been. What had kept the Marshal? For all he admired the man's martial qualities, Kurt could be dangerously unpredictable.

Enough. He wasn't coming. Even if he tried to, the road would be swarming with the enemy. He'd never get through.

'We recovered Grunwald?' asked Schwarzhelm, watching the beastmen working themselves into a frenzy on the plain.

'Yes,' replied Gruppen. 'He'll survive. Though half his command is gone.'

Schwarzhelm nodded.

'And what of that halberdier captain?'

'He's called Bloch. He'll make it too.' Gruppen let a rare smile slip across his lips. 'My men told me he wants to get back to the front.'

'Let him, if he can still hold a blade. And if he survives, I'll want to see him.'

'Very well.'

Out in the mass of churning, chanting bodies, something was crystallising. The random movements were beginning to coalesce into something more regular.

'What are they doing?' asked Gruppen, a note of frustration entering his clipped voice. The man was eager to get back to work.

Something was emerging, a sound. The undisciplined howling was turning into a new chant.

Raaa-grmm.

'They wait for their champion,' said Schwarzhelm. His eyes stayed flinty, his expression calm. The exertion of the ride had been replaced by a grim equanimity. 'Do you think a horde such as this creates itself? He will come soon.'

Across the Cauldron, the rolling of the drums grew even wilder. Fresh thunder growled across the northern rim and the lightning returned. Even the elements were preparing for the final onslaught. The rain poured in rivers from the rock, sluicing down into the ranks of the beasts below.

Raaa-grmm.

'Their standards are close enough to hit,' said Schwarzhelm. 'Tell the archers to aim for the men strung up on them. We can give them a quick death at least. Then instruct the captains to ready the stakefields. It will not be long now.'

Gruppen saluted and left the outcrop. Alone, Schwarzhelm continued to observe, as still and silent as a statue in the halls of the dead.

Raaa-grmm. The massed chant was getting louder, drowning out all else but the drums.

'You will come,' the Emperor's Champion whispered. 'You must face me. And then we will enter the test together.'

Verstohlen pulled aside the entrance flaps to the apothecary's tent, careful not to snag them with the halberd he carried for Bloch, and ducked inside. The place was almost deserted. A dozen wooden pallets lay inside, arranged in two neat rows. Not nearly enough for the wounded of an entire army, but this one was for the officers only. Only if a man like Gruppen or Tierhof were injured would the precious jars of salve and holy water be broken into. The others could take their chances in the less well-appointed medical tents.

'Morr damn you, let me go!'

Verstohlen smiled. Bloch had recovered his voice. And his temper. The man had been wounded by the gor, but Verstohlen had a feeling it wasn't grave enough to keep him from the front.

He walked down to the far end of the tent where the halberdier captain was struggling with a state-employed apothecary and two Sisters of Shallya.

'You can release this man,' said Verstohlen, showing the

apothecary Schwarzhelm's seal. They let him go immediately, and Bloch lurched to his feet unsteadily.

The apothecary, a wizened man with a balding pate and snub nose, shook his head.

'I was instructed to keep him here, counsellor. He's been hit hard.'

'Not as hard as I'll hit you,' growled Bloch. The Sisters took a step back.

'Come,' said Verstohlen, handing Bloch the halberd. 'Your place isn't here.'

With Bloch still grumbling, the two men turned and left the tent.

'I could've handled those leeches,' he muttered. 'You didn't need to fetch me like a child.'

'They would have given you sleepwort, and you'd have missed the whole thing,' said Verstohlen. 'Besides, I feel responsible for you. I asked you to look out for Grunwald, and you've suffered for it.'

Bloch grunted. He still looked groggy and his face was pale. 'How're things looking?'

The apothecary's tent was near the summit of the bastion, shielded by high rock walls and far from the front. As they rounded a column of basalt, shining in the rain, the scene below them unfolded in all its full drama and horror.

The Cauldron was full with rank upon rank of beasts. There were at least thousands of them out there. Perhaps tens of thousands. The drums beat in unison, hammering out a steady, baleful rhythm. It wasn't the mindless thumping of hides that it had been. Some sense of purpose had gripped the entire horde, and Verstohlen could see them swaying in time with the booming rolls. They were surrounded. Besieged.

Then there was the chant, endlessly repeated, throbbing through the rock beneath their feet, filling the air.

Raaa-grmm. Raaa-grmm.

Despite the man's gruff exterior, Verstohlen could see that Bloch was shaken. There was no let-up, no respite. The Cauldron had been turned into a seamless fabric of rage.

'What d'you think that means?' Bloch asked.

'The name of their champion,' replied Verstohlen, looking over the scene calmly. 'We can't see them, but there will be shamans in the forest. They're working on something. All will become clear soon enough.'

Bloch shook his head.

'Well, that's good then.'

Then, down below, there was sudden movement. The front ranks of beasts, which had been milling around the base of the bastion without advancing, began to swarm up the lower slopes. Their stamping, bellowing and chanting was replaced by a massed roar of aggression. The tide, which had been lapping at the defences, surged and broke its bonds.

'I need to be with my men,' said Bloch, grasping the halberd with both hands. At the prospect of fresh fighting, his vision seemed to clear. 'Where do you have to be?'

Verstohlen reloaded his pistol coolly.

'I thought I might tag along with you, if that's acceptable.'

Bloch thought for a moment, clearly in doubt. The sounds of combat rose from the terraces below. Verstohlen couldn't blame him for his hesitation. Bloch didn't know who he was, nor why Schwarzhelm gave him the licence to do the things he did. None of the soldiers did, though some guessed. To most of them, he must have seemed like a strange hanger-on, dragged into the serious business of war on a whim.

'Do as you please,' Bloch said, striding off to where his company were positioned. 'Just don't get in the way.'

Verstohlen followed him silently, his long coat streaming with rain. His blood was still pumping from the ride out on to the Cauldron floor, and he made a conscious effort to calm his emotions. He'd need a steady hand, and an unwavering eye. The beastmen were hunting, and they were the prey.

Grunwald limped along the terrace, still feeling the effects of his flight from the ridge. He hadn't seen Schwarzhelm since his return. All the other commanders were busy with their

own units. He felt curiously bereft, cast adrift. Now that the
assault had begun, there was no time to seek new orders or
plan some new tactics. He'd rounded up all of his men who
could still walk and carry a weapon, and taken them back to
the defensive front. They may have failed to hold the ridge,
but there was still service they could render.

The bastion looked like it had been designed for war.
Above the smooth lower slopes, the rock rose up in a series
of steps. Schwarzhelm had arranged his forces in long ranks
along these natural terraces. An invading force would have
to come at them from below, suffering all the disadvantages
of having to clamber upwards while under attack. Between
the twisting rock ledges, paths had been worn. Some were
natural, others the product of centuries of human footfalls.
These were the weak points. If the invaders managed to force
their way up the paths, then they could get on to the level
of the terraces and cause havoc.

All across the lower reaches of the bastion, commanders had deployed their forces to prevent this. The terraces
were crammed with troops capable of dealing death from
afar: handgunners, archers and pikemen. At the crucial inter-
sections where the rock offered less protection, the heavy
infantry had been stationed, halberdiers mostly, drawn from
the Reikland regiments. In the places of most danger, squadrons of Knights Panther were deployed, grim and immoveable
in their heavy plate armour. Clusters of greatswords were
there too, grizzled warriors bearing the huge, two-handed
blades of their forefathers in gnarled fists. Across the most
accessible routes up the rock, wooden stakes had been driven
into cracks in the stone. Behind these fragile-looking barriers,
the troops stood ready, watching impassively as the beasts
tore up the slope towards them.

'Stand your ground,' roared Grunwald. He knew his men
were in a bad way. They'd already been driven from one battle. Some had been fighting for hours with no respite, and
they all looked drained. 'This is where we make amends!
Give no quarter!'

The beasts surged towards the lines, hollering and whooping in their bloodlust. Grunwald felt the sweat start on his palms. On either side of him, rows of steel blades glinted in the low light. The beasts had followed his men all the way from the ridge, thirsting for their blood still.

The feeling was mutual. Grunwald watched as his first target, a shaggy behemoth with a tusked face, lumbered up the incline towards him. Its flanks were streaked with entrails and its maw dripped with gore. So, it had recently feasted.

'Your last victim,' hissed Grunwald, lowering his blade, fixing the beast with a look of unwavering hate and standing his ground.

Schwarzhelm looked down from his vantage point. He held an ancient-looking spyglass to one eye, sweeping across the grim vista below. His expression was unreadable. As he had done countless times before, he studied the enemy onslaught, watching for weakness, scouring for opportunities. As the battle intensified, functionaries hovered on the edge of his vision. Every so often, men would come running up with reports from the front. He responded with terse instructions.

'Redeploy the Third Halberdiers.'

'Instruct Herr Morgart to withdraw to the upper terrace.'

'The Helblasters are angled too high. And Tierhof's rate of fire is poor.'

The officials would then scurry away into the rain, shepherded by Ferren, his aide-de-camp. A few moments later, Schwarzhelm would observe the adjustment in the response of the army. From his position, he could see across the entire rock. The army was like an extension of his will. When he uttered an order, the shape of the defence shifted. Somewhere, he knew that his adversary was doing the same. The beastmen may have appeared crude and barbaric, but they had their own ways of directing their horde. There was an intelligence out there, guiding the assault, apportioning its resources at the points of greatest weakness.

'Show yourself,' breathed Schwarzhelm, fingering the pommel of the Rechtstahl impatiently.

'My lord?'

Gruppen was back, hovering at his shoulder. His blade was notched and his heavy breastplate had been scored with three great scratches. If their claws could do that to plate armour, then...

'Report,' said Schwarzhelm.

'Two terraces have been lost,' replied Gruppen. He was a military man and spoke dispassionately. There wasn't a trace of fear in his voice, just realism. 'We need more knights. The state troopers don't have the armour for this fight.'

'Damn Helborg,' spat Schwarzhelm, giving away his exasperation.

He turned around slowly, letting his eyes take in the sweeping panorama of war. On every front, the beastmen were assaulting hard, scrabbling up the slope and throwing themselves at the defenders on the terraces. Despite the advantage of higher ground, the lines were being beaten back. Slowly, it was true, but his forces were being driven ever higher up the slopes. The beasts could afford to lose twice the number of fighters he could in every engagement, and still outnumber them for the final assault. All around the base of the bastion, the landscape was lost in a seething maelstrom of monsters.

'Tell the artillery captains to throw the last of the shot at them. I don't care if they run out. We need to blunt this thing now.'

Gruppen hesitated.

'Will you not descend, my lord? The men–'

Schwarzhelm fixed the preceptor with a dark look. Gruppen, who faced monstrous gors without a second thought, swallowed.

'Do not question my judgement, master knight,' warned Schwarzhelm. 'I will descend when the time is right.'

As if to reinforce his words, a fresh chorus of *Raaa-grmm* echoed up from the battle below. The beasts could sense their master's presence. Schwarzhelm could sense his presence. But, for the time being, he didn't show himself.

Gruppen bowed and descended from the vantage point back to the fighting. Schwarzhelm listened to the clink of his armour against the stone. He wasn't worried about being thought a coward. No one in the Empire would dare to make such a claim, and he had long stopped caring about what other men thought of him.

No. His place was here, marshalling his forces, squeezing out the last ounce of defence from his beleaguered men. They would stand their ground, grinding out every foot of surrendered stone with blood and steel. Not until the rock lay heavy with the corpses of beasts would his adversary be drawn out. And then the clash would come, the battle that would decide the fate of all of them.

'Show yourself,' hissed Schwarzhelm again, scouring the battlefield for the movement he yearned to see. 'Face me.'

But the rain snatched his words away and the skirling wind mocked them. Across the plain, the beasts tore at the defences, their lust for human flesh unquenched.

Bloch arced his halberd downwards with a cry of exertion. The blade lodged deep in the neck of the gor scrabbling at his knees. The creature howled, shaking its head, spraying blood into the air. Bloch felt his grip come loose. The beast was powerful.

'Die, damn you!' he growled and twisted the halberd deeper. The struggles ebbed, and the gor tried to withdraw. From Bloch's side, a second blade plunged into its flank. The growls were silenced and the beast slid back down the slope. Others leapt up to take its place immediately. Even with the advantage of the stone ridge, it was hard going keeping them out.

Bloch kept hacking, ignoring the protests from his gore-splattered arms. His round helmet was dented, his heavy leather jerkin ripped by claws and teeth. Dimly, he was aware that his wounded shoulder was throbbing again. The hot sensation of blood was creeping down his midriff. Something had come unstuck. Had that damned apothecary stitched him up cock-eyed?

A bull-headed gor, only slightly smaller than the one which had nearly killed him in the Cauldron, tried to leap on to the terrace. It took two arrows in the throat before its hooves touched the stone, and it was pushed back into the heaving press of bodies below. The halberdiers were holding their ground. Their fear had been replaced by a resigned, workmanlike determination. Every thrust was met with a counter-thrust, every strike with a deter-mined parry.

'Herr Bloch,' came a familiar voice. Bloch felt his spirits sink. Not now.

He swiped the halberd back and forth, a difficult manoeu-vre in the tight space. For the moment, the beasts before him withdrew. The foremost of them limped back down the slope. But already larger creatures were massing.

'What is it?' snapped Bloch, made angry by fatigue and the pain in his shoulder.

'The companies on the terraces either side of us have withdrawn,' said Verstohlen. 'We are exposed. I thought you should know.'

Bloch looked hurriedly either side of him. It was true. The beasts were forcing men back up the slopes of the bas-tion, step by step. Two terraces had been abandoned and the defenders were digging in higher up. Soon his own flanks would be left open.

'Is that what you do with yourself all day, Verstohlen?' he asked. 'Spot isolated command groups?'

'Amongst other things, yes.'

Bloch scowled. Who *was* this man? Why did he never get angry?

'Fall back, men,' he cried, pushing the counsellor out of the way. 'Up to the next terrace!'

It was difficult work, made harder by the rain-washed stone. The halberdiers knew enough not to turn their backs to the enemy. Warily, they filed along the terrace, making for the paths at the end of the ridge, backing up carefully.

The beasts were slow to spot the movement, but when they

did, the roars of attack started up again. The gors powered up the slope, heads low, cleavers swinging.

'Keep together!' roared Bloch, raising his halberd. He'd be the last to leave. Only when every man was up on the next level would he join them. They were almost there.

The beasts clambered up on the vacated terrace-end, howling with victory. One of them came straight at Bloch. He ducked under the wild cleaver swipe, and planted the tip of the halberd into the monster's leg. A twist and the bone was broken. The beast staggered, but there was another behind it, horse-faced and crowned with stubby antlers. Bloch withdrew, swinging his blade defensively. Too many. He began to back up. From behind him, he could hear his men safely occupying the terrace above. That was good, disciplined work. He was proud of them. Now he needed a little support.

He began to pick up the pace, shuffling backwards, swinging the halberd deftly. Horse-face advanced slowly, but then sprang, launching itself right at Bloch's face. The beast was quick, far quicker than it looked. Bloch parried a blow from the cleaver, but the force of the impact knocked the blade from his hands.

'Damn.'

Weaponless and isolated, there wasn't much to do. Bloch scrabbled up the slope as fast as he could. Hands from the upper terrace reached down to pull him to safety. His hand grasped one of them and he felt himself hauled upward. His legs kicked at the slavering mass below. He felt his iron-tipped boot connect with something. A jawbone, maybe.

But horse-face was still after him. Springing powerfully, the creature launched itself up the incline, clawing at his legs. The beast's cleaver swung down, just missing Bloch's thigh as he scrabbled to get out of the way. The next blow wouldn't miss. Bloch screwed his eyes up, waiting for the agonising blow.

A shot rang out. Horse-face spun back into the horde beyond. Its fall knocked several beasts from their feet, and the assault up to the terrace faltered. In the brief hiatus, fresh hands grabbed Bloch and pulled him over the lip of the higher ridge.

For a moment, he sat stupidly on the stone, catching his breath. That hadn't been a good experience. Verstohlen came up to him, his pistol smoking.

'I could've handled it myself,' Bloch muttered.

Verstohlen smiled briefly.

'This is a common theme with you, I observe.'

The respite was brief. New, larger gors were making their way to the front. There were no higher terraces left to withdraw to. The halberdiers took up their weapons again. Bloch clambered to his feet, seized a fresh blade and steadied himself. His shoulder was killing him, every inch of his body was bruised and the ice-cold rain was beginning to chill him to the core.

'Come on then!' he roared, baring his teeth and waving his halberd over his head like an ale-raddled savage. From either side of him, his men burst into foul-mouthed support, hurling defiant obscenities into the air. For a moment, they looked more bestial than the monsters that attacked them, a skill no doubt learned in the alehouses on a beer-soaked festival of Ranald.

Despite everything, Bloch felt a glow of pride. They were his lads. Rough as old leather, to be sure, but his lads all the same. Finest men in the Empire. The beasts would have to clamber over every last one of them to get where they wanted to go.

He lowered his blade, located his target and waited for it to come to him.

Schwarzhelm narrowed his eyes. A change had taken place. Out on the plain, something was moving towards the bastion. Hidden, to be sure. His eyes couldn't quite focus on it. It wasn't a shadow as such, more a slippery patch of nothingness. Whenever his gaze fell on it, it seemed to slide to one side. And it was picking up speed.

'Ah,' he said. He knew enough of dark magic to recognise it. The shamans were old, wily and powerful. Only a fool believed the beasts had no art of their own. Their ways were those of the forest, the dark places where the nightmares of men were given shape.

The path of no-vision crept closer. There were gors all around it, huge creatures, bull-horned and carrying massive spears of iron. Whatever was at the centre of that sphere of disruptive magic, it was greater than they were.

Schwarzhelm drew the Rechtstahl. In the rain, the steel shimmered. No dark magic would ever stain its flawless surface. Only the runefangs themselves were purer. He had carried his blade beside him for all the years he'd been Emperor's Champion. His predecessor had done the same, as had his. For generations, the sacred sword had been borne into battle at the side of Ghal Maraz, and the departed souls of those great warriors who had wielded it in ages past were still present. At times, Schwarzhelm could sense their power imprinted on the cold metal. The best of humanity, forged in war, tempered by righteous wrath, locked into the spirit of the blade for eternity. In such things did true power lie.

He let the rainwater run down the edge, watching the liquid sheer from the flat and on to the stone. Was he worthy to carry it? He knew the doubt would never leave him, no matter how many horrors he slew. Only in death, the final tally reckoned up, would he have his answer.

Schwarzhelm turned from his vantage point to see Gruppen climbing up to meet him again. He looked as haggard as before. His helmet had been knocked from his head and an ugly weal ran across his brow.

'My lord,' he said, breathlessly. 'We can withdraw no further. We are penned in on all sides. What are your orders?'

Schwarzhelm's expression was wintry.

'He is here,' he said, watching the meagre light glint from the surface of the Rechtstahl. 'His pride draws him on. Too early. By such misjudgements are battles lost.'

Gruppen looked perplexed.

'I do not–'

'Enough. Rally your knights. The doombull is approaching. I will contest him. Follow me.'

* * *

Grunwald fought on, though his strength was nearly spent. It felt like they'd been retreating from the very beginning of the engagement, step by bitter step. The bastion was now entirely encircled. All ways down had long since been blocked by the horde. The lower terraces were gone, covered in swarming crowds of jubilant monsters and heaps of bodies. Amid them, the larger gors strode, lost in a fog of blood-drunkenness. The bodies of men lay trampled under their hooves. That sent them into still higher levels of fury. The stench of the creatures was as overpowering as their noise. Even above the blood, the aroma of death, the powerful musk of the wild forest rose in his nostrils.

He could no longer feel afraid. Nothing but a blank fatigue had taken over. His arms worked automatically, swinging the blade as heavily as he was able. By his side, his men were the same. Pale-faced, listless, driven into the ground by the remorseless advance. The beasts seemed to know no weariness. On they came, hammering at the lines of steel, desperate to sink their teeth into flesh and crush the hated trappings of the Empire into the mud.

Grunwald grasped his halberd and made ready for yet another charge. For all he knew, it would be his last. He didn't know how many men had died. The army had been horribly diminished by the assault. Perhaps a third of those who had marched to the bastion had made it their grave. Half of those left were barely able to wield a weapon. They remained, like Grunwald, trapped in the narrow terraces, fighting for their lives. The proud campaign to purge the forest was in tatters. He crouched low, trying to still the shaking in his hands. He was cold to the marrow, and his clothes hung from his exhausted frame in heavy, sodden bunches. This was it. The final assault.

But it never came. Against all hope, the gors withdrew. Grunting and shuffling, they pulled back down the slope. It was the same all along the front. Grunwald looked down the lines on either side of him. Men, all as weary as he, looked out across the seething mass of beastmen. None cheered.

None rushed out to press home the advantage. They all knew that the movement presaged only some fresh horror. So they stayed where they were, hunched in the rain, leaning against their weapons.

Then the reason became apparent. The chanting started out again.

Raaa-grmm. There was no fervour in it this time, just a low, mournful dirge. Grunwald listened carefully. A name? Ragh-ram? That sounded as close to a name as a beastman ever got. He peered into the gloom. Something was approaching.

Far down the dark slopes of the bastion, a shifting cloud of shadow drew near. It hurt the eyes to look at it. It wasn't dark exactly, just an absence of anything. To stare into such a thing was to look into one of the aspects of Chaos. It had no place in the world of matter. It was an aberration, a cloak of madness. All along the crowded terraces, men drew back slowly. There were muffled cries of dismay from further up, quickly stifled.

On either side of the approaching terror, ranks of bull-horned gors strode in silence. They made no noise. No bellows of rage, no earth-shaking growls of menace. In silence they swung their iron spears. In silence they stared up at the fragile rows of human defenders. In silence they marched in unison, their knotted muscles evident under thick coats of twisted hair.

Behind them, the beasts fell into a trance-like state, chanting their endless mantra. The stone beneath Grunwald's feet began to reverberate from the dull, repetitious sound. Even the rain seemed to lessen in the face of the grinding aural assault. When the water impacted against the swirling no-vision, it bounced off in steaming gouts. The very elements were horrified by the approaching outrage.

With a terrible certainty, Grunwald knew he was staring at defeat. No human could stand against such a creature. He felt his skin begin to crawl with sweat. His men were succumbing to panic. So this was the end. The battle had all been about this. With the defences strung out, weary, ready to crumble, Raghram had come. As the unholy vision drew nearer, he grasped his halberd with unsteady fingers. Though he knew it was hopeless, he prepared to leave the terrace and charge the monster. At least he would atone for his failure at the ridge.

'No further!' came a voice. It was as clear as a great bronze bell. Grunwald spun round.

Further up the slope of the bastion, men still stood their ground. The Knights Panther, dismounted, naked broadswords in hand, barred the way. Their numbers had been thinned by the fighting, but Leonidas Gruppen was still among them, his uncovered face savage in the failing light. The preceptor was surrounded by his brothers in arms, all still encased in their dark, battle-ravaged armour.

At their head was Schwarzhelm. The wind whipped his cloak about him as he stood, feet planted heavily, sword resting on the stone.

'You have come too soon, beast of Chaos,' he said. His deep voice seemed to come from the heart of the bastion itself. Even the gors halted, gazing at the human with a sudden doubt. 'This blade has drunk deep of your kin's blood before. It will do so again. You know its power. Look on it, horror of the void, and know despair.'

A sudden thrill ran through Grunwald's body. On every side, halberds were raised into the air. Schwarzhelm was with them! Despair was replaced by a wild, desperate hope.

But then Raghram unveiled himself. The shroud of nothingness slipped from his shoulders, dissolving against the stone like smoke. He rose to his full height, towering over even Schwarzhelm's mighty frame. He was vast and old, reeking of death and corruption. His eyes blazed blood-red and his leathery fingers clasped an axe the size of a man. Cruel horns, four of them, rose like a crown over his heavy brow and tusks hung from his ruined face. He wore twisted iron armour over his shoulders and breast, crudely hammered into place and daubed with the foul devices of the Dark Gods.

In that face there was malice, ancient malice, the long, slow bitterness of the deep wood. To gaze into that expression was to see the tortured, endless hatred of the primal world for all the doings of man. Nothing existed there but loathing. Nothing would quench its fury but death.

With a thunderous roar, Raghram cast off the last of his unnatural cloak and charged. The gors fell in beside him. Under the lowering sky, desperate and valiant, the knights stood to counter the assault. Schwarzhelm threw his cloak back and his blade flashed silver. Then all was lost in shadow.

CHAPTER THREE

Crouched in his terrace, Bloch saw the change coming, felt it in the stone beneath his feet.

'Why have they stopped?' he hissed.

All down the line, the gors had ceased their attack. They pulled back from the terrace, leaving several yards of cold stone between them and the defenders. The narrow gap was dark with blood. Once withdrawn, they hung back, lowing ominously. Flickers of bone and steel glinted amongst the dull hides. It was getting dark. At the summit of the bastion, braziers had been lit, but the flames did little to lift the gathering gloom. The stench remained powerful.

'They're watching something,' said Apfel, a young Ostlander in his company. The boy looked pale under his sodden hair. Bloch peered into the shadow. The lad was right. The gors were holding back, craning their bull-necks over to the right. The low, grinding call started up again. *Raaa-grmm*. What in the underworld *was* that?

Verstohlen crouched beside him, cleaning his pistol absently while looking into the face of the horde.

'I'm needed elsewhere,' he said.

'Again?' said Bloch. 'Where do you need to be now?'

'You can see the change. The architect of all this is here. They defer to him. The honour of the first kill will be his.' The counsellor smiled softly. 'How ironic. We do the same thing on our hunts. To the victor, the prestige of the mercy stroke. An interesting parallel.'

Bloch shook his head irritably. He had no idea what the man was going on about.

'Their commander's here?' he snapped. 'Is that why they wait?'

Verstohlen nodded, finished cleaning his weapon and stood up again.

'He thinks we're broken. So now he shows himself. But Schwarzhelm still stands. And I must stand beside him.'

Bloch looked Verstohlen up and down, failing to suppress a sneer of disbelief. The counsellor was slim, urbane, civilised. More importantly, he wore no plate armour. He looked like he'd snap in a light breeze.

'You think he'll want you with him?'

'Always.'

Verstohlen made to stride off towards the source of the most intense chanting. Bloch felt a sudden qualm.

'Wait!' He put his burly hand on the man's shoulder. 'If this thing's to be settled, I should be there too.'

Verstohlen cast a glance at the ranks of beasts below, just a few yards distant.

'This respite is only temporary, Herr Bloch. They will come at you again soon. Stay with your men. Your place is here.'

Bloch felt his blood rising. Something in Verstohlen's simple, clipped tone of command made him furious. He could cope with orders from a military man, but not from, well, whatever Verstohlen was. He raised his fist, searching for an appropriate insult.

He never found it. The beasts started to advance again. The chanting continued, ominous and in unison. Without saying another word, Bloch turned back to the defence. Behind him, unnoticed, Verstohlen slipped away. His leather coat flicked in the gloom and was then gone.

Bloch hefted his halberd. The staff was slick with rain. It suddenly felt heavy and hateful to him. The rush of battle-joy had long departed.

'One more time, lads,' he exhorted, trying to raise the spirits of his men. But in his heart, he knew they were running out of time. From below, snarling and growling, the scions of the forest came for them again.

Schwarzhelm readied himself as Raghram came at him. The doombull was massive. The musk around him was thick and cloying. Beneath his hooves, spoor clung to the rock, stinking. The wide bull-mouth bellowed. The axe swung, spraying rain. On either side of him, the Knights Panther took up their positions against the doombull's entourage of gors. The elite troops of the two armies came together on the slopes of the bastion, and the fury of the storm above was but an echo of the savagery of their encounter.

Schwarzhelm met the onslaught full on, blunting the full force of the charge. Coarse iron clashed with pure steel, sending sparks spinning into the shadows. The blow was heavy, far heavier than that of a man. Schwarzhelm judged it carefully, dousing the momentum without aiming to stop it. When the moment was right, he withdrew the blade, sprang aside and plunged a stabbing blow at the monster's flank. It connected, and black blood pumped down the beast's twisted legs.

On either side of him, Schwarzhelm could sense the presence of the knights. They were locked in combat with the gors. Dimly, right at the edge of his vision, he could see the ebb and flow of battle. A knight would fall, pierced with a cruel horn-tip. Or a beast would stumble, its chest opened by an Imperial blade. It was finely balanced.

But these were just the ghosts of images, flitting at the periphery. Ahead of him, roaring its rage, the doombull came again. Again the axe fell, again it was parried. Schwarzhelm wielded the sword expertly, making play of its speed and keenness. As it worked, the failing light flashed from the steel.

Schwarzhelm let the Rechtstahl guide his hand. He was a master swordsman, second only to one other in the entire Empire, but you could not wield a holy blade as if you owned it. The sword was its own master, and he was but the most recent of its stewards. Only after half a lifetime of wielding it did he understand some of its secrets. Most would never be uncovered.

Raghram maintained the charge and the axe swung like a blacksmith's hammer. In the massive, bunched arms of the doombull, it looked like a child's toy. Schwarzhelm saw the feint coming and angled the sword to parry. At the last moment, he shifted his weight. The blades clashed once more. Feeling the camber of the slope beneath his feet, adjusting for the force of the attack, he pushed back.

His arms took the full momentum of the doombull's weight. For an instant, Schwarzhelm was right up against the monster. The ruined face was above his. The eyes, kindled with a deep-delved fire, blazed at him. Strings of saliva drooled down from the tooth-filled jaw. Raghram wanted to feast. He was drunk on bloodlust.

Then Schwarzhelm's foot slipped. The rock was icy with surface water and he felt his armoured sabaton slide on the stone. The axe weighed down, the blade-edge hovering over his torso.

Schwarzhelm gritted his teeth, pushing against the weight. The power of the doombull was crushing, suffocating. But Schwarzhelm was no ordinary man. Tempered by a lifetime of war, his sinews had been hardened against the full range of horrors in the Old World. He'd stared into the rage-addled faces of greenskin warlords, the horror-drenched gaze of Chaos champions, the cruel and inscrutable eyes of the elves. All had met the same fate. This would be no different.

He twisted out of the encounter, arching his body to deflect the secondary blow, using the power of the beast to drag it forward. He could still sense the battle raging around him. There was no way of telling who was winning. All his attention was bent on the monster before him. This was the fulcrum of the battle. If he failed now, then they all died.

He pulled back, but Raghram was upon him. The axe swung down again. The obvious choice was to step back, evade the curve. But the Rechtstahl seemed to draw him on. Inured to hesitation, Schwarzhelm plunged inside the arc of the axe, crouching low. He was within the grasp of the beast. Twisting the blade in both hands, he brought the tip up. With a savage lunge, he thrust it upwards, aiming beneath the doombull's ribcage.

The tip pierced its flesh, driving deep. Fresh blood coursed over his face, hot and rancid. The doombull roared afresh and pulled back. Schwarzhelm withdrew the blade, ducking under flailing fingers, feeling the monster nearly grasp him. He pulled back again, feeling his breathing become more rapid. There was no fatigue, no weariness, but the sheer power of the beast was impressive. He would need to do more than stab at it. From somewhere, the killing blow would need to be found.

Now the creature was wary. It lowered its head. The horns dripped with rain. The axe hung low against the ground. When it growled, the earth seemed to reverberate in warped sympathy. Schwarzhelm held his position, sword raised. His eyes shone in the dark. Every movement his opponent made, every inflection, needed to be observed. He would wait. The Rechtstahl felt light in his hands. On either side, the savage cries of battle still raged. His knights were holding their ground. No gor would get to him while any of them could still wield a blade. The duel would be undisturbed.

Raghram charged again. Even as the hooves pushed against the rock, Schwarzhelm could see the energy exerted. The muscles in the goat-shaped thighs bunched, powering the massive creature forward. The head stayed low, trailing long lines of blood-flecked drool. As the doombull moved, its horns swayed.

Schwarzhelm adjusted his stance. His armour suddenly felt like scant protection. Keeping his eyes on the swaying axe-blade, he braced for impact.

It was like being hit by a storm. A human, however strong, had no chance of halting such a monster. It was all Schwarzhelm could do not to get knocked from his feet. Bringing all the power he could to bear, he traded vicious blows from the axe with the Rechtstahl, giving ground with every one. Raghram let slip a crooked smile as it advanced. Deep within that deranged face, something like amusement had emerged. He was being toyed with.

Schwarzhelm leaped back, clearing half a yard of space, and let the Rechtstahl fly back in a savage backhanded arc. If it had connected, it would have spilled the monster's guts across the bastion floor. But Raghram was too old and wily for that. With a deceptive grace, it evaded the stroke, its momentum unbroken.

This was dangerous. Schwarzhelm felt his balance compromised, but there was no room to retreat. The axe-blade hammered down, and he barely parried it. His blade shivered as the full force of the axe landed on it, and he felt the power ripple through his body.

He gave ground again, losing the initiative. Raghram filled the void, hacking at his adversary even as it roared in triumph.

Then the axe got through. Whether it was skill or luck, the doombull's blade cut past Schwarzhelm's defence. It landed heavily against his right shoulder, driving deep into the metal of the pauldron. He felt the plate stove inwards. An instant later sharp pain bloomed out, and he staggered back from the blow.

Raghram leapt up. The axe was raised, and a look of scorn played across the bull-face. Schwarzhelm raised his sword in defence, watching the advance of the monster carefully. The doombull came on quickly. Too quickly. In its eagerness to land the killing blow, its axe-blade was held too far out.

Schwarzhelm swept his sword up, twisting it in his hands

as he did so. He left his torso unguarded. That was intended.
The manoeuvre was about speed. Raghram reacted, but
slowly. The Rechtstahl cut a glittering path through the air.
Its point sliced across the beast's face, pulling the flesh from
the bone and throwing it high into the storm-tossed air.

Raghram staggered backwards, a lurid gash scored across
its mighty cheek and forehead. The great creature lolled,
stumbled and rocked backwards, blinded by its own blood.

Schwarzhelm recovered his footing. The Rechtstahl glistened eagerly. Taking the blade in both hands, he surged
forward. The tip passed clean between the beast's protruding
ribs, deep into the unholy torso and into the animal's heart.

Raghram screamed, and the last veils of shadow around it
ripped away. The sudden lurch nearly wrenched the blade
from Schwarzhelm's grip, but he hung on, twisting the sword
further into the monster's innards. It bit deep, searing the
tainted flesh like a branding iron on horsehide. The doombull attempted to respond, flailing its axe around, searching
for the killer blow.

But its coordination was gone. Slowly, agonisingly, the
pumping of the mighty heart ebbed. The light in its eyes
went out. With its throat full of bubbling, foamy blood,
Raghram, the master of the horde, sank down against the
stone. The iron axe-head clattered against the rock uselessly.

Schwarzhelm pulled the Rechtstahl free at last. He stood
back, lifted the blade to the heavens and roared his triumph.

'Sigmar!' he bellowed, and his mighty voice echoed from
the stone terraces around him.

Even in the midst of their close-packed combat, the cry
reached the ears of man and beast alike. The Knights Panther knew what it portended immediately and redoubled
their efforts. Under Gruppen's grim leadership, they began
to hammer the gors further down the slope. Raghram's body
slumped down the dank stone, its rage silenced. Step by
step, yard by bitter yard, the tide began to turn. Bereft of the
guiding will of the doombull, the assault on the rock citadel foundered. The dark-armoured knights pursued them

ruthlessly, their longswords biting deep into the beastmen's hides.

Schwarzhelm sank back against the stone, his breathing heavy. For the moment, the counter-assault was conducted by others. The respite would be short, but after such a duel it was needed.

'Nice work,' came a voice from higher up the rock. Verstohlen emerged from the shadows, his pistol cocked ready to fire. 'I'm glad of it. Not sure this thing would have been much use against that.'

Schwarzhelm didn't smile. He never smiled.

'Its hand was forced. Something new has arrived.'

Verstohlen followed his gaze. Far off, beyond the sea of beastmen out on the Cauldron floor, there was a change. It was hard to make out in the failing light, but there were flashes of steel out in the gloom. Then, as the beastmen finally ceased their chanting, the sound gave it away. The clear horn blast of an Imperial host. There was no noise like it in all the Empire. After a hundred battlefields, it was as familiar to Schwarzhelm as the rain on a thatched roof.

'Reiksguard,' he said. 'Helborg. At last.'

Verstohlen gave an appreciative nod.

'That is welcome. We're still outnumbered. This will turn the balance.'

Schwarzhelm shot him a disdainful glance.

'Don't make excuses for him,' he snapped. 'He's overdue. And if he tries to claim the credit for this victory, I'll string him up myself. We did this, and paid the price in blood.'

Verstohlen raised an eyebrow. He looked genuinely taken aback by Schwarzhelm's vehemence. He started to reply, then seemed to think better of it.

Schwarzhelm finished wiping Raghram's gore from the Rechtstahl in silence, then drew himself up to his full height. Around them, the knights had regrouped and were beginning to pursue the remaining gors down the slope. The beastman advance was dissolving into confusion.

'Go back to the summit,' growled Schwarzhelm. 'Someone'll be needed to keep the army together.'

'If you wish. Where are you going?'

Schwarzhelm gave him a flat look. His expression was murderous.

'Hunting.'

Hours later, Grunwald leaned on his halberd. He was near the summit of the bastion, and had long withdrawn from the fighting. The spires of rock at the pinnacle reached into the sky like fingers. Night had come, and the flickering light of the braziers cast long shadows across the stone. At last, the rain had lessened. Now that the battle was nearly over, he felt the chill enter his bones. His clothes were sodden. His armour and weapons needed cleaning.

That could wait. It was all he could do to keep standing.

Morgart came up to him. Like all of them, the commander looked drained.

'Andreas,' he said. Grunwald nodded in acknowledgement. 'A fine victory.'

Grunwald felt hollow. There were victories he had enjoyed, too many to remember. This was not one of them. His task had been to guard the road, to enable the Reiksguard to ride to the Cauldron unimpeded. He had failed, been driven from his position. Being rescued, even by the Emperor's Champion himself, was a bitter potion to swallow.

'How goes the battle?' he asked.

'Helborg's broken them,' said Morgart. 'The bodies of the beasts lie two-deep across the Cauldron. They'll take years to recover from this.'

'Schwarzhelm killed the doombull,' said Grunwald. 'That was the turning point. I was there.'

Morgart laughed.

'This isn't a competition, Grunwald.' Then his face darkened, as if humour so soon was inappropriate. 'The day's been barely won. We'll return with fewer than half the men we brought. The halberdiers have suffered most. Just be content that we didn't all die here.'

Grunwald suddenly thought of Ackermann. The man's

body would never be found now, never be buried. He deserved better.

'Believe me, I'm content,' he lied.

There was a commotion on the terrace below. Men were moving up to the pinnacle. Gruppen was among them, leading a squadron of battle-ravaged Knights Panther. There were less then twenty of them with him. Grunwald also recognised Tierhof and other commanders. This was a general's retinue. But there was no general to lead them.

The captains strode into the light of the braziers. Noble faces all, streaked with blood and mud. Their fine armour was dented and scored. Some had looks of triumph on their faces, others blank weariness. Their labours were over for the night, and now they came to confer on the clear-up.

Then a new group arrived. Their armour was battle-scarred, but nothing like that of the Knights Panther. They wore no pelts or other elaborate garb. Their plate armour was simple and effective. Their colours were black, red and white. That livery was known all across the Empire. Reiksguard.

They strutted with the supreme confidence of the Emperor's elite. Unlike Schwarzhelm's forces, who had been fighting for hours without respite, they looked fresh. Grunwald could see Morgart and the others try to make themselves look more respectable. He rolled his eyes.

Then their commander arrived. All knew who he was. His face was the third most recognisable in the whole Empire, after that of Sigmar and Karl Franz himself. Miniatures of his profile adorned the lockets of maidens, and were painted into tavern signs across the provinces. Songs were sung about him by all loyal troops, most of whom would have given their own daughters away just to serve under him. To utter his name was to invoke the saviour of the Empire, the hero of mankind, the master of the Emperor's numberless armies. Loyal wives would forget their vows the moment he rode into town, and their husbands would forgive them for it.

He was Kurt Helborg, Kreigsmeister, Hammer of Chaos, Grand Marshal of the Reiksguard. Unlike Schwarzhelm, he cut an elegant figure. His armour shone brightly, glinting in the flames. Despite his ride through the heart of the beast-man horde, it seemed like he'd barely suffered a scratch. His equipment was pristine. Even his famed moustache, carefully oiled and stiffened, was immaculate. He could have walked straight from one of the Empress's balls and he would not have looked out of place.

But this was no court dandy or effete noble. Helborg's name was spoken of with reverence by all fighting men. Though they respected Schwarzhelm, they knew little of him. Helborg's deeds, by contrast, were the stuff of legend. So much so, that he carried not the weapon of a mere general, but the blade of an elector. The Solland runefang, one the ancient twelve. It had many names, across many realms. In the annals of Altdorf it was known as Grollhalter, the Grudgebearer. Others called it the Lightshard, or Helbringer, or Warpsbane. Helborg himself only used one title for it. Klingerach. The Sword of Vengeance. Thus was it whispered of across the homesteads and households of the Empire. When all seemed bleakest, it was Helborg and Klingerach the common folk prayed to see.

As the Marshal approached, the knights and commanders fell silent. Helborg strode into the centre of the gathered men.

'Where is General Schwarzhelm?' he asked. His voice was as weathered as the granite of the bastion.

No one knew. Seeing the indecision around him, Grunwald came forward. He was as senior a commander as any of the others.

'He fights still, my lord,' he said, bowing deferentially. Helborg turned to face him. His glance was piercing, unforgiving.

'The day is won,' said Helborg. 'What fighting is there to do?'

Grunwald hesitated. Making excuses for his master was a dangerous game. Schwarzhelm spoke for himself. He felt caught between two titans.

'While beasts remain alive, there remains fighting to do,' came a deep voice from the shadows.

Schwarzhelm emerged from the gloom beyond the brazier light. He looked terrifying. His armour dripped with dark blood and his heavy beard was caked in gore. His blade was smeared with it. It looked as though he'd waded through a well of entrails. Even Helborg seemed taken aback.

Schwarzhelm approached him, leaving his blade unsheathed. As he came, he tore his helmet from his head. His expression was hard to read in the dark. Grunwald had witnessed his savage departure after the death of Raghram. He looked scarcely less angry now.

Awkwardly, the two men embraced. That was as it should be. Brother warriors, congratulating one another after a crushing victory. But all present could see the stilted movements, the grudging hand clasp. Schwarzhelm still smouldered with resentment, and the fire would not be put out easily.

'This is your victory, Ludwig,' said Helborg. None but he could have used Schwarzhelm's given name.

'That it is,' snapped Schwarzhelm, and turned away. None but he could have shown his back to the Marshal. Grunwald looked at Tierhof, who looked at Morgart. None knew what to do. Even Gruppen seemed uncertain.

Then, from far below, a trumpet sounded. Three notes, long and mournful. The signal for the end of the battle. The last of the beasts had been killed or driven into the trees. That seemed to break the spell.

Helborg's granite face broke into an unconvincing smile.

'Yours will be the honour, my friend,' he said, addressing Schwarzhelm's viscera-smeared shoulders. 'You may count on it.'

'It'd better be,' muttered the Emperor's Champion, as he stalked back off into the dark.

Dawn broke cold and cheerless. The watery sun crested the eastern horizon, but did little to banish the heavy, low cloud. Though the worst of the rain had passed, the air was still chill. With the destruction of the beasts, the combined forces of Schwarzhelm and Helborg had camped as well as they could on the rock of the bastion. Out of a combined force of more than seven thousand, fewer than three thousand remained. The heaviest casualties had been amongst those who had manned the pitiless walls of rock. Despite the cold, the surviving troops had slept as heavily as the dead. Grunwald himself had drifted into unconsciousness as soon as his head had hit the gravel of the terrace. When he awoke, the sunrise was long gone and preparations for the march home were already far advanced. The amalgamated forces would head back to Altdorf and report the utter destruction of the latest beastman uprising. They would say it had been shattered between the hammer of Helborg and the anvil of Schwarzhelm. They would say nothing of the botched preparations that had left half the army fighting on its own for the best part of a day, nor how many lives that had cost.

Rubbing his eyes, Grunwald sat bolt upright. He could have happily slept for hours more, but he should have woken earlier. There were things to do, things to organise.

He struggled to his feet and looked around. Across the wide bowl of the Cauldron, bodies lay in heaps. Some were those of men, most those of the beasts. Already vultures were circling above. The stench was ripening. As the day waxed, it would only grow. Even now, he thought he could make out figures picking their way among the cadavers, looking for something they could use. There was a woman, young and slim with short dark hair, merely yards away from him down on the floor of the Cauldron. She was oblivious to his presence. He was too tired to be angry. Too tired for anything.

Grunwald shook his head to clear it. He was still groggy. His clothes clung to his limbs, cold and deadening.

'Good morning, Herr Grunwald,' came a familiar voice.

Andreas turned to face Pieter Verstohlen.

'Counsellor,' he replied, and there was warmth in his greeting.

Verstohlen came over to him, and the two men embraced.

'I'm told I have you to thank for my life,' said Grunwald.

Verstohlen shrugged.

'I had some small part in it. Schwarzhelm can be persuaded, if you know the right means. But there was a halberdier captain out there too, a man named Bloch. If you owe anyone thanks, it is he.'

'Aye, I know him. Did he make it back to the bastion?'

'I was fighting with him before the doombull arrived. If he's alive, then the general will seek him out. Battle may be the making of a man. Bloch has advanced his reputation.'

Grunwald felt a sudden pang of shame.

'Where I failed,' he said, almost to himself.

Verstohlen frowned.

'In what way? You held the ridge for as long as anyone could have asked. It was foolish of the commanders not to send relief earlier, and I told them so. There's no whispering against you, Andreas.'

Grunwald found scant consolation in those words. He knew that he'd held out for as long as he could. Any longer and his entire command would have perished. But Schwarzhelm was a harsh taskmaster. He'd been ordered to keep the road clear. He had failed. Helborg had made it through at last, but how much sooner would he have arrived if the ridge hadn't fallen to the beasts?

'I worry not about whispering,' he said. 'The verdict of my peers means nothing. But Schwarzhelm... He doesn't forgive easily.'

'He doesn't forgive at all,' said Verstohlen, grimly. 'But there's nothing to berate yourself for. The field has been won. The beasts are scattered. Trust me, Grunwald. We will ride out with Schwarzhelm again, just as we always have done. You've won his trust a hundred times before. He'll remember that.'

Grunwald looked away, back over the grim vista of the Cauldron. Columns of men were picking their way across the stone, stripping weapons from the fallen. There was heavy labour ahead. Swords were precious, and would be recovered for the Emperor's armouries. The beastmen would be left to rot where they fell. This place would be a scene of carnage for months, even when the last of the bones had been picked clean.

'So you say,' he muttered. 'So you say.'

Clearing the battlefield took many hours. Troops, still wearing the armour they'd fought in, were ordered out onto the Cauldron to retrieve items of value and prepare the bodies of the slain for their mass immolation. The work was grim. Amidst the heaps of twisted, bestial enemies, every so often a trooper would discover the face of a man he knew, cold and staring. For them, victory had come too late.

As the lines of men gradually picked their way across the battlefield, others piled wood high for the pyres. There would be two of them. No beastmen would share the same honoured burning as the human dead. Priests chanted over both sites. Prayers of benediction and thanks were offered up over the pyre reserved for the honoured slain. Litanies of exorcism and damnation were chanted over the beastmen's pile. As the morning wore on, the kindling was ignited and pale flames leapt up into the air. One by one, arduously and with much effort, bodies were dragged to the pyres and thrown on the wood. Gradually, the noisome stench of crackling flesh began to mask that of the putrefying cadavers. Two columns of smoke, each black and heavy, rolled up into the grey air.

Restored to his vantage point on the pinnacle of the bastion, Schwarzhelm watched the grisly task unfold. With the cessation of combat, he had withdrawn to his general's position. His armour had been wiped clean of blood and his sword shone again unsullied. His mood, however, remained dark. The Reiksguard had retreated to a position down in the Cauldron on Helborg's orders. Despite the scale of the task, the two men avoided one another. Schwarzhelm's own commanders, sensing his anger, mostly busied themselves with their own tasks. Only Gruppen, driven by necessity, had dared to disturb his isolation. Now even he was gone, organising the Knights Panther for their ride to Altdorf.

Schwarzhelm stood alone, lost in thought. Why did

Helborg rile him so? Was it fatigue? Or something more deep-seated? The ways of war were fickle. There could have been a thousand reasons why the Reiksguard had been held up. Their route had been blocked by beasts, despite his best efforts. But had the Marshal ridden with all the haste he could muster? It had happened so often, this last-minute charge to save the day. Surely the man didn't deliberately plan these charges, just in the nick of time, to bolster his reputation. And yet...

'My lord,' came a nervous voice from his shoulder.

Ferren, his aide-de-camp, was there. His face was pale with fear.

'Yes?'

'The man you were seeking. Bloch. He's been found.'

That was good news. Schwarzhelm felt the worst of his mood begin to lift. He could worry about Helborg later. He had his own men to worry about first.

'Show him to me.'

Ferren withdrew, and Bloch took his place. The man looked unprepossessing. He was short in stature. Fat, even. His features were crude. A squat nose, crooked from repeated breaks, sat in the middle of a peasant's face. The brow was low, the mouth tight. He had the look of a tavern brawler, a common thief. And yet, as Schwarzhelm knew from his own experience, a man's worth was only measured in his deeds, not breeding. Without Bloch's intervention, he would have lost Grunwald, one of his most trusted allies. That alone made up for any roughness around the edges.

'Herr Bloch,' he said, trying to keep the habitual gruffness out of his voice. 'Do you know why I wished to see you?'

The man looked unsteady on his feet. He'd been wounded several times and there was a patch of dried blood on the jerkin over his shoulder. To his credit, he kept his posture as best he could and his eyes were level. Not every man could meet his gaze.

'No, sir.'

Schwarzhelm was used to being address as 'my lord'. It

was a proper title for his rank and station. No doubt Bloch was unaware of this. He liked that. The man was a warrior, not an official.

'The commander of the southern flank was forced to withdraw. Your actions saved his life and that of many of his men. I would have arrived too late. That was a brave thing you did, captain.'

Bloch looked uneasy. Like many of his kind, he could cope with insults, threats and banter. It was compliments that really threw him off guard.

'Ah, thank you, sir,' he stammered, clearly unsure how to react.

'How long have you been in the Emperor's service?'

This was easier to cope with.

'Ten years, sir. Joined as a lad in the militia. Accepted into the state halberdiers when I turned twenty. Promoted to captain last year when Erhardt was killed at Kreisberg.'

Schwarzhelm nodded with approval.

'Good. You've learned your trade the way I did.'

Schwarzhelm studied the man as he spoke, gauging his character from the way he carried himself, the way he responded, the almost imperceptible inflections that indicated a fighting temperament. It was similar to the way a trainer might select a horse.

'There is much wrong in the way that the Empire runs itself, Bloch,' said Schwarzhelm, permitting himself a digression. 'Many who rule do not deserve to. Many who are ruled could make a better fist of it. You're a fighting man. You've seen armies commanded by fools and good men led into ruin by them.'

Though he said nothing, Schwarzhelm could see the recognition in Bloch's eyes.

'But there's opportunity in battle. Mettle will always show itself. There are men in the Empire who know how to reward talent and how to ignore low birth. The Emperor, Sigmar keep him, is one. It is to him I owe my station, not to my breeding. And so it is with me. I need good men around me. I'd like you to be one of them.'

Bloch blinked, clearly struggling to take the speech in.

'Yes, sir,' was all he said.

'There are a number of captains I place my trust in. Not many, since only a few deserve it. In my judgement, you may prove worthy. I'm offering you a chance. Leave the employ of Reikland and join my retinue. The pay's no better, and you'll be campaigning more than you've ever done before. But there's glory in it, and service. Many men would leap to serve me. Others would leap to avoid it. Which of those are you, Herr Bloch?'

The man didn't hesitate.

'I'll serve you,' he said.

Schwarzhelm narrowed his eyes.

'Be careful,' he said, warningly. 'This offer will only come once. Danger follows me. I'll not think less of you if you refuse. A life in the state halberdiers is an honourable one, and you'll stand a better chance of seeing your children grow up.'

To his credit, Bloch didn't flinch. His assurance seemed to be growing. A good sign.

'With your pardon, sir, I've never been one for changing my mind. I know a chance when I see one. I'll fight with you, and you'll not find a better captain in the Emperor's armies.' Then he looked worried, like he'd overreached himself. 'And I'm grateful for the chance. Really grateful.'

Schwarzhelm kept his gaze firmly on him. Nothing he saw contradicted his initial assessment. Here was a leader of the future.

'Very good,' he said. 'For now, remain with your company. They've fought hard, and you should reward them. When we're back in Altdorf and your hangover has cleared, report to Ferren. He'll sort out the papers of commission. Then you'll report to me.'

Schwarzhelm didn't smile. He never smiled. But something close to a humorous light played in his eyes.

'I like you, Bloch,' he said. 'I wonder if you know what you've committed yourself to? Never mind. We'll see soon enough. Return to your men and prepare for the journey home.'

Bloch, his uncertain confidence looking a little dented, bowed awkwardly and limped away. From some distance away, Schwarzhelm heard Ferren begin to confer with him. He ignored the noise of their conversation, and turned to face the Cauldron. For the moment, his brooding on Helborg had lifted.

Out on the plain, the columns of smoke rose ever higher. Another victory. The army would decamp before nightfall. And then it would start over again. The endless test, the endless struggle. Only now, in these brief moments, could any satisfaction be taken. He crossed his arms over his burly chest. The head of Raghram had been stuck on a spike near the summit of the bastion. It would be taken to Altdorf and presented to Karl Franz. And that would be an end to it.

For now.

By late afternoon, the fires began to go out. Huge piles of charred flesh lay strewn across the Cauldron. While the army remained on the bastion, the vultures steered clear of the smouldering carrion. But not all of the bodies could be retrieved and they knew that rich pickings remained. As soon as they left, the birds would descend. They would feast on the beasts only when the juicier remnants of the men were scraped clean. They knew the difference between wholesome flesh and the warp-twisted fodder of the deep forest.

Gradually, as the worst of the carnage was cleared away, the army began descending from the bastion to start the march from the Cauldron to the forest road. As they went, the state troopers glanced at the distant trees darkly. None of them relished the journey back under the close eaves of the forest. Only the foolish among them believed the beastman menace to have been extinguished. It had only been deferred. Perhaps a year, maybe two, and then they would mass again. Who knew how they replenished themselves? There were bawdy stories of mass ruttings in the shadowy heart of the woods, driven by crude ale and bestial fervour. All knew the tales of witches heading out into the darkness on the festival days of the Dark Gods, prepared for unspeakable rites. And then there were the children, the ones touched by the Ruinous Powers. When they were left in isolated clearings to die, who knew what happened to them? Did they find refuge amongst the twisted beasts, ever ready to fan the flames of their hate towards the unsullied scions of humanity? If so, it was a dark secret to hide, and one the mean folk of the Empire would never admit to.

The Knights Panther were the first to ride out, with Gruppen at their head. They had restored their armour as best they could and went ahead to clear the road home of any residual beastmen. Behind them marched the ranks of halberdiers, archers and other state troopers. Every company was depleted. Some were leaderless and attached themselves forlornly to other companies. Some of the regiments had lost their standards in the fighting, and their shame hung heavy over them. Only a few carried themselves proudly. The fighting had been too bitter to take much satisfaction from. All the men cared about was getting back to the city in one piece. Their payment would stand for a few beers in a tavern and a night at the whorehouse. That would be enough for them to forget the horror, however briefly.

Verstohlen watched them silently as they passed. It seemed a poor reward for all their heroism. And yet what else would they want? Would a king's ransom really make them happy? They would just drink it away all the same. They were the Emperor's fodder, nothing more, nothing less, and all knew it.

He sighed and turned away from the sight. Such thoughts depressed him. He wondered, not for the first time, what he was doing amongst them. Better, perhaps, to have stayed in the more genteel world of lore and study. But he had made his choice, and the reasons for it hadn't changed. Every man had his fate mapped by the gods, and he knew what his was.

He began to pack his belongings away in his slim leather

bag. The pistols were safely cleaned and holstered, his blade sheathed.

'Verstohlen!' came a familiar voice. It was Bloch. The man strolled up to him, looking like he'd inherited the fortune of Araby, and then drunk it. 'It looks like you have some use after all. Get used to having me around. The big man's promoted me!'

Verstohlen feigned surprise.

'That's truly impressive, Herr Bloch. My congratulations to you. It makes me feel a little better for having drawn you into Grunwald's rescue.'

Bloch grinned. He must have found some ale from somewhere.

'I won't forget it,' he warned. 'Next time we're in a tight spot, I'll call in the favour. You keep your wits about you, Verstohlen!'

Then he was off, walking unsteadily down the bastion. He, at least, had found something worth celebrating.

'Enjoy it while you may, my friend,' whispered Verstohlen to himself.

Then he pulled his coat about him, slung his bag over his shoulder and made his way down the slopes of the bastion, back into the Cauldron, ready to start the journey home.

CHAPTER FOUR

Altdorf. Greatest city of the Old World.

Marienburg may have been larger, Nuln older, Middenheim more warlike, Talabheim stronger. But none of those pretenders could compete for sheer exuberance and unruly majesty with the home of the Emperor Karl Franz. At the mighty confluence of the Talabec and the Reik, where the pure waters running down from Averland mixed with the silt-laden torrents from the heart of the Drakwald, the spires, towers and crenulated bridges all jostled for space. Ships rubbed up against each other in the crowded harbours, rocking gently on the grey, filmy waters. Vast warehouses stood on the quaysides, rammed with goods both legal and contraband. Tenements crowded next to one another along the twisting alleyways and stairwells. Like the long-forgotten forest that had once stood on the ancient site, the buildings competed with each other for the light, strangling and throttling one another as they strained ever upwards.

The lower levels had been left behind by the race towards the sun. They were now half-drowned in bilge and the haunt of none but brigands, cut-throats or worse. And yet somehow, amidst all the violence and squalor, buildings of an awesome grandeur and vision had been raised on such foundations. The Colleges of Magic, varied and inscrutable, towered over the streets around them. The Imperial University, unwittingly built on the site of human sacrifices in the pagan days before Sigmar, stood proud and austere in the bright sunlight. Huge garrisons broke the skyline, each stuffed with arms and the men to wield them. Slaughterhouses, temples, marketplaces, mausoleums, scriptoria, merchants' apartments, monasteries, brothels, cattle pens, counting-houses, all ran up against one another. Like a priest caught in bed with a prostitute, the high and noble rubbed shoulders – sometimes more than shoulders – with the filth and desperation of the gutter.

The narrow towers rose high over the lapping waters of the Reik. Chimneys belched out steady columns of muddy brown filth, staining the whitewashed walls a dirty flesh colour. Yet none of these buildings was more than a footnote to the mightiest of them all. The sprawling, ancient, ever-changing, ever-evolving Imperial Palace stood in the very heart of the city. Like the city it dominated, the palace was an architectural mess. Gothic arches of dark stone rubbed up against graceful elven-inspired gardens. Huge fortifications, some semi-ruined, were piled up against flimsy wattle and daub outhouses. Immaculate baroque halls of gold and copper were placed right next to boiling ceremonial kitchens, stinking with cooking fumes and slopping with goosefat.

No single man knew the full extent of the Imperial Palace. It descended into the bowels of the earth for nearly as far as its squat towers rose above the city. Many rooms within it had been left to fall into ruin, or were flooded, or had been locked in ages past to keep some terrible secret from the hands of the unwary. Few ventured into those uncharted areas at night unless driven by some awful need. There were strange things buried in the deep places, accumulations of generations of Emperors and their servants. When the candle-flames went out, not all the shadows were natural.

Even in the normally habitable regions, officials guarded their little kingdoms with obsessive jealousy. Vicious feuds, some stretching back across many lives of men, dominated the corridors of power. Behind the artful politesse and diplomacy, access to the Emperor and his court was ruthlessly sought. When it was secured, it was clung on to. The entire place was a microcosm of the world outside, complete with its civil wars, power struggles, dynastic manoeuvrings and applications of subtle poison in the dark.

And yet, somehow, out of all this ceaseless intrigue and politicking, the business of the Empire was conducted. From the gilded salons and audience chambers, orders were given. Inscriptions were made on parchment and vellum, and scribes passed them to officials and commanders. Though no one could track the paths these orders took, far less trace them back to their author, laws were made and decisions were taken. Trade agreements were entered into, appointments were made and broken, lands were granted and taken away. Most importantly, the armies of the Empire were deployed. From the stroke of a quill deep in the candlelit study of some grey-skinned scribe, a thousand men on the other side of the Empire could find themselves sent on campaign, or disbanded, or ordered back to barracks. Thus, imperfectly and with many detours, was the will of Karl Franz enacted across his domains.

So it was that weeks after the victory at the Turgitz Cauldron, a homecoming parade was ordered in honour of the Emperor's Champion. Gold was procured for the event by means both legal and dubious. Hundreds of officials left their regular tasks to bend all their attention to it. Times were harder than usual across the Empire. Ceaseless war had taken its toll and the people were weary. When a great victory came, it needed to be celebrated. For no more than a moment, the impoverished masses would believe that all their troubles were over. For as long as the procession lasted and the ale flowed, they would think humanity the undisputed master of the world, and their leaders the wisest and most benevolent of men.

In any case, all those dwelling in Altdorf knew that
Schwarzhelm was no ordinary general. He had the Emperor's
favour more than any other (with the possible exception of his
great rival), so the officials took especial pains to make sure all
passed off as it should do. Less money than usual ended up
disappearing between the coffers and the merchants' guilds,
and habitually slovenly workers found new reserves of diligence and attention to detail. Whole streets were cleared of
their usual clutter. Market stalls were swept away, mounds of
refuse dumped in the river, and fragrant oil-burners placed
over the most noxious open sewers. Most impressively of all,
the mighty thoroughfare leading from the Wilhelm III garrison to the grand gates of the palace was cleared. When the
great flags were scraped clean of filth, men were amazed to
discover that some of the graffiti still marking the stone dated
back hundreds of years. Some less than flattering references
to the Imperial ruling family and their proclivities were hastily scrubbed clean, though not before copies had been taken
and circulated around the shabbier sort of tavern.

After many weeks of frenzied preparation, the great day
finally dawned. Workers were given the day off by their
employers and the streets filled with cheering crowds. Perhaps half of them had no idea why they were there. All they
knew was that the drink was plentiful and the militia didn't
seem to mind. Many others knew exactly what they were witnessing. The Great Schwarzhelm. Children were shoved by
their parents to the front of the teeming crowds. Normally
placid men pushed and gouged their way to get a better
view. A rumour went round that if he touched you then all
illnesses would be banished. As the result the front ranks
were dominated, aside from bewildered infants, by the lep-
rous, the feverish and the consumptive.

When the procession came, it was no disappointment.
Units of Reiksguard, resplendent in glittering armour, headed
the cavalcade. That was no accident. Should any of the enthusiastic crowd get too carried away then the stern glances from
the knights quickly restored some sense of order.

Behind them, ranks of soldiers marched in full regalia. Most had never been so finely kitted out and were determined to make the most of it. The younger men's chins were laced with cuts where their shaving had been too vigorous, and the older ones had their facial hair arranged into ever more outlandish configurations. Each infantryman was cheered wildly by the crowd, even those who had no idea what they were celebrating. Flowers were strewn at their feet and kisses blown from maidens leaning from balconies. It didn't matter that the flowers were half-rotten from storage and that the 'maidens' generally charged half a schilling for their time. It was appearances that mattered.

When the commanders emerged, the cheering became even louder. Moving steadily up the causeway in full ceremonial armour, mounted on fine warhorses, Schwarzhelm's retinue rode stiltedly between the baying mob. None of them looked comfortable. Leonidas Gruppen, accustomed by noble birth to feigned adulation from his subjects, was the most at ease. He wore his full battle armour minus the helmet, and raised his gauntlet now and again to acknowledge the shrieks all around. Andreas Grunwald was far less assured and picked nervously at his collar. Fighting beasts was one thing. Facing the full unleashed force of Altdorf's citizenry was another. His companions looked equally unsure what to do. They went as quickly as they could, nudging their steeds impatiently, desperate to get the whole grotesque charade over with.

Finally, carried aloft on a ridiculous open carriage decorated with stucco images of Karl Franz vanquishing various breeds of monster, came the star attraction. Ludwig Schwarzhelm, Slayer of Raghram, Emperor's Champion and dispenser of Imperial justice, had somehow been persuaded to wear armour made of what looked like pure ithilmar. It probably wasn't any such thing, but it blazed in the sun nonetheless. The only thing fiercer than the sheen of the fake silver was Schwarzhelm's scowl. If he hadn't owed his allegiance to Karl Franz above all others, he would never have allowed such a farrago to take place. As it was, his loyalty had barely survived the test, and he suffered the foolishness in silence.

Ahead of him, the severed head of Raghram was carried aloft on a long pole. As it passed, it was pelted with missiles from the crowd. Some thought it nothing more than a bull's head, placed there for no better reason than to provide some sport for them. Others, more accustomed to the life of the forest beyond the city walls, recognised it for what it was and gaped in renewed awe at Schwarzhelm as he passed them. A doombull was a mighty prize.

So it was that, slowly and with as much pomp as the Imperial bureaucracy could muster, the victory parade made its way from the lower quarters of the city to the gates of the palace itself. When the various dignitaries had passed through the massive bronze-inlaid doors, mighty wheels within the stone walls were turned. The gates closed with a clang. Dried flower petals showered down from murder holes above the gatehouse and a flock of baffled doves lurched into the air. The crowd surged forward, eager for more. At the edges of the mob, scuffles broke out. Some thought that was the end of their entertainment.

Sadly for the military commanders, the ordeal was not yet over. Above the mighty gates was a stone portico. Carved out of the heavy facade was a wide balcony, supported by flamboyant gargoyles with the wings of griffons and lined with a balustrade of fluted sandstone. One by one, the members of Schwarzhelm's retinue emerged on to the space to receive the adulation of the crowd. There they stood, gazing with a mix of embarrassment and contempt at the raucous mob beneath them. The horde cared nothing for that. Most were too far gone with ale to reliably recognise their own children, let alone the disdainful expressions on the face of each Imperial commander.

Just as the beasts had done at the Cauldron, a chanting began to take over. The people wanted to see their hero.

'Schwarzhelm!' came the cry, over and over again.

Eventually, with a face like thunder, he answered their call.

Still dressed in his blazing silver armour, Schwarzhelm strode onto the balcony. The horde of people below broke into wild cheers. The flowers, by now broken and foetid, were hurled up to the railing, where they showered back on to the people directly below. Schwarzhelm gazed over the scene impassively. Had any of the people been close enough to see his face, they would have recoiled at his studied look of distaste.

For a few moments longer the party on the balcony acknowledged the applause of the crowd. Eventually, clearly anxious to escape, they made to leave. But there was a final surprise. A new figure joined them, also clad in a suit of improbably polished armour. Immediately, the mob below changed their chant.

'Helborg!' came the cry. Men and women alike surged forward, desperate for a glimpse of the hero of the Empire. The Grand Marshal was happy to oblige, and raised a gauntlet in salute. That sent them even wilder. The press at the gates began to become acute. The Reiksguard captain stationed on the walls discreetly gave the signal to begin the dispersal. Troops began to emerge from the side streets, some very heavily armed. The commanders began to shuffle from the balcony. From a distance, all looked as it should be. The glorious heroes of the Empire, arrayed together for all to see their splendour. An observer would have had to have been very close by indeed to witness the frosty look that passed between Schwarzhelm and his great contemporary as they left the balcony to enter the palace.

But then they were gone, and the doors closed for good. The militia commanders ordered their troops steadily into the thoroughfare, making sure their weapons were raised and visible. All but the most beer-addled celebrants took the hint. The last of the petals drifted down from the murder holes, and the Reiksguard took guard in front of the closed gates. The party was over.

'Morr damn this nonsense!' spat Schwarzhelm, feeling his temper fray at the edges. The Emperor Karl Franz sat back in his heavily upholstered chair and looked with amusement at Schwarzhelm as he struggled out of his armour.

Aside from two manservants helping Schwarzhelm with the heavy plate armour, the two men were alone, cloistered together in one of the Emperor's many private chambers. From the south wall, the warm summer sun streamed through large mullioned windows. Thick embroidered carpets adorned the wooden floors and gaudy portraits of Karl Franz's illustrious ancestors hung from the panelled walls. The Emperor himself looked supremely at ease. He ran a finger around the edge of his gold-rimmed goblet, his dark, acute eyes glistening. He had the harsh features of all the Holswig-Schliestein line. His neck-length hair shone glossily in the filtered light, framing a battle-ravaged, care-lined face. Few of his subjects would ever have seen him thus, clad simply in a burgundy robe and soft leather shoes. A heavy gold medallion hung across his broad chest was the only sign of his high office.

Within the palace, the Emperor had no need for the finery of state. One look from his grey eyes gave away his mastery of the place. This was his lair, his seat, the wellspring of all his immense temporal power. Freed from the endless gaze of his people for a few precious moments, he could be something like himself. He could be amused.

'Don't tell me you didn't enjoy it just a little bit,' Karl Franz said. 'I know you too well, Ludwig. You need the adulation. We all do.'

Schwarzhelm didn't reply, but pulled the last of the frippery from his body. One of the manservants took up the piece reverently and placed it next to the carefully arranged stack of pauldrons, greaves, cuirass, cowter, poleyns and other sundry components of the armoured knight's wardrobe. With the final elements retrieved and wrapped in cloth, the two hunched figures withdrew, closing the ornate doors behind them as they went.

Schwarzhelm pulled on a white robe and flexed his fingers. In the corner of the room, a great clock gently ticked.

It was one of the newest innovations from the College of Engineers, presented to the Emperor in thanks for his long years of patronage. They'd said it had Ironblood workings inside, but they were probably lying about that.

'So. Now you're free of all that, come and have a drink.'

Karl Franz was a genial host. Unlike his guest, he was clean-shaven. His voice was that of a statesman, calm and controlled. A lifetime spent in the higher echelons of the Empire's ruling classes had given him easy manners. And yet the polished facade hid a mind of utter, ruthless determination. If it had not done so, the Empire would have long since succumbed to its many enemies. Karl Franz was the strand of iron that held the fractious realms of men together, and all those close to him knew it well.

Schwarzhelm sat heavily opposite him, traces of his scowl still present. Unlike his master, his social graces were rough. The battlefield was his home, and all other places were unnatural to him. He grasped a goblet from the table beside him and poured a large measure from the decanter.

'I'm sorry you had to go through that,' said the Emperor, letting the last of his amusement drain from his face. 'The people need to see their heroes from time to time. Without that, they lose faith. And faith is everything.'

Schwarzhelm took a long swig.

'I'll leave the politics to you. You know how to keep the crowds happy.'

'Don't scorn that talent. You should trust my judgement.'

'I do. Why else would I go through with it?'

Karl Franz smiled.

'Never have I tested your loyalty more,' he mused. He placed his goblet down on the table next to him. 'But that charade is over now. We need to discuss more serious matters.'

Schwarzhelm let the wine sink down his gullet. Here it came. The next assignment. The scant days of reprieve had passed too quickly.

'I make no apology for publicly celebrating your victory at Turgitz,' said Karl Franz. 'The beasts will be back, that we know. But not for a while, and that frees up resources for other things.'

He looked directly at Schwarzhelm.

'My mind has turned to healing old wounds,' he said. 'One in particular. Ludwig, we need to do something about Averland.'

So that was it.

'Averland. Why now?'

'Why not?'

Karl Franz leaned forward in his seat. His eyes sparkled. It was the only outward sign he ever gave of excitement.

'We may never get a better chance. For the moment, our northern borders are free from threat. Though I will not say the war is over, it has abated for a season. There are matters left hanging, threads to be tidied away. Leitdorf's seat is empty. A province must not be left without a master.'

'Maybe so, but that's not in our gift to alter.'

'You disappoint me. How long have I known you? Have you learned nothing of the arts of state?'

Schwarzhelm said nothing. Even a gentle rebuke from the Emperor felt like a stain on his honour. That was his peculiar gift. He didn't inspire loyalty. He inspired *devotion*.

'I recall when you were a young man,' continued the Emperor, picking up his wine again and rolling the liquid around in the crystal. 'Leitdorf was still alive, but even then his mind was disarranged. He couldn't be left to run things alone. You had no qualms about imposing the Imperial writ then.'

'That was different.'

'Not really,' said Karl Franz.

'We can't interfere with the coronation of an elector. It's never been done.'

Karl Franz let slip a sly smile.

'I don't believe you really think that, Ludwig,' he said. 'But hear me out. I have nothing underhand in mind. It's in our interests – in the *Empire's* interests – for Averland to have a strong man at the helm. The situation cannot be left to

fester. There are plenty in that province who have no desire
to see restoration of an electorship, but none of them can
see beyond their own selfish noses. Even now we hear of
greenskins in the passes, remnants of Ironjaw's ravagers. The
integrity of the Empire is at stake. The runefang must be
wielded.'

Schwarzhelm pursed his lips. This sounded like politics
already. He loathed politics. The only word he liked in that
monologue was 'greenskins'. Those, he knew what to do with.

'I'm waiting for you to tell me how I fit into this.'

'You are the dispenser of the Emperor's justice,' replied
Karl Franz. There was the faintest trace of irritation in his
voice. 'You carry the sword. Just as you did twenty years
ago, I want you to go to Averheim. Oversee the succession
of a new count. They can't be allowed to drag their feet any
longer. Take an army with you. If you have to use force, do
it. The other electors won't like it, but they have their own
worries. I don't care who ends up with the title, as long as
it's legal and as long as it happens soon.'

It was getting worse. Electoral law, the most fiendishly complicated legislation in the Old World. This wasn't just politics.
It was high politics. The kind that men lost their souls over –
or their minds.

'My liege,' began Schwarzhelm, struggling to find the correct form of words, 'are you sure I'm the right person for
this? There are legal scholars in Altdorf, men steeped in...'

He trailed off. The Emperor looked at him with a disappointed expression.

'I have a thousand legal scholars here. Averheim has them
too. Can any of them do what you can? Do any of them
embody my Imperial power? What are you telling me? That
you're *afraid* of this?'

Ludwig felt the burning spark of shame kindle. He knew
what the Emperor was doing. Karl Franz knew how to find a
man's weak spot. He was being tested. Always being tested.
The examination never ended.

'I fear nothing but the law and Sigmar.'

'Then do as I ask.'

'Are you ordering me?'

'Do I need to?'

Schwarzhelm held the Emperor's gaze for a few moments. This was the tipping point. He'd never queried an order. Never even queried a request. But this felt wrong. Some sense deep within him resisted. He could already see a host of possible outcomes, branching away from him like the tributaries of rivers. None were good. He should decline.

'No,' he said, giving in to duty. 'Of course not. I am your servant.'

The Emperor smiled, but the gesture had an edge of ice to it.

'I'm glad you remembered.'

Far from the Imperial Palace and the grandeur of its associated institutions, a special area of elegant housing had been devoted to a single purpose. There had never been an official edict authorising the quarter to be so given over, but over many years a number of quietly influential people had started buying up portions of land and letting them to various other quietly influential people. A complicated series of trusts had been established, and some recalcitrant undesirable tenants had it discreetly but firmly made clear to them that they were no longer welcome in the area. Older structures were demolished, including a rare example of Mandred-era stonework, and handsome townhouses took their place. These were somewhat more desirable than the ramshackle Altdorf norm and were all constructed of solid oak beams and well-laid brick.

Whenever anyone tried to make enquiries as to the legal basis of all this change, they were met by an impenetrable wall of ownership, cross-ownership and counter-ownership. It was surprisingly difficult to discover who owned what and how the money had been unearthed to build such a fine collection of handsome dwellings. Over time, however, it became clear that all of the new inhabitants were peculiarly similar. They were all men, all old and all retired from the highest reaches of the Empire's armies. Unlike the rank and file, who mostly died on the field or sloped back to a life of penury in the villages whence they'd come, these were wealthy men. Generals, regiment commanders, grand masters and master engineers. They had the resources to fund a comfortable retirement and the connections to snare the best of the available property in the city. They could have gone anywhere, but they liked being with their own kind.

As soon as the quarter began to fill up with such types, the rest of Altdorf knew it was pointless to pursue any further legal challenges. The various organised criminal syndicates had nothing on the quiet muscle of this old officers' club. And as the new arrivals were mostly eccentric old codgers with their potent days far behind them, no one minded very much. The area became renowned for a kind of faded, civil gentility. That was a rare thing in Altdorf, and city-dwellers in less enlightened districts would occasionally pay a visit, just for a glance of another, more refined, way of life.

There were many famous old names who'd ended up in the General's Quarter, as it became known. Klaus von Trachelberg, the Butcher of Bohringen, now spent his time constructing bird cages from discarded walking canes. The fiery Boris Schlessing, renowned for his bloody defence of Skargruppen Keep during the incursion of Gnar Limbbreaker, had created a garden made entirely of fabulously expensive Cathayan miniature trees. This he watered every morning, clipping the edges of the tiny branches with a pair of silver scissors while humming tunes from his childhood.

Not all the residents had descended into senility or dotage. Many noble reputations had been preserved in the quarter, and a steady stream of disciples made their way into it from time to time, looking for guidance and inspiration. So famous did it become, that the expression 'to go to the Quarter' entered into common use, meaning to take time to seek some measured opinion from a wiser head.

Schwarzhelm paused before entering the house. It was on

the edge of the Quarter, in sight of the river but far from the worst elements of the quayside. It was modest by the standards of the area, but had a well-kept look about it. The seal of the Emperors hung over the main doorway, carved in granite. Schwarzhelm stared at it for a moment. He'd fought under that seal for nearly thirty years. He knew every line of its intricate form. The paired griffons rampant, the sable shield, the initials of Karl Franz and the devices of his Reikland forebears. It might as well have been branded on to his chest.

'You can stare at it as long as you like. It won't change.'

The door opened. From inside, the speaker emerged. He was an old man, clad in a simple robe of pale grey. Though stooped with age, he still bore himself proudly. Something in the way he carried himself, the fearless manner in which he looked up at Schwarzhelm, gave his old profession away.

'Master,' said Schwarzhelm, simply.

'I suppose you want to come in?'

The Emperor's Champion nodded like a callow youth.

'Do you have time?'

'Of course. For you, always. Mind the mess as you enter, though. I've been brewing, and there are hops all across the scullery floor.'

Ducking his mighty head under the low doorway, Schwarzhelm entered the house of Heinrich Lassus, and the door closed behind him.

The two men sat in the old general's drawing room. It was cluttered, filled with the residue of a long career in the saddle. Two wolfhounds slumbered in front of the empty fireplace. They hadn't raised an eyebrow at Schwarzhelm's entrance. They were old dogs, and his smell was familiar enough. Like their master, they'd seen better days.

A row of battle-honours hung over the imposing marble mantel-piece. Some were old indeed, long superseded by more modern tributes. Few scholars would have recognised Wilifred's Iron Hammer for anything other than a pleasing trinket, though most would have realised the importance of

Lassus's papers of commission, now placed behind glass to preserve the cracking vellum. Even the illiterate would have recognised the florid initials of the Emperor and the Imperial crest stamped in faded red.

The greatest honour of all, though, was not on display on the walls. Schwarzhelm saw that Lassus still wore it himself. He was a humble man, but some gifts were beyond price and all soldiers had their weaknesses. As he always did, Lassus had the Star of Sigmar pinned to his robes, just above his heart. The greatest military honour in the Empire. As his chest moved, the iron comet emblem rose and fell with the fabric.

'So it's Averland,' he said.

Lassus's eyes drifted out of focus. His white hair looked almost transparent and his fingers shook a little as he cradled them in his lap. The proud features which had once inspired such devotion and terror had softened with the years. Schwarzhelm thought his skin looked more fragile than it had done the last time he'd called. When had that been? A year ago? More? The demands of the field were endless. For every night he spent in his bed in Altdorf, he'd lived through a week on campaign. He felt stretched. Drained. One day, something would break. He'd prove unworthy of the blade he carried. One day.

'It had to come at some point, I suppose.' Lassus's gaze returned to focus. Old he may have been, but his mind was still working fast, teasing out the possibilities.

'I can't see the wisdom of it,' said Schwarzhelm, sullenly. Ever since his audience with the Emperor, his mood had been sluggish. There was something about the task ahead that chilled him, something indefinable. Facing doombulls was something he could cope with, even take a kind of enjoyment in. War was what he was built for. Politics was for lesser men.

Lassus smiled tolerantly.

'You're going to lecture Karl Franz on statecraft now, Ludwig?' The old man looked at him fondly. 'You haven't changed. Not since you walked into my training ground for the first time. Even then, I knew you were something special. But you've always doubted yourself. You've never shaken that off. Your one weakness.'

From another man, those words would have invited swift retribution. Schwarzhelm's reputation was fearsome. On the battlefield, he was the very image of implacable, terrible resolve. To have that quality questioned was verging on heresy. And yet, Lassus remained free to ruminate unmolested. That was the honour given to the teacher. Even now, Lassus was the master and Schwarzhelm the pupil.

'He's sent me on many such missions in the past,' muttered Schwarzhelm. 'Never have I even given the faintest hint of reluctance. But something about this turns my stomach. Averland has always been...'

'Your home,' interrupted Lassus. 'You have the blood of the Siggurd in your veins, my boy, though you've probably forgotten it. The Emperor isn't stupid. He needs someone who understands the ways of your strange province. That's why he sent you to stamp down on Leitdorf before, and it's why you're the only one to do it now.'

Schwarzhelm listened to the words, but they brought him no comfort. Was comfort what he'd expected? That was for babes and women. He needed wisdom, even if it proved hard to hear.

'So what would you do?'

Lassus laughed. The sound was dry in the man's leathery throat.

'If I were young enough to still do my service? I'd go. You have no choice. But be careful. You've just been given a triumphal procession. Few men are afforded such an honour. That makes you enemies amongst the many who will never see such nonsense delivered in their name. Those whom the gods wish to destroy they first give a triumph. There may be those who will use this situation to harm you.'

'Let them try,' growled Schwarzhelm.

'I did not say: be defiant. I said: be careful. This manoeuvring is not your strength, my lad. You can fight your way out of almost anything where a sword is called for. But there are other ways of harming a man. Subtle ways. And there are plenty in Altdorf who would like to wield the Rechtstahl in your place.'

Schwarzhelm felt his sullen mood return. Lassus had never been one to tell him what he wanted to hear. That was why he'd been the greatest fightmaster in the Reikland and before that one of her greatest generals. It was why he had been given the Star, and why he still wore it. No lesser man would have been able to tame the young Schwarzhelm, full of anger and dreams of conquest. And even then, the youthful Ludwig had given Lassus a hard time. Like an unbroken Averland colt, he'd been hard to teach without a fight. Hard, but not impossible.

'I don't say this to dishearten you,' the old man continued. 'The first step in avoiding a plot is to know it's there. The world is changing. The Emperor knows it. New powers are rising. So he tests all his servants. You must prove yourself again, and this is the exam.'

Schwarzhelm remained silent, pondering the words as Lassus spoke them.

'And of course, he's right about Averland. If the war hadn't come, something would have been done earlier. It can't go on, this uncertainty. A few merchants will get fat off it, and the luck of Ranald to them, but all good things come to an end.'

Schwarzhelm stirred himself. It was clear that there was no escape from the onerous task. He had to take what wisdom he could from the old man.

'It's been too long since I was in Averheim,' Schwarzhelm said. 'Much has changed in twenty years. My agent Verstohlen has some contacts there, and he's doing work on my behalf, but what would your judgement be? Where is the balance of power?'

Lassus looked pleased to be asked. No doubt in his retirement, studying the politics of the provinces was a welcome exercise for his subtle mind.

'There are only two men who can take the runefang. Ferenc Alptraum has neither the stomach nor the support to do it, much to the chagrin of his formidable grandmother. The Alptraums would rather poison their own children than see another Leitdorf occupy the elector's chair, so they'll rally behind Grosslich, the pretender. That's a powerful card for him to play. Grosslich's popular with the masses. I hear he's handsome. He's also a bachelor, which holds the promise of a political marriage. That'll bring other noble families to his side, at least those with eligible daughters.'

'Heinz-Mark Grosslich,' said Schwarzhelm, repeating the name of the upstart contender for the vacant electorship. The man had emerged from relative obscurity to challenge for the prize. Where his gold had come from was shrouded in uncertainty. His family had never been particularly influential. The man had done well to carve out his claim. 'Can he do it?'

Lassus shrugged.

'That's your task to determine. The peasants love him. He knows how to play to them. There's not a drop of noble blood in his body, but maybe that's the way things are going. You're no aristocrat yourself, after all.'

Schwarzhelm grunted. He didn't need reminding. 'And Leitdorf?'

'Rufus? He has the weight of tradition on his side. His father may have been mad, but he was an astute old fox in his way. There are many in debt to that man, even now. If the older son, Leopold, hadn't died at Middenheim, maybe this would never have come up. But Rufus is a different breed of thoroughbred. Second sons never expect to inherit the seat. He's spent his youth whoring and gambling, and it shows. I met him once, here in Altdorf. He didn't impress me then, but that was while his father still ruled, and they say he's married since. A woman can change a man, just as surely as a blade can. The Empire's a conservative place. He remains the favourite.'

Schwarzhelm digested the information. It was more or

less the same as Verstohlen had told him. But the spy had named his wife, Natassja Hiess-Leitdorf. Where she'd come from was as opaque as Grosslich's gold. That would have to be looked into. There were many things to be looked into.

'Any others?'

Lassus shook his head.

'With the Alptraums behind Grosslich, there are no other challengers. This is a two-man race. But it won't be simple. There are wheels within wheels. The guilds are still powerful, especially the horsemasters. Some would rather have no elector, some are desperate for one to be appointed. And watch out for the city fathers. Von Tochfel, the steward, is known here at the palace. He's acquired a taste for power, like most men do when they're allowed to sample it. He may find reasons not to stand aside.'

Tochfel was another of Verstohlen's names. As was Achendorfer, the loremaster. There were plenty of power brokers to contend with. Schwarzhelm let slip a long, grating sigh.

'This is not the kind of fight I relish,' he said. 'They say there are greenskins massing in the mountains. I hope they come. Cracking their heads will make this assignment a little less dull.'

Lassus gave him a shrewd look.

'Be careful what you wish for. A wise man does not seek to multiply his problems. The Emperor knows you can wield a warhammer. He's looking for finesse on this occasion. Prove that to him and you need worry about Helborg no longer.'

At Kurt's name, Schwarzhelm felt his heart miss a beat. Was he that transparent?

'Why mention him?'

'Come, now. I mean no dishonour to the Marshal. You two hold the Empire aloft together. But don't try to conceal the rivalry between you. I've watched it unfold for thirty years. All of Altdorf sees you sparring, and that's just how the Emperor likes it. It keeps you both fresh. Helborg would have to be a saint beyond reproach not to wish to see you stumble, just a little. And from what I hear, he's no saint.'

Schwarzhelm scowled. This was too close to the bone.

'I could use your counsel in Averheim,' he said, almost without meaning to.

'Don't be stupid.' The voice was his old fightmaster's, berating him for sloppiness. Schwarzhelm could have been right back on the training yards, his wooden sword heavy in his blistered hands. 'I'm too old. I was leading armies out across Ostermark when you were suckling at your mother's breast. This is your time, Ludwig. None is held in higher esteem than you. Get this right and you will leave all your rivals behind. For good. There is nothing more I could do to aid you.'

He fixed Schwarzhelm with that old look, at once savage, at once paternal.

'This is your fate, my boy. Seize it, and magnify the honour due to you.'

Schwarzhelm heard the words, but they gave him little comfort. The dark mood that had plagued him since his meeting with the Emperor was slow to lift. He found himself wishing to change the subject, deflect attention from himself.

'You tell me to seek honour,' he said. 'You never did.'

Lassus looked shocked. Suddenly, Schwarzhelm felt rude and ignorant. That was what he was, at the core. Just another peasant from the provinces. No matter how long he stayed in Altdorf, he'd never learn the manners of Helborg.

'Direct, as ever,' Lassus said. 'Do you really think I ever wanted the kind of standing von Tochfel has? Or, Sigmar preserve us, the Leitdorfs? There are more ways than one to make a success of one's life. Maybe when you're as old as I am, you'll see that. My battles are over. I've been granted the grace to retire from the field and see out the rest of my days in peace. Whatever the result of this affair, do you think Rufus Leitdorf will ever know such satisfaction?'

Lassus looked at Schwarzhelm with poorly concealed affection.

'I'll take my pleasure in the achievements of others now, Ludwig. I have faith in you, even if you don't. I'll pray for you when you're gone. And, when all is concluded, I'll be here to welcome you back.'

Schwarzhelm saw the look of trust in Lassus's eyes. His old master had complete confidence. That was touching. Another man might have smiled back.

'I'll keep you informed of progress,' Schwarzhelm said gruffly. He rose from his seat and made to leave. 'I fear it may be months before a decision is made.'

Lassus remained seated.

'Not if I know you,' he replied. 'But do not be too hasty. Your enemies know of your quick temper. They will use it against you. Be careful, Ludwig.'

Schwarzhelm looked down at the frail old man. It was a ludicrous scene. Schwarzhelm, even out of his armour, looked almost invincible. And yet it was Lassus who was most at ease, most in command.

'I will be,' said Schwarzhelm. Then he turned, ducking under the low ceiling, and left the house of his master.

CHAPTER FIVE

Pieter Verstohlen lay back in the bed, arms behind his head. The morning sun slanted through narrow windows, throwing bars of golden light across the sheets. It wasn't long after dawn, and the noises of the city were beginning to filter up from the street outside. They weren't the usual raucous obscenities. This was an affluent district, far from the worst of the rabble. The University was nearby, and its spires were just visible from the window. After the long campaign, it felt good to be in luxury again. He always missed it.

'Awake, then?'

Julia returned to the side of the bed, her long dark hair falling around her face. She was wearing one of his shirts. She looked good in it. Very good. When she passed in front of the window, the sunlight picked out her silhouette through the fine fabric.

'Just about. Why don't you join me?'

Verstohlen reached for the remains of his wine from the night before. He took a sip as Julia slipped the shirt off and lay beside him. The wine had turned vinegary in the night, but was still drinkable.

'You were talking in your sleep.'

Verstohlen felt a sudden spike of concern. That was unprofessional. The anxiety didn't show on his smooth, open face, though. It never did.

'Oh yes? Whispering undying love?'

Julia sighed.

'No such luck. I couldn't make it out. But you looked worried. I almost woke you.'

Verstohlen wriggled his arm under her and feigned indifference.

'It's been a long campaign,' he said nonchalantly. 'A man forgets the pleasures of the city.'

'I hope I've reminded you.'

'Oh yes.'

Julia was a whore, to be sure, but a very good one. Verstohlen had impeccable taste in all things, and women were no exception. She was educated, well-connected and discreet. All three were important to him. That said, she probably knew far more about him than she ever let on. Occasionally, he wondered who her other clients were. Generals, dukes, magisters, maybe a prince or two. He'd never asked, and he knew she'd never tell.

'You're going off again soon?' she asked, nuzzling against his shoulder comfortably.

'How do you know these things?'

'Schwarzhelm is going to Averland. Everyone knows that. And where he goes, you're bound to follow.'

Verstohlen smiled ruefully. That was true.

'In a couple of days. The Emperor has decreed that the succession must be decided. Schwarzhelm will pass judgement on the claims.'

'That's a quick way to make enemies.'

'You're an astute judge, my dear.'

'Thank you.'

Verstohlen didn't need to ask her where she got her information. That would have been indelicate. But she was right. It suited many Averlanders not to have an elector in place.

With no incumbent in Averheim, they could get on with the business of cattle-rearing and horse-breeding without those inconvenient Imperial levies. They were far enough from the front line not to care too deeply about the demands of war. Life was good in the south, and they were milking it for all they could get.

'So which way do you think it'll go?' she asked.

'You're asking me to predict the outcome before we get there? Have you so little regard for the Imperial law?'

'Imperial law,' she scoffed. 'If you cared anything for that, you wouldn't be here.'

'True enough,' he said. 'But no, I have no idea which way the thing will turn. I'd say they were evenly matched, Grosslich and the Leitdorf heir. And, before you ask, we're not under orders to pick one of them. This is a genuine contest. Schwarzhelm's just there to force a decision.'

'If you say so.'

'I do.'

As he spoke, Verstohlen realised how unusual that situation was. In any normal assignment, there'd be some clandestine objective. He might have to slip some misinformation here, or place a modest bribe there. On occasion, the cause demanded more drastic measures, and he knew his poisons. He was good at it all. That was why Schwarzhelm trusted him. That, and many other reasons.

This situation was odd. His role was to gather intelligence, and nothing more. That alone unnerved him. Perhaps that's why he'd been talking in his sleep.

'Are you travelling with him alone?'

'Oh no. It'll be the family. Schwarzhelm likes his own people around him. He's good like that, picking up us waifs and strays.'

'The family. Quaint.'

'It keeps us out of mischief.'

'So it's you, Grunwald and Gruppen?'

Verstohlen turned his head to give her a suspicious look. That was very well-informed, even for her.

'Did you really not hear what I said last night?'

Julia shrugged.

'Come on. There's no secret about his lieutenants.'

'If I didn't know my secrets were as safe with you as they would be with Verena herself, I'd begin to get worried. You could destroy my reputation.'

'And lose my best customer?' she said. 'I don't mean the money, either. You're a handsome man, Pieter. I'd miss these special visits.'

Verstohlen laughed.

'Oh, you're good,' he said. 'But to answer your question, Leonidas won't be there. His chapter's been called to the front. The order came from high up. *Very* high up. Andreas will be going, though. And a new man. Bloch. I like him. He's dangerous, but in the best way. Schwarzhelm sees something of himself in him, I reckon.'

'He sees something of himself in all of you.'

'In Grunwald, maybe. Not me. That's why he trusts me. I'm Morrslieb to his Mannslieb.'

Julia chuckled at that. As she laughed, Verstohlen admired the rise and fall of the crumpled sheets around her.

'I'll miss you, Pieter,' she said, wistfully.

'What do you mean? I'll be back. I can't keep away from you.'

'Don't mock me. I mean it. You're getting too old for whoring. You need a wife. And when you get one, that's the last I'll see of you. I know it. That damned sense of honour.'

Verstohlen felt the good humour suddenly drain out of him. How was he going to respond to that? Perhaps with the truth, that most elusive and valuable of prizes. But there were only so many ways you could tell the story without sounding bitter. And where would he stop? Just with the fact that he had been married? Or with the fact that Leonora was dead? Or with the way that she'd died, at the hands of those monsters? Or with the fact that he'd loved her so much, so painfully and so completely, that there would never be another woman in his life again, not even if an avatar of blessed Verena herself descended and begged him to take her in blissful matrimony?

The appetites of the flesh were one thing. He was a man, after all. But his soul belonged to another, and that would never change. He was no longer, as they said, the marrying kind.

'Don't trust too much to honour,' was all he said. His voice was bleak. 'It has a way of letting you down.'

Julia, with all the grace of her profession, sensed a nerve had been touched. Smoothly, expertly, she ran a finger down his cheek.

'So serious,' she whispered. 'I could help with that. How long before you have to leave?'

Verstohlen rolled over, looking her in the eyes. He didn't like to remember the past. Anything that helped him forget was welcome. And Julia certainly helped him forget.

'Long enough.'

'That's good news,' said Julia, pulling him towards her.

Much later, Markus Bloch relaxed against the wooden bench, feeling good. He was full of ale. So full, it felt as if it would soon start running out of his eyes. It was Altdorf filth, not as good as he'd get back home in the sticks, but it did the trick. His vision was blurred, his gut over-full, his head heavy. He felt fantastic.

What made it better was sharing his fortune with his best friends. To be fair, they had only been his best friends for the past few hours. It was uncanny the way a man could strike up such close relationships after walking into a tavern with a purse full of schillings. If he was cynical, he might put it down to the generous rounds he'd been able to stump for. But that would be churlish. These men were the finest in the world. His kind of people. The salt of the earth.

Bloch let his gaze sweep across the interior of the inn. He couldn't remember its name. Something like the Seagull, although that would be odd, since Altdorf was hundreds of miles from the sea. The bar was crowded and acrid clouds of pipesmoke hung heavy in the shadows. The smells were reassuringly familiar. Beer, straw, sweat, piss.

Most of the patrons were human, though there were dwarfs skulking in the shadows. Altdorf was a cosmopolitan place, and no eyebrows were raised at their presence. They drank from massive iron tankards carved with runes while the men knocked back their beer from rude pewter cups.

You had to hand it to the dwarfs, thought Bloch. They cared about their beer, and they knew how to put it away. He hadn't seen one of them drunk under the table in all his many happy years in the inns of the Empire. He'd tried to achieve the feat himself. Twice. It hadn't ended happily on either occasion. The first time he'd lost his dignity, the second his wallet. Still, it had been worth it. One day he'd do it. He just needed more practice.

With that thought in mind, he downed the last of his drink. The beer became unpleasantly silted at the base of his cup, but you had to drain it to the end if you wanted to get a fresh one. House rules, and damned good ones they were too.

'Renard!' he bellowed, feeling the liquid swill around his insides. 'I'll have the next one now.'

His Bretonnian companion, beer-bellied and greasy like the rest of the drinkers, grinned. The man had done well out of the evening so far and seemed happy to stand for another drink. Unlike most of his effeminate countrymen, he was content with proper man's ale. That was what Bloch had always liked about him. Ever since he'd first met him. An hour ago.

'You can handle it, Bloch, I'll give you that,' said the Bretonnian. He was smiling. Bloch smiled back. His benevolence knew no bounds. 'Tell us more stories. They're entertaining.'

Bloch looked around the table. All eyes were on him. There was Clovis, the travelling peddler from Bogenhafen. He looked shifty and sallow, and hadn't bought a drink all night. Walland was a better man. Thick as a giant, but generous and ready with a dirty laugh. His eyes were drooping now. And then there was the builder's mate Holderlin, and the halfling Tallowhand, and Bruno the hired muscle. All fine men. His kind of men. He felt like telling them he loved them.

'All right,' he slurred, watching his next drink arrive with approval. The serving wench had an appealing set of curves, but she moved too quickly for him to grab anything. Anyway, she was badly blurred. 'I've saved the best till last. You're going to love this.'

He took a long swig. Bilge water. All eyes were on him.

'I told you about the Turgitz campaign, when I killed the doombull,' he continued, wiping his mouth. 'But that's not the best of it. After I'd pulled the halberd out and cleaned it, I noticed the general was in trouble. That's right lads, the general of the whole bloody army.'

Bloch noticed with satisfaction that they were hanging on his every word. Marvellous men, they were.

'Another man would've looked after himself. After all, I'd just killed the bull, and I was pretty bloody tired. But no, I thought. Damn it, the general's a fine man. The finest of men. Just like you fellas. So I hoisted my blade and launched in. I was pretty fired up by then, and I tell you, you don't want to get on the wrong side of me when I'm angry.'

He might have imagined it, but it looked like Renard shot a low glance at Clovis then. What was that about? Never mind. He was in full flow now.

'So I launched in, like I said. You don't want to get on the wrong side of me when I'm angry. Like I said. One, two, and he's done. I've stuck him. Right in the guts. Not the general, mind. He's a fine man, the best of men. I've killed the gor. That bloody great gor that was giving him some trouble. And when it's all over, he turns to me – the general, that is – and he says, "Bloch, that was the finest fighting I've seen in my fifty years in the Emperor's armies. Forget your service with the Reikland halberdiers. Come and join my retinue". So I did. And that's what's brought me back here. I told you I was a halberdier captain. No bloody longer, mates. I'm the general's man now. And he's a fine man, I tell you.'

There it was again. Renard was definitely up to something. Clovis was looking shifty. But Holderlin was hanging on his every word, as was Bruno.

'Which general?' said Tallowhand, looking suspicious. Damned half-breeds. This was difficult. He knew he should keep names out of this. Ferren had told him to. But the story was running out of steam. Clovis looked bored. They needed something big. Something to impress them.

He took a long, gulping swig.

'You're not going to believe it, mates,' he said, wiping his mouth. 'But it's the truth. I swear it on Sigmar's holy mother, it's the truth. I wouldn't lie to you.'

He leaned forward, milking the moment for all it was worth. Holderlin was wide-eyed, and even Walland had woken up.

'He's the foremost general in the Empire,' he said, his voice low. 'The Emperor's right-hand man.'

He sat back, folded his arms, and waited for the gasps.

'Helborg!' exclaimed Holderlin.

Bloch nearly spilt his drink.

'Damn you!' he bellowed, all thought of secrecy forgotten. 'Not that prancing pretty boy. Schwarzhelm. You know, the Champion.'

That silenced the room. Bloch felt a twinge of unease. Why were they so quiet?

'You shouldn't have said that about Marshal Helborg,' said Walland in a low voice. His slow face looked surly. That annoyed Bloch. What did these peasants know about Helborg? They were idiots, the lot of them. He couldn't recall what he'd ever seen in them.

'Oh yes?' Bloch said, a sinister note creeping into his voice. 'And why's that?'

Holderlin was nodding in support of Walland.

'He's the hero of the Empire, that's why,' he said. His voice was thin and annoying. Bloch felt his temper rising.

'He's nothing compared to the big man. Gods, you weren't there after he killed the doombull. He was like Sigmar reborn!'

'I thought you killed the doombull?' said Clovis, obsequiously.

Bloch got angrier. These people were scum. Real scum.

'Yeah, we both did, all right? And then we carved our way through the rest of those damned beasts. And where was your pretty boy Helborg? Riding around the Drakwald on his own, lost! He's not half the man Schwarzhelm is, and I'll fight anyone who says otherwise.'

That changed things. At the mention of the word 'fight', Tallowhand and Holderlin finished their drinks and quietly slipped away. Bruno was close behind, but Walland remained. His expression had lowered further, and he looked surly. Renard and Clovis stayed in their seats, watching.

'You don't know nothing 'bout Helborg,' Walland growled. Bloch saw him reach down to his beltline. This was getting nasty.

'I know a damn sight more than you, fat man.'

Walland stood up. He had a knife in his hand and his flabby cheeks were flushed.

'No one calls me fat,' he said.

Bloch felt a surge of hot blood rush to his temples. He didn't have a weapon, but he was more than capable of taking on a drunken provincial hick like Walland. He rose in turn, pushing the bench back. As he did so, the inn lurched uncomfortably and he had to grab the table for support. This ale was damned strong stuff. Perhaps more than he'd thought.

'Gentlemen,' interjected Renard, rising quickly. 'You don't want to be ruining a pleasant evening like this. We're all friends here.'

He pressed something shiny into Walland's palm and whispered something in the man's ear. Walland grunted and retreated, glowering at Bloch all the while.

Though he wouldn't have admitted it to anyone but himself, Bloch felt relief. He wasn't that steady on his feet. The tavern interior was pitching alarmingly. They really ought to fix that.

Renard came to his side, supporting him. Somehow, Clovis ended up on his other arm. Bloch blinked furiously, trying to clear his vision.

'Another drink?' he suggested cheerfully.

'I think you've had enough,' said Clovis. The man wasn't smiling. Bloch felt himself being manoeuvred towards the tavern entrance. That was a shame. The evening had just been getting started.

'So what are we up to now, boys?' Bloch asked, noticing how cloudy his eyesight was even as they left the tavern and staggered out into the street beyond.

Renard smiled again, but said nothing. The man was always smiling. Bloch didn't like that. You couldn't trust a man who smiled too much. That was one of the many great things about Schwarzhelm, Sigmar preserve his soul.

'Did I tell you about how I rescued Grunwald?' Bloch asked, hoping another story would rekindle the bonhomie between them. 'He's a damned pansy, if you ask me. Lost his position and ended up being chased by the beasts all the way to me. He'll be my superior officer, more's the pity, but he won't have anything on me. What's he going to do when I refuse to follow orders? I saved his life! That's a pretty good position to be in, don't you think? Lads?'

They didn't reply.

'Lads?'

'You can stop talking now.' The voice was Clovis. He'd stopped even pretending to be civil. Bloch looked around him. Everything was in shadows. Where had they taken him? It looked like an alley of some sort. It was quiet. Very quiet.

Damn.

'Forget it,' Bloch said, with as much bravado as he could muster. 'I've handled worse than you before. If you step away now, we'll call it…'

He felt the cool metal of the blade against his neck. It pressed in close. He felt a line of blood form on his skin. It trickled down the inside of his jacket.

'We've heard all about it,' said Renard from his shoulder.

The man's face was close, and Bloch could smell the cheese on the man's breath. But not ale. Had he been the only one drinking? 'You're an entertaining fellow. I'd hate to end your stories for good. So why don't you hand over those shiny schillings you've been so free with. We know you've got more. The Emperor's Champion pays handsomely.'

Bloch felt his fists balling instinctively. Could he fight his way out of this? For a moment, he weighed up the options. Clovis had a blade too and looked anxious to use it. He didn't share his companion's friendly manner.

The knife pressed harder against his skin. Bloch felt the skin part. The pain cut through his drunken haze. There was no chance.

'Just stick him, Renard,' spat Clovis, looking eager to be gone.

'All right!' said Bloch, hurriedly rummaging through his pockets. The pouch with Schwarzhelm's payment was still there. Still nearly full. He pulled it out and threw it to the ground. Clovis darted after it.

'Everything there?' asked Renard, still pressing the knife to Bloch's neck.

There was a coarse laugh from the shadows.

'Oh yes. This'll do nicely. Very nicely indeed.'

Renard twisted the blade into Bloch's flesh.

'You're a lucky man,' he said. 'Taking money puts me in a good mood. And I never kill when I'm in a good mood. But if you weren't lying about your new employer, you'd better wise up fast. You're not as impressive as you think.'

The blade was removed. Bloch whirled around, trying to catch Renard, but the movement made him feel sick. Everything span, and he couldn't see a thing. He stumbled forward, trying to catch at least one of them.

He saw the fist too late. With a crunch, it hit him square between the eyes. He fell heavily, feeling the last of his vision give out. From somewhere, Clovis's laughter echoed up the narrow alleyway. With the metallic taste of blood in his mouth, Bloch tried to rise, failed, then passed out.

* * *

The vast corridor in the Imperial Palace was empty. Even the guards that had escorted Grunwald down the six levels from the South Gate had left. Their echoing footfalls had ebbed into nothing, and the shadows in the empty space hung heavily. That hadn't improved Grunwald's nerves. All around him were depictions of great military engagements of the past. Over the doorway he was facing there was a massive frieze of the relief of Praag. The artist had really made an effort with the daemonic hordes. That didn't improve his mood.

Part of him didn't understand why he was so nervous. He'd worked with the big man for years. As far as one ever got with Schwarzhelm, they were close. Grunwald had proved himself on the battlefield countless times. They were both common soldiers, both had risen through the ranks. And yet, there had never been a failure like Turgitz. Before, he'd always met the challenge, always found a way. Perhaps that had raised expectations.

There was no use delaying things. He'd been summoned, and the big man cared about punctuality. After a few heartbeats more, Grunwald swallowed and knocked on the door. The raps resounded down the vaulted passageway.

'Come.' Schwarzhelm's voice was unmistakable. He didn't sound angry. But it was the first time he'd been summoned since the failure at Turgitz. You could never tell with the big man.

Grunwald pushed the door open. Inside, Schwarzhelm sat at a huge desk. It was covered with parchment maps and documents of requisition. More charts hung on the walls. They covered all the provinces of the Empire. Some even went further afield. There was one ancient-looking sheet of vellum with a depiction of what looked like a massive, circular island hanging on the far architrave. Sigmar only knew where that was.

'Sit,' ordered Schwarzhelm. Grunwald did as he was told, taking a low chair opposite the desk. Was the Champion still in a bad mood? By the expression on his face, yes. The man's face looked more lined than usual and there were grey bags under his eyes. The huge beard, normally a source of pride, looked unkempt. He had the look of a man who hadn't been sleeping.

Grunwald didn't ask why he'd been summoned. He knew better than that. He sat and waited.

'You'll be leaving with a detachment of my personal forces tomorrow,' said Schwarzhelm at length. He pushed the chart he'd been studying aside and looked at Grunwald.

'Yes, my lord.' That was a relief. Grunwald had been wondering whether he'd be included in the Averland assignment at all.

'There've been more reports of greenskins massing in the east,' continued Schwarzhelm. 'From Grenzstadt. And now close to Heideck. Too many for comfort. Averland's got lazy without an elector. If we have to, we'll do their work for them.'

'I understand.' He knew what the score was. The incursion would have to be kept away from Averheim while the legal process was expedited. That was all that mattered. 'Do the Averlanders have forces of their own?'

Schwarzhelm made a dismissive noise.

'Plenty. But the two sides are keeping them back in case the selection turns ugly. I've already sent letters of requisition. We'll see how far we get with them.' He shook his head. 'They're my countrymen, so I ought to understand them. But when they've got an incursion on their doorstep, you'd have thought–'

He broke off, looking disgusted.

'They've forgotten about Ironjaw already,' he concluded.

Grunwald stole a glance at the maps on the desk. Schwarzhelm had scrawled all over them. Supply lines, possible attack routes, staging posts, he'd got it all worked out. That was no surprise. He always had the alternatives mapped out. Grunwald would have to study them himself later.

'You'll be taking Markus Bloch with you,' said Schwarzhelm. 'He'll be under your command.'

Grunwald let the ghost of a frown pass across his face before suppressing it.

'Bloch? The halberdier?'

'You have a problem with that?'

'No, my lord. Except... he's not worked with us before.'

Schwarzhelm looked calm. He could be intolerant when his decisions were questioned.

'He's proved his worth already. Or had you forgotten who guarded your retreat?'

Grunwald felt his ears go red, despite his long training. The shame of his failure still hung heavy on him.

'I know,' he mumbled. 'And I should say... I mean, I'm sorry. We lost the ridge.'

Schwarzhelm didn't respond with words of comfort. Nor did he add condemnation. He looked implacable.

'You did your best,' he said. 'The day was won. But maybe we need some new blood. New ways of doing things. We can always learn.'

The criticism was implicit. Grunwald should have found a way to hold out longer.

'Yes, my lord,' he acknowledged, working hard to keep the resentment from his voice. No one knew how hard it had been on the ridge except him and Ackermann. And his deputy was dead, now to be replaced with a halberdier captain he hardly knew.

'I've completed the commission documentation,' continued Schwarzhelm, turning back to his piles of paper. 'There's money to pay the men and warrants of supply with agents in Averheim. When you get there, make sure to keep me informed. I'll be no more than a few days behind you. There are things to arrange here, and I don't want to arrive in the middle of a greenskin plague. I can trust you to handle this?'

Grunwald felt the flicker of resentment bloom into a flame. Why was he asking him this? When had he ever proved wanting, except at Turgitz?

'You can rely on me, my lord.'

Schwarzhelm nodded.

'I hope so. Now come and look at these deployment plans.'

Grunwald rose to study the annotated charts. As he did so, he was already thinking forward to the campaign ahead. This was his chance for vindication. The only one he'd get. He stood beside Schwarzhelm, and the commander began to reel off his orders and recommendations.

Silently, efficiently, Grunwald committed them all to memory. He wouldn't fail again.

A day later, Bloch still had a headache. He sat uncomfortably in the saddle, watching Schwarzhelm's army take shape. The grey morning light breaking over the wide parade ground made him wince. All across the space below him, regiments of men shuffled into position. He'd been able to conceal the wound at his neck well enough, but there was no escaping the black eye. Every time he passed a row of soldiers, he could feel the suppressed humour. When he was gone, they'd be laughing at him. He could understand that. As a halberdier in the ranks, he'd have done the same. As long as they thought he'd picked up the marks in some honest fight, he'd be fine.

He adjusted his position, trying to find the least discomforting position, and surveyed the scene before him. The muster yard, several miles south of the city, was full of men. Schwarzhelm's army, the Fourth Reikland, had come together again, ready for the long march south. They'd been at Turgitz, though you'd hardly have known it to look at them. A few weeks' rest, plenty of ale and a wallet stuffed with copper coins, and they'd recovered most of their energy for the fight. The gaps in the ranks had been filled quickly. There was never a shortage of men willing to fight under Schwarzhelm. They trusted him, which you couldn't say about some Imperial commanders. They may not have liked him, but they knew his reputation. Better to fight under a grim bastard who never smiled than a flighty aristocrat who'd ride off at the first sign of trouble.

The bulk of the army were halberdiers, just like him. Four

thousand of them. They'd been arranged in their marching detachments. Even as Bloch watched, the sergeants were making last minute adjustments to formations, bawling out any troops with defective equipment or misaligned livery. They were all in the Reikland colours of white and brown, and they'd scrubbed up pretty well.

Not so many years ago, Bloch would have been one of those men himself. His elevation had been quick. That was fine by him. He was a born fighter, and the men around him knew it. They were already responding well to his orders. If he could keep out of trouble in taverns, he'd have no problems.

He scanned the rest of the deployments. There was little artillery. A few light pieces and one middle-sized iron-belcher. Since the war had broken out in the north, demand for the big guns had risen. If even Schwarzhelm couldn't commandeer more, then that told its own story. There were no knights, nor pistoliers. This was an infantry force, a holding army. A few companies of handgunners gave them a little ranged support, and there were archers too. That was good, though not as many as he'd have liked. He'd faced orcs before, and they were tough opponents. He'd have preferred to have more heavy armour.

'Like what you see?' came a familiar voice. Bloch turned to see Grunwald coming towards him. The man looked rested. Bloch couldn't help notice the finery of his garb, the close fit of his leather jerkin and mail. The man looked like a proper commander. He guessed that he cut a sorry figure in contrast. He really needed to cut down on the ale and meat. He was getting fat.

'They're in good order, sir,' he said, hiding his misgivings.

'I agree. Are any units still to report ready?'

'No. All the sergeants' papers are in.'

Grunwald nodded with satisfaction.

'Then you may give the order to march, Herr Bloch. They've been drilled here long enough. Averheim awaits.'

'Yes, sir.'

Bloch barked an order to a waiting messenger, who ran off to the signallers. A few moments later, trumpets blared out across the muster yard. Halberds were hoisted and the detachments smoothly moved into position. Regimental standards swung upwards and rippled in the breeze. With admirable efficiency, the regiments started to move from the yard and on to the road.

Grunwald and Bloch rode to the vanguard, where the remainder of the commanders waited on horseback. For a moment, Bloch felt like he had no place among them, that he should be back in the ranks with the company captains. He pushed such thoughts to the back of his mind. Schwarzhelm had picked him, and that was good enough for him. When the greenskins came for them, then he'd show his worth. He'd a damn sight more bottle than Grunwald, anyway. That had been proven already.

He kicked his horse onward, joining the vanguard as they made their way into position. The time for pondering, reflecting and drinking wages away was over. They were on the road again, back on campaign. Just the way he liked it.

'Have another glass. It's good stuff,' said Verstohlen.

Orasmo Brecht was happy to take another. The man's cheeks were rosy in the candlelight. It was the last of Verstohlen's haul from the cellars of the heretic Alessandro Revanche. He was sorry to see it go, but this was in the cause of business. The exquisite vintage had a way of loosening guarded tongues. He didn't even need to add any truthpowder. That was a good thing, as he was running low on that too.

Verstohlen poured himself a smaller glass of the same stuff and sat back in his seat. The two men were at dinner in Verstohlen's small but elegant apartment. The dining room was decorated in the latest style. Fine wax candles burned slowly in silver candelabras. The food was served on china rather than metal, something hardly ever seen outside the homes of the very wealthy. Verstohlen wasn't exactly wealthy, but he did know the right people. His stuff had come from a Cathayan junk via about a dozen intermediaries and handling agents. The path of the import documentation was obscure, but that didn't matter. Verstohlen had contacts down in the harbourside. He had contacts everywhere. Like Orasmo Brecht.

'My wife won't thank you for making me so fat,' said Brecht, dabbing at one of his many chins with a napkin. 'If I eat here again, that might be the end of our marriage.'

Verstohlen smiled. The man was a glutton. He'd eaten twice the portions that Verstohlen had and hadn't even noticed. No matter. What Brecht lacked in table manners he made up for in political knowledge, and he'd just come back from Averheim after two years there working for an importers' cartel. Good timing.

'I hope not,' Verstohlen said. 'I'd miss these little chats. It would be a shame to lose you to Averland for good.'

Brecht belched, and shook his head. 'Worry not. I'll not be going back. Never again.'

'Really?'

'Absolutely. Averheim leaves a nasty taste in the mouth. I prefer it here. Altdorf's filthy, but at least it's honest filth. And the food's better.'

Verstohlen played with his fork absently. No one seemed to have a good word to say about Averheim. That was odd. It had a reputation as one of the Empire's more civilised places.

'You're not the first to tell me that,' he said. 'I'm thinking of going there myself soon. I'd be interested to know what's so bad about it.'

Brecht helped himself to another leg of duck before replying.

'D'you know, I can't quite put my finger on it myself,' he said, chewing carefully. 'I liked the place when I first got there. The people are decent enough, if a bit rural. And the city's cleaner than Altdorf. I can't tell you when it all began to change.'

Verstohlen stayed silent, letting the man drift into a

monologue. When a contact was happy to talk, it was best to leave him to it. You never knew what would come out.

'If I had to pick something,' said Brecht, 'it might be the joyroot. That's certainly a part of it.'

This was new. And interesting.

'I've not heard that name. What is it? Some kind of narcotic?'

'So I believe. You never saw any of it a few years ago. Now it's becoming a problem. They smoke it. You've seen what the poppy'll do to people? Joyroot's not as bad as that. They get listless. I've been told they don't sleep so well. Nothing too dreadful. But I don't like it. It makes business difficult. There are only two drugs a man should take: wine and women. And they're dangerous enough.'

Brecht laughed at his own joke and his jowls wobbled. Verstohlen smiled politely.

'So the militia haven't impeded the import of this... joyroot?' he asked.

Brecht shrugged.

'Maybe they're on top of it. I don't know. It's probably not that important to them. That's what happens when you don't have a good man at the top. The little things slip.'

Verstohlen nodded absently. Brecht was right. But maybe this wasn't such a little thing. You could never tell.

'Then we must hope for a speedy resolution to the succession.'

Brecht snorted disdainfully.

'You'll never get that. The merchants' guilds have no interest in it. Believe me, they run Averheim. Anyway, both the Leitdorf pup and this Grosslich have legal problems with their claims. Many make out Rufus is illegitimate. Whispers are that he's the son of one of Marius's housemaids, and that she's been packed off to the family estate with a wad of gold and an armed guard. Grosslich's no better. He's got papers proving his noble birth, but no one thinks they're real. He's got scholars poring over them for him, trying to prove it. Leitdorf's people are doing the same, trying to discredit them. These arguments will run for months. Maybe years. It'll take a war for Averland to sort it out.'

Verstohlen listened carefully, taking note of everything. None of this information was new to him, but it was useful confirmation. Much might turn on the validity of the genealogical records.

'They may get their war, if they're not careful,' he said grimly.

Brecht laughed. He didn't seem to think the prospect was that alarming.

'They'll be all right,' he said, munching on the last of the duck. 'The summer's coming, and the weather's good down there. They'll be getting the harvest in soon, and they say it'll be a good one. Whatever happens in the rest of the Empire, the Averlanders will look after themselves.'

He paused.

'Maybe that's why I don't like it down there,' he mused. 'They're just a little... self-satisfied. Something's not natural, anyway. Better to be here among honest thieves.'

He laughed again. This time Verstohlen couldn't share the amusement. Too many people from Averland had used that phrase, 'not natural'. He didn't like that at all. The words had presaged trouble for him in the past. It was probably nothing more than the casual xenophobia of Reiklanders, but it still rankled. This joyroot was something else to worry about. Schwarzhelm would have to be told.

'Anyway, you're very interested in all of this, Pieter,' said Brecht, washing down the duck with the last of his wine. 'How long are you going away for?'

'Oh, not long,' Verstohlen said, reaching to top him up. 'At least, I hope not. From what you say, I'm not sure I'd like it.'

Brecht shrugged, and looked around the table for more food. His eyes fell on a pig's cheek in jelly and he reached for it eagerly with his fork.

'You'll be fine,' he said. 'They like their food down there. You'll fit right in.'

He began to eat again and his fat face radiated happiness.

Verstohlen sat back and nursed his wine. He knew he should eat some more. He and Schwarzhelm were due to leave in the morning, and the ride was a long one. But for some reason, his appetite had gone.

Schwarzhelm awoke. He was in Averheim. It was still night. The sickle moon, Mannslieb, rode in the deep sky. The stars were familiar to him. The stars of his homeland. Even in Altdorf, they were different.

He felt sick. He'd not slept well. He reached for the table by his bed, where an iron goblet had been placed. Gratefully, he placed it against his lips and took a long draught.

Immediately, he spat it out. He tasted the blood before he saw it. He threw the goblet to one side, hands shaking. He looked down. The sheets were splattered with blood. He pulled the sheets aside. There was blood everywhere, hot and sticky. From outside his chamber, the sound of laughter rose into the night sky. He looked up at the moon. It was disfigured, changing. A face was forming. He felt terror grip his heart. He tried to cry out, but his mouth had stopped working. There were men in the room, laughing at him. How had he missed them? He didn't recognise all of them. But there was Helborg, right in the middle of the crowd.

'You've failed,' he crowed, preening his moustache. 'They should have sent for me! You've failed!'

Schwarzhelm awoke with a start, properly this time. His sheets were drenched with sweat. He was in his chamber in one of the palace towers. Moonlight, real moonlight, streamed through the window.

Breathing heavily, he swung his feet to the stone floor and padded over to the window. Naked, he stood before the open pane and looked across the city below. His heartbeat was returning to normal. Another nightmare. Where were they all coming from? He hadn't had an unbroken night's sleep for a fortnight. It wasn't good for him. He could feel his tiredness growing during the daylight hours.

He took a deep breath and gazed out over the rooftops. It

was the deep of the night. Altdorf slept, at least in patches. A few fires still burned here and there, and the towers of the Celestial College retained their habitual blue aura. The memory of the dream was fading. The cool night air was clearing his head. Amidst the foul odours of the street, there were new smells. Summer was gradually coming, and even in Altdorf that sweetened the air.

He turned from the window and looked grimly at his disarranged bed. He knew he'd get no sleep now. Not for the first time, he regretted living on his own. He'd had women in the past, of course. The last had been Katerina, the Amethyst wizard. Perhaps he'd been wrong to break it off with her. Perhaps he hadn't. He'd never been good with women. That was another kind of warfare he was no use at. He never knew what they wanted from him and they never knew what he wanted from them.

Just then though, with his mind plagued by the memory of the nightmare, he couldn't help but think it would have been good to have a warm body in the bed beside him. Someone to protect. And maybe, though it was harder to countenance, to protect him. That was what nearly every man in the Empire, no matter how mean and baseborn, had. Something to care about. Something to make the fighting worthwhile. Something to come home to.

He sat on the bed. In the corner of the room, the Rechtstahl had been hung. It was sheathed and the scabbard shone dully in the moonlight. The runes of its dwarfen makers were picked out in lines of silver. It was as impassive and uncaring as ever.

Schwarzhelm lay back on the sheets. He was due to ride in the morning. He needed some sleep. Verstohlen would want to ply him with the information he'd gathered, and his mind would have to be alert.

He let his great body relax, feeling the wooden frame of the bed creak under the weight. He closed his eyes, blotting out the moonlight, wrapping himself in darkness. He let his heart rate slow. Like any warrior, he was used to grabbing rest where he could. Normally, he'd be able to drift off in any situation. He tried all the tricks.

He knew it was useless. Even if he found sleep, his dreams would be vivid. He couldn't relax, couldn't let go.

Just like all the others, this would be a long night.

CHAPTER SIX

The city of Averheim rose above the River Aver some three-hundred miles south-east of Altdorf. By the time a traveller had passed from the Reikland, through the free city-state of Nuln and into the province of Averland, the country had changed drastically. Gone were the powerful, ancient and gnarled forests that dominated the heart of the Empire. The south-eastern reaches of Karl Franz's domain were formed of rolling hills and wide rivers. The earth was rich, the grass lustrous. In a fertile triangle between the Aver, the Upper Reik and the Worlds Edge Mountains, the people of Siggurd had carved out a prosperous way of life. Their cattle were the finest in the world and their horses not far behind. The province was studded with small, self-contained villages. Each of them sat amidst acres of productive land. So complacent had the populace become that many of the settlements had let their protective walls fall into ruin. Without an elector to coordinate the defence of the realm, the fractious militia were a tithe of their former strength.

Most Averlanders saw little reason to change this. Apart

135

from mild irritations, such as the unfortunate rampage of a rogue ogre in the outlying regions the previous year, war came to the province only sporadically. The barons sent gold for the Emperor's armies and made sure token forces of men-at-arms were maintained in their ancestral manor houses to keep down the irregular beastmen or greenskin raids. Otherwise, trade was good. Demand for iron and tin was high, and the mines in the east of the province provided more of that than anywhere else. More trade moved down the River Aver since the Stir and Talabec had become more dangerous. Some even whispered that Averland should consider going the way of Marienburg. Perhaps then, freed of the onerous Imperial levies, the Grand County would rise to become richer than Reikland itself.

Wiser heads knew such talk was ludicrous. If it were not for the vast armies of Talabecland and Middenheim, nothing would have stood between the rich, fat south and the gibbering hordes of Chaos. Though many barons resented the taxes imposed from Altdorf, and the high-handed manner of the officials that came with them, they knew the money paid for the shield they sheltered behind. And so they stayed loyal. At least, as loyal as any other province in the bickering realms of men.

There were few cities in the huge, open land. Averheim was four times as big as the nearest rival. It had been built on a wide curve of the river where the land rose up in a great steep-sided mound. More than two millennia ago, Sigmar himself had founded a fortress on the site. Or so the locals liked to claim. Even though that boast was possibly futile, no one disputed the settlement was old. Some of the stones at the base of the massive Averburg fortress on the east bank of the river were so large and so beautifully laid that many called them the work of dwarfs. Over the wearing years, the Averburg had been added to, amended, part-demolished, rebuilt and extended with the waxing and waning enthusiasm of successive counts. Despite everything the war-conscious Imperial architects had thrown at it to make it strong, it retained a certain elegance.

Though the Averburg, with its sheer-sided walls and heavy ramparts, dominated the centre of the city on the east bank, there were other notable features within the snaking walls. To the north, where frequent flooding had prevented large-scale building, huge cattle showgrounds had been constructed. Visitors from less fortunate parts of the Empire had been known to gape in awe during the height of the showing season. The massed collection of Averland herds was one of the wonders of the Old World. It was said that when the first hammer of the season fell, there were thirteen cows in Averheim for every person. Those kinds of statistics were liable to provoke suggestive rumours from outsiders, but in truth they were jealous. The animals were valuable and had made Averland extremely rich.

Those riches showed in Averheim's mighty townhouses and guild-chambers. Most of these were many storeys high, constructed of warm brick and decorated heavily. On the richer east side of the river, elegant squares had been embellished with the bequests of rich men. Fountains gurgled even in the height of the hot summers, and there were fewer slums than in most Imperial cities. Though there was poverty, especially on the western fringes of the city where the migrant workers from Stirland and Tilea congregated, a careful visitor could ignore it. Such a thing was impossible in Altdorf.

Since leaving the city of Karl Franz, Schwarzhelm had made good progress. The journey had taken many days, first along the Reik to Kemperbad, then by land across the Stirhugel Massif in the Lower Stirland. Being away from Altdorf had had a cleansing effect on his mind. The fresh air was invigorating. As he travelled with his entourage, the weather grew steadily warmer. The dank, shadowy world of the Drakwald gave way to the flower meadows of the Lower Aver. Even a man of war such as himself was not immune to their restorative effects. It was some compensation for the rigours of the road.

Schwarzhelm reached the city on a typically fine morning. A cool breeze ran across the big man's face as he crested the final rise before the Aver valley fell away in tumbled heaps of grassland. The river itself lay serene, glittering in the warm sun. In every direction, deep green fields stretched away. In the distance, the pinnacles of the Averburg rose high into the clear sky.

'Bringing back memories?' said Verstohlen, reining in his horse alongside.

'I've been here since I came to call Marius to heel,' said Schwarzhelm. 'But yes, I am reminded of that.'

Verstohlen flicked the reins and his steed came to a standstill. Ahead of them, the armed escort fanned out down into the valley. They were arrayed in the colours of Karl Franz and bore his coat of arms. In the strong sun, their weapons sparkled.

'So much trouble, for such a pretty place,' mused Verstohlen, admiring the view.

Schwarzhelm grunted.

'A pretty face can hide a dark heart,' he said. 'Don't be deceived by appearances.'

He kicked his horse back into motion and the heavy charger began stepping down the descent into the valley. There'd be time to admire the view on the way back. Until then, he was impatient to arrive. As far as he was concerned, this assignment couldn't be over quick enough.

'Welcome, my lord. Or, I should say, welcome back! Though it has been many years indeed since you were last among us as the ambassador of His Imperial Majesty. We are – the city is – extremely glad to have you among us again.'

Verstohlen worked hard to suppress a wry smile. He knew how much Schwarzhelm hated flattery. True to form, the man looked as grumpy as hell. The ride had been a long one, and court pleasantries were the last thing any of them wanted.

They were standing in the great hall of the Averburg. It was tall and narrow. The bare stone walls soared upwards to a hammerbeam roof into which bosses with the devices of past counts had been embedded. The place was crowded with nobles, knights and the richer sort of merchants. They'd done their best to make a good show of it. Bright coloured cloth from Ind and Tilea mixed with highly polished ceremonial armour. Banners hung from the roof with the emblems of the Grand County and its many guilds. Verstohlen felt like he'd stumbled into some kind of pageant. It was a bit garish for him, but one had to make allowances for rural tastes.

The speaker was the Steward of Averheim, Dagobert Matthias Rauch von Tochfel. He was an unassuming character with a balding pate and grey skin. He looked like the kind of man who hunched over papers by the light of candles, totting up expenditure and income balances into the small hours of the night. Verstohlen couldn't have imagined a figure less likely to impress Ludwig Schwarzhelm, a man who had driven armies of thousands to victory by the sheer force of his will.

Predictably enough, Schwarzhelm gave him short shrift.

'That's fine, Steward,' he muttered. 'But we've had a long journey, and there's work to do. When do we get started?'

Tochfel looked taken aback.

'Well, we had rather hoped that you would join us for a banquet in the hall this evening. The claimants are not yet in Averheim, and there are formalities to ob–'

'Damn your formalities,' snapped Schwarzhelm. 'I'll eat with you and your court, and then I'll want to see your records of the legal process. You've kept the Emperor waiting for too long already. And send messages to the claimants to hasten their progress to the city. I won't wait forever.'

Tochfel looked like he'd been slapped in the face.

'V-very well,' he stuttered.

Schwarzhelm ignored him and turned to the commander of his honour guard, a flint-faced veteran named Kraus.

'Take your men and examine our quarters. When you're content they're secure, place a man at the entrance and organise a watch.'

'My lord,' said Kraus, bowing. He and his men filed out of the audience chamber, roughly pushing aside any curious nobles who got in their way.

'When do we eat?' said Schwarzhelm to Tochfel, who now looked pale.

'Whenever you wish, my lord,' said the Steward. Verstohlen noted that the man was getting the hang of things.

'Good. How about now?'

Tochfel looked around the assembled throng nervously. No doubt they'd been promised some kind of access to the great man.

'Of course. I'll have the high table laid.'

Schwarzhelm grunted something inaudible, then stalked off in the direction Kraus had taken. All around the hall, a low murmuring broke out. The Emperor's Champion had not been quite what they were expecting.

'So that was Ludwig Schwarzhelm,' mused a man standing close to Verstohlen. A legal scholar by his look. He wore a charm with the figure of Verena over crimson robes. 'Something of a disappointment. I'd expected more.'

Verstohlen gave him a contemptuous look. As the crowd started to disperse, he made his way to the dejected figure of the Steward.

'Herr von Tochfel? I'm Verstohlen, Lord Schwarzhelm's counsellor. If you'd contacted me prior to this meeting, I could have warned you of the likely result. But never mind. Do you have somewhere private we can go? We need to discuss the itinerary.'

Tochfel looked at Verstohlen like he was some gift from the gods.

'Did I offend him somehow?'

'No more than usual,' reassured Verstohlen, taking the man's arm and guiding him smoothly through the milling figures around them. 'He doesn't like ceremony. There'll need to be some of that, of course, but we'll have to manage that together. The important thing is to get Leitdorf and Grosslich here as soon as possible. Can you do that? Good. If you give me the names of your officials, I'll ensure the messages get through. He wants to meet both of them in private before the legal arguments are heard. That's not entirely usual, but it's perfectly within his rights as the Emperor's Judge. Again, if you can give me some names, I'll get that done. And there's the matter of security at the Averburg…'

Verstohlen spoke quickly but firmly. He guessed that Tochfel wouldn't be used to presiding over more than cattle fairs. If the assignment was not to unravel before it had started, then work needed to be done.

As they neared one of the side doors to the hall, Tochfel hesitated. He looked like he was having trouble taking everything in.

'So who's in charge here?' he said. 'You, or him?'

Verstohlen stopped in his tracks, genuinely amazed. Were the deeds of the Emperor's Champion really not known here? What kind of backwater was this?

'Don't be a fool, man,' he snapped. 'Lord Schwarzhelm is the Emperor's right arm. I merely arrange. You'd do well to remember that, or this visit will be more painful for you than you can possibly imagine.'

With that, he half-guided, half-pulled Tochfel through the door and into the corridor outside. The door shut behind them, and the grumbling of the crowd beyond was silenced.

Schwarzhelm sat at the long table in one of the Averburg's many gilded reception rooms. He felt weary and irritable. His sleep at night was still erratic. The air was getting too hot for comfort and flies plagued his room. He was aware he'd become irascible, even with his own men. They'd have to live with it. Two days waiting for the claimants to turn up was beyond insolent. He didn't believe the excuses. They were lazy and arrogant, the pair of them. If he hadn't been bound by the strictures of his office, he'd have ridden out to meet them himself. As it was, he was forced to wait. The delay was maddening.

Apart from the ever-present Verstohlen, calm as ever, the chamber was empty. Tochfel's flunkies had departed and Kraus's men guarded the doors. They wouldn't be disturbed.

'Have we heard from Grunwald yet?' Schwarzhelm asked. The long wait with no news was preying on his mind.

'Nothing.'

'You've sent out fresh messengers?'

'As you commanded.'

That was troubling. There should have been something by now. He knew the army had arrived in Averheim two days before he had. Grunwald had then departed immediately for the east, following new intelligence on massed orc raids in the mining country beneath the Black Fire Pass. That was just as he'd been ordered to do, but the lack of communication since his departure was unusual. Grunwald was normally scrupulous about such things.

'How many men are garrisoned here?' asked Schwarzhelm. 'If we don't hear soon, I may have to do something myself.'

'Give him time,' said Verstohlen. 'He'll send tidings when he's able. Worry not. He's your finest commander.'

Schwarzhelm grunted. That might have been assent, or it might not.

'Which one of the bastards are we due to see now?' he asked wearily.

'Leitdorf arrived in the city this morning. He's on his way now.'

'Marius's brat. Anything more I should know about him?'

'He's bringing his wife. They're devoted to each other. The one never leaves the other's side. That's been a source of friction with those you'd expect to be loyal to him. We don't know where she comes from, and neither do they.'

'That's not like you, Pieter. Find out.'

'I'm working on it. If it's any consolation, Tochfel's as much in the dark as we are. That goes for his loremaster too, Achendorfer. Her presence makes them uneasy. It makes everyone uneasy. But Rufus has inherited his father's pigheadedness. He can't see that such things damage his cause. This is a conservative province.'

'That it is.'

From the far end of the chamber, beyond the closed doors, noises broke out. Someone had arrived.

'What's her family name? Hiess? Does that mean anything to you?'

'Nothing. I've got people making enquiries.'

There was an exaggerated knocking at the far doors. Schwarzhelm stood and smoothed the juridical robes over his massive frame. His head was feeling heavy. He really needed some sleep soon. When this was over, he might ask Verstohlen for some sleepwort.

'I hope they're good people.'

The doors opened. In the antechamber beyond he made out the figure of Tochfel, hovering in the background as ever. Kraus had prevented him from entering. Good man.

Only two came into the room. No doubt they'd come with a retinue, but those too had been detained by Schwarzhelm's honour guard. That made things even.

The foremost was Rufus Leitdorf. He was dressed in a ludicrous burgundy-coloured outfit, replete with a floppy hunting hat and spurred boots. As he walked across the stone floor, the spurs clattered. He wore his hair long. Like his father's, it was brown, fading to grey prematurely. He had the Leitdorf eyes with the famous hooked nose. Rufus had already run to fat, though, and had none of his father's swordsman's poise. He didn't look like he could hold his own in a fight. Maybe Leopold had been given the fencing lessons, for all the good that had done him.

Despite this, Rufus carried himself with all the natural-born arrogance of the Empire's coterie of noble families. His swagger told Schwarzhelm all he needed to know about the man. He regarded the Averburg as his personal possession, and all those who stood between him and his rightful prize were his enemies.

As he approached, their eyes met. Leitdorf stared at Schwarzhelm with disdain. The Emperor's Champion was baseborn. All knew that. Schwarzhelm met the gaze and held it. For a few moments, Leitdorf managed to keep his head up. Then he looked away. Disappointing. Most could manage just a few moments longer.

'My Lord Schwarzhelm,' Leitdorf said, extending a hand limply. His father's ring was on the fourth finger of his glove. What did he want him to do? Kiss it?

Schwarzhelm grasped the man's hand and gave it a shake that would have crushed wrought iron. It was important this dandy knew who he was dealing with. Schwarzhelm had made his father learn the fear of the law. His pup would be no different.

Leitdorf grimaced.

'Herr Leitdorf,' said Schwarzhelm coldly, letting the hand go. 'I'm glad you could make it at last. We may speak freely here. My counsellor, Herr Verstohlen, is in my confidence.'

Verstohlen bowed. Leitdorf ignored him.

'As is my wife,' he said.

Schwarzhelm nodded his head towards her. So this was the famous Natassja. Reports of her beauty hadn't been even close to the mark. She had the kind of cold, superior physical presence that he'd seen men go mad for. Unlike her husband, she was dressed impeccably in a nightshade blue gown. Her dark hair had been gathered up by a silver lattice and an elegant ithilmar pendant graced her neck. She moved with the simple economy that was taught in the best finishing schools of the Empire. A native of Altdorf, by her look and manner. Far too good to be languishing out here in the provinces.

Natassja inclined her head in response and they all took their seats.

'I won't waste your precious time, Herr Leitdorf,' said Schwarzhelm. 'But there are a few things you need to know. I have no view on the merit of your claim, nor that of your rival. But the arguments have gone on long enough. The Emperor has run out of patience. One way or another, before I leave here, the matter will be determined.'

Leitdorf was transparent. He couldn't conceal the depth of his contempt for Schwarzhelm, or the legal process, or anyone but himself.

'The Emperor's concern for the health of Averland is touching,' he said artlessly. 'If he'd come himself, I might have been impressed. Sending his lackey will do nothing to advance this cause.' He gave Schwarzhelm a look of pure loathing.

'Very soon I shall be elector of this province. You'd do well to remember that. In my current position I cannot punish insolence. That will not be the case forever.'

Schwarzhelm felt a deep sense of weariness sink into his bones. For his whole long, honourable career he'd had to deal with the sons of nobles. They were all the same. If they'd had any sort of upbringing at all, they'd have been horse-whipped to learn some respect for their betters. This fool had no idea of the power at his command, nor quite how far Karl Franz trusted him. If Schwarzhelm chose to crush the insolent dog's skull then and there, the Emperor would find a way to forgive him. The image was a tempting one. He curled his fist up under the table, enjoying the sense of strength coiled within it. One day, maybe. But not now.

'That's your prerogative,' Schwarzhelm said, keeping his voice low. Forceful, not outright threatening. 'But for now, I am the Judge of the Succession. Under Imperial law, you are bound to answer my summons. You will come when I call you. You will leave when I dismiss you. You will abide by any ruling I arrive at. Failure to do so will render your claim void. You may not like that. But such is the law.'

Rufus's cheeks filled with blood. He was used to lording it over terrified servants. He'd probably never been spoken to in such a manner in his life. Schwarzhelm was amused to see his podgy fingers open and close. He was angry. But also intimidated. Good. That was as it should be.

'You… *dare* talk to me like that,' he started. 'By what authority–'

Schwarzhelm stood from the table, pushing his chair back. In a single fluid move, he drew the Rechtstahl. The blade was dull. It knew it would not be drinking blood, and it resented being used for show.

'By this,' hissed Schwarzhelm. 'As long as I carry it, you're under its shadow. You, and the man you're competing with. Never forget it.'

Rufus shrank back into shock. He pushed his own chair backwards, the rush of blood fading from his cheeks.

'You wouldn't dare!' he stammered.

Schwarzhelm felt like giving him a grim smile. But he didn't. He never smiled. He looked at Natassja. She'd remained calm and was watching him from under her dark lashes.

'You're under edict too, Frau.'

'You needn't worry about me, my lord,' she said. Her voice was languid, poised, untroubled. Unlike her husband, she knew what she was doing. So this was the one to watch. Intriguing.

'I'm glad to hear it,' said Schwarzhelm, sheathing the blade and taking his seat. 'Now we've established the rules, there are some more things to discuss.'

Verstohlen brought a sheaf of parchment from his bag and began to hand copies out. For the moment at least, Rufus had been cowed. He took the documents meekly. Verstohlen began to explain what they were and where he needed to sign. As he did so, he let a significant glance slip towards Schwarzhelm. The purpose of the meeting had been achieved. One candidate had been tamed. Now they needed to do the same to Grosslich.

The thunder rolled in the distance. There was a heavy storm somewhere over the Worlds Edge Mountains. Even from many miles away, its force was evident.

Grunwald wiped his brow. The air was thick and heavy. He'd welcome a downpour. Though it was close to evening, the heat was still uncomfortable. It made the army fractious. On the march from Averheim he'd had to discipline three of the company captains for brawls in their commands. He felt the sweat running down the inside of his jerkin. It took some doing, keeping four thousand men marching in something like formation. When he'd first been made commander, over ten years ago, he'd taken a positive enjoyment from goading his forces into action. Now, after so much campaigning, it had become a chore. He wondered if he'd passed his prime. Perhaps Turgitz had been a sign. It was a commonplace, but still true enough: command was a lonely business.

Grunwald placed the spyglass to one eye and trained it on the distant peaks to the east. The land marched up towards them in a steadily rising patchwork of craggy rises. His gaze swept across broken foothills, twisting for miles, before the first of the huge granite cliffs soared into the air. Tough country. No movement. Perhaps the reports had been mistaken. They'd been trudging for miles with no sign of orcs. No sign of people, even. The land was empty. A wasteland.

He pondered his options. The last of the errand riders had gone. Despite sending regular reports to Averheim of his progress, nothing had been heard back. Grunwald could only assume that Schwarzhelm knew where he was and how the assignment was going. Until he received fresh orders and fresh horses, there was nothing for it but to keep heading east in the hope of engaging the enemy. Assuming, of course, that one even existed. He was beginning to wonder whether the stories they'd been told in Heideck had any truth to them at all.

Bloch came up beside him.

'See anything, sir?' he asked.

Grunwald shook his head and stowed the spyglass away.

'Nothing. Not a damn thing.'

Bloch looked up at the heavens uneasily.

'It'll be dark soon. What do you want to do?'

Grunwald looked back over the army. The bulk of the detachments had been stood down. They were arranged across a long, shallow hillside in their regimental groups. Some were sitting on the grass, cradling their weapons. Others stood, leaning on the shafts of halberds or spears. The columns had lost their pristine shape since leaving Heideck. The men were tired, bored and frustrated. If there was one thing worse than stumbling across the enemy, it was not stumbling across them. Marching up into the foothills would be dangerous. If the quest continued to be fruitless, it would have to be done sooner or later.

'We'll withdraw,' he said. 'At dawn we'll strike out for Grenzstadt and the passes. We've been sold stories. Something's very strange here, and I want some answers.'

Bloch nodded.

'Aye, sir.'

Grunwald looked at him carefully. Bloch always spoke carefully around him, but he couldn't shake the sense that the man didn't give him the respect the subordinate officers did. It was a difficult situation. Bloch had saved his life at Turgitz. He might feel that gave him some kind of special licence. If he did, he'd have to disabuse himself of that quickly.

'Order the captains to break for the march. We're being fed false information. When we're in Grenzstadt, that'll need to be addressed.'

Bloch hesitated before replying.

'Yes, sir.'

'Was there something else?'

The lieutenant was looking up to the broken country stretching away to the east, dotted with twisted trees, scrub and gorse.

'If they're anywhere, they'll be in there.'

Grunwald gave a wintry smirk.

'Itching for a fight, Herr Bloch?'

Bloch glowered. The man disliked being talked down to.

'When it's warranted, aye.'

'Good instincts. But be careful what you wish for. This is not the place.' Grunwald looked back over the way they'd come. 'The light's failing and we're too close to that cover. We'll fall back west to the last open ridge and make camp. The morning may bring new counsel.'

'Yes, sir,' said Bloch, but he looked distracted. He was still looking east.

Grunwald followed his gaze. For a moment, he saw nothing but gradually rising grassland, punctuated by dark conifers and rows of low gorse bushes. Beyond them the first of the low hills rose, jagged with tumbled rock. The dying sun threw golden light across the stone. It was a peaceful scene.

'You see something?'

Bloch narrowed his eyes. Absently, he took up his halberd.

'You're right, sir,' he said. 'We need to fall back. Now.'

Then Grunwald saw them too. Far off, creeping close to the ground, dark shapes. They were half-lost in the wasteland, but moving quickly. Just a few bodies visible, hunched low, before dropping behind cover. More emerged, then slipped away again. They didn't move like humans. Only one breed of warrior moved that way.

Grunwald's heart lurched.

'Get them moving,' he hissed.

Bloch ran back to the massed ranks behind them. Soon shouts rose into the air as the sergeants began to knock the regiments into defensive formations.

Grunwald stayed where he was for a moment longer, screwing his eyes up against the weak light. The shapes were still distant. It was hard to make out numbers. Maybe just a scattered band.

Or maybe not.

He turned and hurried back to the army, drawing his sword as he went. He wasn't taking any chances. They'd fall back to the ridge. Only a madman would attack in the dark across such treacherous country.

As he made his way back to the heart of the army, Captain Schlosser, one of his more experienced commanders, approached him. His heavily moustachioed face was grim.

'More sightings to the north, sir,' he reported.

Grunwald stopped. 'How many?'

'Not sure, sir. Lots.'

Grunwald felt a cold sensation enter his stomach. Had they been drawn on? Had the orcs kept to cover long enough to pull them between two arms of a greater army? It wasn't like them. A greenskin would normally attack at the first opportunity. To use such stealth was strange. Very strange.

'Keep the companies together,' he snapped, not wanting to think he'd made another mistake. 'We'll make the ridge. Then we'll see what we're dealing with.'

Schlosser saluted and headed back to his regiment. All around him, the army was pulling itself back into some sort of order. Men were beginning to set off, locked in their

company formations. Massed spear-tips glowed gold against
the setting sun. Any expressions of boredom had been banished. They had the tight, expectant faces of men about enter
battle.

Grunwald looked along the ranks, watching for any laggards. One figure stood out. Bloch. His voice was louder
than the rest of the captains put together. His company had
moved to the rear of the army. The position of greatest danger. Even as the other captains hastened their men to march,
Bloch kept his in a defensive unit, waiting for the rest to
leave before following on.

Grunwald smiled coldly. The man would get his fight. At
least that was certain. After so long hunting shadows, the
wait was over. They'd found the greenskins at last.

The countryside immediately north of Averheim was particularly beautiful. The river ran in wide curves, sparkling under
the sun. On either bank, the turf was lush and verdant. In
the distance, scattered herds of longhorn cattle grazed. The
summer was hotter than anyone could remember. It made
everyone languid.

Verstohlen pulled his hat down to shade his eyes. His steed
shifted irritably under him. The beast was too hot. That went
for all of them.

He looked across at Schwarzhelm. The big man looked
tired. He'd complained of not sleeping. Verstohlen knew
what he meant. The air was close and humid, even at night.
There wasn't much anyone could do about it. He found
himself missing the cooler climes of Altdorf. Then again, it
could get unpleasantly steamy there too. There was no escape
from the elements.

Aside from the two of them, the hunting party was small.
Just Kraus and half a dozen of the honour guard. They hadn't
caught anything yet. Then again, that wasn't really the point
of the exercise. The invitation to hunt had come from one
of Grosslich's supporters in the Alptraum family. These were
Ferenc's estates. Their real quarry was human.

Schwarzhelm's steed looked restive. He calmed it with a word. Despite his bulk, there was no finer horseman in the Empire. He seemed to understand beasts more easily than he understood scholars.

'He's late,' Schwarzhelm growled. Verstohlen could see the lines of sweat on his temples. 'Is this an Averlander habit?'

Before he could reply, Verstohlen finally caught sight of the other party riding towards them. Six horses, all arrayed in magnificent gear. Even as they approached it was clear who the leader was. Heinz-Mark Grosslich was taller than those around him by several inches. Just as Schwarzhelm was. In fact, they looked somewhat similar. Though Grosslich was clean-shaven he was a bear of a man. His cheeks were ruddy and wind-bitten and his blond hair was been clipped short, just as a warrior's should be. He handled his horse well.

At his side rode a shorter man with dark hair and a weasel face. That would be Ferenc. The others were retainers and guards. As the party drew near, the escorts fell back.

'My Lord Schwarzhelm!' cried Grosslich, pulling his horse up. 'You have my apologies. Had I know you were in Averheim so early, I'd have ridden sooner myself. We were told you were not due for another week.'

'Leitdorf's doing,' muttered Ferenc.

Schwarzhelm was unmoved by the greeting. He was as impervious to friendliness as he was to intimidation.

'You should cultivate more reliable sources,' he said.

Grosslich nodded in agreement.

'Indeed. My adviser has been dismissed. I regret the delay extremely.'

Verstohlen watched the man carefully as he spoke. He had an easy manner and a commanding presence. There was none of Leitdorf's evident arrogance, but still that palpable impression of self-belief. Grosslich looked like a man who could command an army. That wouldn't sway the loremasters too much, but it would stand him in good stead with Schwarzhelm.

'We'll say no more about it,' said Schwarzhelm. 'You know why I wished to see you?'

Grosslich laughed.

'You wish to lay down the law,' he said, looking unconcerned by the prospect. 'We've been taking too long making up our minds, and now the Emperor wants to see results.'

'You think the matter is something to smile about?'

Grosslich looked into Schwarzhelm's unmoving face and his laughter quickly died.

'Forgive me. Though you must understand, the lengthy process has nothing to do with me.'

Ferenc nodded enthusiastically.

'That's true, my lord,' he began. 'It's that Leit–'

Schwarzhelm fixed the noble with an acid stare.

'When I wish for your opinion, Herr Alptraum, I will most certainly ask for it.'

'The problem does lie with Leitdorf,' continued Grosslich, letting an irritated glance slip towards his companion. 'I have the support of the province by dint of my deeds, not my heritage. And yet that is still not enough. Leitdorf has the scholars in his debt, and they perpetuate his arguments. Give me an honest judge, or a sword, and I will settle it for them.'

Schwarzhelm continued to look darkly at Grosslich, but Verstohlen could tell he had some sympathy. All those who battled against the rigid hierarchy of the Empire had at least one thing in common.

'You have an honest judge now,' Schwarzhelm said. 'And I warn you as I warned Leitdorf, any attempt to sway my verdict will result in your claim becoming void. I care nothing for your history with him, nor his with you. All that matters is the law.'

'That is what I wish for too,' said Grosslich. 'But you must know how far he has perverted this place. His wife, that bitch Natassja, controls his every move. She is as corrupt as she is deceitful. I don't doubt that you've met her. Be careful. She is the power behind his campaign.'

Schwarzhelm raised an eyebrow.

'You think I'd be swayed by a woman?'

'Many men have. She's poison.'

Verstohlen noted the man's vehemence. That hatred was not feigned. Schwarzhelm remained unmoved.

'Your warning has been noted. Was there anything else you wished to tell me? From dawn tomorrow the court of succession will be convened. Thereafter, we'll have no chance to confer in private.'

Grosslich looked at Ferenc, but the Alptraum heir said nothing. The smaller man looked crestfallen.

'Only this,' said Grosslich, turning back to Schwarzhelm. 'All looks well in Averland. The harvest has been good and gold is plentiful. The war is not much more than a rumour to us. Do not be fooled. There is a sickness here. No one knows where all the gold comes from. The law is laughed at and honest men suffer. I know your reputation, Lord Schwarzhelm. Perhaps you can bring an end to this. But beware. There are traps here for the unwary.'

Schwarzhelm maintained his implacable expression. Perhaps only Verstohlen saw it. The faintest flicker of uncertainty, swiftly extinguished.

He'd never seen that before, not from Schwarzhelm.

'Fear not,' the Emperor's Champion said, pulling his steed's head around and kicking it into a walk. 'I do not waver, and the Emperor's will shall be done. But there's been enough talking. My limbs need stretching. We came here to hunt. Are you with me, counsellor?'

Verstohlen nudged his horse to follow Schwarzhelm, as did the rest of the party.

'Yes, my lord,' he said, though there was little enthusiasm in it. Chasing after boars in the deep forest was not his idea of a well-spent morning. And the longer he spent in Averland, the more he began to suspect that something darker was at work beneath the sunlit facade. Only time would tell.

CHAPTER SEVEN

'Form up!' roared Bloch.

On either side of him his men shifted into position. Just like the detachments strung out along the rest of the ridge, Bloch's men had arranged themselves in the time-honoured Imperial defence form-ation. A rectangle of men, each of them armed with a halberd, four ranks deep. Bloch and the most experienced troops stood in the centre of the front rank. The rest of the soldiers clustered close by, shoulders grazing one another as they shuffled into their stations.

Bloch could smell their anticipation. After days out in the wild, they were filthy-looking. Their faces were streaked with dirt and sweat. Though night had fallen, the heat still rose from the earth in waves. Averland was like a furnace and the darkness brought little respite. He could feel the slickness of his palms against the rough wood of his halberd shaft. His heart was thumping. Not long now.

'Blades up!' he bellowed. 'Hold your positions!'

All along the Imperial lines, steel flashed as halberds were hoisted. Bloch stole a look along the ridge. The moon was full and high, and the land around was bathed in silver. Not a cloud in the sky.

Grunwald had driven the army hard to reach the ridge. As they'd marched towards it, the truth had become slowly apparent. The orcs had been engaged in a sophisticated exercise, drawing them further and further east while never letting themselves be detected. That was astonishing. Bloch had never heard the like. Now the greenskins were closing. From all directions. They were at the centre of the storm. Grunwald had barely had time to arrange the regiments along the ridge before the first of them had been sighted. He'd done well to get them into formation, and the few artillery pieces they'd brought had been assembled and primed. It was a good position to occupy, and the Imperial army had the high ground. It's what Bloch would have done.

Now it all came down to numbers. Just how many of the bastards were there?

He'd find out soon. The front ranks of greenskins were coming into view, charging up the slope towards them. The artillery cracked out, flaring across the battlefield.

'Pick your targets. Remember you're men! No quarter for these Sigmar-damned filth!'

That brought a half-hearted cheer from his men, but they were busy watching the charging figures tearing towards them. In the moonlight, the orc skin looked sickly and pale. Like green-tinged ghosts, they surged up the incline. The gap closed.

Behind the front ranks, more and more orcs streamed into view. This was bad. There were more than he'd imagined. Where had they been hiding?

From the far side of the ridge, sounds of battle broke out. They were surrounded. Then the time for speculation ended. The first of the orcs hurled themselves forward, swinging their cudgels and cleavers. Bloch saw their red eyes burn as they raced towards him. They chopped the turf up under their heavy feet, now mere yards away.

'For Sigmar!' he roared, watching the eyes come for him.

Then the lines crunched together.

Bloch punched his halberd forward viciously. The orc before him staggered backwards. Those on either side of it crashed into the defenders. One man was sent hurtling back into his fellows by the force of the impact. Fresh men struggled to take his place. Halberds thrust up and out. The detachment buckled, but held. Bloch worked his own blade expertly, using the cover at his shoulder to maintain the wall of steel.

More greenskins joined the attack. Bigger warriors shoved their way to the front, panting heavily from the run up the slope. Their stench stained the air, their bellows filled it. The warriors hurled themselves forward, hammering away at the defences. Still the detachment held. When a man fell, another took his place. They knew their business.

Bloch worked hard, feeling the sweat pool at his back. It was heavy fighting. The orcs were at least as big as the gors he'd faced at Turgitz, but their armour was better than he'd ever seen greenskins wearing. It was close-fitting and heavy. Their blades were good, too. He'd seen orcs bearing rough axes and cleavers before, but these had broadswords and halberds. Sigmar only knew where they'd got them. They were as good as his own men's.

The force of the assault began to waver. For all their ferocity, the orcs were still attacking up the slope and the determination of the defences had blunted the full force of the charge.

'No mercy!' Bloch roared, feeling the shift of momentum. He lowered his halberd and prepared to push back. To his satisfaction, the men around him immediately shifted their weapons to compensate. The orcs may have had savagery and strength, but the Empire troops had iron discipline. The long line of halberds, each trained on a target in the gloom, was a formidable obstacle.

'Hurl them down!' Bloch bellowed, and the line of men surged forward. The footing was treacherous on the churned-up grass, but the row of halberds stayed in formation. The orcs responded to the challenge in the only way they knew how, with a counter-thrust of their own. The larger greenskin warriors lumbered to meet the blades, smashing the metal aside and roaring their defiance.

The slaughter was immediate. Well-directed halberds lanced through the orcs' defences, skewering their victims. Other blades glanced from the heavy plate armour, the staves shattering from the impact. Any defenders pulled from the lines were torn apart in an instant, their blood thrown high into the night air. The order of the assault was soon lost in a frenzy of hacking and slashing.

Bloch thrust his own weapon straight through the face of an oncoming monster. The orc dragged the halberd from his hands in its death throes, so he drew his shortsword. Another warrior came for him, its distorted mouth agape and eyes flaming red. He deftly stepped aside, blunting the force of the charge, then slashed with all his might. The aim was good, and he drew thick blood. Further enraged, the greenskin came at him again, its mighty axe whirling. Bloch parried the blow and nearly lost his sword to the force of it. He stumbled back, and the greenskin leapt after him. In its eagerness to crush his skull, it left a gap between those grasping arms. Bloch ducked sharply under them, switching his sword to his left hand. He plunged it upwards. He felt it bite deep, then blood cascaded all over him. The roaring orc slumped across his shoulders, its fire extinguished.

With difficulty, Bloch shrugged the heavy corpse off and it crashed into the ground. He stepped back, sword raised, looking for a fresh challenge.

It never came. The assault had been broken. In every direction, the orcs were falling back.

'After them!' came a voice from further down the line.

'Hold your ground!' panted Bloch. To charge off into the gathering gloom would be madness. The orcs had withdrawn, but had not been routed. That in itself was strange. It wasn't their style.

From further up the hill, a lone trumpeter gave the order to maintain position. From his command position, Grunwald had obviously seen the danger too. Slowly, reluctantly, the defensive perimeter re-established itself. His breathing heavy, Bloch backed up the slope with his men. The detachment re-formed. The orcs passed into the shadows, their fury abated for the time being. They'd left behind a score of human dead, but hadn't dented Grunwald's defences. Yet.

Bloch took up a fresh halberd as he resumed his position in the front line. First blood had been drawn. But the green-skins would be back. This fight had just got started.

Schwarzhelm's temples throbbed as he studied the parchment before him intently. It was the thirteenth document he'd been asked to read that morning. He'd been sitting at the same desk in the Averburg's scriptorium for what seemed like hours. At least the place was cool. The chamber was buried deep within the lower levels of the keep, and only a weak light entered via narrow windows. The walls were lined with leather-bound tomes of law and the chronicles of the province. Some looked older than the stone behind them. Beyond the bookshelves, passages led to further repositories of scrolls and sealed cases of documents.

After a while, the narrow blackletter legal script had started to swim before his eyes. The depositions and statements were all written in the kind of dense language that seemed to defy sense and encourage obscurantism. Wading through this stuff was its own kind of torture.

He could see the loremaster waiting impatiently for him. He decided to let the man wait. Like Tochfel, Uriens Achendorfer was grey and insignificant. He looked marginally healthier than the Steward, but that was only due to his less advanced years. A few more winters locked in his cloisters scratching out contracts on parchment and his last bloom of health would disappear. Schwarzhelm loathed men like that. Officials. They were all mean creatures, the least of the Empire's many servants. Give him an illiterate spearman who knew how to hold his ground in the face of an enemy any day.

He kept reading, trying to keep his irritation and fatigue under wraps. The text was something to do with the claim against Leitdorf's legitimacy. Several witnesses' reports had been collated by a Verenan arbiter who had visited the Leitdorf estate in eastern Averland some years ago. The accounts were contradictory and vague. Not for the first time, Schwarzhelm began to suspect deliberately so.

'I can't admit this evidence,' he said at last, putting the script down on the desk in front of him.

Achendorfer cleared his throat nervously. He'd already been on the wrong end of some choice words that morning. 'May I ask why, my lord? It is a warranted document and has been catalogued in the–'

'This testimony is years old,' said Schwarzhelm. 'The arbiter is dead. It cannot be verified. The verdict is inconclusive.' He fixed Achendorfer with a withering look. 'Everything is inconclusive. There's not a single document you've given me with an unambig-uous claim. No account is complete. The authority is always disputed. A more suspicious mind than mine would conclude that a deadlock has been allowed to develop here.'

Achendorfer looked genuinely offended, despite his fear. 'We've done what we could within the boundaries of the law,' he complained. 'We are required to conduct ourselves with an even hand. Much depends on the result of this appointment. The traditions of Averland require that all competing claims are heard in full.'

'The traditions of Averland be damned,' muttered Schwarzhelm. 'Money has changed hands here for too long. How many more of these submissions are there for me?'

'There are twenty more depositions to cast judgement on. Then there are six cases of genealogical research carried out by the College of Heraldry. This sets out the case for the two candidates as clearly as we've been able to establish. Then there are the credentials for the Grand Jury to be cleared and some ceremonial documents that require your seal to ratify. To start with.'

Schwarzhelm looked at the wizened man carefully. Was he deliberately doing this to rile him? Or were all of his kind so in love with parchment? Achendorfer must have noticed the dark look cast in his direction and stammered an apology.

'You see, my lord, it is highly irregular for the Emperor's representative to intervene in such matters. The Averland Estates would normally pronounce itself. To transfer the authority, protocol must be followed.'

Schwarzhelm was about to say exactly what he thought of Averland's protocol when there was a knock at the door to the chamber. The sequence of beats was unusual. Verstohlen. And he had news he wished to keep private.

'Go,' snapped Schwarzhelm. 'Deliver the scripts I've ratified to the Estates secretariat. I'll do the rest later.'

Looking grateful for the excuse to escape, Achendorfer scuttled away. He passed Verstohlen as he slipped through the door, his arms full of parchment rolls. The counsellor took his place in the chamber, closing the door behind him firmly.

'Is this place secure?' he asked, sitting on Achendorfer's chair and pulling it closer to the desk.

'As much as anywhere. What do you have for me?'

'I sent men to Heideck, as you commanded. I've had word back today. Grunwald passed through the town some days ago. He pressed on towards the mountains, where there are now many reports of orc attacks. No one can explain how they're getting through the passes.'

'Why hasn't he sent reports back?'

'He has. Messengers were sent from Heideck to Averheim. Perhaps more were dispatched later. There are witnesses who can attest to it. They never arrived here. Some of my own men are missing. Though I'm loathe to believe it, it may be that someone's watching the roads.'

Schwarzhelm frowned. There were many dangerous roads in the Empire. Losing messengers was not unheard of. But in Averland?

'What news of Grunwald after he left Heideck?'

'None. I'll keep working on it, but we must accept that the

countryside is a dangerous place for us now. At least until some other explanation can be found.'

Schwarzhelm felt his inner weariness begin to reassert itself. This was a complication he could do without.

'I don't like it. Grunwald has a large force, but we know little of the orcs. This business here is killing me. I should ride out to aid him.'

'Perhaps,' said Verstohlen. 'But consider the motives of those who wish to see no resolution. For such men, this is a very helpful incursion. They'd rather see you chasing greenskins across the countryside than forcing the Estates to come to a decision.'

For a moment, Schwarzhelm had a vision of himself riding across the wide fields of Averland, the wind in his hair, scattering the orcs before him and scouring the land of their foul presence. It was an appealing image. He could feel himself going stale, cooped up in the dungeons of the Leitdorfs.

'Maybe you're reading too much into this.'

Verstohlen reached into his clothes and handed him a scrap of parchment. It had been part-burned, but a few words remained legible.

'I've been making enquiries in Averheim too. We've made some progress. Messages have been sent from the Averburg to Altdorf. It's been going on for some time. The replies were burned before Kraus could track down their source. The man responsible took a draught of deathflower before I could get to him. We don't know what was passed on. These scraps are all we have. But they're getting help from outside.'

On the fragment, beside some illegible scrawls, was a single word. 'Schwarzhelm'. He looked at it dispassionately.

'This proves little,' he said. 'My visit here has hardly been secret.'

'Maybe. But if the communication was innocent, then a man's died for no reason. These are all small things. Messengers may be waylaid. Correspondence on the Estates may be kept secret. There are even stories of youths disappearing from the streets. People are scared, my lord.'

Schwarzhelm pursed his lips, pondering the news. Verstohlen was usually reliable in these matters.

'What do you recommend?'

'I do not think we have the forces we need. Grunwald should be sent reinforcements immediately. The road from here to the east should be guarded. We can't do that without help. I've taken the liberty of making enquiries. There's a garrison of Reiksguard at Nuln. Helborg is with them. We could–'

'Helborg?' The name was like a shard of ice. 'What's he doing there?'

'I've no idea.'

Schwarzhelm felt old suspicions suddenly stir. 'So he's waiting there. For what, I wonder? What if the messages weren't going to Altdorf, but to Nuln? Can he really be so jealous?'

Verstohlen gave Schwarzhelm a startled look.

'I'm sure there's a reason for his being there,' he said, carefully. 'Whatever it is, it gives us an opportunity. Ask for his aid. A regiment of Reiksguard to secure the Averburg and the roads would release the troops we need to make contact with Grunwald. I'm sure he'd agree, given the situation.'

'No.' Schwarzhelm felt a surge of anger building up within him. He kept it down, but only barely. Helborg was unreliable. A glory-seeker. If he arrived now, fresh from his last-gasp charge at Turgitz, they would all say that Schwarzhelm couldn't handle the Emperor's bidding. That had to be avoided. At all costs, that had to be avoided.

Verstohlen made to protest, but Schwarzhelm cut him off.

'These are rumours. Fragments of information. I'll not divert the Grand Marshal for such trivia. We have the men we need. Maintain your enquiries, but the decision on the succession will not be delayed any further.'

Verstohlen looked at him steadily before responding. He was one of the few men who dared to meet his gaze. Schwarzhelm could see the counsellor was unhappy.

'Very well,' Verstohlen said at last and rose from his chair. 'I'll do what I can.'

He turned to leave, then hesitated. 'My lord,' he said, his voice uncharacteristically halting. 'I mean no disrespect, but is all well with you? You do not seem... quite yourself.'

Schwarzhelm did his best to look equable. In truth, he felt terrible. His headache was now ever-present, and he'd grabbed only the barest snatches of sleep for the past three days. When he did drift off, his dreams were terrifying. The stress of the legal work also bore down heavily. He could feel himself starting to fray. It was another reason to bring this thing to a conclusion as soon as possible.

'I'm fine. I could do without this heat, but I've been in worse.'

'I have some sleepwort with me,' said Verstohlen. 'Perhaps a tincture of that, now and again, would help? The nights are humid in the Averburg.'

It was a tempting offer. He'd considered it earlier. Verstohlen knew his poisons, as well as the cures.

'I'll ask you if I need any,' Schwarzhelm said. 'Now I need to finish reading these papers. Report back when you hear anything certain of Grunwald.'

Verstohlen bowed and left the chamber. With his departure, the scriptorium felt more like a prison cell than a reading room. The door closed with an echoing thud. Schwarzhelm looked around. The books looked down at him from their shelves. It was like being surrounded by enemies he couldn't fight.

With a weary sigh, he pulled the parchment towards him, and starting reading all over again.

Dawn had broken. Grunwald looked around him in desperation. The orcs were everywhere. In the distance, he could see a fresh mob, mixed in composition and running steadily, making its way to his position. How had they coordinated so well? This was getting difficult. Very difficult.

The greenskins had attacked all through the night, throwing themselves at the increasingly exhausted defenders with the fearless abandon typical of their race. Until the dawn, he hadn't been able to tell whether the waves of attackers were different tribes, or whether the same bands had been charging the rise again and again. With the rising of the sun, the truth became apparent. This was no isolated collection of warriors. It was a major incursion, and fresh reinforcements were arriving all the time. His forces on the ridge were already outnumbered. They would soon be heavily outnumbered.

He looked west, as if some help might come from that direction. There was nothing. Just the endless rolling fields, empty of anything but the beating sunlight.

Bloch came to his side. His armour was dented in several places. For a moment, Grunwald recalled Ackermann. He'd looked similar, back on the ridge. Everything was horribly similar.

'They're preparing to charge again,' Bloch said grimly. 'What are your orders?'

'We have no choice,' Grunwald replied. 'We're too far out. We'll hold them here.'

Bloch looked exasperated.

'If we stay, we'll soon be outnumbered two to one.' Grunwald noticed he'd stopped using 'sir' automatically.

'What do you suggest, Herr Bloch? That we withdraw across the fields? They're not going to let us walk out of this.'

'Then we'll fight our way back to Heideck!' Bloch spat. 'The men need some direction. Keep us here and we'll all die on this hill.'

The man's voice was raised. Troops nearby started to look around. There was a murmur of assent from the ranks further down the slope.

'We have the high ground,' insisted Grunwald, keeping his own voice low. 'I'll not see my men cut to pieces as they try to run for safety. I have my orders.'

'Damn the orders!' Bloch was now red-faced and angry. 'We've been drawn out here by cock-and-bull stories. Even you can see that this has been planned.'

Grunwald hesitated.

'What do you mean?'

'Have you seen the weapons those orcs are using? Have we heard a *thing* from Averheim since we set off? We should have stayed at Heideck. We're useless this far out.'

The man was beginning to ramble. It was probably the lack of sleep, or the heat. It was getting to them all. Even Grunwald could feel it begin to affect his judgement.

'Keep your voice down,' he growled. 'I'll not give you orders twice. We'll hold the ridge. My instructions were to meet the incursion head on. I won't run back at the first sign of trouble.'

Bloch gave a bitter laugh.

'So that's it,' he said, shaking his head. 'You're trying to make up for Turgitz. Schwarzhelm's ordered you to hold the ridge and you're damn well going to hold it. Even if it kills us all.'

'Enough! Get back to the front, lieutenant. I'll not tell you again.'

Bloch was still smiling, but there was no humour in his face. He looked as bitter as wormwood.

'Yes, sir,' he said sardonically. 'I'll do my duty. But don't come running to me this time when you need bailing out.'

Grunwald's hand leapt to his sword. That was too much. But then fresh shrieks of alarm rose up from the lower slopes of the hill. The orcs were back in the assault. With a final backward glance of despair, Bloch ran to his position amongst the halberdiers. He didn't say another word. Grunwald called his personal guard to his side, drawing his sword as he did so.

'Watch for the breach,' he said, trying to push the dispute to the back of his mind. 'On my mark, we'll enter the melee.'

The artillery spat out again, spinning shot high over the ranks of the defenders and into the advancing orcs. It did little to halt the tide. On every side, greenskins surged towards the defensive lines. Grunwald watched them as they came, looking for a weak point to exploit. The orcs were unusually tightly-formed. He had a sick feeling in his stomach. There were so many. They looked well armed indeed. Perhaps Bloch was right.

He grasped the grip of his broadsword with both hands. There was no time to reconsider now. Battle had come again.

The long day waned over Averheim. It was still hot. Verstohlen looked up into the sky. There wasn't a cloud in it. The sun remained strong. He'd never known a summer like it. Now he realised why southerners were so flaky. It was the heat that did for them.

He was standing on one of the seven bridges across the Aver. Long ago, Averheim had consisted solely of the Averburg and its attendant residences. As the Empire had grown, the city had sprawled out across the whole valley. As a rule, the richer dwellings were still on the southern shore. The poorer quarters, some of them legally inside Stirland, were on the north-west bank. They were crammed close together, like all impoverished tenements in all cities of the Old World. There were none of the wide parks and elegant avenues that graced the Old City on the east side. That made it far less edifying to spend time in, but, for his purposes, much more interesting.

Verstohlen walked across the bridge and into the maze of streets beyond. The air was thick and unmoving. Out of the evening sun, beggars slumped in the shadows, their mouths open like dogs. Flies droned lazily in the open doors to shops and taverns. There was no sign of the militia that seemed to patrol the Old City's streets incessantly. Verstohlen made sure his pistol was safely stowed under his jacket, ready to be withdrawn quickly. The atmosphere seemed reasonably benign, but it did no harm to be careful.

He pressed on, walking away from the river and further into the rows of mean houses. The more he walked, the less obviously cared-for the architecture became. The streets passed from having stone flags and proper gutters to being dirt tracks. Piles of refuse were deposited at the ends of streets. Rats openly scuttled across them. Everything looked slumped, weary. The heat didn't help. The people dragged their feet as they walked, leaving trails behind them in the dust. They looked shabbier than he'd expected. There was an air of casual degradation about the place.

Verstohlen walked further into the suburb. He knew what he was after. After a long trail up a winding cobbled street, he turned into a narrow alley and found himself in an enclosed square. On the far three sides, old stone buildings lurched haphazardly into the air. They'd seen better days. Clothes hung from the windows, heavy in the listless heat. If they'd been laundered and left to dry then the washerwomen had done a poor job, and there were still stains all over them. Naked children squatted at an open sewer, playing some kind of game in the filmy water. Their parents were nowhere to be seen. The only visible adults were in a shadowy doorway on the far side of the square. One of them, a fat man wearing no shirt, stared at Verstohlen with little interest. He looked half-asleep.

Verstohlen walked up to the doorway. There was a strange aroma on the air, detectible even over the reek of the sewer and clumps of refuse. One didn't need to be a bloodhound to be able to follow it.

'Greetings, friend,' said Verstohlen, taking off his hat. 'Can a man get a drink here?'

The man looked as if he didn't understand Reikspiel. After a pause, he grunted and motioned for Verstohlen to enter the house. They went in together. If the stench had been bad outside, it was worse inside. Used cooking pots had been discarded at the back of the room. Scraps of food, rags and other clutter littered the floor. A flight of wooden stairs led up to the next floor, and a doorway at the rear of the room indicated there were more chambers set further back.

As Verstohlen had guessed, this place served as an inn of sorts. It didn't sell ale, but that wasn't what the patrons were after. The strange aroma he'd detected outside permeated the place.

'You're a stranger here,' said the man, bluntly. As he spoke, his jowls quivered. There were a few others in the room, mostly propped up against the walls. Their eyes were blank.

One of them, an older man in reasonably expensive clothes, looked like he'd been there a long time. A glittering line of drool ran down his chin from his open mouth. Every so often, his fingers would twitch.

'I am,' said Verstohlen coolly. He'd need to keep his wits about him, though none of the residents of the den looked capable of sudden movements. 'Just passing through. I'd heard about the fine ale you people sell. Perhaps I could try some of it?'

The man's senses seemed to have been permanently damaged. He'd obviously forgotten the first rule of the peddler of contraband and had indulged himself. After a while, he realised what was being asked of him and ducked under the doorway. From the chamber beyond there was the sound of something heavy being dragged from its place. Verstohlen looked around him. The clientele were lost in another world. It was as if he wasn't there at all. He squatted down and waved his hand in front of the old merchant's face. Nothing. The man was still breathing, but he might as well have been dead.

The owner came back. He had a collection of objects in his hand. They looked like ginger roots, but were a darker brown. Even from a couple of yards away the aroma was pungent.

'How many?' he asked.

Verstohlen picked one up and rolled it between his fingers. The outer skin came off in his hands easily. It felt strangely caustic. Underneath, the flesh of the root was a pale pink colour.

'How much do I need?'

The fat man laughed, a strangled sound that had little mirth in it.

'First time? Half a root. You'll be back. Three schillings.'

The price was low. That was a worry. If such dissolute characters could get hold of it, then it was more widespread than Brecht had believed.

Verstohlen gave him the money and took one of the roots. He slipped it into his pocket. The fat man laughed again.

'You'll love it,' he gurgled. 'You'll love her.'

Verstohlen paused.

'Who?'

But the fat man couldn't stop laughing. He shuffled back into the rear of the house, shaking his head at some joke. Verstohlen watched him go. He suddenly felt nauseous. The squalor around him was overwhelming.

He walked back out into the sun. Once in the courtyard, he drew in a mouthful of air. It wasn't the purest in the world, but it was less noxious than it had been inside the house. The last of the sunlight still lay golden on the stone. The light was fading quickly. With more purpose than he'd shown on the way out, Verstohlen began to retrace his steps. He knew it would be unwise to be on the west bank when night fell.

His haste was not just a matter of prudence. This thing needed to be investigated. An uncomfortable thought had occurred to him. The words were still etched on his mind.

You'll love her.

That could mean nothing. It could be innocuous. It could have been mistaken.

It could be horrifying.

Schwarzhelm woke suddenly. His eyes flicked wide open. For a moment, he had no idea where he was. Then the real world clarified. He was in his bedchamber in the Averburg. As ever, he was plastered in sweat. As ever, the dream had been bad. The sheets were clammy, wrapped up around his powerful legs like bonds. He looked down at his hands. They were still shaking. He took a deep breath, forcing his heart to stop racing.

Schwarzhelm swung his feet on to the floor, shoving the flimsy silk coverlet from his body. He rubbed his eyes roughly. The last of the images, Bloch's accusing face, steadily receded. He felt like he was losing his mind.

As he had done in Altdorf, he walked over to the window of his tower room. He stood at the open sill, waiting for his heart to stop thumping. He looked out and down, willing the images in his mind to recede. He could see all of the Old City laid out before him. The night had done little to cool it down, but the place slumbered. The streets were silent, and the river ran quietly under the moon.

When he'd been a boy, many years ago, Schwarzhelm had called this place his capital city. Growing up in rural Averland, the word 'Altdorf' meant little. Though it was hard to recall now, he'd only had the vaguest idea what the Empire was or who ruled it. His life had been permeated by simple things. The rhythm of the harvest. The intense politics of village life. The need to learn a trade.

His father had wanted him to be a blacksmith. Even as a lad, he'd had the arms for it. If he'd taken that advice, he'd no doubt still be in the village. Wenenlich. He barely even remembered the name. When he'd first come back to Averland to rein in Marius, he'd not visited. That kind of sentiment had never been his style. For all he knew, the villagers might still boast of their famous son. They might have forgotten he ever came from there. Either was possible. It didn't really matter.

He leaned further out on the sill, letting the warm breeze run across his skin. Since those days, he'd travelled the length of the Empire and beyond. He'd fought marauders on the far shore of the Sea of Claws, orcs in the Grey Mountains, ratmen in the sewers of Middenheim, traitors in Ostland, undead in Stirland, beastmen all over the Empire. Now nowhere was his home – and everywhere was. He'd become one of that select, strange band for whom the whole Empire was their concern. Few men ever achieved such a feat. Karl Franz, of course. Gelt, Volkmar, Huss. And, of course, Helborg.

The name reminded him of his recent sensitivity. It was unworthy. He'd allowed himself to get caught up in the game of prestige. Wasn't that what Lassus had warned him against? The old man's lesson was simple. He'd served his time. When it was over he'd allowed himself to leave the stage, honoured by all and hated by none. That was the way a man's life should be. Getting drawn into these rivalries was foolish and dangerous.

Perhaps Schwarzhelm's own time was drawing to a close. Maybe, after thirty years of constant service, he'd become trapped in that endless, fruitless struggle for mortal honour. All things came to an end, after all. Maybe that was what the Emperor was testing for. Whether the old dog had any life left in him.

The memory of the nightmare began to fade. Schwarzhelm felt his equilibrium gradually return. The still of the night brought a certain clarity to his thoughts.

Lack of sleep was getting to him. The nightmares were unnatural. He'd had them in Altdorf, but they'd been worse since getting to Averheim. He'd seen enough of the world to know that such things always had their causes. There were forces at work, hidden for the moment, determined to see him fail. Maybe they were already in the city. Maybe they would show themselves in the days to come. But, as surely as he'd known that Raghram would come to the bastion, he knew his enemies would scuttle from their cover at the last. Until that moment, the torment would continue. His spirit knew what his mind could not. It sensed their presence.

'You will not break me,' he whispered. His words melted into the night. 'You cannot break me.'

For a few moments more he remained at the window's edge, watching the city sleep, reflecting on its fate. Then, finally, he felt the drag of weariness again. The dawn was still hours away.

Schwarzhelm walked back to the bed and lay on it. Eventually, slowly, his eyes closed. Hung in the corner of the chamber, the sheathed Rechtstahl looked coldly, silently on. Outside, high in the night sky, the full moon rode untroubled above Averheim.

CHAPTER EIGHT

Bloch roared his defiance. The men around him did the same. They were brave lads. They hadn't given up. But the situation was getting hopeless. Hundreds of men now lay trampled into the turf. All around the beleaguered army swarmed a maelstrom of greenskin fury. The artillery rounds had given out, the last of their shot spent in a futile effort to stem the rising tide. Two nights of fighting stranded on the ridge and no let-up in sight. The rotations had become unbearable. Sleep had been nigh impossible amid the constant series of assault and counter-assault.

The second dawn, hot and humid, brought no comfort. Grunwald's army, sent so proudly south from Altdorf, was facing ruin. The orcs came at them again. They scented victory.

'Hold your positions!' bellowed Bloch, though his voice was beginning to crack. His halberd felt heavy and blunt. 'Pick your targets!'

His men were now using whatever weapons they could find. Some still had their halberds, others swords, others hunting knives. The defences held, but they were being run ragged. Bloch had ordered a withdrawal further up the slope just to avoid fighting knee-deep in their own dead. As the beating sun rose higher up into the sky, the pungent smell of the corpses began to strengthen.

That only seemed to spur the greenskins on. Their attacks were coordinated, but they were also feral. They'd lost none of their energy for the fight, despite the casualties they'd taken. As the balance of numbers had shifted they'd started picking off men in gangs. Bloch had seen single troopers borne down by three or more greenskins, their bodies trampled into the mud until they were little more than slicks of blood.

He focussed on the charging orc lines. That wouldn't be his fate. He lowered his halberd, gritted his teeth and braced for impact.

The orcs thundered into the human ranks again. There were too many gaps in the line of steel, and some broke through. Swordsmen immediately raced to engage them. The combat was close, murderous and heavy. There was barely room to swing a blade, let alone wield a halberd properly. This kind of intense melee suited the greenskins better. The defenders were being butchered.

Bloch traded vicious blows with his target, a brutal-looking warrior orc with three tusks protruding from its maw. It was far heavier than he was and carried a crude warhammer in both hands. As the hammer came down, Bloch's broken halberd shaft shivered. The warrior advanced, swinging his weapon wildly. If it connected just once, the game was over. Bloch swayed out of reach, thrusting back with his halberd when he could. He was driven back. The men at his shoulder were pushed up the hill alongside him. They couldn't hold the charge.

He heard the spearman beside him go down rather than saw it. A spray of hot blood splattered down his cheek. For a moment, the man's scream drowned out the rest of the battle clamour. Then he was gone, and another defender took his place in the line. They were being thinned out.

The prospect of defeat maddened him. Bloch charged forward, no longer worried about becoming exposed. Something needed to be done to break the momentum. His blade moved with speed, flashing in the sun. The warhammer-wielder was too slow. Bloch sliced through his defences, carving the green chest open and throwing up gouts of blood.

He could sense men following his lead. He wasn't alone. In every direction, humans pushed back against the orc assault. The cries of pain told him they were being cut down. The defenders didn't have the numbers to back an assault up. The orcs were stronger, fresher and better-armed. A strange, guttural sound rose up into the air. They were laughing.

'Sigmar!' yelled Bloch, trying to conjure something, anything up. He whirled his blade around, cutting down any orcs who strayed into its path. With hopelessness came savagery.

Then, from the summit of the hill, a lone trumpet rang out. Grunwald had ordered the retreat. At last.

Bloch stood his ground. He could hear the clatter of arms as men on the far side of the ridge broke through the thinnest point in the orc ranks and attempted to break the ring of iron around them. They should have done it hours ago. Even now, they risked being cut down as they fled.

'Hold your positions, you swine!' roared Bloch, wielding his halberd with renewed vigour. 'Give them time to get away. We leave last!'

His words were wasted on some, those who had already turned tail. His was a diminished company that fought its way steadily back up the hill. They gave ground a yard at a time, never breaking, never losing shape. Bloch fought with a steady, controlled anger. He was damned if he could see a way out of this, but wasn't going to run yet.

Then, all around him, fresh troops arrived. Grunwald's personal guard, thrown into the melee to shield the retreating men behind. The commander was at the forefront, slicing through the orc ranks with his broadsword. The strokes were expert. Deadly. Bloch had never witnessed that side of him. The man knew how to wield a blade.

Bloch fought his way to Grunwald's side.

'How many can we get away?' he shouted, felling an orc warrior with a savage stab from the halberd even as he came alongside the commander.

'What're you still doing here?' grunted Grunwald, grappling with a huge red-eyed monster. It took three of them to drop the orc. Behind its toppled corpse, more greenskin warriors rushed forward.

'Flee!' Grunwald snapped at Bloch, his eyes wild with desperation. 'The men need leading!'

For a moment, Bloch didn't understand.

'Are you not–'

Grunwald turned to face him for a brief instant. His face was grim. The man had been in heavy fighting, and his leg had been hastily bandaged. He wouldn't get far.

'I'll hold them here as long as I can. Rally the men. Head for Heideck. That's an order, Herr Bloch.'

Then the orcs charged again. Grunwald raised his sword.

'Sigmar!' he roared, and his men echoed the battle cry. They were hopelessly outnumbered.

Bloch looked around, struck by indecision. All those who could were running, sprinting down the far side of the rise. They were strung out, no formation at all. They'd be picked off like flies.

He looked back over to Grunwald. Every fibre of his being wanted to stay. He'd never walked away from a fight in his life, not when he could look his opponent in the eye. He was caught in an agony of indecision. That was dangerous. He was still in the middle of the fighting.

A greenskin lumbered up to him, maybe seeing the torment in his eyes. Snapping back into focus, Bloch ran at it, swinging his halberd into the warrior's flank with all the strength he could muster. The blade bit, lodging in the green flesh. He ducked under the counter-stroke and punched the orc square between the eyes. Once, twice, three times, each with an armoured gauntlet, quick and brutal. The orc slumped to the earth, its face a mess of broken bones. Bloch pulled a knife from his belt and finished the job.

He looked up. There were orcs everywhere. The shape of the battle had dissolved. Whole companies of men were streaming down the far side of the hill. A few yards away, the last knot of resistance on the ridge still held out. Grunwald's men were tough, but it couldn't last forever. An orc warrior got through, but Grunwald met the charging creature, parried two blows, but his back was unprotected. A fresh warrior leapt up to take advantage.

'Commander!' shouted Bloch, powerless to prevent it. The orc blade plunged deep. Somehow, Grunwald managed to finish off his opponent, but the blood was already beginning to gush. He fell to the ground, still grappling with the second warrior. Then his body passed from view, hidden by the press of men and orcs around. He was gone.

For the moment, the orcs were still consumed with the need to bring down Grunwald's defensive formation. They were drawn to it like wasps to a honeypot. Bloch hesitated, aware of the danger, unwilling to leave.

It was hopeless. The field was lost. His duty was to the men that remained.

'Sigmar forgive me,' he spat, as he turned tail and headed down the hill, tearing after the fleeing column of men ahead. There were orcs swarming everywhere, and their attention was rapidly turning to the retreating human forces.

Bloch felt sick. He'd left behind the chance of an honourable death, but he might still meet a dishonourable one. The only thing that would make up for that was if he could rally the fragments of Grunwald's command and get them away. He gripped the broken halberd tightly, looking for fresh targets. There'd be plenty more killing before the day was done.

Schwarzhelm lowered the gavel, and the noise echoed around the chamber. Immediately the crowd ceased their chatter. Those still standing took their seats. The first session of the Estates Tribunal was convened. At last, the process was underway.

The chamber was in the largest audience room in the Aver-burg citadel. It was one of the oldest parts of the ancient castle still in use, as indicated by the worn stone of the walls and the archaic narrow windows. The space was barely big enough for all those who were entitled to attend. The appointment of an elector was a major event in the province, and the hall was stuffed with every notable who believed they had a right to be there. Schwarzhelm suspected that Dagob-ert had been weak in his admissions policy, and many who sat on the long wooden pews were simply rich enough to be able to buy a seat. That irritated him. This was a serious procedure, not a bear-baiting spectacle.

Aside from the noble onlookers, there were dozens of lore-masters, scholars and other legal experts in attendance. This was the kind of debate they lived for. Some of them were in the pay of Leitdorf, or Grosslich, or – if they were very clever – both. Others were simply there for the joy of witnessing a long and turgid academic debate on the finer points of law.

Schwarzhelm had in front of him a list of names Verstohlen had prepared. They indicated what each of them was likely to say and why. Not for the first time, he was glad to have the ser-vices of such an able man. There had been a time when the Temple of Sigmar might have taken him away. Verstohlen would have made a formidable witch hunter. Operating as the personal agent of the Emperor's Champion seemed to suit his tempera-ment better, which was something to be thankful for. He knew why that was, of course. He'd never forget why that was.

Schwarzhelm sat behind a heavy wooden desk on a raised dais. Below him, scribes were poised to record the events of the day. On the front row of pews before him, Leitdorf sat with Natassja. He looked bored. He wore a turban-like headdress and was draped in an ostentatious purple robe. It did nothing but display his rotund stomach. Clearly, the man had never lifted a sword in his life. If he hadn't been so wealthy, and potentially so powerful, surely a capable woman like Natassja wouldn't have had anything to do with him.

On the other side of the room, Grosslich's delegation had gathered. Heinz-Mark sat apart from the others, dressed in ceremonial armour. Unlike his rival, he looked like a future elector. His supporters, including the weasel-faced Ferenc, were set some distance behind.

'My lords,' said Schwarzhelm, his rolling voice echoing around the room. The scribes below him immediately started scraping. 'This Estates Tribunal is now in session.'

At a hidden signal from Tochfel, a priest of Sigmar stood up and delivered a lengthy benediction. After him, an Ulrican did the same. Schwarzhelm felt his spirits begin to sag. There was no prospect of this being either quick or easy. As far as he could tell from the legal papers, both candidates had equally flawed cases. Rufus was rumoured to be illegitimate and came from a family in which madness had been proven. Many powerful families had threatened to leave Averland if he were crowned. Grosslich, on the other hand, had dubious claims to being a member of the ruling elite at all. He'd bought his support amongst the Alptraums. If it were not for his extreme popularity with the lower classes, his candidacy would have foundered long ago. His was an intriguing story.

When the prayers had taken their long and dreary course, Schwarzhelm returned to the business of the day.

'According to the articles of the court, I will now hear the opening statements of the candidate's advocates. As the son of the late Count Marius, I now give the floor to–'

'My lord!' came a cry from the floor. A lawyer stood up. Schwarzhelm thought he recognised the man from Leitdorf's delegation. 'I wish to lodge an objection. The business of determining an elector is for the authorities in Averland. The Emperor can have no say in the matter. According to the learned Jeroboam of Gruningwold, since the year 1345 the Procurators Legal have ruled that...'

The man droned on for some time, outlining the case for provincial self-determination. Schwarzhelm looked down at Leitdorf. The odious little man was smiling to himself as his lackey reeled out the arguments. There would be more such interruptions as the day went on. Too many people wanted the tribunal to fail. Too many had the money to sponsor interruptions.

Eventually, the lawyer finished his argument.

'Your objection is noted and overruled,' said Schwarzhelm. He worked hard to keep his voice level. He was already getting a headache. The objection had been anticipated, and he had the counter-arguments ready to hand. 'My learned friend will be aware of the Drusus Precedent, dating to the time of Mandred. The summary of the principal is contained in the Volksfram Chronicles. Under the articles contained therein, I invoke the extraordinary right of the supreme governor of the Imperial executive. I am his representative, and the tribunal will continue.'

The lawyer sat down, looking pleased with himself. No doubt he'd earn himself a few crowns for the intervention.

'If we may continue?' said Schwarzhelm, sweeping his gaze across the packed chamber. It was early morning, but the room was already getting hot.

'My lord!' came a cry from further back. Another lawyer rose. 'You will of course be familiar with the prescriptions contained in the Averland Charter of Freedoms of 1266, under which the jurisdiction of the Imperial representative may be limited in the following cases...'

Schwarzhelm sighed. There'd be a number of these to get through before the tribunal could get underway. Leitdorf had sat back in his pew, legs outstretched, and looked like he might be planning a snooze. Grosslich appeared frustrated and had turned to his own advisers. They'd no doubt start chipping in with points of their own.

Schwarzhelm fingered the pommel of the Rechtstahl as the lawyer droned on. It hung at his side, useless and decorative. He'd have given anything for an excuse to draw it. But for now he was a captive of the arcane mysteries of Imperial succession law.

He let the blade alone and tried to concentrate on what the man was saying. It was going to be a very, very long day.

* * *

Bloch felt as if his heart would burst. If not that, then his lungs would. He'd been running for longer than he'd ever done in his life. Just as at Turgitz, all those years of ale and offal-pies now felt like a very bad idea. He could feel the sweat running down the inside of his jerkin in rivulets. He'd long since cast off his helmet and the heavier items of plate armour, but he still felt bogged down.

'Enough!' he gasped, and came to a stop. All around him, men fell to their feet, panting like dogs. They were at the end of their strength, both from the retreat and from the hours of fighting that had taken place before it. Though they'd escaped the pursuing orcs for now, there wasn't a triumphant expression among them. They knew the greenskins would be hard on their heels. It was only a matter of time before they'd have to turn and fight again.

Bloch could feel his vision begin to cloud at the edges. Fatigue was beginning to weigh him down. Not yet. He needed to keep going just a little longer.

He looked around. Somehow, against all likelihood, some of them had outrun the orcs and made it into the cover of woodland. They were barely a mile west of the site of the massacre. Under the scant cover of the trees, they at least had some chance of remaining undetected for a while. It wouldn't last for long. Though Grunwald's last stand had taken the brunt of the greenskin assault, the respite had only been brief. The pursuit would already be underway. They'd have to start running again soon.

More men arrived, crashing heavily through the under-growth. Some carried their halberds, while others had discarded everything in their panic. The remnants of Grun-wald's army he'd managed to gather together from the rout were pitiful. Three hundred or so had made it to the woods. Perhaps others had found other ways to escape. If they still were out on the open country, they'd be easy pickings for the orcs.

For a moment, Bloch was utterly at a loss. He was exhausted, his men were exhausted, and there was nowhere to go. Heideck was miles away. They'd be lucky to get halfway there before being overtaken. There were no obvious choices.

'Sir?' came a voice. Bloch turned round. A young spearman was looking straight at him. He seemed in better physical shape than many of the rest and his cheeks weren't hollow with fatigue. The benefits of youth. 'What do we do now?'

Bloch stared back. He'd always prided himself on his ready answers, his quick tongue, his self-command. During his years as a company captain, he'd never been placed in a position where his best course of action seemed uncertain. There had always been the strategic picture handed down from above. He'd just had to look after tactics. After Grunwald's death, things were different. There was no one left to give the orders but him. He remembered his disdain for Grunwald. It was the same casual contempt he'd always had for senior officers. If he'd known then what he knew now, maybe that quick tongue would have been sheathed more often.

He took a deep breath. Something needed to be done. If he didn't act now, then they were all dead without so much as a fight being offered.

'Any officers make it out?' he said, addressing all the men around him. More soldiers were arriving every moment, staggering through the bracken. For the time being, there was no sign of the pursuing orcs. That was one small mercy.

'Schlosser was first away,' said one. 'He drew a lot of orcs. I reckon they'll have got him.'

'Rasmussen's dead,' said another.

Not very encouraging. The men around him were state troopers. Some experienced hands, but none who could share the burden of command.

'So be it,' Bloch said, trying to sound more authoritative than he felt. 'We can't stay here. Anyone still with heavy armour, get rid of it. Take one weapon only, the lightest you have. We've still got a long way to go before we get out of this, and those monsters don't tire quickly.'

All around him, men hurried to obey his orders. Bloch felt a degree of confidence return. He'd commanded soldiers for years. He knew what he was doing. If they stuck together, kept their discipline, there'd be a way out. Somehow.

'Any Averlanders among you?' Several men came forward. 'I want guides who know the woodland. We'll head for Heideck, but not by the straightest route. Between you, come up with a trail we can follow that keeps us under cover.'

The Averlanders began to confer animatedly.

'Do it quickly. We set off in moments,' said Bloch, growing in confidence. His spirit began to disseminate through the men, and they started to stand straighter. Like most soldiers, they could cope with almost anything if they understood the plan. It was when they didn't know what was expected of them that morale collapsed.

Bloch started to plot possibilities in his mind. Perhaps he'd been too pessimistic about numbers. As he'd been speaking, more stragglers had found their way to their position. Maybe others had got away too. The orcs were still nowhere to be seen. If Grunwald's men had held them up for longer than he thought, they might have a chance.

'Horseman!' came a cry from the edge of the ramshackle group. Bloch hefted his weapon instinctively. After a few moments, he saw it. A man, leading his steed through the trees. He looked nearly as exhausted as his own men. After a few moments, Bloch recognised the errand rider Grunwald had dispatched two days ago.

'What are you doing here?' he snapped, waiting for the man to come to him. 'You should be halfway to Averheim.'

The rider shook his head.

'I had to turn back,' he said. 'Commander Grunwald needs to know that his messengers haven't been getting through. I found bodies. Two of them. They'd not bothered to hide them. The corpses were barely out of sight from the road, and the crows were still busy. So I came back to let him know. Only to find this–'

Bloch regarded him suspiciously.

'How did you find us?'

'Luck,' he said. 'I nearly rode into the greenskins. I had to seek shelter somewhere. There are orcs roaming all over the fields to the east of you. Most are heading north, from what I could see. I think some other survivors have tried to make it to Grenzstadt, and they're being pursued. You chose well to head this way.'

If that was true, it gave them some breathing space, though there was little comfort in achieving that at the expense of the remaining survivors. And if this messenger ended up drawing greenskins to their position, Bloch would kill him himself.

'I'll need a fresh rider,' said Bloch, turning to the men around him. 'Someone fast, and who knows the land between here and Averheim.'

After some discussion, the young spearman came forward. He looked nervous, but there was some steel in his gaze.

'What's your name?'

'Herren. Joskar Herren.'

Bloch looked him directly in the eye.

'You've heard what this man said. The road is watched. I need you to find a way through. Averheim must be warned of what happened here. You need to ride fast, faster than you've ever ridden before. Can you do that?'

Herren nodded.

'Run this horse into the earth if you need to. Take a weapon. If you need a fresh steed, there are farms between here and the city. Use your wits and stay out of sight when you can. It'll be dangerous. I'll say it again. Can you do this?'

Herren held his gaze.

'Yes, sir.'

Bloch clapped him on the shoulder.

'Good lad. Go now, and Sigmar be with you.'

The young spearman mounted. He pulled the horse round expertly, and with a kick of hooves and a flurry of earth, he was gone. Bloch watched as the soldier galloped off under the trees. He'd be lucky to get through. Then again, they'd all be lucky to get through.

He turned back to his men. His expression was bleak. They looked back at him, waiting for instruction. That was good.

They trusted him. Perhaps more than they had Grunwald. He'd have to work to ensure that trust wasn't misplaced.

'This isn't over yet,' he said, looking hard at each of those nearest in turn. 'There are greenskins all over us. But we have one thing left to us. We're men, and men of the Empire at that. They'll have to work for our hides if they want them. They'll have to earn them in blood.'

The survivors hung on his words. As he spoke, Bloch felt his confidence growing. They were his kind of men. And now he was responsible for them.

'Stay close together. We'll go quickly but quietly. If we follow the valleys and stay under the trees, we'll make it. Get to Heideck and everything changes. Schwarzhelm won't leave us out here. We'll regroup and come back fighting. And then we'll pay the greenskins back double the pain they've caused us. It'll be hard. Hard as nails. But keep your minds fixed on that. Vengeance. We'll pay the bastards back.'

The men responded to that. The horror of the chase was fading. They knew what the odds were, but at least they had a plan, something they could work to.

Bloch turned to the Averlanders.

'Now show your worth,' he ordered. 'Find me a route out of here.'

Verstohlen looked deep into the eyes of Artoldt Fromgar. The man was terrified. Verstohlen couldn't blame him for that. If he'd been shackled to an interrogator's chair in the dungeons of the Averburg and surrounded by men like Kraus, he'd be scared too. He almost felt pity for him. Whatever was going on in Averheim, Fromgar was nothing more than a small part of it. He probably had no idea what was going on beyond his petty activities. But if Verstohlen's suspicions had any foundation to them, then he couldn't allow pity, or any other emotion, to guide his actions.

'Do you want me to remain here, sir?' asked Kraus. He'd plucked Fromgar from the street with admirable efficiency.

The captain of the honour guard was a capable man. Schwarzhelm knew how to pick his lieutenants.

'No, that will be all, captain. Place a man on the door and see that we're not disturbed.'

Kraus bowed, withdrew, and the door slammed shut. There were no windows. Candles burned in lanterns around the narrow chamber. They threw flickering shadows across the dark stone walls. Verstohlen walked away from the man bound in the chair. He could smell his fear. That was good. The more afraid he was, the easier this would be. Verstohlen didn't enjoy this work. It brought back too many memories of the past. The sooner it was over, the better.

He walked over to a chest of drawers and took a bundle of instruments from the top drawer.

'Do you know why you're here, Herr Fromgar?' he asked coolly, masking his own nerves, unwrapping the tools.

The man could hardly get the words out of his mouth.

'N-no, my lord,' he stammered. 'No idea. No idea at all.'

He was beginning to babble. Verstohlen arranged the steel items on the desk, one by one. They made an echoing clink as they were placed. Some were sharp. Some were twisted. Some were crudely blunt. They all had their purpose.

'I've been asking around,' continued Verstohlen. 'Your name came up more than anyone else's. You've been doing well for yourself. How much have you sold in the past month? Enough to buy you those expensive clothes, I see.'

Fromgar began to whimper.

'It's a lie,' he blurted. 'I've got rivals in business. They're not above slander. I'm a wine merchant. It's all a lie!'

Verstohlen finished arranging the tools. He selected one. It was old, forged long before Karl Franz had taken up the throne. Such deadly finery wasn't produced any more. He would have appreciated the artistry if its purpose hadn't been so black. Despite himself, he loathed it. With the instrument in hand, he walked back over to the chair. The candlelight reflected from the polished metal.

When Fromgar's eyes saw it, they went wide. A trickle of liquid collected at the legs of the chair. He was incontinent with fear.

'Are you absolutely sure about that, Herr Fromgar?' asked Verstohlen, coming up to him and trailing the tip of the device down his cheek. The man was sweating heavily. He already smelled bad. It would soon be a lot worse.

'I– ah– I...'

Verstohlen withdrew the slender shard of steel to give the man a better view. Fromgar's pupils followed it all the while. 'W-who are you? What are you going to do?'

That was a good question. Few people knew who Verstohlen was. It was kept secret for a reason. A reason hidden in the past, in deeds too terrible to bring to the surface.

Leonora.

Verstohlen winced and turned his mind back to his work.

'That depends on you, friend. You shouldn't doubt my resolve. I want to know where you get the joyroot, how much you pay, and where it's coming from.'

Fromgar swallowed nervously. The sweat was now shining all over his face. He looked like he might be sick soon.

'And if I tell you? Can I go?'

Verstohlen smiled grimly. The man was in no position to bargain.

'Tell me what you know and you'll never see me again. I'm after answers, Herr Fromgar. That's all. Answers.'

He brought the instrument back to bear, placing it carefully just under the man's right earlobe.

'Enough!' Fromgar screamed, going rigid in the seat. Verstohlen withdrew the blade. 'I don't know where it comes from! That's the truth. I'd tell you if I did. By Sigmar, on the souls of my daughters, I'd tell you if I did.'

Verstohlen stepped back and leaned on the edge of the desk. He kept the instruments in full view. The man was talking now. They'd served their purpose.

'I get my supply from a man called Lepp. He brings them down the river, from the east. We've got an arrangement.

Exclusivity. There's stuff that comes in from elsewhere, but it's not as good.'

'Is this Lepp in the city now?'

'No. He comes and goes. He could be anywhere now.'

'How do you get in touch with him?'

'He sends a message to me when he's in town. I collect the gold from my clients and pick up the stock.'

'Sounds like dangerous work. His cargo is valuable.'

Fromgar didn't know what to do unless he had a direct question. He froze, eyes still staring.

'I guess. I've been careful, though. Not like some of the others.'

'Not careful enough,' mused Verstohlen, running his finger along the edge of the instrument. 'Have you taken the root yourself?'

Fromgar shook his head.

'So you're happy to let others pollute their bodies, but not your own?'

'It's their choice,' he mumbled miserably. 'I never forced it on anyone. No one. It's them that comes back for more.'

Verstohlen felt a swell of disgust. A petty kind of evil, though destructive enough. He began to lose any residual sense of pity for Fromgar.

'I don't doubt it,' he said. 'If I'm right, this is powerfully addictive stuff. Perhaps more so than the poppy. What would it do to a man, the first time he took it?'

Fromgar was still scared, but something in Verstohlen's manner seemed to have assured him that he wasn't in immediate physical peril. He even managed a nervous smile.

'It makes them happy,' he said. 'That's all. Takes away the cares of the world for a while. Lifts their burden. It's helpful.'

Verstohlen walked over the chest of drawers again. Fromgar stiffened in the chair.

'Would I be right in thinking that a novice user would experience a particularly powerful reaction?'

'I guess so. Maybe. I don't know.'

Verstohlen retrieved another cloth-wrapped bundle, the size of a fist, and returned to the chair.

'I think you do,' he said, unwrapping the bundle. 'I think you've forgotten your pledge to tell me everything you know.'

Fromgar lapsed back into a state of fear.

'Yes!' he cried, his voice rising. 'It can have the effect, in the beginning. It depends on your strength of mind to start with. Some don't take to it. Some do. That's just how it is.'

Verstohlen paused. That was interesting.

'Strength of character?' he mused. 'Did you mean to say that? Perhaps you're referring to physical strength?'

Fromgar shook his head. His shirt was sodden with sweat.

'It's their minds,' he said, looking warily at the bundle in Verstohlen's palm. 'It's all in the mind. How virtuous, or not how virtuous. It makes a difference.'

Verstohlen nodded, filing the information away. That might prove useful.

'Very well. You've been most helpful.'

Fromgar's eyes lit up.

'That's it? Can I go?'

Verstohlen gave an ice-laced smile. He felt his own heart begin to beat a little faster. Here came the real experiment. This was where his suspicions would be allayed or confirmed.

'Go? Oh no,' he said. 'You see, I brought you here for another purpose. I've purchased some of this joyroot. It might have even come from your own stock. It's very interesting. I've had it ground down. Now, though I've some alchemical knowledge, I'm no expert. I have a feeling I know what its powers are, but of course I'm not stupid enough to try it myself.'

Fromgar began to struggle against his bonds. He wasn't entirely stupid either.

'You can't!' he said. 'Once you're hooked—'

Verstohlen reached up to the man's face and grasped his nose with his left hand, closing the nostrils. Being so close to the gutter-rat made him feel slightly nauseous. The stench was now acute.

'I'm aware of the effects,' he said coldly. 'Just as you were aware when you peddled it.'

Fromgar struggled for breath. His head lashed one way, then the other, but Verstohlen kept the grip tight. Eventually, the man had to open his mouth. As he did so, Verstohlen slapped his other hand over it. Fromgar immediately coughed the powder back up, gagging on the plume of pink vapour.

Verstohlen withdrew, placing a silk handkerchief over his own mouth. The man had managed to splutter some of it out, but he'd taken in enough. Verstohlen sat back against the chest and waited.

For a moment, nothing much changed. Fromgar breathed heavily. He said nothing, though he continued to sweat profusely. His skin was an unhealthy pallor, but that could have been through fear as much as anything. The remains of the powder streaked his shirt, turning an ugly purple where it soaked up the moisture.

Then, it started working. Verstohlen watched intently, his body taut with expectation. Fromgar's muscles began to relax. The grip of terror left his features. His fingers went limp in their bonds. His breathing slowed and a gentle sigh escaped from his lips.

'Feeling better?' asked Verstohlen.

Fromgar nodded listlessly.

'Heh,' he gurgled. 'This really isn't so bad.'

'Tell me what you're seeing.'

Fromgar looked like he was having trouble concentrating. 'Ah, well, I'm not really seeing anything. I'm just feeling a lot better. Sigmar, I've not felt this good since...'

He drifted off into unintelligible mumbling. A childlike smile spread across his face.

'Do you know where you are?'

Fromgar nodded. 'In the Averburg.'

So he retained some sense of the real world. The root could just be a harmless relaxant. There was always that chance.

Verstohlen stood up again and went to the chest for a final time. There was one more item he needed to deploy. Of all of them, it was the most proscribed. It was why Kraus couldn't stay in the room, and why the interrogation couldn't be disturbed. If the witch hunters knew he had it, he ran the risk of facing interrogation himself. He retrieved it and went back to Fromgar.

'Can you hear me, Herr Fromgar?' he said, quietly but firmly. He clasped the object in his hidden hand carefully. The metal felt hot against his skin already.

Fromgar's head was beginning to loll. With some effort, he looked up.

'I can see you,' he drawled.

'I am going to show you something. You must look into it. Do this last thing for me and I'll leave you alone with your dreams. Do you understand? This is very important.'

Fromgar nodded. The joyroot seemed to make him both suggestible and benign. There was no resistance.

Verstohlen took a deep breath. There were dangers associated with this. He drew out the object. It was an amulet. On the silver surface the design of a serpent had been inscribed. On the reverse face a script had been engraved. There were none now who could read it. It belonged to a realm that had long since been scoured from the face of the world. But Verstohlen knew what it had been made for. And he knew what power was still bound within it.

He thrust the amulet before Fromgar's eyes.

The change was immediate. The benign smile was replaced with a malignant leer. Fromgar's tongue flickered across his exposed teeth. His body went rigid again, his fingers scrabbling at their bonds. Flecks of spittle flew from his mouth.

'Ach!' he cried, writhing against the rope that held him. 'Herself! Ah, so beautiful!'

The convulsions began to accelerate. Verstohlen withdrew the amulet. Fromgar began to spasm. He looked wracked between some kind of ecstasy and crippling pain. The chair started to shuffle across the floor as his feet kicked out. That shouldn't have been possible. It was solid oak, bound with iron.

Verstohlen watched carefully, reaching for his pistol. Pricks of sweat burst out across his palms. This had always been the danger. With such work, there was always this danger. He primed the weapon, his eyes fixed on Fromgar the whole time.

The foaming got worse. The man was drifting into a seizure. He began to shriek. His voice sounded strangely feminine, like an adolescent boy's before it broke.

'She *is* coming!' Fromgar wailed, then his speech drifted back into gibberish. Verstohlen watched carefully, trying to make sense of the words. They were nonsense. Or some language he didn't understand.

Suddenly, he realised what was going on. Fromgar's eyes snapped open and the man stared at him. The pupils were gone. In their place, lurid pink spheres blazed out. Lines of blood ran down his cheeks. A deranged grin distorted his face. The language wasn't nonsense. It was as ancient as the amulet.

'She is coming!' he said again in Reikspiel.

The chair began to rise from the floor.

The pistol rang out, twice. The first shot went through Fromgar's heart, the second through his forehead. The chair fell back to earth with a clang. Fromgar slumped in his bonds, drool and blood running down his chin. His fingers clenched, then relaxed. The light went out from his eyes.

Verstohlen looked on for a moment, his heart still beating heavily. His hands shaking slightly, he reloaded the pistol, watching the corpse all the while. There was a knock on the door. The guard.

'Sir? Everything all right in there?' came the muffled enquiry.

'Yes. You may come in now,' said Verstohlen, putting the amulet away and doing his best to restore a facade of calmness.

Kraus's man entered. He glanced at the body in the chair. The merest flicker of surprise crossed his solid features. No doubt he'd seen much worse.

'This man was a heretic,' said Verstohlen, putting his instruments carefully back in their wrapping. 'I was obliged to silence his blasphemy. His body will have to be burned, as will his clothes and the perishable items in this room.'

The soldier nodded smartly.

'It will be done,' he said.

'Ensure a priest is present, and alert the Temple of Sigmar. They'll want to make their own enquiries. Tell them what I told you, but do not delay burning the body. If they have any complaints, they can speak to me.'

The soldier bowed, then rushed away to make arrangements. When he was gone, Verstohlen looked back on Fromgar's body. Despite all his training, the sight of it turned his stomach. His assessment hadn't changed. The man had been a crooked fool, no more. He'd had no real idea of what he'd been mixed up in.

But Verstohlen did. And as he contemplated the possibilities, the thought of it chilled his blood.

CHAPTER NINE

Gerhard Muller gripped the cudgel tightly. It wasn't as easy to do as it should have been. His vision was still clouded with drink. The men around him looked unsteady on their feet too. That was predictable, of course. If you gave a bunch of thugs a handful of coins and told them to prepare for trouble, they were bound to drink it away. That was what thugs did when you indulged them. Averheim was a much friendlier place for his kind than it used to be. And it was getting even better.

He looked at the boys around him. He knew most of them. Some had been dragged out of some hole by Drucker, others looked entirely unfamiliar. They might just have been coming along for the ride. As far as Muller was concerned, they were welcome to. The more, the bloodier.

The gang of men rounded the last corner before the square. The targets were right in front of them, celebrating in the evening sunlight outside the inn on the far side. They looked pretty well-lubricated. Muller surveyed the scene quickly. Leitdorf's men numbered about fifty. Maybe a shade more. They were relaxed. He didn't see any weapons. Some of them had already passed out. It was just as Alptraum had told him. 'Charge!' he bellowed, waving the cudgel wildly over his head. All around him, his mates did the same. They made a pretty terrifying spectacle. In a disorganised tide, Muller's band of brothers swept across the square. With satisfaction, Muller saw Leitdorf's mob scramble to their feet. They were completely unprepared. That was sloppy. Really sloppy.

Then they were among them. Muller swung the cudgel with abandon. Most of Leitdorf's men were unarmed. He enjoyed the way the heavy wood crunched against bone. One particularly vicious swipe audibly caved a man's skull in. Muller liked that. He made it an ambition to do it again. There was something gloriously satisfying in the sound, the squishy, liquid squelch of brains being redistributed.

A man swung a table leg in Muller's direction. It was a pretty pathetic sight. Muller hammered the cudgel into the man's midriff, knocking the wind out of him. He collapsed, and the table leg skittered across the stone. The cudgel rose and fell quickly. Two, three blows and the man was out cold. Muller stood over him, feeling the surge of victory in his blood. He took aim and plunged the cudgel down at the prone man's skull. It cracked, caving in like a chicken's egg.

'*Yes!*' he cried, looking around to see if anyone had noticed. This game was getting better and better.

Drucker swayed up to him. He looked drunk, both on violence and on ale. He had a trail of blood across his mouth. Even Muller didn't really want to know how he'd got that.

'We should torch this place,' Drucker said, grinning.

'That's what we're being paid for. Who's got the flints?'

'Thought you did.'

Muller laughed. As much as he liked his ale, he couldn't deny that getting plastered got in the way of proper planning.

'Damn it. What are we going to do now?'

That question was answered more quickly than he expected. From the other side of the square, more men had arrived. They were bearing weapons. Just like Muller's men, they were pretty crude. Meat hooks, hammers, blacksmith's tongs, even rocks. Leitdorf's people weren't entirely unarmed after all.

'Excellent!' exclaimed Muller, licking his lips. 'They're up for a fight.'

Drucker grinned savagely.

'I'll squeeze their eyes out,' he wheezed, fingering his meat chopper lasciviously. Muller looked at the man uncertainly. He liked a good scrap as much as anyone, but Drucker could be a little alarming.

There wasn't time to dwell on it. Muller's men left their looting and charged the newcomers. The two groups met in the middle of the square. They were evenly matched. Soon the blood was flowing again. Muller began to really enjoy himself. He took a deep cut from a flailing knife. That was fine by him. Credit to the man who managed to land a blow. It all made for a more entertaining evening. Especially once the lad in question, a meek-faced boy with freckles and a tuft of light brown hair, was lying on the floor with his jaw knocked clean from his head. He made an appealingly ago- nised yelping as he crawled along the ground, a slick of blood and saliva in his wake. Muller walked after him cas- ually, swinging the cudgel. He lined it up with the boy's head, and wondered if he was likely to make it three skull cracks in a row.

Then there was the sound of trumpets blaring. Muller looked up, a horrible sinking feeling in his stomach. This fun could soon be about to end. The square began to fill with mounted warriors. Knights. They were wearing the liv- ery of the Averburg garrison, wearing armour and carrying longswords. That was completely unsporting. He looked around, trying to see if there were any escape routes. The way they'd come was still open. If he ran, he'd make it.

Leaving the lad to choke on his blood, Muller broke into a sprint. The ale still swilling round his head made the going difficult. Running in a straight line was far harder than it should have been. He stumbled at one point, tripping over a prone figure on the ground. It might even have been Drucker, but he couldn't stop to check. He picked himself up and carried on running. He was going to make it. The horsemen were busy mopping up the laggards behind. The side street beckoned.

Then something very hard and very heavy hit him on the back of the head. That really caused him problems. He fell down again. Getting up was difficult. The world was swimming. Something hot and wet ran down his back.

Muller pushed himself to his feet, trying to keep his legs steady. He looked up. There was a horseman looming over him. He couldn't focus on the figure well. The man looked massive. He was wearing heavy armour and had a grey beard. His blade was unsheathed and it blazed silver. The man's face in the open helmet was contorted with anger. It looked oddly familiar, though he couldn't think why.

Muller could feel his awareness slipping away. The scrap was over. He'd had his fun and spent his money. That was really all a man like him could expect out of life. With any luck, this militia captain would give him a break and he'd spend a day or two in the stocks. After all, brawling was something that happened all over the Empire.

'You've got me, sir,' he drawled, dropping the cudgel and holding his hands up shakily. 'I'll come quietly.'

The horseman leaned forward, pulling his blade back as he did so.

'No, you won't.' The voice was humourless, as cold as iron.

Muller looked up, just in time to see the sword sweep towards him. His last thought was how magnificent it looked. There were runes on the steel. That must have cost a packet.

Then it bit, and the game was over for good.

Schwarzhelm pushed open the door to his chamber and sat down heavily in his chair. His sword arm ached. It had been out of practice. Though he'd craved some action to offset the tedium of the tribunal hearings, there was no satisfaction in breaking up the mobs of Leitdorf's and Grosslich's supporters. Three more days had passed. The daylight hours were filled with legal arguments, the nights with suppressing the electors' unleashed violence.

It was grim, depressing work. The gaols were full, and still the candidates found willing hands to do their sordid work. They were both as bad as each other, though each was careful to distance themselves from the trail of gold. It was getting worse. The city was drifting into lawlessness. The whole situation was listing out of hand.

Schwarzhelm poured himself a flagon of ale from the jug on his desk. He drank deep. He hadn't slept for any of those three days. Even drink made no difference. It was making him fractious, paranoid. Something would have to change. Somehow, he'd have to turn things around. As it was, he felt like he was slowly going mad.

There was a gentle knock at the door. Verstohlen again. The man was like a bad schilling.

'Come!' he roared.

The agent entered. His face looked grave.

'I've not been able to contact you,' he said. Was there reproach in that voice? There'd better not have been.

'I've been busy,' Schwarzhelm growled.

'I heard about it. That's the second night of disturbance in the Old City.'

'They've both got their hired boneheads out in force. I had to adjourn this afternoon's hearing. These men are powerful, and they know what they're doing. We can't run the tribunal while the city burns.'

'You're halting it?'

Schwarzhelm shook his head. 'It'll continue. We're making progress. They'll accept the Imperial decree. They'll have to.'

'I'm glad they're coming around. But the closer you get to a decision, the worse things will get on the streets.'

'You think I don't know that?'

Verstohlen paused.

'There are other options.'

'I know what you're going to–'

'You should give it some consideration.'

Schwarzhelm's eyes blazed. His anger seemed to come so readily. He had to keep a lid on it. Verstohlen was only doing his job.

'You're questioning my authority,' he said, warningly.

'I'm doing no such thing. I'm questioning your judgement.'

Only Verstohlen could have said that. Kraus or Grunwald would have died before such words could have passed their lips. That was the difference between soldiers and ordinary men. Soldiers knew when to shut up and take orders.

But Verstohlen wasn't ordinary, in any sense.

'I won't debate with you,' Schwarzhelm said bluntly. 'I don't want Helborg brought into this. You know my reasons.'

Verstohlen held his ground for a few more moments, looking like he was going to argue. Then he clearly thought better of it. 'Heard from Grunwald yet?'

Schwarzhelm shook his head.

'Nothing.'

'And that doesn't concern you?'

'He can look after himself. When things are more stable, I'll send more men.'

Verstohlen didn't look happy. He was a professional spy and could project any demeanour he wanted to. He didn't bother hiding the way he felt with Schwarzhelm. That, at least, was a minor courtesy.

'I think things are more complicated here than may be apparent,' Verstohlen ventured, choosing his words carefully. 'If this were just a matter of the electors-in-waiting fighting amongst themselves, maybe I'd agree with you. But I no longer think it is.'

Schwarzhelm found himself getting impatient. If his agent had a flaw, it was a tendency to see hidden schemes in everything. As a soldier, he took the world as it appeared. He listened, though, quelling his bubbling irritation.

'This joyroot,' continued Verstohlen. 'The substance I told you about. I've been conducting some experiments. It's tainted.'

'Poisonous?'

'No. *Tainted.*'

Schwarzhelm paused. 'You've seen evidence of this?'

'As firm as it ever gets. The narcotic is relatively harmless on the surface, but I no longer believe its traffickers are interested in money alone. Its spread has been carefully planned. My estimate is that it's been distributed here for a year or more. I don't know its ultimate function, but you cannot have missed the sense of wrongness here. It's undermining Averheim. No one has a good word to say about the place. The city is sick.'

Schwarzhelm nodded slowly. He found himself reluctant to follow the implications of Verstohlen's report. There was no time to get bogged down in an investigation. But corruption was corruption. It couldn't be ignored.

'What do you propose?'

'You know my counsel.'

'Witch hunters.'

Verstohlen looked surprised.

'How long have you known me? I despise them.' There was a shard of vehemence in the quiet man's voice. 'They'd blunder across the trail, destroying everything. No, I can get to the bottom of this.'

Schwarzhelm looked at him carefully. 'Don't let your past interfere with your judgement, Verstohlen. Sooner or later, they'll have to be brought in. If you're right about this, that is.'

Verstohlen looked back at him defiantly.

'They will. When I've traced this back to the source.' He seemed unwilling even to countenance their employment. Schwarzhelm didn't feel like pressing the point. He knew why. 'In the meantime, we should send for reinforcements from Nuln,' continued Verstohlen. 'Recall Grunwald. The city must be secured. I can't work through this anarchy.'

Helborg. For the first time, Schwarzhelm felt his will began to waver. There would be a price to pay if he sent for the Reiksguard. He'd never be allowed to forget it. What was worse, the suspicion that Helborg had stationed himself at

Nuln for just such an eventuality still hadn't left him. The man was clever enough. He was also ambitious.

Schwarzhelm looked at Verstohlen carefully, putting the tankard down beside him. Perhaps the man was right. The situation was becoming hard to contain. Perhaps it was time to summon help.

Suddenly, there was hammering at the door outside.

'My lord,' came a voice from the other side. It was Kraus. 'Word from the east.'

Schwarzhelm leapt up from his seat and wrenched the door open. Kraus stood in the corridor beyond, looking even grimmer than usual.

'A messenger has arrived. He's half-dead from riding, but we've got tidings out of him. Grunwald is dead, my lord. His army is broken. Herr Bloch has assumed command of what remains and is aiming for Heideck. Grenzstadt is cut off. What are your orders?'

For a moment, Schwarzhelm stood stunned. Grunwald slain. His army destroyed. The news felt like a series of hammer blows. He reached for the door frame and leaned against it. The stone was cool under his fingers.

'My lord?' asked Kraus again.

Schwarzhelm felt his heart begin to race, just as it had been doing in the silent hours of the night. A sweat broke out on his brow. His policies were unravelling. Every decision he made seemed to be foundering. For the first time in his long and distinguished career, he didn't know what to do. He was surrounded by men who wished to see him fail. He remembered Lassus's words in Altdorf. *There are other ways of harming a man. Subtle ways.* They couldn't best him in battle, so they were striking at those close to him.

Kraus said nothing, though Schwarzhelm could see the concern in his face. The captain had never seen indecision from his master before. The look in the man's eyes struck at his heart.

'My lord?' This time, the voice was Verstohlen's. 'Are you all right? You look sick.'

That was it. He was sick. Something had been poisoning him. Eating away at his mind. Ever since Turgitz. What was it? Why couldn't he fight it?

'Enough!' he roared, pushing himself away from the door frame. He strode back into the chamber, looking for his sword. 'Enough of this skulking in the shadows!'

He retrieved the Rechtstahl and buckled the scabbard to his belt. Kraus and Verstohlen looked on worriedly. Let them fuss. The time had passed for intrigue and plotting. Blood had been drawn, and it needed to be matched.

'Gather the men,' he said to Kraus. 'We'll muster the remainder of the garrison here and ride out tonight. Grunwald will be avenged.'

'Yes, my lord.' The man bowed and hurried away. Kraus looked reassured. All he wanted was leadership. That was all any of them wanted.

Except for one.

'Is this wise?' hissed Verstohlen. He followed Schwarzhelm out into the corridor. 'You can't leave the city like this. With you gone, there'll be nothing–'

'Damn the city,' snapped Schwarzhelm, striding down the corridor towards the armoury. 'They've brought it on themselves. I've stayed cooped up here too long.'

'They *want* you out of the city,' insisted Verstohlen. 'These attacks aren't random. Why do you think the roads are blocked? Who's doing that?'

Schwarzhelm whirled around to face Verstohlen, his face a mask of anger. Grunwald's death was sinking in. A deep, dark anger had been unleashed within him. Justice would have to wait. Vengeance demanded it.

'Silence!' Schwarzhelm snarled. Even the agent, used to his temper, shrank back. 'Pursue your theories if you want to. Good men have died, and I should have been with them. Tochfel can handle the mobs. Keep an eye on him. And warn those warring fools: when this is over, I *will* return.'

For once, Verstohlen was speechless. In the face of Schwarzhelm's cold ferocity, it was all he could do to nod weakly.

Schwarzhelm swung round and resumed his march to the armoury. A black mood consumed him. Deep down, part of him knew he was being drawn into this. Part of him knew that his judgement was impaired. He needed sleep. Part of him knew that he might be making a terrible mistake.

It didn't matter. His blood pumped vigorously around his body. The Rechtstahl hung reassuringly at his side. Soon the fields of Averheim would feel the thunder of his wrath. If the enemies of the Empire had intended to provoke him, they'd succeeded. Now he would teach them the true meaning of fury.

Dagobert Tochfel looked from his window gloomily. Even from so high up in the spires of the Averburg, he could see the city burn. A hundred small fires sending their smoke rising into the warm night, lit by the mobs of the electoral candidates. They were running riot. Though their energy was aimed at each other, it was the city they were destroying. The city he'd served for three years, ever since Ironjaw had slain the last count.

He'd put off a contest for as long as he could. He'd always known what it would bring. While Leopold remained alive, there had been the hope that a succession would pass off peacefully. But Rufus was a different proposition. The era of great men was over. Those who remained were like squabbling children. The days when the Empire could produce a Karl Franz, a Volkmar, a Todbringer, were gone. When the older generation passed on, there would be nothing left.

Tochfel watched the fires burn for a little longer. Then he closed the window and turned away. It sickened his soul.

His chamber was small and modestly proportioned. Pious icons of Sigmar and Verena hung over a simple desk. Candles burned in iron holders. A narrow bed, hard and unyielding, stood against the plain stone wall. Every inch a scholar's room. Not much to show for a lifetime's service, perhaps, but it reflected his character well enough. As things had gone, the very plainness seemed like an indictment. Averheim was drifting apart. Perhaps he should have devoted himself to a different cause. The law was no longer the protection the city needed.

There was a knock at the door. Tochfel sat down at his desk. 'Come.'

A man entered. Achendorfer. He looked tired too. He'd borne the brunt of organising the legal procedure for the tribunal. Neither Schwarzhelm nor the opposing counsels had given him much room to manoeuvre. His normally pallid skin looked as white as death.

'The papers you asked for, Steward.'

Achendorfer placed a sheaf of parchment documents on the desk. When he spoke, his voice wheezed slightly. This thing was taking its toll on all of them.

'Good,' Tochfel said. 'The tribunal will start on time tomorrow?'

Achendorfer shrugged. 'I've been told it will. We've much to do before then.'

Tochfel smiled, but there was little warmth in it.

'Try to get some rest. In the end, it will come down to Schwarzhelm's word. Precedent will not decide anything.'

'In that case, there's little point going through the motions.' His voice betrayed his irritation. He ran his hands through his thinning hair. 'But that's not why I'm here, Herr Tochfel. I've been approached by men from both camps. There's more money floating around this than I've ever seen. I'll not lie to you. I've been tempted. Others may have given in.'

Why was the man telling him this? Could he really believe Tochfel didn't know it all? Was it to vouch for his own probity?

'I'm doing all I can, Uriens. I have my hands full with the riots. We need more militia. Even the Lord Schwarzhelm can't quell it by himself.'

Achendorfer looked sidelong at him. 'The mighty Lord Schwarzhelm,' he mused. 'You've spoken to him much?'

Schwarzhelm spoke to no one much. When not locked away in the tribunals, he kept to his chambers in the tower.

His movements were unannounced, his decisions arbitrary. Only the captain, Kraus and that enigmatic counsellor seemed included in his deliberations. It was like having an oddly powerful ghost controlling events in the city.

'He consults me on everything. Why?'

'There are whispers in the Averburg. There have been noises heard from his chamber at night. The man's not well. You can see it yourself. We may have reached the point where–'

He broke off.

'Say what's on your mind, Uriens.'

Achendorfer still hesitated. He was an official, not used to rocking the boat.

'Has he the confidence of the Grand County still, Steward? Can we trust the decision he comes to? I do not say this lightly, but…'

He trailed off again. That was as far as he dared go. Tochfel didn't reprimand him. All who were close to the process were thinking the same thing.

'They do things differently in Altdorf,' was all he said. 'He has the trust of the Emperor. That's enough for me.'

Achendorfer was about to say something else, but there was a second knock at the door. As if the noise reminded him of his timid nature, the loremaster retreated into his robes.

'Very well, Steward,' he said. 'Perhaps we'll talk about this again soon.'

Tochfel stood and showed him to the door. Standing outside was Verstohlen, Schwarzhelm's counsellor. Achendorfer bowed, and slipped away into the gloom of the corridor. Verstohlen barely seemed to notice him.

'Do you have a moment?' he asked. He looked distracted.

'It seems to be my night for visitors. Will you come in?'

'No. I can't stay. But there are things you should know right away. The Lord Schwarzhelm has been called east on urgent business. The cavalry forces in the city garrison have been requisitioned. You'll have to maintain security without them.'

Tochfel felt as if someone had knocked the floor from

under his feet. Things were already bad. Now they would become impossible.

'How... *could* he?' he exclaimed, incredulous. He now regretted his even-handedness with Achendorfer. The appointment process was descending into a farce. 'How will we keep the mobs apart?'

Verstohlen gave him a look that indicated he sympathised, but his hands were tied. 'You have the rest of the militia, the city watch. They'll have to suffice. I have my own business to attend to. The tribunal will have to be suspended. If you want my advice, you'll try to persuade the two parties to withdraw from Averheim until it can be reconvened.'

Tochfel felt light-headed. Matters were spiralling beyond his ability to deal with them. Neither Leitdorf nor Grosslich were in a mood to respond to persuasion. Their blood was up, and he wasn't sure whether they could rein in their supporters even if they wanted to. With Schwarzhelm gone, the two men might easily resort to more direct means of gaining power.

'This is madness, counsellor,' he said. There was an edge of bitterness in his voice. 'We were promised Imperial aid to ensure a smooth transition. Is this the best you can do?'

'Feel free to take it up with Lord Schwarzhelm when he returns. In the meantime, you have some decisions to make.' He gave Tochfel a significant look. 'There are options. Not all the Empire's armies are away in the north. When trouble looms, a wise commander looks for help close to hand.'

Tochfel wasn't reassured. Gnomic utterances were the last thing he needed.

'I'll bear that in mind.'

Verstohlen bowed. 'I'll be in contact when I can.' Then he was gone, following Achendorfer into the cool depths of the Averburg.

Tochfel left the door open. He stayed standing where he was for a moment. The tidings were the worst he could imagine. The prospect of the city tearing itself apart suddenly looked real. He ran over the possibilities. None looked good.

He was not a proud man. The stewardship had always been an unwelcome burden. He wilted under the demands of power. Always had. That made him an uninspiring leader, but it prevented some of the worst vices of command. He knew when he was overmatched. This was one of those times.

Tochfel stirred and reached for a small bell hanging over his desk. Almost as soon as the echoes of its ringing had died away, a functionary appeared. The man looked nervous. The unrest in the city had threatened to spread even to the Averburg, and everyone was looking over their shoulder.

'Tell the stables to make an errand rider ready. Then return here to collect a message. I'll inscribe it myself.'

The functionary hesitated. 'Where will the message be sent, Steward? Some will refuse to ride east. They say the greenskins are roaming free.'

Tochfel barely noticed the rank insurrection implied in that. His mind was already working on the contents of the missive. It would have to be worded carefully.

'Tell them Nuln,' he said. 'The Reiksguard garrison and Lord Helborg.'

Schwarzhelm kicked his horse into a gallop. It responded immediately. In the night sky, Mannslieb remained low on the eastern horizon. It was waxing to the full, but its light was uncertain. Clouds drifted across the sky, the first he'd seen for days. The harbingers of storms, perhaps, driven from the Worlds Edge Mountains.

Around him, the cavalry responded. Five hundred head of horse. The best that Averheim had to offer. Kraus and the honour guard were at the forefront. They'd accepted their orders without question. They always did. It had taken them mere moments to check their equipment and mount up. Even in the night shadow they looked magnificent, the moonlight glinting from their armour. They were as fine as Reiksguard. Maybe finer. Every man in the company had been picked by him. Their loyalty was unquestionable.

The Averlanders had been slower to organise. He'd had to

storm into the stables himself to get them in a suitable shape to ride. There was no excuse for such slovenly behaviour. It was true that some of them had previously been pressed into controlling the mobs in Averheim, but such work was nothing compared to the rigours of campaign. The whole province seemed to have gone soft. This was what happened when scholars took over. The Empire had always been ruled by military men, men who knew how it felt to lead a cavalry charge into the heart of an enemy. When that order was subverted, it was no wonder that sickness took hold. Sigmar had been a chieftain, not a loremaster.

As the hooves hammered on the hard ground, the mounted troops left the Averburg stables behind. They tore through the streets of Averheim. Any men still out quickly ducked into the alleys as the company of knights thundered along the thoroughfares. As he went, Schwarzhelm saw how many fires still burned in the squares and crossroads. The elector candidates had eschewed the last of their restraint. That was too bad. Tochfel would have to deal with it until he got back.

For some reason, that made him think of Grunwald again. A shard of pure pain entered him. Andreas had been a good man. A brave commander. The last time the two of them had spoken, he'd given him nothing but harsh words. If the tidings were true, he hoped he'd died honourably. That would be at least some consolation.

Schwarzhelm shook his head, trying to clear it. His mind was forever dwelling on failures. That wasn't like him. Why was his mind so troubled?

The gates were approaching rapidly. The horses didn't slow. A trumpet blared from further back in the column. Frantically, the drawbridge was lowered and the mighty doors swung open. They were out, past the walls and into the Averland countryside. Kraus's honour guard fanned out on either side of him. The men rode in unison, hooves beating on the road in a thudding rhythm. Further back, the Averlanders struggled to keep up.

Schwarzhelm gave them no quarter. The pace would be

hard. They'd ride through the night and ride through the day until they made Heideck. Then onwards, into the countryside, hunting the greenskins. He'd known he should have attended to the incursion as soon as he'd arrived in Averland. Now was the chance to make amends. This kind of combat was what he was born to do.

He grasped the hilt of the Rechtstahl, feeling the weight of it as he crouched in the saddle. It was eager to be drawn. Schwarzhelm had felt the spirit of the weapon sicken, just as he had, imprisoned in the stultifying heat of the tribunal chamber. It would be wielded soon enough, just as its makers had intended, on the field of battle.

For the first time in days, Schwarzhelm began to feel invigorated. He urged his horse on. The hooves thundered. The countryside began to slip by faster. This was what he needed. The chance to revive his animal spirits, shake off whatever malady had been afflicting him.

He looked towards the eastern horizon, shrouded in darkness. The air was no longer still and humid. Storms were active in the far distance and lightning flickered against the serrated line of mountains. The clouds had cleared from the face of the moon and pale light streamed across the silent fields.

He looked over his shoulder. Averheim was already some distance behind. Thin towers of smoke still rose into the sky. It looked lost, forlorn, vulnerable. He remembered Verstohlen's words. *They want you out of the city.*

He turned back, setting his face like flint. Averheim would have to look after itself. His duty drew him to Heideck, to Grenzstadt, to battle and vengeance. He kicked his horse again and the pace quickened once more.

Like a storm wind, the cavalry tore through the sleeping countryside. Even while Averheim burned, the Rechtstahl rode east.

CHAPTER TEN

Verstohlen crouched down. The trail had taken him close to the river on the east bank, down amongst the forlorn warehouses and goods yards. The alleyway he squatted in stank, and he covered his nostrils. The air was still warm, even in the deep of the night.

The two men he'd been following had stopped and were conferring with one another. They looked nervous. They had every right to be. Gangs of rogues were still roaming the streets. Whether or not the mobs were being actively controlled by Grosslich or Leitdorf was immaterial if you were caught by one of them. The two candidates had unleashed lawlessness on Averheim, and Verstohlen doubted if they knew the true effects of their actions.

He regretted Schwarzhelm's decision to leave deeply. It was the worst possible decision. While the Emperor's Champion was in the city, there was at least a chance that the situation could be brought under control. Rufus Leitdorf may have hated him, but he was easily scared. Grosslich was tougher, though Schwarzhelm was still more than capable of cowing the man. Schwarzhelm was capable of cowing anyone.

When he was himself, that was. Verstohlen had never seen him so ground down by an assignment before. For the first few days, he'd put it down to the heat. That explanation would no longer suffice. Maybe his best years were behind him. After so many years in the saddle, maybe the great old warrior had finally lost his nerve.

That wasn't it either. Schwarzhelm was a great man. One of the greatest in the Empire. Verstohlen had reason to be grateful for that. For Leonora's memory. Schwarzhelm hadn't been able to save her, but he'd ensured that those responsible had died. For that alone, he deserved Verstohlen's unwavering loyalty. He'd commanded it for ten years, and he'd have it for the rest of his life. There was little enough left to him to attach any allegiance to.

Verstohlen snapped back into focus. He was tired. His mind was wandering. The men began to move off. They walked with exaggerated casualness, the way a thief does when he has something to hide.

Leaving a few moments to let them get ahead of him, Verstohlen crept after them. Wrapping his dark coat about him, hugging the shadows, he maintained a safe distance. He wasn't close enough to hear what they were saying, but some energetic conversation was clearly taking place. They were on edge. At least one of them wasn't happy with the plan.

Then they seemed to relax. They'd reached the river's edge. Dark water lapped quietly against the quays. No one was around. Moored boats gently bumped against the stone. The still air was only punctuated by the creak of ropes and the distant crackle of the fires. Verstohlen shrank back again, waiting. This was what he'd been expecting. Now he'd see if the information he'd worked so hard to get had any substance to it. There was only so much one could do with a single name.

The men hung around at the water's edge for a few moments. Time passed. They began to get impatient.

Verstohlen wasn't. He settled back against the stone wall of a nearby storehouse and checked the knife at his belt. His pistol was with him, as ever, but for this he'd need stealthier tools.

Eventually, something changed. The men perked up. Verstohlen leaned forward. Even with the moonlight on the water, it was dark.

A boat drew up to the quay. It was a small one, a dinghy used by the river pilots. Somewhere, perhaps several miles upstream, a larger cargo barge would be moored, no doubt heavily guarded. There were several men on the dinghy, their faces masked. The two men on the quayside helped to moor the craft, where they were joined by the cloaked figures. There was a brief, low-voiced conversation and two packages changed hands.

Their business transacted, the two groups separated. The cloaked men climbed back into the dinghy, and the oars creaked. With a commendable lack of noise, the sail was hoisted and the vessel glided back off into the night. The men on the quayside, looking more relaxed than they'd been previously, started to walk away.

Verstohlen waited, keeping his body flat against the stone. They approached his position, oblivious to his presence. He let them pass. They got close enough for him to smell their breath. Then, as they walked off, he slipped out. The knife flashed, plunging deep into the back of the man on the left. Verstohlen pulled him round, twisting the knife as he did so.

His companion was slow to react. By the time he'd realised what was happening, he was pressed up against the wall, the blade at his neck. Verstohlen had the cargo in his hands, a carefully-wrapped oilskin package. He didn't need to open it to know what was in it.

'Where are you taking this?' he hissed into the man's ear. The smuggler froze. He was nearly paralysed with fear. At his feet, his accomplice was expiring in a frothy pool of blood. Just like Fromgar, they were hardly hardened criminals. Just small-time vagabonds drawn into a network of powerful men who preferred their couriers expendable. 'Your friend is dead. If you do not wish to join him, tell me where you're taking this.'

'H-Hessler's townhouse,' he stammered. 'Old City. Below the tanner's.'

Verstohlen listened carefully, judging whether he was being told the truth. The man was clearly afraid. He pressed the knife into his neck further, feeling the point penetrate the flesh. 'Think carefully, friend. I'm coming with you. Give me the wrong information and I'll make sure your death is unpleasant.'

'I'm telling the truth!' he spluttered. He was near tears. He was young, not much more than a boy. Clearly they hadn't found a reliable replacement for Fromgar yet. 'The barred door near the base of the loading platform.'

'What's the password?'

'Wenenlich.'

'What's that?'

'I don't know.'

The knife pressed harder.

'I don't know! Some place up the river, I think. It's just a word. That'll get you in.'

'That'll get us both in. Take me there now. Try to escape and the blade will find a resting place between your ribs. Do what I say and you'll live to do this again. If you can bear it.'

Verstohlen pushed the lad roughly forward. His feet dragging slightly, the smuggler kept walking. He was still scared. Verstohlen could feel the sweat on his neck, despite the cool night air. That was good. Every so often, he pressed the knife a little more firmly against his skin. It didn't hurt to be reminded. Well, not very much.

Helpfully, the dark obscured their halting passage up from the quayside and back into the inhabited areas of the town. There was almost no one around. Houses were boarded up, thick shutters locked shut. Even the rival gangs seemed to have gone to ground. Anyone who was still creeping through the echoing streets would have no doubt seen them as two drunks, supporting each other after a long night out.

'Wenenlich,' whispered Verstohlen to himself. The name was familiar, though he couldn't recall why. It sounded like a place, or possibly a name. Maybe nothing turned on it.

They continued their strange, limping journey. After a few minutes of shuffling down the dark, winding alleyways they reached their destination. The smuggler came to a halt before a nondescript door at the base of a silent townhouse. There was nothing to distinguish it from any of the others in the street. There were no lights, no sounds. The district was reasonably smart, but not too exclusive.

A good choice.

'What happens here?' he hissed.

The boy was getting scared again. This time, it wasn't Verstohlen making him anxious. 'Knock on the door six times. The grille will open. Say the password and he'll open the door.'

Verstohlen grinned in the dark.

'Nice try. You'll be doing the talking. Remember, the blade'll be at your back. You know what you have to do.' The lad took a deep breath. His hands were shaking. He was trying hard to hold things together. He knew his life depended on it. That tended to concentrate the mind. 'Off you go. I'll be right behind you.'

The smuggler went forward nervously. Verstohlen stayed at his shoulder. The package was stowed under his coat. It felt heavy. The roots must have been tightly packed.

The boy knocked six times on the door. The sound was flat. Verstohlen suddenly realised the significance of the six. So *that* was the nature of the organisation here.

An iron grille in the centre of the door suddenly slid back. The grate of metal against metal made Verstohlen jump, and the point of the knife pricked into the boy's back. That was sloppy. The tension was getting to him. Commendably, the boy didn't move.

'Password,' came a rasping voice from the other side. It was thick and unnatural sounding, more like a dog than a man. His voice trembling, the lad gave the answer. The grille slammed shut.

'Stand back,' warned Verstohlen. A light had appeared in the cracks at the door's edge. He wondered if the boy had done this before, or if he was simply acting on instructions. Either way, this was the risky part.

The door opened inwards. A sweet smell rushed out of the open portal and into the night air. It contrasted strangely with the dank stench of the street. The light within was dim and vaguely tinged with purple. A bulky figure emerged, his face still in shadow.

Verstohlen pushed the smuggler out of the way. The lad sprawled in the dirt and scampered off into the dark. Verstohlen ignored him and went for the doorkeeper. His knife flashed, aiming for the eyes. It connected with yielding flesh. He pressed forward, using his other hand to stifle a scream. His fingers closed on something clammy and tooth-filled. It felt like no human mouth.

Gurgling in agony, the doorkeeper slumped to the ground. Verstohlen withdrew the knife quickly and stabbed him in the neck and the heart. Each time, the blade plunged beneath the skin with almost no resistance. If the man had been wearing armour, that might have made things more interesting.

Verstohlen dragged the man inside and closed the door. He was in a narrow antechamber constructed of ordinary-looking stone. The light was coming from below. On the other side of the chamber, a stairwell led down steeply. There were no other openings. The place was silent. There was no sign of movement.

He pulled the body to the side of the door and leant it against the wall. The man's face looked horribly distorted. His jowls were longer than any normal human's, and long scars ran from the corner of his mouth up to his ears. They looked like they'd been made by sutures. One of the incisions had come open where Verstohlen's knife had plunged in. The flesh underneath was pale and glistening, like roast pork.

Verstohlen shuddered and turned away, wiping his blade. Despite his long service, something about the house was beginning to have an effect. He felt the first beads of sweat on his palms. Nothing wholesome had a guard like that. Whatever the secret of the joyroot was, there was some part of it hidden here.

He pondered what to do with the package in his hands. It had served its purpose in getting him in, and carrying it with him further seemed pointless. There was nowhere to hide it, though, so he kept hold of it for the moment.

Verstohlen crept forward, making sure his soft leather boots made no noise on the stone. The stairs ran steeply down. Torches had been placed in the walls, the source of the unusual light. Some substance had been placed in them that gave the flames a lilac edge. The aroma came from them too. The smell was an elusive cross between cinnamon and jasmine. Just on the edge of sensation, there was something else too. It might have been putrefaction. Or maybe that was his imagination.

As the base of the stairs there was a corridor running from right to left, as well as a double doorway leading straight on. From beyond the doors, there were noises. They were too dim to make out clearly, but they might have been voices.

Verstohlen could feel his heart pumping heavily. He was alone, vulnerable. Perhaps he ought to withdraw. Now that he knew the location, he could commandeer help from Tochfel. A raid could be organised in the morning, when the sun was up and men's hearts were stouter. Much as he loathed them, this was witch hunter work.

It was tempting, but it was the fear talking. He was after information, not to destroy the cartel. Blundering in now would undo all he'd worked to discover. He'd do as he always did, go silently and invisibly.

He made the sign of the scales over his chest. 'Merciful Verena, ward all harm.' His voice shook as he breathed the words.

Then he went on. Ignoring the doors, he crept along the corridor leading to the right. After a while, it curved round. It looked like he was tracing a route around a central circular chamber, one into which the double doors must have opened. The light was still dim, but enough to see by. It was near-silent. He began to hear his own breathing echoing in his head.

Ninety degrees around the circle from his starting position, a narrow stair ran up the outer wall. Beyond it, the corridor continued onwards. The doorway at the top of the stair was open. The ascent to the next storey. Verstohlen paused, looking back. Nothing.

He climbed the stair carefully, keeping his blade loose in his hands. As he went, his eyes scoured the gloom. The chamber at the top was small and empty, but it was well lit. The light wasn't coming from inside, but from an archway which opened up in the interior wall of the circle. Clearly this was some balcony above the central chamber. There were others of the same kind leading off in either direction. Like the boxes in a Tilean opera house, the antechambers overlooked whatever was in the centre of the building. That was where the murmuring voices came from. That was where the light came from. That was the heart of it all.

Verstohlen crouched down low, placing the package down carefully in a shadowed alcove and creeping to the edge of the antechamber. His heart had begun to hammer in his chest and he had to wipe the sweat from his knife-hand. Something was definitely happening. Beyond the railing of the antechamber, there were voices rising. The smell of jasmine was powerful. He looked over the edge.

The chamber was bathed in a lilac glow. It was circular, just as the external walls had suggested. Iron-framed braziers had been placed around the edges. They gave off light, heat and the strange, cloying aroma. Within the dark metal frames, flames writhed like snakes. The floor was a dark, polished stone. In the centre, a dais had been raised. The light reflected from the surface dully.

Verstohlen was barely twenty feet above the level of the chamber below. He kept as low as he could. For the first time, he could make an accurate assessment of the danger he was in.

In the centre of the chamber a throne had been constructed. It was made of the same stone as the dais. The artistry was astonishing. Verstohlen found his eyes drawn to it. Once there, it was almost impossible to pull them away again. There were figures carved into the high back, writhing in and out of one another. It looked as if a crowd of lissom youths had been fused into one tangled mass. Each member of the cluster was achingly beautiful, but their faces were contorted into expressions of exquisite agony. It was a warped mind that had created such a thing, though a gifted one. Despite himself Verstohlen's aesthetic sense was drawn to it.

Then he noticed that slowly, almost imperceptibly, the bodies that made up the throne back were moving. This was no cunning sculpture. The limbs were real, as was the agony of their owners. His appreciation vanished. He chided himself silently for expecting anything else. He'd known what he'd find in the house. The nature of the enemy never changed.

Around the edges of the chamber, more youths were scattered. They moved scarcely more than those trapped in the throne. Most were dressed in diaphanous robes that concealed little. All of them, men and women alike, seemed strangely listless. Their movements were miniscule, and ended almost as soon as they'd begun. With a spasm of distaste, Verstohlen saw that in place of eyes they had blank metal plates. The surface of the plates were polished, making it look as if they had mirrors sewn into their faces. One young girl seemed to be trying to crawl to the doorway. Every tiny shift of her body got her just fractions of an inch closer. Then it became clear that she had no idea where the door was. She started to head away from it. She was blind, aimless as the rest.

The tortured youths weren't the sole occupants of the chamber. The throne wasn't empty. Perched elegantly on the seat was a woman Verstohlen recognised all too well. She wore a long, elegant gown, slit to the hip. Her pale skin seemed to glow in the lilac light. Even more so than she had been before, Natassja was flawless. Her beauty was so absorbing, so utterly captivating, that it couldn't be anything other than unnatural. Nothing in the real world had a perfection of form like hers. Safe from the eyes of the world outside, here she was able to display herself in her full majesty.

Verstohlen narrowed his eyes. Prostrate before her was a man. He wore the robes of a loremaster.

Natassja regarded her devotee coolly.

'You may get up now,' she said at length. Her voice rolled around the chamber like a soothing balm. It was at once lustrous and spare, arch and disdainful. Despite his fear, Verstohlen felt the hairs in his neck rise. He clasped the knife more tightly. This was dangerous. He should leave.

He couldn't leave.

The man was Achendorfer. He slowly clambered to his knees. Lines of blood ran down the front of his robes. He'd been lying on a bed of wickedly curved spikes.

'How do you feel?' asked Natassja, looking at the wounds with mild interest. Achendorfer was clearly in a lot of pain. His face was contorted with it, though somehow he managed to keep his voice reasonably steady.

'To suffer for you is ecstasy, my lady,' he said through clenched teeth. It didn't look much like ecstasy from where Verstohlen was perched.

Natassja didn't appear impressed. She swept her eyes around the chamber.

'Do you know what these young people are?' she asked. Achendorfer shook his head, still kneeling before her. 'They're my latest toys. Since Rufus has been so busy with the great project, I've had to amuse myself. They're really coming on. I'm quite proud of these ones.'

As she spoke, Verstohlen could see a cruel delight play across her magnificent features.

'They're from all over the place. Serving girls from Rufus's estate. Street urchins. All beautiful of course, but poor enough not to be missed. Once we get them down here, we can get to work on them. Here's the game. They know they have to escape. They hate it here, of course, as I'm so cruel to them.

But you'll notice we've taken their eyes away. So they've no idea where the way out is. And – this is the amusing part – their bones have been rearranged. Very carefully rearranged. You've no idea how hard that is to do without killing them. Every movement they make is agony. *Excruciating* agony. So they have to go very, very slowly. It might take them forever to get out. I can't tell you how entertaining it is to watch them try.'

Achendorfer looked grimly at the slowly moving bodies. He had the look of a man who'd stumbled into a nightmare but couldn't free himself of it. Verstohlen suddenly realised why his skin had always been so pallid.

'An ingenious entertainment, my lady,' he said, doing his best to sound enthused. 'Have any of them made it yet?'

'Not yet. When they do, I'll have to think of some other gift for them. Some kind of reward. I suspect I'll have plenty of time to ponder what that will be.'

Achendorfer looked nauseous. 'An excellent plan.'

Natassja gave him a contemptuous glare. 'I hope you mean that, loremaster. If I detect a lessening of your enthusiasm again, you know what awaits.'

He glanced at the rack of spikes and a shudder visibly passed through his body.

'Yes, my lady,' he mumbled.

'Enough entertainment. Are you making progress?'

'Yes, my lady. He's left the city. He's at the end of his strength. Your influence is having its effect. He lasted longer than I'd expected, but it's turning his mind. The dreams have driven out his sleep. And there's the root. The air's full of it. He's finished.'

'Don't be sure. He will resist until he cracks. Does he have the numbers to defeat the greenskins?'

Achendorfer gave a nervous laugh. 'He could defeat them on his own. He's got days of frustration locked in him. I've seen to that.'

Natassja didn't smile. What amused her and what didn't seemed arbitrary.

'Good. That gives us the opening we need. Go back to the Averburg. Continue your work. The time has come for my husband and I to make our move. I'll send word to him and we'll make the final preparations together. When the moment comes, you will perform the final rite. Do not fail.'

Achendorfer shuddered.

'No, my lady.'

Then Natassja suddenly paused. She cocked her head to one side, as if listening for something. Verstohlen tensed and drew back from the railing.

'Oh, how delightful,' Natassja mused. 'I think my games have just got even better.'

Achendorfer looked around the chamber, confused. The youths still crept around in their agonised state. 'I don't understand.'

'There's someone in the building,' she said, licking her lips. 'A new companion for my pets, perhaps. We'll see.'

Verstohlen felt his heart jump. He had to get out of the chamber. Suddenly, something kept him frozen in place. A heavy reluctance to leave came over him. He gripped the railing of the balcony, heart hammering.

'Free yourselves, children,' said Natassja indulgently, looking at the miserable wretches crawling on the floor around her. 'Just for the moment, I'll let you go. But you know what you have to do. You know the rules. Stand!'

As one, the mirror-eyed youths stood up. Their limbs seemed to snap into action, though the movements were strangely jerky. It was as if a puppet master had suddenly picked up the strings.

Their mirrors went dark. Then, one by one, a purple light kindled in them. The youths started to smile. Their lips pulled round in ugly, tooth-filled grins. It stretched their faces horribly. Verstohlen guessed it wasn't really them smiling.

That sight helped break the spell. He pulled his hands from the railing and drew back from the edge. He left the package where it lay, going as quietly as he could. His fear was mounting. He had to keep under control. Every muscle in his body was screaming to run.

'Bring him to me!' cried Natassja. From below, her slaves started hissing, and there was the sound of doors slamming open.

Verstohlen felt panic overtake him. He gave up on stealth and turned to speed. He burst from the antechamber and careered down the stairs. The sound of the oncoming slaves echoed along the corridor. They were coming for him. The double doors had slammed open. His route back was blocked.

Hoping there was a way out somewhere at the rear of the townhouse, Verstohlen turned to his right, back into the depths of the building and broke into a sprint. From behind, he could hear the noise of his pursuers. They'd lost their immobility. They were able to move. Like spiders.

He gritted his teeth, tried to quell the panic within him. He tore down the curving corridor. As he went, he pulled the flintlock from its holster. His fingers felt clumsy. He cocked the hammer, feeling the cool metal respond instantly. Two shots, then he'd be back to knife-work. The blade in his favoured left hand, pistol in his right, he ploughed on.

The corridor ended in another set of double doors. Without pausing, Verstohlen barged into them. He could hear the rattling pursuit behind him, metal against stone.

The doors were unlocked, and slammed open. There was a large chamber beyond, lit by more of the jasmine torches. He had the vague impression of long tables, all covered with joyroot. Further back, giant vials boiled with liquid. They were refining it. There were six copper kettles. Naturally.

As he burst into the chamber, the figures within turned slowly to face him. They were clearly Natassja's creations. They'd all been altered. Most had no mouths or nostrils left. How they breathed was a mystery, but it must have kept them from sampling the stock. They stared at him with hopeless, empty eyes. Those who had eyes left.

He ignored them, barging his way past the drying tables. The hissing was close behind. The pets were gaining. Despite having their bones rearranged, they were quick.

A drone worker lurched into his path. Using his knife-hand, Verstohlen punched him in what was left of his face and pushed him aside, barely breaking stride. Those poor wretches were scarcely alive and were no threat to him. The far end of the chamber loomed. There were two doors in the far wall, one on the left, one on the right. Both were open, gaping like mouths.

Which one?

Verstohlen felt the scales pendant dangling at his neck.

'Ward all harm,' he whispered.

He chose left, pushing his way past three shambling, mouthless drones. From behind, he heard one of Natassja's pets leap on to a table, scattering joyroot essence across the floor. The hissing was getting louder.

Then he was through the door, back into another corridor, back into the shadows. He ran as fast as he could, ignoring the fact he could barely see. His heartbeats echoed in his ears. His heavy breaths turned to ragged, frightened panting. The joyroot dust was in the air. It intensified the panic. This whole place was laced with insanity.

He burst into another chamber. It was narrow, high-ceilinged. Up above, windows let in natural moonlight from outside. An external wall. On the far side of the room, there was another door, heavy and lined with metal. Weapons had been stacked in the corner and the Leitdorf banner hung over them. Arms for Rufus's men, ready to be deployed.

There were men in the room, lounging around a low table. Even as he ran in, Verstohlen could smell the sour beer, see the crude playing cards. This was a guardroom. Perhaps his last obstacle before outside.

One of the guards leapt up, reaching for a sword. Like the doorkeeper, his face had been stretched. Misshapen teeth stuck out at unnatural angles from his dog-jaw. The others, four of them, had been altered in the same way. They came at him.

Verstohlen didn't miss a stride. The first shot rang out, slicing straight through the dog-warrior's face, knocking him backwards. His knife finished a second, emptying his innards across the floor with a wicked swipe. Then he spun away, out of the reach of their crude blades, switching to the second barrel as he went.

They came after him. Verstohlen kept moving, leaping on to another low table, scattering flagons of ale. One nearly caught him. The knife flashed, and the guard lost his fingers. He howled in pain, before Verstohlen plunged the blade into his swollen eye socket.

The last of them withdrew warily. Verstohlen flicked his eyes to the card table. There were keys on it. From the corridor beyond, scuttling noises came. The pets. They were nearly there. He sheathed his blade. For this, he'd need a free hand.

He leapt towards the remaining dog-guard, kicking his boot out as he did so. The guard swung his blade clumsily to intercept, but the move was a feint. Verstohlen swerved away from the swipe easily and gained his real objective. The keys were heavy, strung on a loop of iron. He grabbed them and scrambled across to the door.

The pets burst in. Like insects, they swarmed across the floor. One, confused perhaps, leapt on to the dog-guard. The frail youth tore his throat out with his teeth, swinging his head from side to side like an animal. The others came after Verstohlen.

He slotted the key in the lock, then spun around. A pet reared up at him. A slim girl. Her robes bloomed out as she attacked, exposing the naked alabaster flesh beneath. Like all of Natassja's victims, she'd been beautiful once. Now her eyes burned with lilac light, and her mouth extended wide for the feast. Her teeth were pointed, tipped with steel, and her tongue was forked.

Verstohlen fired, feeling the heavy recoil of the pistol. The horror was hurled back. Her lithe body bunched up, limbs curled round like a wounded insect. Then he was through the door, out into the warm night.

The door slammed shut behind him, but in his haste he'd left the keys stuck in the other side. He cursed his stupidity and kept running, kept facing forward, kept going. The fresh air cleared his head, but the panic was still with him. They'd followed him out. How many? Maybe three. Maybe more.

Verstohlen couldn't look back. All he had was speed. No bullets left. He stowed the pistol and pulled the knife from its scabbard again. He wasn't sure it would be much good against those horrors.

He risked a look over his shoulder. Purple eyes, swaying in the shadows. They were scuttling still, hissing for his blood. So Natassja was prepared to risk them being seen on the streets. That was bad.

Verstohlen turned back, legs pumping, trying to exhort more speed from his burning muscles. There was no one abroad at this hour. For all important purposes, he was alone and far from help. More so than at Turgitz, more so than at any point in his life, he was afraid.

He careered down the alleyway, breath ragged. A nightmarish sequence of streets and silent squares passed. There was no noise bar the hoarse rattle of his own breath and the distant hissing of the pets. He was lost. He had no time to stop, no time to gain his bearings. Around every corner, he expected to stumble into the arms of a grinning horror, sharpened teeth ready to tear out his throat.

Then he saw it. The spires of the Averburg, vast against the night sky. The citadel was still distant, but its silhouette rose reassuringly large. If he could get there, he'd make it. With a redoubled effort, he sprinted down the street towards it. With a shriek of frustration, the pets saw his purpose.

But they were far from the controlling will of their mistress. Verstohlen couldn't risk another glance backwards, but the truth soon became apparent. They were falling behind. Whatever terrible perversions had been committed on their bodies had taken their toll. As Natassja's power waned, so their altered bodies began to give out.

Verstohlen careered around a corner and into a wide square. The windows were all dark or shuttered. But he knew

And they'd made one mistake. Up until now he'd been doing his job dispassionately. Now that had changed. They'd drawn something out of him that his countless victims, perhaps misled by his generally phlegmatic demeanour, had discovered was the very worst thing they could do.

They'd made him angry.

CHAPTER ELEVEN

Schwarzhelm brought his steed to a standstill on the ridge. The stallion pulled up reluctantly, stamping and rolling its eyes. The beast was exhausted, its flanks shivering and wet. The ride through the night had been punishing and the day had barely dawned. Dew still hung heavy on the lush grass. In the valleys, pale mist rose lazily from the rivers. As ever in Averland, the scene was one of peaceful beauty.

Behind him, he could hear the vanguard come to a halt. Further back, the detachments of Averheim cavalry were still riding to catch up.

Kraus pulled alongside him. He was as impassive as ever.

'Heideck,' said Schwarzhelm bluntly, gesturing ahead.

Averland's second city lay in the valley below, surrounded by its low, thick walls. Like most of the substantial settlements in the province, it had been made rich from trade. The Old Dwarf Road from Averheim to the mountain passes, the great artery of commerce in the southern Empire, ran right through it. Heideck had grown fat on the passing traffic. Its agents were known even outside Averland for being quick to spot the potential for a percentage. Despite being surrounded by lush pasture, few of the richest men in the city were farmers.

In normal times, the thoroughfares would have been laden with the wains and caravans of the trading guilds. The greenskins, even the rumour of them, had finished all that. As the dawn waxed into early morning, the last of the watch fires smouldered on Heideck's ramparts. There was no sign of fighting. The road ran down the slope before them, looping over broken ground and the ancient stone bridge crossing the River Pegnitz. It looked calm, prosperous, neat. The red tiled roofs of the merchant houses glowed in the early morning sun.

'So the greenskins haven't got this far west,' Schwarzhelm muttered. 'If those bastards kept their swords to themselves while Grunwald protected them, I'll–'

He didn't finish and kicked his horse back into motion instead. The animal whinnied in protest, but complied grudgingly. The column started moving again. The stragglers at the back would have no rest at all. Served them right.

The cavalry picked up pace, travelling swiftly from the high ground down into the Pegnitz valley. As they neared the city, Schwarzhelm sent a pair of buglers on ahead. The drowsy gatekeepers would no doubt need some warning of his presence. He didn't plan on knocking on the door.

Schwarzhelm felt tired but alert. His mind had cleared a little since leaving Averheim. Verstohlen was almost certainly right. He should have stayed in the city. But it was too late for second thoughts. He'd made his decision, and that was an end to it. The greenskins were his only concern now.

As they rode, Kraus said nothing. The honour guard captain never gave anything away. He never questioned orders, never looked askance. Perhaps that was a failing. Schwarzhelm's reputation made it hard to disagree with him. Grunwald had never done so. Nor had Gruppen. That was a weakness. His decisions had not been tested enough, and that left the door open to mistakes. He'd become intransigent. Intolerant, even.

It was not a quality he liked seeing in himself. It wasn't one he'd been born with.

Verstohlen was the only one who ever stood up to him. It was one of the many reasons he valued the spy's service. The man would have made a good witch hunter, if he hadn't despised them so much. Too much independence of mind was never a good thing in a Templar of Sigmar. The young Pieter would have probably ended up in their employ anyway if Schwarzhelm hadn't seen his potential. Verstohlen hated Chaos enough to be a witch hunter. He probably hated Chaos more than any man Schwarzhelm knew. For Schwarzhelm, the great enemy was one among many foes of mankind, each as foul as the next. But Verstohlen reserved a special loathing for the traitor, the heretic and mutant.

Schwarzhelm knew why, of course. He'd seen Leonora's body himself after she'd been retrieved from the pits. Back then he hadn't known who she was. Just another victim of the insanity of a cult, another innocent soul sacrificed on the altar of misguided fervour. The memory of the corpse still made him shudder. She hadn't given in to them, even at the last, even after all they'd done to her. That level of bravery had been astonishing in one so young. Verstohlen had been destroyed. A young man on the cusp of a scholar's career. All his learning had been impotent in the face of the raw sadism of the cults. And what was worse, they'd been Templars of Sigmar. The very men charged with hunting down corruption. The watchdogs had turned on those they'd been employed to protect.

After the cabal had been exposed, Schwarzhelm had hunted the men down personally. All of them. It hadn't been much consolation, but Verstohlen had been grateful. Grateful enough to devote the rest of his life to Schwarzhelm's service. The spy had since paid back any debt a thousand times over. Money was no motivation to him, neither was prestige. Schwarzhelm reckoned that nothing much drove him anymore except that one, burning quest. He wouldn't stop until every last den of heresy was extinguished, every corrupted cabal purged.

A futile quest, of course. Even Volkmar didn't believe that
the great enemy would ever be truly defeated. All they had
was resistance, the endless struggle against an infinite foe.
Perhaps Verstohlen knew all that, deep down. If he did, he
never admitted it. Every man needed a purpose, a way to
keep the nightmares from taking over. That was his.

The gates of the city drew nearer. The buglers had done
their work, and the archway was open. Beyond the gatehouse, Schwarzhelm could see frantic activity. They were
unprepared. Any watchmen they had on duty must have
been asleep. That summed up the entire province. Drowsy,
lazy and disorganised, even in the face of turmoil in Averheim and greenskins in the east.

Schwarzhelm picked up the pace, driving the cavalry column into a gallop. By the time the column reached the gates,
they were travelling fast. The hooves thundered on the old
road, throwing dust high into the air. He didn't pause at the
gatehouse, but continued straight on up the main thoroughfare. The streets were half-empty. The few townspeople out
and about rushed to get out of the way, pressing themselves
up against their neatly whitewashed houses. They looked fat.
Slow. Lazy. This place had sheltered behind the protection
of better men for too long.

Flanked by Kraus and the honour guard, Schwarzhelm
swept through the town and towards the main square. He
didn't need directions. The place had barely changed since
he'd last visited it.

The centre of Heideck was dominated by its merchant
guild-funded Halzmann Platz. The wide space was framed
on all sides by towering buildings, each decorated with
guild symbols and intricate stonework. All the fraternities
were represented. Tanners, miners, importers, landowners,
money-changers. Each had their own brotherhood, sucking
in money from the healthy flows of trade. All of them had
spent vast sums on their ornate frontages, and the crests of
the wealthy and powerful were all over them. Schwarzhelm
recognised the Alptraum coats of arms in more than one

place. So they were still powerful here, despite Leitdorf's best efforts. That boded well for Grosslich.

Once in the centre of the Platz, he called a halt and dismounted. Around him, his guard did the same, their armour clattering against the stone. From the guildhouses, men were beginning to emerge. Some were rubbing their eyes, seemingly uncaring of how ridiculous that made them look. It was too early for them to be at their desks. They must have lived in the huge mansions too.

From the largest building, a huge baroque edifice of fluted stone with rare coloured glass in its windows, a delegation of sorts filed out to meet him. Its members were dressed in the robes of town officials. At least most of them seemed awake. Schwarzhelm felt distaste stir in his frame. Officials. They were the same across the Empire. Tochfel, Achendorfer, Ferren. The names changed, but their characters never altered.

The leader of the delegation came up to him and bowed low.

'My Lord Schwarzhelm. You honour us. If we'd known–'

'Be silent. There are orcs on your doorstep. Where are your men?'

The man's face went grey. Next to Schwarzhelm, standing tall in his heavy armour, he looked little more than a child.

'We have maintained a garrison here, just as we are required to do.'

Schwarzhelm gave him a disdainful look. He felt like grabbing him by the neck and shaking him.

'My commander passed through here days ago. What help did you render him?'

'He asked for none. He was not here long. He headed east.'

'I know that. What forces did you give him?'

The official looked confused.

'None. There were no orders. I don't–'

Then Schwarzhelm snapped. His temper always seemed to be on the edge of breaking in recent days. Something about the petty man's manner, combined with the dull ache of Grunwald's death, pushed him over. He struck the man viciously with the back of his armoured hand. The official tumbled to the ground, squealing with pain and fright.

His companions started. Some made to intervene, then crept back, daunted by Schwarzhelm's presence. Kraus said nothing. Schwarzhelm leaned over the miserable figure of the official. Worm-like, he looked like he was trying to squirm away.

'You filth,' Schwarzhelm hissed, his face iron-hard. 'My commander is dead. He rode out to protect you. If you weren't so feckless you'd have done the job yourself. No doubt your troops are well fed and watered here while better men died to keep you safe from harm.'

The man looked up at him, clearly terrified. Schwarzhelm took no enjoyment in his humiliation. The official was nothing. A parasite. Like so many of those in positions of power across the Empire.

'You'll release your men into my command immediately. You don't need papers. You don't need orders. Anything my men need, you'll provide. You'll show Captain Kraus the keys to your treasury chamber. I'll need gold and supplies. You'll provide it all. You'll do it quickly. And you'll think yourself supremely fortunate you caught me in a good mood this day.'

The official's face was fixed in a kind of half-comical terror. Not many men could stand up to Schwarzhelm in full flow. This man wasn't one of the few that could.

'Y-yes, my lord,' he stammered. 'You'll get everything you need.'

Schwarzhelm turned away in disgust. His point had been made. Just looking at the man made him feel nauseous.

'What next, sir?' asked Kraus.

'Rouse the garrison. I want them ready to march within the hour. Find fresh horses and re-form the cavalry. Whip those Averlander dogs if you need to. Just get them ready to leave. We don't have much time.'

Kraus bowed smartly and set to work. Across the square, orders rang out. Schwarzhelm watched it impassively. Somewhere out there, in all the empty land to the east, the orcs were waiting. If Sigmar willed it, Bloch would be there too, still on his feet. Schwarzhelm knew he needed more men, knew he needed to give the horses water, but all of this would take time. The frustration burned at him. He felt his fingers creep towards the hilt of the Rechtstahl. The spirit of the weapon was eager to be drawn.

'Soon,' breathed Schwarzhelm, anticipating the slaughter ahead with a grim relish. 'Very soon.'

Ferenc Alptraum gazed out across Averheim. He was high up in his chambers. The ancestral castle, owned by the Alptraums for as long as anyone could remember, was second only to the Averburg in size. It offered him a commanding view. From the curve of the Aver up to the dominating bulk of the Old City, the landscape was studded with fires. The fruit of the power struggle he'd helped to create.

That wasn't what he'd wanted. It had never been what he'd wanted. If Rufus hadn't been so hell-bent on violence, it could all have been avoided. His own men had died. Most were hired scum, but some were not. Members of his family entourage, dragged into the city from Heideck. This wasn't their fight. The loss of a single one of them grieved him.

He stepped away from the window. The destruction was depressing. For all that, he couldn't withdraw. Not now. He'd committed himself to Grosslich. If he let things slip, showed even the slightest sign of weakness, it would be over. Averheim would be ruled by a mad elector again, and the Leitdorf grip on power would be resumed. It could not be allowed to happen.

In the past, of course, an Alptraum had wielded the runefang. His grandmother, the formidable Ludmila, had governed the Grand County with a silken glove over a fist of iron. Perhaps she'd been too intransigent, too belligerent, trodden on too many people. Even the guilds had no desire to see an Alptraum back in the Averburg. That sad fact had become clear years ago, back when Ferenc had still had designs on the throne himself.

But he was nothing if not resourceful. When Grosslich emerged, seemingly from nowhere, Ferenc was astute enough to spot a winning horse. Power was a fluid thing. If he could not be the figurehead himself, then he would have to be the next best thing. Grosslich was no man's fool, but he was a provincial and could be moulded. He needed Alptraum money and Alptraum manpower. Ferenc had provided both.

He thought of it as a business investment, the kind his family had made for centuries. For all he was supporting Grosslich now, the time would come when the debts would have to be repaid. The fact that the Alptraum name was on the gilt-edged bills would ensure the proceeds flowed directly to him.

It would be worth it. Anything would be worth it to prevent another mad Leitdorf ruling from the Averburg. Rufus and his damned wife both. Natassja was clever, but she had the looks and morals of a courtesan. There had been rumours about her for months. Where had she come from? What hold did she have over Rufus? The marriage was an embarrassment. The woman dominated him despite her dubious lineage. Though Marius had never been an ideal count, he'd at least married into nobility and not brought his ancient line into complete ridicule. With Natassja, Rufus had made his final mistake. For every addled noble who'd been seduced by her, there were two more who'd do anything to see her banished from the province. Why Rufus couldn't see that was something only he could answer.

There was a knock on the door. Ferenc glanced at the elaborate clock mechanism on the wall, one of his proudest possessions. It was early. He wasn't expecting Heinz-Mark until later. Instinctively, he made sure his dagger was in easy reach. You could never be too careful.

'Come.'

The door opened and a manservant appeared.

'You have a visitor, highness. Schwarzhelm's counsellor. He craves an audience.'

That was odd. Ferenc had had almost nothing to do with the elusive Pieter Verstohlen since the selection process had started. Grosslich seemed to think he was nothing more than a functionary. Maybe not.

'Show him in.'

The servant withdrew. A moment later, the counsellor appeared. He looked terrible, like a man who hadn't slept for several days. When Ferenc had last seen him, the man had seemed well groomed, urbane. Now he appeared more like his master, hollow-eyed and dishevelled.

'Counsellor,' said Ferenc, showing him to a chair. 'This is unexpected.'

Verstohlen said nothing but sat heavily in one of Ferenc's expertly carved chairs. There was a decanter of wine on the table to hand, and he poured himself a goblet. He took a long draft, then refilled it.

'I hope you don't mind,' he said, wiping his mouth.

'Not at all.' Ferenc sat opposite him. 'Have as much as you like.'

'A Heissmuller, I see. Very nice,' said Verstohlen. He was referring to the chair. Not many men would have known the marque. Despite his appearance, the man had refined tastes.

'That it is. Fifteenth Century. It's older than the castle.'

Verstohlen nodded appreciatively. The wine seemed to have restored his equilibrium, though Ferenc noticed that his hands shook slightly as he replaced the decanter stopper.

'What can I do for you, counsellor?'

'I'll come to that. First I must enter into confidence with you. Is this place secure? Can we be overheard?'

'This is my family house. You may speak freely.'

Verstohlen looked only partly satisfied. His eyes continued to flicker, as if hunting for unseen pursuers. He took another draught of wine.

'I am a member of Schwarzhelm's inner circle,' he said. 'I use the title counsellor, but my true functions are somewhat more specialised. A man like Schwarzhelm is recognised across the Empire. There are times when he needs information a public figure could never openly obtain. That's the service I perform for him. Among other things.'

A spy, then. That in itself was unremarkable. All powerful men had agents working on their behalf. But it was rare
for one to voluntarily declare themselves. Verstohlen didn't
look stupid or indiscreet, so there must have been a reason.
Ferenc listened carefully.

'My master is out of the city at present. I suspect he has
been drawn there deliberately by those who wish to see the
succession battle continue indefinitely. Until recently, I might
have suspected you of such motives. Maybe you still have
them. As things transpire, it matters not.'

Ferenc paid close attention, giving nothing away. Verstohlen
was speaking frankly. A lesser man might have been offended
by the suggestion that the succession had been deliberately
prolonged, but Ferenc wasn't put out in the slightest. They
were both men of the world. In any case, it was perfectly true.

'As part of my work here, I've made certain enquiries. They
began with rumours concerning joyroot. This led to other
things. I'm now certain that my earlier suspicions were correct. There are forces at work that wish to see the Emperor's
Champion removed from the city. They also wish him harm.
Their general purpose is clear. The succession will be subverted.' Ferenc poured himself a glass and crossed his legs.
Everything the spy said hinted at more. Despite his candour,
Verstohlen was still being careful. Something had scared him,
and for all his polished manners he couldn't conceal that
entirely.

'Interesting,' said Ferenc, keeping his voice controlled. 'I
hope you're not casting your gaze in our direction. For our
part, there has never been anything but full cooperation with
the Estates and with Lord Schwarzhelm.'

Verstohlen looked briefly amused, and his worried features lifted.

'Naturally. You needn't worry, Herr Alptraum. If I thought
you were behind the attempt to divert my master, I'd be having this conversation with your opponents. As it turns out,
however, that would be impossible. I'll not waste your time
with evasion. The Leitdorfs have turned to the great enemy.

They're traitors, and their claim to the electorship is now void. Were Schwarzhelm here, he would declare the contest over and enlist your help in destroying them. In his absence, that task is left to me. So I have come to you, through no small peril, to deliver the verdict. Grosslich will be the new Elector of Averland. If he is not, then the province will be given over to damnation.'

Ferenc felt his heartbeat quicken. He had to work to control it. The spy spoke calmly and with authority. He felt his fingers loosen on his goblet and grasped it more tightly. This was news indeed. If true, it would change everything. The battle would be over. Grosslich would gain the Averburg, and his own long plans would come to fruition at last.

Ferenc took a deep breath. He'd need to play this carefully. The game of power was a subtle one. Verstohlen might be lying. He might be mistaken. He might be a dozen other things, none of them helpful.

'Why come to me?' As Ferenc spoke, his mind raced ahead, considering the possibilities. All things being equal, having the Emperor's Champion onboard was a priceless opportunity. But in politics, things were rarely equal.

'You're the gatekeeper to Grosslich, just as I am to Schwarzhelm. I could no more gain an audience with him than you could with the Emperor. If I judge things right, then you're the real power behind his campaign. The Alptraum coffers are still full, and you've always known how to use them.'

Ferenc smiled. The flattery didn't deceive, even if the man was right.

'Your insinuation that Grosslich is anything less than the leader of our campaign distresses me. But you're right to come to me in the first instance. He listens to my counsel. If he's to take me seriously, though, I'll need more from you than a rumour. These are serious allegations. I'm loathe to believe them without some form of proof.'

In actual fact, the more Ferenc thought about it, the more sense Verstohlen's story made to him. Natassja was surely at the heart of it. She had the look of a witch. Rufus was no doubt the dupe in all this. He couldn't bring himself to feel sorry for him. The spoiled brat had it coming.

'I can give you none,' said Verstohlen. 'My own testimony is all I have, and I've seen the corruption with my own eyes. But consider this. You've nothing to lose by answering my call for aid. In Lord Schwarzhelm's absence, I speak with the authority of the Imperial warrant. The city is in peril. Help me save it, and Karl Franz won't forget it.'

They were convincing words. Inwardly, Ferenc found himself persuaded. Grosslich could be brought around. Heinz-Mark would need little argument to mount further attacks on Leitdorf's forces. As things stood, the turn of events was welcome. Very welcome.

'You've given me much to think about,' Ferenc said, masking his growing enthusiasm. 'In the interim, I'll send word to Heinz-Mark. I can't speak for him, but, between us, I think you needn't worry. We all have a duty to protect against corruption.'

Verstohlen nodded.

'Good. But time is short. Leitdorf knows his secret has been discovered. Even now, he'll be mobilising. I don't know how deep the rot runs. He may have allies. For our own part, we're in great danger the longer we hesitate. I urged the Steward to summon aid from Nuln before Schwarzhelm left. Even if he's done so, we'll need more help. We must summon Schwarzhelm back.'

'It will be done.'

'Send a heavily-armed party. The roads are no longer safe.'

'Worry not. My family's estates are in the east. I have messengers who know the hidden routes to Heideck and beyond, and there are no faster messengers in Averland. Your message will get through.'

Verstohlen took another swig of wine. The lines of worry across his brow seemed to be receding somewhat.

'I'll stay here for the time being, if I may,' he said, looking slightly sheepish. 'The Leitdorfs have a renewed interest in tracking me down, and the Averburg will offer no protection.

If Grosslich has any sense, he'll arm his men quickly and secure this place. We're on a precipice here.'

Ferenc sat back in his chair, exuding confidence. The news was dramatic, to be sure, but it boded nothing but good for his prospects. A few cultists could be snuffed out with ease. Grosslich was a formidable commander, for all his political naïveté. What was really valuable was the seal of Imperial approval. He, Ferenc Alptraum, could do great things with that.

'Never fear,' Ferenc said. 'You did the right thing to come to me. We've restrained our forces until now out of respect for the law. But all that's changed. We've arms, and men, and funds to pay them. Trust me, we'll have that traitor Leitdorf run out of the city before the week is ended.'

Verstohlen looked straight back at him. His eyes still bore the signs of some great fear.

'I hope so, Herr Alptraum,' he said, his voice shaking with vehemence. 'By holy Verena, I hope so.'

The forest was about as cool as anywhere out in the baking eastern countryside. Even under the leaves of the trees, the air was heavy with heat. Flies circled lazily in the ambient warmth.

Bloch leaned on his halberd, welcoming the shade. He'd got used to the never-ending sun, but he was tired to his bones. The harrying of the orcs, day and night, had strained his nerves and his sinews. He'd lost count of the days. Three? Four? They'd had some luck, it was true. The bulk of the greenskins had indeed turned back to Grenzstadt, just as the messenger had said. But the last of Grunwald's forces in that direction must have been long since destroyed. Now bands of orcs roamed the whole eastern marches of Averland, pillaging as they went. The damage they wrought was terrible.

Bloch looked over the ragtag army he'd managed to salvage from the ruins of Grunwald's campaign. They were snatching a few moments' rest under the shade of the trees. Over the past couple of days his forces had grown. More men had got away from the orcs than he'd first thought, and they'd been able to rescue further scattered groups as they'd headed west towards Heideck. There were maybe five hundred of them now, arranged into makeshift companies of a few dozen each, headed by the most experienced soldiers among them. Not much, maybe, but better than nothing. As the orc bands had splintered into smaller packs, they'd even been able to extract some measure of revenge.

Their bravery was beginning to cost them, though. The orcs weren't stupid. Despite his best efforts, Bloch couldn't hide his forces from them forever. Word had got out that a kernel of resistance still existed, and the hunt was on. He didn't have enough men to stand against them in the open. The only chance was to keep going to Heideck, to consolidate there with whatever forces remained in that garrison and then strike back.

It wasn't something he put all his faith in. The men of Heideck, from memory, were soft-bellied fools. But it was all he had.

'What are your orders, sir?' came a voice from beside him.

Bloch shook himself out of his introspection. Lars Fischer, his hastily promoted lieutenant, looked at him with weary eyes. The man was an Averlander and had proved invaluable so far. If they ever got to safety, it would be down to the local knowledge that had guided them down hidden paths in the woods and gorges.

'How far d'you reckon we are from Heideck?' Bloch asked, running his hands through his hair. He felt exhausted. No doubt they all did.

Fischer shrugged.

'Another day's march. No more than two. But the country's open there. Nowhere to hide. If there are orcs, we'll have to fight them.'

'There'll be orcs. They're on our trail now. Maybe it's better to come out and fight them. I'm fed up of this sneaking around.'

Bloch took another look across his men. They didn't look

ready for a fight. The constant running and skirmishing had muted the brief flame of defiance they may have felt at the beginning of the trek. Many of them slumped over their weapons, half-asleep in the middle of the day. The heat, the dust, the lack of sleep. It all took its toll.

'We'll give them a few moments,' said Bloch. 'They've already been driven too hard. But then we need to move.'

Fischer was about to reply when there was a crashing sound from deeper into the woods. Arrows whined across the clearing, thudding into tree trunks. The greenskins were back.

'Form up!' cried Bloch, springing into action immediately. He grabbed his halberd. His men rushed to form into defensive detachments.

The crashing became louder. From the shadows of the trees, the orcs burst into view. Bloch saw their leader before he saw the rest. Huge, bunched muscles, raging eyes and dripping tusks. There were dozens behind him, all heavily armoured like the ones they'd faced on the ridge.

He lowered his halberd. How many this time?

'Keep to your companies!' he roared. All around him, the men were falling into their detachments. The movements were expert, skilful. But they needed to move quicker.

The orcs closed, and the space under the trees filled with their battle roars. Bloch felt his fellows cluster around him. Even now they stuck to the defensive square. The familiarity was reassuring. As if by instinct, the leader of the greenskins made straight for Bloch. Its broad legs churned up the leaf matter on the forest floor, throwing it in all directions as it ploughed onward. Bloch adjusted his stance, legs apart, braced for the impact.

'Steady, lads.' he warned. 'Blades up!'

The lines came together, and the world descended once more into a storm of desperate combat. Bloch was knocked backwards by the force of the charge, but those on either side of him held the line. He recovered, hacking powerfully with his halberd. The greenskin screamed at him, covering his face with stinking trails of saliva.

Bloch grimaced, recovering his balance and pushed forward. His arms ached. His hands were calloused and bleeding. Like the others, he fought on. Any sign of weakness now and it would be over. They looked to him. He needed to stay strong, give them something to believe in.

With a mighty heave, he swung his halberd upwards, aiming to catch the greenskin in the face. The blade connected, slicing through the thick hide, spraying black blood into the canopy above. The monster staggered back, blundering into those around him. Even in the midst of their efforts, the men at Bloch's shoulders broke into a coarse cheer.

'Enough of that.' roared Bloch, readying himself for the next thrust. 'Keep your discipline!'

The orcs came again. There were dozens of them. Perhaps more. The leader was gathering himself for a fresh assault, its face streaming with blood.

Bloch made eye contact with it. He held it. This fight wouldn't be over quickly.

'Come and get me then, you green bastard,' he snarled, his halberd running with gore. The invitation was accepted.

Tochfel hurried through the corridors of the Averburg. The feeling of unease he'd endured for days was getting worse. With Schwarzhelm and Verstohlen both gone, any semblance of order to the proceedings had vanished. He'd had to deal with frantic messages from both Leitdorf and Grosslich, each demanding to know when the next session would be. In Achendorfer's absence, he had no idea. In fact, he had no idea where Achendorfer even was. The grey-faced loremaster wasn't much of a companion in times of need, but at least he had an idea of the protocol for such things. Tochfel didn't.

The Steward burst into his chamber, half-expecting to see the man waiting for him. Instead, he was confronted with the toppling pile of parchment documents he'd left from the previous day. All of them required answers, but only Sigmar knew what they might be.

Tochfel sat down at his desk. He could feel his whole body

tensing. The city was on the brink of anarchy, and there was nothing he could do about it. The few troops he'd had left at his disposal had been requisitioned by Schwarzhelm. He ran his hands through his hair. As he released the fingers, he saw loose strands of it twirl to the floor. He was getting old, tired and fractious.

There was a sharp rap on the door.

'Come!' Tochfel's voice sounded reedy and quavering. He hoped it would be Achendorfer. Instead, it was Morven.

'Steward, I bring a message from Lord Grosslich,' the aide-de-camp announced. His expression gave away the fact this was going to be bad news.

'I'm not going to like this, am I?'

'I'm charged to inform you that the Grosslich candidacy for the Estates has been withdrawn. His lordship accuses the Lord Leitdorf of turning traitor to the Empire and has declared himself elector in order to preserve the integrity of the Grand County. He wishes to inform you that his forces have been mustered and that they have begun their assault upon the city. None of the citizens therein will be harmed unless they have declared for Leitdorf and bear arms in his cause. However, any person resisting his just crusade will not be spared. The Lord Grosslich will not cease until the traitors have been destroyed and the city returned to the rule of the electors.'

Tochfel listened with growing despondency. So that was it. The mastery of the city had been taken from him at last. The passage of the law, so dear to his heart, had been utterly subverted. Whichever man eventually took up the runefang, Leitdorf or Grosslich, it would be as a result of might, not legal procedure. Such was the way of the wilderness, not the greatest realm of men in the Old World.

'What grounds has he for these claims?' asked Tochfel, trying to maintain an outwardly calm demeanour.

'I don't know, Steward. I only report.'

'Where is the Lord Leitdorf? Still in the city?'

'He cannot be reached. But there are reports of fresh fighting in the Old City. Grosslich's men are moving. It may not be safe here. We should consider abandoning the Averburg.'

That wasn't worth contemplating. The citadel hadn't been given up to an enemy in two thousand years. Even Ironjaw hadn't penetrated the outer walls.

'What about Schwarzhelm? Or his counsellor?'

'Still missing. Though I have reason to believe Herr Verstohlen has lent his support to Lord Grosslich. It may be a sign that the allegations against Leitdorf have foundation.'

Tochfel shook his head.

'Allegations? They're nothing more than rumours. Grosslich has used Schwarzhelm's absence to seize his chance. They're vagabonds, the pair of them, whatever noble blood they claim to have.'

As he spoke, Tochfel began to feel a strange sensation well up within him. The constant slights, the endless struggle to maintain authority, had all begun to take their toll. For once, he found that resignation wasn't what he felt. It was anger.

'This farrago has gone on long enough,' he said, balling his fists on his desk. 'All of them, Schwarzhelm, Grosslich, Leitdorf, have treated this place like their private fiefdom. No more. The rot stops here.'

Morven looked shocked, but said nothing. He was no doubt unused to being addressed by Tochfel in such a manner.

'We will *not* surrender the Averburg,' continued Tochfel, feeling more assertive the more he spoke. 'to either faction. Until I hear from the Emperor's representative himself, I remain the lawful keeper of this city. We will arm the men with what weapons we have. The gates will be barred. Grosslich and Leitdorf can hammer on them all they like. These walls were built to keep out worse foes than them.'

'We're not soldiers, Steward,' protested Morven, looking appalled. 'The garrison has been–'

'Don't tell me what has happened to the garrison!' snapped Tochfel, his eyes blazing. 'I know exactly what happened to it. But we still have men at our command and weapons in the armoury. Distribute them. See the gates are guarded. Go now, and report back to me within the hour.'

Still looking startled, Morven bowed hurriedly and scuttled out. Tochfel, his blood still hot, slammed the door behind him and strode over to the window. He looked over the city, just as he did every evening. The fires still burned. They were growing in number. He even fancied he could hear the noise of Grosslich's forces marching through the distant streets.

As he watched, his sudden anger was steadily replaced with a grim, implacable resolve. The city was descending into war. The Averburg, home for most of his adult life, would soon be an island in the midst of the fighting. In times past, Tochfel might have found the prospect terrifying. Now, he took a strange kind of comfort from it.

At last, the pretence of the legal process had been removed. The succession in Averland would be determined through strength of arms and force of will. Perhaps that was the purer way. In any case, at least his task was clear.

The Averburg must be preserved. That, and that alone, was his concern now.

Kurt Helborg, master of the Reiksguard, bowed low. He felt his forehead touch the cold marble floor. He stayed in position for a few moments, prostrate. The position was one of penitence, of humility. Before such a judge, there was no other attitude to adopt.

Heartbeats passed in the silence.

Then, his observance done, Helborg rose to his knees once more. The altar of Sigmar soared above him. He made the sign of the comet on his chest and clambered to his feet.

The Chapel of the Lord Sigmar Martial was one of the oldest and grandest in the Empire. The citizens of Nuln were justly proud of it. The floor was chequered with patterns of black and white marble imported from Sartosa, the very best gold could buy. The columns that sprung up to hold the distant ceiling had been carved into a host of intricate shapes. Some resembled tree trunks, complete with branches and leaves. Others had been shaped into dizzyingly complex geo-metrical figures, a fitting compliment to the mathematical heritage of the city. Aside from the light given by the massed racks of candles, the massive nave was clad in darkness. Hulking statues to various ancient warriors and dignitaries brooded in the gloom. The Imperial religion was not one of light and beauty. It celebrated steadfastness, gravity and bitter resolve.

Helborg liked that. He liked the whole place. Its evident riches, its seriousness of purpose, its ancient foundations. This was what a chapel should be. This was what the Empire should be.

With a final bow, he turned from the towering altar of Sigmar. The brass cherubs surrounding his effigy, each bearing a mechanical crossbow or repeater handgun, gazed back blankly.

He walked from the transept into the long nave of the chapel. The place was nearly deserted. A few priests shuf-fled in the shadows, tending to the candles and the votary incense burners. No ordinary people would ever come here. It was reserved for the mighty of the Empire. Despite himself, Helborg enjoyed that feeling too. Hierarchy was everything. Control was everything. Discipline was everything. As long as they were maintained, mankind would continue to dom-inate the ancient lands of Sigmar. If they were forgotten, the end would come swiftly.

As he neared the exit, he caught sight of a lone figure waiting for him just inside the porch. The shape was unmis-takable. Years of fighting alongside a man made his armoured profile almost as familiar as one's own. Leofric von Skarr, Preceptor of the Ninth Company of the Reiksguard. One of his most trusted men. Honest, capable, utterly brutal. Just as he preferred his officers.

'My lord Helborg,' Skarr said, keeping his voice defer-entially low. Even in whispers, the words echoed eerily in the vaults of the chapel. 'My apologies for disturbing your prayers.'

'It's fine. Come outside.'

Skarr opened the gigantic brass bound doors of the chapel for the Marshal, and warm sunlight flooded into the shadowy nave. The two men stepped through it.

They were high up on the north side of the city. The courtyard before the east front of the chapel offered a sweeping panorama. Around them, the greater mass of Nuln spread out in all its confused, tumbled majesty. The sound of the forges, ever-present even during the night hours, filled the air. Huge columns of black smoke rose into the summer sky from several quarters. The buildings were stained with soot. Below their vantage point, the River Reik ran dark and polluted. It would take miles before the filth of the forges was washed from its water again.

Such things mattered not. Nuln had not been built for beauty. The hammers of the blacksmiths fashioned weapons for the defence of the Empire. That was the city's function. The greatest foundry and workshop of war west of the Worlds Edge Mountains. Helborg loved it.

'So what is it, Skarr?' he asked, retrieving the sheathed Klingerach from the chapel warden and donning the ancient runefang.

'A messenger, my lord,' said the grizzled preceptor. His face was heavily scarred, as befitted his name. He'd lost an eye at the siege of Urkh five years ago, and the leather patch made him look half-feral. He had an angular face and his long hair hung dark and lank about it. There wasn't an inch of fat on his severe features. Everything was taut, muscular, spare. 'From Averheim.'

'Ah,' said Helborg, the ghost of a smile on his lips. 'Ludwig's little project. How goes it for my unsmiling brother?'

'Not well, I fear. The Steward has requested aid. The factions for the electorship have resorted to arms. He doesn't have enough men to keep order.'

Helborg frowned. 'How many men does he need? He has Schwarzhelm. That ought to be enough.'

'Lord Schwarzhelm isn't in the city.'

'Not in the city? Where is he then?'

'In the east. The message says no more than that.'

Helborg felt a sudden qualm of unease. That sounded wrong. Schwarzhelm was a stickler for the law. When given orders, he stuck to them until the bitter end. Such unbending devotion was what made him so formidable. It was also what made him such a pain in the arse. The fact that he'd left his duty for some other purpose was out of character, and that alone was a cause for worry.

'Are the Reiksguard in readiness to march?'

'Always, my lord.'

'Then I'll study this message myself. I don't like the implication in it.'

'Yes, my lord. The message bearer is still lodged at the garrison. I'll summon him to your chambers.'

'Do it.' Helborg's voice was as it always was when dealing with subordinates. Clipped, gruff, solid. But his mood of contentment had been punctured. Something was wrong in Averheim. Deep within, like a fleck of rust amidst the smooth workings of a cannon bearing, the germ of suspicion had lodged. Schwarzhelm had been behaving oddly recently. Maybe the man's judgment was failing.

As Skarr departed, Helborg looked out over the city again. The sun was high in the sky. Its warmth bathed the spires of Nuln generously. The manufactories were working at full tilt, hammering blades and gun-workings for the war in the north. He could have spent weeks in the city, ordering the production to best effect. The need for arms had never been greater.

Helborg shook his head. Whatever the messenger reported, his instinct told him his services would be called on. His work in Nuln would be cut short. His devotions would have to wait. As it ever did, duty called for the Reiksguard.

CHAPTER TWELVE

Schwarzhelm and the Averheim garrison had reached the wide pasturelands east of Heideck. In the far distance, the Worlds Edge Mountains were just visible, jagged and low against the horizon. For miles around them, the undulating countryside ran unimpeded, lush and green under the ever-present sun. In the distance, warmth shimmered from the deep grass. The light was blinding from the honour guard's polished armour.

The army had broken into a gallop. Schwarzhelm tensed in the saddle. He made a minute adjustment to his posture, eking out a fractional increase in speed from his charger. The knights on either side of him worked to keep up. He looked over his shoulder quickly. They were still in close formation. Kraus and his men in the front rank, the Averlanders behind. Some distance in their wake, hundreds of footsoldiers from Heideck streamed across the fields. All had weapons drawn. In combination with the elite guard at his disposal, he now had the tools he needed. More importantly, he had the will to use them.

He turned back to the chase. Prey had been sighted. Like the predators of the wild, his army had responded to the quarry. Clods of turf flew from the horses' hooves as they accelerated into a fully-fledged gallop. Lances were lowered. As they charged, the warriors looked like they were wreathed in a halo of light.

The heat was crippling. Schwarzhelm felt the sweat pool under his breastplate. He didn't care. For the first time in weeks, he felt fantastic. This was what he was born to do. His face was twisted into a cry of pure, unbridled aggression. As he roared his fury, his knights bellowed their defiance alongside him. The crescendo of noise thrilled his heart.

The orcs were running, loping like animals across the grass. It was a large mob, but no match for his forces. The sun flashed from their armour as they went. They looked better equipped than usual. He thought he could make out straight swords and halberds amongst their ranks. That was more than rare.

On either side of him, the knights moved expertly into formation. The honour guard were flawless, controlling their mighty warhorses with almost unconscious ease. The Averlanders, good horsemen all, kept close behind. Lances extended, the cavalry formed a single sweeping row of steel.

Now only yards remained. The greenskins had been taken by surprise. Their polluting stench rose over the pristine fields, wafted over the charging knights by the warm breeze. Some larger warriors turned and stood their ground. Silently, one by one, they were singled out by the knights. Near the centre of the mob, a larger monster prepared to meet the assault. He had a near-black hide and his bodyguard were clad in what looked like plates of armour. Clearly the leader.

'That one's mine!' roared Schwarzhelm.

Hooves churned. The distance shrunk further. Details came into focus. The final few yards vanished in a blur of speed. Schwarzhelm grasped his lance tightly and took aim. With a crash of metal, bone, hoof and muscle, the knights crashed into the orc lines.

The defence broke. Any pretence at formation was swept away with the first charge. Schwarzhelm's lance plunged into the breast of the foremost orc, lifting the massive warrior clean from the ground before the shaft snapped. Blood sprayed into the air, sparkling like rubies in the sun. All along the line, the knights scythed their way through the greenskin ranks, driving great wedges into them and throwing them into confusion.

Schwarzhelm let the broken lance fall and pulled the Rechtstahl from its scabbard. As the metal withdrew it seemed to shimmer with light. It knew it would taste blood. He pulled his stallion around, searching for the leader. A lumbering greenskin half-heartedly attempted to engage him. Schwarzhelm rode straight at it, his blade whirling. The warrior crumpled to the blood-soaked earth, spine severed. There were more behind him. Dozens of them. Fodder for his holy blade.

'For Sigmar!' Schwarzhelm roared, feeling the coppery taste of blood in the air. 'For Grunwald!' After weeks cooped up in the cesspit of Averheim, the Sword of Justice had been unleashed at last.

And it felt good.

Verstohlen ran along the streets of Averheim's Old City, maintaining an easy pace. The hunt for Leitdorf had begun in earnest. All around him, Grosslich's men kept their formation. There were two dozen in the warband, and they'd been well trained. Some were dogs of war, paid handsomely for their services, others were taken from the Alptraum estates. None of them had the stench of joyroot about them. That, more than anything else, reassured him.

'Was this the way?' asked the captain, holding the pace steady as he spoke.

'We're nearly there, Herr Euler. This is the district.'

All across the city, similar bands of Grosslich's supporters were fanning out. Up until now, the fighting had been sporadic. Now all the cells across Averheim had been mobilised.

The battles had been notched up a level. Alptraum had offered Verstohlen a place beside him with the forces attacking the Averburg. Verstohlen had refused. He had business of his own to deal with.

The warband rounded the final corner. There were men ahead. A few of Leitdorf's hired thugs. They didn't stay to fight. They ran off into the side streets, and a couple of Euler's soldiers made to go after them.

'Leave them,' snapped Verstohlen. He looked down the street they'd cleared of men. At the far end of it, a narrow alleyway stood. He knew what lay down there. Part of him dreaded going back, but the contagion had to be cut off at the source.

'Follow me,' he said grimly, drawing his pistol from its holster. Euler and his men fell into close formation around him. Without saying another word, the warband advanced towards the unassuming-looking townhouse at the end of the alley.

Out on the fields of Averland, Schwarzhelm drew his horse up, feeling the beast shiver from fatigue. He'd ridden it hard. His hands were streaked with the dark blood of the orcs. All around him, the butchery was in full flow. He shaded his eyes from the sun, trying to get an overview of the fighting.

The orc warband leader was close at hand, hurling threats in its obscene tongue. The initial charge of the knights had carved through the disarranged ranks of greenskins like a dagger through flesh. There would be no respite. They would press on until every last one of them was dead or driven back over the mountains. Grunwald's memory would be honoured.

Schwarzhelm turned back to face the enemy. They were massing for a counter-attack. Scattered bands of orcs nearby had somehow got wind of the battle and were streaming across the fields to reinforce their kin. That was all good. There was no point picking off the fringes of the contagion. The heart of it had to be cut out.

'To me!' Schwarzhelm bellowed to his honour guard, raising

the Rechtstahl aloft. Kraus was at his side instantly, along with a dozen of the honour guard. Averlanders followed in their wake looking hollow-eyed and murderous. Any pretence at holding detachments had long gone. This was melee fighting, close and packed-tight. That was fine. They had the numbers, and they had the leadership. Schwarzhelm's fury had been roused, and there wasn't a warrior on earth, greenskin or not, who could stand against him.

With a kick of his spurs, Schwarzhelm swung his charger around to renew the charge. Kraus fell in alongside him. Fresh lances were brought up, and the assault was marshalled anew.

The orc leader saw the danger. Like of all its cursed race, it showed no fear. With a low growl, it stamped on the earth, rousing its followers into a frenzy of defiance.

Schwarzhelm rode straight for it. He lowered his lance, watching the steel tip swing into position over the approaching orc's eyes. He could sense Kraus riding hard at his shoulder, feel the momentum of the charge all around him. The orcs could see it too. Despite their bravado, despite their dogged willingness to stay and face the onslaught, their roars of defiance were less pronounced than usual. They feared the cavalry.

The gap closed in seconds, and then they were among them. The orc leader, a head bigger than its nearest rival, swung a spiked club in a wide circle, aiming to take out the horse's legs as it thundered towards him. Schwarzhelm pulled the reins and the beast swerved comfortably to avoid the swipe. Then he was on top of it, hooves kicking out. The orc leapt to the ground, rolling across the grass before springing up with surprising agility. Schwarzhelm's lance missed it by inches. His steed careered onwards before he could pull it round for the return run.

The evidence of the charge's devastation was all around him. Kraus and the other knights had carved straight through the heart of the orc horde, and the surviving warriors were in disarray. In the gap opened up by their assault, Averlander footsoldiers were hurrying to catch up and consolidate the won ground.

But the monster, the guiding force behind the orc's movements, still lived. Schwarzhelm kicked his horse back towards the huge figure of the greenskin commander, watching carefully as the creature prepared itself for the next pass.

In a split second, he determined his tactics. He was too close for another full charge. At such a range the lance would be more of a hindrance than a weapon. As the powerful horse lurched forward, he let the long shaft fall to the ground and drew the Sword of Justice. The orc saw the change of strategy and braced itself, hurling insults at the oncoming Schwarzhelm in its dark and obscene tongue.

They came together again. The orc reared, scything its spiked weapon, once again aiming at the horse. This had been expected. The warhorse had been trained for combat, and was more than just a mere mount. As it closed on the orc, Schwarzhelm pulled sharply up on the reins. The charger reared, kicking its front hooves out viciously before they fell back down to earth. One of them connected with the orc's face, knocking one of its tusks out and cracking bone. The warband leader staggered back, roaring in pain.

Then Schwarzhelm was on it. He brought the Rechtstahl down in a sudden plunge, burying the tip of the steel deep into the orc's hide. The warrior howled, twisting to escape the agony of the blade. Like all of its kind, it was strong, nearly wresting the sword from Schwarzhelm's hands.

But Schwarzhelm was too expert a swordsman for that. He withdrew the blade while pulling the horse round, keeping it close to the stricken creature below. The orc tried to match the move, turning on its squat legs clumsily and raising its club more in defence than attack.

Schwarzhelm ignored the threat, watching for the opening. It came soon enough. He spun the sword rapidly in his grip, switching so the blade pointed down from his clenched right fist. As it whirled into position, the sunlight blazed from the holy steel.

Mustering all the power in his arm, Schwarzhelm stabbed the Rechtstahl down. The tip of the sword punctured the orc's flesh between shoulder and neck, and kept going.

The greenskin screamed, an unearthly sound that echoed over the whole field of battle. With a fury born of desperation, it tried to tear itself away from the pain, lashing out blindly with its club. The blows were ill-aimed, and Schwarzhelm evaded them easily, keeping the blade in position, turning it and pushing it down, aiming for the heart. For a moment they struggled together thus, their strength pitted against one another.

Eventually, the blood loss was too much. The mighty creature sank to its knees, the fire in its eyes extinguished. Schwarzhelm withdrew his sword. The orc's gore flew into the air as he reverted to his usual grip. With a rattling sigh, the greenskin keeled over on to the pristine turf.

Schwarzhelm looked around him. In every direction the honour guard were slicing apart the orc defences. In their wake the Averlanders were rushing to make good the gains made. The assault was progressing well.

But the greenskins were numerous. Some signal must have been given, as more were running to reinforce them from all across the plains. Schwarzhelm's forces were taking losses as they advanced, and even as he watched one of the knights was dragged from his steed by the press of orcs around him. They still needed discipline, still needed formation. If this thing slipped into a shapeless scrap, then all their advantages would be gone.

'To me!' he cried, his powerful voice echoing across the battlefield. The horsemen began to fight their way back to his position. They would need to re-form the wedge, set up another massed charge, punch the orcs into submission. They would have to do it over and over again. More than most, Schwarzhelm knew how stubborn an opponent the orcs were.

They would have to be. Now his fury was roused, there was no place for them to hide.

* * *

Euler's party ran down the narrow alleyway towards the townhouse. Verstohlen reached the door first. It was just as he remembered it. In the daylight it looked, if anything, even more innocuous. There was no handle, no decoration.

'Break this door down,' he ordered.

Euler gestured to his men, and two of his larger soldiers came forward. They slammed their bodies against the wood. Once, twice, three times, then the frame buckled. A fourth heave and the planks splintered. Euler hacked the broken wood aside and reached in to unlock the door. It swung open. The familiar aroma of jasmine wafted from the chamber within.

'Keep together,' warned Verstohlen. 'Do not be deceived by appearances. Kill anyone inside you see, fair-seeming or foul.'

Some of the men were looking uncertain. Their stock in trade was street fighting and campaigns against rival magnates. Even they could sense that there was something very wrong about the townhouse.

Verstohlen didn't have time to pity them. If Rufus's allies were allowed to take root, there'd be plenty more such establishments in Averheim to give them nightmares.

'Let's go.'

He went inside, pistol drawn. There was no one in the antechamber. The stone was bare and the lanterns had been extinguished. The body of the grotesque dog-warrior had been removed. Where his corpse had been slumped, Verstohlen thought he could see a faint brown stain against the plaster.

He went on, down the stairs and towards the central chamber. Euler followed close behind. The men had trouble squeezing into the narrow way, and their weapons clanged against the stone. Fighting in such close quarters would be difficult.

Verstohlen reached the bottom of the stairs. The corridor was empty and silent. To his right was the route he'd taken last time. Ahead of him were the double doors leading straight into the chamber.

Euler stood beside him, breathing heavily from the earlier exertions.

'Which way?' he asked.

Verstohlen nodded in the direction of the doors.

'Straight to the heart of it,' he said.

With a faint tremble that he couldn't suppress, Verstohlen reached for the handle. He pushed firmly, and the doors to Natassja's throne room swung apart.

Bloch lowered his blade and grinned. After days of fighting, he knew they must be close to Heideck. The fact that they'd run into yet another splinter band of orcs wouldn't stop them achieving their goal. The days of endless combat had begun to blur into one long procession of fighting, but he'd somehow managed to keep it together. His forces were intact, morale was as good as could be expected, and they were nearing their destination. They'd turned from mindless running from the enemy and started to engage them at will. Something had got the greenskins worried, and the feeling was infectious. From every direction he could hear his men laying into the enemy, hurling themselves into combat with a commendable ferocity. He was happy to join them. He'd even started enjoying himself.

The orc before Bloch looked drunk with fatigue. Its slab-muscled shoulders slumped, and its chest heaved. The end would not be long now.

'Is that the best you've got?' he taunted, swinging his blade and advancing towards his enemy. The orc stared back at him stupidly. The fire in its red eyes was nearly out. Blood as thick and dark as oil ran from a dozen wounds. Like a bull in the rings of the Estalians, it had been ground into the dirt.

Bloch laughed and swung his halberd directly at the monster's head. The orc parried, lifting its spike-studded cudgel to block the path of the blade. Bloch pulled back and swung again, probing for the weak spot. The orc, its breathing heavy and uncertain, matched the strokes. Bloch began to hammer his weapon down more quickly, using the shaft of the

halberd as much as a club as a blade. The orc staggered backwards, desperately fending off the blows.

Bloch didn't relent. He felt a surge of exhilaration course
through him. The greenskins had killed too many. They'd
had it their own way for too long. This was their chance to
even the score a little.

With a final, limb-jarring thud, his halberd found a way
through the greenskin's defences. It bit deep, slicing into the
thick flesh of the orc's neck. The stricken creature bellowed
a final time and sank to its knees. Bloch withdrew the blade
and hacked downward again. And a third time. The creature
collapsed on to the ground, limbs twitching. Bloch raised his
weapon in triumph, angling the point over the orc's prone
heart. With a savage cry, he brought it down with all his
might. The tip pierced the greenskin's heart, ending its rampaging forever. Bloch twisted the metal, watching the blood
bubble from the wound like spring water. It wasn't much to
celebrate, but it gave him some satisfaction.

At last, he pulled the halberd from the still twitching body
of the orc. He stepped back and looked about him. The
enemy were routed. His men still stood their ground. They'd
run the orcs out of the forests and into the open country.
For the first time since Grunwald's last stand, they had the
initiative.

'What's got into them?' came a voice from behind him.
Fischer. The lad had taken a nasty wound to his forearm
and carried his weapon in his left hand. He looked pale
but defiant.

Bloch shaded his eyes against the violent sun and tried to
make out where the fleeing greenskins were heading. The
countryside was open. They were all loping in the same direction, as if called by a signal beyond his hearing. They didn't
look like they were running mindlessly or in a panic. Something had summoned them away.

'Sigmar only knows. They've been all over us for days, and
now…' He trailed off. He strained against the haze, trying
to make out what was happening.

'What do you want to do?' asked Fischer. 'We're out of cover here.'

'Wait a minute,' said Bloch. He peered into the distance. The heat made the ground shimmer. On the horizon, everything was indistinct. It looked, though, as if there were another orc warband in the distance, kicking up dust from the parched earth. A big one, by the cloud they threw up. As big, perhaps, as the one that had defeated them in the foothills. And, unless his eyes deceived him, it was already fighting.

He turned to Fischer. This was getting interesting.

'They're not running from us,' he said. 'They're mustering to face a greater threat. That's why they're falling back. Something bigger has got them worried.'

Fischer looked blank.

'From Heideck?'

Bloch snorted derisively. 'Those milk-fed weaklings? No. You'd have to have balls of gromril to take that mob on.'

He hefted his halberd, ready for another long trek across the fields. This time, however, the objective was more than just survival.

'Ready the men,' he ordered. 'We'll form up again and follow that pack. Carefully, mind. Nothing reckless. But I've a feeling we're all headed towards the same place. And I've a feeling I know who's there too.'

Fischer still looked clueless. Bloch grinned at him.

'Trust me. We're not done fighting yet.'

The doors of the townhouse's central chamber swung open. Their motion was noiseless. For a moment, Verstohlen thought he saw movement within. He swung his pistol round swiftly.

Nothing. The chamber was empty.

He walked in, keeping the weapon raised. Euler and his men followed, fanning out across the wide circle.

'Send men up to the next level,' said Verstohlen. His voice sounded very loud against the echoing silence. 'They may be hiding. No man is to enter any room alone.'

While Euler relayed the orders, Verstohlen took a good look around. There was no throne, no dais, no iron braziers. The place had been stripped bare. The floor was wooden, the stone unadorned. If it were not for the lingering smell of jasmine, he might have begun to doubt his own recollection.

He crouched down and examined the floor. There were no scraps of cloth, no remnants of Natassja's spiked toys. They'd done a good job. As good as he would have done.

'See anything, counsellor?'

Verstohlen stood up.

'No, Herr Euler. Not a thing. That may be a cause for satisfaction. They are not yet so bold as to leave traces of their presence behind. But we must not be complacent. Let us explore further.'

Euler nodded, but Verstohlen could see the doubt in the man's eyes. None of his band wanted to believe that there were cultists in Averheim. Without tangible proof, they were always likely to distrust the word of a stranger. For the time being, though, they were not ready to question his orders.

From up above, Verstohlen could hear men going through the antechambers on the next level. There was the noise of crates being shifted and doors slamming. No fighting, though. No unnatural hissing, or warped barking. That was something to be thankful for.

'Come,' he said, turning round and heading back to the corridor outside. He led them out of the circular chamber and along the way he'd fled before. The smell of jasmine grew stronger as they went. Months of processing joyroot couldn't be erased overnight.

Verstohlen entered the hall with the drying tables. As before, everything had gone. The refining kettles, the stacks of raw root, nothing remained.

'Have your men search this place closely,' said Verstohlen, letting his eyes roam across the scrubbed surfaces. 'They may have left something behind.'

He pressed on further, studying every bare floorboard, every blank stone wall. Behind him he could hear Euler's men

clumping around, pulling apart anything they could prise
from its fastenings. They were too clumsy for this work. With
a twinge of regret, Verstohlen realised that they were as likely
to destroy any evidence as discover it. The mission had been
fruitless. Natassja and her horrific court were long gone.

He turned back, ready to order Euler to stand down. Just as
he did so, something caught his eye. Once he'd seen them, he
wondered how he'd missed them. Hung on the wall, two of
them. Verstohlen walked over to them and took one down.

Euler came to his side.

'What are these?'

Verstohlen picked up the second and held the two together.
They were masks. The faces had been artfully carved. In every
respect, they resembled their real-life counterparts. The fidel-
ity was remarkable. He found himself looking at the simulated
flesh, marvelling at the detail and precision. The face in his left
hand was his own. The one in his right was Schwarzhelm's. In
the low light, he could almost have been staring into the big
man's features. Only the eyes betrayed the origin of the masks.
They were caked with blood and had been crudely rammed into
the sockets. No doubt retrieved from Natassja's long-suffering
pets. Sigmar only knew what had happened to them.

'They are a warning, Herr Euler,' said Verstohlen, standing
up. He let the ceramics fall to the floor. 'Frau Leitdorf has a
fondness for surgery. No doubt she wishes us to know the
fate of those who stand against her husband.'

Euler looked down at the masks warily. They gazed back
blankly from their unseeing eyes. Verstohlen stamped down
heavily, shattering the fragile artistry.

'Ignore them,' he said, turning away from the scattered
shards. 'There's nothing more to see here. It was a mistake to
think there would be. Gather the men and prepare to leave.
Grosslich will need our support.'

With that, he turned on his heel and walked towards the
exit. He hoped he projected an aura of casual disregard. Deep
down, though, he knew he didn't.

* * *

Out on the fields of Averland, the orcs continued to cluster. More and more had streamed into combat, drawn from miles around. Schwarzhelm and the Averlanders had pushed them steadily east, wearing them down with a series of heavy cavalry charges followed up by ranks of footsoldiers advancing across the trampled turf.

As ever, Schwarzhelm was at the heart of it. All around him, ranks of orcs and men struggled for mastery. Readying his steed once more, he charged straight at the cluster of heavily-armed greenskins before him. With a sickening clatter, he smashed into their midst. The Rechtstahl swung down, slicing the hands of the nearest grasping warrior clean from its wrists. His horse whinnied frantically, clutched at from all sides by the orcs. Schwarzhelm kicked out against them, trying to turn the steed round. He could hear the cries of the honour guard as they fought their way to his position. For the moment, he was isolated, cut off by a sea of slavering orcs. There were too many. As the orcs hacked and dragged his steed down, he felt the noble beast give out a final shudder. He twisted free of the stirrups and leapt from the saddle as the horse was pulled to the earth.

Then they came for him. Finding his feet, Schwarzhelm whirled around. The warriors here were massive, clad in heavy iron plates and wielding cleavers and crude halberds. They surrounded him, clamouring to get close. One jumped right in front of him, swinging a long sword in a wide arc. Schwarzhelm ducked under the swipe, feeling the soft earth give under his heavy armour. They were all around him, slavering with bloodlust. They knew who he was. More than anything, they wanted to take down the Emperor's Champion.

He almost felt like smiling. Almost. Many orcs had vied for that honour. The result had always been the same.

Schwarzhelm clenched his gauntlet and punched the nearest adversary in the face. The metal bit deep, slashing even the tough orc hide open. Schwarzhelm kept moving, shifting balance, parrying blows and counter-striking with his own blade. More cudgels and blades swung in his direction.

The Rechtstahl flashed. Howls of agony showed it had found its mark.

One brute, four foot wide and weighed down with burnished plate armour, charged straight at him. Schwarzhelm waited for the impact, then turned aside at the last moment. The orc brought down its cleaver in a heavy arc. Schwarzhelm swung the Rechtstahl back to meet it. When the metal met, a resounding clang rang out.

He pushed back, heaving against the bulk of the greenskin with all the strength that remained in him. The monster staggered back. A look of amazement passed across its grotesque features. It couldn't have been often that a human had held such a monster up.

Schwarzhelm ignored it, turning quickly to meet the attacks coming at him from all directions. His sword moved ever more quickly, spark-ling radiantly in the powerful sunlight. Even in his full armour, he could move faster than the orcs around him. Years of endless combat, honed and polished in the best training grounds in the Empire, had left their mark. Though his frame was battered and his body scarred, he was still more than a match for these lumbering foes. Steel clashed against iron, and the greenskin blood flowed freely.

Slowly, painfully, their bestial will began to break. Single-handedly, Schwarzhelm began to hammer them back. Some wavered, loath to concede the field to a lone human warrior. They were the first to fall. The Rechtstahl cut through their armour as if it were made of mere scraps of parchment. Like a master blacksmith pounding at a forge, Schwarzhelm waded into the throng, fearless and resolute.

Then Kraus and the honour guard broke through. The whole company of knights fought in the same style as their master. Swift, precise, controlled. Their blades like a wall of whirling steel, they slammed into the ragged orc ranks.

That was the final blow. Faced with Schwarzhelm and his retinue working in concert, the greenskins fell back, then broke. As the knights pursued them remorselessly,

Schwarzhelm finally relented. His guard drove the orcs back, creating a window of calm amid the fury of the battlefield.

Breathing heavily, Schwarzhelm lent on his sword. His arms ached. His body ached. Sigmar had been his protector, as He always was.

'You were cut off, sir,' said Kraus, coming to stand beside him. There was a touch of reproach in his voice.

'An orc respects only one thing,' replied Schwarzhelm, ignoring the tone. 'Bravery. If they see you're willing to take the fight to them, and do it in a way they recognise as their own, they'll know doubt. That's the way to crush the greenskin.'

Kraus looked doubtful, but said nothing. Schwarzhelm was tempted to smile at his concern. He didn't, though. He never smiled.

'Anything else to report?' he said, wiping his blade clean and looking around. The knights had cleared a space around him, but it wouldn't last long.

'We're holding our own. They've mustered in numbers, but we can match them. I'd like to have tougher men under my command than Averlanders, but there's nothing I can do about that.'

Schwarzhelm shaded his eyes against the glare and tried to make sense of the fighting. His army had initially formed up in lines along the high ground to the west. The detachments were still intact and were now steadily advancing across the undulating grassland. The orc horde had become more ramshackle in its defence. Frequent charges by the cavalry had punctured the greenskin ranks, pushing them back further. The orcs were all footsoldiers, and they had no answer to the heavy cavalry assault. The greenskins had decent wargear, and fought with all the savagery of their race, but they were losing ground. The footsoldiers now scurried to follow the breakthrough up, labouring under the hot sun to keep the assault moving and secure the ground won.

Schwarzhelm looked back at the greenskin army, squinting against the morning sun. The nearest ranks of orcs, separated from him only by the swords of the honour guard, were still howling in a mass of incoherent rage. But beyond them, something else was happening. Incredibly, hidden by the press of bodies, there was the sound of more fighting.

So that was why the orcs were in trouble. There was a second front to the east. They were being attacked from two directions.

'Find me a fresh horse,' he said, suddenly filled with an unexpected hope. 'Then re-form the cavalry detachment.'

'We're consolidating?'

'Mother of Sigmar, no. Can't you see it? We're not the only men at work here. We'll cut our way through to them, right through the heart of the horde. They'll be gutted like a fish. We'll take a detachment of the heavy cavalry. Fast and deadly. I want those men relieved.'

Kraus looked out across the heaving rows of bodies uncertainly. Striking out again risked breaking their formation, leaving the mass of halberdiers and spearmen behind them unprotected. Schwarzhelm knew the manoeuvre was dangerous. But everything worthwhile was.

'Who do you think it is?'

Schwarzhelm hefted the Rechtstahl once more, relishing as always the solid weight of steel.

'Only one man it could be,' he said. 'And we're not leaving him to fight alone.'

Bloch reeled backwards, knocked almost from his feet by the blow. The orc warrior before him roared in triumph, pressing home the advantage. Bloch desperately tried to parry, but his halberd was ripped from his hand. On either side of him, his men were being pushed back. Perhaps the decision to charge after the orcs hadn't been such a good idea after all. The horde was still massive. He'd always been guilty of taking too much on.

He staggered backwards, weaponless, as the orc charged him again. With a sudden sense of despair, he realised he stood no chance. He had nowhere to go, no way of warding off the killing blow.

Balling his fists, he acted in the only way he knew how in such situations. He let fly with a torrent of filthy invective, every obscenity he'd collected over a long career in the Emperor's forces and hostelries and prepared to fight with his bare hands. It was pointless, and he'd be dead in seconds. But at least he'd go down scrapping.

Then the orc shuddered, stumbled and keeled over to one side. With a crash, the heavily armoured warrior slumped to the earth.

Bloch stood nonplussed. That hadn't been expected.

'I should swear more often,' he mused.

Fischer emerged from the shadow of the fallen greenskin. His spear was in two pieces. One end remained in his hands. The other protruded from the orc's back, still shivering as the massive creature died. The spearman threw Bloch a sword. For a young man in the thick of the fighting, he looked remarkably assured.

'That's one I owe you,' Bloch cried.

'I'll hold you to that.' Fischer looked like he was enjoying himself.

'Come on, boys!' bellowed Bloch, his vigour restored. 'One last push!'

All around him, his men cheered, but the cries were muted. They were fighting hard, going toe to toe with the rearguard of the orc horde. The fighting was bloody and confused. It was hard to retain tight formations in the close press, and the attack was at risk of turning into a disorganised melee. That handed all the advantages to the heavier, stronger orcs. If this wasn't to end in disaster, he needed to act.

'To me!' he roared, waving his new sword around his head and trying to pull his men around him. 'Shoulder to shoulder. Don't get drawn out!'

Being overheard above the din of the battlefield was hard, and not all his troops heeded the command. But those closest to him did, and they began to draw together. Soon they were formed up in something like proper Imperial ranks. Bloch himself kept in the thick of it. Ignoring his wounds, he led from the front. On either side of him, his men were kept busy, hacking and thrusting against the stubborn orc resistance.

Bloch was no different, stabbing with his sword against the greenskins. He didn't enjoy using the blade. A halberd was his weapon, the one he'd been trained to use since he was a boy. The sword was for noblemen and princes. It cut through greenskin flesh all the same though, and the blades working in tandem on either side of him gave him some protection.

'No mercy, lads!' he roared. 'No respite! Keep at them!'

They were holding their own. They were maintaining their formation. But it couldn't last forever. This warband was far bigger than the ones they'd been pursued by over the past few days. Either he was right, and a relieving army was fighting on its western flank, or he'd made a terrible mistake.

From the heart of the greenskin mass, a series of roars rose into the air. They were gearing themselves up for a final push. Something had got them angry. Bloch hoped to Sigmar that was what he thought it was.

But then his vision was blocked by yet another greenskin warrior, tusks lowered and eyes raging. They weren't giving up. They'd keep fighting until the last one of them fell to the ground. Bloch respected that. He felt the same way.

With a feral look in his eyes, he raised his sword and got stuck in.

Euler's band had returned from the Old City. Going quickly through the backstreets, they'd reached the bridges over the Aver at last. Verstohlen had kept tight-lipped since leaving the townhouse, letting Grosslich's captain make the decisions. He was eager to find the core of the fighting. That was as it should be, but still not reassuring. Chaos was always stronger than it appeared. Weakness was always fleeting. Even as Grosslich's men drove the traitors from the Old City on to the western bank, his mind was unquiet. Far too easy.

Captain Euler brought the warband to a halt. The men looked like they needed a break. Though late in the afternoon, the sun was still strong. Truly, Verstohlen had never known a summer like it. The whole province was baking.

'This is the place?' asked Verstohlen.

'It is, and the hour. He should be here soon.'

Verstohlen looked around. They were on a wide boulevard that ran along the eastern bank of the river. The street was cobbled and warehouses rose up behind it. The smell of the water was rank. Under the blistering sun, the water looked green and sickly. With no wind to drive the smells away, the air was heavy with the stench of gutted fish and refuse. The few boats moored nearby sat low in the water, their sails and ropes slack.

Further ahead, Verstohlen could see the bulk of the Averburg rise up against the empty sky. He couldn't tell whether it was still manned. The standard of Averland hung from the flagpole at the summit, but that meant little. Surely Tochfel had surrendered it to one of the warring parties by now. The question was, which one?

Verstohlen put his knife away. In the daylight, with the enemy flying before them and the Old City nearly locked down, it was hard not to become complacent. He knew that would be a mistake. Verstohlen was no coward, but he was no fool either. Deep down, he was still afraid. Mortally afraid. The consequences of what he'd seen were terrible enough.

'He approaches now,' said Euler, breaking Verstohlen's concentration. He looked along the quayside.

Heinz-Mark Grosslich in armour looked even more the picture of a commander than he had done in civilian robes. The sun shone from his exposed blond hair. He appeared calm, confident and in command. The self-appointed elector was surrounded by greatswords from the Alptraum estate. Their notched armour betrayed the fighting they'd been in, but they bore no resemblance to the scruffy mercenaries who formed the bulk of the fighting men on both sides. Ferenc had given him the best to work with.

As Grosslich came up to him, Verstohlen bowed politely.

'Did you find anything, counsellor?' the count asked.

Verstohlen shook his head.

'As I feared, they'd long flown the nest. They'd worked hard to cover their tracks, too.'

'Any sign at all? Any signal?'

Verstohlen thought of the masks.

'No, my lord.'

Grosslich nodded grimly. 'Then we'll keep hunting.' He motioned for his bodyguard to stand down. 'Walk with me,' he said to Verstohlen and moved towards the water's edge. Verstohlen fell in beside him. Euler and his men, grateful of the respite, put their weapons down and began to talk amongst themselves.

'I'll confess that Ferenc's news came as a surprise,' said Grosslich, keeping his voice low. 'I've never hidden my dislike for Rufus and his slut, but if I'd known about the–'

'It is in the nature of corruption to be hidden,' interrupted Verstohlen, wanting no mention of the details. 'Do not trouble yourself.'

'The joyroot is at the heart of it. This I suspected for many months. Leitdorf is not as wealthy as his lineage suggests, and it is I who have the support of the guilds. Only through this trade could he have armed his men. I won't let those in my employ touch it.'

Verstohlen wondered if that was true. Joyroot use seemed to be endemic across the city.

'Very wise.'

Grosslich paused before speaking again. He seemed to be weighing something up.

'Ferenc tells me you're an agent of the Lord Schwarzhelm,' he said. 'I assumed – forgive me – that you were merely an official.'

'It's an impression I work hard to cultivate.'

'Then you'll be an astute judge of politics. You'll know, for example, that Herr Alptraum wishes to use me as a figurehead. He cannot succeed to the electorship himself, so he uses me as his proxy.'

Verstohlen had to admire the man's judgement.

'Then why maintain your alliance?'

'I need him. His money, his connections, his arms. I have none of these. The only thing I have linking me to the electorship is a long forgotten blood-tie to an ancient count, and even that is contested. If there were better candidates than Alptraum and Leitdorf, I'd never had stood a chance.'

'You make it sound as if you do not wish to succeed.'

Grosslich stopped walking and looked at him seriously. 'I wish for nothing else. This province has wallowed in indolence for too long. Sigmar willing, I *will* restore it to glory. We must no longer be the rich weakling amongst the Empire's realms.'

'Ferenc Alptraum is an old hand at this game,' said Verstohlen. 'Be wary of taking him on.'

'That is why I needed to speak to you. My victory here is almost at hand. Rufus's men have been driven from the Old City and on to the western bank. We will hunt them down, and then I shall be crowned. But then the real battle begins. Alptraum cannot be allowed to rule through me. If that were to happen, nothing would change. We'd have swapped one tyrant for another. I need your help, counsellor. You have the skills for this work, whereas I am but a soldier.'

Verstohlen raised an eyebrow.

'Are you offering me a job, Lord Grosslich?'

Grosslich looked uncharacteristically uneasy.

'Not exactly. Some kind of advisory role, perhaps. I'm not a proud man, counsellor. I need help. You could provide me with it.'

Verstohlen smiled sadly.

'I appreciate your predicament. Be assured that while the taint of Chaos remains in Averheim, I will help you root it out. But after that, I'm Schwarzhelm's servant. That, I'm afraid, is not something I can change. Not even for the Emperor himself.'

'Your devotion commends you,' said Grosslich, keeping his expression level. If he was disappointed, he hid it well. 'Let me speak candidly, though. There are many here who wonder if the Lord Schwarzhelm deserves the services of one such as you. He is a son of Averland, but–'

Verstohlen raised his hand.

'Say no more. I will not hear this. If it were not for Schwarzhelm, Marius would have driven your province to ruin twenty years ago. Even now he fights to prevent it falling apart. He has been targeted by those we fight against, and a lesser man would have cracked long ago. Whatever you think, he is the greatest hope for your cause.'

Grosslich inclined his head in apology, withdrawing the criticism gracefully.

'Forgive me. I should perhaps have more faith.' He looked back along the river. In the distance, the great bridge over the Aver had begun to burn. The fighting had evidently reached the crossings, and the fires spread with it. 'I wish I could discuss this at greater leisure, but I should go back to my men. You are to be commended, Herr Verstohlen. Your tidings given to Alptraum have set this in motion, and victory is at hand.'

'Does Leitdorf lead his forces?'

'He's not been seen, but it's not his way. He'll be skulking in some cellar, letting his peasants lose their lives for him.'

'That concerns me. We're driving them back too easily.'

Grosslich grinned. He looked supremely unworried.

'Worry not, counsellor. In an honest fight, there is only one winner. Whatever dabbling Leitdorf has been doing in spells and potions, it won't make up for his poor judgement. Even his own men hate him. The city will be ours before nightfall tomorrow.'

Verstohlen looked at the burning bridge darkly. Something was wrong here. Though he couldn't put his finger on it, every instinct he possessed warned him that they were winning too quickly. The ways of Chaos were subtle, and uprooting the contagion was never as simple a matter as this.

'I will come with you,' he said. 'You could use a good shot, and I want to see Leitdorf's forces with my own eyes. Something has eluded me here, I am sure of it.'

Grosslich smiled confidently. 'It'll be an honour. We'll drive them out together.'

CHAPTER THIRTEEN

Bloch felt his resolve begin to flag at last. The sun was failing. The fighting had been fierce and unrelenting for too long. His men were surrounded on all sides. They'd taken heavy losses. Of the several hundred he'd led in the orc rearguard, perhaps two-thirds remained on their feet. They'd driven hard into the orc lines, but the greenskins had swallowed them up. This was beginning to look more and more like a mistake.

Even his arms, hardened by years of incessant combat, were near the end of their strength. Wielding the sword was hard. He'd already sustained several wounds due to the unfamiliar weapon. A halberd was more difficult to use in a confined space, but it served as both attack and defence. Without the long stave to use, Bloch found the hooked weapons of the orcs getting through his guard too often. He'd taken a flesh wound to his leg and only narrowly avoided being skewered by an unusually nimble greenskin warrior.

Too many of his men hadn't been so lucky. Fischer was gone, dragged down by the combined attack of several orcs

working in tandem. Bloch had reached him too late. After
so many days on the run, his men were flagging. The battle with the orcs had ebbed and flowed, but it seemed as if
they'd finally run out of the fortune that had preserved them
since Grunwald's demise.

'To me, lads!' he shouted, desperately trying to rally the
men that remained. His voice cracked as he urged them on.
The halberdiers and spearmen around him kept their heads
down, desperately trying to stem the assault of the orcs. The
formation still held, but only just. With every backward step,
every orc assault, Bloch's detachment was beaten back. They
were surrounded, cut off from help.

Bloch raised his sword a final time. The men on either side
of him looked drained. The orcs hung back for a moment,
taking the chance to jeer at them before they charged. They
swung their crude weapons wildly, relishing the impending
victory. Bloch couldn't make out what they were saying, but
the gist was obvious enough.

Gritting his teeth, he prepared for the onslaught. He'd
had a good run. He couldn't complain. It'd been worth the
gamble.

Then, before his astonished eyes, the orc ranks were torn
apart.

From nowhere, crashing through the press of greenskins,
armoured knights charged straight through the mocking warriors. Heavy plate armour flashed in the sun as a wedge of
horsemen tore through the orc resistance. No more than two
dozen of them, an arrowhead of steel amid a sea of foes. But
they were superb horsemen. Bloch saw one sweep a greenskin warrior from its feet on the charge, drop the lance, take
up a sword and swing it round to decapitate another. All at
speed, all in a heartbeat.

At their head was a figure he knew all too well. Schwarzhelm
was like a force of nature. His armour was battered and
dented all over, but his momentum on the charge was irresistible. He roared his defiance in that familiar resounding
voice, hacking left and right with the Sword of Justice as he

came on. In that moment, with the sun glinting from his armour like a halo, he looked like one of the heroes of old, the companions of Holy Sigmar who cleansed the Empire of the orc menace when the world was young and purer. With every mighty stroke, every hammer blow, the will of the greenskins to resist was thrown down.

In an instant, the situation was reversed. The orcs were smashed to one side. Bloch could see more knights galloping to join the assault. They had the colours of Averheim. Bloch was transfixed for a moment, hardly daring to believe what he was seeing. The orcs sca-ttered, ridden down by the knights. Suddenly relieved of the pressure of constant defence, his own men began to break out of the stricture. The greenskins, caught between two forces, broke under the assault.

Not all of them ran. Some of the larger warriors stood their ground, bellowing in frustration at the denial of their prize. A huge orc lurched up to Bloch, eyes blazing, axe swinging low against the ground. A halberdier charged straight at it, but was swatted away with a casual swipe of the monster's vast claw-like hand. The creature fixed its pig-like eyes on Bloch. Somewhere deep within its violence-addled mind, it singled him out. With a guttural roar, it charged. Bloch tensed, waiting for the impact.

It never came. A knight rode between the two of them, cutting off the orc's attack. There was a blaze of sunlight as the rider's sword plunged downwards. The greenskin crashed to the ground, decapitated, its severed neck pumping blood. The ruined corpse rolled several times before coming to a halt, its claws still twitching. The knight tore onward, hardly pausing to regain his balance. Ahead of him, the rest of the orcs were being driven away. The horde had been smashed. In the wake of the knights, Averlanders poured into the breach. They rushed over to Bloch's beleaguered men, sweeping the orcs from their hard-pressed lines and pursuing them as they broke and ran.

Finally, the relief had arrived.

Bloch felt his sword arm go weak at last. He'd been fighting with barely a break for days. It had taken its toll. He felt his vision begin to cloud, and he felt suddenly light-headed.

Then a shadow fell across him. Shading his eyes against the sun, he looked up. Schwarzhelm towered above him. His charger's flanks were glossy with sweat. The man's massive armoured form must have taken some carrying. Schwarzhelm's presence was like the return of a welcome dream. There was the familiar armour, the laurel-wreathed helmet, the massive breastplate with the Ghal Maraz pendant swinging from it.

'My lord!' cried Bloch.

Schwarzhelm pulled his horse around and dismounted in a single movement. The blood of the orcs sluiced down the Sword of Justice. He walked up to Bloch. The Emperor's Champion was as grim-faced as ever, but there was an icy satisfaction in the man's eyes.

'You survived,' said Schwarzhelm. 'I knew you would. I am not too late.'

He clasped Bloch on the shoulder. The grip was as heavy as any blow he'd received on the battlefield, and he had to work not to stagger under it.

'It's becoming a habit, sir,' said Bloch, his worn face breaking into an expression of pure relief.

'What is?'

'Riding to the rescue. Just like in the legends.'

More Averlander troops were arriving every moment, striding across the battlefield. In the face of the reinforcements, the remaining orcs were driven back further. All around them, Bloch's men were falling to the earth in exhaustion. Their places were taken by fresh footsoldiers, backed up by the ever-present knights.

'Can you still wield a blade?' asked Schwarzhelm, clearly itching to be after the remaining greenskins.

Bloch grinned. His energy returned in an instant. Even after everything, the prospect of fighting alongside the great man was something he relished. There were men who would have given their own families into slavery to have the honour of marching beside Schwarzhelm.

'Give me a proper weapon to wield and I'll fight with you till the End Times come and we're all damned together.'

Schwarzhelm nodded with approval.

'Get this man a halberd!' he roared. 'Then we finish this thing.'

Kurt Helborg drew his horse to a standstill. The armoured bridle clinked as the beast shook its head impatiently. On either side of him, Reiksguard knights took up position. One hundred of them, all in full battle array despite the stultifying heat. The Reiksguard livery of red and white looked pristine in the sharp, clear light, and their weapons glistened with menace. It was a formidable contingent. If the reports coming out of Averland were true, they would be needed.

Skarr pulled up beside him. The man's lank hair was slick with sweat. Flies buzzed around the muzzle of his horse. Everything was dank, warm and humid.

'What do you think?'

'Looks peaceful enough.'

They looked from their vantage point into the valley beyond. The road ran on for a few hundred yards before dipping sharply to follow the contours of the land. Perhaps a mile or two in the distance lay the town of Streissen, roughly halfway between the industrial might of Nuln and the rural backwater of Averland's interior. As befitted a town on the border, it reflected a mix of regional styles. The walls were high and crenulated. They'd been whitewashed in imitation of Altdorf's naturally white stone, though the long years had stained the surface a dirty grey. There were high watchtowers at regular intervals along the protective barrier.

The River Aver looped around the southern edge of the town before running west, and there were landing stages all along the bank. They didn't look busy. The water was still and sluggish under the sun. There was very little traffic on the road. The place looked half-asleep.

'This heat,' complained Skarr, wiping his face with a rag. The cloth was already sodden.

'Do you sense anything?' asked Helborg, looking at the town before them intently.

'What do you mean?'

If he was honest, Helborg couldn't quite place what he meant. There was an air of something about the countryside around them. Perhaps the heat was part of it. Perhaps it was just the effects of the long ride from Nuln. But something put him on edge. It felt wrong. Just on the edge of sensation, he thought he could smell jasmine, though they were far too far north for the flowers to bloom.

'I don't know. Ignore it. Have we heard anything from Averheim?'

Skarr shook his head. Messengers had been sent on ahead to the capital, but they hadn't returned. There were any number of explanations for that. The Empire was a dangerous place.

It was still strange.

'Let's press on,' said Helborg, nudging his horse back into motion. 'This place isn't worth bothering with. We'll carry on to Averheim.'

Tochfel hurried along the ramparts of the Averburg. The situation couldn't last much longer. Any sense of defiance he'd felt over the past two days had melted in the face of the sustained assault on the city. Just as he'd feared, the citadel was now an isolated spot of sanity amid a swirling torrent of violence. He had no idea who was winning the war for the streets. From his vantage point, the destruction was senseless, whoever was causing it.

He turned a corner rapidly, only to bump into Morven. The man was carrying a stack of arrows. They scattered across the stone. He was about to burst into a furious string of expletives when he saw who'd caused the accident.

'M-my apologies, Steward,' he stammered, reaching for the arrows. 'I didn't know it was—'

'What are you doing, carrying these?' asked Tochfel, helping him retrieve them. 'Aren't there others for this kind of work?'

Morven gave him a look of despair.

'They're all on the walls, Steward,' he complained. 'We barely have enough to give even the pretence of resistance. If they want to storm the walls, they can do so whenever they please.'

Tochfel rose to his feet. He walked up to the parapet and risked a look down between the battlements. Far below, men clustered around the gates. They were well armoured and arrayed for an assault. He guessed several hundred were stationed along the ramp leading to the gatehouse, and more looked to be arriving from the Old City all the time. All they required was a ram for the doors and the attack would surely begin.

'Which one of them is it?'

'Ferenc Alptraum.'

Tochfel rolled his eyes. Of course. His family had once ruled from the Averburg. No wonder he wanted it back. He stole another look over the edge. There were seasoned troops down there. If the Averburg had been manned they'd have posed no threat at all, but the hastily arrayed guards of the citadel were mostly scribes and junior loremasters. There were mere dozens of them on the walls and scarcely more waiting on the inside of the great doors to repel intruders. The charade wouldn't fool anyone for long.

'Keep them out for as long as you can,' said Tochfel, handing the aide-de-camp his bundle of arrows and turning back the way he'd come.

'Where are you going?' came the querulous voice of Morven.

Tochfel ignored him. He descended into the castle swiftly, following routes he'd known since childhood. Once inside the cool stone, he began to think more clearly. The end would come soon. Alptraum must surely have realised how meagre their defences were, and he'd waste little time taking over once he was inside. That could not be prevented, but there was one service he could render before he lost control of the citadel.

The records. The precious records of the succession battle. They must not fall into either Grosslich's or Leitdorf's hands. Though it would probably prove futile, Tochfel knew that he had to preserve them. One day the law would be restored and the chronicle of these times would be required again.

He went down the narrow spiral staircase that led to the archives. The repository of Averland's history was in the oldest part of the ancient citadel, locked behind walls many yards thick. He was as familiar with it as he was with his own chambers. Over his life, he'd probably spent as much time in there.

He reached his destination. He was far below ground level, and the only light came from torches clamped to the stone walls. Some of them had gone out, and the shadows hung heavy on the stone flags.

The thick oak door to the library was open. That was unusual. It should have been locked. Only two men had the keys to the archives. He was one of them. Achendorfer was the other. He felt a sudden sense of wariness take him over. From far above he could hear muffled sounds. Perhaps the attackers had broken in at last. Time was running out.

Tochfel crept forward, looking around him carefully. The library looked deserted. The stone ceiling was low, built in the style of a crypt. Passages and antechambers led off in all directions, dark under narrow arches. Cracked leather tomes lined every wall. Their spines were inscribed in formal Reikspiel, but in the flickering light most were unreadable. It was cold. Even in the height of such a summer, the warmth of the sun never penetrated this far down.

The archive had many departments, and even Tochfel didn't know them all. The one he wanted was straight on, down into the bowels of the scriptorium. He went quietly, his soft leather shoes making no noise against the stone. As the light from the torches ran out, he took the last one from the wall and held it as a brand. Its glow was warm and comforting, but it didn't extend far. He didn't like the way the flickering shadows reared up on the walls. They danced at the edge of his vision in an unnerving fashion.

He was getting closer. He passed more bookshelves, groaning under the weight of their heavy loads of parchment, vellum and leather. The noises from the corridor outside had died away. It was as if he'd entered a dark sanctum of calm, buried deep within the eye of the storm raging outside.

Then he saw it. Another light. In the chamber ahead, no more then twenty yards away. His heart stopped. Perhaps one of the loremasters had had the same idea. In these troubled times, one could never tell. He wished he'd brought a knife, a rod, anything to defend himself with. Suddenly, his brand felt flimsy in his grip. Not much of a weapon.

Tochfel swallowed.

'Achendorfer?' The words echoed mockingly through the empty vaults beyond. There was the sound of a book being slammed shut and the light guttered. Tochfel rushed forward, holding the brand aloft, trying to throw more light across the chamber.

There were more sounds, as if someone was hurriedly pushing something to one side. Then a face lurched up out of the shadows of the arch.

'Achendorfer!' cried Tochfel, feeling relief well up inside him. His heart still thumped heavily. 'Mother of Sigmar, you scared me.'

The loremaster looked terrible. His ashen grey face was distorted by fear, and his forehead was shiny with sweat. Tochfel noticed the man's hand shaking as he tried to re-light his own brand.

'Sorry, Steward,' he mumbled, striking the flint clumsily. His voice sounded thick and strained, as if he had a heavy cold.

'What are you doing down here?' asked Tochfel, holding his own light up high, trying to illuminate some more of the cramped chamber. The volumes in here were obscure ones. Tochfel couldn't remember if he'd ever ventured into this part of the library himself. The air was dank and unwholesome.

Achendorfer looked evasive. He was breathing with difficulty. He finally got his brand re-lit, and the orange light of the flames bathed him with a lurid glow.

'I could ask you the same thing.'

Tochfel looked at him carefully. There was something strange about his eyes. The man looked like he'd been taking something. Surely not the joyroot. That was only used by the gutter filth. He felt his fear return. Why was Achendorfer staring at him like that? Almost without thinking, he took a step back.

'Uriens?' he asked, feeling more unsure of himself with every moment. 'Are you all right?'

Achendorfer came after him, his eyes shining in the torchlight. He seemed like he was trying to come to some kind of a decision, like a boy caught with his fingers in the honeypot and looking for an excuse. Tochfel clutched his brand more tightly. If he had to, he'd use it.

Achendorfer stared at him. His expression was tortured.

'I'm sorry, Dagobert,' he said. 'For everything.'

Then there was a sudden crash behind them. Fresh light bloomed down from the main body of the library. Achendorfer looked panicked and scuttled back, away from the intrusion. Tochfel, grateful for any interruption, whirled around to face it.

Men were piling into the chamber. They were all bearing torches. The place was soon filled with firelight. Tochfel watched them fan out across the archive with alarm. It would only take one spark.

'Be careful!' he cried out, knowing how pathetic he sounded. The instinct of the official in him was strong, even in such terrible times.

'Don't worry, Steward,' came a familiar voice. One of the men walked into the pool of light cast by Tochfel's brand. He was dressed in armour, but it looked more ceremonial than anything else. The Alptraum crest was embossed on the breastplate, a rampant lion flanked by laurels.

The speaker took his helmet off, revealing the thin face of Ferenc Alptraum.

'No doubt you're here to secure the safety of the succession documents,' he said, smiling widely. In the distorted light, it looked more like a grimace. 'I'm glad I arrived when I did. Now my men can help you.'

Tochfel didn't know whether to feel relieved or terrified. Where had Achendorfer crept off to? And what had come over him? What was he sorry for?

'Am I a prisoner, then?' said Tochfel, trying to strike as dignified a pose as he could.

'Only if you want to be. It was foolish of you to try and hold the Averburg against us, but I don't keep grudges. There's been little blood spilled. Be thankful it was us that reached you rather than Leitdorf. There are things about him you should know.'

Tochfel felt his spirits sink. The propaganda of the victor. No doubt Grosslich's faction had discovered some 'dark secret' about their opponents. Tochfel wouldn't believe a word of it. He was too old for such games.

'You can save your speeches, Herr Alptraum. As far as I'm concerned, you're a usurper and a traitor to Averland. When the law is restored, I shall testify to that effect.'

Alptraum laughed, and the sound echoed from vault to vault.

'How noble. I'll bear that in mind. But now you need to come with me. There are things to discuss, whether you wish to hear them or not.'

As Alptraum spoke, two of his men moved quietly to Tochfel's side. Aside from their brands, they also carried naked swords. Tochfel finally saw the danger he was in. His bravado melted away.

'There are laws in Averheim still,' he said, but his voice sounded shaky and terrified. 'You may not assail me. I am still the Steward.'

Alptraum came towards him, still smiling. There was cunning in his expression, but little malice.

'Oh, we'll respect the laws, Steward. You need not fear for your own skin. This is a peaceful transition of power. I'll need

you at my side to ensure an orderly succession.' He looked
around him with interest. 'But I'm sure you know that some
erroneous documents have found their way down here over
the past few months. This collection is long overdue a little
selective culling. We'll be careful. *Very* careful.'

Tochfel felt the bitter taste of his failure. He'd been too
late. If he'd retrieved the documents just an hour earlier, he
might have been able to salvage something. Now it was over.
The Grosslich version of events would be preserved, everything else destroyed.

'So you say,' he muttered.

'Now you'll go with my men,' said Alptraum. 'You'll show
them your private papers, while I shall also study. Then you'll
resume your duties, working under me. If you're sensible, nothing need change for you, Herr Tochfel. The parchment will keep
on coming across your desk. All will be well with the world.'

Tochfel glared at him for a moment, wondering whether to
believe him. It didn't matter very much if he did or didn't.
He had no power to resist. The vainglorious attempt to hold
the Averburg had ended pathetically.

'It shall be as you command,' he said. With a deep sense of
despondency, Tochfel allowed himself to be led off by Alptraum's men. Ferenc himself took a final look around the
archives before withdrawing and leaving a couple of guards
on the door.

In the absence of the soldiers' torches, the vaults sunk
back into complete darkness. Heavy footfalls echoed along
the spiral stairwells as they ascended and then dwindled to
nothing. Everything was silent.

Except, hidden in the shadows, there was a faint, barely
audible wheezing. Alone, forgotten, Achendorfer still
crouched.

When the others had all left, he rose and made his way
back to where he'd been hiding. He retrieved something from
the antechamber, then hurried off into the darkness, following routes into the bowels of the citadel that only he knew.

* * *

Morning broke over the rolling grassland of eastern Averland. Bloch awoke suddenly. For a moment, he had no idea where he was. He couldn't even remember falling asleep. Then it came rushing back. Some of it, at least.

The orcs had been destroyed. It had taken the entire day to finish them off, and they'd fought until dusk. But they had no answer to Schwarzhelm. He'd carved through them, giving them no respite or mercy. Every attempt by the greenskins to rally had been destroyed by him, every retreat pursued ruthlessly. Only with the coming of the dark had the army at last been able to sink into an exhausted rest. The rank and file halberdiers, spearmen and irregulars were clustered on the east-facing slopes of the hill they'd fought over so hard into the night. With the eventual destruction of the orc horde, that was where they'd spent the night, clustered together in a state of half-watchfulness, half-exhaustion.

Bloch still couldn't remember how the battle had ended for him. At some point he must have given out, fallen to the earth with fatigue like those around him. It was all so hazy.

He rolled over, still in his full armour, and staggered to his feet. Immediately he felt the stabbing pain of the wound in his leg. He looked down. It had been bandaged. Had he done that? He didn't remember doing it. He didn't remember anyone else doing it either.

It wasn't just his leg that ached. Every muscle in his body protested as he moved. He could barely walk. There was a low, hammering headache behind his eyes. He needed something to drink. How long had it been since he'd eaten properly? Sigmar only knew.

All around him, the rest of the army looked in the same kind of shape. Schwarzhelm had pushed the Averlanders hard, and many of them were slumped in exhaustion in the grass, their eyes hollow and staring. The survivors of Grunwald's command were in even worse condition. Some were still on their feet, but many had collapsed during the final stages of the battle. Even after the orcs had been routed and the field won there had been no celebration.

The heat didn't help. Bloch fumbled at his collar, trying to release his jerkin. He felt grimy, caked in old sweat that had never truly dried. The sunlight, still low in the east, hurt his eyes. This whole province was too damnably *bright*. Not like the wholesome grey skies of the Reikland or the brooding forests of the north. No wonder Averlanders were so strange. Their country was fit for cattle, not honest humans.

As his senses gradually returned, he saw that the army around him had been put in some kind of order. The footsoldiers were arranged in companies and there were watchmen on the edges of a makeshift camp. Wains had caught up with them, full of provisions from Heideck. There were tents, which must have gone up during the night. There were even fires, their thin pillars of smoke curling into the blue sky. From such a scene of desolation just the day before, the place was starting to look something like a proper camp.

'Herr Bloch.'

The voice came from further up the slope. Bloch turned to face it. It was Kraus. The honour guard captain looked almost unscathed, though his gait betrayed his weariness. It had been a testing campaign for all of them.

'Lord Schwarzhelm is back from orc hunting. He asked me to find you. Can you walk?'

Bloch grimaced. Every time he moved, a sharp pain shot up his thigh. He was damned if Schwarzhelm would know about it.

'I'm fine. Show me to him.'

Kraus walked up the slope. As Bloch limped alongside him, he took a look at the faces of the men around them. Some of the men must have got some sleep in the night. Others still slumbered, prostrate on the grass where they'd fallen after dragging themselves back from the fighting. They were still perhaps a day's march out from Heideck and further still from Grenzstadt. That was a long way from anywhere, given the condition of the men. For the time being, they'd have to make this place their own.

At the summit of the hill the Imperial standard had been

planted. It had rarely flown over such a hastily concocted and dishevelled army, thrown together in haste and with no proper planning for its deployment. But, held together by little more than Schwarzhelm's will, it had succeeded in its task. The horde had been destroyed and its remnants scattered. Heideck was no longer threatened, and the way was clear to rid the rest of the province of the greenskin menace. Not a bad result. To the extent he'd played a part in it, Bloch felt proud. It could have gone very differently.

Only one man stood beside the standard. His massive bulk against the horizon was familiar. His plate armour still glinted, though it had been ravaged by blows. The longsword still hung from his belt, decorated with the comet motif and engraved with runes of warding. As Bloch approached Schwarzhelm, Kraus tactfully withdrew. The general looked up from a sheet of parchment he'd been studying. His face was lined with concern. When he saw the halberdier captain, his expression lightened a little. Only a little.

'Herr Bloch,' he said, rolling the parchment up and putting it away. 'I trust you slept well? The bedding was to your liking?'

Bloch didn't know quite how to respond to that. Was that what Schwarzhelm called a joke? It was impossible to read the expression on that vast, scarred, bearded face. He decided it was probably meant to be amusing.

'Not bad. Could have done with a few more feathers in the bolster.'

Schwarzhelm grunted. He didn't look amused.

'In any case, you deserved some rest. It was heroic, to last so long out here. I've served with men who'd have given in long before I found you.'

Again, Bloch hardly knew what to say. He'd still not learned how to cope with compliments. They were strange things, alien to his whole way of being.

'Forgive me,' he stammered. 'I don't exactly recall–'

'You don't remember the final hours? It was an honour to have you alongside me. When I finally ordered you to

retire, you could hardly see. By then, the worst was over.'
Schwarzhelm gazed down on the ranks of men below, most
of them lying on the grass as Bloch had been doing, utterly
drained. 'This is still a formidable army. The men need rest,
but they'll recover. We lost many, but the orcs lost more.
The tide has turned.'

Bloch followed his gaze, trying to gauge how many men
they had left. Still more than two thousand capable of bearing arms, he estimated. A serious contingent. He didn't like
to estimate how many were from his own command. It
would be too few. They'd suffered badly in that last assault.

'Tell me,' said Schwarzhelm, his tone a little less confident,
'how did Grunwald die?'

In a flash, Bloch saw it in his mind's eye. The commander,
borne down by a whole pack of orcs, shouting at him to flee.
He winced. That vision would haunt him.

'Well, sir. He held the line while we withdrew.'

Schwarzhelm looked at Bloch intently. Those eyes, set deep
into the lined face, were penetrating. Bloch felt an overwhelming urge to look away. With effort, he held Schwarzhelm's
gaze. It was always a mistake to look away.

'A good commander,' was all Schwarzhelm said, though
there was an edge of bitterness in his words.

'He was, sir.'

'You know that his requests for reinforcements never
reached Averheim?'

'I'm told the road was blocked.'

'It was. Greenskins, maybe, though it seems unlikely. Perhaps men allied to one of the candidates.'

'Whoever it was, they knew what they were doing. We
heard nothing from you either. Grunwald wasn't even sure
you'd made it to Averland.'

'It's something to be investigated. If I had the time and
the men, I'd scour the highways now. Rest assured, when I
find those responsible…'

He trailed off. Bloch waited. Schwarzhelm seemed more
troubled than he'd ever been. After witnessing him at the

crushing victory at Turgitz, the change was remarkable. He was still dominating, but he looked tired. Huge bags hung under his eyes and his pupils were dull. How much rest had he had in the last few weeks?

'As it happens, I have neither the time nor the men for what needs to be done,' Schwarzhelm said at last. 'We've achieved a great deal here, but the task is not finished. But I've had word from Averheim. An armoured party from Ferenc Alptraum, of all people, has caught up with us. My counsellor has been speaking to him, it would seem. They're calling me back.'

Bloch didn't know what to say to that. He'd not been party to any of the events in the city. Saying anything risked exposing his ignorance.

'How goes the succession?' he asked, hoping that wasn't a stupid question.

Schwarzhelm snorted his disdain. 'They're fighting openly now. But it's worse than that. The Leitdorf candidate's a traitor. Verstohlen's message found me just this morning.' He looked west and his lungs filled with a huge, weary sigh. 'I'll have to return. If he's right, this can't be ignored.'

Bloch looked back down at the army uncertainly. The orcs had been defeated, but there would be splinter bands still at large. To turn back now would risk all that had been achieved.

'Does Verstohlen say how serious a threat Leitdorf is?' asked Bloch. 'We still have–'

'I know. You want to finish the task at hand. There are greenskins left alive.' Schwarzhelm pursed his lips in thought. 'We are being stretched. Do you not think it odd that, just when my presence is needed in Averheim, an incursion of orcs comes through the most heavily guarded pass in the Empire to cause havoc? And that when I have been drawn out here to snuff out that threat, then it's Averheim that dissolves into civil war? We are being played with, Herr Bloch. Verstohlen warned me we were being manipulated. They're assaulting us on all fronts.'

Bloch felt the truth of that. The more he learned about

the situation, the less he liked it. They needed more men, more time, more supplies. For all its beauty, Averland was turning into a swamp. He couldn't see a solution. To ignore the situation in the city was impossible. To ignore the orcs was irresponsible.

'We have a choice,' said Schwarzhelm. 'West to Averheim, or east to Grenzstadt and the passes? Which of them appeals to you, Herr Bloch? Which would you choose?'

Was he being tested? Bloch couldn't believe that Schwarzhelm didn't already know what he wanted to do. Bloch's mind worked quickly, assessing the options, the manpower, the distances.

'Do we have to choose? We still have many men here. The orcs are mostly routed. If you need to return to Averheim with half the troops, I can lead the men who remain.'

Schwarzhelm looked at him shrewdly.

'That had occurred to me,' he said. 'But we'll be stretching ourselves thin. Maybe too thin.'

'But if the orcs have been scattered…'

'They're still dangerous. We don't know how many remain.'

'A damn sight fewer than there were.'

And then, it almost happened. For a split second, Schwarzhelm's face twitched. His eyes glittered mischievously. Some men might have called that a smile. Bloch wouldn't have dared, but it was certainly something damn close to one.

'That there are, Herr Bloch,' Schwarzhelm said, a kernel of savage satisfaction in his voice. 'That there are.'

He looked west again, as if by peering in the direction of Averheim he'd get some kind of confirmation of his decision.

'I'll be honest with you,' he said at last. 'Since arriving in Averland I've not felt myself. It's been as if some force has turned against me, weighing down on my mind. The city is at the heart of it. If Verstohlen's right, then it may be that Averheim is perilous for me. It's only out here, doing the honest work of a soldier, that I've come even close to remembering who I am. I can think clearly here.'

Bloch said nothing. Schwarzhelm was speaking candidly.

Amazingly candidly. It was as if the big man needed someone to confide it. In the absence of Verstohlen, it seemed to
fall to Bloch to fulfil that role.

'Your offer of leading the men east to seal the passes while
I respond to Verstohlen's missive scares me.' Schwarzhelm
turned back to Bloch. 'Does that surprise you? That a man
like me would be scared of anything?'

Bloch began to feel very uncomfortable. Before Turgitz,
Schwarzhelm had been like a name from the time of legends, a figure of such transcendent power that the very idea
of him having emotions or anxieties as a mortal man did
would have been laughable. And yet here he was, laying
them out as plain as day.

'You shouldn't be,' Schwarzhelm continued. 'Only a fool
claims to fear nothing. I've heard the Emperor himself confess fears. It makes us stronger, to acknowledge the fear
within us. The question, Herr Bloch, is what one does with
that knowledge. Does fear become the master, propelling us
forward like puppets, or do we test ourselves against it? Do
we embrace our fear, or run from it?'

'I can't imagine you running from anything, sir,' said Bloch.
As soon as the words left his mouth, he wished he could
reel them back in. He sounded clumsy and obsequious. He
was not built for such talk.

'I did not say *run*. It's a question of choice.'

Schwarzhelm fell silent. Bloch, worried about saying something equally stupid, kept his mouth shut. For a few terrible
moments, Schwarzhelm remained unmoving, lost in thought.
The wind around them lifted the grass gently. Below them,
Bloch could hear the men of the army stir themselves. As the
sun climbed higher, the need to move on would grow. They
needed direction. As he had done in the woods after Grunwald's death, Bloch felt the burden of command keenly. He
had an inkling that Schwarzhelm felt it too. For some reason, he knew the decision he was wrestling with was vitally
important. It was more than tactics, more than strategy. If
Schwarzhelm went back to Averheim, then something was

going to happen. He was the key to all of this. All of them, friend and foe alike, wanted him there for some reason.

'I will go,' Schwarzhelm announced at last. His voice had assumed its habitual tone of clipped command. 'Verstohlen has never been wrong about these matters before. We'll divide the army. I'll ride back to Averheim with an escort, and the infantry will follow when they can. You will take the remainder of the men to Grenzstadt. Your orders are to head to Black Fire Pass. There is a garrison there that should have stopped this incursion before it reached the interior. Find out what happened, and above all else make sure the gap is sealed. Only when that's done do I want to see you in the city. Do not disappoint me.'

'Yes, sir,' said Bloch.

'You will take the bulk of the footsoldiers and some of the Averlander cavalry. That's over a thousand men, and you can resupply at Grenzstadt and take on reinforcements. I'll send Kraus with you, and warrant documents. The rest of the men will come with me to Averheim. I'll ride ahead with an advance guard; the remainder can follow on foot when they're rested.'

Bloch felt relieved. Listening to Schwarzhelm agonise over the options had not been easy. Being given a task to perform, no matter how difficult or dangerous, was far preferable to having to second-guess an outcome.

'Who'll command the forces sent east?'

Schwarzhelm gave Bloch a shrewd look.

'That, at least, is something I am clear about. I took a risk bringing you, Bloch, and it's been rewarded. You'll take them up to the passes. I'll speak to the captains and to Kraus. You should be proud. I'm giving this army to you, Bloch. Use it well. You're in command.'

CHAPTER FOURTEEN

Verstohlen was standing on the west side of the river with Grosslich's men amidst a cluster of low buildings. He checked to see that his pistol was loaded and primed to fire. The campaign was going well. All the major bridges were now in Grosslich's hands, and they'd made inroads into the poorer parts of the western bank. It seemed that wherever they chose to assault, they had the victory. Leitdorf's men were demoralised and divided. By contrast, Grosslich's were disciplined and effective. Verstohlen's regard for the man as a commander had only grown.

'Keep it quiet,' whispered Euler. 'Let's make this quick and easy. One den at a time.'

The fighting here was house-to-house. No one knew where Leitdorf was holed up. The race to find him was intense. Grosslich had promised a hundred gold crowns for his head, which had encouraged a good deal of enthusiasm for finding him. Following a vague lead, Euler's band had ended up in one of the smelliest alleys in the poor quarter. The walls were tall and narrow. As they crept down it, even the dominating Averburg was lost to view, as were the baking rays of the sun. That would have been a comfort had it not been for the refuse piled knee-high at alleyway's base. In some sections it felt like they were wading through slurry.

The men went watchfully. Their numbers had swelled since the start of the campaign, and there were now thirty of them in the company. Euler crept up to the door at the end of the foetid alleyway. Rubbish was piled up against it and the wooden frame looked half-rotten. A terrible place for a hide-out, but Leitdorf was no doubt running out of boltholes. Plenty of terrified citizens of the poor quarter had pointed them in this direction. For the most part they didn't care which of the warring factions won control of the city. They just wanted the fighting to end.

Euler listened at the door for a few moments. Stepping carefully, regretting the mess the grime had made of his expensive Zellenhof boots, Verstohlen joined him. He placed his ear against the pitted surface of the wood. There was some noise from within, but too faint to make out. Movement, perhaps.

'You're sure about this?' said Verstohlen, his voice low.

Euler shrugged. 'It's a lead. Got any better targets?'

'None. Let's get it over with, then.'

The two men stepped back from the door. Euler placed his foot over the flimsy lock and kicked savagely. The door swung open on rusty hinges and they charged in.

There was a dingy chamber beyond, lit by dirt-streaked windows on one wall and a series of tallow candles on another. The smell was overpowering. Several men sat around a table in the centre. They were armed, if poorly, and jumped up as soon as Euler and Verstohlen burst in. In such an irregular war it was impossible to tell at first glance who was fighting for whom, but they had the look of Leitdorf's men, holed up away from the fiercest fighting.

Verstohlen stepped to one side, took careful aim and sent a bullet spiralling in the face of the nearest man. The man spun backwards, his cries of surprise cut cruelly short. Euler flew at the next nearest, knocking him back with a furious swipe of his sword. Then the rest of the men were in the chamber, tearing at the inhabitants. Blades flashed in the semi-darkness, and blood splattered on the filth-strewn floor.

There was no way out, no rear exit. The fighting was mercifully brief. Leitdorf's men put up a token struggle, but they were outnumbered and taken unawares. Verstohlen took little part in it and put his pistol in its holster.

'Do not kill them all!' he cried.

By then there was one survivor, cowering in the corner. He had no weapon and seemed older than the others. Euler held up his hand, and the assault stopped. Six men lay dead on the floor, five of them Leitdorf's.

Euler went over to the man in the corner. He was skinny, almost emaciated, with lank hair that hung to his shoulder. His skin was a pale grey, almost blue in the folds of flesh under his eyes. He looked utterly wretched. As Euler stood over him, the man scrabbled to get even further back into the corner, like a trapped animal in a cage.

'Leave this to me,' said Verstohlen, walking over to the corner.

Euler shrugged. 'As you wish. We'll have a look around.'

Verstohlen squatted down facing the trembling figure. The man smelled as bad as everything else. The heat had turned half of Averheim into a cesspit.

'What's your name?' asked Verstohlen, keeping his voice calm.

The man stared back at him, wide-eyed, and said nothing. He seemed to be having trouble focussing. Verstohlen leaned forward and sniffed. Somewhere, buried beneath the layers of body odour, halitosis and excrement, there was an element of jasmine.

A joyroot user. Verstohlen had begun to wonder whether Leitdorf had stamped the trade out amongst his followers.

'Where do you get your supply?'

The man shook his head, still trembling. It was as if his mouth had been glued together. Verstohlen couldn't decide

whether the man was terrified of him, or just generally terrified. The narcotic was certainly capable of inducing paranoia.

'There's nothing more for us here,' said Euler, coming to
stand at his shoulder. 'You think it's worth questioning this
one?'

'I do. Will you wait outside for me?'

Euler nodded. 'Don't be too long. There are more leads to
follow. I could use those gold pieces.'

The men filed out of the chamber and back into the alley.
The last one to leave pulled the door closed behind him.
Verstohlen and the man were alone.

'I think you understand why I'm asking you these things,'
said Verstohlen, fixing the ruined figure with a hard stare.
'If you choose to give me answers, it will go better for you.'

The man shook his head, keeping his mouth clamped
closed. Then, as if as an afterthought, he spat in Verstohlen's
face. He shrank back after that, looking even more scared
than before.

'So be it.' The spy reached into his coat. As ever, when he
retrieved the amulet, the metal was hot. It knew when it was
near corruption. Indeed, the device was part of that corruption, just a shard of the horror that still existed at the roof
of the world. It was a dangerous thing to use. Dangerous,
but invaluable.

As Verstohlen withdrew the amulet, the man looked at him
sidelong. He could obviously sense something, but didn't
seem to know what it was.

'Look at this,' ordered Verstohlen and thrust it before the
wretch's eyes.

Just as had happened with Fromgar, the change was
instantaneous. The blurred eyes became sharply focussed.
The bluish lines around them seemed to pulse with a lurid
light, as if thick veins had suddenly generated around the
lids. The man tried to get up, scrabbling at the stone. His
breath started to come in thick wheezes.

Verstohlen stood and withdrew a few paces. He pulled the
pistol from its holster and aimed it at the man's face.

'Speak to me,' he commanded.

The red-rimmed eyes blazed.

'You cannot command me!' the man cried, and spittle flew from his mouth. The voice was strange and twisted, like a cross between a man's and a woman's.

'I have the power to kill you. You'd do well to speak to me.'

The man laughed, and his skeletal chest shuddered with the effort.

'And what? You'll spare my life?' He nearly choked on his laughter and broke into a racking cough. 'I don't think so. You have no idea about life and death anyway. You're ignorant, human. As ignorant as the rest.'

'Maybe so. Why not enlighten me?'

'What do you wish to know? How the six dimensions of pleasure are interwoven? How the nexus of desire derives from the kernel of a nightmare? How the world will end? I can tell you all of this, human. All of this and more.'

Verstohlen ignored the ravings. All cultists thought they had privileged access to arcane secrets. That was what made them so pathetic. To acquire genuine knowledge was a long and difficult process. Expecting it to be handed over on a silver platter in exchange for performing a few rites over a pentangle was tedious in the extreme.

'Nothing so grand. Tell me about Natassja. Where's she from?'

The man grinned widely, and his tongue ran around his cracked lips. For the first time, Verstohlen noticed how long it was. It looked forked.

'Ah, the queen. Have you not guessed it? She's a rare one.'

He seemed to be passing into some kind of rapture. He ran his bony fingers over his body as he spoke. It looked like a grotesque parody of a lover's caress.

'Why do you call her the queen?'

'You'll see. You'll see!'

'Where is she? Where is Rufus?'

'Nearby. And they have their pets with them! You've seen them already, haven't you?'

Verstohlen felt a twinge of anxiety. That was what he feared. There were still horrors being held in reserve. Grosslich's men were pushing on too quickly. They didn't know what they faced.

'Tell me where Rufus is.'

A wicked look passed over the man's face.

'I don't know where he is. But I can tell you where someone else is. Someone you haven't seen for a long time.'

'I'm listening.'

The cultist reared up like a snake, his hands stretched out in a twisted motion. He looked suddenly delighted, as if a new game had occurred to him. His tongue flickered out. As he rose, his rags fell from his body. Verstohlen saw with disgust how diseased his filthy flesh had become. The joyroot had become everything to him, more important even than food. He kept the pistol trained carefully. He should have tied him up before applying the amulet.

'She is in torment at the feet of the master of pain!' he cried, his voice increasingly shrill. 'Her soul writhes in delicious agony under the weight of his glorious debauchery!'

Verstohlen primed the weapon to fire. There was an unholy gleam in the cultist's rheumy eyes.

'Cease this nonsense. Where is Leitdorf?'

'I've seen her in my dreams, Pieter Verstohlen. Your lovely wife, shriven before the altar of his infinite lust!'

'Do not speak of her.'

'She's damned, Pieter Verstohlen!'

'Be silent!'

'Damned to an eternity of torment! And there's more. Do you know the worst part?'

Verstohlen stepped forward, his hand shaking. He felt sick.

'I will fire. Cease this now!'

'She has been corrupted! They corrupted your Leonora! She enjoys it! She–'

The pistol rang out. The cultist was instantly silenced, flung back against the dirt-caked wall. He slumped to the ground. From his forehead, thick blood pumped from a neat round hole. It was nearly purple.

Verstohlen stood motionless for a moment, the gun still in position. His hands were trembling.

Slowly, with difficulty, he brought his emotions under control. The cultist lay at his feet like a crushed spider, his tortured limbs bent in every direction. Verstohlen replaced the gun in the holster and carefully backed away.

That had been a mistake. It was foolish to think he could bring an end to this through such means. It had all been a mistake.

He withdrew, opened the door and stepped outside. Euler was waiting. His men had moved to the far end of the alleyway.

'Are you all right?' asked the captain, looking at him with concern.

'I'm fine.'

'You look like–'

'I'm fine.'

Euler gave him a doubtful stare, then let it drop.

'Find out anything useful?'

'No. He was mad. We need to keep moving.'

Euler shook his head resignedly.

'Very well. There's another lead we can follow.'

He began to walk off down the alley. Verstohlen followed close behind, his breathing gradually returning to normal. The cultist had been raving. It was nonsense. They said whatever came into their diseased head. They wanted to unsettle you. That was their mission, their miserable purpose. Best to ignore.

As he went, though, one thought remained lodged in his mind. It wouldn't leave, even when he emerged once more into the sunlight of the open street.

It knew my wife's name.

Even before Helborg had ridden into the outskirts of Averheim, he'd been able to smell the burning. He brought his steed to a halt. Around him, his men did likewise. The ranks of Reiksguard controlled their mounts perfectly. They stood for a moment, looking at the city before them. The thin columns of smoke hung over Averheim, staining the clear sky. It looked like the place was under siege, yet there was no army camped around the walls.

'Mother of Sigmar,' Helborg spat, looking over at Skarr. 'We should have ridden harder.'

Skarr gave him an expression that indicated he didn't think it was possible to have ridden faster, Reiksguard or not.

'The west gate is nearest,' was all he said. 'We'll have to ride through the poor quarter.'

Helborg nodded. He knew Averheim. He'd visited as little as possible in recent years. All the Empire knew of his enmity with the late Marius. As far as Helborg was concerned, the elector had been an arrogant, raving fool. He'd brought his own death about through foolishness and lack of foresight. If Schwarzhelm hadn't curbed his worse excesses twenty years ago, there would surely have been a coup against his authority then. Perhaps that would have been better. In Helborg's experience, it was generally better to cut out an infection at source than let it grow. Now, twenty years on, they were still dealing with the legacy of the mad count, and it looked like even Schwarzhelm had failed to grapple with it.

Then again, Schwarzhelm himself was another problem. The man was becoming irascible and difficult, even by his own standards. His behaviour at Turgitz had been embarrassing. If it had been another man, Helborg might have run him through for such impertinence. He could admire the man for his martial prowess, and there was no more steadfast ally to have on the field of battle, but Schwarzhelm didn't understand politics. He made enemies too easily, was too quick to spot a slight or suspect a campaign against him. That was a serious flaw. One had to understand that military might was always subordinate to the demands of politics. There would always be intrigue, always be conspiracy. The trick was to understand it, get inside it, cultivate the right allies. Schwarzhelm never did. He was as clumsy with diplomacy as he was with women.

Between them, Helborg and Schwarzhelm were the two might-iest warriors of the Empire, unmatched by any other. And yet they so often worked alone, driven apart both by the endless demands of the Emperor and by the differences in their essential character. It was foolish, wasteful, unnecessary. Maybe that would have to be rectified. The low-level feud was becoming damaging. When this was over, a summit would have to be convened. Schwarzhelm, Helborg and the Emperor would have to meet, thrash out some kind of accommodation. The bad blood could be drained from their triumvirate with a little imagination. The stakes were too high to let it continue festering.

'Let's go,' Helborg said, taking up the reins. There would be plenty of time for reflection when the two men met again. For now, the Reiksguard were clearly needed. Averheim had the look of a city that had drifted into anarchy. That could not be allowed to continue.

The day was waning to dusk. In the west, clouds barred the setting sun. Averheim was still distant.

As he rode, Schwarzhelm felt the effects of a long day in the saddle begin to wear on his battle-ravaged body. The landscape around him looked eerily familiar. He knew he'd travelled along the same road just days before at the head of a conquering army. Now he was riding back with an escort of less than a dozen riders, consumed with a mix of alien emotions. The certainties he'd enjoyed while pursuing the orcs had receded again. The further west he went, the more his mood began to return to one of darkness. The city was a curse for him, the home of the sickness that had blighted his sleep and impaired his judgement. And he was going back.

The hooves of the horse thudded on the hard dirt of the track. The incessant rhythm began to have a soporific effect. Schwarzhelm shook his head, trying to clear the strands of sleep from his eyes. There were many miles of riding ahead. Neither he nor his bodyguard would rest more than they needed to. They all knew time was of the essence.

Even as the light weakened, the rolling hills passed by. The uplands beyond Heideck were now far behind them. All around, the cattle-country extended. The grass was still deep green despite weeks of beating sun. This country was blessed indeed. The folk of the Drakwald, huddled around their meagre fires and living amongst their skinny animals, would have given anything to live in such rich plenty.

But there was always a flaw, always an imperfection. Amid all the majesty of the Empire, there was corruption. Averland was no different. He'd felt it every night of the mission. How many days had he gone without proper sleep? Too many to keep a count of. A man could only go so long before he started to lose his mind.

Perhaps he *was* losing his mind. Others thought it. He'd heard the whispered rumours, seen the sidelong glances in his direction. Half of Averheim probably doubted his state of equilibrium.

There was a shout from further ahead. One of the outriders, mounted on a sleek mount of Araby picked for speed, was riding back along to the road to meet them. Schwarzhelm called a halt. Freed from the tyranny of the whip, the horses stood shivering in the balmy air, flanks shiny with sweat.

The rider came amongst them. As the man approached, Schwarzhelm noticed the gentle hiss of the grass around them. The fronds moved in the warm breeze like waves on the sea. The tips were tinged with the golden light of the sun, though the roots were hidden in darkness. All around them, as far as the eye could make out, they were surrounded by an ocean of grassland. It was like a scene from one of his dreams. Everything was moving, everything was quiet.

'My lord,' cried the rider. His voice sounded suddenly harsh against the soft backdrop of the scene. 'I've found something.'

'It'd better be good,' Schwarzhelm growled. His voice sounded thick and sullen, even to him. The scout, experienced by the look of him and from the Averheim garrison, swallowed nervously. 'All the same, my lord. I think you should see this.'

Schwarzhelm looked into the west. The sun was still above the horizon. There would be perhaps half an hour of light. Just enough.

'Lead on,' he ordered, kicking his horse into motion once more.

The scout turned, and the party followed him further along the road for some distance. No one spoke. The only sound was the faint noise of the grass in the breeze. In the east, far behind them and over the distant line of the Worlds Edge Mountains, the first of the stars became visible. Night was drawing on fast.

Schwarzhelm knew where they were headed long before he could make out exactly what the scout wanted to show them. A few hundred yards from the road, a narrow track curved away and off into the fields. The earth was rutted and uneven, and the grass on either verge had been flattened recently. Without needing to ask for directions, Schwarzhelm nudged his steed to follow the branching path. He soon saw why the scout had turned from the road to follow the path. Carrion crows. Dozens of them. They looked as large and ragged as vultures against the darkling sky. Some wheeled around, black in the dusk, moving in lazy circles. Others perched on the branches of the trees, looking at them intently with their glossy eyes.

None of the birds uttered so much as a caw. They had the air of sentries, silent watchers of the night. Crows were as common as the pox all across the Empire, but these had an unsavoury look. Perhaps it was the unnatural heat in the air, or the silence, or their size. Whatever it was, the effect was unnerving.

'I saw them from the road, my lord,' said the scout. He kept his voice low, eyes watchful. 'There it is.'

A ramshackle shed, isolated in the dark grassland. The fading sunlight leaked through the gaps in the wood. It had only half a roof and one of the walls had slumped into ruin. Perhaps it had been an old barn.

Schwarzhelm halted. He felt as if an icy fist had clenched around his heart. He could feel his pulse quicken.

'Are you all right, sir?'

'We'll dismount,' he said gruffly. 'From here, we go on foot.'

The men did as they were ordered. They swung stiffly from
their saddles, legs sore from hours of riding. Schwarzhelm
felt his own frame creaking as he landed heavily on the earth.
The ground was baked hard. He could feel the waves of heat
rising from it. Even as the sun edged towards the horizon,
Averland still sweltered.

The men waited for him to move. Schwarzhelm could sense
their fear. He stalked towards the ruined barn. Above him,
the crows circled. Their loops seemed to compress. They
were inquisitive. He ignored them, but kept his hand on
the sword.

On the northern wall of the barn, a wide opening gaped.
It was hard to see much of what lay beyond the stone door
frame. The shadows were now long. A sickly sweet smell
wafted across the air. For a moment, Schwarzhelm couldn't
place it. Was that jasmine? He went closer. The aroma was
more familiar than that. It was the mark of battlefields across
the Old World. The reek of death, of bodies rotting in the
mud. That was what the crows were there for.

Schwarzhelm looked up at them grimly. He'd deprived
them of their meal. That, at least, was something.

'You've been inside?' he asked the scout.

The man shook his head, looking ashamed.

'I… it seemed…' he began, then trailed off.

For once Schwarzhelm couldn't bring himself to reprimand him. A cold vice of dread was wrapped hard around
his own breast. Nothing, not the last golden rays of the sun
nor the warming balm of the dusk air, could shift it. He
merely nodded in response.

'Be on your guard, then,' he said, drawing his sword. It
gave a metallic rasp as it left the scabbard. 'Stay watchful.'

Turning back to the barn, he took a deep breath and
ducked under the lintel. Inside, the stench was thick and
cloying. Schwarzhelm felt his gorge rise and clasped his hand
over his mouth. For a moment, he couldn't see anything at

all. Then his eyes adjusted to the gloom. Gaps in the ruined roof and the part-collapsed walls let in enough of the evening light to begin to make some sense of the interior.

He couldn't see how many corpses there were. Perhaps a dozen, maybe more. All men. Soldiers, by the look of them. Some of their armour still remained on them. Grunwald's men, some Averheim troops. Here and there a sword-edge glinted. There was little flesh visible. One cadaver, strewn across the rough earth floor on his back, lay in the middle of a pool of weak light. His skin was grey. His eyes had long been pecked out by the crows and there were holes in his cheeks and neck. His expression was fixed in agony. His death had been painful. Possibly prolonged. Not all his injuries looked like the work of carrion fowl.

Schwarzhelm felt his heart begin to beat harder. He consciously quelled it. He'd seen hundreds of bodies in his time, many in more terrible places. This was no different. Outside the barn, the grass continued to hiss in the breeze. It was as if the place was surrounded by a host of whispering ghosts.

He looked away, down at the floor for a moment, trying to collect himself. He could feel his composure fraying. The days without sleep were getting to him. Something about this whole scene was getting to him. He turned back to his men. A couple of them had followed him in and were gazing at the piled bodies with ill-disguised nausea. Others held back, unwilling to enter the stinking interior.

'Come,' said Schwarzhelm, feeling sick at heart. 'There's nothing more to see here.'

Once outside again, he took a deep draught of pure air. It did little to lift the sense of corruption he felt about him. His bodyguard looked at him expectantly.

'Was it as I feared?' asked the scout, looking nervous. 'They were Commander Grunwald's troops?'

Schwarzhelm nodded. He knew exactly what they'd been. The riders sent back along the Old Dwarf Road to request reinforcements. Each of them had been waylaid, killed, their bodies dumped in a forgotten barn a mile from the trade

route. Schwarzhelm himself must have ridden past the place
on his journey east, oblivious to the secret contained within.
Stumbling across it now was a rare chance. Perhaps more
than that.

'Anything else?' he asked.

'Men have camped nearby. They're long gone.'

'We'll take a look.'

The scout led them further from the road. Several yards
down the track, there was a collection of trees, isolated in
the endless miles of rolling pasture. They rose tall and dark
against the sky. At the base of the trunks, there were signs
of fire. Schwarzhelm bent down and placed his hand over
the ashes. Cold. He looked around him.

'Whose lands are these?' he asked.

One of the Averlanders answered. 'We're close to Leitdorf's
estates. This is his family's country.'

Schwarzhelm looked over the deserted campsite. There
were more blackened circles of old fires around the edge
of the trees. The grass was heavily trampled. At one stage,
many men had come and gone here. The exercise had been
well planned. Perhaps other bands had been active too. In
his mind's eye, Schwarzhelm saw Leitdorf's fat face, running with arrogance and scorn. He remembered his bitter
words. *In my current position I cannot punish insolence. That
will not be the case forever.* Perhaps even then his forces had
been mobilising.

He shuffled further into the camp, studying, watching.
There was little left. No weapons, no discarded clothing.
He turned to leave.

'Sir, this one's still warm.'

One of the Averlanders had walked off towards the edge of
the field. At his feet lay another charred circle. Schwarzhelm
came up to it. It was different. It was further from the camp,
hidden by the whispering grass. They'd dug a hole in the
parched earth and stuffed it with refuse. This hadn't been
a fire for food.

Schwarzhelm bent over it. The ashes were barely warmer

than the air around him. The faintest impression of heat lingered over them. It looked like a sack had been flung into the fire-pit. Scraps of fabric, black and curling, lay amidst the spent fuel. He thrust his hands into the ashes, scattering them, combing through the white flakes. Here and there, fragments of parchment. Nothing large enough to make out. Orders, perhaps, sent by courier from Averheim. They'd been thorough when they left. Nothing could be made out on them.

Then he saw it. Mere inches from the fire, a scrap of dry parchment, no more than two inches long. Eagerly, he grasped it. The light was poor, and there was nothing much on it. It looked like a strip torn from a page. There were five words visible on it, scribbled hastily. Part of something larger.

...forces to RL from Nuln...

That was the name he needed, not that he'd been in any doubt. But it was the final word that chilled his blood. He remembered Verstohlen's words, days ago. *They're getting help from outside.* He'd assumed it was Altdorf, someone at court, an Averlander exile with a stake in one of the contenders. But Nuln. That was much closer.

It was probably nothing. Probably part of routine orders.

But the ice around his heart had returned. He knew who was at Nuln.

'Let's go,' Schwarzhelm said gruffly, standing up again and walking back to the horses.

His men hurried to comply. The last of the light was failing, and there would be hard riding ahead before they could rest. They walked back past the ruined barn, through the fields and on to the road. As they went, Schwarzhelm said nothing. He didn't look back. His mind was working, running through the possibilities. He felt the return of that great pressure, the presaging of the nightmares that he knew would come as they approached Averheim.

He took a deep breath and mounted his horse. The others did likewise, and soon they were heading west once more.

Behind them, lost in the night, the barn stood alone. Lazily,

the crows descended to the rafters. Their meal had been interrupted, but it could now commence again.

CHAPTER FIFTEEN

Holed up in his temporary command post deep in the poor quarter of Averheim, Rufus Leitdorf raged. He could feel the spittle form at the corners of his mouth. The room was malodorous and squalid. Ancient plaster hung from the walls of the second storey chamber, curling with mould. The heat and filth were everywhere. He hurled the pile of maps to the corner of the room, watching the parchment curl up and slide across the floor. His captains, what was left of them, cowered.

'You pack of useless dogs,' Rufus spat, running his accusatory eyes across them in turn. 'We *knew* Grosslich would move against us. Where are your tactics? Where is the counter-attack?'

One of the captains, a thick-set, swarthy man named Werner Klopfer, was brave enough to respond.

'It happened sooner than we anticipated, highness. Schwarzhelm has given Grosslich his blessing. It's drawn more support to his side.'

'Schwarzhelm isn't here! He's been taken away. That's the whole point. We should have had this place to ourselves.

Now it's all gone to ruin. The trade's in tatters, we've lost control of the Old City, and we've barely got the money left to pay our miserable fighters another day.'

Rufus could feel his anger begin to get the better of him. He had to calm down. He knew he couldn't lose it entirely in front of the men. They all knew the reputation of his father, and it hung heavily over him. The Mad Count of Averland. Rufus wouldn't go down that road. That's why he'd made the choices he had. Difficult choices. Not many would have made them. But he needed the power. He had to have the power. Without Averland, his life was nothing. Nothing at all.

'Where's my wife?' he asked, his voice sullen.

There was a series of blank looks from the assembled captains. Natassja hadn't been seen for days. That alone was enough to drive him mad. He needed her. She'd planned all of this. It had all been her idea, even from the very beginning. Now, just when their plans were beginning to unravel, she was nowhere to be found.

'Damn her,' he hissed, banging his fist on the table before him.

'Grosslich has moved quickly across the river,' ventured another one of the officers. 'She may have become cut off in one of the root houses. There's still fighting in the Old City, whatever they say on the streets.'

'What good is she to me from there? Don't tell me about things I have no control over.'

One of the officers shot another of his companions a weary glance. That made Rufus even angrier, but he pushed the fury down. They were despairing of him. His rages, his tantrums, his impossible demands. He knew they were losing faith. His instinct was to have them all dismissed, to lead the rest of the men himself, to sweep all resistance before him into the Aver.

He knew that was a fantasy. He was alone. His allies had deserted him. The Alptraums hated his whole family, and they were still powerful. The only sure support he had was Natassja, and now she too was missing. He could only hope that she was working on some means of recovering their position. She was resourceful, that one. Devious. Intelligent. Beautiful. Even a day without her was torture. He needed her back.

'Very well,' he said wearily, trying to keep his voice under control. 'We need to decide what to do.'

'Leave the city, highness,' urged Klopfer. 'Grosslich controls all but a fragment of it. We cannot fight him here.'

Rufus looked at him disdainfully.

'Flee? Is that your only advice?'

'We can regroup at your family estates. Restore the trade along the river. Hire more men. If we stay here, we'll be discovered. Sooner or later, our positions will fall to them.'

There was a nod from one of the other captains. Rufus failed to control a sneer. They were weak. None of them had the slightest idea what was at stake, what had been sacrificed for the goal of power. If they'd been privy to his and Natassja's full plans, then they wouldn't have dared to roll their eyes in his presence or doubt his commands. He was playing for higher stakes than they could possibly imagine.

'Do you understand nothing? The succession is being decided now. Grosslich has declared himself elector. Once he has control over the city, the Emperor will crown him. As things stand, we remain in contention. If we leave now, it will all go to dust. To dust!'

He looked Klopfer in the eye. Did the man have an ulterior motive? Why was he so keen to concede defeat? Perhaps he'd better see about removing him. Not that there were many left to replace him.

'And there's Natassja,' he added, his voice fervent. 'I'll not leave her. We'll fight until she's found and that bastard Grosslich driven back into the Old City.'

For a moment there was silence. None of the captains wished to assent. None of them wished to pick a fresh fight. They looked dejected, half-beaten already. Rufus felt his scorn for them grow. Natassja was worth a hundred of them. Where *was* she?

Then there was a commotion in the hall outside the chamber. A soldier burst in, panting from exertion. One of his own men, bearing the Leitdorf colours. More trustworthy than the mercenary scum he'd been driven to using.

'Your pardon, highness.' he blurted.

'Speak quickly.'

'We've been discovered. Grosslich has sent an advance detachment here. The rest of his army follows. They'll be here soon.'

Rufus shot a glance at Klopfer. The man had a smug look of vindication on his face.

'This is it, then,' Rufus said. 'We'll meet them.'

Klopfer met his gaze. Still defiant.

'With respect, that is madness, highness,' said Klopfer. Bold words. When this was over, the man might live to regret such candour. 'We no longer have the numbers to take on Grosslich's men openly.'

On another occasion, Rufus might have raged at him, thrown objects at him, ordered him to fall on his sword. Not this time. The knowledge that the net was closing in on him brought a strange sense of resignation. There would be no retreat. The Leitdorfs might have been many things. Mad, unpredictable, feckless. But they weren't cowards. Not when it really mattered.

'We've spent months buying this army,' he said. His voice was strangely quiet, unusually firm. 'They've failed us so far. It's only fair to give them a chance to redeem themselves.'

He turned to Lars Neumann, the one lieutenant he still felt some degree of confidence in.

'Get the word out. Muster everyone we still have. Promise them double the gold. We'll meet them in the Vormeister-platz. The retreat stops here.'

Neumann hesitated for a moment, then bowed and hurried from the room. Rufus ran his gaze across the remaining captains. None of them looked convinced.

'If any of you are thinking of getting out of this, I warn you there will be no forgiveness from me. There are forces at work here that you have no idea about. Once I'm elector, I'll remember any treachery.'

He drew his sword. His father's old blade, the Leitdorf Wolfsklinge. It was an ancient weapon, studded with the symbols of his house. Not as prestigious as the runefang lying in the Averburg, but still potent. There were old runes on the steel, just as on the weapons of the electors.

'Gather your men,' he said, gazing at the blade with fondness. 'This isn't over yet.'

Schwarzhelm and his escort reached the Aver valley. All about them the countryside stretched away in serene curves of pasture. The river at the base of the incline was as wide and turgid as before, green with blooms of algae. The city itself lay ahead at the end of the road, sweltering under the midday sun. The fires were still visible, staining the open sky with lines of smoke. It looked like more of them than when he'd left. Even the noise of the fighting was faintly audible. So Averheim had truly descended into anarchy.

This was what he had been appointed to prevent. Schwarzhelm let his fingers clench around the hilt of the Rechtstahl. It wasn't too late.

'What standards are those?' he asked, pointing to the flags hanging from the distant Averburg, just on the edge of sight.

One of his bodyguards, a young man with keen eyes called Adselm, came forward.

'Hard to make out, my lord. The standard of Averland no longer flies. Maybe Grosslich's devices.'

Schwarzhelm grunted. That was good. If Verstohlen was right, then Grosslich was now their only chance. It would be some time before the rest of Schwarzhelm's army could make its way back to Averheim from Heideck. In the interim they'd need Heinz-Mark's men to keep order.

'Let's move,' he said, taking up the reins.

The riders around him did likewise, but their movements were sluggish. They were exhausted after the punishing ride. For a moment, Schwarzhelm felt their weariness infect him. He felt like he'd been in the saddle for weeks, hurtling back and forth, trying to keep order as Averland gradually pulled itself apart.

He knew he was tired. He knew his judgement was impaired. But there was no time. There was never any time.

'Follow me,' he said, and kicked his horse into movement once more. As he did so, he had a low sense of foreboding. Things were drawing together. There was a canker at the heart of Averheim, something rotten and concealed. It had been eating away at him for weeks. One way or another, it would be uncovered soon.

Helborg and the Reiksguard rode up to the west gate of the city. It was open. The guards had long gone. The courtyard beyond, normally bustling with traders and cattle merchants, was deserted. The handsome buildings flanking the open space stood empty, their rich owners having fled the fighting soon after it had got out of control. The elegant glass windows had been smashed and the interiors looted. It was a scene of desolation.

As the Marshal rode under the parapet, a few scavengers looked up, eyes wide with fright. They darted into the shadows like rats, their rags fluttering behind them.

Helborg stopped. On either side of him, the front rank of the knights formed up. Their visors were down and their swords were drawn. There were few more formidable sights in the Empire than a whole company of Reiksguard in full battle-gear. They looked grim and deadly. The noonday sun flashed from their polished armour and naked blades. The horses stamped in the heat, impatient to move on.

Still Helborg paused. Skarr drew alongside him.

'Where now?'

Helborg inclined his head, listening. 'There's fighting. I can hear it. This thing must be ended quickly. We'll make an example of them.'

'As you command.'

'Tell the men to kill on sight. I don't care which faction they belong to.'

'What of Lord Schwarzhelm?'

'If he makes an appearance, then we'll worry about him. Until then, assume we're the Imperial authority here.'

With that, he drew his sword. The Klingerach glittered in the sunlight. The runes on its surface blazed as if lit from within. Once again, the Solland runefang had been called on. For a blade that had cleaved the armour of Chaos warlords and vampire counts apart, it felt almost churlish to draw it in such circumstances. But Averheim needed to be cowed. If insurrection was tolerated anywhere, it would soon spread like a cancer across the whole Empire. Whatever Schwarzhelm had tried in order to stem it, he had failed. Helborg would not repeat those mistakes.

'Reiksguard,' he roared, pointing the sword straight ahead, 'to battle!'

After a resounding shout of acclimation, the knights kicked their steeds into action. With a thunder of hooves on stone, the company rode from the courtyard and into the interior of the city.

Grosslich's scattered warbands were being drawn together on the east bank of the river. Hundreds of men had been assembled and more were arriving at every moment. Above them all, the vast bulk of the Averburg towered over the preparations.

Leitdorf had been found. Everything else could be forgotten. Once they had the renegade in their hands, dead or alive, then it would be over.

Verstohlen pushed his way through the throng towards Grosslich. When he found him, the man already looked flushed with the prospect of impending victory.

'You're joining us?' asked Grosslich, buckling the last of his armour with the help of his squire and preparing to mount his horse.

'Perhaps. I'm worried about this.'

Grosslich gave him a weary look.

'Counsellor, your advice has been invaluable, but do you

not think your fears have been allayed now? Leitdorf is finished. Even his own men no longer obey him.'

'You know what I fear. The great enemy always looks weaker than it is.'

'We've caught them too soon,' insisted Grosslich, donning his open-faced helmet and smiling confidently. 'They haven't had time to respond. That's your doing, Pieter. You should be proud.'

Verstohlen wasn't consoled. Ever since the encounter with the cultist, he'd been feeling like he'd missed something. How had he known his name? What dark purpose was being enacted here?

'Is Natassja with him?'

As the mention of her name, Grosslich couldn't prevent his face twisting into a sneer of disgust.

'The witch? They never leave one another's side. If we kill one Leitdorf, we'll kill them both.'

'I hope that's so. She has powers of her own. I've seen her servants. They are deadly.'

'Then I'll hunt her down myself. We need to ride. Euler has already gone ahead with the vanguard to pin them down.'

'Very well. I'll join you when I can. Be careful, Heinz-Mark. The enemy has subtle powers. Verena be with you.'

'And Sigmar with you, counsellor.'

With that, Grosslich dug his spurs into his steed's flanks and the horse sprung forward. Behind him, the mounted troops followed suit. The mounted column clattered off towards the poor quarter, blades drawn and standards unfurled. For all their mixed livery, they were an impressive sight. In the wake of the cavalry, Grosslich's infantry companies struggled to keep up. They ran down the streets, their boots thudding on the stone. They looked eager, keen to be involved in the final struggle.

Verstohlen watched them go. He was torn over whether to join them. It had been days since his message had been sent to Schwarzhelm. Had he received it? If he had, would he answer the request for aid? For all Verstohlen knew, the greenskins still controlled the east of the province. Battle was unpredictable, and the roads remained dangerous.

'They cannot handle this on their own,' he breathed, talking to himself in his agitation. 'They haven't seen the horror in their midst. They need the Emperor's Champion.'

He drew in a deep breath. Mumbling like a madman would do nothing to bring Schwarzhelm back.

Still plagued by doubts, Verstohlen took a horse from one of Grosslich's stablehands. He mounted quickly and drew his pistol from its holster. The time for running skirmishes in the streets was over. The forces had come together at last. Now in earnest, the battle for Averheim had begun.

Captain Euler charged into the Vormeisterplatz. He was on foot, as were all his men. In his hand he carried a broadsword. Those around him had an assortment of weapons: halberds, cudgels, spears, halberds, even kitchen knives and skewers. Grosslich had worked hard to equip his men properly, but this was still a semi-irregular war. For every trooper kitted out in full Imperial regalia there were many dogs of war, wearing and wielding whatever they could get their hands on.

It didn't matter much. If they knew how to use their weapon and follow orders they were helpful. Euler had been put in charge of the entire vanguard. That comprised several hundred men, all champing at the bit for a first look at the hated Leitdorf. It was nothing personal, but the promise of a hundred gold crowns had a way of inflaming the passions.

Once in the wide square, Euler had little time to take in the surroundings. The Vormeisterplatz was huge, nearly the same size as the famed Plenzerplatz in the Old City. It had been constructed for similar reasons, to allow the huge trade caravans within the city walls for the great seasonal shows. In more peaceful times, the great squares would have been full of covered wagons proffering delicacies from all corners of the Grand County. Averlanders liked their food and drink, and the ale-fuelled fayres would last long into the night.

No more. The Vormeisterplatz was a rubbish-strewn mess.
Two huge piles of refuse at either side of the massive courtyard burned steadily, casting an angry red light across the
flagstones. The afternoon sun was beginning to weaken, and
its amber rays blended with the flames. It looked like the
hearth of some monstrous kitchen.

Towering buildings rose up on all four sides of the square.
Most were trader's warehouses, bleak and utilitarian. All had
their windows smashed or doors broken in. Other buildings, merchant's houses and official institutions, had fared
similarly badly. It hadn't taken long for the citizens of Averland's capital to take advantage of the anarchy in the streets.

On the far side of the square, Leitdorf's men had arranged
themselves. There were more than Euler had expected. They
were arranged in rough-looking detachments. Some of them
looked pretty well-equipped. He guessed they were Leitdorf's
own family regiments, drafted in from his estates further
east. They would have had feudal obligations to the count
and would fight for him even when his gold ran out. No
one else would.

The mercenaries were another matter. They looked even
more ramshackle than the very worst of Grosslich's men.
Some had no armour at all, not even a helmet. Their mixture of weapons was just as eclectic as Euler's own troops.
Leitdorf had placed them on the flanks of the army where
they belonged. Only in the core did he have any number of
regular soldiers.

'This is it, lads!' Euler shouted as he ran, willing his men
onward. His forces were outnumbered by Leitdorf's men, but
that mattered not. He had faith in his soldiers, and Grosslich
would not be far behind them. Then the game would truly
be up. 'Keep in formation. A hundred crowns for the head
of Leitdorf!'

That brought a cheer. It always did. They streamed across
the open space, leaping over broken flagstones and running
through the patches of refuse.

But Leitdorf's men were not there just to cower in the

shadows. With a shout of aggression nearly as loud, they surged forward in their turn. None were left in reserve. There were no elaborate tactics or manoeuvres. Just as it had been for the last few days, this was the fighting of the gutter, hard and vicious.

The gap narrowed quickly. Euler could see the eyes of his opposite numbers as they charged towards him. They looked mad with rage. They weren't going to back off this time. He began to swing his blade, building up momentum for the crash.

'The protection of Sigmar,' he whispered, making the sign of the comet with his free hand.

Then the two forces slammed into one another. The lines broke into a confused mess of stabbing, hacking, punching and hammering. The voices of captains rose above the fray, trying to impose some kind of order on the murderous encounter.

It was futile. The melee soon descended into a vicious series of lethal struggles. In the thick of it, Euler worked his broadsword skilfully. He and his men punched their way toward the heart of the enemy. It might have been terrible tactics, but there was method in their recklessness.

Euler respected Grosslich and wanted him to prevail. But more than that, he wanted the money. A man could do a lot with a hundred gold pieces.

'For Grosslich!' he bellowed, and hacked his way into the centre of the fighting.

Helborg heard the fighting before he saw it. Even over the thudding of the horses' hooves, the tumult was audible from several streets away. There was no sound quite like it, a mix of frenzied shouting, the clash of steel against steel, screams of agony. It didn't sound like an isolated skirmish. They were heading into a major engagement.

He crouched in the saddle, riding his horse expertly across the hard surface of the street. The windowless buildings and burned-out warehouses passed by in a blur. Ahead, the street looked like it opened on to a wide expanse beyond. That was where the noise was coming from.

'Keep it tight,' he cried to Skarr, who was on his left flank. 'Sounds like a lot of them.'

Skarr grinned.

'They picked a bad day for a fight.'

'That they did. We'll divide the company. I'll take the Leit-dorf pup, you try to find his rival. If we can get them out of this, we'll break it up quickly.'

'Yes, sir.'

Then they were out of the streets and into the Vormeister-platz. The space was huge. Across the far side, two forces, each several hundred strong, were locked in what looked like a mass brawl. There was little sign of formation or tactics. It wasn't even clear from the liveries who was whom. This would be tricky to unpick. The battle was framed by two enormous fires, and the smoke drifted in rolling gouts across the flags.

Helborg kept up the pace, trying to sort out the confusion as he went. Near the centre of the fighting he caught sight of a tight knot of men standing in clear ranks, four deep. They were wearing Leitdorf's own colours, blue and burgundy, rather than the standard yellow and black garb of Averland. Once the personal livery of Marius's house had been something men had looked to with pride and envy, but since the old count's descent into madness, it had become a laughing stock. Still, it was distinctive enough, and that was all that Helborg cared about.

'I'll take that detachment!' he shouted at Skarr, who was still close at hand. 'You wheel around for the others.'

The preceptor nodded and his men, half the company, peeled off to the left. They were closing, but the mass of Averlanders still hadn't seen the Reiksguard at their backs. Only a few caught sight of their peril and tried to scuttle away. Helborg smiled coldly. It was pointless to run. If he'd truly cared about such small fry, he could pick them off at ease.

Then he was into the bulk of the struggling armies. He

crashed into the seething pack of warriors. His steed, trained for war, ploughed straight through the rival groups of men, hardly breaking stride. Some laggards were dragged under its hooves, others cut down by his sword. Their screams were added to the general cacophony.

Once in their midst, Helborg began to slice his way towards the Leitdorf mob at the centre. Any soldiers in his way were slammed aside or carved down with the Klingerach. The noble blade was wasted on such scum, but it bit through their flesh just the same.

His men stayed at his shoulder, arranged into a tight wedge. Such a charge from the Reiksguard had been known to crush whole regiments of heavily-armed Chaos warriors. Smashing aside these mere dogs of war was, by comparison, hardly worth breaking a sweat over.

One of Leitdorf's sergeants, a bulky man wearing the blue and burgundy of the bloodline, tried to organise some kind of resistance. A row of spearmen began to form in the midst of the melee, clearly intended to frustrate the cavalry charge. They didn't realise who they were up against. Helborg rode straight at him. That was just insolent.

As he neared, a couple of spear-tips were lowered in his direction. He evaded them with ease and caught up with the portly sergeant. A single thrust of the Klingerach was all it took, and the man slid to the ground, his neck severed. That seemed to dim the enthusiasm of the rest, and they dropped their spears and ran. Leitdorf's defences had been torn apart. Helborg allowed himself a grunt of satisfaction.

His prey was in sight.

Schwarzhelm was back in Averheim, his steed's hooves clattering on the stone. Behind him, his bodyguard struggled to keep up with him and began to fall back. They didn't matter. His escort was little more than a formality in any case. He needed no protection. Since seeing the city again, he was in no mood to let them catch up.

As soon as he'd passed the eastern gate and entered the Old

City, he could feel the sense of oppression settle in his bones again. He hated the place. He hated its loremasters and their obsession with procedure, he hated the sleepless nights in the sweltering heat, but most of all he hated the arrogant electoral candidates with their lust for power. Both could have learned something from Lassus, a man who had achieved everything but coveted nothing. There were none like him left in the Empire. They lived in a debased generation.

Schwarzhelm pressed the horse hard, urging it harshly onward through the empty streets. Signs of destruction were everywhere. The citizens had either been pressed into the armies of one of the rival counts, or cowered in their homes, or had left the city entirely. It lent Averheim an eerie, semi-populated feel.

He passed beneath the Averburg swiftly, not bothering to detain himself there. It was obvious where the fighting was. Huge columns of smoke rose into the air from the western end of the city, across the river and into the poorer areas. That was where he'd be needed.

As he rode, he drew the Rechtstahl from its scabbard. It was late afternoon, and the warm sun reflected in its surface like flame. Schwarzhelm gazed along its unsullied length. The blade had already tasted much blood since his arrival in Averland. It would do so again. The greenskins had suffered under its keen edge. Now its wrath would be reserved for the great enemy, the bane of mankind.

Ignoring the increasingly ragged breathing of the horse, he kicked his steed on faster. Though ground down by days of fighting, his spirit sapped by sleepless night and visions of terror before dawn, he was still the wielder of the Sword of Justice. In the mood he was in, there were few who could stand before him. Perhaps only one other in the entire Empire.

Schwarzhelm knew the decision to leave had probably been a mistake. He knew he'd endangered the city. But that was behind him now. He was back, and he could finally put his anger to good use. There would be no more debates, no more tedious discussions of the law. The time of the loremasters was over. Now the matter at hand would be decided by the warriors, just as in the days of Sigmar.

Helborg smiled and brought his steed to a halt. Around him, the Reiksguard did the same. They were in the heart of the fighting, but none dared approach them. Ahead of them, Rufus Leitdorf was still surrounded by his bodyguard. They had the best of the armour he was able to afford. The man himself looked terrified, but there was nowhere for him to go. Frantically, he pushed his protectors forward, urging them to form a barrier.

That was fairly pointless. A footsoldier in their position stood little chance against a fully-armoured knight. And Helborg was no ordinary knight. He pondered spurring his charger straight through them, scattering them and riding down their master. It was an attractive thought.

No. Leitdorf deserved more than that. For all his youthful arrogance, the man had noble blood in him. That counted for much with Helborg. When the Empire lost its respect for rank, for the discipline of social standing, then all would be lost. If there was one thing he couldn't stand, it was the rabble and their pathetic aspirations. Even a mad count was better than a sane peasant.

With a flamboyant swing he dismounted, landing easily and bringing his horse to a standstill. Around him, the rest of the Reiksguard did the same. Leitdorf's men made no attempt to engage them. Most stood open-mouthed, staring at the knights as if Sigmar himself had come to visit. Several of them fled, preferring their odds against Grosslich's rabble.

Rufus Leitdorf was less visibly cowed by Helborg's arrival. To his credit, he didn't back away but strode up to Helborg, sword in hand. As he did so, he pulled his helmet from his head, revealing his sweat-streaked face. He looked furious. In another man it might have been impressive. In the face of Kurt Helborg it merely looked petulant.

'What is this?' he spat, jabbing his finger at the Marshal. 'What are the Reiksguard doing here?'

Helborg took off his helmet, making a concealed gesture as he did so. His troops fanned out around him, forming a cordon within the centre of Leitdorf's makeshift army. For the moment at least, the count had been taken out of the fighting.

'Perhaps you don't know who I am,' said Helborg, fixing him with a cold stare.

Leitdorf, against his best interests, didn't seem deterred in the slightest.

'I know exactly who you are, Grand Marshal. And I ask you again, by what right do you intervene in this affair?'

Helborg checked the progress of the fighting all around them before replying. Behind the steel shield of the Reiksguard the struggle between the opposing groups still went on.

'Word reached me in Nuln that the succession here had descended into anarchy. I've seen it for myself. You should thank me, Herr Leitdorf. It doesn't look like things are going your way.'

Rufus looked to be working hard to control his anger.

'So this is how the just and fair Imperial authorities conduct themselves,' he spat. 'Is it not enough that the madman Schwarzhelm sides with my rival, in defiance of all law? Must I contend with the both of you? Are there not wars in the north to fight, Marshal?'

Helborg stopped in his tracks. That didn't sound like Schwarzhelm. He was scrupulously fair. Annoyingly so.

'The Lord Schwarzhelm does not take sides. He is the Emperor's representative.'

Leitdorf gave him a contemptuous look.

'Is that so? Then tell me why his adviser has been offering them his exclusive counsel. Tell me also why he's been spreading lies about my loyalty to the Empire and why he went to Ferenc Alptraum to incite him to this violence. Believe me, general, I wanted none of this. Why would I provoke a war with Grosslich when he has such men working for him? It would be madness. It *is* madness.'

Helborg turned to the knight on his left, a tall Nordlander with a shock of blond hair.

'Can you make out Skarr? Grosslich?'

'No, my lord. Not yet.'

Helborg turned back to Leitdorf. His expression was dark. He didn't like feeling as if he'd been dragged into something under false pretences. Whatever Schwarzhelm had done here, he'd better have a damned good explanation for it. The whole thing was a shambles.

'Herr Leitdorf, I am taking you into my protective custody,' said Helborg, motioning for the Reiksguard to assume the place of the man's own bodyguard. 'I don't know the rights and wrongs of this, but I won't stand by and let you butcher each other on the strength of rumours. This thing ends now.'

Leitdorf laughed, though the sound was bitter and shrill.

'So you say. But you might have more on your hands than you think. Here comes my rival. I don't think he likes what your men have done to his army. Will you fight him too, or is this all just for show?'

Helborg whirled round. On the east side of the Vormeister-platz, trumpets had been sounded. Over the heads of the men around him, Helborg could see fresh cavalry charging into the fray. At their head was a tall man in full battle armour. Beside him was a squadron of armoured riders. In the front rank was a man wearing a leather coat and a wide-brimmed hat. He looked far too familiar for comfort.

Schwarzhelm's man, the counsellor. Could Leitdorf have been telling the truth?

'Damn them all,' he muttered, before turning back to the Nordlander. 'This is getting ridiculous. Find a horse for the elector. He comes with us.'

'We're withdrawing?'

Helborg gave him a shocked look. 'Are you mad? Skarr needs reinforcing. We've taken the head from one army. It's time we did the same for the other.'

With that, he pulled himself back into the saddle. All around him, his guard did the same. Leitdorf's troops looked on helplessly as their leader was plucked from their midst. They seemed unsure whether to keep fighting at all.

Unfortunately, their choice was being made up for them. Grosslich's men were pressing home the advantage. The brawl was becoming a massacre.

'Follow my lead,' growled Helborg, lowering the Sword of Vengeance and pointing out Grosslich amid the advancing cavalry. 'Kill those around him if you have to, but we take the leader alive.'

The Reiksguard swung their horses round as one. With a single command, the phalanx moved off, smashing aside any foolish enough to get in their way.

As he rode through the sea of men, all struggling against each other in an increasingly pointless battle, Helborg felt his mind racing. The whole situation had descended into farce. Dark farce.

'Damn you, Schwarzhelm,' he muttered, keeping his eyes fixed on the approaching front rank of Grosslich's troops. 'What have you *done* here?'

Verstohlen caught up with Grosslich just as the cavalry vanguard thundered into the Vormeisterplatz. As he rode alongside the elector, Heinz-Mark flashed him a wide grin.

'You catch up fast!' he cried.

Verstohlen said nothing in reply. His pistol felt reassuringly heavy in his hand, but his heart still misgave him. Grosslich's forces looked impressive, but they'd be no match for the servants of Chaos. At each turn, at every corner, he still expected to see Natassja's horrors burst into view. He earnestly hoped he was wrong.

'There they are!' cried Grosslich as they careered around the final bend and galloped into the square. Behind them, trumpets sounded. The cavalry vanguard streamed into the Vormeisterplatz. Three hundred horsemen, all armed with the best weapons Alptraum money could buy, all eager for the hundred crown bounty. When they sighted Leitdorf's beleaguered army, a cry of scorn and mockery broke out across their ranks.

'Euler's done well,' shouted Verstohlen, his eyes scanning

the battle before them. Leitdorf's troops were pinned back, locked behind ranks of Grosslich's men. The fighting was already fierce. It would be mere moments before they were plunged into the thick of it.

'That he has. We'll finish this today!'

Grosslich looked carried away by his battle-rage. As he rode, he swung his heavy broadsword around him. His eyes glittered with the strange joy that some men took in killing. Unlike Leitdorf, this man was every inch the warrior.

'What are those riders?' asked Verstohlen. They were closing fast. Amid the press of infantry, mounted knights were heading in their direction. 'Mother of Sigmar, they're Reiksguard!'

He looked across at Grosslich in alarm. How did Leitdorf come to have Reiksguard fighting for him? The gap between the riders closed further. They were less than a hundred yards away.

'Grosslich, those are the Emperor's troops! Pull back!'

Grosslich shot him an impatient look. The light of battle was in his eyes. With a terrible certainty, Verstohlen suddenly realised he wasn't going to stop.

'I don't care who they are,' he roared. 'If they're protecting Leitdorf then I'll kill them too! This is my province, and my war!'

With that, he kicked his horse savagely and thundered towards the approaching knights. Helpless to prevent him, Verstohlen followed in his wake. His finger slipped from the trigger. He suddenly remembered his advice to Tochfel, and began to realise what was happening. This wasn't what he wanted at all. If Grosslich took on the Reiksguard, there could be only one result.

He spurred his horse on, tearing across the remaining ground. With teeth gritted, unsure what he'd do when he arrived, Verstohlen charged into the heart of the combat.

Schwarzhelm finally felt his strength begin to flag. Perhaps he'd pushed himself too far. Even with the sun dipping in the sky, the heat dragged at him. This was the end of the long trek. He was in the heart of the city, less that a mile from his destination. Whatever had transpired in his absence he'd soon find out. Something told him he wouldn't like what he found.

His bodyguard still followed, but they were lagging. If things hadn't been so pressing he'd have stopped to give them some respite, but there was no chance of that. Averheim was aflame, and there was no time to attend to the weakness of the body. They would have to catch up when they could.

Schwarzhelm passed quickly over the bridges and into the poor quarter of the city. The streets were narrower there and clogged with the effects of the rioting. Some buildings had been half-ruined, their broken walls tumbling into the street. Refuse was everywhere, some of it smouldering where the gangs had set it alight, all of it stinking.

He knew exactly where he was going. Two huge palls of smoke hung heavily over the west of the city. The sound of men clashing echoed down the narrow alleyways. Whatever Leitdorf had unleashed had been cornered in that place. The sooner he arrived there to snuff out his heresy, the better.

As he neared his destination, the sounds of battle grew louder. The air was thick with the acrid smoke of the fires. He passed men running down the streets, some towards the fighting, some away. He ignored them. They themselves seemed to have very little idea what was going on. As was ever the case, when men of the Empire fought amongst themselves, allegiances were quickly confused. There was no honour in such fighting, just the petty satisfaction of the few noblemen who benefited. It sickened his heart.

He was nearly there. Just a few more streets, passing in a flash, and he emerged into a wide square. He took the scene in. Two forces, each numbering many hundreds, were fighting at close quarters on the far side of the space. He recognised the livery of both Leitdorf and Grosslich, though he could see neither of the rivals. The combat looked vicious and disorganised. The mass of infantry was locked together in a bloody melee. It was unclear which side had the mastery. To his relief, Schwarzhelm neither saw nor detected any sign of Chaos. These were mortal men struggling, the kind that had been fighting sporadically in the city ever since he'd arrived.

He pressed on. Every lurch of the horse carried him nearer. Faces began to come into focus, formations began to clarify. He needed to find Verstohlen. The spy would be at the thick of it, no doubt with Grosslich. Schwarzhelm stood up in the saddle, craning to make out what was going on. Everything was fluid, everything was in motion. Some men ran up to him, trying to waylay him before he could join the fray. The Rechtstahl cut them down with almost contemptuous ease. He whipped the horse faster, bearing down on the core of the fighting.

He saw Leitdorf first. The flamboyant armour was hard to miss. The man still wore a cape of blue and burgundy, just as his father had done. He didn't ride alone. He was surrounded by a bodyguard of knights. They looked terrifyingly efficient, carving their way through Grosslich's troops with a cold precision that reminded him of...

Reiksguard. Schwarzhelm felt his heart nearly stop. He pulled his horse to a standstill. The beast skidded to a halt, whinnying in protest. Even in the midst of the conflict, with men fighting and falling on either side of him, Schwarzhelm stood as still as a graven image. A terrible feeling had come over him, as if the nightmares of his past had suddenly caught up and become real before his eyes.

Helborg was there. Fighting with the traitor. His mind flashed back to the eyeless corpses in the barn. *There are plenty in Altdorf who would like to wield the Rechtstahl in your place.*

It couldn't be. He wouldn't believe it.

He nudged the horse into a walk, still unsure, still hesitant. The battle around him passed into a blur. All he could see was his great rival, master of the Reiksguard, laying into Grosslich's men with his familiar gusto. And at his side was Rufus Leitdorf, the architect of Averheim's ruin, grinning stupidly, surrounded by an honour guard he scarcely deserved.

Anger welled within him. Schwarzhelm kicked the horse

into a canter. The slaughter was sickening to watch. He remembered Turgitz. The endless slights, the sneering, the manoeuvres at court. The man was jealous of him, insanely jealous. But this?

Schwarzhelm picked up the pace. The Rechtstahl blazed red in his hands, reflecting the light of the fires. He was alone, caught between the two armies. The dull rage began to flare.

Helborg would have to be a saint beyond reproach not to wish to see you stumble, just a little. And from what I hear, he's no saint.

Still Schwarzhelm pulled back. The Rechtstahl thirsted for blood, but he resisted it. The two of them were brothers, the twin pillars on which the Imperial armies depended. It was impossible.

Messages have been sent from the castle to Altdorf. It's been going on for some time.

Still he hesitated. Still his hand was stayed.

Then Grosslich appeared, charging from the midst of his army, heading straight for Helborg. Schwarzhelm felt like calling out a warning, but the look on the count's face told him it wouldn't be heeded. It was suicide. No one took on Helborg in single combat. No one.

The two men converged. Both were committed. That broke the spell.

Schwarzhelm sprung into action. Grosslich could not be allowed to die. Grand Marshal or not, Helborg would not be permitted to subvert the outcome of the succession. Schwarzhelm hefted the Rechtstahl, feeling the taut metal hum with anticipation. The spirit of the blade remained near the surface, goading him onward. It sensed blood. Rivers of blood.

And then, from nowhere, careering from behind Grosslich's outriders, came a figure Schwarzhelm knew all too well. The wide-brimmed hat, the long leather coat. Verstohlen was there, right beside Grosslich, knife in hand.

In a second, Schwarzhelm saw what he was trying to do. He was attempting to get between them, to prevent Grosslich from engaging.

'Pieter!' cried Schwarzhelm. He was still too far away. Verstohlen was a deadly swordsman, but no match for Helborg.

The spy achieved his goal, heading Grosslich off and forcing his steed from the engagement. But his flank was exposed. Helborg was on him in a second. Schwarzhelm saw the Klingerach, the Grudgebearer of legend, flash in the firelight.

Then it fell. Verstohlen tumbled from his horse, hitting the ground hard.

Schwarzhelm felt the tide of his rage break.

'Helborg!' he roared.

Even above the sound of the battle, the rush of the flames, the cries of the dying, Schwarzhelm's mighty voice echoed around the square. Men in the thick of the fighting halted in their slaughter and turned to see what was going on, shaken by the resounding cry. Kurt Helborg himself, blood running down his sword, paused. He looked up at Schwarzhelm, and their eyes met. Across the tangled, confused press of fighting men, the ruin of Averheim, the twin titans of the Empire saw one another for the first time since Altdorf.

A heartbeat passed. The sounds of battle seemed to recede into distant echoes. Even the cries of agony were muffled, indistinct.

Then Schwarzhelm snapped. His rage, building up for weeks, fuelled by nightmare, driven by fatigue, became his master. Nothing, not even all the armies of the Emperor, would have been capable of stopping him then.

He raised the Sword of Justice, blood-red in the failing light, and charged.

CHAPTER SIXTEEN

Helborg felt the thrill of the chase. Leitdorf had been dealt with. Now it fell to him to do what Schwarzhelm had been unable to. He sped towards Grosslich. The Averlander rode towards him at a similar speed, sword drawn.

That was brave. Not many men chose to take him on in the knowledge of who he was. He liked that. It would be a shame to kill such a warrior, but he wouldn't shirk from his duty. Averheim had been brought low by these feuding noblemen, and if they forced his hand he'd have no qualms about passing down the ultimate sentence.

He brought the Klingerach up into position. He could hear the thunder of Reiksguard hooves behind him. They were keeping pace, dragging the unwilling Leitdorf with them. Where was Skarr? There was no sign of the preceptor.

Grosslich neared. The fool kept his blade raised. Helborg felt the ghost of a smile flickering across his lips. Just a few more strides...

Then came a new figure, hurtling in from the side and riding between them. Helborg pulled on the reins, immediately adjusting his trajectory. He recognised the distinctive coat and hat again – Schwarzhelm's spy. With phenomenal horsemanship, the man headed Grosslich off, pushing his steed away and shoving it off into the wrong direction. An impressive manoeuvre. It had saved the man's life. So Schwarzhelm was in league with Grosslich after all. Leitdorf had been right. The damned fool.

The spy's horse was now careering towards him in place of Grosslich's. Pushed off-balance by his last manoeuvre, the man was headed right into his path. Helborg could see him struggling with the reins. One traitor for another, then. The result would be the same.

Helborg brought the Klingerach round in a decapitating blow. The man saw it at the last minute. He was quick. A long dagger rose to meet it, and the blades clashed.

But the spy was still reeling from his centre of gravity. The power of Helborg's stroke knocked him back from the horse and on to the stone below. He rolled over, head in his hands, desperately warding it from the stamping hooves around him.

Helborg wheeled his horse round to finish the job. As he looked at the cowering figure on the ground below him, he felt nothing but contempt. The man had forgotten his duty. He'd been drawn into the feud rather than protecting against it. There was no pity for that breed of weakness. He raised his blade.

'Helborg!'

The shout resounded across the square. Men stopped what they were doing. Even the Reiksguard, inured to all but the most powerful presences on the battlefield, looked up from their rampage.

Helborg sought out the source of the sound. The voice was one he knew intimately. He'd fought alongside the owner of it for years.

Schwarzhelm was charging straight for him. The man looked terrible. His beard was matted with blood. His armour was dented and streaked with the evidence of fierce fighting. Even under the shadow of his helmet, the madness and rage in his eyes was evident. He looked like a man who'd been dragged out of the Chaos Wastes and let loose on the realms of mortal men. His horse seemed half-crazed with fatigue. Foam streamed along its muzzle. The blade, the famed Sword of Justice, swung wildly as he approached. As the metal carved through the air, blood flew from the shaft like a shower of rain.

There was no time to react. No time to protest. A lesser man than Helborg would have been smashed from his saddle by the impact, driven into the ground and trampled under the hooves of Schwarzhelm's crazed beast. As it was, it was all he could do to bring the Klingerach up to parry the sweep of the Rechtstahl.

With an explosion of sparks, the two holy blades, each forged at the birth of the Empire, clashed together. The resounding clang swept across the courtyard, drowning out all other sounds. A blaze of light burst from the crossed swords, as if some powerful force within them had been unleashed after centuries of slumber.

Helborg felt the massive power of Schwarzhelm's blow shudder down his arm. He gritted his teeth, using all his strength to hold his ground. He held it. Just.

The horses spun away from one another, pushed apart by the force of the impact. Schwarzhelm's steed staggered. Its legs began to give way underneath it. With a strangled cry of distress, the overworked beast sank to the ground, its flanks heaving.

Schwarzhelm leapt from the stricken animal and strode towards Helborg. He pointed his sword straight at him. There was a fire in his eyes Helborg had never seen before, even in the many sparring contests they'd had as young men. This was different. Schwarzhelm wanted to kill him.

'What are you doing, man?' Helborg cried, keeping his own mount under control with difficulty. Despite its training, the beast shied away from the armoured figure walking towards it. Schwarzhelm was projecting a terrifying aura of hatred.

'Come down and face me,' growled Schwarzhelm. His voice was thick and snarling. As he spoke, Helborg could see his features twitching. He looked exhausted. Still he came on, inviting the contest between them.

Helborg looked around. The Reiksguard were fully occupied and badly outnumbered. Grosslich's riders had engaged them and more of his footsoldiers were arriving all the time. He caught a glimpse of Skarr with his company before they plunged into battle. Leitdorf still looked contained, but Grosslich's men were clawing at his guards. The fighting was everywhere. They were in the heart of the storm.

The two masters of the Emperor's armies squared off against one another. Helborg couldn't see where Grosslich had been driven to. It didn't matter. Only one battle mattered now.

'What have you done here, Schwarzhelm?' asked Helborg, keeping his voice level.

'My duty, as always.'

'You've forgotten your duty. This city is burning.'

'I'll not bandy words with a traitor. Come down and face me.'

Traitor. The words stung. Something terrible had happened to Schwarzhelm. He bore the look of a man who'd suffered some kind of prolonged torture.

'Do not use that word in my presence.' Helborg felt his own anger rising. There was an aura of violence in the air. He'd need to be stopped. Somehow, Schwarzhelm would have to be brought down. But how, without killing him?

Then Schwarzhelm smiled.

Of all the things that had happened in Averheim since Helborg's arrival, that spoke most clearly of some terrible twisting of the great man's mind. Schwarzhelm never smiled. Now his mighty face, the scourge of the Emperor's enemies across the endless expanse of the Old World, distorted into a mocking, sarcastic leer of savage intent. His eyes flickered with a baleful gleam. The blade rose again, glittering coldly. The afternoon sunlight was failing, to be replaced by the angry heat of the huge fires. In their crimson glow, Schwarzhelm looked half-daemonic.

'Come down and face me,' he repeated, looking eager for the fight. 'I know you, Kurt. Refuse me now and all will know you for the traitor you are. Face me!'

Helborg let his eyes flick around him again. His men had their hands full keeping Grosslich's men at bay. None of them could match Schwarzhelm. Reiksguard or not, they'd be dead in seconds if they as much as moved towards him.

Only one man alive had the power to contest him in combat. It felt as if fate had brought him to Averheim for this purpose alone. Wearily, feeling a sickness enter his heart, Helborg prepared for the duel that only he could undertake. Schwarzhelm had been driven to the edge of ruin and had to be stopped.

'So be it,' he said, dismounting heavily. 'If this is how you want it. Your mind has been poisoned, Ludwig. I warn you, if I have to, I will cut you down.'

Schwarzhelm snarled. The strange half-smile still twisted his face.

'That's what you've always wanted, Kurt. At least now the truth of that is out.'

Then he charged, the Sword of Justice held high. Helborg raised his own blade, focused on the weapon before him and waited for the impact.

The duel had begun.

Verstohlen came to his senses. He'd hit his head hard on the stone. There was a black corona around his vision and the world about him was blurred and indistinct.

With difficulty, he dragged himself up on to his knees. Everything was in motion. His horse was long gone. In all directions, men struggled against one another. He saw one burly trooper drag another to the ground, tearing at the man's eyes. Another throttled his opponent, rolling with him in the filth as each strove to finish the other off. There were scraps of skin on the ground about him, tufts of hair and knocked-loose teeth.

What was going on? Even for such debased kinds of combat, the very air seemed heavy with a deranged, fervid stench. There was no shape to any of the fighting. This was a mass outpouring of rage; a messy, maniac brawling.

Verstohlen clambered to his feet. For a moment, the world swung around him. Then, slowly, it clarified. The evening was waning fast. In the east, stars had appeared. The sunlight seemed to have bled from the sky surprisingly fast.

Then he saw it. Morrslieb. Just a sliver of the Chaos moon was visible, jutting out from behind the dark towers of the distant Averburg. Its sickly light was barely visible in the glittering of the swords. How long had that accursed moon been in the sky? It explained some of the madness around him. When the dark moon was abroad, men's minds were altered. Perhaps this whole city had cradled its sickness for too long. Maybe it had affected him too. Maybe it had affected all of them.

Verstohlen shook his head, trying to clear his mind of the rambling thoughts. He retrieved his knife shakily. All around him, the fighting continued unabated. How had he been wounded? He couldn't remember. He had to find Grosslich.

Verstohlen began to stumble through the milling bodies around him. One of Leitdorf's thugs staggered into his path. The brute lunged at him. Verstohlen dodged the blow casually, feeling sluggish and nauseous. His knife felt unbalanced in his hand. He returned the attack, letting the blade guide him. It plunged deep into the man's stomach. Verstohlen pulled it sharply to the right. Hot blood and viscera streamed over his wrist. The gobbets of flesh, glistening in the firelight, slipped over his hand and fell, plopping and slapping, to the ground. The soldier, face fixed into a frozen scream of agony, crumpled to the stone.

Verstohlen withdrew his knife, watching the man enter his gasping death throes. For a moment, a savage joy filled his heart. He looked around him. The knife was hot in his fingers, glowing like a brand. The shapes of the men around him flickered and shuddered, like a candle flame caught in a sudden gust. A curious musk was mingling with the stench of blood and sweat. He recognised it immediately. Welcomed it. It was sweet, as sweet as death. Like jasmine.

He raised his hands to his face, uncaring of the flow of carnage around him. His hands were steeped in gore. Dark trickles ran down his arm, staining the leather of his coat. He felt an overwhelming urge to lean forward, press the still-hot viscera against his face...

Verstohlen jerked his hand back. What was happening to him? What was happening to all of them? He drew in a deep breath. The air was hot. It wasn't the sun. The fires were burning higher. Their flames danced into the dusk. They writhed like snakes. Against the red tongues of flame, a faint lilac flickered.

Joyroot. Tons of it. Leitdorf had chosen his battleground well. At last, the dark sorcery at the heart of his campaign had become manifest.

Verstohlen wiped his sleeve in disgust. Even now, he could sense the beckoning lure of madness. Weaker minds had little defence. Where was Grosslich? He needed to be warned.

He started to stumble through the press around him. There was a knot of knights a few yards away. They seemed to be protecting something. For a moment, he thought he saw Leitdorf's livery hidden amongst them. The man was smiling smugly, arms crossed over his flabby chest. Why were they protecting him? A surge of hatred ran through Verstohlen's body, and he lurched unsteadily forward towards him.

Then another warrior blundered into his path. Verstohlen couldn't tell what his allegiance was, but the man looked ready to take on anyone. His eyes were wild and starting. A bloody weal ran across his neck. Seeing Verstohlen in turn, he launched himself forward, sword waving wildly.

Verstohlen met the attack, parrying with his knife and pushing the lurching soldier back. He worked quickly, trying to recover his balance. The nausea and confusion were beginning to wear off. Deep down, though, he was worried. More worried than he'd been since arriving in the accursed city. What was driving the attacks? Where was Grosslich?

He dispatched the clumsy attacker with a double-back swipe of his knife. Behind him, more men were approaching. For some reason, they seemed to have latched onto him.

Verstohlen stayed low and gritted his teeth. He didn't have time for this. The stench of Chaos was everywhere. He had to get to those knights. The soldiers came for him, stumbling and tripping as if in a drunken stupor.

Verstohlen hefted his knife lightly, whispered a prayer to Verena the Protector, then charged into their midst.

The two swords danced around one another, flickering like flames in the dusk. Each blade moved with breathtaking precision. As he worked, Schwarzhelm felt the fatigue fall from his arms. His concentration was absolute, his movement perfectly controlled. Just as Lassus had taught him, he let the sword become an extension of his being. He was a plain man, but it was in such moments that he got as close as he ever came to the sublime. The Rechtstahl responded. The heavy shaft of steel swung through the air as if made of a weightless shard of ithilmar. The metal shimmered, glorying in its impeccable balance and poise.

Before him, Helborg kept pace perfectly. He was a master swordsman. The best in the Empire, they all said. His technique had always been just a fraction ahead of Schwarzhelm's. When they'd sparred in front of the Emperor in their youth, he'd won all their contests. Only by a shade, only by a fraction. There had been so little at stake then. Now things were different.

Schwarzhelm took a big step forward, swiping heavily with the Rechtstahl to draw the defensive push, switching direction at the last moment.

Helborg was alive to it, and parried watchfully. For a moment, they came together. The blades locked.

'Why are you doing this, Ludwig?'

Schwarzhelm didn't reply. He broke away, back into the duelling posture. As he moved, he thrust the Rechtstahl upwards jerkily, nearly twisting the runefang from Helborg's hands.

He could hardly bear to look at his old rival. Of all the men to turn to the great enemy, this was the most bitter blow. He'd always known Helborg had secretly envied his closeness to the Emperor. Whatever men said, being master of the Reiksguard didn't compare to the honour of carrying the Imperial standard into battle. Now his mask had slipped. The man's treachery had been revealed.

He spun round, scything the Sword of Justice through the fire-flecked air. Helborg gave ground. His face was intent, careful. He wasn't pressing forward. He was trying to contain Schwarzhelm's attack.

That was a mistake. A master swordsman always attacked. Schwarzhelm pressed home the advantage, hammering away at Helborg's defences with growing speed and assurance.

Dimly, he was aware of the men around him. He could hear the continued sounds of fighting as the darkness gathered. There was a mood of savagery in the air. The entire space seemed to have been given over to the settling of petty feuds. Somewhere close by he knew that Leitdorf was amongst the Reiksguard. Maybe Grosslich too. Perhaps they watched. Perhaps they fought amongst themselves.

No matter. Such paltry squabbles were no longer his affair. The greater battle lay before him. The architect of his misery was in his hands at last. He remembered the corpses by the road, the death of Grunwald, the sense of powerlessness.

Schwarzhelm shifted his grip, letting his left hand take the greater weight of the sword. He fell back, opening up a small gap between him and his adversary. Helborg filled it quickly, his runefang whirling with deceptive speed. It was the orthodox response. The one he'd expected. Helborg wasn't fighting at his full potential. For some reason, the man held back.

Too bad.

Schwarzhelm drew the attacking thrust, then countered with his left-handed grip bringing the Rechtstahl in lower. Helborg was slow to close it down. The blade shot under his defence, taking only a glancing parry from the Marshal's sword. Schwarzhelm felt the edge bite deep into Helborg's thigh before he pulled it away again.

Schwarzhelm stepped back out of range, easily fending off the resultant flurry of blows. Helborg still moved quickly, still kept his guard up. But now blood trailed down his left leg. It looked black in the twilight. As a traitor's blood should be.

'Your heart's not in this, Kurt,' he growled. 'Guilty conscience?'

It was Helborg's turn to stay silent. The Marshal stepped up his swordplay. The runefang spun into the attack again, glimmering darkly. But Schwarzhelm could see he was troubled. For the first time in his long and illustrious career, the Marshal knew he was being matched. The Swords of Justice and Vengeance met again, and sparks showered the stone as if from a blacksmith's forge.

It was then that Schwarzhelm knew he would win. Helborg's guilt slowed him down. The traitor was always weakened by his crimes. Schwarzhelm alone fought for the Empire now, he alone guarded the flame of faith. He shifted his weight into an attacking posture, feeling strength coursing through his sinews, and launched into the assault again.

Leofric von Skarr tried to fight his way back to Helborg. He was surrounded by riders. Even as he attempted to turn his own horse, two more engaged him. He swung his sword in the face of one of them, forcing a swerve. Then the Reiksguard around him pushed forward, driving Grosslich's men away a few yards.

Skarr looked around him, trying to make sense of what was going on. The whole square was crawling with men. The cavalry were all Grosslich's troops. Between them and Leitdorf's mob, the Reiksguard were heavily outnumbered. Despite their superior skills, they couldn't hold against a melee of hundreds forever. This was not going according to plan.

He tried to spot Helborg and Schwarzhelm, but they were lost in the flickering light. Until the tide of battle had pushed him away, he'd seen their ruinous duel start up. He hadn't expected to witness such a scene in his worst nightmares. Skarr had had a long career in the Reiksguard and had seen many things he'd rather not have done, but watching Helborg and Schwarzhelm batter one another into submission was horrifying. His horse shifted uneasily under him. Even the beast could sense the sickness in what it saw.

He looked over to where his men guarded Rufus Leitdorf. The knights held their formation, holding out against ferocious attacks from Grosslich's troops. The man himself was raving about something, waving his arms from the saddle and trying to break their grip. He stood no chance. The man was a typical effete nobleman, and the troops around him were as tough as any in the Empire.

Grosslich was of more concern. After the first clash, the rival elector had been driven off, perhaps to rally what remained of his entourage. Despite Leitdorf being taken into custody by Helborg, his own men still fought with an unexpected savagery. Something in the very air around them seemed to be goading them on. Holding both sets of combatants off was beginning to become difficult. Though they were Reiksguard, the finest soldiers in the Empire, they were but one company. If the anger of the masses were to be turned on them, he wasn't sure how long he could hold them back.

Skarr hefted his broadsword. His knights were becoming strung out, drawn into the undisciplined brawl around them.

'Reiksguard!' he roared. 'To me!'

Some of the knights were able to cut their way to his position. Others remained isolated, trapped in a sea of enemies. It didn't matter whether the massed brawlers fought for Leitdorf or Grosslich, they seemed equally intent on bringing as many knights down as they could.

'Sir, it's getting hard to hold them back.'

The voice at his shoulder was that of a young knight, Dietmar von Eissen. He was a good soldier, already tested in the fires of battle, but his eyes betrayed uncertainty.

'Remember your training,' Skarr hissed. 'You are Reiksguard. Hold the line.'

Even as he finished speaking, a gang of Leitdorf's men piled towards him. They looked drunk with bloodlust. Three of the closest Reiksguard moved to intercept. Two of them felled their men, but the third was borne from his saddle by the frenzied charge. More hurried up behind them, a whole mob of them. There were too many. The fighting had become a quagmire.

Skarr kicked his horse into action. He reached the first of the attackers, pulling his sword back and letting it swing back. The blade took the head clean off the nearest combatant. The bloody mass span off into the night, spraying gore across the struggling bodies beneath it. A second thrust eviscerated the soldier's companion. That cowed Leitdorf's men, but still they held their ground.

On either side of Skarr the knights were beginning to form up. At last, they were carving some kind of formation out of the mess. They'd been driven into disorder by Grosslich's intervention, but that was slowly changing.

'Charge them!' he bellowed, pointing his sword directly at what looked like the ringleader.

The line of horses sprang forward, hooves ringing out against the stone. The Reiksguard moved as a unit, bearing down any infantry in their way. Faced with a concerted wall of steel, Leitdorf's motley collection of fighters broke and fled. Those too slow to turn were dispatched, either by the blades of the knights or under the churning legs of their steeds.

'Halt. Re-form the line!'

Already Grosslich's riders had seen the danger and were massing to attack them. If it wasn't one, it was the other. What had got into these people?

Skarr looked across the fragile line of knights. His men were still being drawn into the melee around them. This couldn't last forever. At least Grosslich appeared to have been taken out of the fighting for the moment. Despite his best efforts, Skarr could see no sign of him. Nor could he catch a glimpse of where Schwarzhelm and Helborg were.

Somewhere, hidden by the sea of men around him, they still fought. He had to get to them.

'What are your orders?' asked Eissen, pulling his mount up beside him. The man's sword was running with blood.

'Find the Marshal,' said Skarr, looking at the approaching horsemen grimly. 'We'll cut these fools down, then we sweep back.'

He turned back to face the approaching riders. Around him, those knights that could had formed a defensive line. The footsoldiers kept coming at them. The world had gone mad. This was wasting precious time. He needed to get back to the Marshal. He didn't know what madness had come over Schwarzhelm, but Helborg couldn't be left to face it alone.

'Raise your blades,' Skarr shouted, seeing the knights around him take up their swords. The metal gleamed. 'Kill them all.'

Helborg felt the Sword of Vengeance become heavy in his practised hands. Every move he made with it seemed to come a little too late. Schwarzhelm was fighting like a man possessed.

He drove the image from his mind. That possibility was too grim even to entertain.

Helborg let the sword curve round to meet the latest flurry of blows from Schwarzhelm. Each impact felt like a hammer blow. As the shocks ran through his body, he was forced back. Schwarzhelm had always been strong. Now he was quick. Breathtakingly quick.

Helborg leapt back, making half a yard of space. He whirled the sword around, shifting the balance to his right side. Schwarzhelm advanced, his own blade darting after him. The light was failing. It was hard to keep up with the flickering path of the steel.

The blades clashed again, and fresh sparks sprung into the air. For a moment, Schwarzhelm's face was lit up in savage relief. His eyes were wide and staring, like a wild cat's. This was not about pride or prestige, or even the debacle in Averheim. Schwarzhelm wanted him dead.

Helborg dropped down to his left, letting the guard down, inviting the stroke. Schwarzhelm was too sharp for that. He brought the Rechtstahl tearing down against his protected right flank, trusting the force of the blow to deliver the result.

Helborg spun against it, using the Klingerach as a shield. The Rechtstahl bit deep, tearing a notch from the runefang. The splinter spiralled from the blade. Too late, Helborg ducked out of the way. The shard lodged in his cheek, searing like a snakebite. He staggered backwards, teeth clenched, frantically warding off the cascade of blows from Schwarzhelm.

The pain was agonising. He kept his eyes fixed on the swipes and feints of the Sword of Justice as it angled to penetrate his defences. Helborg kept it out, but only barely. His arms began to wilt as the blades clashed again and again. The rest of the battle around him drifted out of focus. There was only one thing in the world, only one thing that mattered. He slipped into that strange place that swordmasters occupied in the heat of combat, the realm where all reality was composed of the movement of blades, the shimmering play of metal against metal.

Eventually, even Schwarzhelm tired of the attack. He withdrew, panting heavily. Helborg kept his sword held high. The assault had been horrifying. He'd never had to endure such a sustained period of brilliance, even from Schwarzhelm.

'Your blade is notched,' said Schwarzhelm.

Helborg stole a quick glance at the surface of the Klingerach. The runefang hadn't been so much as scratched in all the days he'd worn it at his side. It was one of the twelve forged by Alaric, one of the dozen mightiest talismans of mankind, bound by runes of warding, infused with spells of ruin and destruction. Nothing could break a runefang. Only its wearer could be harmed.

And yet, the sword was notched. Even now, he could feel the shard buried in the flesh of his cheek. The pain was like a brand of fire. The trail of blood ran hot down his neck. Schwarzhelm, of all men, had been the one to break the symmetry of the Klingerach. After more than two millennia, the sacred blade had been marred at last, not by a Chaos warlord or beast of darkness, but by the Emperor's Champion himself.

Maybe only Schwarzhelm, alone in the entire Old World, carried a sword capable of doing such a thing.

Turning away from the desecrated shaft, Helborg felt the last of his restraint leave him. He'd been unwilling to let himself go until that moment. Schwarzhelm was clearly under some kind of madness or paranoia, the knowledge of which had stayed his hand. But now the final bonds had been broken.

With a roar of anger, Helborg swung the Klingerach into position once more. Ignoring the pain of the wounds across his body, he tore into Schwarzhelm, wielding his blade with all the ferocity his years of training had embedded in every sinew. The Klingerach whirled in a tight arc, perfectly balanced, perfectly aimed. As the last of the natural light faded, all that was left to illuminate the clash of the two men were the flames rising higher on either side.

With Morrslieb riding high and the Vormeisterplatz echoing with the sound of slaughter, Kurt Helborg launched his assault on Ludwig Schwarzhelm. It had the air of a final push. One way or another, only one of them would walk free of it.

Verstohlen punched the soldier in the stomach, putting every scrap of energy he had into the blow. The man reeled backwards but stayed on his feet. He looked like one of Leitdorf's irregulars, and wore an archaic leather jerkin and iron skullcap for a helmet. Most of his teeth had been knocked from his jaw and his nose was broken. As Verstohlen hung back he grinned, exposing the holes in his mouth. This kind of vicious struggle was the thing such scum lived for. He'd probably have joined in even if he wasn't being paid for it.

Verstohlen gripped his knife tightly. The pointless combat was draining. He needed to get out of it, clear his head, come up with some kind of a plan.

The mercenary charged, brandishing a heavily notched short sword. Wearily, Verstohlen prepared to meet the assault.

It never came. Before he could close on Verstohlen, the man was knocked violently to one side. He swung into the air, his arms flailing. He staggered for moment, looking confused and angry, before he saw the spider of crimson spreading across his chest. He fell to his knees, coughing phlegm and blood, before finally toppling on to his front.

Verstohlen looked up, waiting for the next challenger to fend off. Instead, Grosslich was there, mounted, surrounded by horsemen of his household. Amidst all the confusion, his company was a rare island of order.

'I've found you, counsellor,' he said, motioning for his men to fan around them. A spare horse was brought forward. Recovering himself, Verstohlen mounted quickly.

'About time,' he said. 'Where've you been?'

'Since you diverted me into Leitdorf's men? Fighting my way back to you. I could have you run through for that treachery.' He smiled. 'Glad you're still on your feet.'

Suddenly, the memory came rushing back. Helborg. That was why he'd spurred his horse into the path of Grosslich's, to prevent the clash that would have undoubtedly killed him.

'Leitdorf has the Reiksguard fighting for him,' said Verstohlen, feeling his earlier fear and confusion return. The joyroot in the air was addling his mind. He couldn't think straight. He knew he was missing something.

'That he does,' said Grosslich grimly, wheeling his horse around and preparing to carve his way back into the melee. 'What devilry has passed between them is anyone's guess. But Leitdorf still lives. Helborg is distracted. We have a chance to strike.'

Verstohlen kicked his horse into a canter, keeping up with Grosslich and his horsemen as they began to cut their way through the ranks of fighting men.

'Helborg distracted? With what?'

'You'll see, counsellor. Ride with me. All will become clear.'

Verstohlen held the reins tightly, willing his tired body to stay in the saddle. He reached into his coat and withdrew the pistol. He still had one bullet left. Not much, but better than nothing. Ahead, the press of Reiksguard knights waited. They'd seen the threat, and were moving to meet it. In their midst, the pathetic figure of Leitdorf cowered. He knew it was over.

Verstohlen kept the gun cradled at his side. He'd wait. If nothing else, it would suffice for Rufus.

The sun had set. Over the Vormeisterplatz there was only the red light of the fires and the ivory sheen of Morrslieb. Leitdorf's forces, bereft of their leader, had finally begun to buckle. Many of the mercenaries had started to flee where they could, streaming out of the square and into the dark alleys. Grosslich's men pursued them hard, and the sounds of bloodshed soon filtered into the winding passages of the poor quarter. Under the baleful light of the Chaos moon, the death and pain was spreading throughout the city. Soon nowhere would be free of it.

Schwarzhelm ran his finger along the edge of the Sword of Justice. Even with the lightest of touches the blade drew blood. It was the perfect sword, a flawless instrument of death.

He looked up at Helborg. The Marshal stood in a defensive posture a few paces away. He was ashen-faced. With satisfaction, Schwarzhelm glimpsed at the shard of the Klingerach lodged in the man's cheek. It was a badge of shame, the mark of treachery. The scar would be with him forever.

'So what price did he buy you with?' Schwarzhelm asked bitterly, letting Helborg recover himself for his next assault. 'Or was the prospect of seeing me fail here enough reward for you?'

Helborg was breathing heavily.

'You're really that insecure? Look around you, Ludwig. This is your doing.'

As Helborg spoke, a sliver of doubt entered Schwarzhelm's mind. Somewhere, deep within, he could hear a small voice of warning. Like glimpsing the sun through a gap in the clouds, the Marshal suddenly seemed to him the way he always had. Upright, stern-faced, the embodiment of Imperial martial pride. They were brothers, the two of them. They'd always been brothers.

And yet.

The stench of Chaos was everywhere. Leitdorf was stained with it. Verstohlen had seen the evidence of it. From the first hours he'd spent in Averheim, Schwarzhelm had been aware of it. The visions in the night, the terrors and portents. They'd been trying to break him. They'd all been trying to break him. They'd failed.

He lifted the Rechtstahl a final time. Overhead, lost in the gathering darkness, there was a distant rumble of thunder. The weather, so unbearably hot for so long, was breaking at last. A storm was coming.

'No more words.'

He lunged forward. He kept the Rechtstahl high, holding it two-handed, unmindful of his defence. Helborg met him, swinging the Klingerach heavily to meet the incoming downward plunge. The blades met again. Again, they were forced apart.

Schwarzhelm pressed home the attack. He could feel raw power coursing through his sinews. His wrath was what propelled him now. After so many days of frustration, of fatigue, of whispering against him, of weasel-worded legal arguments, the canker at the heart of Averheim had been unveiled.

He kept the sword moving, adjusting his body minutely to compensate for its every stroke. They said the elven Sword Masters felt like this, lost in the perfect symmetry of stroke and counter-stroke. He and the weapon were fused together, each an extension of the other.

The time had come to finish it. Schwarzhelm went for the kill. His blade whirled, blood-red in the firelight. Helborg fought back, meeting the heavy blows expertly, warding what he could. But the Marshal was weakened. He'd lost blood from his thigh. He wasn't fighting with his full commitment.

Something was holding him back. Something weighed him down. This wasn't the Helborg who'd bested him a dozen times on the training grounds of Altdorf.

The opening came. Helborg brought his sword up in another defensive move. As he drew back, his foot turned on the stone. He stumbled and the blade dropped out of the position.

A whip of lightning scored across the heavens. For a split second, Helborg's body was illuminated in stark relief. The chance was there, beckoning him.

Schwarzhelm pounced. Summoning all the energy that remained to him, he plunged the Sword of Justice downwards. As if drawn by the prospect of blood, the blade nearly flew from his hands.

It bit deep, carving through armour and into the flesh beyond. The metal sheered between spaulder and breastplate, unerringly finding the weak spot in the Marshal's exquisite armour.

Helborg roared with pain. His whole body tensed. Blood spurted high into the air. Schwarzhelm felt it splatter against his face. The liquid seared him as if it had been boiling oil. He withdrew the blade and staggered back, wiping his eyes.

Helborg slumped to the ground, clutching his shoulder. His sword clattered to the stone harmlessly. The Marshal shot Schwarzhelm a final glance, one of mingled anger, pain and betrayal. Then he collapsed face down on to the stone, his blood spreading across the flags.

A peal of thunder boomed across the city. It felt like the arch of the sky was cracking. Schwarzhelm suddenly felt his store of violent energy drain from him. He stood like a graven image, staring at his stricken brother.

The man was broken. And he had done it.

The world around seemed suddenly insubstantial and shifting. Rage was replaced by guilt, violence with grief. It was as if a mask of madness had fallen from him. He started forward; hands outstretched towards his old rival, his sparring partner, his friend.

His victim.

'Marshal!' The voice belonged to one of the Reiksguard. They'd seen their master cut down too.

Schwarzhelm whirled around. There were knights backing up towards him. They were being attacked in their turn. He could make out horsemen wearing Grosslich's colours bearing down on the steel lines. They would break. They were breaking.

Schwarzhelm felt the indecision paralyse him. He didn't know what to do. There was movement all around him. His certainty had vanished, his will had snapped. He stood immobile.

I have killed him, he thought. The mantra repeated over and over in his head, paralysing him. Sigmar forgive me. I have killed him.

Then the Reiksguard lines broke. Grosslich was breaking through, and the Imperial knights fell before the onslaught. They ignored Schwarzhelm. Several galloped over to the stricken Helborg. With peerless horsemanship, they swept him up into the saddle. The Klingerach stayed on the stone, forgotten.

Schwarzhelm watched it all take place impotently. Horses veered past him on either side. His fingers felt loose around the hilt of the Rechtstahl. The events before him unfolded as if in one of his nightmares. He was just a spectator.

Grosslich's men streamed across the square, pursuing the fleeing Reiksguard. Leitdorf rode along with the Imperial knights, surrounded by stern-faced protectors. He cast a fleeting look at Schwarzhelm as he was carried away. His expression was one of terror, like a child caught up in games it doesn't understand.

Then they were gone, riding into the night and towards the flames. Grosslich's men thundered after them, Heinz-Mark at their head. So many.

Schwarzhelm remained unmoving. His face dripped with blood. Helborg's blood. Amid all the tumult, still no one approached him. As if warned away by some unnatural force, the swordsmen stayed away.

All except one. Verstohlen dismounted. The spy walked up to him, concern etched on his face.

'You answered my call,' he said.

Schwarzhelm didn't reply. He couldn't take his eyes off the Klingerach, lying discarded on the stone. He walked over to the sword and picked it up. He held the blades together for a moment, comparing the lengths of steel. They were so alike. Only the notch in the Sword of Vengeance marked it out. Otherwise, they were sister weapons.

Verstohlen came to his side.

'You were right to stop him, my lord. Even the mightiest can turn to darkness.'

Schwarzhelm turned to face him. All around them, men streamed from the square. The remainder of Leitdorf's forces were being hunted down. What fighting remained was brutal and self-contained. The murderous chase had begun through the streets and alleys of Averheim.

'Darkness has been at work here,' said Schwarzhelm thickly. The words left his throat with effort. 'Your words bring me no comfort.'

'They should. Leitdorf would have turned this place into a slaughterhouse. You can feel it in the air.'

Schwarzhelm looked off into the distance. His eyes swept the square, now littered with bodies.

'He was the mightiest of us all, Pieter. Never have I regretted a kill to this day. And now…'

He felt his voice begin to break, and tailed off. If this was victory, it left a bitter taste. He lingered for a moment longer, staring at the spot where Helborg had fallen. Then he finally turned, allowing himself to be led from the scene by Verstohlen. Slowly, haltingly, the two men walked from the battlefield. Behind them, the last of the fighting in the square limped to its bloody conclusion. None hindered their passing.

Through war and treachery, the succession of Averland had been decided. Heinz-Mark Grosslich would take up the runefang, and Leitdorf would be cast into damnation.

CHAPTER SEVENTEEN

Hundreds of miles away at the other end of the province, Bloch looked up at the looming peaks of the Worlds Edge Mountains, darkening quickly as the sun went down. Though his army was still in the pasture country of Averland's eastern marches, the land was now rising steeply. Soon they'd be in the foothills, the treacherous, uneven landscape they'd surveyed before encountering the orcs. Then their path would take them higher, far up the winding gullies and coombs towards Black Fire Pass.

He felt a shiver pass through him. After so many days of unremitting heat, the weather had begun to turn at last. With the sunset, the air had chilled appreciably. He pulled his cloak around him. Perhaps the summer was finally coming to an end.

'Cold, commander?'

Kraus had a look of mild amusement on his weather-beaten face. The man didn't say much, but Bloch was still glad to have him at his shoulder. Schwarzhelm had been generous to lend the honour guard captain to him for the remainder of the campaign. Either that, or he didn't quite trust Bloch enough to lead an army on his own.

'Not as cold as I'm going to be,' he muttered.

He looked back over the column behind him. Over two thousand men, all well rested and resupplied, followed him and Kraus along the Old Dwarf Road. The men had proper weapons and armour again. They looked in good spirits. A baggage train, stocked with food and barrels of ale, trundled along in their wake. The folk of Grenzstadt had been grateful for the relief from the orc attacks. To provision the army that had saved them was the least they could have done, but the stocks were still appreciated. After all those days living hand-to-mouth in the wilderness, it certainly made a change.

Beyond the toiling figures of the troops, the wide landscape of Averland yawned away towards the horizon. Even in the failing light, Bloch could see for miles. The road ran like a ribbon across the gently rolling hills, heading west towards Grenzstadt. The town itself lay in the distance, looking peaceful and prosperous. Unlike Heideck, the place had defended itself well from the remnants of the orc raiders and the task of relieving it had been straightforward. Now the few greenskin stragglers had been driven up into the hills and the campaign had entered its final stages.

After Grenzstadt the plains gradually disappeared into the haze of the gathering sunset. Far on the western horizon, it looked like rain clouds were gathering. A storm, even. That would be welcome for those who'd endured the oppressive heat for so long. Maybe things were changing at last. Out here, Schwarzhelm's pessimism seemed strangely misplaced.

'Have you traversed the pass before, Herr Kraus?' Bloch asked, turning from the view.

'Many times. But not always to fight. It is a holy place, after all.'

Bloch knew what he meant. For all the cathedrals to Sigmar across the Empire, the high pass through the Worlds Edge Mountains was still the place where children learned of the deeds of their God-Emperor. It was in the narrow defiles, lost in the wearing years, where the race of men had teetered on the edge of oblivion and had been pulled back by the actions of a single man.

'Aye, that it is.' For once, Bloch couldn't think of a wry comment. There were some things a loyal Empire soldier didn't joke about.

He turned back to the march. They had a long haul to get past before the first of the many massive granite crags that reared above them, flecked with white and scored with a thousand cracks and gullies. Beyond that, the way would get harder. These roads weren't travelled lightly, even in summer. He felt the shiver return, and worked to quell it. It wouldn't do to look weak before the men, many of whom had fought as hard as he had to get there alive.

But there was one nagging feeling in the back of his mind that wouldn't leave him. The Black Fire Pass was heavily guarded. As the only route into Averland from outside the Empire, a whole garrison of seasoned soldiers was stationed at the mouth of the pass in order to seal the narrow passage. They should have been able to hold the greenskins back. That was what they were there for. Either there was some explanation for the incursion, or the keep in the mountains would be full of bodies. Neither of those choices filled Bloch with enthusiasm for the climb ahead.

He put his head down and kept walking. There was nothing for it but to keep going. Schwarzhelm had charged him with discovering what had happened at Black Fire Pass, and he wouldn't return before he'd uncovered the mystery.

Pieter Verstohlen awoke late. He shifted and immediately felt the stabbing pains in his muscles. For a moment, he didn't register where he was. Then the events of the previous night came rushing back. He could still taste the ash from the fires on his lips. He lay still for a moment, remembering. They were not pleasant memories.

After a while, he pushed the covers back with stiff hands. It was nearly midday, but his chamber was still dark, shuttered against the bright sun. His chest was clammy from the heat. Even after the thunderstorm during the night, Averheim was still warm.

Gingerly, he swung his legs from the sheets and limped over to the window. He pulled the shutters open and sunlight flooded in. His chamber was high up in the western front of the Averburg. He had a commanding view over the entire city. The Aver lay far below, glittering in the sun. It looked somehow cleaner. The last of the fires had burned themselves out. The palls of smoke that had hung over the city had cleared. The storm had done some good in dousing them.

There was a pitcher of clear water by the sill. Verstohlen took a long swig. He felt the cool liquid run down his throat, soothing his parched flesh. He reached up and carefully felt for the bloody lump on the side of his head. His hair was matted with dry scabs and the flesh beneath was tender. That had been a hard fall. Not a very distinguished way to receive a battlefield wound, even from so mighty a hand.

There was a quiet knock on the door. Verstohlen reached for a robe and wrapped himself in it.

'Come.'

Tochfel entered. The man looked tired. How long had it been since Verstohlen had last seen him? Many days ago. The last hurried conversation they'd snatched seemed like an age away.

'I've tried to see you twice already,' the Steward said. 'I wondered if you'd sleep all day.'

Verstohlen smiled politely. If the old fool had been in the midst of the fighting himself, he might have been less snide.

'Take a seat, Steward. How have you been?'

Tochfel pulled a chair from by the wall. Verstohlen sat on the side of bed. As the straw mattress yielded, he found himself wishing he could crawl back under the sheets. The rest had been too short.

'There've been some… adjustments to make here.' Tochfel looked rueful. 'Ferenc Alptraum runs this place now. He's retained my services in the meantime. That's something, I suppose.'

'There've been many hasty decisions made recently,' said Verstohlen. 'Some of them may have to be rescinded. Where is the Lord Schwarzhelm?'

'He sleeps still. Since you both returned, none have dared to rouse him. Perhaps you'd noticed that beforehand he'd not seemed to be sleeping too well. We can hope, perhaps, that the rest will make him less... unpredictable.'

'He's always been unpredictable. And there have been forces working against him that would have killed a lesser man. Against all of us. Verena willing, we've ended that now.'

Tochfel nodded. 'I think that is becoming apparent, even to those who doubted him.'

'And where's Grosslich?'

'The Elector Designate still rides. Leitdorf has not been found. But the city is being purged of his followers. The witch hunters have been summoned.' At that, Tochfel gave Verstohlen a look of reproach. 'Perhaps they should have been summoned days ago, when some of you first had suspicions.'

Verstohlen raised an eyebrow. 'A criticism, Herr Tochfel?'

The Steward quickly averted his eyes. 'I'm sure you acted as you thought best. In any case, Lord Alptraum has commissioned Odo Heidegger, an experienced hand in such matters. Our own Temple in Averheim seems to have been... disturbed by the recent events, and there are no witch hunters to be found in the city.' Tochfel gave Verstohlen a significant look, as if to suggest that fact was hardly coincidental. 'Heidegger is master of the Temples on the Alptraum ancestral lands. He'll be in Averheim soon. Then the rooting out of heresy will begin in earnest.'

Verstohlen felt his heart sink at the prospect. It could hardly be opposed, given what had happened, though the thought of more savagery being unleashed depressed him.

'Ferenc's moved quickly. Until Grosslich receives the rune-fang, Schwarzhelm is still the authority here.'

'What would you have him do? It is the great enemy we're dealing with here.'

Again, the tone was accusatory.

'You seem to have come around to his mastery with some speed, Herr Tochfel,' said Verstohlen, looking at the Steward carefully. 'Grosslich will replace you as ruler of this city. Do you not mind that?'

Tochfel smiled sadly.

'Such is life. The right choice has been made.'

'And what of Alptraum?'

'As I say, he commands the Averburg. He was marshalling the defences here while Lord Grosslich was fighting last night. I gather that decision did not go down well. Alptraum thought it important to ensure that certain records in our archives were... looked after. His family has a long history in this place. Perhaps there are facts he would rather weren't widely available.'

'Understandable.' Verstohlen began to cast his mind forward. The worst of the fighting was over but there was still much to do before Averheim could return to normal. Grosslich would have to be invested. The witch hunters, regrettably enough, were best qualified to root out the last of Leitdorf's heresy. A court of inquiry would no doubt be set up. And of course there were still mysteries to uncover about the Reiksguard.

'You say Leitdorf is still at large. Where is his wife?'

'Nothing has been seen of her. Troops are moving through the city as we speak, hunting her down.'

'I should be with them,' said Verstohlen, rising from the bed.

Tochfel raised his hand warningly.

'There will be time for that, counsellor. If you place weight on anything I say, I'd counsel you to rest a little longer. The coming days will be hard on all of us. Enjoy some respite while you can.'

Verstohlen hesitated. The man spoke sense, though it was not in his nature to rest while others laboured.

'Very well,' he said, relaxing. 'I'll dress and be with you shortly.'

Tochfel rose awkwardly. It looked like he'd aged years over the past few weeks. No doubt such excitement was not what he'd hoped for out of life.

'Perhaps we can talk again later,' he said, moving to the door. 'There are some things about this affair I still don't understand.'

Verstohlen knew what he meant.

'That would be good, Steward,' he said, trying to keep his voice untroubled. 'No doubt we shall have much to discuss.'

Schwarzhelm sank further into the deep, deep pool of sleep. He felt like he was floating in a vast, warm abyss. The layers of water pressed down on him, enveloping him, imprisoning him, protecting him. The outside world was a lifetime away. Its cares, its terrors, were all hidden. As long as he languished in the deep places, they couldn't reach him. He was alone, forgotten, safe.

He dived down further, pushing against the languid water, feeling it slide past his battered body. There was nothing around him. No fish, no drifting plants. This was the isolation he had always craved, the sense of being alone he hadn't enjoyed since being a child.

Then he saw it, far below. A shape, tumbling down into the infinite darkness. It spun lazily in the current, twisting and falling. Schwarzhelm kicked his legs and plunged towards it. His powerful limbs pushed him through the water. Long before he reached the tumbling form below, he knew what it was. He tried to stop then, but his momentum carried him down and down. The water grew darker and colder. Suddenly he became aware how far he'd come. He might not be able to return, even if he wanted to.

Then the body rolled over. Its motion was sluggish. Helborg's limbs dragged in the water like trailing weeds. The flesh was pale, reflecting the last of the sunlight filtering from the surface. The mouth was open, fixed in a stare of outrage and accusation.

Schwarzhelm flailed, trying to swim back up, away from

the corpse. He was dragged down, faster and faster. The current had him now. The water became icy.

Helborg's empty eyes stared at him. They'd been pecked out, just like the soldiers' eyes in the barn. His flesh was bone-white. Parts of it had begun to flake away, drifting off into the abyss like fragments of china.

Schwarzhelm felt the horror well up within him, choking him. He could no longer hold his breath. He felt his lungs begin to ache. Whatever he did, he couldn't push himself up.

Helborg's shoulder rotated into view. The wound was still there, still pumping blood into the water. It would never heal, never be made right.

Schwarzhelm felt the ache turn to a sharp pain. He couldn't take a breath. He was drowning. He rolled over, desperate to look away from the cadaver below. Far up above, he could see the play of sunlight on the surface. He'd never reach it. It was too far. He was too tired. Too weak. His guilt weighed him down like lead. It dragged him down.

His lungs gave out. He opened his mouth. The water rushed in.

Schwarzhelm lurched awake. With a warrior's instinct he sat bolt upright, hands searching for his weapon. His bedclothes were tangled across him. Some had been thrown to the floor. His palms were dripping with sweat. He breathed heavily, drawing in the air with relief.

He was safe. He was in the Averburg. He wasn't alone.

Opposite him, sitting on a low stool at the foot of bed, a man was waiting for him.

'Bad dreams?' he said.

Schwarzhelm still felt disorientated. The dream still hadn't quite left him. For a moment, he didn't recognise who was speaking.

Then Verstohlen's face crystallised. Schwarzhelm felt his memory return. For the first time in weeks, he'd slept through the night. Though his dreams had remained vivid, they hadn't shaken him awake. Something had changed. The mental oppression that had plagued him for so long had lifted. The air felt purer. He took a deep breath, feeling it fill his mighty chest.

'What are you doing here?'

'Forgive the intrusion. I was worried about you.'

'That's not your job.'

'It's always been my job.'

Schwarzhelm scowled. He didn't like the protective tone in Verstohlen's voice. He pushed himself from the bed. There was a robe hanging nearby, and he donned it. Despite the heavy slumber, he felt strangely alert. His body was still filthy. As he moved, he could feel the crack of the dried blood across his skin. His beard felt heavy and matted. How had he let himself get into such a state?

'How long have I been asleep?'

'The day is nearly past. I'd say you needed the rest.'

Schwarzhelm grunted. He walked over to a pitcher of water and doused his face. The liquid dripped back red. He scrubbed at his eyes and old blood streamed back into the water below. None of it was his.

'How stands the city?'

'Grosslich's still hunting Leitdorf's men down. They've rounded up some of his captains who were too slow to get out. There's a witch hunter court of inquiry being set up.'

Schwarzhelm's face creased with disapproval. Like his counsellor, he hated witch hunters. Every right-thinking man hated witch hunters.

'Things seem to be in hand, then.'

Verstohlen gave him a significant look.

'Yet you still look troubled.'

Schwarzhelm gave him an irritated look. Verstohlen could be like an old woman at times.

'Grosslich had better remember who put him in this position,' he growled. 'I want no further actions taken until I've given the orders for them.'

'He'll be back in the citadel tonight.'

'Good. We'll talk then.'

'And is there anything else you wish to discuss, my lord?'

Schwarzhelm paused. Verstohlen was his counsellor, not his confessor.

'Helborg.'

There was a long silence. The Swords of Vengeance and Justice hung next to one another by the bed. One had a scabbard, the other was naked. Schwarzhelm felt the grief rush back, as if it had been unlocked by saying the name.

'He was riding with Leitdorf,' said Verstohlen, quietly. 'A proven traitor.'

'I only have your word for that, Pieter. In the heat of battle–'

'You didn't see what I did.'

'Exactly.'

Verstohlen looked agitated then. That was strange. The man was normally so calm.

'We did the right thing, my lord. The Leitdorfs were damned! Whatever Helborg was doing supporting them is his affair. The enemy has corrupted greater men.'

As Verstohlen spoke, Schwarzhelm remembered the scraps of parchment by the road. They had planted the seed of doubt in his mind, the suspicion that had come to such dreadful fruition in the Vormeisterplatz. Strange to have stumbled across the proof of treachery so far out into the wilds. Perhaps it had been Sigmar guiding him. Or maybe some other force.

He didn't want to discuss it any further. The pain was too raw. He needed to think, to reflect.

'I feel like I've not been myself these past few days,' he muttered.

'And how do you feel now?'

Schwarzhelm paused.

'Better.'

'Then there is your proof. We have broken the hold of that witch over Averheim. Do you not sense it in the air? There had been corruption here for far too long. Subtle corruption. There are things a sorcerer can do, ways of influencing the mood of a place. They have been attacking you, my lord, maybe even before you arrived. You know the truth of this.'

Verstohlen looked at him earnestly as he spoke. He was as fervent as ever in his denunciation of Chaos. 'We have beaten them. The court of inquiry will vindicate us. Leitdorf and his bitch will be found. Then the truth will emerge. Take comfort in this. We have beaten them.'

Schwarzhelm began to reply, but then changed his mind. Verstohlen was right. Something did seem to have changed. And yet, deep within, like a worm coiled around the core of a ripe apple, the seed of doubt had been laid. If he'd been wrong about Helborg, if it had been his pent-up jealousy that had truly wielded the Sword of Justice, then he would never forgive himself.

'I trust you're right, counsellor,' was all he said.

Skarr called the knights to a halt. Night was falling and they needed somewhere to lay low for the night. It had been a hard ride to escape Grosslich's men, and the horses shivered with exhaustion.

The young knight Eissen rode up to him. He looked ready for fresh fighting. Like all Reiksguard he hated flying before the enemy, though he'd understood the need to withdraw. In the aftermath of the fighting at Averheim, Grosslich had been able to send hundreds of troops after them. In the battle to get out of the city many of the Reiksguard had been cut down. Skarr's company now numbered less than fifty, half the number Helborg had led into combat.

More importantly, they couldn't fight while the Marshal remained so close to death. As long as Helborg remained unconscious, they would act to preserve him. That was the only task left for them. Averland politics, and vengeance, could wait.

'How is he?' asked Skarr.

Eissen shrugged.

'The same, preceptor. The wound is deep.'

Skarr looked over to Helborg's horse. The Marshal had been strapped to the saddle, propped up by a knight riding behind him. His face was white, his eyes closed. The bandages he'd hastily tied over the wound were soaked with blood again.

'We can't ride further tonight,' said Skarr. He looked over to an isolated copse in the field beyond. It wasn't much, but at least it was cover. 'We'll set up camp there. Bring the Marshal down carefully.'

What remained of the Reiksguard company rode across the field and dismounted under the eaves of the trees. Helborg was borne from his saddle with all the reverence given to the remains of an Imperial saint and placed carefully on the dry earth.

Skarr knelt over him with fresh bandages. There were not many left. Working quickly, he untied the blood-soaked cloth. Though hardened by years of battle injuries, the wound in Helborg's shoulder was still a shock. Schwarzhelm's sword had pierced deep, lifting up the flesh and boring beneath the shoulder plate. It was bleeding profusely, though thankfully not as strongly as it had done when he'd first tended to it. Many men would have perished from a blow as severe. Even Helborg looked near death, his breathing shallow. He had drifted into a fever. His pale forehead was clammy.

'Make a fire,' ordered Skarr, tearing fresh strips of bandage. 'I don't care if we're seen. I need hot water.'

He set to work, cleaning the wound and picking out the old scraps of cloth around the angry weal. Thankfully no metal had broken off in the flesh. The Sword of Justice had bitten true and the laceration was clean.

As Skarr worked, Helborg began to wince. The pain seemed to half-revive him. His eyes flickered open. He tried to speak, but no words came from his parched throat.

'Give him water,' ordered Skarr. A knight came forward bearing a gourd. The man managed to tip a few drops into Helborg's mouth. The Marshal swallowed a few before breaking into an anguished coughing. 'Enough. Tell me when you have boiling water.'

The brushwood on the copse floor was dry after weeks of heavy sun, and the fire crackled into life quickly. A helmet was filled with some of the scarce drinking water and placed over the flames. After a few minutes it reached boiling point and was brought over.

Skarr took a needle, gut thread and a pouch of dried herbs from the saddlebag of his mount. He emptied the contents of the pouch into the boiling water. Immediately a caustic aroma sprang up, making his eyes water. In its fresh state, healwort was an effective ward against contagion setting in. It was less efficacious when dried and stored, but still better then nothing. Skarr cleaned the wound with the infused water, sluicing the last remnants of foreign matter from the blood-red flesh. Then he threaded the iron needle and placed it against the edge of the broken skin. Helborg looked like he'd drifted back into unconsciousness. Skarr began to sew, pulling the flaps of skin tightly. He was accustomed to such work, having acted as a makeshift apothecary for years. All Reiksguard knew how to stitch up a blade wound.

With the laceration closed, he began to wind fresh sheets of bandage across it. He finished with a layer of leather strapping before replacing the jerkin on top. Even before he was finished he saw the spider-like tendrils of crimson begin to appear again.

Skarr stood up, putting the needle and thread away. He felt no confidence in his work. Helborg needed the services of a real apothecary. The longer they stayed out in the wilds, the worse his condition would get.

'What are we going to do about him?' Eissen had come to his shoulder. He gestured towards the sullen figure of Leitdorf. The deposed count huddled far from the fire, watched over carefully by his guards. Skarr felt a sudden flush of anger. This was all because of that wretched figure.

'Douse the fire,' he ordered. 'Organise a watch party. I'll speak to him.'

He strode over to Rufus, his expression dark. As he approached, Leitdorf shrank back even further, looking like he'd seen a wraith.

'Now then, my lord,' said Skarr, lacing his words with heavy

irony. 'I think it's time you explained what in Morr's name
happened back there.' He crouched down opposite the shaking figure and looked him directly in the eye.

'Tell me everything.'

Bloch shaded his eyes. The cold had grown steadily. Ahead
of him, the Worlds Edge Mountains reared their lofty peaks
towards the sky. The flint-grey cliffs soared ever higher, flecked
with frost and lingering snow at the summits. The walls of
rock were massive, far higher than those of the Drakwald or
the Mittebergen. Truly, Bloch saw how the range had earned
its name. As he gazed at the mist-shrouded peaks in the distance, piled atop one another in an endless series of stone
faces, gullies and terraces, it seemed indeed that they marked
the limits of the realm of mortals. Whatever lay beyond such
vast pinnacles must have been shut out for a reason. This
was where the jurisdiction of the Emperor ran out. The lands
on the far side could surely be nothing but blasted wastes.

The army had already climbed far. As they'd travelled,
storms had passed over them, moving swiftly westward. As
if to compensate for the weeks of unbroken sun, now the
world threw heaps of storm cloud at the lush pastures of
Averland. The wind was biting. Bloch found himself missing the hammering heat of the lowlands. He'd cursed it
when he'd been marching through it, but even that sweltering weather was better than the endless swirling gusts of
ice-wind in the high peaks.

He looked up. Even so high up, the road was wide and well
ordered. The engineers who had carved the way had been
artisans of the highest order. That didn't prevent some perilous passages as the path twisted up into the heights. Ahead
of him, the route passed under a cliff edge on the right-hand
side. To his left, the stone fell away sharply. A deep ravine
had been carved into the living rock and the sound of running water echoed between the buttresses of stone. Beyond
that the landscape dissolved into a tumble of windblasted
outcrops and crags on either side of the path.

Kraus came to stand at his shoulder.

'We loop around that cairn?' Bloch asked, pointing to a conical pile of rocks at the summit of a typically fractured rise. On either side of it, the going looked tough. Scree littered every exposed surface.

Kraus squinted up at the rising stone. The sunlight reflected harshly from the cold rock, and his old face wrinkled as he studied the way ahead.

'Aye. There'll be a way-fort soon. But we're still far from the passes.'

'How far?'

'A day. Maybe two.'

Bloch felt his heart sink. They'd already spent more time than he'd have liked hauling themselves up into the mountains. The sooner they reached the fortress at the head of the pass, the better.

'You're not filling me with confidence.'

'Two days, then. I'd bet on it.'

'How much?'

'A schilling.'

'You're a tight bastard, Kraus, and you're still not filling me with confidence.'

Kraus laughed. It was a tough, grating sound. The man looked almost as battered as the stone around him.

Then Bloch saw the shadow against the rock. He tensed immediately.

'See that?' he hissed, grabbing his halberd.

Kraus was ahead of him. He dropped into a half crouch, pulling the sword from its scabbard with a swift movement.

'Aye,' he whispered. His eyes narrowed.

Bloch turned and frantically signalled to the men toiling up the ridge behind him. They halted, and the order passed down the ranks quickly. The only sound was the serried drawing of weapons. They'd already encountered the last fragments of the orc army in the foothills. Bloch had assumed they'd finished off the last of them. Perhaps not.

He looked back up. The wind moaned against the granite. Everything looked empty.

'What d'you think?' he whispered, peering up at the cliffs.

Kraus shrugged. 'Maybe noth–'

He never finished his sentence. From the cliff above them, dark forms fell. Bloch tried to get his halberd in position, but he was far too slow. Before he knew what had happened, Kraus and he were surrounded by nearly a dozen men. They were dressed in Imperial garb modified for the cold. Most had fur-lined jerkins, cloaks and heavy leather boots. The colours suited the mountains around them; grey, pale, drab. From a distance, one would never have known they were there.

Bloch froze. He found himself staring down the bronze barrel of a long gun. At the other end of it, carefully shielding the cord, a man with a grey moustache and thin lips was staring at him. He didn't look friendly.

'State your business,' he growled. His voice sounded almost as harsh as Kraus's. At the edge of his vision, Bloch could see the other intruders move to disarm the guard captain. Three of them had guns. The rest carried crossbows, all loaded with bolts.

'Who's asking?' said Bloch, working hard to maintain his dignity. He didn't like having a gun pointed in his face. He also didn't like people being rude to him.

The man smiled coldly.

'You're not in a position to be asking questions, master halberdier.'

'Oh yes? You might want to take that up with the men behind me.'

'They'll not attack while we hold you.'

'Don't be so sure. I'm a tyrant. They might be pleased to see me dead.'

The gunner smiled again. He let the gun drop.

'Something tells me you're not like the others.'

Bloch relaxed his shoulders. His fingers had been clenched tight around the halberd, ready to swing it up in a sudden movement. He let them loosen. All around him, the other gunners lowered their barrels. But they kept the guns to hand.

'What others?'

'First tell me who you are. This is my country.'

'Fair enough. I am Commander Markus Bloch, charged by the Lord Schwarzhelm to drive the greenskins from Averland and reinforce the passes. This is Captain Kraus of the general's honour guard. You'd better introduce yourself now. Some of my men have itchy trigger fingers of their own. I'd hate you to take a stray bullet now we've become such good friends.'

'Schwarzhelm, eh?' said the man, looking impressed. 'I'd heard he was headed for Averland.' He gestured to his men, and they stood down. He extended a gnarled hand to Bloch. 'Captain Helmut Drassler, bergsjaeger of the passes.'

Bloch looked blank.

'The what?'

'Mountain guard. Since the greenskins came through, we've been stretched. There aren't many of us left up here.'

'You saw them come through? Then you can explain how they got past the defences.'

Drassler gave him a bleak look. 'Aye, that I can. The news can wait, though. We're not far from shelter. I'll guide you there and your men can rest. Then I'll tell you what you need to know. But I warn you, you're not going to like it.'

'Tell me something I don't know,' muttered Bloch.

'You wish to know everything?'

Skarr studied Leitdorf's face carefully. The man's expression was a mixture of contempt, confusion and fear. He seemed to oscillate between the emotions quite freely, as if he couldn't quite believe his aspirations had entirely been taken from him.

'That's what I asked for.'

'Give me a reason why I should speak to you, Reiksguard. You deprived me of my moment of triumph.'

Skarr rolled his eyes. This was going to test his patience.

'Perhaps I should set out the facts as I see them. We were

summoned to Averheim to reinforce the forces of the Steward. He claimed, rightly as it turned out, that the city was descending into civil war. This is the war we rode into. The war you instigated.'

'That's a lie.'

'You can give your excuses later. All I know is that I saw you fighting at the head of your troops. It didn't look much like legal debate to me. The troubling question is this. Why was Schwarzhelm fighting with your enemy? What had you done to provoke his anger?'

Leitdorf let slip a sly smile.

'You really expect me to answer for him? The man is mad. You saw that yourself. If he wasn't, your Marshal would still be walking on his own two feet.'

'There was madness in the air that night, I'll grant you. But I've fought alongside the Emperor's Champion before. There's something you're not telling me.'

Leitdorf snorted derisively.

'Must I know the contents of every man's mind?' He leaned forward. A strange, rather frantic light was in his eyes. 'If you'd been in Averheim these past few weeks, you'd have seen what your precious Emperor's Champion was like. He'd become a laughing stock. Averland has always had a weakness for mad governors. Schwarzhelm was no exception. I heard tales of screaming from his chambers. *Screaming*. Even his own men couldn't control him. He was like a man possessed.'

Skarr remembered how Schwarzhelm had looked in the Vormeisterplatz. The image was uncomfortably close.

'I don't know what Grosslich did to subvert him,' continued Leitdorf. 'Really, I don't. If I knew, I might have tried it myself. But don't be taken in by my rival's good looks and charm. He has no claim to the electorship at all. He's a front, a screen for the ambitions of the Alptraum family. His blood is as common as a milkmaid's. In fact, his mother probably *was* a milkmaid.'

Skarr began to feel troubled. He was used to receiving the

testimony of captives, and Leitdorf didn't have the look of a man lying to save his skin. The man was arrogant, cowardly and prickly to be sure, but the words had an uncomfortable air of truth about them.

'Listen to me, preceptor,' Leitdorf went on, moderating his tone somewhat. 'I'll not try to deceive you. I'm no saint of Shallya. My wife and I have been involved in the importation of some slightly illicit substances. Since Leopold died it's been the only way to raise the funds we needed. And I won't try to pretend we didn't hire men of dubious origin to help defend our people. But Grosslich was no different. That's how politics has always been done here. The fact of the matter is that it was *he* who started this war, backed up by Schwarzhelm and his entourage.' Leitdorf looked suddenly reflective. 'Perhaps I hadn't appreciated quite how much certain people didn't want to see a Leitdorf back in power. That might be something to think about.'

Skarr looked across at the prone body of Helborg, lying between the roots of a great oak. His breathing looked painfully shallow.

'Grosslich hunts you still,' said Skarr grimly. 'Though I can scarcely believe it myself, they want Lord Helborg dead too. We've been drawn into this madness. If there's been deception, then we're now a party to it. We must return to Nuln before the Marshal's condition worsens. Wiser heads than mine must decide what to do about Schwarzhelm.'

Leitdorf looked scornful.

'Is this Reiksguard tactical thinking? No wonder the war goes badly. Listen, you're deep into Averland. We've been driven east. The routes to the river are crawling with Grosslich's men. Even fifty Reiksguard can't take on a whole army. If you try, your man will surely die.'

'I take it you have an alternative suggestion.'

'Of course. My estates are closer than Nuln. Far closer. I have men there I can trust. We can remain hidden there until the Marshal has recovered. I can build up my strength. Trust me, this affair is not over yet. Whatever the Estates decide, I *am* the rightful heir of my father. I intend to claim the rune-fang for my own.'

'Grosslich will move against you soon. He'll know where your loyal subjects are.'

'He can't do everything at once. Averheim will take time to pacify. He'll expect us to flee for Nuln. That's what I'd do, in his place.'

Skarr paused. The man was probably right. There was no way they could fight against Grosslich's men with Helborg in such a condition. If they tried to force their way north, he would surely die.

'Do you have healers?'

'Petrus Glock is the finest physician east of Altdorf. He'll be there. If he can't restore your Marshal to health, then no one will.'

'How far?'

Leitdorf shrugged.

'With a fast horse, two days. But more if we need to stay hidden and keep the Marshal alive. That's still half the distance to Nuln though, and it's my family's country. We'll be amongst friends.'

Skarr looked down at his hands. The choice was unappealing. Leitdorf was flighty and erratic, but he could hardly deny that the situation was desperate. For all he knew, Schwarzhelm himself led the search for them. If that was true, then trying to fight their way west would be worse than folly.

'I'll make my decision in the morning,' he said, standing once more. 'This requires thought. In the meantime, keep your head down. I've been given the order to protect you, but if you give away our position or try to escape, don't expect any mercy from me.'

Leitdorf nodded. He looked chastened.

'Of course. And I'll remember this when I come to be elector. I never forget a kindness, preceptor.'

Skarr looked at him in disbelief.

'You still think, after all of this, you'll end up with the runefang?'

Leitdorf smiled broadly. There was a pale gleam in his eyes.

'Fear not,' he said. 'There are forces at work the likes of Schwarzhelm have no idea about. One in particular. She's still in Averheim. They haven't found her yet. They won't catch her. I'd know if they had.'

Skarr almost asked him what he was talking about, but then decided against it. Night was falling fast, and there were things to organise. Leitdorf had the look of an obsessed man, drifting into raving. He'd listened to enough of those in his time.

'So you say, Herr Leitdorf,' he said, walking back to his men. 'So you say.'

CHAPTER EIGHTEEN

Schwarzhelm stood in one of the Averburg's many audience chambers. The walls were panelled with an austere dark wood and candles burned in ornate brass fittings. Tapestries marking the province's military history had been hung from the hammerbeam roof. There were imaginative renderings of past orc incursions among them.

Schwarzhelm suppressed a wry snort of disdain when he saw those. Perhaps in ages past the Averlanders had been more capable of defending their own soil.

Verstohlen leaned over towards him. There were just the two of them in the chamber.

'He's coming.'

Schwarzhelm nodded. A moment later, the twin doors at the far end of the chamber swung apart. Grosslich walked in. He was flanked by four of his commanders. They were dressed in full battle armour, some of it scarred from use. They were all wearing colours Schwarzhelm hadn't seen before. Red lined with gold. An ostentatious choice for the new dynasty.

'I asked Herr Alptraum to join us,' said Schwarzhelm.

'He is indisposed at present,' said Grosslich, coming to stand squarely in front of the Emperor's Champion.

'That may be. He's still been summoned.'

'I'll remind him of the importance of following orders when I next see him,' said Grosslich. He placed a particular emphasis on *following orders*. Schwarzhelm saw Verstohlen raise an eyebrow.

'Do that. Have your men discovered Leitdorf?'

'His forces in the city have been utterly destroyed. We uncovered six safe houses in the poor quarter from where the joyroot trade was administered. They have all been burned and their contents destroyed. The supply lines–'

'That's all very interesting, Herr Grosslich. It's not what I asked you.'

Grosslich appeared to flush. He had a straightforward manner about him. That was good for a soldier, less good for an elector.

'Not yet. The Reiksguard took him with them. All the roads to the north-west are watched. I have horsemen sweeping the countryside.'

'He has estates to the east, is that not so?'

'He does, my lord, but–'

'He will head there. You're wasting your time guarding the river.'

'Your pardon, but there are at least two dozen Reiksguard with him. We can't watch every possible route. It seemed best to me to prevent his flight from the province.'

'You've given him time to regroup. Send your men east at once. If you don't destroy the nest, the viper will return.'

Grosslich looked chastened. Schwarzhelm gave him no respite. The man had assumed that taking on the mantle of elector would be straightforward. He had to be disabused of that.

'Are the witch hunters in the city yet?'

'They are, my lord. The courts of inquiry have been placed in session.'

Schwarzhelm felt a tremor of distaste. He knew what that meant. The instruments of agony. Still, such were their methods. The great enemy could not be defeated with pleasant words and gentle persuasion.

'You will instruct them to meet me this evening. You're not elector yet, Herr Grosslich. Until you have my word on it, I still carry the Imperial authority here.'

'Of course. I didn't presume–'

'What are your plans for securing the city? There can be no coronation until the traitors have been rooted out.'

Grosslich looked on firmer ground then. Tactics were something he understood. They both did. At the simplest level, the two of them were soldiers and nothing more.

'Those who served closest to Leitdorf have been disarmed. The captains have been surrendered to the witch hunters for examination. The ordinary troops, including those with feudal ties to my rival, have been released. I will have no bloody reprisals here. The city has suffered enough.'

'You're confident you can maintain order?'

'I have a thousand men-at-arms already in the city. More are on their way. Herr Alptraum has been most generous with his family's wealth. As long as they've not served in Leitdorf's inner circle, I will turn no willing recruit away. Averland's army needs rebuilding.'

Schwarzhelm grunted with approval. That was certainly true.

'You will send me documents concerning your revenue and deployment plans. Only when I'm satisfied that the city is secure will I set the investiture in motion. I want regular reports on progress. And while Leitdorf is at large, the eyes of the Emperor will be closely watching you here.'

Grosslich bowed.

'I understand.'

'Have you found Natassja?' interjected Verstohlen.

Always Natassja. The man seemed obsessed with her.

'She remains free, I regret to say, but I have as many men searching for her as I do for her husband. We've taken your warnings seriously, counsellor.'

'I'm glad of it. She is at the heart of the whole thing. Perhaps even Leitdorf doesn't know what her full plans are.
There's no doubt she remains dangerous. Do not be complacent. The great enemy is ever stronger and more enduring
than it first appears.'

Grosslich couldn't resist a smile. The man was flush with
victory, and such warnings must have seemed pointless.

'So you've been telling me ever since this affair began,'
he said. He looked amused, but there was no malice in his
voice. 'Trust me. I've been fighting against these people for
two years. Their powers have already proved weaker than
they hoped for. She will be found.'

Verstohlen didn't look reassured.

'Make sure of it,' he said. 'She may be in the city still.'

Schwarzhelm turned back to Grosslich.

'That is all for now,' he said. 'You may return to your men.'

Grosslich made to leave, then hesitated.

'My lord,' he said, looking uncertainly at Schwarzhelm. 'I
haven't thanked you yet.'

Schwarzhelm scowled. This was unnecessary.

'Herr Grosslich–'

'Please. Hear me out. Perhaps I didn't give you the credit
you deserved when you first arrived. It's clear to me now
that not all was as it appeared. I wouldn't have believed
that a man like Helborg could turn, not if I hadn't seen it
myself. We couldn't have stood against him. In my arrogance
I thought to challenge him myself. Now that my blood has
cooled I realise it would have been my death to do so. Had
you not arrived when you did–'

'Enough,' snapped Schwarzhelm. He knew the man meant
well, but to even think of it caused him pain. 'We will not
speak of it. Is there anything else?'

Grosslich hesitated, then shook his head.

'I understand,' he said.

'Then return to your duties.'

Grosslich and his captains turned and headed from the
chamber. As they left, the heavy doors closed behind them

with a clang. Schwarzhelm and Verstohlen were alone again. For some moments, neither of them spoke.

'Have we done the right thing here, Pieter?' asked Schwarzhelm. He made no effort to hide the concern in his voice.

'I have no doubt of it. You're letting your friendship cloud your mind. Do not dwell on it.'

'Friendship? It's not been that for years.' Schwarzhelm frowned. 'He was a great man. It will break the Emperor's heart.'

'None of us are immune.'

'That is the truth,' said Schwarzhelm. 'Though I wish with all my heart it were otherwise.'

The great hall of the Averburg was dark. Even though the sun blazed outside, drapes had been hung over the tall windows. Each of them bore the symbol of the comet embroidered in scarlet thread. Braziers had been set up at intervals along the nave. They gave off an acrid smell and sent plumes of black smoke curling up into the rafters. The place had been turned into something more fitted to the tastes of its temporary occupants.

It had been less than a day since the witch hunters had arrived, and they'd wasted no time in setting up their tribunal. Grosslich's men worked hard to supply them with a steady stream of suspects, all dragged from the poor quarter, all members of Leitdorf's inner circle. The investigation had been typically thorough. Where the taint of Chaos was even suspected, the questioning was always rigorous and applied without mercy. The methods were ancient, honed by the master interrogators of the Temple of Sigmar over generations. Some were subtle, preying on the weaknesses of men's minds. Others were brutal, playing on the frailty of men's bodies. Both had their place. Both had been employed in Averheim.

Witch hunter Odo Heidegger looked down at his latest subject with a mix of pity and scorn. He knew what other men thought about his profession. That they were sadists, butchers who enjoyed their work, fanatics and zealots. No

doubt some of his colleagues were. He'd met many others of
his kind, particularly in the remoter reaches of the Empire,
who had depressed him. There was nothing more saddening
than seeing a man charged with the most holy offices of the
Imperial hierarchy turn to brutishness. Heidegger prayed to
Sigmar nightly that such a fate would not befall him.

He was, after all, a cultured man. He enjoyed lyric poetry,
so long as the subject matter was suitably reverent. He had no
time for tavern singing, but revelled in the soaring music of
the Imperial Chapel in Wittenburg, justly famous for its cho-
ral tradition. In another life, perhaps he would have become
a musician himself. He'd always wondered what it would be
like to play the lute, to dance across the strings with his delicate fingers, producing the kind of gentle, strumming sound
that pleased even the hardest of hearts. He had the sensibility for it. He also had the delicacy of touch, honed over
years of dedicated practice.

He tried not to think too closely about the screams, of
course. They clouded out the images of harmony running
through his mind. It was important to concentrate on this
kind of work. He didn't take any pleasure in the pain he
caused. That was just a means to an end. But he did take
pleasure in the skill. Sigmar would forgive him that sin of
pride. It was pursued, after all, for His ends.

Thankfully, Werner Klopfer had stopped screaming. He
was now engaged in a kind of frenzied panting. The man
was naked, strapped to a table in the centre of the great hall.
His right arm had been turned into a cacophony of gore.
The muscle was visible in patches, shining in the candlelight. Aside from a diligent scribe and a couple of deaf-mute
guards standing watch at the doors, they were alone together.
It was a pleasing, intimate scene.

Klopfer's breathing became more ragged. The poor man
was panicking. Heidegger took a damp cloth from the bench
beside him and pressed it to his subject's brow. Klopfer shivered under the touch. His skin glistened with sweat. His
whole body stank with it. Like most of the subjects brought

before him that day, he had lost control of his bowels with terror. That was certainly unfortunate, but one couldn't blame the wretches for that. It was an arduous business, this uncovering of the truth.

'Now then,' said Heidegger in his soft, almost feminine, voice. He put the cloth to one side. 'Do not concern yourself with the physical pain you feel, my son. This is just the necessary prelude, the means by which your soul may be cleansed. Pain will pass, even if in death.'

He reached for another bowl, this time filled with clear water, and washed his hands. Everything he needed had been laid out on the bench, just as he liked it. There was his battered old prayer book, the leaves flaky and ancient, his vials of holy water, the icons of Sigmar and Magnus the Pious, the litanies of exorcism. And of course, the instruments of inquiry. The clamps, barbs, scalpels, gouges, pins and all the rest. All lovingly catalogued and labelled, ready for use. Most of them shone brightly in the firelight, polished to a high sheen and resting on soft cloth. The others, the ones that had already seen action, were covered in a second skin of crimson. He would look forward to cleaning them again in the evening.

'W-what do you want to hear?' sobbed Klopfer. 'I'll tell you anything. Anything!'

Heidegger folded his arms and tutted.

'That will not do. Have you not been listening to anything I've been saying? I want the truth from you. The whole truth. Tell me what you know, and your soul may be spared.'

'I worked for Leitdorf!' Klopfer cried. His anguished voice echoed from the high rafters. As he spoke, the scribe diligently transcribed his words. Alrich was a good servant. He never lost his place, never asked for a repetition. Whenever a session was over, he would present his sheaves of parchment, all neatly inscribed with the black letter Reikspiel record of the conversation. Heidegger was really very fond of him. So many scribes lost their minds as the long years wore on that it was a relief to find a true professional.

Klopfer's voice began to quicken. 'I was one of his captains. We knew that Grosslich was arming his men, so we did the same. Some of our troops came from his estates. They were carried in by river, under cover of night. Others we bought.'

'How did you acquire the funds for this work?'

'We had many sources. Leitdorf had money from his inheritance. His wife was rich too. Then there was the root. We imported it. Leitdorf's men had control over the cartels. There were rival gangs in Averheim, but he controlled them all in the end. The money was good. They couldn't stop buying it. I don't know where the rest came from.'

'I've heard about the joyroot from others. Was it part of your corruption?'

'Corruption? I don't–'

Heidegger reached for another instrument.

'Yes! Yes, it was! Please no more!'

Heidegger took up a fresh tool. It was a piece of real artistry, as elegant and refined as an elven maid's ankle. He didn't really want to use it. There was always the chance of snagging on a tendon and interfering with the mechanism. Perhaps later, if the conversation was beginning to flag.

'So the joyroot was part of your corruption. That is indeed the consensus I've picked up from others. Did you take it yourself?'

'No! Never. It was only ever given to those outside the organisation. Some of the mercenaries took it. Leitdorf gave us strict instructions never to touch it.'

'And why was that?'

'We saw what it did to the others. It made them lazy. He wanted us ready to fight.'

'Did you not question these orders when you realised that the joyroot was a tool of the great enemy?'

Klopfer looked at Heidegger with new terror. Tears started in his eyes. He was clearly struggling to know what to say. Admitting guilt was always difficult.

'You can confess all to me, my son,' said Heidegger kindly. 'Though I know it doesn't seem that way at present, I am here to help you.'

Klopfer began to break down into bitter sobs. That was disappointing. They so often did that when he offered them the benefit of his spiritual wisdom. Why were so many men deaf to the insights of the Temple, to the potential for salvation? Mortification of the flesh was only temporal. Damnation, on the other hand, was eternal.

Heidegger gave Klopfer a moment to recover himself.

'Speak to me, my son,' he said at last. He let a firm edge enter his voice then. Heidegger was a patient man, but his benevolence only stretched so far.

Klopfer brought his sobs half under control. He had a resigned, broken look about him. That was good. The penitent spirit would enter Sigmar's halls.

'I knew there was something about it. Something wrong. I thought it was her doing.'

'Leitdorf's wife?'

'Yes. We were all scared of her.'

'Fear is no excuse.'

'I know! I know now. Believe me, I regret everything.'

Heidegger felt a warm glow of satisfaction bloom within him. This was what made his vocation such a blessed one.

'This ordeal is nearly over for you now. There is just one last thing.'

Klopfer looked up at him. There was a sudden, desperate hope in his tear-stained face.

'What is it?'

'I have been asked to enquire about the role of the Grand Marshal of the Reiksguard, Kurt Helborg. He is a powerful man. Of all the troubling aspects of this case, that is the most grave. The truth must be ascertained.'

As he spoke, Heidegger brought the instrument, his favourite, down gently against Klopfer's face. The man stiffened and began to shake violently. Thankfully, he had been shackled expertly. His head could only move a fraction of an inch. With the tender touch of a lover, Heidegger rested the tip of the device on the skin below the man's left eye.

'You will tell me the truth of this, will you not, my son? Was

Helborg involved in this affair? Was he directing it from Altdorf, and then Nuln? Was he, along with Rufus Leitdorf and Natassja Hiess-Leitdorf, the true architect of this shameful episode?'

For a moment, Klopfer looked so stricken with terror that he could hardly speak. He tried to look at the device resting on his face but it was too close. He could feel it, though. And he could guess what it did.

'Speak quickly.'

Klopfer looked up into Heidegger's eyes. There was a pleading there. An agonised pleading. He would say anything. Anything to avoid the pain. They always did, sooner or later. That was the genius of the exercise. They would come to the truth in the end. Whether it was the truth as they saw it, or the truth as he wanted it to be, it didn't matter. Everything was relative, after all. All ways led to glory, to the greater praise of Sigmar, the origin of all beneficence.

'H-he was, my lord,' stammered Klopfer. As he spoke, fresh tears ran down his cheek. They glinted from the surface of the metal as they splashed over it. 'Helborg was one of them. I saw the letters that passed between them. They were all traitors. Leitdorf, his wife, the Reiksguard Marshal.'

Heidegger sighed gently. Another confession. How quickly they came, once all the work had been done. Another soul had been saved. Another piece of information had been collated. His work was done. He withdrew the instrument. As he did so, Klopfer broke down again, slack against his bonds.

'There, now,' said Heidegger soothingly. 'Does that not feel better? Confessing one's sins is a cleansing process. Your soul is now free of the taint you have carried for so long. You should be proud.'

He placed the instrument back on the cloth. It clinked against its fellows gently as he rolled the covering up.

'That's it?' asked Klopfer. The desperate hope had returned. 'I'm free to go?'

Heidegger nodded. This was the part of the process he really didn't like. It always seemed such a shame after all they'd been through together.

'There is no more. The ordeal is over. You are free to go.'

He picked up a cloth and dabbed his hands. They needed a wash. He'd been working too hard. Perhaps he needed a break.

'You have done well, my son,' said Heidegger, placing the cloth back on the table. 'The information you have provided will root out this heresy.'

Klopfer didn't seem to be listening. He was lost in some kind of reverie. That was ungrateful. This was for his benefit, after all. Heidegger felt deflated. He always did when the process was over. It was at this stage that his faith was weakest. In the darkest moments, he sometimes wondered whether he wouldn't have been better employed in the Chapel at Wittenburg after all. Perhaps then his sleep wouldn't have been as troubled as it was. Maybe then he wouldn't find himself weeping for no reason at all, wracked by the inexplicable terrors that came to him when he was alone.

Enough. These periods of depression were a test. Everything was a test. He walked away from the table, turning to the scribe as he went.

'Did you get it all?'

'Yes, my lord.'

'Including the testimony on Lord Helborg?'

'Yes, my lord.'

Of course he had. Alrich never missed a thing. Heidegger sighed. He was a diligent servant. They were both diligent servants.

He kept walking, snapping his fingers to attract the attention of the guards. Using the hand signals they understood, he gave them the only order he ever gave them.

Kill him. Then bring in the next one.

Verstohlen stood on the terrace above the lower levels of the Averburg. The wind had picked up again. It made the city feel healthier. Since Leitdorf had been driven from the place, the air had changed. The lingering sweetness, the hint of rottenness, had gone. Grosslich had brought order to the

place quickly. Of course, he'd been aided by Schwarzhelm.
The man seemed back to his old self, if a little more withdrawn than was usual. He went about his business with the
grim-faced efficiency for which he was known.

That alone convinced Verstohlen that their actions had
been justified. The Leitdorfs might have succeeded for a
time in driving Schwarzhelm from the city, in tying him
up with legal paperwork, in using the subtle poisons of the
mind to cloud his judgement, but all that was over now.
Had their plans not been discovered when they were, they
might have succeeded. Verstohlen was in no doubt they'd
used the greenskins somehow. The precise mechanism was
still hidden from him, but it would emerge. With the witch
hunters given full rein to investigate, few secrets would
remain hidden for long.

He looked out over the city. It seemed as peaceful as it had
done when they'd arrived. There was little obvious sign of
the scarring which had taken place since then. The merchants
had come back. The streets had been tidied up. People were
sick of the fighting. Even those who had previously sided
with Rufus seemed resigned to the accession of Heinz-Mark.
Anything was better than the gathering anarchy which had
plagued them over the past few weeks.

There was a sound behind him. He whirled round in an
instant, blade at the ready.

Tochfel stood before him, arms raised in surrender.

'Apologies, counsellor,' he said, looking at the knife
nervously.

'Forgive me,' said Verstohlen, putting the dagger back in its
sheath. 'It's been a difficult time.'

Tochfel came to stand next to him on the terrace.

'Think nothing of it. We must hope things have changed
for the better.'

'You don't sound convinced they will be.'

'I am cautious by nature.'

'I'd noticed.'

Tochfel smiled ruefully. The two men stood for a while in

silence, watching the city breathe below them. Some life had already returned to the river. Where there had been nothing but stagnant water, a few barges now plied their trade. It would take time for the bustle to return, but it was a start.

'I feel some measure of guilt for what happened, of course,' said Tochfel.

Verstohlen raised an eyebrow.

'It was I who summoned Helborg from Nuln.'

'At my suggestion, as I recall.'

'Even so.'

Verstohlen made a noncommittal gesture. All of Averheim seemed to be lost in introspection.

'You could not have known his role in this. None of us did. Only Schwarzhelm suspected his motives. At the time, I put it down to... professional rivalry. Perhaps he saw further than any of us. Of course, even he doubts himself now.'

Tochfel looked down at the stone balustrade. Like most of the architecture of the Averburg it had survived the fighting unscathed. Men had died, but the city remained intact.

'The witch hunters have concluded their investigations. The traitors all name Helborg in their confessions. Schwarzhelm need have no doubts.'

'Good,' said Verstohlen. 'I'm sure the Templars have been very thorough. This paves the way for the coronation.'

'It does. Preparations have been made.'

'You don't sound entirely happy with that either.'

Tochfel shrugged. 'It's not how I wanted it to happen. But what's done is done. A tragedy has been avoided. I think I can work with Grosslich.'

'Good,' said Verstohlen. 'There's not a drop of noble blood in him, whatever he says, but he's clawed his way to the top.' Verstohlen smiled to himself. 'He rode straight at Helborg. By Verena, that's bravery. He's still not forgiven me for heading him off, even though it saved his life.'

Tochfel didn't smile in return.

'I hope we can move beyond such things now. Averland is reeling. We need a leader who can govern, not a warlord.'

'He has the advice of Ferenc Alptraum and others like him. That's a powerful alliance.'

'Have you seen Alptraum recently?'

Verstohlen paused. Now that Tochfel mentioned it, he hadn't. In fact, he hadn't seen Alptraum since leaving for the battle at the Vormeisterplatz.

'Has he left the city?'

'I don't know. Nobody knows. Just as nobody knows where Achendorfer, my loremaster, has gone.'

'When did you last see him?'

'Just before Alptraum took control of the citadel. He was acting... strangely.'

Verstohlen looked at Tochfel carefully. Was he trying to insinuate something? The man didn't look like he had an agenda of his own.

'What are you telling me, Steward? Should I be worried about this?'

Tochfel shrugged. 'Perhaps there's been enough intrigue. I don't wish to reopen wounds. But I thought you should know.'

'Thank you. I'll make enquiries.'

As the words left his mouth, Verstohlen realised how empty they were. His cover had been blown. All the players left in Averheim knew who he was, what he did and who he worked for. He had no function any longer beyond Schwarzhelm's errand runner. If there were secrets to uncover still, then someone else would have to find them.

'I should go,' said Tochfel. 'Coronation preparation.'

Verstohlen nodded.

'I don't envy you.'

The Steward withdrew, leaving Verstohlen alone again. He remained silent. His hair lifted in the breeze. Below him, the Aver glittered in the sun. All was as it should be. The mission was concluding and a decision on the succession had been made. When they left Averheim, it would be safe in the hands of a new elector.

He should have been content. Happy, even. But then he'd

never been very good at being content. Not since Leonora's death. Even in periods of victory, his mind still worked apace, seeking out the potential for danger, fearing the potential for loss. It was not a quality he liked in himself, but he could no more change it than change his past.

After the coronation Schwarzhelm would leave. The big man wanted to give the news of Helborg's treachery to the Emperor in person. Verstohlen had been ordered to stay to oversee the remaining work of pacification. There was much to do. Bloch's army had to be contacted with the news. Leitdorf and Natassja had to be tracked down. The roads had to be made safe again. It was interesting work. Demanding work. Normally, he'd have jumped at the chance to ensure it was done well.

But not this time. After all that had happened, Verstohlen was sick of Averheim. Though his sense of duty would never let him admit it, he had come to loathe the place. The sooner he could leave and return to Altdorf, the better.

He continued to look over the cityscape for a few moments longer. Then he turned and headed back into the citadel. The terrace was empty once more, buffeted by the cold wind from the east. There was no corruption in it, but no comfort either.

Just as it had been for Schwarzhelm's arrival, the great hall of the citadel was lined with people. The finery was not quite what it was, but given all that had taken place, the noble citizens did as well as they could. If some of the silk had been hastily patched up, and some of the jewellery hanging round the necks of the court ladies seemed slightly tarnished, then people were prepared to look the other way. There was a general sense of relief in the crowds of nobles. Many had only just been able to return to their opulent townhouses after retreating to their country estates. Now they were back, they were eager to see no repeat of the anarchy that had driven them away.

The great hall had been decorated with banners holding the symbols of Averland. Most were in the black and yellow

of the province, decorated with a stylised sun image derived
from the lost realm of Solland. There were the devices of
the noble families too, as well as the ubiquitous comets
and Imperial eagles, griffons and lions. The symbol of the
Alptraums was prominent among them, though Verstohlen
could see no sign of Ferenc in the crowds.

The new addition to the rows of standards was the newly
embroidered battle-flag of the Grosslich line. It was a gaudy
affair. A black boar's head, surrounded by gold laurel leaves
set on a blood-red field. The new elector clearly hadn't
been chosen for his aesthetic sensibility. Still, if that's what
he wanted, that's what he'd get. No elector had ever been
deposed for having a silly flag.

As the time dragged on, the crowd began to get restive.
With the paraphernalia of the witch hunters having been
cleared away, the great hall had been restored to its habitual sunlit state. The strong sun lanced through the high
mullioned windows. With so many people gathered, the
temperature soon started to rise. Verstohlen felt a certain
dampness under his collar and eased it open. Grosslich was
keeping them waiting. He'd learned a few tricks of the trade,
then. Arrive late, leave early.

Verstohlen turned to glance at the double doors. They
were heavily guarded. Grosslich's personal troops, decked
out in the same outlandish livery, stood three-deep at the
exit. Leitdorf had still not been found, and no one was in
the mood to take any chances. Verstohlen knew that hundreds of Grosslich's men were prowling the corridors of the
Averburg even as the ceremony was due to take place.

He looked back at the high dais. The members of the Electoral Council had taken their seats. Some of them were old
hands. He recognised Tochfel, looking uncomfortable in his
new crimson garb. Most of the rest seemed to be members
of Grosslich's inner council. Euler was there. That was to
be expected. He'd have been foolish not to put those closest to him in positions of power. A good elector knew how
to cover his back.

The crowd grew more restive, and the smattering of gossip began to rise in volume. It was then that the trumpets finally blared out. The brazen notes echoed uncomfortably in the enclosed space, and Verstohlen found himself wincing.

Then the doors slammed open. A procession of citadel guards strode down the central aisle. As they came, the standing crowds shuffled to make room for them. The soldiers took up their places and turned to face the throng. They placed their spears on the stone in unison.

Then Schwarzhelm arrived. Verstohlen couldn't suppress a smile of amusement when he saw him. He knew how much the great man hated ceremonial occasions. He was wearing his full suit of armour, freshly cleaned for the coronation. The metal which had been dented, scarred and covered in gore so recently now shone like starlight. He carried the Rechtstahl in its ancient scabbard and the pendant of Ghal Maraz swung from his neck as he walked.

Knowing his reputation for irascibility, the nobles crept even further back as he strode towards the dais. Schwarzhelm didn't make eye contact with any of them. He had the look of a man who would have given money to be anywhere else.

He took his place at the head of the hall and turned back to face the crowd. There was an expectant hush. For a moment, the only sound was the faint echo of soldiers' boots as they patrolled the corridors outside.

Then he arrived. Grosslich emerged in a robe of red lined with gold. That was clearly his favourite combination, though not an obvious choice for a soldier. He wore a loremaster's cloth cap. Chains of office hung around his neck. Perhaps he was sending a subtle signal here. The time for war had passed, and he was as at home in the garb of a scholar as he was in the armour of a warrior. If that was so, then it boded well for Averland.

He strode confidently down the aisle. As he went, there was a general murmur of acclimation. Verstohlen might have imagined it, but there were semi-audible sighs from some of the younger women in the chamber. Grosslich was unmarried, and they all knew it. The situation was unlikely to remain the case for long.

Grosslich approached the dais. Schwarzhelm waited for him like some brooding idol in the jungles of Lustria. Grosslich knelt down. He was showing the proper degree of humility. That was wise.

'People of Averland,' announced Schwarzhelm. His heavy voice rolled round the chamber. For the first time, Verstohlen noticed the faint Averland accent to it. Strange that he hadn't before. Perhaps the big man had returned to his roots after all. 'By the authority vested in me by the Emperor, and according to the Imperial Law of Succession, I hereby crown Count Heinz-Mark Grosslich the new Elector of Averland. May his reign be long and prosperous. May he be blessed by Sigmar in battle, uphold the law, protect his people and smite the enemies of mankind.'

With that he took up the gold crown of the Electors of Averland. Grosslich removed his scholar's hat, and Schwarzhelm placed the jewel-encrusted circlet on his head. The elector remained kneeling. The crown was unimportant. That was just a symbol. The artefact he really wanted was still to come.

From the rear of the dais, Tochfel shuffled forward carrying a heavy item draped in gold cloth. It was nearly as tall as he was and he looked weighed down with the burden.

Schwarzhelm took it from him in one hand and swung it around lightly.

'Behold,' he announced, sweeping the cloth from the blade beneath. 'The runefang of Averland, the Sword of Ruin, the holy blade of the people of Siggurd.'

He brandished the blade. Like all the runefangs, the sword was a work of peerless craftsmanship. The steel glinted in the sunlight, exposing the intricate runes engraved on to the metal. As the runefang was revealed, a sigh of satisfaction passed across the crowd. That was what they had longed to see for so long. The runefang of Averland would be wielded once more.

With reverence, Schwarzhelm handed the sword to Grosslich. The count stood to receive it, taking it in both hands. For a moment he remained motionless, staring at the sacred sword. Schwarzhelm stepped back, letting him savour the moment.

Then Grosslich rose and turned to face the crowd. The sunlight from the sword reflected onto his face. He looked the very image of an elector count. He held the runefang aloft in both hands.

'For Sigmar!' he roared. His eyes were alive with jubilation. 'For the Empire!'

'For the Empire!' cried the crowd before him, before bursting into rounds of cheers. Verstohlen kept apart from the excitement, watching carefully as was his habit. He couldn't blame them. After years of enduring the mad count, then the painful experience of hiatus, they deserved something to cheer about.

Verstohlen looked up at Schwarzhelm. Though he wasn't smiling – which was to be expected – he did have an expression of grim satisfaction on his battered features. That was good. The big man had suffered more than the rest of them. He deserved his triumph. When he returned to Altdorf, he would no doubt receive the full credit for all that had happened here, and Verstohlen knew how much that meant to him.

Letting his habitual reserve slip for just a short while, Verstohlen joined in the cheers of the crowd. It would have been churlish not to. This was a great day.

The party had taken a while to die down. After the crowning ceremony, there had been a series of legal procedures to endure. Then the crowd had retired to the grand ballroom in Alptraum's mansion for a feast of epic proportions. The wine had slopped from crystal buckets all night.

As he recalled the evening, Elector Count Heinz-Mark Grosslich couldn't prevent a smile from creasing his broad face. He had done it. After all those months warring against the bastard Rufus, he had done it.

He trod heavily back to his private chambers, feeling the weight of the runefang against his thigh as he climbed the spiral stairs. He could get used to that. The sword was palpably ancient. He could sense the latent power within the blade. It felt like it was eager to be drawn.

He arrived at his chambers. Two guards stood to attention as he approached.

'You can go now, lads,' he said to them.

They looked back at him blankly.

'We were ordered to remain here all night, sire,' said one of them.

Grosslich looked at him benevolently. On another occasion he might have berated them for not following his orders instantly. But he was in a good mood. All had come to fruition. A bright future lay ahead.

'I don't think we need worry about my safety tonight,' he said, looking significantly at the sword hanging from his belt. 'There's wine left over in the ballroom. Enjoy yourselves. We've all earned it.'

The two men looked at each other, then grinned.

'Thank you very much, sire,' one of them blurted, then they were gone, hurrying down the stairs before the rest of the banquet was consumed.

Grosslich pushed the door open. He smirked a little as he remembered the number of propositions he'd had that night. It wasn't as if he'd had trouble attracting women before, but it was amazing what an Imperial title did for one's amorous prospects. He'd almost been tempted to take one of them up on it.

Almost, but not quite. There was only one woman for him.

'You're back late,' said Natassja, drawing the bed curtains aside and rising from the bed.

Grosslich locked the door and turned to face her. He drew the runefang with a flourish.

'Look at it, my love,' he said, gazing at the sword with undisguised relish. 'Finally.'

Natassja smiled tolerantly. She was clad in a black

nightdress. It clung to her in all the right places. Suddenly, Grosslich couldn't decide which of the two prizes he was more interested in.

'Very nice. Now come here.'

Grosslich put the sword down and approached her. They embraced. As they did so, the candles in the room flickered and went out. A lilac glow replaced the natural flame, throwing lurid patterns across the massive four-poster bed. That was more like it. He began to feel at home again.

'It's been too long,' he said, gazing into her dark eyes.

'Have you found Leitdorf yet?'

Grosslich felt a little wounded. Was she going to talk business now? This was his hour of triumph. She could show a little appreciation.

'Not yet, my love. It's only a matter of time. I've hundreds of men searching for him.'

'Perhaps I can help.'

'Not until Schwarzhelm's left.'

'Indeed. But you'll like my latest experiments. They may prove useful.'

Grosslich shivered with anticipation. Natassja's imagination was terrifying.

'How did you stand being with that fool for so long?'

Natassja smiled coldly.

'He was easy to deceive. Most men are.' She looked into his eyes. Her pupils were mirrored like a cat's. 'Most men. Not all.'

From somewhere, the aroma of jasmine filtered into the room. The musk was thick and heady.

'We should be thankful for that. All of this has traded on deception.'

'There were unexpected factors. I didn't foresee Helborg. That nearly ruined us.'

Grosslich laughed then. He couldn't help it.

'Of all the ironies. It was Schwarzhelm who cut him down.'

'You sound surprised. Don't forget the long hours I spent walking in his mind. I have never been so tested. I couldn't break him. Not after using spells that would have destroyed a normal man. All I could do was plant the suggestion. Do not be too eager to celebrate. Just as it was with Marius, I couldn't break him.'

Grosslich pulled her closer to him. He could feel her body under the nightdress. The anticipation almost made him sick.

'Enough talking. I *am* eager to celebrate.'

Natassja gave him a savage look. With surprising ease, she flung him on to the bed, pinning him down. As her face lowered over his, her feline eyes were filled with a lilac flame. The glow in the room darkened and became more intense.

'And so you shall. Just remember who's in charge here.'

Grosslich grinned.

'As you wish, my love,' he sighed. 'Everything shall be just as you wish.'

CHAPTER NINETEEN

Schwarzhelm waited. That wasn't something he was used to doing. The mirrored corridor ran for over a hundred yards, and he was the only one in it. Not even the Reiksguard came down here to disturb the peace. The Emperor knew he was there. And still he waited.

He ran his mind over the past few days. At times there were gaps in his memory. Half the time it had felt as thought he'd been fighting against his own nightmares. The moments he remembered vividly were the deaths. Grunwald. Helborg. Although maybe he wasn't dead yet. The body hadn't been recovered. He didn't know what to hope for.

After the trails of the past few weeks, the journey back from Averheim had been easy. As Schwarzhelm had ridden north, the weather had turned. The open skies had been replaced with slate-grey cloud. Altdorf was sodden with rain. The gutters were overflowing, the roofs dripping, the river turgid and filthy. It felt just as the Empire should feel. Averland was a strange and unsettling place in comparison. He was glad to be away from it.

'Come!'

The voice echoed down the mirrored hallway. As he answered the summons, the Sword of Justice clanked on his belt. He carried the Sword of Vengeance in his hands. Helborg still had the scabbard, for all he knew. The bare metal was almost flawless in his hands. He'd washed the blood, his own blood, from it carefully. The only blemish was the notch. The one he'd caused.

Schwarzhelm walked to the gold-lined doors at the end of the corridor. The Imperial seal had been inscribed on them in ithilmar. They must have been fabulously expensive. He pushed against them and they swung open smoothly.

The chamber beyond was completely different. It was vast, dark and old. Rows of bare stone columns marched along its flanks. The windows were tall and narrow, like those of a fortress. The grey sky outside only let a meagre light bleed into the shadowy space. At the far end of the chamber, hidden by the gloom, a massive altar of Sigmar had been carved. Unlike the gilt images in most Imperial chapels, it was simple. The stonework was crude. Schwarzhelm could just make out the brooding face of the God-King looming above him. The long-dead sculptor had chosen to accentuate the unforgiving aspect of the Imperial deity. He brooded over the mournful space like a wronged patriarch.

The Emperor sat on a simple chair in the centre of the nave. There was no other furniture in the room. His robes were dark and simple. Like the image of Sigmar above him, he did not smile.

Schwarzhelm approached the chair and bowed. The Emperor said nothing.

'There is an elector in Averland, sire,' said Schwarzhelm. His voice echoed around the vaulted chamber. 'The task has been accomplished.'

Karl Franz nodded. Still he said nothing.

'There is other news.' Schwarzhelm offered him the runefang. The Emperor took it and placed it on his lap. He stared down at the dark blade. In the poor light it looked dull, as if carved from obsidian.

'I know why you bring me this,' said the Emperor. His voice sounded hollow. All the easy diplomatic charm of their last meeting had gone. He looked like a bereaved father.

Schwarzhelm should have known better than to hope he could break the news. Karl Franz had ways of gathering information that were unknown to all but himself.

'I had no choi–'

'There is *always* a choice.' The Emperor's face shook with grief and anger. He locked eyes with Schwarzhelm. In them was grief. Bottomless grief. 'Are you *absolutely sure*? Is there any room for doubt?'

For a heartbeat, Schwarzhelm paused. Of course there was doubt. Every waking moment since the Vormeisterplatz there had been doubt.

'He was fighting for Leitdorf, whose corruption has been verified by those close to him.' As he spoke, the words sounded cold and officious. 'The witch hunters have confirmed what we feared. I am sorry. He was working against us.'

The Emperor stood up. The sword in his lap clanged to the floor, and the echoes ran into the dark recesses of the chamber. He'd never have treated the sacred blade thus had its wearer been present. Besides the loss of Helborg, clearly nothing else mattered.

He walked up to Schwarzhelm. Though his body remained still, his eyes blazed with a cold fire.

'I don't care what the witch hunters say,' he said, his voice low and fervent. 'I've fought with him. You've fought with him. He led my armies. If there is any doubt at all, even the slightest possibility you're wrong–'

Then it was Schwarzhelm's turn to feel the anger boil over within him. He towered over the Emperor. He could understand his grief. They all grieved. He hadn't been there. He hadn't seen the sickness.

'What do you want me to say?' Schwarzhelm cried, balling

his fists impotently. He felt like he wanted to strike out at something. 'I carry out every task you ask of me! Averheim was a den of Chaos. We have rooted it out. The greenskins have been destroyed. A new elector sits on the throne. What more could I have done?'

Karl Franz withdrew half a pace. His eyes betrayed his surprise. No one spoke to him like that.

Schwarzhelm felt his iron-hard voice crack with emotion. 'He was my brother. Do you think, if I didn't believe it...'

Then there was nothing else to say. He saw Helborg's final look again in his mind's eye. *Why are you doing this Ludwig?* The betrayal.

The Emperor didn't reply. He turned slowly, bent down and retrieved the sword. He looked like an old man then, bereft of his habitual assurance. The years had not been kind.

Schwarzhelm stood stiffly, as cold and solid as the columns on either side of him. The silence filled the chamber.

'You're not sure he's dead,' said the Emperor at last.

Schwarzhelm shook his head. 'The Reiksguard took him. The ones he rode with.'

'My Reiksguard. That is something.' The Emperor sat in the chair once more. His expression remained dark. 'If he still lives, he must be taken back alive. I want him brought here. I will examine him. None but I shall examine him. Leitdorf doesn't matter. But Helborg...'

Schwarzhelm felt the old shame return. Like a boy, he'd always been competing with Helborg for his master's attention. Even now, with his rival declared a traitor and struck down, he was still competing.

'You want me to go back?' Schwarzhelm couldn't conceal his hatred of that idea. The Emperor shook his head.

'I think you've done enough, don't you?'

That cut deep. The Emperor seemed to regret it as soon as he said it. He drew in a deep sigh, and looked at the dark blade again.

'You think I'm being harsh on you, Ludwig,' he said softly. 'I do not mean to be. But he was like a son to me. You both were. Even his death in battle would be preferable to this... corruption. While there's the slightest shard of doubt, I'll not let it rest.'

Schwarzhelm hung his head. He wondered how many interrogations had been performed here. The Emperor chose no audience chamber lightly.

'Maybe I have erred,' said the Emperor. 'Your rivalry was useful to me. I liked the fact you competed. It kept you both strong. I should have realised the potential for harm.' He ran a finger down the cold length of the runefang. It paused at the notch in the blade. 'Perhaps he delved too deep for a way to best you. If so, then I am to blame.'

The Emperor looked up at Schwarzhelm. Some of the rage had left his expression, but the grief remained, scored across his face.

'I trust your judgement, Ludwig. I always have. You've done as I asked you. None could have done more. I want you to take some time to yourself now. The war continues in the north. You'll be needed there soon. But do not leave straightaway. I have kept you too busy. You need some rest.'

Schwarzhelm began to protest. Rest was the last thing he needed. The Emperor held a warning hand up.

'Enough. I will not debate this with you. Return to your lodgings in Altdorf. I'll see to the remaining business in Averland. Perhaps I should pay a visit to this Grosslich. Or maybe summon him here.'

He looked directly into Schwarzhelm's eyes. The gaze was not without sympathy, but it was iron-hard.

'I'll call for you when you're recovered. In the meantime, do not leave the city. That is an order.'

Schwarzhelm thought about protesting. There were things he could do, services he could render. He thought of Turgitz, of the greenskins. Without his expertise, the armies of the Empire would be weakened. They'd already lost Helborg.

It was no use. He'd seen similar expressions on the Emperor's face before. As he'd always known, there were some kinds of warfare he would never win at.

'Yes, my liege,' he said, forcing himself to keep his voice level.

There would be no victory parade this time.

Skarr looked down at Helborg's face. The stricken Marshal lay amid piles of the finest goosedown linen. His old bandages, stiff with dried blood, had been taken from him and replaced with fresh ones, expertly wound. Fragrant herbs and salves had been crushed into the wound. Prayers had been said by the priest and passages of holy scripture recited over him.

For the time being at least, it had done no good. Helborg was barely alive. But at least he was off his horse and out of the wilds. It had taken them two days to ride to the first of Leitdorf's safe houses. Then they'd moved on, heading further east after every rumour of Grosslich's pursuit. Now, deep in the countryside, far from the well-travelled roads, they were hidden. For now. The Leitdorfs had more than one great house in Averland, but Grosslich would find them all in the end.

No colour had returned to the Marshal's cheeks. The wounded man looked like one of the undead. Skarr pressed his finger against the carotid, feeling carefully. There was a faint pulse. So faint, it was easy to miss. He was on the border between life and death. Skarr withdrew his hand. Helborg's eyes remained closed. His breathing was thin and ragged.

Skarr stood up from the bed.

The wound on Helborg's cheek had closed at last. After the apothecary had finished, Skarr had taken the shard of the Klingerach and kept it. Probably a useless gesture, but the runefang was sacred. He could sense the ancient metal against his skin as it hung from the chain around his neck.

Skarr withdrew from the bedside. A fire blazed in the hearth even though the sun still shone warmly outside. The apothecary had advised them to keep the room heated. He reached for a log and threw it into the flames. The wood crackled as it settled, spitting sparks.

'What do you think?' asked Leitdorf. The man sat in an

extravagantly upholstered chair in the corner of the room. This whole place was extravagant. His father had clearly had money to waste on it, even though it was just one of many country houses kept in his name. Marius's portrait hung from nearly every wall in the mansion.

'He's strong. But I don't know.' Skarr sat down opposite Rufus. 'How long before Grosslich's men come after you here?'

Leitdorf shrugged.

'There are other places, even more remote. When he can travel, we can move again. None of my people will talk.'

Skarr smiled humourlessly. 'They will, if Grosslich sends interrogators worth anything.'

'We have some time yet. Word has already got out. There are many who'll bear arms for me in this part of the world.'

Skarr suppressed a snort of derision. He placed more faith in his own Reiksguard than in whatever forces Leitdorf could still muster. Still, the safe houses were essential.

'What are you going to do now?' asked Leitdorf.

Skarr paused. He'd given it a great deal of thought as they'd ridden east, away from the harrying of Grosslich's troops. If he'd learned one thing, it was that they were still in mortal danger. For whatever warped reason, the entire province had been raised against them. Schwarzhelm must have been a part of it. That was terrifying enough. If even the Emperor's Champion could turn traitor, then something was horribly awry. He could still see the blood-streaked face, the staring eyes.

'We'll give the Marshal time to heal. I don't know what's happened here to make us fugitives, but I'll not risk harming his recovery.'

'And if he doesn't recover?'

Skarr looked at him darkly.

'If that comes to pass,' he said, choosing his words carefully, 'then I will hunt down the one who has done this. I will hunt him across the Empire, and I will hunt him across the length of the Old World if I have to. And then, Sigmar and the fates willing, I will do to him what he has done to my master.'

Skarr looked at Leitdorf, not bothering to hide the murderous feelings stirring within him.

'Vengeance *will* come. You may count on it.'

Schwarzhelm knocked on the door. Lassus's house was just as he remembered it. Neat, orderly, unassuming. The rest of the Generals' Quarter was similarly unprepossessing. The weather had turned cold and blustery, and the topiary in the generals' gardens looked more fragile than ever.

After a few moments, there was a heavy click as the door was unlocked. Then it swung open, revealing Schwarzhelm's master. Heinrich Lassus looked, if such a thing were possible, a little older. His face was more lined, his skin drier. Only the eyes still gave away his essential vitality. They still glittered with the acute edge that had made him such a feared general in his day.

'So. You're back.'

Schwarzhelm ducked under the lintel.

'I said I'd call.'

'You're always welcome.'

Lassus led him through into one of his private rooms. Leather-bound books lined the uneven walls. A fire burned in the grate. The wooden floor was hidden with a series of fine rugs. Over the mantelpiece hung some mementos of Lassus's time marching under the Emperor's banner. A ceremonial dagger. A fine Boccherino pistol. A beast's skull, lovingly cleaned and hung.

'You were successful, then?' asked Lassus, lowering himself carefully into a low chair. Schwarzhelm sat opposite him. The warmth from the fire was welcome. After so long in the heat of Averland, the damp of Altdorf took some adjusting to.

'Grosslich was appointed. What else have you heard?'

Lassus shrugged. 'Some news came my way. I know there was trouble.'

Schwarzhelm wondered why he'd come. He didn't need

a confessor. Or perhaps he did. The enforced inactivity was driving him to distraction.

'Something like that. Have you heard the news of Helborg?'

'Nothing reliable. He's not been seen here for weeks. I was told he was in Nuln.'

'Then you've not heard. He was implicated in it all. With Leitdorf. There's testimony from the witch hunters.'

Lassus paused.

'What are you saying?'

'That he was a traitor, master. That's what I'm saying.'

A flurry of emotions passed across the old man's face in rapid sequence. Amazement. Disbelief. Anger. Confusion. Schwarzhelm had been there ahead of him. He'd expected nothing less. Helborg had been the golden boy. It would take time for people to get used to the idea.

'You must be mistaken.' The tone was a familiar one. It had been used when Schwarzhelm had made a mistake on the training ground. Or not tried hard enough. Or lied.

'He tried to kill my counsellor. He rode against us in battle. If I'd not been there, he'd have killed Grosslich too.' Schwarzhelm felt suddenly weary. This had been a mistake. He'd not come here to rehearse the arguments again. He'd been running them through his head for days already. 'We fought. The two of us.'

Lassus was looking at him with a kind of horrified, rapt attention.

'And?'

'I'm still here.'

The old man shrunk back in on himself, looking horrified.

'Blessed Sigmar!' he whispered, shaking his head. 'By all the saints.'

'Chaos was at work in Averheim. Leitdorf and his witch were behind it. I don't know how Helborg was dragged in, but it matters little now. They are all destroyed.'

'And Grosslich?'

'He is safe. My agent is still with him. Bloch, my commander, remains in Averland. I'd hoped to join him, to organise the rebuilding. That won't be possible now.'

'Why not?'

'I am forbidden to return. The Emperor wishes me to have nothing more to do with the affair.'

It was only then that Lassus seemed to notice the anguish on his face. Schwarzhelm knew he hid it badly. The trust of the Emperor had been everything to him. The knowledge that it had gone was a bitter taste to take. As bitter as gall.

'I had no idea.'

'Of course not. We spoke in private. I should not be talking to you about any of this.'

'I'm glad you did, Ludwig. Did I not warn you there would be treachery in Averland? But you have prevailed. Can you not take some pleasure in that? You have done what was asked of you.'

Those were the words that were hard to take. Not the scorn, not the criticism. Sympathy was the most painful gift of all.

'But at what price?' Schwarzhelm felt as if he was back on the training fields, holding a sword for the first time. He was sick of the doubt, sick of the uncertainty. It was as if a part of him had been wounded in Averheim and had never truly recovered.

Lassus rose from his chair with difficulty. His hands shook slightly. He limped over to a cabinet on the far side of the room and poured himself a goblet of wine.

'Will you have one?'

Schwarzhelm shook his head. Lassus took a swig, then refilled the goblet. As he retook his seat, the shaking had reduced somewhat.

'I'd not expected this news,' he muttered. 'Helborg gone. Could things be worse?'

'They could. He might not have been discovered. He might be in Averheim with Leitdorf now. With the Emperor's armies occupied in the north, what would there be to stop him? It could have been much worse.'

Lassus nodded and took another sip of wine. 'Of course. You're right. This is much to take in, though. Very much to take in.'

He looked up at Schwarzhelm.

'I'm sure you did the right thing, Ludwig. You've been vindicated by Grosslich's election. You were there. You saw his actions. You saw the message on the parchment. The evidence was before you.'

Schwarzhelm took some comfort from that.

'Indeed,' he said. 'Those were the things that I–'

He stopped.

'What parchment?'

'You said it yourself. On the road to Averheim.'

'I said no such thing.'

Lassus frowned.

'I'm sure you mentioned it. That was the thing that finally confirmed your suspicions, was it not? That's what you told me.'

Schwarzhelm felt a sudden chill strike at his heart. He didn't want to believe it. He couldn't believe it.

'I've not told you of it,' he said, feeling a mounting wave of dread within him. He felt like being sick. 'I've not told anyone of it. Even Verstohlen.'

Lassus seemed suddenly nervous. He let out a weak laugh. 'Well perhaps I did hear from somewhere else. I'm not as young as I used to be. Sometimes I forget.'

Schwarzhelm rose from his seat. His hand crept down to the hilt of the Rechtstahl.

'How could you know that, master?'

Lassus looked scared.

'Sit down, Ludwig,' he snapped. 'Don't tower over me like that in my own house. What are you doing?'

'How could you *possibly* know that?' He suddenly remembered Verstohlen's discovery of the letters. Weeks ago. *Messages have been sent from the castle to Altdorf. It's been going on for some time.* Lassus tried to rise in turn, but his hands were now shaking uncontrollably.

'I think you'd better leave.'

Schwarzhelm felt his confusion begin to crystallise into anger. 'It was you. Of all the horrors. By Sigmar, it was you.'

Then Lassus's face stretched into a snarl. 'Don't be stupid, Ludwig. I've known you since you were a boy! Sit down!'

Schwarzhelm drew the Rechtstahl. The blade slipped from the scabbard easily. As the sword flew out, the steel hummed. The spirit of the weapon was roused. It thirsted.

Lassus staggered back, knocking over his wine. At the sight of the sword his eyes went wide with fear.

'What are you going to do? Kill me? Have you lost your mind?'

Schwarzhelm felt a dark clarity come over him. Though the man made him sick to the pit of his stomach, killing Lassus would solve nothing. There were mysteries here still. The secrets had not been uncovered.

'Kill you?' he said, his voice like scraped steel. 'No. You'll come with me. You know what's been happening here. Your secrets will be wrung from you. Every last one of them. I *will* find out what happened in Averheim.'

At that, Lassus seemed to lose control of himself. His fingers flew to his neck, scraping at his windpipe. He let out a shriek of horror. The dry skin began to crack at the edges of his mouth. He tried to clamber past the chair, out in the hallway beyond.

He was too slow. Schwarzhelm grabbed his cloak with his left hand. It felt like his fingers had closed on a sack of bones.

'Don't do this,' begged Lassus. There were tears of fear in his eyes. 'Kill me if you must, but do not make me talk!'

Schwarzhelm loomed over him, digging his fingers into the frail old man's shoulder. 'Why not?' he hissed. He was angry enough to kill him. It would be better than he deserved, but the truth was more valuable even than vengeance.

For a moment, Lassus stared back at him, lips trembling. His whole body had started shaking. He was in mortal terror.

'She won't let me talk! She won't permit it!'

Schwarzhelm let the wretched figure drop to the floor.

'What do you mean? Who are you talking about?'

But the truth was already becoming apparent. Under Lassus's loose robes, a transformation was taking place. Whatever information he possessed, his dark patron wasn't about to let him divulge it.

Schwarzhelm backed away. He'd seen this happen before. He brought his sword up, ready to strike.

Too late. With a shudder, Lassus's cloak shrunk back on itself. The fabric sucked inwards, like water running down a drain.

Then it exploded. Fragments of cloth spun out in all directions, ripped apart by the detonation at their core. Beneath the shredded fabric, Lassus had disappeared. In his place, an obscene ball of pulsing flesh had appeared. With breathtaking speed, the orb began to change. Growths shot out in different directions, latching on to objects and sucking them into the growing mass. Jaws opened, lined with mucus, then snapped shut and sank beneath the fleshy folds around them. Limbs burst out, wrapping themselves around furniture before snapping off and wriggling blindly back to their origin.

The spawn began to grow. A vast maw, ringed with pin-sharp teeth, opened up in its midriff. Eyes popped out all around it, hundreds of them. They glowed purple. The flesh around them was as white as teeth and ink-dark veins throbbed under the surface.

Lassus had gone. His mistake had been a costly one.

Schwarzhelm pulled the Rechtstahl back, preparing the strike. It was hard to know what to aim for.

'Do not cut me!' cried the spawn. The voice was like Lassus's. It sounded as if he was still there, buried deep within the flexing glands.

Schwarzhelm ignored the pleas. There was nothing he could have done to save him even if he'd wanted to. And he didn't want to.

The Sword of Justice arced downwards. As it bit into the mutating flesh, a foul stench burst from the bulging sacs. Sharp musk spurted into the air, splattering against the walls.

The spawn screamed. Tentacles, each laced with purple barbs, shot out from the heart of the maw. They latched on to Schwarzhelm's clothes, clutching and binding. He swung round, tearing them free, slicing the hooks from his leather jerkin and cloak.

'You killed Helborg!' screamed the spawn from mouths that rapidly formed and then closed again. 'You killed him, Schwarzhelm!'

Schwarzhelm ploughed towards the heart of the tentacle swarm, hacking each one down as it snaked towards him. For every barb that was cut down, two more shot out, aiming for his eyes, his throat, his fingers.

Schwarzhelm held his ground, letting the sword find its path through the flailing lengths of extended flesh. He had to keep calm. The thoughts rushing through his head weren't helping. This was no longer the Lassus he knew. Perhaps that man had died long ago. All that lay before him was a twisted amalgam of dark magic and ruined matter.

The contest continued for some time, but then the swarm abated. One by one, the tendrils fell to the ground, either severed or withdrawn. The orb of flesh remained, shivering and weeping. The maw was there too, surrounded by eyes. As it drooled, the pupils popped in and out.

'Very good,' mocked the voice. It sounded scraped and warped, as if the vocal cords within were undergoing radical rearrangement. 'You've been taught well.'

Schwarzhelm ignored the taunts.

'Why?' he said, keeping the blade high, watching the remaining tentacles as they slithered across the floor.

'Who are you asking? Heinrich Lassus? He's in here. But not much of him. His soul has been taken to another place.'

'But you know why he did it.'

'Of course. I know many things.'

'Who are you?'

The maw expanded rapidly, and a choking sound slopped out of it. The flesh flapped and fresh eyes burst out across the moving skein. That might have been something like a laugh.

'You know who I am. I've been in your dreams for weeks. Your mind is an interesting one, Schwarzhelm. So full of anger. If you knew the damage those emotions caused, I doubt you would think so highly of yourself.'

Schwarzhelm began to advance once again. He knew not to listen to the ravings of a spawn. Perhaps the speaker was a fracture of Lassus's consciousness. Or maybe something worse. Whatever it was, only a fool listened to the blandishments of Chaos.

'I will discover the truth behind this,' he said, choosing his moment to attack with care. The spawn, seeing the blade come nearer, withdrew in on itself again.

'Be careful what you wish for. The truth can help you, or it can drive you mad. Which do you want?'

'Neither. I wish to uphold the law.'

'As you did in Averheim, then! I look forward to mocking your failure. Just as you have done already. Helborg is dead, and his soul is in torment. You have ruined Averland, Emperor's Champion. Soon daemons will roost in the eaves of the Averburg and the streets will be lined with screams. This is all your doing. You were our instrument. You were our tool! Hail, herald of Chaos! The Lord of Pleasure salutes you!'

That was enough. Schwarzhelm let rip at last, swinging the Rechtstahl with ferocious abandon. Ignoring the fresh tentacles sent darting in his direction, he hacked and thrashed at the disgusting bag of slime and sinew. The blade rose and fell with astonishing speed and power. There was no pretence at precision, no semblance of control. Like a farmer with the grain flails, he surged through the spawn's defences, cutting down everything that reached for him.

As the blade carved through the gelatinous surface of the orb, the maw split in several pieces. One mouth let out an unearthly screaming. The others grew spine-like fangs and snapped at him.

Schwarzhelm went straight for the mouths, plunging the sword into each one in turn. Blood the colour of sapphires and garnets spurted out, drenching his hands and chest. Where it touched naked skin it burned like hot wax. He ignored it.

The spawn began to weaken. Its vital essence sluiced across the floor, splashing up against the walls. What little coherence it possessed began to dissipate. Schwarzhelm didn't relent. He whirled the sword in tighter circles, cutting through the trembling miasma. He was soaked in foul-smelling fluid. The tentacle barbs had lefts welts on his hands and neck. His exposed flesh was scored with pinpricks from where the teeth had bitten.

All were superficial wounds. None of them mattered. Soon the spawn could no longer muster even token attacks. Its flesh slopped from the edge of the Rechtstahl like slurry. The eyes went dark, hard and rolled across the floor like marbles. The screaming subsided to a whimper.

In the end, all that remained amid the pools of liquid was a quivering pile of semi-transparent muscles and sinew. Twisted blood vessels curved around a mockery of a heart. There were a few tufts of human hair and what might once have been a voice box. All of it was distorted and perverted. Even as Schwarzhelm watched, the pathetic creature tried to mutate further, to shape itself into some kind of viable form. It looked like it was trying to speak again. The voice box trembled, and new sinews formed on its outer reaches. Something like a fluted mouth began to emerge.

Schwarzhelm raised the Sword of Justice a final time. The edge glinted. He plunged the tip down. It pierced the heart. The remainder of what had been the spawn burst open. In the centre of the pools of plasma and fluid lay a single object. Lassus's Star of Sigmar. The small iron token lay amid the filth like a mockery.

Ignoring the stench, Schwarzhelm picked it up and cleaned the slime from its surface. He looked down at the reeking mire contemptuously.

'For the Lassus I knew,' he said.

There was no time for either anger or mourning. Schwarzhelm's mind worked quickly. A clarity had descended over him. There were things he had to do.

He retrieved the decanter of wine from where it lay, still

intact and half-full. He poured the contents over the jellied remains of the spawn. He didn't think of Helborg. To do so now would be fatal. The time for remorse would come later. He left the room, heading for the chamber on the next floor.

Schwarzhelm swept through the narrow house, uprooting chests, emptying boxes, lifting up floorboards. As he did so, the remains of the spawn gurgled in isolation. The fluids ran between the cracks in the floor, seeping into the rugs, pooling in the dark places under the finery.

Eventually, after much searching, Schwarzhelm took only one item from its place. An old iron key, found in a rosewood box under Lassus's austere single bed. Perhaps it meant nothing. Perhaps it didn't. There was nothing else of any note.

With that done, he returned to the lower chamber. Everything was as he'd left it. The spawn continued to gurgle. Slowly, unbelievably, some of the liquids were beginning to coalesce again. Schwarzhelm took a flint and struck a spark on to the oily pool of wine and plasma. The mixture kindled immediately, throwing off a strong scent of jasmine.

Schwarzhelm didn't wait to see the results. Making sure he had the Star of Sigmar and the key with him, he turned on his heel and walked from the room. Behind him the flames caught quickly. On the edge of hearing, he thought he could hear the ghost of screams, an old man crying out in agony.

He kept walking. As he left the house, smoke began to curl from the upper window.

Schwarzhelm passed from the General's Quarter and headed for the river. A kind of cold resignation had seized him. The guilt was finally rushing back. He saw Helborg's face. *Why are you doing this, Ludwig?*

Because of the deception. Because the great enemy clouded all things.

Because they'd known how to exploit the jealousy that lay there already, untouched, ready to be used.

He reached the river. The water was thick, grey and fast moving. Rain whipped at the surface, mottling the surface scum into foam. Far out, industrial barges plied their heavy trade. On the other side, half-lost in the haze of rain and smoke, factories rose into the air. Their brown smoke rose into the polluted air, adding to the stain of the elements. Everything was tainted, old, tired.

His emotions surged through him, as fluid as the spawn's flesh. It had been Lassus, not Helborg. *Lassus*.

Schwarzhelm stared into the water for a long time. The brown water stared back. The torrent was heavy, bolstered by the storms upriver. He wouldn't last long. Not even he, the Emperor's Champion, defender of the Empire, mightiest general of the Old World. His heavy jerkin would drag him down. The silt would clog his lungs.

He carried on staring. The quayside was deserted. A chill wind, laced with rain, gusted at his coat.

Then his hands slipped to the pommel of the Sword of Justice. His fingers closed around the hilt. He drew it. The metal glinted grey in the filthy light. The insignia of the comet glistened along the long blade.

It was ancient. It had been wielded long before he'd been born. It would be carried on to the field of battle long after he'd gone. His only task was to be a good steward, to carry it faithfully in the time allotted to him.

Schwarzhelm drew the steel surface closer to him. He could see his reflection looking back at him. His expression was savage. The lines of loss were still vivid. All those he'd been close to had gone. He'd been wrong. He had failed. He was alone.

So be it.

He sheathed the sword once more. With a final, parting shot at the mighty Reik, he turned away from the torrent. Any man could fall into error. The test was what he did to rectify it.

As he strode, Schwarzhelm felt some sense of purpose return. His limbs regained some vigour. His mighty heart began to beat again with strength.

He would use the key. He would find a way to contact Verstohlen. He would return to Averheim somehow. He would seek out Helborg, if he still lived. There was atonement to be made. Restitution. Forgiveness.

He had to go back. Schwarzhelm now knew he'd been wrong about many things, but one above all. He'd thought the battle for the soul of Averheim had been averted, that the corruption had been cut off at source. That was what he'd tried to achieve.

It was not so. His master's house was burning. People rushed out to see the blaze, gawping and gesturing like puppets. He ignored them. As he strode past the smouldering wreckage and back to the centre of the Imperial capital, he knew the truth of it at last.

The war for Averland had only just begun.

SWORD OF VENGEANCE

CHAPTER ONE

Running didn't help. They were faster, unnaturally faster, and they didn't give up. Anna-Helena tore round the corner of the old bakery, dragging snatched breaths into her overworked lungs, her fingers scratching against the stone as she grabbed at it. The alley beyond was dark, far darker than it should have been. She couldn't see the end of it. Panicked, she started to twist back around.

Then they were on her. Three of them, wheezing like animals. She broke free of the first grasp, hearing the fabric of her dress rip and come away in shreds. There was nowhere to go but further down into the shadows, away from the horror, deeper into the cool valley between the silent buildings.

'Mercy of Sigmar!' came a voice, her own, shrill and panicked, on the edge of hysteria. The sound sank deep into the uncaring stone. There was no one awake to hear her, no one to come to her aid. It had been foolish, *stupid*, to cross the river after dark. She'd heard the stories. Everyone had. But the woman with the deep eyes had whispered such kind words, and she'd promised root.

Her bare feet, criss-crossed with lacerations, made no sound as she sprinted across the filthy cobbles. Her fear made her fast, even as her tattered dress hugged at her thighs.

Not fast enough. She felt the first grip dig in deep, talons sinking into the flesh of her shoulder. She was pulled up, dragged back. She whirled round, ignoring the pain, trying to shake them off. Her heart raced out of control, flooding her body with hot, terrified blood.

'Get off me!' Her voice was almost bestial with horror, the cry of a prey animal.

Another of them seized her other shoulder, pinning her down. Their weight was crushing, forcing her to her knees. She fought back, panting and ineffectual. A blank helmet gazed down at her, distended into a muzzle. Broken wheezing came from behind the closed grille.

'What are you?' she sobbed, slumping in defeat as the grip tightened. They towered over her, the three of them, saying nothing, holding her down. 'Love of Sigmar, what *are* you?'

A fourth man appeared then, walking between them. She'd not seen him earlier. He was short, hunched-over with age. He had the grey skin of a scholar and black rings around his deep-set eyes. He pushed one of her pursuers aside and grabbed her chin, holding her face up to the scant moonlight. She gazed, trembling, into a cold and pitiless face.

'Let me *be...*' she protested, feeling hot tears run down her cheeks.

The man ignored her, pinching her flesh and rocking her face from side to side. He was looking at her like a housewife buying fruit, assessing suitability.

'She'll do,' he said at last. He had a thin, scraping voice. 'At last, we have three of them.'

She was dragged to her feet by the helmeted warriors. They started to haul her back down the alley, back the way they'd come, back to the building site and its hidden workings.

'Where are you taking me?' she screamed, jerking pointlessly against their iron-hard clutches.

The hunched man smiled sadly at her. It had been spirited

of her, to run, but not much more than that. None of them got far.

'Into another world, my child,' he whispered, watching her disappear back into the night. 'Into another world.'

Averland had sweltered under the beating sun for too long, and the weather had turned at last. Cold air tumbled down from the peaks of the Worlds Edge Mountains, ruffling the long grass of the plains and stirring the waters of the rivers. The herds of cattle felt it as they grazed, as did the peasants in their hovels. The wind had changed.

Averheim looked perfectly serene in the golden light of the afternoon. The recent battles in its alleyways and squares had done little to dent the facades of the elegant streets. More damage had been caused by the months of dereliction beforehand, during which men had lain in the streets half-sensible, their mouths open and drooling from joyroot. Back then thoroughfares had succumbed to piles of filth, and sewage had been left to gather in the heat, crawling with flies. Now discipline had returned, and the drift of the past was being expunged.

After his coronation, Heinz-Mark Grosslich had moved his seat of power from the ancestral Alptraum castle to the Averburg, the ancient citadel that dominated the east bank of the river. Now the gold-rimmed device of the boar's head hung from every battlement. Signs of conflict, most notably in the Vormeisterplatz, had been scrubbed clean by an army of drudges. The fires had gone. Companies of armed men walked the streets at night, the merchant guilds had come back, and trade along the river had returned.

Dagobert Tochfel, Steward of the Averburg, walked down the wide avenue from the citadel to the Griffon Bridge, the oldest crossing over the river. He could smell the water as he drew near, dank and cool. The worst of the scum on its surface had been cleared away and the barges had come back. As he went along the quayside, he could see at least a dozen of them, jostling and bumping as they jockeyed for position by the warehouses.

He allowed himself a smile of satisfaction. The days had been hard, and the memories bad. Like everyone else, he needed to believe the worst of it was over. Every sign of renewal was seized upon, welcomed and documented. Averheimers wanted their city back. They wanted their lives back.

Tochfel's skin was now a shade less grey, his eyelids a little less red, but he still had the hunched look of a scholar. His life before the affair with Schwarzhelm had been dominated by parchment ledgers and legal depositions. It was much the same now. Rulers might come and go, but the real business of governing changed little.

Ahead of him, dressed in the crimson and gold of the Grosslich hierarchy, Captain Erasmus Euler was busy overseeing the unloading. A dozen of his men lounged nearby, their halberds casually leaning against the warehouse walls. The scene was relaxed. Merchants haggled in small groups around them, exchanging bills of lading.

Tochfel walked up to the nearest barge, the *Rosalinde*. She was ugly, dark and low in the water. Most of her crew were ashore. The cargo was obvious – building materials, and lots of them. Every day brought a fresh consignment from somewhere. Granite from the mines in the east, marble from Sartosa, iron from Nuln. Averheim was sucking it in, and Tochfel didn't even want to think about how much it was costing. It wasn't on his ledger, and that was the important thing.

'Good day, Herr Euler,' he said, waving to the captain.

Tochfel thought he caught a flash of irritation on the man's face.

'Good day to you, Steward,' Euler said, handing a sheaf of documents to one of his men. 'What can I do for you?'

'Thought I'd take a look at how the project's coming on. Even I feel stale eventually, cooped up in the citadel.'

'It's going fine.' Euler's voice was semi-hostile, but Tochfel was prepared to cut him a good deal of slack. Before Grosslich's elevation, the man had barely commanded more than a dozen men. Now he was in charge of hundreds.

The Steward looked out across the river. Behind the *Rosalinde* there were two more barges in line for the berth. More were visible under the wide arches of the Griffon Bridge. The queuing had become a problem. 'How many more are we expecting this week?'

'Couldn't say. Get used to it, Steward. They'll be coming in for weeks.'

Tochfel gave a rueful look. 'Oh, I am used to it, captain. Though I can't pretend I don't have my concerns.' He checked to see if Euler was in a tolerant mood. He'd heard the man had developed a temper. 'These landings are used for more than building materials. There are supplies for the citadel that are now two weeks late.'

'Then land them further down.'

'I would do so, Herr Euler, if you could show me one clear berth. The elector's project – important as it no doubt is – seems to have taken things over somewhat.'

He tried to keep his voice deliberately light – there was no point in provoking a fight over this. Euler ran his fingers through his hair. He looked tired.

'Things have changed,' he said. 'There's business you're not in command of any more. You'll have to talk to the elector yourself.'

'You think I haven't tried that? I can't get near him. I can't even get near to Herr Alptraum, whom I've now not seen for over two weeks. I thought perhaps this might be best coming from you.'

For a moment, just a moment, there was a flicker of fear in Euler's eyes. Tochfel could see the hollowness in his cheeks, the tightness around his mouth.

'The elector's busy. If you want to bother him with this, then feel free. I've got more important things to see to.'

Tochfel decided to take that as a warning. It was a troubling thought. If even men like Euler disliked bringing things to Grosslich's attention, then dealing with the elector would be difficult. For all the stories they told about Marius Leitdorf, he'd at least known how to keep trade flowing along the river.

'I see,' was all he said. He turned to look across the water. Half a mile distant, peeping over the crowded roofs of the poor quarter, was the object of all this work. With astonishing speed, Grosslich's grand project was going ahead. The wooden scaffolding was already higher than the buildings around it. Beneath the cages of oak, the frame was starting to take shape.

Tochfel couldn't suppress a shudder of distaste. Of course, he didn't know what it would look like when complete, but the early signs weren't promising. What kind of an architect came up with a tower made entirely of iron? Perhaps it would all become clear later. Perhaps he'd be surprised by it.

He hoped so. Just for once, it would be nice for the surprises to be good ones.

Heinz-Mark Grosslich sat on the electoral throne in the audience chamber of the Averburg. He was draped in crimson and the crown of his office sat heavily on his brow. The late afternoon sun slanted through the narrow windows, bathing the dark wood of the walls. As with every part of the citadel, banners with the Grosslich device hung along the room's flanks. The more traditional emblems of Averland and Solland were nowhere to be seen.

There were two other men present with him. At his side sat Schwarzhelm's aide, the spy Pieter Verstohlen. He was dressed in his habitual garb – a long leather coat, waistcoat and breeches, linen shirt, all beautifully tailored. His slender, handsome face gave little away.

Grosslich avoided making eye contact with him. The man's continuing presence was an irritation. Schwarzhelm's leftovers would have to be dealt with at some stage, but for now the need for a respectable front remained acute. The eyes of Altdorf were on him. The eyes of the Empire were on him.

That fact was demonstrated by the presence of the second man. A messenger from the Imperial Palace, kneeling on the stone not five yards from him. It had taken longer than Grosslich had expected, but had been bound to happen eventually. This was the beginning, the start of the tussle between elector and elected. Even if he'd been an ordinary provincial governor with ordinary provincial aspirations, the balance of power between Altdorf and Averheim was always fraught.

But he was no ordinary governor, and his ambitions went beyond anything the Emperor was capable of imagining. Soon even Karl Franz would realise it.

'Rise,' he drawled.

The messenger clambered to his feet. He was armoured and wore the red and white Palace livery. His tunic was emblazoned with the Imperial griffon, and he carried a heavy sword at his belt. The man's grey hair was cropped close to the grizzled scalp, his shoulders were broad, and he looked like he knew how to use his weapon. A knight, then, seconded to the Palace's messenger corps. When he looked at Grosslich, there was no fear in his seasoned eyes.

'I bring word from His Most Imperial Highness, Emperor Karl Franz I von Holswig-Schliestein, Grand Prince of Altdorf, Count of the Reikland, Protector of the Empire.'

'That's nice,' said Grosslich. He felt Verstohlen stiffen slightly at his side. Perhaps he should resist the temptation to mock. The vermin around him needed humouring for a little while longer, as tedious as it was to do so.

'The Emperor has instructed me to congratulate your lordship on the succession to the throne, achieved though it was at such a high price. As war has conspired to prevent an assemblage of the Estates in recent months, his highness begs me to enquire of your lordship when your entourage intends to travel to the Palace, so that his highness may pay his respects in person.'

The stilted language was that of Imperial diplomacy, and to the untrained ear might have sounded like a gentle request. Grosslich was worldly enough to know what it really conveyed: he was being summoned to Altdorf. Karl Franz wanted to see if his intervention in Averland had brought him what he wanted.

'Convey to his highness my profound thanks for his gracious concern,' replied Grosslich. 'He'll be aware of the difficult circumstances of my inauguration. The traitors who conspired to ruin this province remain free from capture. There is work to be done on the city, and need for more men under arms. I trust he'll understand that I cannot leave the city for the foreseeable future. When all is placed in order, I'll be honoured to accept his magnanimous invitation.'

The messenger remained stony-faced. He could interpret the response as well as any of them. Grosslich might as well have told the Emperor to run along back to his stinking Palace and wait for him to turn up in his own sweet time. Grosslich allowed himself to enjoy the moment.

'May I ask your lordship if there might be a more... precise indication of how long the work will take? You'll appreciate that the Emperor has many and pressing concerns of his own, and his highness has a personal interest in bringing this to a satisfactory conclusion.'

The translation being: think carefully what you're doing. Karl Franz doesn't tolerate insolence from anyone. He helped put you here, he can help remove you too.

The naïveté was almost touching.

'When Helborg is dead and the Leitdorfs are on the rack,' said Grosslich, speaking deliberately, 'then I will come.'

For the first time, a shade of disapproval coloured the messenger's face.

'No doubt you remember the order made by his highness concerning the Lord Helborg. He is to be recovered alive.'

'Yes, I noted the request. If it falls within my power, Helborg shall be preserved.' He gave the messenger a sly look. 'If it falls within my power,' he repeated.

There was a pause.

'I understand. This shall be conveyed.'

Grosslich didn't reply, and his silence concluded the appointment. The messenger bowed and backed down the length of the audience chamber, never turning his face away from the dais. As he reached the heavy double doors at the far end, they opened soundlessly and he withdrew.

'So what did you make of that?' asked Grosslich, turning to Verstohlen with a satisfied smile.

The spy didn't look amused. 'A dangerous game to play. I don't see the advantage in goading Karl Franz.'

Grosslich laughed. 'Ever cautious, Verstohlen,' he said. 'That's good. It's what I employ you for.'

'You don't employ me.'

'Ah. Sometimes I forget. Perhaps you'd better remind me what your intentions are here. I get used to having you around.'

'As soon as I hear from Schwarzhelm, I'll let you know,' said Verstohlen. 'I find it odd that I haven't had word already.'

Grosslich kept his impatience well concealed. Verstohlen's usefulness had long since expired. If he didn't find a reason to leave the city soon, then something might have to be done.

'Until then, your counsel will be invaluable,' he said.

'Any news of Leitdorf?'

'Which one?'

'Either.'

'There have been reports of Rufus from the east,' said Grosslich. 'I have men on his trail, but the country is wild and we can't cover everything. Don't worry. It's only a matter of time. Their power is broken.'

Verstohlen shot him an irritated look. 'So you evidently believe. But time has passed, and evil seeds will spring up anew.'

Grosslich found himself getting bored of the man's piety. Verstohlen had no idea about the potential of evil seeds. No idea at all.

'We'll redouble our efforts,' he said, looking as earnest about it as he could. 'The traitors will be found, and justice will be done. Believe me – no one wants the Leitdorf line terminated more than I, and it *will* happen.'

Markus Bloch leaned on his halberd and shaded his eyes against the harsh sun. He was high in the passes of the

Worlds Edge Mountains, far from the warmth of Averheim. Around him the granite pinnacles reared high into the empty airs, heaped on top of one another like the ramparts of some ancient citadel of giants. To the north and south, the summits soared even higher, crowned with snow the whole year round, glistening and sparkling under the open sky. The passes were clear, though the air was still bitter. It didn't matter how balmy the summers were in the land below; here, it was always winter.

The army he'd brought to the mountains with such labour was installed a few miles away in one of the scattered way-forts that lined the road to Black Fire Pass. Even though the way-forts were capacious, many of the lower ranks had been forced to camp in the shadow of its walls. He had over two thousand men under his command, the kind of force that only Black Fire Keep could accommodate with ease.

The place where he stood was far from the road and the way-forts. It was a desolate spot, a patch of wind-blasted stone in the heart of the peaks. A wide flat area, perhaps four hundred yards across, was bounded on three sides by sheer cliffs, cracked with age and flecked with mottled lichens. The piercing sun made little impression on it, and there was a dark aspect to the rocks.

Bloch didn't speak for a long time. This was the third such site he'd been shown. It never got any better.

He turned to his companion, the mountain guard commander Helmut Drassler. The man was tall and rangy, and like all his kind wore a beard and was dressed in furs. Drassler looked over the site with a kind of blank distaste. After seeing so many of them, perhaps there was little other reaction.

Aside from Bloch and Drassler, only Kraus, Schwarzhelm's honour guard captain, was present. His expression was as hard, cold and unreadable as his master's.

'This one's the worst,' muttered Bloch. Drassler nodded, saying nothing.

The site was a natural killing place. The cliffs on all sides turned it into a cauldron of death. For any forces out in the

middle of it, there was only one escape – back through the
narrow gap where the three of them stood. If that route were
blocked, then there could be no hope for any trapped within.

So it had proved for the men lying on the stone in front
of them. They had been dead for a long time. Their skin had
been dried and bleached by the wind and hung in tatters
from exposed bone. Their eyes had long gone, taken by the
scavengers of the high places. Even now, carrion crows circled
in the icy airs, waiting to feast again. The banner of Averland, crested with the golden sun of Solland, hung limply
against the far cliff. The standard was surrounded by heaps
of bodies, as if that was where they'd made their last stand.

It hadn't done them much good. Obscene images had
been daubed across the precious fabric, obscuring the proud
record of past conflicts. The figure of the sun had been transformed into the leering face of a corrupted moon.

Bloch couldn't tell how many bodies lay there. Hundreds, certainly. Probably far more. The way they lay atop
one another, rammed together in death as they had been in
their final hours, made it hard to tell.

'They took plenty with them,' said Kraus.

That they had. For every man who lay on the stone, there
was an orc too. The greenskins' flesh had weathered better.
The two armies were intertwined with one another, locked
in an embrace that had lasted far longer than the fighting.

Despite the numbers of dead greenskins, it was clear who
had won. The human bodies had been despoiled and their
armour plundered. There were signs that goblins had crawled
down the cliffs like swarming insects, no doubt raining barbs
down on top of the defenders. One goblin corpse still hung
forty feet up, its hand trapped in a crack, its lifeless body
twisting in the wind.

It would have been a massacre. The soldiers must have
known they were going to die. They would have fought for
pride, but nothing else.

Bloch felt sickened. Just like the other sites Drassler had
shown them. They'd come up here to be killed.

'*Why?*' he said, bitterly, not expecting any better answers than last time. 'Why leave the forts? These places are murder-traps.'

'I told you,' said Drassler. 'We had orders. You'll see it all at the Keep.'

Bloch shook his head despairingly. He hadn't been a commander long, but he'd fought in the Emperor's armies all his adult life and knew how they worked. There were some orders you didn't follow.

He crouched down and took a closer look at the bodies near his feet. The corpses of the Black Fire Keep garrison stretched away across the site, their clothes torn and flesh rent. Empty eye sockets gazed up at the sky, laced with dry, crusted blood.

He wasn't interested in them. He was interested in the orcs. Before him lay one of the smaller breeds. Perhaps a large goblin – it had the hook nose and long yellow fangs of the kind. It had been skewered on the tip of a sword and the blade still stood, lodged in its scrawny chest. Dead claws clutched at the air, locked in the final throes of agony.

Bloch studied its armour. Like all the greenskins it was wearing close-fitting mail. It had been carrying a short sword of its own rather than a gouge or a flail. The workmanship was good. Just as with the orcs he'd encountered in Averland while serving under Grunwald, the greenskins had excellent wargear. Imperial wargear.

He shuffled forwards and took a closer look at the creature's face. Even in death it had a horrifying aspect. A long black tongue lolled from its cruel mouth, and its thin face was set into a scream of rage. The expression was so vivid, so locked in malice, it was hard to believe that some flicker of life didn't still exist within it.

The sun flashed from something shiny. Dangling from the goblin's earlobe was a coin. Bloch pulled it from the flesh and it popped free. An Imperial schilling, embossed with the image of Karl Franz and stamped with the date and place of manufacture. It was new, minted in Altdorf that year. Coins like that were rare – they took time to come into circulation. All the ones he'd seen in the death-sites were the same. Somehow, this horde of orcs had come across Imperial armour and a batch of newly-minted coins.

He stood up again, keeping the schilling in his hand.

'Same as before?' asked Kraus.

'Same as before.'

Bloch turned to Drassler. 'I've seen enough of this. We'll head to the Keep.'

'They're still camped in there,' warned Drassler. 'I don't know how many.'

'I don't care how many,' growled Bloch, clenching his fist around the coin and squeezing it tight. 'We'll kill 'em all.'

CHAPTER TWO

The Iron Tower was not the only building being raised in Averheim, but it was by far the largest. A whole district of the poor quarter had been scoured to allow its creation. Some of the demolished houses and streets had dated back to the time of the first Emperors, before the city had grown large enough to reach over the river and absorb the villages along the western bank. They were gone now, mere whispers in the long march of Imperial history.

The building work had taken place quickly. So quickly that men marvelled at it as far afield as Streissen and Nuln. Though the Leitdorfs and the Alptraums between them had erected plenty of follies in their long years of rule, each had taken years to complete. In a matter of weeks, the Iron Tower's foundations had been laid and the skeleton metal frame had shot up into the sky.

Despite the wonders of engineering, the Tower was not popular. Soon after work had started, ordinary folk of the poor quarter had learned to give it a wide berth. Few willingly walked under the shadow of the great iron spurs that marked out its future outline. Any who had to pass close by scratched the sign of the comet on their chests. It had an evil rumour, and in private many started to call it Grosslich's Folly.

No one knew for certain *why* the Tower was so hated. After all, the new elector was wildly popular. Order had been restored to the city, and the gold was flowing again through the merchants' coffers. It was even hissed in quiet corners that joyroot could be found again, though its trade had been heavily curtailed.

Still, the stories kept coming. A baby had been born in sight of the Tower with three arms and no eyes. Milk curdled across the city when the foundation stone had been laid. No birds would fly within a mile of it, they said, turning Averheim silent at dawn and dusk. All fanciful tales, no doubt. All unreliable, plucked from the gossipy lips of old wives with nothing better to do.

But the world was a strange place, and old wives weren't always wrong. What no one could deny was that, from time to time, attractive youths were still going missing. Not many – just one or two, here and there – but enough to attract attention. That had been going on even before the days of the Tower, and folk had put it down to the evil times with no elector. Grosslich had even issued an edict on the matter, promising death for any found engaged in the grisly removal of Averland's next generation.

It didn't stop the disappearances. Like the slow drip of a tap, they carried on. It was worse around the Tower, some said. Many believed the rumours, even though there was no proof. It was all hearsay, conjecture and idle talk.

Heinz-Mark Grosslich, still dressed in the robes he'd worn to receive the Imperial messenger, found himself enjoying the irony of it all as he headed towards the Tower. The foolish, the ignorant and the savage were quite capable of seeing what was going on under their noses. Only the wise were blind to the horror that lurked around them. Blind, that is, until it was far too late.

Night had fallen. The Tower building site was heavily guarded by men of the elector's inner circle, loyal soldiers who'd seen the fight against Leitdorf through from the beginning. As he approached the perimeter of the works, Grosslich saw half a dozen of them leap to attention. They looked surprised to see him walking on his own. They shouldn't have been. He'd been back and forth between the Tower and the Averburg several times a day for the past couple of weeks. When the work was completed it would become the new seat of power in Averland. The Averburg would have to go. The city needed a fresh start, a new way of doing things.

He nodded to the guards as he passed their cordon and entered the site. None of them would ever go further inside – their job was to patrol the fences. That didn't mean the interior was unguarded, just that the guards there were of a more specialised type.

Once past the fences, the building came into view properly. It had the appearance of an upturned claw. Huge iron shafts had been sunk into the earth, on top of which the structure was now being raised. When finished, the Tower would resemble a giant dark needle, soaring up into the high airs and dominating the land around it. There would be a turret at the very pinnacle sending six spikes out over the cityscape, each twenty feet long. At the centre of those spikes would be his sanctum, far above the rolling plains. That would be the heart of it all, the fulcrum about which the realm would be moulded to his will.

There was still so much to do. The lower levels of the Tower were little more than a tangle of naked metal. Piles of beams, trusses, stone blocks, nails, rods and other paraphernalia littered the churned-up earth. The disarray offended Grosslich's refined senses, and he made a mental note to order the workers to take more care.

As he neared the centre of the works, a door loomed up out of the darkness. It was imposing – over twelve feet tall and nearly as wide – and decorated with friezes of pure, dark iron. Here and there, a face of tortured agony could be made out in the night air, lost in a morass of limbs and torsos. The iron doors themselves were covered in a filigree of sigils and unholy icons, all traced with formidable skill and delicacy. Grosslich had no idea what they all signified, but he knew he would soon. His abilities increased with every passing day.

The wall behind the door was barely started and rose no more than a few feet above the iron frame. Beyond it, the bone-like scaffolding was obvious. It was a door that seemingly led nowhere. And yet, for all that, it was guarded by two heavily-armoured soldiers. They wore strange armour, quite unlike the standard gear his men in the citadel were given. Each was clad in a suit of segmented plates, glossy and polished. The soldiers carried double-bladed halberds, though the steel had been replaced with what looked like polished crystal. Both were short and stocky and stood strangely, as if their legs bent the wrong way and their shoulders had been dragged out of place. Most disconcertingly, their closed-face helmets had long snouts, carved in the shape of snarling dog's muzzles. No unaltered human could have fitted into those helms. These were Natassja's creatures, the product of her endless experimentation.

As he gazed on her progeny, Grosslich felt a surge of love for Natassja bloom up within him. She was everything to him, the one who had taken him from a minor landowner in the border country with Stirland and turned him into the most powerful man in the province. Her imagination and beauty were beyond those of anyone he had ever met. Particularly her imagination.

'Open the doors,' he said. The soldiers complied without speaking, though there was a strained wheezing from their helmets. So many of them died after having the alterations made. That was a shame, but a small price to pay for art.

The iron doors swung inwards, revealing a staircase that plunged down into the foundations of the Tower. The smell of jasmine, Natassja's smell, rose up from the opening. There were other delights too, such as the pleasing chorus of screams, just on the edge of hearing. Things were so much better now that she had the time and freedom to truly give rein to her inclinations. This was just a foretaste of what was to come. Soon, the screams would be ringing out across all Averland.

Grosslich smiled and descended into the depths of the Tower. Behind him, the doors clanged closed.

Ludwig Schwarzhelm finished writing and placed the quill next to the parchment. He sat back in his chair, rolled his massive shoulders to relieve the ache, and looked up from his desk.

The walls of his study in Altdorf looked alien in the candlelight. He'd hardly visited it in the past decade of constant campaigning. Now they were an indictment of him. He'd been ordered to stay in them, to keep out of Imperial affairs for as long as it took the Emperor to forgive him for what had happened. However long that might be.

The rooms were minimally furnished. Most men of his rank would have lived in opulent state chambers, attended to by scores of servants and surrounded by priceless treasures from across the known world. That had never been his way. His dwellings were close to the Palace, but they were simple. He had a single manservant to keep an eye on the place when he was on campaign and employed the services of an aged charwoman, the mother of one of the many men who'd died serving under his command. They were both devoted to him, but since coming back from Averland he'd found he could hardly look them in the eye. He was diminished, and felt the shame of it keenly.

Night air gusted through the shutters. The fire had burned low in the grate. The rain continued to plague the city, and he could hear the constant drum of it outside. He'd been working for hours, and was not an eloquent scribe. Composing the letter to the Emperor had taken him the best part of the day and all of the evening. Even now he wasn't sure everything was ordered correctly. He found himself wishing Verstohlen was around. He'd have been able to advise. He'd always been able to advise.

Schwarzhelm brushed sand over the parchment and folded it up. He slipped it into an envelope, reached for the candle of sealing wax and tipped a gobbet of it on the join. As the wax hardened he pulled his personal seal from the drawer at his side. That too was hard to look at. The Sword of Justice entwined with the Imperial seal atop the initials L.S. Once it had been a source of pride to him. Now, like everything else, it had been sullied.

He pressed the seal onto the wax, watching as the red fluid solidified, then placed the letter on the desk in front of him. Beside it was the key he'd taken from Heinrich Lassus's house. It had taken a while for him to discover which lock it opened, but he still had friends in the city. The old traitor had been careful, but not careful enough. He'd trusted in his reputation, and that alone had been sufficient to fool everyone. Even now, only Schwarzhelm himself knew of the man's treachery. The fire had concealed evidence of his transformation, and men assumed that the old general had suffered from a terrible accident. For the time being, that was how Schwarzhelm wanted it. The truth would emerge in good time.

He took up the key and ran it over his fingers. Iron glinted in the candlelight. Even after much time had passed, he still had no idea why Lassus had done it. As far as he knew, the old swordmaster had no connections in Averland and no interest in the succession. He'd never had any concern with matters of rank or promotion. That was precisely why he'd been so admired. *I've been granted the grace to retire from the field and see out the rest of my days in peace.* That's what he'd told Schwarzhelm, back before he'd ridden to Averheim. Such an effortless, professional lie, so smoothly delivered.

With an effort of will, Schwarzhelm turned his mind back to the present. The longer he lingered on his many failures, the less useful he could be. Deep down, the tidings of Verstohlen nagged away at him. The spy had seen the mark of Chaos in the city, and his reports had been vindicated by the horrific manner of Lassus's death. Schwarzhelm had to assume that Natassja was still alive. Perhaps Rufus Leitdorf was too. In any event, for as long as Verstohlen remained in Averheim, the counsellor was in terrible danger. Schwarzhelm had sent coded messages by secret courier, but had little hope of them getting through. The only course left to him was to return there himself. Amends had to be made, debts settled, secrets uncovered.

He'd tried to seek an audience with the Emperor to explain his worries, but that had proved impossible. Never before had any request of his to meet Karl Franz been turned down. That hurt him more than anything else that had happened. Perhaps the Emperor was still angry. Perhaps he was trying to protect Schwarzhelm from any further involvement, thinking it best that he recovered from his trials. Or perhaps there was corruption even in the heart of the Palace, blocking his missives from reaching their target.

In any case, it didn't matter now. His mind was made up. He would leave for Averheim as soon as his work in Altdorf was done. There were only three things he needed to do first.

He rose from the table, taking the key and the letter with him and placing them in his jerkin pocket. He took a dark cloak from the hook in the wall beside him and wrapped himself up in it. At his side he felt the cool presence of the Rechtstahl. He hadn't drawn it since returning from Averland, and he dreaded seeing the rune-carved steel again. The spirit of the weapon was sullen and accusatory. Like all dwarf-forged master swords, it cared about the nature of the blood it spilt.

Schwarzhelm turned to leave the room. Three simple tasks. To leave the letter where the Emperor would find it. To enter Lassus's private archives in the Palace vaults. To retrieve the Sword of Vengeance, ready to return it to its master if he still lived.

Simple to list, difficult to do. With a final look around his study, Schwarzhelm blew out the candles and left to break in to the most heavily guarded fortress in the Empire.

* * *

Grosslich reached the bottom of the staircase. The echoing screams had now become a gorgeous cacophony, rising from the depths of the crypt and snaking through the many passages and antechambers of the whole foundation layer. For a moment, Grosslich paused to take in the sound. He could almost smell it. That wonderful mix of fear, desperation and utter hopelessness. They had no idea how lucky they were to be shown such exquisite varieties of sensation. Their minds were being expanded. Involuntarily, it was true, but expanded nonetheless. Sometimes literally.

At the bottom of the stairs, a long gallery ran ahead for two hundred yards. Far below the surface of the city, Natassja had been able to indulge her peerless sense of design. The floor was glassy and smooth. A gentle lilac light rose from it, picking out the detail of the baroque walls, each carved with the same care and intricacy as the doors above. The themes were the ones she loved – lissom youths of both sexes, locked in what looked like a ballet of agony. The artistry was such that the iron figures could almost have passed for real bodies, locked into eternal stasis and bound into the foundations of the Tower.

At regular intervals along the gallery, archways had been cut into the walls. Each of these was decorated in the same fashion, with sigils dedicated to Pleasure engraved over the keystone. The noises came from beyond these arches. Grosslich hadn't had time to explore all the rooms in person, but he knew they were where Natassja carried out her works of artistry. On the rare occasions when he'd felt able to peer within their confines, he'd found the experience difficult. He knew that a part of him was still mired in human weaknesses. Even now, after so much transformation, to see some of those... *scenes* made his flesh shiver. He'd have to work on that. The weakness in him, small as it was, was the last remaining impediment to glory.

At the far end of the gallery a large octagonal chamber had been hewn from the earth. When the Tower was completed, the chamber would sit directly beneath the centre of the mighty shaft. For now, all that stood above it was an iron cat's cradle.

Grosslich walked across the glass floor, enjoying the echoing click of his boots. The sound produced a pleasing counterpoint to the sobbing whimpers coming from door number four. As he passed it, he was pleased to see Natassja already waiting for him in the octagon.

'My love,' he said, marvelling as he always did at her splendour.

Natassja sat on an obsidian throne at the centre of the chamber. Her skin, once ivory, was now a shimmering pale blue. Her eyes had lost their pupils and become pure black jewels in her flawless face. Her teeth still shone as white as they'd ever done, even if the incisors looked a little longer. She wore a sheer gown of nightshade silk, and a necklace of ithilmar spikes now graced her neckline. Her hair, black as pitch, hung loose around her shoulders.

At Grosslich's approach, she rose from the throne.

'What word from Altdorf?' she asked, descending from the dais to meet him. Her voice was cool, though a sibilant undertone had been added to it.

'The Emperor summoned me. I played for time.'

Natassja looked thoughtful. 'He won't remain patient forever,' she said. 'Schwarzhelm will tell him the truth soon, if he hasn't already.'

Grosslich frowned at that. Everyone was always so worried. It was inexplicable, given the position of strength they were in.

'You're *sure* Lassus gave much away?'

'He was weak,' spat Natassja. 'Even now his soul is shriven. I have seen it. A thousand years of torment to ponder a slip of the tongue.' Vehemence made her voice shake. 'And yes, he did give much away. His presence in this has given us all away. Schwarzhelm is damaged, but he's still powerful.'

'Then I've no doubt you've plans in place.'

'We still have agents in the Palace,' she said. 'For as long as possible we must maintain the illusion that Rufus was the traitor here. In the meantime, there are two men we have to kill. One is Schwarzhelm, though that will be difficult at such a range. The other is closer to hand.'

'Verstohlen.'

'Quite. See to it.'

'Of course,' said Grosslich. That would be a singular pleasure – the man's bleating had become insufferable.

'And then there's the pursuit of Rufus. That troubles me.'

Natassja spoke quickly but clearly. There was no trace of mania in her eyes. Back when he'd been a normal man, Grosslich had assumed all cultists were raving fanatics. Natassja had her moments, but her demeanour habitually remained as smooth as onyx. Perhaps that shouldn't have surprised him. She'd been active in this, after all, for centuries.

'Any more news from your men?' she asked. 'How goes the hunt?'

'It's difficult, my goddess,' said Grosslich, not bothering to hide the truth. 'He's in his own country, protected by his own people. I send more men east every day, but we can't search every house.'

Natassja shook her head. 'Not quick enough. Come with me. I have something to show you.'

She led him back into the long gallery. With a faint shudder, Grosslich realised they were heading for one of the antechambers. Number one. He'd never been allowed in that one.

'The one uncertain factor in this is Helborg,' said Natassja as she walked. 'He was not part of the original plan, though we were able to make use of him. My senses tell me he still lives.' She turned to face Grosslich before entering the chamber, and her expression was intense. 'I fear his presence. He was not foreseen from the beginning. It might have been better if he had never come.'

She ducked under the archway. As Grosslich followed into the darkness his eyes took a moment to adjust.

'I thought you used him? To goad Schwarzhelm further?'

Natassja nodded. 'We did. Lassus and I had discussed the contingency. At every stage, we made it appear as if Helborg and Rufus were working in tandem. But that was always in addition to the main objective. I was never sure it was the right decision.'

Grosslich's vision began to clarify. The antechamber retreated far back into the darkness of the earth. He couldn't see the far wall for shadow. On either side of him were long wooden tables with leather restraining straps. There were vials of a lilac-coloured liquid and gut tubes leading from them. Surgical instruments had been placed on a separate table, and they glistened in the low light. Across every surface, parchment made of human skin had been draped, painstakingly inscribed with tight-curled script. There were diagrams, etched in blood so old it had turned black. The floor, hidden in the gloom, was sticky. In the darkness beyond, he could faintly make out a rattling sound. Something was moving.

'I saw the blow that felled him,' said Grosslich, trying to concentrate on the task at hand. 'He may yet die from it.'

'Possibly. But we have to be sure. Come forwards.'

The last command hadn't been directed at him. The rattling grew louder. Something was shuffling into the light.

'What is this, my goddess?' asked Grosslich. He was nervous. Despite all his training, all his immersion in the world of the Dark Prince, he was still nervous. He still had some way to go.

'A new toy,' she replied, eyes fixed on the approaching shape. 'A refinement of the creatures I was working on before. I call them my handmaidens. What do you think?'

The figure that emerged had been a woman. She had once been beautiful, perhaps. She was slim, pale-skinned, with mouse-brown hair arranged in long plaits. Maybe in the past she had moved with an easy grace, laughing in the sun and trying to catch the eye of the troopers marching to war.

Now she moved silently. Her once flawless skin was covered in incisions and sutures. Her eyes were gone, replaced with blank brass plates. Black rags had been draped over

her naked shoulders, but they did little to obscure the surgery that had scored her body. Exposed bone glinted from
her hips, her knees, her neck. Most strikingly of all, her fingers had been replaced with long curved talons. They shone
coldly in the dark. What was left of her face was contorted
into a silent, frozen howl of agony. It was unclear if she could
still speak. It looked like she could barely walk.

'Impressive,' said Grosslich, trying not to imagine the full
horror of the transformation. 'What can she do?'

'There has been extensive replacement,' said Natassja
coolly. 'At her heart there burns an iron casket containing a shard of the Stone. That keeps her alive, despite the
removal of the spine. Once given an instruction, she will
never stop. These ones no longer need to be near me to
retain their power.'

The handmaiden shuffled closer. It seemed blind as well
as crippled. Every movement it made was tight with pain.

'It doesn't move fast.'

Natassja smiled and ran a finger gently down the handmaiden's scarred cheek. 'Do not be fooled by her current
state. When given the proper command, she will change.'
Natassja looked at her tenderly, like a proud mother. 'For
now, she only has her own private world of pain. That can
be altered by giving her a name.'

'A name.'

'A name is a mystical thing, Heinz-Mark. It has resonance
in the aethyr. They can use it to find their prey. When they
are ready, I will give it to them.'

'She's not ready?'

'Not yet,' said Natassja, stroking the handmaiden's remaining hair. 'There will be three of them, at least to begin with.
Their creation is long and difficult. Then I will send them
out. They will sweep across Averland like crows, never pausing, never resting.'

She looked back at Grosslich, and her eyes were shining.
'All they need is the name. *Helborg.*'

* * *

Rufus Leitdorf looked down on the stricken face of Kurt Helborg. The Marshal slept still, propped up on bolsters of duckfeather. The two men were alone in the bedchamber of one of his father's houses, far out in the eastern reaches of Averland. The room was typically grand, with a high plastered ceiling and heavy wooden furniture against all four walls. The bed itself was larger than some peasants' hovels, with fanciful images of dragons and crested eagles carved into the headboard.

The night was old. Candlelight made Helborg's face look even paler. The craggy features, so admired and feared across the Empire, were now haggard, and the proud moustache hung in lank strands across his cheeks. His breathing was shallow, and a thick layer of sweat lay on his skin.

Leitdorf took up another towel and began to dab the moisture away. Only a few months ago he'd never have stooped to minister to another man's discomfort, even a man as famed as Helborg, but things had changed. He was now a fugitive in his own land, hunted by men he had once aspired to command. There seemed little point in retaining old pretensions of grandeur.

He replaced the towel on the low table by the bed. Leitdorf sat for a while, watching the man's breast rise and fall under the coverlet. Helborg fought with death. The wound in his shoulder had closed, but some profound struggle was still going on within him.

There was a knock at the door. Leitdorf rose from the bed, smoothing the sheets from where he'd been sitting.

'Come.'

Leofric von Skarr, preceptor of the Reiksguard, entered. He was still in full battle armour and looked as grim and wolfish as ever. His dark hair hung around his face, criss-crossed with the scars that so suited his name.

'Any change?'

'None.'

'He hasn't woken?'

'Not while I've been with him.'

Skarr nodded. Around his neck hung the shard taken from Helborg's sword. It had become something of a totem for the depleted Reiksguard company who still guarded their master, the emblem of his future recovery.

'There was another patrol out there, beyond the line of the hills,' said Skarr. 'We killed them all, but they were getting close. They're going to find us.'

'Then we move again.'

'You haven't run out of houses?'

Leitdorf gave a superior smile. 'My father owned more houses in Averland than there are whores in Wurtbad.'

Skarr snorted.

'It's no solution, this endless fleeing,' he said dismissively, leaning against a fabulously expensive Breugsletter sideboard as if it were a country gate. 'They'll catch up with us eventually, and we don't have the men to fight them all.'

'I've been thinking about that.' Leitdorf walked over to a writing desk by the window. Across it lay a vellum map of Averland, lit by more candles. It bore the crest of Marius Leitdorf in the corner and was obviously a private commission. Each of the old count's many manor houses and fortified places was marked. 'Look at this.'

Skarr joined him.

'We're here,' said Leitdorf, pointing to a country mansion several days' ride from Averheim. 'Far, but not far enough. We should be aiming *here*.'

He indicated a blank spot on the map. The nearest landmark was a patch of scratchily-drawn highland called Drakenmoor.

'I don't see anything.'

'I know,' said Leitdorf. 'This is one of my father's own maps, and it isn't even displayed here. That's how secret he kept it. His last retreat. The place he went to in order to escape the dreams.'

Skarr looked sceptical. 'A hideaway.'

'Something like that.'

'How do you know of it?'

'There were *some* family secrets to which I was privy,' said Leitdorf, affronted. The Reiksguard treated him like a spoiled, feckless dandy.

Skarr continued to frown. 'You can't hide a castle.'

'Of course not. Those who live locally know of its existence. But there are few villages in the region, and fewer staff in the retreat. My father set great store by having somewhere no one could find him.'

'How far is it?'

Leitdorf pursed his lips. 'In the Marshal's condition, maybe three days across country. Once we get there, we'll be isolated. Even if Grosslich sends his men after us, we'll see them coming from miles off. In any case, he's sure to send his men to the houses he knows about first.'

Skarr hesitated, studying the map carefully, weighing up various options. Leitdorf began to get frustrated. There *were* no other options.

'Come on, man!' he snapped. 'Surely you can see the sense of it?'

Skarr whirled back to face him, his eyes bright with anger. Leitdorf recoiled. The preceptor had a quick temper.

'*Never* give me orders,' hissed Skarr. There was a dark expression on his face, drawn from years of expert killing. 'It's down to you and your games that we're in this damned mess.'

Leitdorf felt the blood rush to his cheeks. 'Remember your station, master kni–'

'Remember yours! It is *nothing*. You may think you're the elector of this blighted province, but to me you're just the man who's brought this whole thing down on us.' Spittle collected at the corner of Skarr's mouth. He was consumed by rage. Leitdorf backed away from him.

'Maybe I should leave you to Grosslich's men,' Skarr muttered, turning away in scorn. 'What they want with the Marshal is still a mystery to me.'

Leitdorf, for once, found himself lost for words. His mouth opened, but nothing came out. He stood still, heart pounding, trying to think of a response.

'Skarr,' came a croak from the bed.

The preceptor turned quickly, wild hope kindling across his face. Helborg's eyes were open. They were rheumy and ill-focussed, but they were open.

'My lord!'

'I heard enough,' rasped Helborg. His voice sounded as if it had been dragged over rusted iron. 'Do as Leitdorf says.'

'Yes, my lord,' replied Skarr, suddenly chastened. For his part, Leitdorf didn't know whether to feel relieved or not. His position was still precarious.

'And we take him with us,' continued Helborg. The effort of speaking produced fresh sweat on his brow. 'We need him.'

'Yes, though I–'

Skarr didn't finish. Helborg, exhausted by the effort, drifted back into sleep. His head sank deep into the bolster, his breathing ragged.

Leitdorf turned to Skarr in triumph.

'I think that's given us our answer.'

Skarr shot him a poisonous look.

'We'll do as the Marshal says. For some reason, he seems disposed to be charitable towards you.' The Reiksguard glared at Leitdorf, every sinew of his body radiating menace. 'But I warn you, Herr Leitdorf, my only task is to safeguard Helborg's life. If you do anything – *anything* – to put it in danger, then so help me I will throw you to the wolves.'

Night lay heavily on Altdorf. The turgid waters of the Reik flowed fast, swollen by weeks of rain. Fires still burned across the city, sending acrid peat-smoke curling into the air. Lights glimmered in the darkness and at the pinnacles of the many towers. As ever, the turrets of the Celestial College retained their thin sheen of blue, glowing eerily far above the compass of its rivals. Any men abroad at that quiet hour avoided looking at the unnatural lights and kept an eye on their surroundings.

Schwarzhelm stole along the Prinz Michael Strasse, keeping his cloak wrapped tight around him and hugging the shadows. He feared no street urchin or cutpurse – the rats of the street went for easier pickings than him. Even stripped of his plate armour and helmet, Schwarzhelm was still a formidable-looking target.

Mannslieb was full, throwing a cool silver light across the cobbled streets through broken rain-clouds. Schwarzhelm reached the end of the street and paused, checking his bearings. The southern wall of the Palace complex lay ahead. From his long acquaintance with the sprawling site he knew it was the least watched. There was nothing much of value at the southern end of the estates – just scholars' dens, storerooms, stables, fodder yards for the menagerie, and other semi-maintained buildings. Despite that, the walls were high and heavy, crowned with battlements and cut from unwearing granite. Along the top of them ran a wide parapet, ceaselessly patrolled by the Palace guards.

Schwarzhelm stepped out from the shelter of the street and turned left, walking close to the curve of the wall. He let his gaze slip over the stone as he did so. There were no gates, no windows, not even a grille or arrow-slit. The surface glared back at him, unbroken and smooth.

He kept walking. From time to time he heard noises ahead of or behind him. Footsteps padding away in the dark, the distant cackle of a cheap strumpet, the barking of a chained dog. He ignored them all.

He reached his goal. A culvert placed at the base of the wall, barred against entry and guarding the outflow of a drain. The slops from the Palace ran straight out into the street, gurgling down the edges of the roads and off into the maze of buildings beyond. The stench was marginally worse than Altdorf's habitual fug of filth. The rains had made all drains in the city overflow, and a torrent of grey water surged from the outlet, filmy and dotted with floating refuse.

Schwarzhelm looked back, watching to see if he'd been observed. The street was empty, and there were no guards on the rampart above. He drew a huge ring of keys from his belt, wrapped in cloth to ward against clinking. There were some advantages to being so high in the Emperor's trust.

But, of course, that was no longer true.

He selected a long iron key. The arch of the culvert rose less than three feet above the surface of the street. Reaching down into the foaming water, he felt around for the lock. It was there, rusted closed. He tried the key.

No luck. He reached for another and repeated his groping. On the fourth attempt, he found the one that fitted. It was not an exact match – he had to force it into the lock and then wrench it round. With a grinding sound, the mechanism snapped open. Schwarzhelm grasped the bottom of the barred gate and lifted it. The heavy iron grille took some shifting, and as he laboured foul water splattered up into his chest and face.

Beyond the entrance, the drain ran into darkness, never more than a few feet high and dripping with noisome fluid. There was enough space between the surface of the water and the roof to breathe, though he'd be half-submerged in the stink. Schwarzhelm lay face-down on the street and began to worm himself into the gap. It was hard work – the grille had to be kept open while he snaked under it. Eventually he made it inside and the door slammed back down behind him. There was no way of locking it from the inside, and it was all he could do to keep his mouth and nose out of the drainwater. Like a beetle burrowing in manure, Schwarzhelm hauled himself along the cramped way, feeling his muscles bunch against the sides.

Darkness pressed against him like swaddling. The uneven stone jagged on his clothes, his sword-belt, his boots. He shuffled forwards, mouth closed against the noxious effluent around him. After just a few feet he felt like gagging and stopped in his tracks, working to control himself. He was hemmed in, crushed by the tons of rock above him. A flicker of panic flared up in his stomach.

He quelled it and pressed on. Working slowly, powerfully, he edged through the narrow space. Progress was slow, and he was almost wedged tight as the drain took a sharp dogleg right before running onwards. As he hauled himself round the angle, he felt his heart thud rhythmically, his hands scrabbling at the cold stone.

Then, ahead of him, he saw the far end of the culvert coming into view. A faint semicircle of open air, barred by a similar grille. He shuffled towards it, keeping a tight grip on the bunch of keys. Beyond was a small courtyard. Through the bars it looked like the rear area of a kitchen, or maybe a washhouse. There were barrels littering the space, some open and on their sides revealing their contents of rank-smelling refuse and spoiled food.

There was no movement in the square, and no light save that of the moon. Schwarzhelm fumbled with the lock. The key worked as before, and the grille clicked open. He shoved it up and pushed his way under it. As he rose, he made sure it was gently lowered back into position. He looked about him warily.

He was alone. His cloak, jerkin and breeches were covered in slurry. He stank worse than an ogre's jockstrap, and looked nearly as bad.

So this was what he'd been reduced to. The last time he'd entered the Palace precincts he'd been wearing ceremonial armour and had been accorded a full guard of honour. Now he looked like the lowest common street thief.

No matter. He was in. Now he had to find what he was looking for.

The fevered nights over Averheim had given way to a more seasonal warmth. Cool airs ruffled the Grosslich standards as they hung from the walls of the Averburg, lit by the full face of Mannslieb.

Tochfel sat in his chamber high in the citadel wanting nothing more than to sleep. The day had been long, and his run-in with Euler had been an inauspicious start. The demands of the new elector were legion. Even though Grosslich was almost impossible to track down in person, his orders, delivered by messenger, just kept coming.

Most of them concerned the new building. Requisitions

were coming in at nearly a dozen a day for everything from masonry and metalwork to wine and silverware. The proud home of the Averlander electors, the seat of the Alptraum and Leitdorf dynasties, was being emptied. Soon it would be nothing more than a cold stone shell, a faint reminder of the glories of the past.

But it was not the tide of paperwork that kept the Steward awake. He had a visitor sitting before him, a thin-faced man with receding hair and a wild look in his eyes. Odo Heidegger, the witch hunter in charge of the purgation of Averheim. He sat before Tochfel, his thin fingers clasped on his lap. He'd eschewed the leather coat and breeches worn by most of his order, and instead wore the ceremonial robes of his office – dark red lined with black. They were coloured that way, no doubt, to hide the blood.

'I do not understand,' Heidegger said again in his reedy, mellifluous voice. 'There was no objection to these names when they were first submitted to your office.'

Tochfel ran his hand through his thinning hair. He was strung out. He really needed to sleep. 'And as I told *you*, Herr Heidegger, I've not seen this list until now. I had no idea there were so many.'

In his hands he held the offending list. At the top was the stamp of the Temple of Sigmar in Averheim. Heidegger had been promoted to the pinnacle of the local hierarchy shortly after Grosslich had been installed. Since then it had been his solemn duty to oversee the remaining interrogations and to arrange suitable punishment for those found to have aided the traitors.

'Yes, it is sad, is it not, that so many chose to fall into darkness,' said Heidegger. He looked genuinely mournful. 'But they all confessed. You can see the signatures.'

Tochfel swallowed as he looked at the series of scrawled names from the literate victims and crosses from those who weren't. All of them were shaky, as if the owners' hands had barely functioned by the time they were called into action. Several were half-obscured by dark-brown smudges.

'Some of these names are known to me,' protested Toch-fel. 'Here is Morven, my aide. What possible reason could you have for–'

'He confessed, Steward. What more do you want? It is there, all on the list.'

Tochfel could read it for himself. *Wantonly held the Aver-burg against the forces of the rightful elector, thus delaying the campaign against the Traitor Leitdorf. Sentence: Death by flame.* That was a travesty. Tochfel had passed those orders himself. At that stage in the campaign, no one knew the scale of Leitdorf's treachery, nor that Grosslich had the blessing of Schwarzhelm. For that matter, he himself could be liable to...

He shuddered.

'I will not sign these,' he said, putting the papers down. 'I need more time. There's been no scrutiny, no examination.'

Heidegger retained his sorrowful expression. There wasn't a hint of anger there. He looked a little like one of those otherworldly Jade magisters, lost in a reverie of gentle regret. And yet Tochfel was judge enough to see the fragility of the man's mind. Most witch hunters went mad sooner or later, and this one would not be long.

'That is regrettable, Steward,' Heidegger said. 'I will have to report it. The elector will not be happy to hear that his quest for justice has been impeded.'

'I don't care,' snapped Tochfel, his fatigue making him unwary. 'There are men on this list innocent of any crime. Why has the court of inquiry not included Templars from other cities? I've not been present at any of your interrogations.'

'You're welcome to join me. Some people find them... distasteful.'

Tochfel shook his head. Going up against the Temple of Sigmar was dangerous, even more so since Achendorfer had gone missing. He was running short of allies.

'I did not say I would block these sentences,' said Toch-fel, speaking carefully. 'I merely wish for more time to study them. Give me until the end of the week.'

Heidegger thought before replying. 'I do not like it,' he said. 'Justice must be seen to be done.'

'There've been enough burnings already,' muttered Tochfel. 'A hiatus will do you good, give you time to buy in more firewood.'

Heidegger shrugged. 'As you wish. I shall inform the elector of your views.'

He rose, brushing at his robes as he did so. His fingers were forever fidgeting, as if they longed to grasp the instruments.

'Goodnight, Steward.'

'Goodnight, Herr Heidegger.'

The door closed, leaving Tochfel alone in the chamber. For a moment, he thought about climbing on to his narrow bed. Then he saw the pile of papers on his desk, and realised just how much more work he had to get through.

'This is getting beyond my control,' he mused, speaking to himself in his fatigue. 'I will speak to Verstohlen. He will know what to do.'

Schwarzhelm moved ever closer to his quarry. He went slowly, keeping to the darkness, watchful for the teams of sentries. He'd cleaned the worst of the muck from his clothes. The rain had started again. It might have been sent from blessed Shallya herself, as it damped down his stench and made the guards unwilling to patrol too zealously out in the open.

The interior of the Palace complex was a vast morass of interconnected corridors and buildings. No living man knew them all, though Schwarzhelm was as familiar with them as anyone. He'd never penetrated so far into the southern wings of the mammoth structure, but he knew that Lassus had had his private chambers there. They were modest, less than would normally have been offered to a general of Lassus's stature. Until recently, Schwarzhelm had been pained by the lack of respect shown to his old master. Now he cursed the fact that he even *had* chambers within such hallowed precincts.

From the courtyard, he'd moved quickly towards the

collection of apartments given to distinguished retired officers. Most were housed in a heavy sandstone monstrosity
covered in eroded gargoyles and overworked copies of the
Imperial coat of arms. In an attempt to mask the grotesque
devices, huge stretches of ivy had been allowed to creep
across the stone, obscuring all but the steep tiled roof with
its iron guttering. Originally the building had been set amid a
pleasant ornamental lawn, though the demands of the Imperial bureaucracy had ensured that it was now surrounded by
three gothic scriptoria and a gloomy vaulted archive.

Schwarzhelm paused, taking in his surroundings. The regular Palace guards were issued with crossbows, and without
his armour he was vulnerable. If he was unlucky enough to
stumble across Reiksguard, his situation would be far graver.
For once in his life, stealth would have to take precedence
over ostentatious bravery.

He crouched tight against the wall of one of the scriptoria. The rain splattered down from the leaky roof, bouncing
from his hunched shoulders on to the uneven stone flags
beneath him. Ahead, maybe thirty yards away, two sentries
walked lazily around the perimeter of the apartments. They
had hoods cast over their faces to ward against the rain and
said nothing. By their manner, Schwarzhelm could see they
weren't the Emperor's finest. They moved off, heading in the
direction of the walls. Schwarzhelm waited until there was
complete silence, then moved.

He crept across the open space quickly, lingering in the
pools of shadow. Zigzagging from doorway to doorway, he
reached the porch of the first set of apartments. The twin oak
doors were flanked by crude sandstone columns, wrapped in
ivy and surmounted by the coat of arms of some long-dead
military commander.

He looked back the way he'd come. Nothing. He withdrew
the keys from his belt and tried several in the lock. None of
them worked. That was unsurprising – there were a thousand keys for different parts of the Palace and most were
jealously guarded by their owners.

Schwarzhelm stowed them. There was a time and a place for finesse, and this wasn't it. He pulled back, gathering his strength, and barged into the doors. They buckled against his massive frame, but held. He slammed into them again, sending a dull thud out into the night. On the third attempt, they caved in, swinging back violently and cracking against the walls. He went in quickly, pulling them behind him.

Inside all was dark. The place was deserted, as were most of the buildings in the outer reaches of the Palace at night. A central corridor ran back into the gloom, marked by regular doorways leading off on either side. Two high windows at either end let in the scant starlight, but little was illuminated. Schwarzhelm reached into his jerkin and retrieved a flint and a fist-sized lantern. The metal frame of the lantern was carved in swirling lines and the clear windows were crystal – the gift of a grateful elven prince after a battle over a decade ago.

He lit the wick of the candle and closed the lantern. The light glowed softly from the crystal, throwing diffuse shadows down the corridor. At the far end of it Schwarzhelm could see a stairway leading to the next floor.

He went quietly and quickly, padding like a great bear on the threadbare carpet. The doorways passed silently, each inscribed with the initials of the official to whom the room within was devoted. Chancellor Julius Rumpelskagg, Magister F. H. Heilstaff, Egbertus Schumann, Under-Scribe of the Fifth Archives. Schwarzhelm knew where it would be, and knew just what he was looking for.

Just before he reached the stairs he saw the nameplate glinting in the flame, its brass old and tarnished. Eryniem Hoche-Hattenberg, Master of the Keys. No official of that outlandish name had ever existed, though Schwarzhelm knew the room had been well used. He slid the key from Lassus's chambers into the door and turned it. The lock clicked open.

Inside, all was orderly and neat. The light of the lantern swept across a spartan chamber. Rows of books lined the walls. Most were treatises on warfare and military training.

Schwarzhelm doubted Lassus had read many of them; the man had known all there was to know about war through experience.

There was a single, draped window at the far end of the room. In front of the window stood the desk, a heavy construction in an archaic style with a polished surface and no drawers. The surface was almost empty, save for an inkwell, a penknife, a blotter and a tray of sand. A few used quills had been discarded in a basket next to the writer's chair. No parchment remained, and there was no sign of any papers stacked up against the bookcases.

For a moment, Schwarzhelm began to doubt his intuition. Perhaps Lassus had been too careful. He knelt down beneath the desktop, running his fingers under the wood. He groped further back, feeling for the telltale switch that would hide a compartment. Just as he was about to withdraw his hand, he felt the slightest variation in texture. He pressed hard. From deep within the desk there came a *thunk*, as if a brass mechanism had shifted into place.

Schwarzhelm clambered to his feet. The right pedestal of the desk had opened, and a narrow door hung ajar on almost invisible hinges. The workmanship was perfect. When closed, the join would have been invisible even in full daylight.

Schwarzhelm shone the light against the cavity, looking for needle traps. Seeing none, he reached inside carefully and pulled out a roll of parchment, tightly bound with leather straps. Without unwrapping the bundle, he could see what they were – letters written in some kind of cipher. Schwarzhelm was familiar with most of the battle codes used in the Empire, but this one looked strange and he could make no sense of it.

He stowed the bundle in his jerkin and closed the door to the pedestal again. The first task on his list had been completed. He left the chamber, locking the door behind him. The corridor was as silent as before. He looked up at the window at the far end of the building. The clouds had parted again, and a feeble moonlight had returned. That would make things more difficult. He knew where the sword was being held, and taking that with him would be far more difficult than stealing letters.

Extinguishing the lantern, Schwarzhelm headed back to the main door. The Chapel of the Fallen, right in the heart of the ancient Palace, awaited him.

Pieter Verstohlen watched the moon ride clear over Averheim. For a change, he wasn't in his tower room in the Averburg. His guest lived several streets away and had kindly offered him the use of her bedchamber for the night. Of course, he'd had to pay for the privilege. Or, to be more accurate, for her company within it.

Visiting courtesans was not something he was proud of. He was careful, of course, and made sure only to procure the services of the higher class of courtesan. His stipend from Schwarzhelm, together with a history of cautious investments, had made him a man of comfortable means. He enjoyed the more exclusive things in life: good food, expensive wine, sophisticated women. Though the notion always seemed trite to him, it was true nevertheless – he valued them for their minds as much as their more regular services. Like many of his kind, solitude became a kind of mania after a while. It needed to be broken, even if that meant giving in to appetites that he'd rather not have had.

He pushed himself up higher against the bolsters, trying to get a better view of the moonlit rooftops through the open window. On his shoulder, Elisabeth stirred. Her flame-red hair fell across her face as her head rose.

'What is it?' she mumbled, brushing it free.

Verstohlen stroked the tresses absently. She had a striking face. Ivory-white skin, dusted with freckles, deep green eyes.

'Nothing. Just looking at the moon.'

Elisabeth frowned. 'Like a madman.'

'Indeed.'

The vista across the city calmed him. Despite all the difficulties, he felt a certain pride in what he and Schwarzhelm had accomplished. The streets were quiet. Averheim felt like a different place from the febrile mess they'd arrived in at the start of the summer. And yet it was strange that he hadn't heard from him. Nothing had come out of Altdorf since the man had left. That wasn't like him. Amid all the contentment he felt at a job well done, that made him anxious.

'You look worried, my love,' said Elisabeth with the astuteness of her profession.

Verstohlen tensed. That was the only thing he ever asked them, not to use the word 'love'. There was only one love for him, and it had been the purest, most sacred thing in his whole life. He made a mental note not to use this one again. She'd provided an acceptable diversion, but he needed companions who could be careful.

'Just expecting a message,' he said. 'Nothing important.'

'Anything I can do to help? I know many influential men in this city.'

'I don't doubt it. Are you this helpful to all your clients?'

'Only the ones I really like.'

'I'm gratified,' said Verstohlen, though he wasn't. It made it more difficult if they liked him.

'I mean it. You know how to treat a lady,' Elisabeth said, seemingly oblivious to the irony. 'There are some brutes out there, believe me.'

'I'm sure.'

'I had one last week. Stinking of root. Almost sent him away.'

'Joyroot?' asked Verstohlen, his interest piqued.

Elisabeth smiled. 'You sound surprised. I had you for a man of the world.'

Verstohlen didn't return the smile. 'I thought Grosslich had outlawed it.'

'That's what he said he'd do. That's what the last one said too. But you can still get it. Even I could get it, if you wanted.'

'No,' said Verstohlen. 'I do not.'

Elisabeth laughed, a girlish, babbling sound. 'So serious! There's no harm to it.'

Verstohlen said nothing. A dark thought had entered his mind. The Leitdorfs had controlled the trade. If it was still coming in, then there could only be two possibilities: they were still active in Averheim, or someone else had taken it over. Neither was an attractive proposition.

'Look, I'm awake now, love,' continued Elisabeth, a mischievous sparkle in her eyes. 'What do you suppose we might do about that?'

Verstohlen ignored her. His mind was now occupied with other things. He needed advice. With Schwarzhelm out of the city and Bloch engaged in the east, he was running short of allies. He determined to speak to Tochfel. He would know what to do.

Schwarzhelm crouched down low, making sure his cloak was close around him. He'd moved towards the heart of the Palace complex. The shabby buildings had been replaced by grand structures of marble and gilt, and the patrols had increased proportionately. Though no one really cared about the half-forgotten cells of a few scholars in the semi-derelict southern wing, the core of the Palace complex contained treasures beyond the dreams of Ranald, and the defences were formidable.

It helped that Schwarzhelm was privy to the secrets of the inner circles. He could take routes that few knew existed, could circumvent places where he knew the guards would congregate, could open hidden doors and slip past traps designed to catch the unwary. There were wards engraved across the many gateways against the powers of Chaos, but he knew what they were and what they were looking for. He passed under them silently, feeling the blank scrutiny of the occluded sigils on his shoulders. It felt as if the arcane magicks could sense the guilt burning in his soul, and he didn't linger by them for longer than he needed to.

He couldn't avoid all the many layers of watchfulness by know-ledge and stealth. Three times since leaving Lassus's old chambers he'd been forced to spring from the shadows to silence an unwary patrol. He'd held himself back from killing, even though the risk of one of his victims coming round made his position ever more precarious. There'd been enough slaying of loyal troops, and he planned to keep the Rechtstahl sheathed unless the need was desperate. It was a mean, dishonourable way of fighting, and with every blow of his mighty fists he felt the shame of it.

In the distance, he heard the eerie call of some fabulous creature. Unearthly shrieks rang out across the deserted courtyards of the Palace. The Imperial Menagerie wasn't far away, and the beasts within were disturbed.

Ahead of his current position, the man-made mountain of the Holswig-Schliestein Hofburg soared into the night sky, a confection of twisted columns and graven images. To his left, the mighty banqueting halls, all eleven of them, had been piled on top of one another, each vying with its companions for tasteless splendour. When one of the many Imperial receptions was in session they were filled with light and laughter, sparkling from the crystal chandeliers and from the diamond necklaces of the noble ladies. Now they were empty and sullen, brooding in the dark like jilted lovers.

Ahead of him lay the vast bulk of the Imperial Chapel, a sprawling cornucopia of heavy plasterwork and staring gargoyles. That was where the daily procession of warrior priests ended up, all hollering their praises to Sigmar and swinging incense-loaded warhammers as they swayed towards the high altar. Within those mighty transepts benedictions were offered and penitent prayers issued on behalf of the wayward citizens of the Empire. Beasts were slaughtered before the eternal flames of the inner sanctum, their blood running down iron channels in the marble floor. Massive censers of brass revolved endlessly from chains set into the distant roof, powered by devices from Nuln and Tilea. Gold-plated cherubs poured a ceaseless torrent of pungent smoke from goblets of bronze, obscuring the tombs of the worthy and turning the stone coal-black.

The holy transepts of the Cult of Sigmar were not

Schwarzhelm's destination, though. At the southern end of the soaring Chapel, a smaller building had been raised. Here there was no gold plate or churning machinery. The stone was blank and unadorned, and pairs of iron eagles gazed darkly out from the guttering. Even during the day the place was kept quiet and dark. Obsidian columns stood sentinel in the gloom, watching over the rows of graves within.

This was the Chapel of the Fallen, the resting place of the honoured protectors of the Empire. The guards were drawn from the priesthood of Morr, as were the attendants of the ranks of tombs. No hymns of praise were sung in that place, only a low dirge of remembrance. Few came to visit it, and fewer stayed to pray there. The heavy pall of death hung over the altars.

Schwarzhelm was close to it, and could make out the blank eyes of the eagles as they stared out across the jumbled squares and courtyards. There was a doorway opposite him, barred with metal and surmounted with a death's head, no more than thirty yards across a cobbled space overlooked on all sides. The low hum of the turning censers in the larger chapel masked his footfalls, and there were plenty of shadows to keep to.

He waited, checking for patrols. Instinctively his fingers crept to the pommel of his sword. The square was quiet. The dawn was still hours away, and none of the priests would be out of their cells for some time yet.

Moving more softly than his bulk suggested possible, Schwarzhelm crept out from the lee of the near wall and headed for the door. He heard his breathing grow quicker as he neared, and brought it under control. The death's head loomed up at him from the night, its hollow eye sockets like wells of ink. As with all doors in the Palace, it was locked at night. Schwarzhelm drew the ring of keys from his belt and began to try them, one by one. Finally, he found one that fitted. The lock rasped open and the door began to swing back.

'What are you doing there?'

Schwarzhelm's heart froze. The voice came from behind

him, close on his right shoulder. He'd been sloppy. He felt the tip of a sword press into his back, hard against the fabric of his cloak. Slowly, he raised his hands, showing he had no weapon drawn. He'd need to pick his moment.

'I could ask you the same thing, soldier,' he said, his voice assuming the habitual tone of command.

He turned as casually as he was able, neither seeking to evade the sword at his back nor getting any closer to its bearer. When he moved, he'd have to be quick.

Two men were facing him, both in the red and white of the Reiksguard. Both had their blades drawn, gleaming dully in the fractured moonlight. The nearest had the grizzled look of a sergeant. His companion, standing further back, was younger. For once, experience proved to be a liability. The sergeant recognised Schwarzhelm's features, and his sword-tip wavered.

'My lor–' he began.

He never finished. Schwarzhelm swung a fist into his face, smashing into the man's temple and sending him staggering to the ground. The youngster rushed forwards, sword poised to plunge into Schwarzhelm's torso. He evaded the stab easily, drawing his own weapon as he stepped away from the strike. The Sword of Justice flickered with an icy fire as it was released. The younger Reiksguard brought his blade up again, this time in a cutting arc. Schwarzhelm parried, and the metal met metal with a shuddering clang.

The sergeant leapt back to his feet. Schwarzhelm worked his sword quickly and carefully, mindful of the quality of his foes. They pressed home the attack expertly, swords working in concert, stabbing and retreating like ghosts.

Schwarzhelm had his back to the door, penned in by the onslaught. With a sick lurch of dread, he knew he'd have to kill them. If one or both escaped to raise the alarm, he'd never escape the Palace. He'd have to spill their blood, and two more good men would die.

Schwarzhelm brought the Rechtstahl round in a crushing parabola. The younger Reiksguard parried, but the blow was too powerful. It drove through his defence, sending him sprawling. The sergeant pressed the attack, raising his blade in the orthodox position. Schwarzhelm knew the moves all too well – he'd coached his own honour guard in the same techniques. The Rechtstahl glimmered as it cut back sharply, meeting the sergeant's blow and knocking the sword upwards. Schwarzhelm punched out with his left hand, catching the sergeant in the torso before swinging back with the sword-tip.

The blades clashed once, twice, three times. The sergeant was good, quicker than he looked and as strong as a cart-horse, but few men could withstand a prolonged assault from Schwarzhelm. As his companion struggled to his feet, Schwarzhelm saw the opening and the Sword of Justice flew into the gap. The blade bit between plates of armour, deep into the armpit. Blood spurted out, and the man crumpled heavily.

Schwarzhelm pulled his sword free, ready for the assault from the other man. He wasn't quick enough. With a cry of rage, the young Reiksguard leapt at him, sword swinging wildly, eyes lit with anger.

Schwarzhelm got his blade up just in time, but the force of the blow sent him reeling. He crashed heavily against the unlocked door. It gave way behind him, forcing him into the chapel beyond.

The Reiksguard plunged in after him, whirling his sword in a series of heavy, ill-aimed blows. The boy had been driven into a fury by the felling of his commander, and the rage was making him dangerous.

Schwarzhelm parried and countered, meeting the ferocity head-on and waiting for it to ebb. He withdrew step by step, containing the threat and drawing the Reiksguard deeper into the chapel. The interior was silent, cold and bleak. The heavy sword-clashes echoed down the long aisles, bouncing from the stone and rebounding like mocking imitations. Schwarzhelm could smell the pungent aroma of myrrh, could hear the clink of metal-tipped boots against the polished marble floor.

As the blades turned and thrust, effigies of the heroes of

the past gazed down from dark altars. It was never going to last long. The knight was capable, but limited. He tried too hard to finish it, and his sword overextended. Schwarzhelm swung heavily at the moving blade, knocking it from the boy's hands and sending it skittering across the floor. Before the lad could react he hauled the Rechtstahl back, driving the metal of his right pauldron in and shattering the shoulder blade. The Reiksguard slumped to his knees, his cry of pain echoing down the transept. Schwarzhelm plunged the blade down a third time, finishing the task cleanly. The knight's lifeless body fell heavily to the marble. Almost immediately a pool of blood began to creep across the pristine surface.

Schwarzhelm gazed down coldly at the scene, waiting for his heartbeats to return to normal. He felt nothing but disgust within him. He half expected the commotion to bring a flurry of Morr priests coming to see what was happening. Part of him even hoped they'd come – that would at least have given some meaning to the Reiksguard's actions.

But there was nothing, no sound, no response. The chapel, lit only by narrow, heavily barred windows, remained cold and unmoving. The last of the echoes died away.

Schwarzhelm stirred into action again. The bodies needed to be hidden.

He looked up. There in front of him, either by chance or some more capricious fate, was the object of his quest. The Magnus Memorial – a vast statue of the greatest Emperor after Sigmar – soared up into the vaulted roof, black as smog. The severe face of that puritan warrior was fixed in an attitude of grim piety, just as it had been, so all the records attested, in life. At its huge armoured feet was the Altar of Remembrance, carved from stone taken from Praag after the great siege and sanctified by a hundred Amethyst magisters at the very dawn of their order.

Above the altar, laid on a chaplet of black silk, was the sword. It was naked, and a notch had been taken from the blade halfway along its length. So Karl Franz had ordered it to lie until Helborg either returned to claim it, or was killed, or was proved to be a traitor beyond the doubt of the Theogonist.

Schwarzhelm took it up in his left hand. For a moment he held the two blades together, the Swords of Justice and Vengeance, just as he had in the Vormeisterplatz in Averheim, when madness had stirred in the air and his mind had been locked into a fury that wasn't his own.

The metal of the Klingerach was sullen, its runes barely visible in the gloom. Something about it spoke of betrayal, of anger, of death. He sheathed the Rechtstahl and took Helborg's weapon himself. Reaching inside his jerkin, he withdrew the letter he'd worked so hard to compose and left it on the altar in its place.

'It is done,' he breathed.

Then Schwarzhelm turned, unable to look up at the stern visage of Magnus, unwilling to gaze back on the bodies of the men he'd killed even as he dragged them into the gloom of the chapel recesses and hid the evidence of the brief, sordid combat.

Moving quickly and quietly, he left. He'd done what he'd come for. His business in the Palace was over, and Averheim beckoned once again.

CHAPTER THREE

Night made the air of the Worlds Edge Mountains even more bitter. Though not as bone-jarringly cold as it was in winter, the passes were still harsh at the end of the summer, and the rock underfoot was shrouded in a cloak of frost.

Bloch, Kraus, Drassler and the senior officers sat around a rough oak table high up in the tower of the last way-fort before Black Fire Keep. Most of the army were sleeping below them, either rammed up against one another in the hard stone halls of the fort or shivering in tents clustered close to the gates. The huge fires they'd built to ward off the cold burned still, denting the worst of the chill. Bloch had ordered that they be kept stoked, even though it would give away their presence in the mountains for miles around. They hadn't come to creep around like thieves.

At dawn they would march again. They knew where the enemy was, and thanks to Drassler's scouts knew the rough strength of the forces that remained to them. The back of the orc army had been broken by Schwarzhelm on the plains of Averland, but enough greenskins had survived to make the

Keep a difficult target. Bloch had two thousand men at his command, including the remnants of the mountain guard that had survived the first days of the incursion. Drassler reckoned a similar number of orcs had made it back to the Keep, but they had the advantage of stone to hide behind.

'We'll need to draw them into the open,' Bloch said, looking over the plans of attack his men had been discussing. 'If they stay behind those walls, we'll never prise them out.'

'Why'd they come out?' asked Drassler. 'They've got supplies, and they've got protection.'

Kraus grinned.

'They'll come out,' he said. 'Give an orc a reason to fight and it'll take it.'

Drassler shook his head. 'Not these ones. They had a plan, and they stuck to it.'

'Just like the ones on the plains,' mused Bloch, remembering the artful way Grunwald had been drawn further and further east.

'It's like I said,' insisted Drassler. 'They've been armed by men, and given their orders by men.'

Bloch had heard this said many times since leaving Grenzstadt. He didn't want to believe it, but the evidence was there. The orcs wore close-fitting amour and carried straight swords. They'd not attempted a wild rampage through the east of the province, but had acted as if explicitly commanded to draw Schwarzhelm from the city. And there were the coins. An orc had little use for gold, but there was plenty of it on their corpses. They'd made the schillings into earrings and pendants, or stuffed them into the throats of their victims for fun. Someone in the Empire had planned it all.

'Tell me again,' he said to Drassler, his chin leaning heavily on his crossed fingers. 'How did you let them get at you?'

Drassler looked irritated. No one liked to recount the story of their failure.

'What more do you want?' he asked. 'We got our orders, just as we always did. Captain Neumann did as he was told. We were told there were four bands of greenskins coming over the passes, none of them more than a hundred strong. The orders from the Averburg were to destroy them before they defiled the memorial sites.'

Bloch knew all of this. He knew that the roving bands of orcs had turned out to be made up of thousands, that they'd worked in concert, and that once the defenders had emerged from the walls they'd been slaughtered. The memory of those killing grounds was still vivid in his mind.

'And who gave you those orders?' he asked, still searching for some clue. Schwarzhelm had told him that one of the contenders for the electorship, Rufus Leitdorf, had been a traitor. If he'd orchestrated all of this, then he deserved everything that the big man had no doubt dished up to him in Averheim.

'They came as they always did. A courier from Averheim, dressed in the livery of the citadel, carrying the scrolls in a locked casket. He had a guard of warriors, two dozen, all wearing the colours of the Averburg garrison. Everything was in the standard cipher, signed off by the Steward. I saw them myself. Nothing was different.'

'And you didn't think *anything* was strange?' asked Bloch, trying to keep the incredulity from his voice. 'Four incursions, all at once, all moving in different directions? What of the defence of the Keep?'

Drassler stiffened. 'Fighting is a way of life up here, commander. We're not like the rest of our kinsmen. When the order comes, we follow it.'

Kraus shook his head. 'You were played for fools,' he muttered.

Drassler slammed his fist on the table. 'How *dare* you?' he hissed. He looked tired. They all looked tired. 'We were doing our duty.'

'Your duty was to defend the Keep,' said Kraus, and his face showed his disdain.

'Enough,' said Bloch, unwilling to see the tension spill over into pointless bickering. He privately shared Kraus's assessment, but nothing would be gained by raking over past failures. 'This isn't helping.'

He held his head in his hands, trying to think. There was so much he didn't know. The idea of Averlanders deliberately sabotaging their own defences was disgusting enough, but perhaps the rot went deeper. The money, after all, had come from Altdorf. Maybe they were still being played for fools. Maybe all of this had been anticipated.

That didn't alter the bare facts. He'd been ordered to retake the Keep. He had a mixed army of Averlanders and Reiklanders, most of them seasoned by weeks of near-constant fighting, no siege engines and little artillery. There had been no news from Averheim since Schwarzhelm's departure for the city, and his supply lines were extended and precarious. A cautious commander might have withdrawn, pulled back to Grenzstadt until the situation in the province had become clear and reinforcements were received. Grunwald's failure weighed heavily on Bloch's mind. There was no sense in fighting a battle that couldn't be won.

'We have a few hours until dawn,' he said. He looked at the officers one by one, gauging from their response how ready they were for the fight. They all met his gaze. 'We'll stay awake until we've hammered out a plan to get the Keep back and the pass secure.'

His eyes rested on Drassler, who stared back at him defiantly. Despite everything, the mountain guard were keen to avenge their defeat.

'I want ideas,' he growled, feeling impatient for action again. 'We need to get them out of the Keep. One way or another, when the sun goes down tomorrow we'll have paid those bastards back twice what they handed out to us. I don't care how we do it, but the passes *will* be back in our hands, and the last of those scum choking on their traitor's gold.'

The Grand Theogonist Volkmar was an imposing sight even when bereft of his immense battle armour. His skin was thick and leathery, tanned tight by a lifetime on the battlefield. Dark, direct eyes peered out from under feathered eyebrows. Like Schwarzhelm, he was not known for his humour. His mouth rarely smiled beneath its drooping Kislevite moustache, and his burly arms remained crossed across his chest when not kept busy swinging a warhammer. His shaven head and forearm tattoos completed the savage picture. He looked properly terrifying, as if he struggled himself to contain raging forces of anarchy within him. Even when at rest, he inspired trepidation. When unleashed on to the battlefield, that trepidation turned to awe.

Those who knew him well had even more reason to be fearful. This was a man who had come back from the dead, who'd passed beyond the barrier between the mortal world and that of Chaos. The pain of it still marked his every word, scored his every movement. No one knew the terror of the great enemy quite as intimately as Volkmar, and the experience had marked him out even more than he had been before. With each gesture, each glance, he gave it away. Under the skein of savage piety, a cold furnace of frenzy forever lurked, waiting for the kindling. Once he had been a warrior. Now he was a weapon.

The head of the Cult of Sigmar bowed to few men, but he did towards the figure before him. His ochre robes fell across his broad shoulders as he stooped, his right hand nearly touching the floor.

'Enough of that,' came a familiar voice. 'Sit. We need to talk.'

The Emperor Karl Franz sat in the same chair he'd used when commissioning Schwarzhelm for the Averland mission. Then, he'd looked at ease with the world, confident and self-assured. Now his skin had taken on a pale sheen and his eyes were ringed with grey. His hair, normally glossy, looked dull. The most powerful mortal man in the Old World was troubled, and he hadn't laboured to hide the fact.

Volkmar rose to his full height, grunting as he did so. The wounds that had ravaged his body during his escape from the daemon Be'lakor had been slow to close.

He sat beside the Emperor, saying nothing. The two men were alone. The fine furniture around them looked heavy and lumpen. Outside, a fine rain still spat against the glass windows, and the morning light was grey and filthy. In the corner of the room, the old engineer's clock ticked methodically.

Karl Franz looked down at some sheets of parchment in his lap. They looked like they'd been read many times.

'Why didn't he come here himself?' the Emperor mused.

'My liege?' asked Volkmar.

'Schwarzhelm. He could have spoken to me. I was angry, but not beyond reason. Now I've lost both of them.'

Helborg. If the Reiksmarshal were found, then Volkmar would be the one priest senior enough to interrogate him. Though hardened by the fires of war and the poisons of Chaos, that was a task he wouldn't relish.

'Perhaps he tried,' said Volkmar.

'What are you saying?'

'That not all your servants are as loyal as he.'

Karl Franz frowned, displeased by the implication. He looked down at the parchment again. 'What do you know of this matter?' he asked.

'A little. Averland is now governed by Heinz-Mark Grosslich. Leitdorf's son is a traitor, and Helborg with him.'

'And do you believe it? What they say of Helborg?'

Volkmar gave a snort of disgust that said all there was to be said.

'Schwarzhelm has erred,' agreed the Emperor, 'and he knows it. Whatever forces were ranged against him have achieved what they set out to do.'

He looked up, and a little of the familiar resolve shone in his eyes.

'We've been granted a second chance,' he said. 'They made a single slip. You know of Heinrich Lassus? He was the man behind them. He betrayed himself. Schwarzhelm has killed him, taken back Helborg's sword, and no doubt seeks to return it to him. Perhaps he is already on the road.'

'So how stands Averland?'

'We don't know. All is clouded. The only thing we can be certain of is that the great enemy is active. They've used this succession to gain a foothold. Nothing has been purged. The stain remains, and it is growing.'

Volkmar let the implications of that sink in. Averland had always been the most placid of provinces, the one furthest from the strife that ravaged the rest of the Empire.

He should have seen this coming. Only in war was there purity; where there was peace there was disease.

'Can Grosslich handle it?'

The Emperor shrugged. 'Who knows? He doesn't answer my summons. That may be pride, or it may be worse. In any event, our response must be the same.'

Here it came. The Emperor's orders. Volkmar didn't need his fine-grained knowledge of statecraft to know what they would be.

'I have tried to manage the affairs of Averland by diplomacy. That has failed. Whether or not Grosslich is a part of this, he cannot be allowed to preside over treachery. It will be rooted out and destroyed.' The Emperor crumpled the parchment in his fist and the knuckles went white. 'You will take my armies, Volkmar. Empty the Reikland if you have to. The gold in the reserves is yours. Take warrior priests and the holiest devotees of Sigmar. Take magisters from the colleges, war engines and artillery. Take veteran regiments and a core of knights. This is no routine suppression of a minor rebellion. This is a new war and needs a new army.'

The Emperor looked into Volkmar's eyes, and his expression was desolate.

'Find out what's happening there,' he growled, his fists still clenched. 'Show the traitors no mercy. Crush them, burn them and grind them into the ground. I would rather see Averland turned into a blasted waste than see it harbour a second front against the enemy. You know what to do. You know it more than anyone else. Can I trust you, Volkmar? Can you succeed where both my generals have failed?'

Volkmar felt a surge of enthusiasm quicken within him, tempered with the fear that had never quite left him. Not since the horrors of Middenheim had he commanded men against the enemy. Now he was being asked to ride again, to take up arms and show his devotion to Sigmar in the way the warrior-god had always intended. He'd failed against Archaon. He'd failed completely. He might do so again, just like the others.

'Yes, my liege,' he replied, his thoughts racing. 'Yes, you can.'

Deep in the heart of Averheim's exclusive jewellery quarter, the merchants had been quick to replenish their stocks. Averland was a province blessed with mines on its borders and Averheim sat squarely on the trade routes between Karak Angazhar and the heart of the Empire. There was money in the place too, and every fat merchant who'd made his fortune shunting cattle from the pasture to the slaughterhouse had wives and daughters who needed draping in lines of pearls or traceries of silver, so the jewellery business had prospered with them.

Some of the craftsmen were Averland-bred, plucked from the rural heartland and put to work at the forges or with the hammer. Over the centuries, the fame of the jewellery quarter had grown and artisans from further afield had settled there. Most came from Nuln, bringing new devices with them and a penchant for mechanical innovation, but there were also dwarfs, drawn as ever by the prospect of making money through the manipulation of the things they loved: steel, iron, gold and gromril. The stunted folk kept themselves to themselves, shunning the company of their human counterparts unless some deal needed to be struck or supplies of stones were running low. So it was that they formed a community within a community in Averheim, locked in their own arcane world of contracts and grudges, tolerated by their hosts but seldom interfered with.

Such isolation brought certain advantages. The dwarfs didn't involve themselves in human affairs, and were as happy serving under a Leitdorf or an Alptraum as they would have been under a Raukov or a Todbringer. Happy, that is, as long as they weren't over-taxed and were given free rein to market their creations.

That made the dwarf-smiths of Averland useful contacts for men of a certain profession. If the gold flowed, then they would be more discreet than a corpse. Of course, getting them to trust anyone but a member of their own clan was hard. It took persistence, patience, a working knowledge of the simpler forms of Khazalid, plenty of money and a formidable power of persuasion. Not many humans could boast all of those. Pieter Verstohlen, on the other hand, could.

So it was that the spy sat, knees up almost against his chest, sitting on a three-legged stool in the forge of the master jewelsmith Rossik Valgrind. Before him the fire glowed angrily, throwing red light across the dark interior. Around the hearth hung metal objects of various kinds. Some were familiar – tongs, clamps, bellows and fine-headed hammers. Others looked like nothing Verstohlen had seen before, and their uses could only be guessed at.

The owner of the forge himself worked at the back of the chamber, ignoring Verstohlen and tapping away at a ring of gromril. His gnarled hands worked with astonishing speed and precision, caressing and moulding the metal as if it were a child's forelock. His naked arms were like corded leather, wound about with brass wire and latticed with tattoos. He smelled of scorched flesh, hot metal and charred oil, and his beard was wiry and truncated from a thousand singes.

He didn't speak, and the only sound to escape his bearded lips was the occasional grunt of satisfaction as the jewellery gradually took shape under his hammers. The deal he'd made with Verstohlen had been for a place to meet only. There'd been no payment for conversation, so he didn't provide any.

There was a tap on the door leading out from the forge and onto the street. Valgrind kept working, ignoring everything but his art. Verstohlen clambered up from the low stool and reached for the latch. Outside, wrapped in a long cloak, stood Tochfel. Verstohlen beckoned him in and closed the door behind him. The afternoon light stung his eyes after the occlusion of the forge.

'Glad you could make it, Steward,' said Verstohlen, pulling

up a stool. The two of them sat before the hearth. In the background, Valgrind worked away as if nothing had happened.

'Safe to talk?' whispered Tochfel, casting anxious looks in the dwarf's direction.

'Absolutely,' said Verstohlen, speaking normally. 'Maybe the safest place to talk in the city.'

Tochfel nodded. 'Good. I'm glad my message got to you.'

'Your concerns and mine may be similar.'

'Maybe. How are things with the elector?'

Verstohlen shrugged.

'I see less of him every day. I suspect my services are no longer of much use.'

'But how does he seem to you?'

'His mood changes. Some days, I see the qualities I saw in him when Schwarzhelm and I first arrived. On others, things are less... clear cut.'

Tochfel nodded. 'That's right. That's what others say. It's harder to get to him. I've not spoken with him for days. He's becoming erratic.'

Verstohlen felt a qualm of recognition. That's what they'd said about Schwarzhelm. Was there something corrupting about the city? He immediately thought of Natassja. The witch had still not been found.

'So what are you saying to me, Steward?' asked Verstohlen. 'I can't believe you've come here to moan about your master's moods.'

Tochfel's hands fidgeted on his knees. By the glow of the hearth, his face looked distorted.

'Something's wrong here, Herr Verstohlen,' he said, his voice audibly shaking. 'I tried to warn you of it before Grosslich's coronation. No one's seen Ferenc Alptraum since the battle for the city. No one's seen Achendorfer. There are other disappearances.'

'Such things are normal when power shifts,' said Verstohlen, watching Tochfel carefully, looking for the signs of dishonesty. The Steward was not a master player of the game, but he could still have been subverted.

Tochfel looked hurt. 'I may not have your skill in such matters,' he said, 'but I'm not entirely naïve. Do you know how many men have been burned at the stake? *Two hundred*. They're not all done in public. I've seen the lists. That's beyond reason.'

'Are there trials?'

'Supposedly.' Tochfel snorted. 'The witch hunter Heidegger has his talons into everything. He even wants my own aides dragged to the stake. None of us are safe.'

At the mention of witch hunters, Verstohlen had to work to suppress a grunt of contempt. The cult members who'd taken Leonora had been Templars of Sigmar. He regarded even the uncorrupted ones as little better than butchers and sadists, and the fact he was frequently mistaken for one of them was a considerable irritation.

Tochfel leaned forwards, his fingers twitching with agitation. 'Can't you *see* it?' he implored. 'We've picked the wrong man.'

Verstohlen shook his head. 'Impossible. I saw Leitdorf's corruption for myself.'

'Now who's being naïve, counsellor? So much has turned on that, and yet you always say that the great enemy is ever more cunning than it seems. Could you not have been *allowed* to see what you did?'

Verstohlen froze.

'Natassja's still not been found,' he said. 'She may be in the city. Her powers are formidable, and while she lives none of us should feel safe.'

Tochfel let slip a bitter laugh. 'You're obsessed with Natassja. Can't you see that *Grosslich* is the enemy? He's duped us all. You've seen that monstrosity he's building in the poor quarter. What sane man builds a tower of iron?'

Verstohlen didn't reply. The more Tochfel spoke, the more anxiety started to crowd around him. He'd been so *sure*. He'd convinced everyone of Leitdorf's guilt. Even Schwarzhelm.

For that matter, where *was* Schwarzhelm? Why hadn't there been any word from Altdorf? Why hadn't there been word of anything from outside the province?

'I won't deny there's something wrong here,' he said, 'but Natassja is the witch, and she's Leitdorf's woman. We need to find her, and her whelp of a husband.'

'What can I do to prove it to you?' asked Tochfel, sounding miserable. 'You won't accept the evidence of your eyes. No one will. I feel like I'm the only man left who can see it.'

'I'll speak to Grosslich,' said Verstohlen, placing a reassuring hand on the Steward's shoulder. 'There are things I'd like cleared up myself. Trust me – if the man has been tainted by anything here, I'll be able to tell. I'm not proud, Herr Tochfel. If I'm wrong, then I'll be the first to come to you to admit it. Then we'll decide what to do next.'

Tochfel didn't look reassured. 'He'll get stronger, the longer we leave it.'

'And what could we do, even if you were right?' asked Verstohlen. 'Could the two of us overthrow an elector? We need information. The Empire will not leave Averheim alone for long. This thing requires subtlety, and outside help.'

For a moment, Tochfel looked as if he'd protest further, but the words never came. He looked slumped and fearful.

'Take heart, Steward,' said Verstohlen, trying to improve both their moods. 'We have already saved Averheim from certain damnation. What corruption remains will be uncovered in time.'

Tochfel gave him a piteous look.

'If you really think that, counsellor,' he said, 'then I do not understand your reputation for wisdom.'

Black Fire Keep dominated the land around it, just as its architects had intended. The pass was under a mile wide at the point where it had been constructed. It had been raised on a hill of granite in the centre of the otherwise flat and featureless rock around it. The pinnacle of the fortress commanded long views both east and west, and in normal times the standards of the Emperor and of Averland rustled proudly from twenty-foot-high flagpoles.

The bare rock stretching away from the Keep on all sides

was not there by accident of nature. After the second battle of Black Fire Pass, an army of men and dwarfs had worked for months to clear the land. Piles of stone were levelled in back-breaking labour, and the few clumps of foliage capable of surviving the blinding snows of winter were cut down and burned. Approaching the Keep undetected was now all but impossible, and bitter experience had taught the defenders to remain vigilant at all times.

The massive walls rose a hundred feet into the clear sky and were as thick as a man's height. Their stone was black from the many sieges levelled against them, and the signs of historical devastation were impossible to remove. For all the blood shed over the wind-scoured stone, it would never be left undefended as long as the Empire stood. Black Fire Pass was more than a trading route, more than a strategic foothold in the mountains. It was the place where the Empire had been born. There was never a shortage of volunteers willing to man the ramparts of the way-forts and Keep, despite the appalling casualties and near-certainty of attack. Indeed, the mountain guard commanders had to pick their men carefully, rooting out the genuine soldiers from the fanatic and deranged.

The cycle of fighting never ended here. Incursions would be followed by a bitter fightback, which would be followed by fresh incursions. The humans would never rid the world of the greenskin scourge, and the orcs would never be allowed to hold the passes. As Bloch looked up at the distant walls, now daubed with the blood of their last human defenders, he knew he was just the latest to contest the site. Whatever the result of his actions, the game would be played out for centuries after he was gone.

He found the thought reassuring. All he'd ever known was war. The idea of a world where it didn't exist felt as wrong as being bought a drink by a dwarf. Both were feasibly possible, but he didn't expect to see either in his lifetime.

He stood with his troops half a mile west of the fortress, in view of the ramparts but far enough away to be untroubled by them. At his side, as ever, were Drassler and Kraus. Behind him, the army stood silently. They were arrayed for battle, divided into companies and standing in well-ordered ranks. They'd held together well. Averlander companies still carried their standards proudly, both those which Schwarzhelm had raised in Averheim and the men of Grenzstadt and Heideck who'd been drafted into action. Amongst them were the Reikland detachments that had marched from Altdorf. They were tougher men, hardened by years of ceaseless combat, proudly wearing the white and grey of the richest Imperial province. The tall staves of the halberds glinted in the severe light.

At the front was Bloch's own detachment. To a man, they were survivors of Grunwald's army. All of them were Reiklanders, tempered in the fiercest of fighting, as unyielding and hard-bitten as any regular troops in the Emperor's armies. No fear showed in their grizzled faces, just a grim determination to see the campaign through. Many of their comrades lay in the rich earth of the pastures below, and the deaths required vengeance.

Bloch looked over the heads of the massed troops to the baggage train at the rear. Reserve companies stood ready, as silent as the main body of the army. Teams of horses stamped nervously, steam snorting from their nostrils as they shook their heads against the chill. Behind them were the few artillery pieces of any size that he'd been able to commandeer. Not much, and little danger to the Keep.

Finally, there were Drassler's mountain guard. No more than two hundred or so remained, the others having been killed or harried into the high peaks by the tide of orcs. The survivors looked as hard-edged as Bloch's own men, their beards ragged and their faces unsmiling. This was their chance for revenge, and perhaps for some measure of atonement.

All were watching him, waiting for the words of command. As they stood unmoving, the harsh wind rippled across the army.

Bloch turned away from them, back to the fortress. He

couldn't make out much from that distance. There was no movement on the plain. The Keep rose tall and stark from the stone, a block of solid rock thrust from the core of the earth. Though there was no sign of the infestation, he knew that the place was swarming with greenskins. Schwarzhelm's orders, given so lightly after the rout on the grasslands of Averland, would not be easily fulfilled. That mattered not. He'd been given them, and he'd carry them out.

He took a deep breath and turned to Kraus. The captain's face was as bleak as the granite around him.

'Give the signal,' Bloch ordered. 'Let's do it.'

CHAPTER FOUR

Noon had passed, and the afternoon sun began to cast long shadows from the branches of the trees. The seemingly endless pastures of long, whispering grass had given way to higher country, dotted with straggling woodland and uncultivated scrub. This was poor land. The soil was thin and the undergrowth tangled. Ever since the devastation of Ironjaw the people of the region had been slow to return to their farms, and abandoned buildings, their roofs white with age, dotted the horizon. Gorse had replaced grass on the verges, and the roads petered out into stone-clogged tracks.

Skarr pulled his horse up and the column of knights came to a halt. He rode at the front of it, accompanied by Eissen, who in the aftermath of the fighting at Averheim had assumed the position of his lieutenant by default. Leitdorf was close behind. Further down the column, protected by ranks of Reiksguard, lay Helborg. He'd been placed in a carriage taken from Leitdorf's last country residence. It was absurdly ornate, decked with florid coats of arms and a golden image of the Solland sun on its flanks. If there had been any less ostentatious choice, Skarr would have taken it. As it was, he was stuck with the late count's extravagance.

He looked over the line of troops with a commander's eye, checking for signs of weariness or indiscipline. There were none. Though they now numbered less than fifty, the company held its order impeccably. The Reiksguard, drilled from their teens to embody the perfection of the Emperor's will, had maintained the condition of their armour and steeds with stoic efficiency. They carried most of their gear and supplies with them, and the trail of baggage mules and spare horses at the rear of the column was short.

Rufus Leitdorf nudged his horse alongside Skarr's. The deposed heir had lost some of the fat around his face over the last few days. He looked better for it, less effeminate. In the face of the Reiksguard's open contempt, some of the habitual arrogance had been knocked from his manner.

'How close are we?' asked Skarr, turning his gaze back to the road ahead. The track wound through the heathland uncertainly, threatening to give out entirely. That wouldn't trouble the horses, but it would make the carriage's progress impossible. Like everywhere in the Empire, there were creatures in the dark places far from the road, ever ready to launch an assault if they sensed weakness.

'Another day,' said Leitdorf. 'No more.'

Skarr grunted. Long hours travelling in the wilds didn't bother him at all, but Helborg's condition did. The Marshal needed time to rest properly. Skarr had witnessed Helborg fighting on after taking wounds that would have laid a lesser man low, but this was different. The man's face remained bloodless. Even when awake, his eyes were glassy and listless. Something seemed broken within him, and it wasn't physical. For long periods the Marshal remained unconscious. His slumber was troubled, and on the occasions Skarr had watched over him, he'd seen Helborg mutter words in his sleep. Chief among them was always 'Schwarzhelm'.

'I'm going to check on the Marshal,' he said, dismounting. Skarr pushed his way back through the mounted knights and made his way to the carriage. The doors had been covered with a black lacquer, much of which had rubbed off during the passage south and east. Now the proud emblems were scratched and faded, and the wood was plastered with grime.

Skarr climbed up on to the footboard and pulled the door open. Helborg was slumped against the far wall of the carriage, swathed in blankets. There wasn't room to lay him flat, and he looked awkwardly twisted in the cramped interior.

Helborg was awake, staring out of the window. Days-worth of stubble covered his sunken cheeks, and his moustache was lank.

'Marshal,' acknowledged Skarr, cautiously sitting opposite him. There wasn't much that scared the preceptor, but Helborg, even in his diminished state, made everyone nervous.

Helborg didn't respond. He kept staring out of the glass.

'How do you feel?' asked Skarr.

As soon as the question left his mouth, he knew it had been a mistake. Helborg didn't want pity.

'Where are we?' Helborg's rasping voice was even worse than usual.

'Near the Drakenmoor. Leitdorf's land. Another day's riding, no more.'

'I should be on a horse. What's this damned haywain you've got me in?'

Skarr didn't quite know how to respond to that. The man looked like he could barely raise his arm.

'I'll see to it,' he lied.

Helborg finally looked at him. His gaze was penetrating. 'My recollection of events is... unclear,' he said. 'What has happened here?'

Skarr cleared his throat. He had no answers.

'We're being hunted. Grosslich has raised the country against us. He's been crowned elector, and there's an army on our heels.'

'Then turn and fight it. You're Reiksguard.'

'There are hundreds of them, my lord.'

Helborg grunted with disapproval, as if to say, *and when did that ever matter before?*

'Schwarzhelm was with them,' added Skarr, and it sounded like a hollow excuse. He'd never run from a fight before, but the events of the Vormeisterplatz had been horrifying. To see the two greatest sons of the Empire come to blows had been bad enough. Becoming fugitives was even worse.

'So what's your plan?' rasped Helborg. At the mention of Schwarzhelm's name, his voice had become tighter.

'Keep you and Leitdorf hidden and find out what happened. Grosslich's treachery can't stay uncovered for long, and I'll find a way of getting a message through to Altdorf.'

Helborg shot him a withering look. Skarr recoiled, recognising the imperious disdain all too well. The Marshal wasn't happy.

'Damn it, Skarr, we'll do more than that,' he growled. Something of his old cultivated savagery had returned. 'You didn't see Schwarzhelm's face. He was mad. They'd all been driven mad. It was in the air.'

He leaned forwards with difficulty. Skarr saw one of his hands slip from the cloth wrappings, and it was clenched into a tight fist.

'We'll gather our strength and strike back,' he rasped. 'Strike hard, and strike fast. Whatever treachery has taken place here will be punished.'

Like a long-cold hearth stuttering back into life, the Marshal's eyes recovered their old fire. Then, and for the first time since the fighting at Averheim, Skarr knew Helborg would live to lead him again.

'We are your men, my lord,' he said, with something like joy.

'Forget that!' Helborg snapped, his voice shaking with fervour. 'Forget your loyalties. This is about vengeance. I will recover my strength, I will return to the city, and I will find the one who did this to me.'

He looked at Skarr directly, and his expression was brutal.

'Sigmar preserves those who *fight*, Skarr. We will fight until the Aver runs dark with blood. We will fight until the last traitor drowns in his own gore. We will fight until that bastard

Grosslich has been cast down and his soul flayed to the five corners of the world. They should have killed me. While a breath remains in my body I'll be too much for them. I'll raise the country against them. I'll tear down their walls and shatter their defences. I'll burn their warped dreams and rip out their traitor's hearts. All this I will do and more, for I am Kurt Helborg, master of the Emperor's endless armies, hammer of his foes, and my name itself is *vengeance*.'

Black Fire Keep was ugly. Pig ugly. The vaguely star-shaped walls jutted out unevenly, and the massive ramparts hung like brooding palls of snow over the sloping walls. Everything had been turned black by age and fire, and even the orcs hadn't found many ways to despoil further what they'd found.

'Form up!' Bloch bellowed, letting the sergeants echo his order through the ranks.

He'd pulled the army in close. The detachments of infantry were now in clear view of the battlements, arrayed in a wide semicircle to the south of the fort. All were deployed in company detachments several ranks deep, Averlanders mingled with Reiklanders. The squares formed a long, ragged line across the stony ground, and there were many gaps between the clustered companies. Pennants flew in the strong breeze, snapping and rippling over the heads of the soldiers. There was no heavy cavalry, and what artillery there was had been hauled into place on the far left flank of the army, south-west of the Keep along a narrow shelf of wind-smoothed rock. Reserves were minimal – just a couple of halberdier companies set back from the main formation.

The troops kept out of bow-range, but only just. If Bloch could tempt the defenders to waste arrows, then that was all to the good. The sun was still high in the sky, and there was plenty of time for an assault. If he had his way, the fortress would be breached by nightfall. It all came down to tactics, expectation and a generous slice of luck.

Bloch shaded his eyes and looked up at the ramparts. There were shapes moving along them, hunched against the stone.

The greenskins were agitated. He knew it wasn't fear. They were cooped up, locked behind walls. They hated that. It was that hatred he had to use.

'Artillery!' roared Bloch, and the signal was sent down the lines.

The firepower wasn't much to boast about: a handful of Helblasters, two Helstorms and a couple of light cannon. Hauling them up the mountainsides had been a miserable task; now they had to prove their worth.

On either side of the artillery, the reserve companies of halberdiers edged away. None of them trusted the gun crews, who worked fast in the cold to get the engines of war ready. Barrels were aimed and last-minute adjustments made. Buckets of water were drawn up and burning rags placed ready next to the wicks. The crew captains looked up expectantly.

'Fire,' growled Bloch.

The order went down the line. With a deafening crack that echoed around the pass, the first guns fired. Cannonballs whined into the air, smashing high up against the walls and sending the gun barrels slamming back yards. They were followed by the swish of Helstorm rockets, spiralling in their wake and exploding in balls of fire. The Helblaster batteries that followed were less effective – they'd been designed to counter infantry units, not batter down solid walls – but Bloch ordered them to open fire anyway. The task was not to reduce the walls to rubble, but to play on the nerves of the orcs. He knew they were itching to strike back. He just had to keep provoking them.

'Aim high!' he roared, reminding them of their orders. 'Dead greenskins, not cracked stone.'

Standing at Bloch's side, Kraus gestured to the commander of the archery companies. There weren't many of them – no more than two hundred – and they didn't have the range or the volume of arrows to seriously trouble the defenders. Nonetheless, they marched forwards, flanked by heavily-armed infantry carrying shields. As they came into range, the first bellows of scorn and challenge came down from the fortress. The orcs were roused.

'Remember your orders!' barked Bloch. 'No arrows wasted.'

The archers settled into position and a stream of enemy bolts began to spin down towards them. The armoured infantry formed protective ranks in front of the lightly armed archers and did their best to shelter them from the deadly hail from above. Once in position, the Imperial bows began to sing and arrows flew up at the heavily guarded battlements and windows. Even as they did so, the second round of cannon fire blazed out.

Kraus watched the flurry of bolts and shot impassively. Bloch did likewise, seeing a soldier in the front rank of the exposed archery battalion crumple to the floor, a black-barbed dart shivering in his chest. The exchange of fire was lethal in both directions, but only one army was in proper cover.

'We can't keep this up for long,' Kraus said grimly.

Bloch knew that as well as he did.

'Keep firing!' he shouted, spittle flying from his lips. The men had to know he was in charge, that this was all part of the plan.

'They'll come out,' he hissed, his voice low so only Kraus could hear.

'And if they don't?'

Bloch didn't answer. He didn't want to think about that.

The day waxed across Averheim, and all along the river barges bumped and jostled for position. Clouds had begun to drift from the east, and the sky was no longer the unbroken arch of blue it had been for so long. A light breeze whipped up the surface of the Aver, throwing flecks of foam against the bows of the vessels in the water.

Men clambered from hold to hold, carrying goods or ticking off items on requisition ledgers. Soldiers were everywhere. The number of men-at-arms in Averheim seemed to have trebled. Some looked like Alptraum's men, given new uniforms and new weapons. Others had an unfamiliar look about them, as if they were new to the city and out of sympathy with its residents.

Tochfel gathered his cloak around his shoulders, feeling the cool air against his skin. He had no business on the wharfs today, and since his meeting with Verstohlen he'd grown wary of any attempts to influence the traffic there. If no one but he could see the problem in suborning an entire province to the demands of a single building, then that was their problem. The time had come to make his protests at the highest level, while he still had the protection of his rank and title. He had no confidence in retaining either for long.

He hurried on down from the quayside, avoiding the glares from the roving bands of soldiers. Grosslich's men had become officious, as if given special orders to stop and search anyone abroad without permission. Even in the middle of the afternoon, some of them were clearly the worse for wear. They were well-paid, that Tochfel knew, and there were only two things a soldier spent his money on. The taverns and bawdy-houses had never done better business.

Striding on from the Griffon Bridge and the embankment beyond, Tochfel made his way to the poor quarter. As he went, the crowds thinned out. Even the patrols lessened, and before he'd gone more than half a mile the roads and streets were eerily quiet. No taverns were open, no hearths glowed behind lead-lined windows, no brothels rang with song and laughter. Everything was buttoned-down, locked-up, shut fast.

Tochfel didn't pause, but kept his head down. He knew what kept the people away. Ahead of him, the Tower rose. It seemed to grow taller with every passing hour. Iron fronds had shot up from the base like plants, curling into the air and branching into new tendrils. The skeleton was gradually being clad, and fresh beams criss-crossed between supporting struts like the bone spurs of a lady's corset. Even at such an early stage it was clear that the final construction would be huge. When completed, the horrific needle of metal and stone would dwarf the Averburg and cast a spiked shadow over half the city. As Tochfel looked at it, he shuddered. Why could no one else see how *wrong* this was? Why was Verstohlen so relaxed about it?

Tochfel pulled his cloak tighter and pressed on. It was time to get to the bottom of things. If Grosslich wouldn't come to see him at the Averburg, Tochfel would have to come to Grosslich at the Tower.

He turned into the long, straight street which led directly to the construction site. The houses on either side of him were almost completely silent. Even in the strong sunlight he felt a strange chill settle on his bones. There were no open windows. A loose door banged in the breeze at the far end, and from somewhere else there came the sound of a rusty hinge being worked back and forth.

At the end of the street the old wooden perimeter fence had been replaced with something more permanent: iron, naturally, hammered into eight-foot poles and elaborately spiked on the top. As far as he could see, it looked like the new fence ran around the entire site, enclosing the workings of the Tower completely.

Where the street met the fence, a high gate had been raised, crowned with a stylised 'G' set amid a crown of thorns. There were other shapes sculpted there, though quite what they were was hard to make out. Despite the strong daylight, lamps burned atop twin pillars on either side of the gates. The flames within them were an odd colour, a deep orange, with the faintest blush of pink at the edges. The fires flickered within their glass caskets like grasping fingers.

Tochfel paused, suddenly uneasy. He'd heard the stories of this place, just as everyone else had. The river was less than a mile away, bustling with life, and yet it could have been left behind in another world. His resolve began to waver. Perhaps coming had been a mistake.

'Declare yourself,' came a voice from beside the gate.

A man stepped from the shadow of one of the pillars, brandishing a spear. Another approached from the opposite side. They were wearing the crimson and gold of Grosslich's army. Tochfel noticed that they were better equipped than the guards at the Averburg and wore a close-fitting breastplate, greaves and a tall helmet. Not very Averland-like. Almost... *elvish*.

'The Steward,' said Tochfel, letting his cloak fall back and trying to keep the fear out of his voice. Now that he'd been noticed, retreat was impossible. The guards recognised him and lowered their spears.

'You're here on your own, sir?'

'What does it look like? Open the gates.'

The guards looked at one another doubtfully. 'Are you expected, sir? The elector doesn't like–'

'Open the damn gates, man. Neither he nor I like being kept waiting.'

The lead guard shrugged. He went back to the pillar and pulled some kind of brass lever set into the stone. There was a hiss, and the gates swung inwards. Beyond them, a wide path had been cut, lined with some kind of thorn-bush at ground level. Dotted clumps of the strange plant were visible beside the path as it ran the several hundred yards up to the unfinished Tower.

Tochfel hurried inside, not giving the guards a second glance. Behind him, the gates sighed closed, coming together with a soft click. Like everything about the place, the motion was unsettling.

Within the fence, the ground had been cleared and flattened. Huge paving slabs of dark stone had been laid. They were interlinked, and traced out some obscure and massively complicated pattern. As Tochfel gazed at it, he thought he caught something of its outline, but the totality eluded him. It was both familiar and deeply strange. The artistry of the stones' placement looked superb, and the joins between sections were barely visible.

He went deeper in the compound. The silence became more absolute. Only his own footfalls, soft against the polished stone, seemed to make any noise at all.

Tochfel looked up as he went. The sky had lost some of its lustre. There was a greyness to it. That was strange. As he watched, the colour seemed to run out of it. He flicked his eyes earthwards, disorientated. The mass of iron loomed ahead, a fraction more distinct than the sky behind it. It was no longer dark. Everything was going grey, as if a mist had rolled across the plain while he walked.

Tochfel could feel his heart thumping strongly. His palms grew sweaty. The air around him smelled strange. There was a metallic taste on his tongue, almost sweet. He felt light-headed and dizzy. This really had been a mistake.

His breathing quickening, he turned and started to head back. The place was cursed, and he had no place in it.

A sudden noise made him start. He felt panic rise in his throat. It sounded like the wheeze of some huge dog, close by, somewhere in the gathering mist. Tochfel hurried back the way he'd come. The scorn of the guards didn't matter now. There was something in the grey light, and it wasn't natural. Perhaps a hundred yards ahead, he could still see the dim outline of the pillars with their flame lanterns. He'd be there in moments.

Then the pillars shrank from view. Both of them. As if some order had been given from within the Tower, the colour-drenching mist swept up and across the compound. Everything but the patterned stone beneath him disappeared. Even his hands looked pale, like a cadaver's.

Tochfel found himself struggling to keep a lid on his bubbling fear. He began to run. To his left there was another dog-like sound, closer than the last, right on his shoulder. He veered away from it, losing his sense of direction. The last shreds of vision merged into the grey fog. It felt like the whole world had been torn from existence. Heart hammering, breath ragged, he stumbled blindly, mumbling prayers to Sigmar in his panic.

Then, from nowhere, a patch of curling vapour ripped from the rest and let a shaft of the world's sun into the cloud. Ahead of Tochfel was a man. No, not a man. It had an armoured snout, impossibly long, plated and dark. It crouched low, as if its joints were twisted backwards. A snarling, grating sound came from its muzzle, and it clutched a crystal-bladed halberd in a pair of clawed hands.

Tochfel screamed. He screamed like he'd never screamed

in his life. Other soldiers emerged from the shifting clouds, each panting and growling like a dog, each limping towards him like a grotesque parody of both man and beast.

Then the beam of sunlight passed, obscured by the grey miasma once more. Tochfel's screams lasted for a moment longer, and were then extinguished, muffled by the mist. Silence rolled back across the construction site. After a few moments the mist sank back to earth, wavering and rippling as it sighed out of existence.

Back at the gates, the guards did their best not to pay any attention. They'd learned it wasn't wise to interfere with what went on in the Tower. They hadn't seen the mist anyway. Only one man in Averheim had seen the mist, and he was gone. Just on the edge of hearing, there was a faint noise. It could have been a trick of the wind, but it sounded like a woman laughing, cool and elegant.

Then it too was gone. The compound looked as it always did, empty and echoing. Across the wide expanse of stone there was no sign of the dog-soldiers, nor of Tochfel. If the human guards had been foolish enough to venture inside the compound, perhaps curious as to his fate, they would have found no body, and no blood.

There was no blood, because he hadn't been killed. That wasn't the way of the Tower. He'd been taken, just as the others had been, alive. And that, of course, was only the beginning.

Arrows flew up at Black Fire Keep, peppering the stone and clattering back to earth. The cannon still boomed, but only the faintest of cracks had been opened up on the ramparts. It was too old, too strong. The orcs stayed clustered in safety, locked out of harm's way. Frustration began to spread across the besieging army.

Bloch sensed it before he saw it. He was barely out of the ranks himself, plucked from being a company captain by Schwarzhelm after the engagement at Turgitz, and knew all the moods of a halberdier detachment. They were getting close to boiling over. They could all see the exposed archers being picked off from the ramparts, all hear the jeers of the capering orcs on the battlements. This was death by attrition.

'Pull them back,' hissed Kraus through clenched teeth. Nearly two dozen archers lay dead, and another score had been wounded. They were having almost no effect.

'No,' said Bloch, watching the carnage blankly. 'It's keeping their eyes where I want them. We won't pull back.'

'Damn you, commander, pull them back!' Kraus looked livid. His fingers itched at his side, eager to draw his sword and exact retribution for the losses.

'Bring out the bait,' said Bloch, clenching his jaw to hide his anguish. His faith in his plan was being sorely tested.

Kraus shook his head, but called out the order. A company of Averlander spearmen rushed from the reserve position to the front ranks of the army. Still out of bowshot, but ahead of the main body of halberdiers, they stopped. Each of them carried a heavy bag on their back. Some were bent double under the weight, and others were carried by two men.

Their captain, a veteran of the Averheim garrison who'd ridden out with Schwarzhelm, looked up to Bloch for confirmation.

'Do it!' Bloch roared, before turning to Kraus. 'Send the word out. The army holds position. Do *not* threaten the gates, d'you hear?'

The orders were passed on. The hail of artillery and arrows was kept up, nearly obscuring the Keep beyond with its drip feed of provocation.

On the plain, in full view of the Keep's massive gatehouse, the Averlanders began their work. All slammed their bags to the ground and pulled the fabric back. Within them were the bodies of fallen greenskins. Most were goblins, scrawny and spiteful-looking even in death. Some of the cadavers were of larger breeds, and there were even a couple of heavy warriors, carried by two or more men and as thick as the bole of a fallen oak.

All of the bodies had been stripped of their armour, and

the naked green flesh looked almost grey in the spare light. The limbs were bound with twine, and there were blood-stains on all the corpses. There were nearly a hundred of them, the best part of a company, all dead. As the carcasses were produced, a howl of anger rose from the Keep.

'It won't work,' insisted Kraus. 'They're obviously dead.'

'They can't see that,' said Bloch, looking at the carnage grimly. 'It'll look like an execution. And even if it doesn't, would you watch while *they* butchered your comrades' bodies?'

The Averlander captain waited until the stricken orcs were all out, then brought his sword down. One by one, working from right to left, the cadavers were dragged forwards. With the maximum ceremony, the captain sliced off their limbs. He didn't work quickly, and lingered over every stroke. If the orc had been alive, it would have been howling in agony. As it was, Bloch hoped the distance would give a similar impression to those watching on the battlements.

More orc corpses were sliced apart. The growling and cursing from the Keep grew louder. Figures could be seen scurrying back and forth against the battlements, and the rain of black-feathered arrows stepped up. They were getting angrier.

'Maintain artillery barrage!' bellowed Bloch. 'Keep those arrows coming!'

He looked at the distance between the front ranks of his army and the gate. There was plenty of space. He'd deliberately kept the ground open and his forces in a loose offensive position. The orcs had to think that he was ill-prepared for a sortie, that he'd left his men wide open to attack. Even now, he could sense the boiling anger from within the castle walls. He knew the orcish commander would be holding them back, but he also knew there'd be hotheaded warriors burning to strike back. If the roles were reversed, he'd have been one of them. Better an honest fight in the open than skulking in the stinking halls of a human hovel.

'Come on,' he breathed, watching the walls intently.

A muffled cry told them that another archer had been slain. A low tide of muttering reached his ears from the halberdiers around him. More orc corpses were cut apart, their limbs thrown towards the gates with scorn. Averlanders capered around with severed heads, throwing them back and forth like children with snowballs. The cannon roared again, making the ramparts shudder with the impact.

'Come *on*...'

The gates stayed shut. The growling from within reached a fever pitch. Bloch was running out of time. Kraus put his hand on his sword, ready to draw it. His face was black with anger. Bloch knew what he was thinking. The madness had to be put to an end. They had to withdraw. The plan wasn't working.

Bloch looked up at the ramparts. The gamble was blowing up in his face, and good men were dying. Another shield-bearer went down in the front ranks, his skull crushed by a rock hurled from the Keep. The cries of agony as he writhed on the stone rent Bloch's heart.

'By Sigmar,' he hissed, knuckles white with tension as he gripped the shaft of his halberd. 'Come *on*...'

Verstohlen waited. He'd already been waiting for some time. It had been hard to gauge how long, but it must surely have been two hours. He was sitting in an antechamber in the Averburg. The room was almost entirely bare. There were marks against the stone where furniture and paintings had once hung, now just bleached emptiness. The one bench that remained was old and battered. The place had been stripped, and was now not much more than a draughty hall of naked rock.

Verstohlen crossed his legs and looked out of the window opposite. Doubts ran through his mind, one after the other. It was the little things that gave cause for anxiety. Traders spoke in hushed tones of a heavy military presence all along the Aver. What little dissent had remained in Averheim after Leitdorf's departure had been ruthlessly crushed. Verstohlen recalled Tochfel's look of disbelief as he'd recounted the burnings. *Two hundred.*

And Natassja was still alive. She had to be. Despite all Grosslich's assurances that she and her husband were being hunted, there was still no result. Only a body would satisfy him.

Now Tochfel had thrown doubt on the elector himself. Part of him couldn't believe the ebullient, golden-haired warrior could have been corrupted; the other part of him dwelt on the possibility endlessly. Averland seemed to have developed a knack for turning the minds of its governors. First Marius, then Schwarzhelm, now Grosslich. There had to be something deeper going on. For all his supposed acumen, all his long experience, he couldn't see it.

Verstohlen sighed, letting his head fall back against the bare stone wall. There was no pleasure in this work any more. There never had been, really. He was just Schwarzhelm's tool, the keenest of his many instruments. With the Emperor's Champion gone, Verstohlen was bereft, like a plank of old wood washed up on the shoreline. Some men made their own destinies. Verstohlen hadn't been like that since Leonora. For all his peerless attributes, the wound of that parting had never closed. He was a follower, not a leader, and the shadows were his home. Now exposed, held out in the open as the architect of Grosslich's rebellion, he was useless, a liability, an anachronism.

'My lord?'

Verstohlen snapped back into the present. He'd been drifting. Reverie was replaced with irritation.

'What is it?' he asked, looking up sharply.

An official wearing the robes of a loremaster had entered. The man's face was curiously white and smooth, rather like a woman's. He was gazing at Verstohlen with a faint air of smugness, as if glad to have caught the famous spy napping.

'I'm sorry to inform you that His Excellency is not able to grant you an audience after all. I regret extremely that you've waited so long for no purpose.'

'*His Excellency*? What in Sigmar's name is that? And who're you?'

'I am Holymon Eschenbach,' replied the official, still as smooth and untroubled as cream. 'The new under-Steward. And His Excellency has issued a proclamation on the titles and ranks to be observed in the new dispensation. You would do well to note them, counsellor.'

Verstohlen felt his frustration begin to rise. He was being snubbed, and crudely so. Or perhaps this was another message. He rose fluidly, pulling his leather overcoat closed around him.

'Well then, under-Steward,' he said, letting a note of contempt sink into that title. 'It seems I have no more business here. Perhaps you would let His Excellency know that I need to see him as soon as is convenient.'

Eschenbach bowed. 'I'll do so.'

Verstohlen made to brush past him when a faint whiff of something familiar caught his attention. He paused.

'I assume you work for Dagobert Tochfel now?' he asked.

Eschenbach couldn't suppress the ghost of a sneer across his full lips. 'Naturally.' In that one, short word, much information was conveyed. Verstohlen caught the meaning perfectly clearly. So this Eschenbach was after the Steward position. Tochfel had better watch his back.

Then he placed it. The aroma wasn't strong, but Verstohlen had spent enough time trying to trace its origins to recognise its presence. Joyroot. The man was either a user, or he'd worked on the trade in it. Grosslich couldn't possibly have missed it. So much for all the promises.

'Are you all right, my lord?' asked Eschenbach, his tone profoundly unconcerned.

'I'm fine,' said Verstohlen. His mind was working quickly, teasing out the possibilities. Tochfel had been right. This Eschenbach was a minor player, but his presence here was no accident. Perhaps the joyroot on his collar was a slip. Or perhaps he was being given a warning, a reward for the work he'd done to drive Leitdorf out and deliver the throne to Grosslich. Verstohlen felt the first stirrings of a deep nausea. More than anyone else, more than Schwarzhelm, he'd done this. He'd brought it about, the man who hated Chaos with a fervour unequalled even by the witch hunters. The irony nearly killed him.

'This has been an instructive conversation,' he said, and pushed the door open. Outside, the guards stood to attention. There was fear in their faces. How could he have been so blind? The fear had never gone away, it had just been hidden for a while. Long enough for the damage to have been done.

Verstohlen hurried down the corridor, anxious to get into the fresh air again. He could still smell the joyroot. A dozen thoughts crowded into his mind at once. He had to find Tochfel. He had to find Schwarzhelm. He had to find help.

And then he remembered Natassja, the masks on the walls, the dreams.

With a pang of fear, he knew then what his principal objective was. They weren't quite ready to kill him in the Averburg, not while his name was so well known and there were loyal personnel still at their stations. They'd come for him at night, when he was alone, when the last of his friends had been despatched. Nowhere was safe now, perhaps not even the forge.

As he passed through the winding passages of the ancient citadel, the message Tochfel had been trying to convey to him became painfully apparent. The corruption had never been defeated, never been banished, never been suppressed.

It had always been there, and now it was coming for him.

CHAPTER FIVE

At last, the rain had stopped falling on Altdorf. The skies remained a low grey, heavy with sodden cloud, but the dull thud of water against stone and tile ceased for a while. That didn't make much difference to the stench hanging over the old city. Though much of the water drained down into the vast network of catacombs and sink-holes far beneath the foundations of the clustered buildings, plenty of the filth and slurry had nowhere to go but the street, and large pools of foetid water sat stinking across the thoroughfares. Folk trudged through it while going about their business, making the sign of the comet to ward off pox and plague. It didn't help much. In the aftermath of the deluge, dysentery and cholera spread with the same speed they always did, and the tight-knit terraces of wattle houses were soon racked with coughs, splutters and phlegmy expirations. The gravediggers and the priests of Morr were the only ones who profited, revelling as they always did in misery.

Set some distance from the sprawl and splendour of the Imperial Palace, as streaked with rain as every other building in the city, was the Cathedral of Sigmar Risen and Transformed. It had been purposefully set away from the Imperial Chapel, whose priesthood were part of the Emperor's retinue and therefore loyal to the master of the throne. The Grand Theogonists, with their long tradition of independent thought, had always seen the danger in letting the Emperor's pet priests monopolise the worship of the warrior-god in Altdorf, so funds had been set aside to create a rival institution within the city. The first stones had been laid in the year 580, before Altdorf had even been recognised as the pre-eminent settlement in the Empire. Successive masters of the Cult of Sigmar had augmented, rebuilt, extended, demolished and refashioned the structure until it came to dominate nearly half a square mile of prime Altdorf real estate.

In a conurbation already rammed with massive, vulgar piles of stone, the Cathedral of Sigmar Risen and Transformed was a serious contender for the most massive and vulgar of them all. The Church was rich, and no expense had been spared on its decoration. Huge murals had been commissioned, some by de Buenosera himself, which adorned every inch of the plastered ceilings. They mostly depicted Sigmar slaying some beast or other, although the famously dissolute Michaelangelico had managed to insert spurious vignettes of buxom Reikland maidens being carried off in various states of undress to a fate worse than death at the hands of improbably proportioned Norscans.

Every pillar was encrusted with bands of gold, studded with semi-precious stones and ringed with ingots of silver. The floor was made up of a dizzying array of marble flags, each a different colour, some engraved with trader's marks indicating passage from furthest Cathay. The windows were a riot of brightly-stained glass, most illustrating moral tales of dragon-slaying, mutant-hunting or witch-burning. In the very centre of the colossal building, where four vaulted naves met under a domed roof nearly two hundred feet high, the Altar of the Ascended Warrior stood in gaudy magnificence, crowned by a thirty-foot-high statue of Sigmar wrestling with the dragon Gauthmir cast in ever-polished bronze and ringed with forty-two censers containing the finest spices of Ind and Araby.

Every day, whether the rain was falling or the pox raging, thousands of pilgrims made their way to the holy site. Some fell on their faces before the splendour, mumbling prayers to Sigmar before being dragged away by the small army of impatient priests. Others fell into silent contemplation, marvelling at the labour required to create such a daunting monument to the human spirit. Still others, perhaps over-educated or seduced by the thin-lipped creed of Verena, found the whole thing mildly distasteful and regretted handing over the three-schilling entrance fee to the heavily-armed zealots at the north gate entrance.

For Volkmar, who had nothing but contempt for the pitiable worship of Verena, that was about the only thing he had in common with such borderline heretics. He hated the Cathedral. He hated the gold, he hated the gilt, and he hated the pilgrims. They were simpering fools, the lot of them. None knew how to wield a warhammer, and hardly any would have been able to read the scriptures or the ordinances. They would come to the Cathedral fresh from whatever petty debauchery they'd been engaged in, thinking that a donation of brass and a few genuflections would save their souls from an eternity of damnation.

Volkmar knew different. He knew what kind of god Sigmar was. Sigmar didn't value excuses, and He certainly didn't value offerings. He needed spirits forged in white-hot steel, hands willing to take up swords, feet willing to march into the cold wastes of the north to pin back the hordes of destruction.

Volkmar also knew about damnation. He'd stared into the face of it, seen the fate awaiting mankind should it falter. On the pitiless plains of the far north, he'd been struck low by the Everchosen of Chaos, Archaon the Mighty. He'd felt his life slip away, had cried out as his soul was ripped from his mortal frame. It was Chaos that had brought him back, had pulled his essence back into his ravaged body and tortured it before the gibbering hosts of ruin. The ranks of the corrupted had stretched from horizon to horizon, filling the northlands with a simmering tide of hate.

Volkmar alone of mortal men knew what it was to die and be forcibly reborn. He alone knew of the utter horror of existence on the planes of madness, and he alone had seen, however briefly, the world through the aspect of a daemon's eyes.

Most would have been driven mad. He sometimes wondered why he hadn't. No doubt there was a reason he'd endured. There was some pattern, some divine intention behind it. He wasn't sure what it was yet. In the meantime, taking the war back to the filth that had caused him such pain seemed like a reasonable way of repaying the debt. They said that familiarity bred contempt. Volkmar, uniquely amongst his peers, was familiar with the great enemy, and Volkmar, uniquely amongst his peers, held it in utter, withering, grinding contempt.

And so it was that he despised the Cathedral. It was showy, a front for the futile rivalry between the Cult of Sigmar and the officials of the Imperial Palace. He preferred the Chapel of the Fallen, or the Cathedral of Sigmar the Avenger in Talabheim, or the Abbey of Sigmar the Destroyer of Beasts in Middenheim, hard under the shadow of the imposing Ulrican temple and carved from solid granite.

He strode down the long south transept, snarling at the shiny flummery around him. Every so often, a priest would see him coming and look for an escape. If none was available, the man would bow low, desperate to avoid the wrath of the Theogonist. Even the brute mass of the populace, as ignorant as they were malodorous, knew well enough to keep out of his way. A six-foot mountain of a man, clad in heavy furs and carrying the ancient Staff of Command, was not someone to be crossed lightly.

Eventually, Volkmar reached his destination: a small door in the outer wall of the transept, barely marked and overshadowed by a tasteless frieze depicting Magnus smiting some worm or other. With a final snarl at the milling crowds around him, Volkmar pushed the door open, ducked under the lintel and went inside.

It led into a small, unadorned chamber. Centuries ago this had been a tomb. Now Volkmar had commandeered it for his private meetings. The walls were made of solid stone and had no windows. Though he was in the very heart of Altdorf, nothing of the plague-ridden, gossip-laced town ever penetrated down there.

There were men already waiting for him. They clustered around the old sarcophagus in the centre of the chamber. All around the walls, torches guttered, throwing sooty smoke curling into the vaulted roof. It was dark, cold and austere. Just how a chapel to Sigmar ought to be.

'Greetings, Theogonist,' said one of them.

Volkmar grunted, slammed the door shut behind him and shot the bolts home. Then he rose to his full height and surveyed the scene.

There were three figures waiting for him. All wore armour, notched and scored by recent fighting. They were nearly as massive as Volkmar himself and had the confident stare of men who'd faced death, or worse, in battle. Two of them Volkmar knew almost as well as he knew himself. The third was new.

On his left was his confessor, Efraim Roll. The man looked as old as the tomb he stood behind. His beard was long and matted, and his skin lined with a latticework of wrinkles. His head was bald, and old wounds decorated the bare scalp. His dark eyebrows jutted out, as did his chin, and he bore himself with the demeanour of a man fighting against a constant stream of rage. His armour was as ancient as any in the Empire, having been forged by dwarfs for the first conclave of Sigmar's personal priesthood. It was hammered from purest gromril and engraved with runes of destruction and damnation. Roll was perfectly suited to it, being Volkmar's confessor and the only man in the Empire apart from

Karl Franz who ever dared to give him an order. In the flickering light of the torches, the innate savagery of his face was amplified.

To his right stood a very different figure. Odain Maljdir was a vast bear of a man, ruddy-cheeked with a blond beard bursting over his enormous breastplate. He wore his hair long, and it streamed in a series of elaborate plaits over his studded pauldrons. His skin was tanned by the ice-glare of the far north and looked as tough as old horsehide. Once the man had been a priest in the service of Ulric and had made his name smiting the Norscans on their endless raids across the Sea of Claws. They said he'd once held back an entire company of them single-handed on the steps of a pagan temple while waiting for an army of state troopers to relieve his position. Soon after that, something had changed. He never said what it was, but he'd ended up travelling south. The first Volkmar had known of it was when the huge man had hammered on his door with his two fists, blurting in heavily accented Reikspiel that he'd come to learn of the ways of Sigmar. Since then he'd been inducted into the secrets of the Cult, and given the warhammer Bloodbringer as his weapon. If he still hankered for the bleak worship of Ulric, he never gave a sign. He'd become as devoted a Sigmarite as Volkmar himself, which was a rare thing in an Empire made up of doubters, heretics and fools.

The final figure stood apart. He looked scarcely less deadly than his counterparts, though he was clearly no Templar of Sigmar. His dark hair was long, and his visage lean. Like the others, his armour was of ancient pedigree, though dented by recent sword blows. He had a haughty, noble look about him, as confident as it was pitiless. This was a man who had been forged in the keenest fires of combat, who had ridden once against the terror-inducing foes of mankind and had the stomach to do it again. He carried a longsword at his belt, sheathed in a scabbard marked with the campaign records of Araby and Tilea. It was the first day he'd been in Altdorf since being ordered to take the fight to the enemy in the wind-scoured wastes of the north. He bore the scars of that assignment in his dour expression. No man fought against the legions of the Dark Gods and was unchanged by it.

In other ways, though, he was still the man he'd been when standing besides Schwarzhelm at the battle of the Turgitz Cauldron. Preceptor Leonidas Gruppen of the Knights Panther had been summoned home, though at that point he had absolutely no idea why.

'Greetings to you all,' grunted Volkmar. 'Now, to business.'

Drassler lay still amongst the boulders, his grey cloak smothering him, barely an inch of room exposed to see out from under. His breathing was shallow and he could feel his heartbeats against the stone. Around him, he knew the rest of the mountain guard, all two hundred of those who remained, were similarly concealed. As the sunlight began to wane, throwing shadows across the broken landscape, their disguise became even more effective. For generations the bergsjaeger had known how to blend into the barren landscape. The skills had originated in the hunting of game but had been perfected over the long years for warfare. Now he waited, face down and sprawled against the ice-hard rock, waiting.

Nearly two hundred yards away, the Keep stood as solid as a peak. The barrage from Bloch's artillery was being maintained and a steady stream of arrows flew up at the battlements. Drassler and his men had crept round to the east side of the castle. The gates were in view now, and he could see the Averlanders continue to goad the orcs with feigned executions and mutilations.

He didn't like the tactic. Drassler had seen too many greenskin armies use the same strategy, driving defenders mad by torturing their comrades in sight of the walls. But he knew what Bloch was doing, and saw how it gave them their chance. The commander had deliberately left his force in disarray, making it look like the overconfident approach of a novice general. The orcs would see that. They would see how far back Bloch had deployed, how little he threatened the gatehouse. The sortie beckoned. If Drassler had been in charge of the Keep, he'd have been tempted.

He wouldn't have taken the bait. Unlike the orcs, Drassler knew of the opportunities for ambush, of the techniques the mountain guard could use for creeping up unawares. All his men were clad in the same stone-grey cloaks, mottled and streaked to mimic the pattern of the terrain beneath them. It had taken hours to work their way around to the east of Bloch's position and then shuffle forwards over the rock, grazing flesh and tearing the stiff leather of their jerkins.

If a watchful orc on the battlements happened to gaze straight at them, then the game would be up. Even their camouflage, as good as it was, couldn't foil direct scrutiny. So it was that Bloch kept up the nagging barrage, doing everything he could to keep the eyes of the Keep on him.

It was a dangerous tactic. A sudden rush from the gates in numbers risked overwhelming Bloch's first lines of defence. The cost of being so ostentatiously out of position was that a determined assault would cause havoc.

It was a risk worth taking. As long as the gates remained closed, the chances of driving the orcs from the Keep were slim. As soon as they opened, those odds shortened.

Drassler moved his head fractionally, looking out at the distant lines of archers. They were being given a hard time by the defending greenskins. Perhaps a third of them had been killed or wounded, and the shield-bearing infantry around them had fared little better. Orcs didn't like using ranged weapons if there was a choice, but they were more skilled shots than many Imperial generals gave them credit for.

He felt his stomach turn in disgust. The gates remained closed. The ammunition for the guns would begin to run down soon. Bloch would have to pull back. If he did so, then all his plan would have yielded would be four-score men dead and a brace of empty gun barrels.

Drassler reached slowly for the sword at his back. At any

moment he expected to hear the signal for withdrawal, closely followed by bellows of derision from the orcs locked up within. Then their own position would become precarious, and they'd have to get clear of the walls. A shambles. A bloody shambles. They were running out of time.

Then came the first sound.

A heavy clang of iron, as something was unhooked from within the gates. A fresh barrage cracked out from Bloch's artillery, harmlessly smashing against the walls. Drassler felt his heart start to pound. At last. They were going for it.

He turned to the nearest of his men. The sounds of more beams being flung to the ground came from the Keep. A thin line of daylight stretched down between the mighty iron-barred doors. From behind them, a rising tide of baying and bellowing came out. Against all hope, they were going for it.

Drassler rose to a low crouch, ready for the breakneck sprint across the rock. This would all still unravel if the mountain guard couldn't close in quickly enough. He saw the massive gates begin to swing open. The noise of the horde rose in volume, a terrifying roar of pent-up aggression and frustration. The orcs had been maddened, and the storm of their emergence would be terrible.

Drassler's hand was damp with sweat as he drew his sword, keeping it under his cloak as best he could. They'd be outnumbered badly until Bloch could get to them. Surprise was all they had.

'On my mark, lads,' he hissed, knowing his men would be as taut as he, ready for the charge, knowing the danger. 'On my mark...'

There was a boom, a scrape of tortured metal, and the gates slammed back against the stone. With a torrent of bellows and roars, the orcs surged out, eyes blazing red, blades swinging, trampling over one another in their lust for combat.

The pretence was over. Now the real fighting had begun.

* * *

Volkmar walked up to the sarcophagus, the heel of the Staff of Command clanking on the stone floor. The other three men clustered around the tomb.

'We don't have long,' said Volkmar. 'The army is gathering, but these things take time.'

'What's the state of it?' asked Maljdir.

'Twenty thousand men promised. We need twice that.'

Gruppen let slip a low whistle.

'That's big.'

Volkmar nodded. 'That it is, Herr Gruppen. I'd like it bigger. I'd like more warrior priests, and I'd like more wizards.'

Roll shook his head, looking disgusted. 'Spell-casters? Sigmar's bones, surely we can do without them this time?'

'We can't, and we won't. Most of the magisters are on duty in the north, but there are some stationed here and in Nuln. We'll take as many as we can find.'

'And the priests?'

'We'll empty the chapels here, and there's a whole company of them in Nuln. They'll all go.'

Gruppen frowned. 'Perhaps one of you would like to tell me why all this is needed?'

Volkmar turned to the preceptor. 'You served with Schwarzhelm, right?'

'Right.'

'What was he like?'

Gruppen looked nonplussed.

'Was his behaviour unusual? Any sickness evident?'

'No. None at all. He slew the doombull.'

'I'm not asking for evidence of his heroics, preceptor. I'm asking about his judgement.'

Gruppen's face flushed. He wasn't used to being talked down to. 'As sound as ever. Why are you asking me? Where is Schwarzhelm?'

'Nobody knows,' said Roll. 'We'd hoped you might.'

'Though it's not hard to guess where he's headed,' said Volkmar. 'He was sent to Averland soon after you were ordered to the northern front. Something happened to him there, and he made a serious mistake. He's now been relieved of his office, and has disappeared.'

Gruppen gripped the side of the tomb. He looked pale. 'What kind of mistake?'

'He cut down Kurt Helborg, possibly to the death. He installed a new elector whom we now believe is in league with the great enemy. He killed the swordmaster Heinrich Lassus and stole the Sword of Vengeance from the Chapel of the Fallen. That enough of a mistake for you?'

'Sweet Myrmidia,' swore Gruppen, shaking his head. Then something seemed to occur to him. 'I remember the name Lassus.'

'He's the one who ordered you north,' said Maljdir grimly. 'We checked. He had no authority to do so, but the habit of command is strong and the orderlies followed instruction.'

'I never understood why my assignment changed.'

'To keep you away from your master,' said Volkmar. 'Lassus knew Schwarzhelm trusted you. When the Emperor's Champion left for Averland, his army was commanded by Andreas Grunwald, a man whose command ability was known to be suspect.'

'He was a good soldier.'

'No doubt. Not good enough.'

Gruppen took the information in quickly. It was a lot to digest, and Volkmar saw him struggling to absorb it. To his credit, the man stayed focussed.

'So how stands the province?'

'We don't know that either,' said Roll dryly.

'Very little has come in or out of Averland since the election of Grosslich,' said Volkmar. 'We believe the new elector is training an army, and that he has gold and weapons. For the time being, his allegiance is still for the Empire, at least in public, but we can be sure that won't last.'

'How?'

'Schwarzhelm wrote a letter before he disappeared, detailing all he'd done and what it meant. We now know the great enemy is active in the city, and Grosslich's actions have left the Emperor in no doubt that we have a rogue elector.'

Gruppen leaned heavily against the cold stone. For an elector to turn traitor was almost unheard of. Minor nobles, yes, even dukes and barons, but the holders of the runefangs were different. All the resources of the province were theirs. The consequences were too dreadful to contemplate.

'And there's been no uprising in Averland?' he asked, obviously clutching for some sign of hope. 'Why have the Estates tolerated it?'

Maljdir gave a snorting laugh. 'That's the problem, preceptor. They don't *know*. If Lassus hadn't given his role in this away to Schwarzhelm, we wouldn't either.'

'Such is the beauty of the scheme,' said Roll. 'They didn't just seize power. They were *given* it. As far as anyone in Averland knows, Grosslich is the duly appointed master of the province and all that lies within it.'

'He'll play for time,' added Volkmar, 'building up his forces, keeping the cloak of respectability for as long as he can. We know he's arming, and there are reports of men being drafted from as far afield as Tilea. We have to act now.'

Gruppen nodded. 'I can see that, but what do you want from me? I'm not Schwarzhelm's physician, and I can't tell you why he did it.'

'You're coming with us,' said Volkmar. 'Schwarzhelm will be there somewhere, and I want your counsel.' He leaned forwards, and his dark eyes glittered. 'You'll bring your company of knights too, preceptor. Their swords will be needed. This is no minor insurrection. This is a new war.'

'Then you'll have them, Theogonist,' said Gruppen without hesitation. 'And as many more as I can muster.' He paused, and his eyes slipped down to the face of the tomb.

'But why Averland?' he asked.

Volkmar's face remained as grim as his appellation.

'We don't know,' he said. 'Yet.'

The gates had opened. With a mighty torrent of screams and whoops, Black Fire Keep began to disgorge its contents. The surging mass of greenskins charged straight towards the waiting ranks of Bloch's army. With frightening speed they closed the gap, loping across the uneven ground like wolves hungry for the kill.

Bloch strode forwards, heart thumping in his breast. This was what he'd prepared for, what he'd wanted, but unleashing the fury of the greenskins was perilous.

'Bring that artillery round!' he yelled, knowing the gunnery captains would already be working. All of this had been prepared, the army knew it was coming, but the impression of disarray would take time to correct. He hoped Drassler was still in position. This all depended on him. 'Archers withdraw! Get back here, you dogs!'

Trumpets blared out, giving the signal over the rising roar of the orcs. The gap between the armies shrank. Rank after rank of orcs thundered from the Keep, swinging their straight swords with furious abandon.

Bloch had fought many orcs over the long years, and he'd always hated their feral enjoyment in bloodshed. They seemed to treat battle as a sport, like a man would enjoy drinking or bear-baiting. These ones, however, had been tipped over into a blind fury. The tactic of mutilating their kin had done the work.

'Halberdiers! Form up!' All around him, slovenly looking groups of men rushed into formation, taking up their spears and halberds and assuming their positions.

The gap closed further. The orcs were tearing towards them. Bloch found himself itching to get stuck in, to tear his blade through the flesh of the scum, but he knew he couldn't. Not yet. This army needed its commander.

The archers rushed back behind the lines of infantry like birds before the storm, leaving their gear on the ground and hurrying to take up heavier weapons. As they did so, the first round shot out from the Helblasters on the left flank. Their ammunition was much more effective against infantry than walls, and the front row of orc berserkers stumbled.

It hardly dented the force of the assault. Huge warriors, roaring with incoherent fury, leapt over their fallen kin, desperate to tear into the waiting human soldiers. Ever more of them poured from the gates. The Keep was emptying.

'Hold your ground!' roared Bloch, seeing the last few yards between the armies dwindle to nothing. 'By Sigmar, hold your ground!'

Then the horde crashed into the halberdiers.

The lines slammed together with a sickening crunch. The first line of defenders buckled, driven back by the force of the assault. Behind them, the second rank was smashed apart in turn, knocked back and hurled into disarray.

The third barely held. Orcs rampaged through the broken human lines, wading into battle and plunging their weapons with abandon. The fighting spread down the long crescent of the besieging army, and soon the entire southern face of the Keep approach was engulfed in desperate combat. There must have been over a thousand orcs in the sortie, all frantically trying to get to the action, all lusting after the blood of the humans who'd taunted them for so long. The greenskins were outnumbered, but they had the initiative and plenty of anger to fuel them.

'Reserves!' cried Bloch, seeing his plans ripping away under the sudden onslaught.

The trumpet blared out and the extra men piled in to staunch the onslaught, desperately trying to blunt the force of the orc charge.

Bloch whirled around, letting his eye sweep across the battlefield. Both armies were fully committed. Fighting was heavy at every point across his long deployment. None of his detachments had broken, but several were close to it. They had to hang on, to weather the storm until they could douse its initial fury.

He turned to Kraus, who was looking over the scene with his habitual bleak expression.

'I'm going in,' he said, buckling his helmet. 'The men have their orders.'

The honour guard captain nodded, unsheathing his own sword and preparing for the melee. 'What about Drassler?'

'Give him the signal. This is when we find out what he's made of.'

Drassler sprang to his feet, casting his cloak aside and taking up his sword. The blade flashed silver in the sunlight. All around him his men did likewise, emerging from the rock like ghosts. Some carried handguns, most swords. They immediately formed up into two companies, one led by Drassler, the other by his lieutenant, Hochmann.

'That's the signal!' he cried, as the trumpets blared out from the rear of the main army. 'Sigmar guide your blades!'

The mountain guard sprinted hard towards the gates. A few hundred yards to their left, the column of orcs had slammed into Bloch's position, no doubt aiming to drive them back so hard they'd be unable to respond. The greenskins had left almost nothing in reserve, as was their wont. The few orcs that remained in the rearguard were clearly itching to pile into combat, and saw Drassler's men coming at them far too late.

The gap closed.

'Fire!' Drassler roared, and a ripple of blackpowder detonations ran across the front rank of his men. With a confused bellow, a dozen orcs at the gate fell, tumbling down onto the rock as they clutched their eyes and midriffs.

Fifty yards to go. Drassler picked up the pace, feeling the weight of his sword as he ran, revelling in the blood pumping round his body. For too long he'd had to creep and scuttle in his own land, prevented by his paltry numbers from striking back at the orcs who'd ripped through his comrades. Now revenge had come, and it felt good.

Twenty yards. The orcs at the gate were trying to form up into some kind of defence. Some called frantically to their kin who'd rushed out to engage Bloch's men, beckoning them back. There couldn't have been more than two dozen ready to meet Drassler's assault, and it looked like there were barely more than that emerging from the interior of the fortress.

Ten yards. Drassler stole a glance to his right, seeing the mountain guard around him surge as one towards the Keep. They cried out curses in the old tongue of the mountains as they came, ancient smiting words that had echoed down the glens since before the time of the Emperors. All of them had hatred in their faces, the kind of naked anger that made a man deadly. Drassler felt pride. They were his kindred, and this was their moment.

Then he was amongst the orcs, slashing, hacking and heaving with his blade. At his shoulder, mountain guard soldiers piled in, bearing down orcs twice their size with the force of the charge and their numbers. Drassler took apart his first victim with a vicious two-handed slash, watching with satisfaction as the mighty figure bent double across the sword-edge before it was finished off by another charging member of his company.

They made the gates. The few remaining orcs broke and fled into the courtyard beyond. Some of his men rushed to follow them, consumed by the need for vengeance.

'Hold fast!' cried Drassler, seeing the danger. The mountain guard were only two hundred strong and there were five times that many orcs on the field. He whirled around, looking back over to where the greenskin column had charged out. He expected to see a morass of entangled combat, with Bloch's men holding the sortie and turning it back on itself.

What he saw was a wall of greenskins charging right back at him, their faces contorted with fury. There was no time to organise a defence. The greenskins had realised their mistake and were coming back to correct it. From inside the Keep came the noise of fresh troops arriving to bolster them. Drassler had taken the gates, but he was caught between the returning sortie and the mustering Keep defenders.

'You take the ones inside, I'll handle the rest!' snapped Drassler to Hochmann, and braced himself for the coming impact.

Around him, his men did their best to form into some kind of defensive arrangement. Under the shadow of the open gates they clustered together, watching as the horde rushed back towards them. There was no escape, and no chance of surrender. If Bloch got his timing wrong, they were all dead men.

'We've done our part,' he muttered, watching as the nearest orc warriors thundered into range. 'Now damn well do yours.'

Bloch charged into the fray, his halberd held low, his throat hoarse from hurling invective at the enemy. He had his men around him, the Reiklanders who'd stood at his side since the march from Altdorf. All did the same, barrelling into the charge, levering the long halberds with expert hands.

There were few armies across the wide earth that could cope with a massed charge of close-serried infantry, and the orcs before them were no different. The steel sliced through them, tearing apart leather, ripping sinew and breaking bones.

'Onward!' Bloch cried, his blood hot with the exhilaration of battle. 'Tear them apart!'

Drassler's charge had done it. The orcs had seen the mountain guard spring up as if from the stone itself, and the force of their assault had wavered. Now Bloch had to press home the advantage, pile on the pressure before they could regroup and take back the gates.

'No mercy!' he bellowed, breaking into a run. All along the lines, his men were doing likewise, striking back at the greenskins and turning the counter-assault into a rout.

Even as he went after them Bloch could see the indecision in the orcs' inhuman faces. Some opted to stay and fight, while others had broken from the horde and were racing back to the Keep. Speed was of the essence now. If Drassler's men were left isolated for too long then all they'd achieved would fall apart.

A hulking warrior loomed up before him. It crouched down low and let fly with a spittle-laced roar of defiance.

'To me!' cried Bloch, calling to the two halberdiers on either side of him. As one, they charged the greenskin, blades

aimed for ribcage, legs and face. The orc was big, clad in plate
armour and swinging a mighty warhammer around its head,
beckoning the charge with wild-eyed relish.

The halberdier on Bloch's right plunged his blade in high,
aiming to catch the shoulder. The orc whirled around, smashing him aside with the hammer, before lurching back to
counter the thrust of the other blades.

Bloch ducked low, feeling the hammer-head whistle above
his ears, before stabbing the shaft of the halberd up. The
blade struck true, halfway up the orc's torso, but deflected
from the armour and left nothing but a long scratch on the
metal. Bloch staggered back, arms jarred from the impact.

The halberdier on his left had better luck, and his blade bit
deep into the orc's muscle-bound arm. The creature roared
in pain, shaking off the fragile shaft and swinging the warhammer round in response. Bloch's companion sprang back,
but too late. The iron head crunched into his ribcage, crushing the bone and sending him sprawling in agony across
the ground.

Bloch was exposed. There were men all around him, grappling with the ranks of orcs, but none were close enough to
come to his aid. He grabbed the halberd from the first soldier
who'd fallen, picked it up on the run and charged straight
back into range. The orc saw him coming and heaved the
warhammer round for the killing blow.

He had to strike hard and true. If he missed, the hammer
would do for him as it had done for the others.

'Sigmar!' Bloch bellowed, plunging forwards with all his
might, keeping the tip of the halberd high and controlling
it with both hands.

The steel bit deep between the orc's breastplate and collar, driving into the flesh beneath and sending up a spray of
hot, black blood. The warhammer flew from the orc's flailing hands, spinning into the air and sailing high over the
heads of the struggling warriors. Bloch pushed the halberd
in deeper, twisting the blade, churning through the flesh and
severing the head from its massive shoulders.

The roars were silenced. The orc crashed to the ground, taking the shaft of the halberd with it, hitting the stone with a dull thud.

Panting, Bloch looked around for a fresh weapon. Time was running out.

'Faster!' he roared, stooping to collect the halberd of another fallen soldier and breaking back into a run. His men were still on the offensive, hammering at the retreating orcs, trying to hack their way through to the Keep. 'Faster, damn you!'

Ahead of him, Bloch could see the Keep looming closer, still cut off by the horde of greenskins. The fighting was frenzied and brutal – both sides knew what was at stake.

Bloch raised his halberd, the blade streaked with blood, and roared his defiance. From every direction men answered his call, hurling obscenities at the orcs and slamming into their disordered defences. The counter-assault was in full swing, the fruit of the tactics he'd spent so long devising. All their hopes were with Sigmar now.

Bloch got his head down, picked his next target and charged.

Drassler's men were hemmed in, surrounded on all sides by the orcs and pinned back close against the open gates of the Keep. The two companies had formed up into ranks three deep on either side, fighting under the shadow of the mighty ramparts and repelling the assaults coming at them from both directions.

The orcs returning from the sortie were the biggest and most aggressive – they'd been the vanguard of the attack and were the most heavily armoured greenskins left. Those remaining on the inside were the weaker breeds, less nakedly belligerent than their larger kindred though nearly as deadly at close quarters. Seeing the danger of losing the gates entirely, scores of them had torn across the courtyard and thrown themselves at the rear of the mountain guard position, heedless of the steel fence waiting for them when they arrived.

Drassler heard the cries of anguish as the lines clashed, but he couldn't pay them any attention. Hochmann had taken the rear ranks, and he was busy enough with his own counter-assault. The first of the returning orcs slammed into the ranks in front of him, tearing their way back to the Keep with desperation. The orcs lived for fighting, but even they could see when their position had become exposed. As savagely as they'd fought to break out of the Keep, they now fought to recover it.

'Form up!' Drassler shouted. In the midst of the ranks of defenders, he'd assembled a detachment of his own. Twenty men, all from his home village, all experienced and tempered by a lifetime fighting the greenskins. As the battle raged around them they formed into a tight column, four men deep and five across. Drassler stood in the centre of the front rank, leading as ever from the front.

'Charge!' he roared, breaking into a run. The men swept forwards, thrusting aside their comrades as they surged to the front. All were swordsmen, carrying the blades of their fathers, handed down from each generation to the next and stained with the blood of countless orcs.

Drassler's unit crashed into the front rank of the enemy, sweeping it aside and ploughing onwards. The greenskins were disorganised, broken up by their headlong race to recover ground. Each of them alone was twice as strong and quick as a man, but by acting in concert a disciplined detachment made up the shortfall.

'That one! Break them!' Drassler pointed to the right, spotting a vast, dark-skinned monster hammering away at the mountain guard's right flank. It was surrounded by a heavily-armoured bodyguard, all wielding human weapons. There were swords, maces and warhammers. Not a curved scimitar or cleaver to be seen.

Drassler's unit swung into battle, keeping their formation as they assaulted the knot of larger orcs. Drassler himself got into position quickly, pulling his sword back to strike, knowing his back was covered by those around him.

His bladed flashed, slicing clean through an orc's extended forearm. The greenskin bellowed with pain and swung a halberd straight back at him. Drassler dodged it, and a swordsman to the left of him leapt in with another strike. The orc, bleeding heavily, turned to face the new threat. Then the man on Drassler's right struck, plunging his blade deep into the orc's back.

Working in unison, swords spinning and jabbing in a united front, Drassler's men carved their way into the heart of the fighting. The greenskins retreated further, knocked aside and bludgeoned into submission by the organised ferocity of the human assault.

But the charge only lasted so long. With nowhere to go, the orcs regrouped and struck back. Dragged into a melee, the detachment formation lost its edge and soldiers began to fall. Whenever a grey-clad swordsman went down, another rushed to take his place, maintaining the line and keeping the pressure on the greenskins. The orcs were strong, though, terribly strong. When they got close, their heavy fists and crushing blows began to tell.

Drassler worked like a blacksmith at a forge, his sword heaving in arcs of destruction. Ahead of him loomed the warlord, the heart of the orc forces. Drassler lowered his sword-point and bellowed a challenge. The language of battle was universal, and the lumbering brute turned to face him. It was nearly as broad as it was tall, covered in bunched muscle and draped in plates of ill-fitting armour. It carried a halberd in one hand and an axe in the other. Seeing Drassler come at it, the orc thundered its defiance, opening its tusked mouth wide and roaring like a bull.

Then they came together. The orc struck first, bringing the axe down hard. Drassler sprang aside, dodging the blow and sweeping his sword back for a counter-thrust. The orc punched the halberd up, and the blades met with a jarring clang. Drassler withdrew a pace, keeping his blade raised, watching for the next blow. The axe fell, followed by the halberd again. The flurry of blow and counter-blow was fast and deadly. Drassler matched it as best he could, but he was driven back.

Then there was another man at his side, jabbing a halberd into the fray, going for the patches of exposed flesh. The orc turned to face him, swinging its own blade to meet the attack.

Drassler joined in, catching the axe with a sharp upward jab and knocking it out of position. Now the orc withdrew, unable to cope with every warrior at once. The halberdier pursued, working his stave with incredible skill and precision. Drassler followed suit, knowing his men around him guarded his flanks.

Together, halberdier and swordsman battered the mighty orc to its knees, raining blow after blow onto its desperate parries. Seeing the danger, it tried to break back out, powering up to its feet with a heavy lunge. The halberdier was knocked back by the thrust, rocking back on his heels and staggering two paces.

That gave Drassler the opening. Leaping forwards, he spun the sword-tip round in his hand, gripped the hilt with his fists and rammed it down. The point sank deep into the orc's ribcage, snaking between plates of metal and lodging deep.

The greenskin bellowed like a wounded ox and whirled round, axe flailing. Then the halberdier was back, scything his blade mightily. The arc swept through the creature's defences and took its head clean off. The severed hunk of flesh and bone flew high into the air, before hitting the rock and rolling to a standstill.

The decapitated body swayed for a moment, pumping hot blood into the air like a fountain, before it too slumped to the earth. Drassler pulled his sword clear as it fell. The orcs weren't bellowing now, and a kind of sullen hush fell over the entire horde.

All around him, mountain guard pressed home the advantage, sweeping past Drassler and tearing into the demoralised orcs.

Drassler turned to thank his comrade. Markus Bloch

grinned back at him, his face streaked with blood. Only then did Drassler notice the swarms of Averlanders and Reiklanders breaking through the mass of orcs and smashing them aside. The relief had arrived. The orcs were broken.

'Good timing,' Drassler said.

'Not finished yet,' said Bloch, heading back into the melee. Before long his coarse voice was raised above the general roar, uttering every obscene curse known to man.

Smiling like a wolf, Drassler plunged after him. There was hard fighting left before the day was over, but the outcome was no longer in doubt. The orcs were in disarray, the halberdiers rampant, and soon the Keep would be theirs.

CHAPTER SIX

Pain. That was all that remained. Sometimes a dull, throbbing ache, distributed evenly across his body. Other times, they made it sharp and sudden. There were long, drawn-out sessions, and mercifully short ones. It all depended on her mood. He'd stopped being able to mark the passage of time, and couldn't truly remember what had brought him here. Maybe he'd been in the Tower for a few hours, maybe a few weeks. Only one thing was certain. The pain.

There was a noise, somewhere close. With effort, Tochfel dragged his eyelids open. He was suspended. He felt the flesh of his wrists, raw and angry, chafe against the rope. The muscles under his ribs had been pulled tight. He should have been dead long ago. He had no idea why he wasn't. Down on the stone floor, beneath his gently swaying feet, he could see pools of his own blood. The sight no longer nauseated him. After a while, the horror became a long, numb dream. There was only so much screaming a man could do.

He moved his head carefully, trying not to inflame the exposed muscles of his neck. The chamber looked much

as it always did. There were tables on either side of him.
One had the instruments. They were astonishingly beautiful,
forged from steel with the precision of a master craftsman.
From time to time, when they came to have their fun, he'd
tried to remember which ones they'd used. It was the little
things, the repetitions and rituals, that kept a fragment of
sanity lodged in his mind.

The other table had the items. Some of them had already
been added to him. Others had once been part of his body.
His extracted organs still sat, glistening and viscid, slopped
in the metal bowls.

Ahead of him was the door, the only way in and out. When
they shut it, it was dark like no darkness he'd ever known.
There, suspended, far from help or salvation, he could reflect
on the variety of pain they'd introduced him to during the
last session. He didn't have the language to describe it all,
but he suspected they did. They knew all the ways of misery. They were geniuses of their craft, masters of sensation. In
comparison to what they'd shown him, his former life now
seemed impossibly stale and drab. He'd had no idea that
existence could be so raw, so unutterably acute, so agonising.

The door opened. Tochfel had trouble focussing. Was it
her? He could no longer decide whether he should scream
or not. Being in her presence was unbearable. Being away
from it was unbearable. He'd been transformed in so short
a time. He felt his mouth hanging open, a line of drool running down to his naked chest.

'You shouldn't have come here, Steward.'

That wasn't her voice. It was a man's voice. A hunched,
slender man, bowed by a curving spine. Tochfel's eyes weren't
working. Everything was blurred. He tried to screw them
into focus.

'Achendorfer?' he croaked, wincing as the tendons in his
throat rubbed against one another.

The man came closer. Uriens Achendorfer had changed.
His skin, always grey, was now as white as snow. The bags
under his eyes hung heavier than ever, purple and pulsing.

His pupils were pin-pricks of red, and lines of sutures ran across his sagging cheeks. He looked heavily altered. His purple robes were loose, but when he moved they gave away the changes that had taken place. Willingly or not, the loremaster had become something more, or perhaps less, than human.

'What were you *thinking*?' asked Achendorfer scornfully. His voice rattled when he spoke. 'You must have known what was in here.'

Tochfel ignored the questions. None of the others had asked him questions. That was the confusing thing. Why torture him, if they didn't want to know anything? It was senseless.

'Where've you been?' Tochfel croaked again.

Achendorfer let slip a thin smile, and his cheeks ran like fluid around his lips. 'Here,' he replied, self-satisfied. 'When Alptraum took the Averburg, that was my signal. I had to bring the book here.'

'Alptraum?'

'He's in number seven, and still not dead. Amazing, given what she's done to him.'

Tochfel felt a tear run down his cheek. That was unusual. He'd thought all his tears had been shed. Perhaps something still lingered within him. That was bad. If they discovered it, there would be more pain.

'Why?'

Achendorfer raised a heavily plucked eyebrow. '*Why?* Do you really need to know that?' He shook his head. 'This is power, Dago-bert. You've no idea what these people are capable of. What *she's* capable of. I was shown a fraction of it. The scrolls, the parchments, they mean nothing to me now. Only one of them was important – the one I could bring to her. There are rewards for those who know how to serve her. There are punishments, to be sure, but rewards also.' The white-faced man grinned, exposing black teeth. 'I am no longer a petty man, Dagobert. She will make me a god.'

Tochfel found he wasn't listening. Speech bored him. Everything bored him. Only pain piqued his interest. That was all there was left. He hated it, feared it, needed it. That was what they'd driven him to.

Another figure appeared at the door. Tochfel had no trouble recognising her outline. There was something curved in her hand, shining in the dark. As she approached him, Natassja patted Achendorfer affectionately on the head.

'That's right, my foul pet,' she said. 'I have great plans for you. Just as I have for all my creatures.'

Achendorfer shivered, whether out of pleasure or fear Tochfel couldn't tell. His vision started to cloud again. What was left of his skin broke out into sweat. His heart, shivering beneath his open ribcage, beat a little faster. Why didn't he die? What malign force kept him sustained in this living hell?

'And what do you plan for me?' he asked, eyes wide with fear, locked on the approaching instrument.

Natassja smiled and began to work. 'Something very special,' she purred. 'Something very special indeed.'

Dawn broke over Averheim. The sun peered through veils of mist rising from the river, taking an age to warm the stone of the quayside buildings. Even before the light made its way down to the wharfs men were busy unloading and loading the endless train of barges. Orders were bellowed out from overseers, and the cranes wheeled back and forth with pallets of iron bars, brick and stone.

Verstohlen watched the activity from his shabby rented room on the east side of the river. From two storeys up he had a good view of the operation. As he watched, he began to wonder how he'd missed the signs. Some of the crates were clearly full of arms. One of them spilled open on landing, revealing scores of curved swords, all wickedly fashioned with trailing spikes. They were no ordinary Imperial manufacture, and he could bet they hadn't come from Nuln.

Verstohlen let his gaze run down the long harbourside, watching as the gathering dawn brought more activity. There were soldiers everywhere. How had he not noticed the increase in their numbers? Where did Grosslich get them from? It seemed like every street corner had a group of surly-faced guards, all wearing the absurd crimson and gold of the elector's personal army. There must have been several hundred of them, milling around, threatening and cuffing the merchants doing their best to unload cargo. The Averlanders seemed to have learned not to talk back.

He turned from the window. He needed to get some sleep. It wouldn't take them long to find out where he'd gone. Even now he guessed that his rooms in the Averburg had been ransacked. Perhaps they'd slipped deathflower into his food. That would be a real spy's death.

Verstohlen rubbed his eyes. The room around him was grim. The sheets were stained and stinking, and there were long lines of grease down the faded walls. He walked from the window and sat down heavily on the bed, ignoring the cocktail of unsavoury aromas that curled up from the linen. All night he'd been kept awake by the shouts of gamblers in the chamber below, steadily getting drunker and more violent. Not that he'd have been able to sleep much anyway. He'd kept his dagger and pistol close to hand and sat watching the door until the dawn.

There was a knock.

'Come,' said Verstohlen, cocking the pistol and placing it under the sheets.

The fat landlord, a man with as many chins as he had rooms, waddled in. He wore an apron that might once have been white, but now had been stained the colour of thin gruel. In his hands he carried a mug of small beer, long past its best and reeking of spoilage.

'You're awake, then,' he grunted, placing the mug on an unsteady table and wiping his hands on the apron. 'You'll be wanting food?'

'No, thank you,' said Verstohlen. If the food was prepared here, then he wouldn't need to worry about assassins. 'I won't be staying another night. Prepare my account, and I'll settle it this morning.'

The landlord looked at him blankly. 'Suit yourself,' he muttered. 'It'll be five schillings.'

The price was exorbitant. He'd have balked at paying it even in a refined inn. For a moment, he considered challenging it, then changed his mind. He needed to keep a low profile until he could get out of the city.

'I'll bring it to you as I leave,' said Verstohlen. The landlord hung around, as if waiting for something. 'Was there anything else?'

The fat man coughed and looked down at his hands. 'Maybe, if you're not having food...' He trailed off.

'Yes?'

'I can get it for you. Cheap price. Best this side of the river.'

Verstohlen looked at him coldly. If joyroot was available even to scum such as this, then the last pretence at controlling the trade must have been abandoned. Grosslich was flooding Averheim with it, just as before. Was he in it with the Leitdorfs? Or had he taken it over? So much still to unravel.

'No,' said Verstohlen, his voice quiet and controlled. 'A little early for me.'

The landlord shrugged and shuffled out again, closing the door behind him clumsily. Verstohlen pulled his pistol out from under the sheets and looked over the workings. It was important that everything operated flawlessly. Unless he could get out of the city soon and find his way north undetected, he knew he'd be using it soon enough.

Rufus Leitdorf watched as the land around him became steadily more familiar. The gorse and heather stretched to the horizon in all directions, rustling gently under a ceaseless wind. The air was sharper than it had been in the lowlands, and in the distance the peaks of the Grey Mountains were just visible, lost in a haze of blue in the far south. A low tide of mist rolled across the depressions in the land, shifting and miasmic, torn into tatters as the breeze across the moors ripped it away. In the far distance there were ruins, tall towers of age-whitened stone marching across the horizon. No human hand had built those places, and no human dwelt among them now. In the vast space between mankind's scattered settlements, there were still plenty of ancient secrets lying dormant. Drakenmoor was replete with them.

Leitdorf had been sent to the secret castle twice in the past, once as a child when there was a threat of assassination against him, and once as a teenager. The second time he'd travelled on his own account, albeit surrounded by household servants, Averburg officials and a retinue of armed guards. Growing up as a prince had given him precious little solitude. He found it hard to recall any occasions where there hadn't been members of the elector's court hovering around, waiting to take orders from him or pass on new requirements from his father.

That world, the one of privilege and prestige, had slipped away so fast. Less than a month ago it had seemed like the trappings of true power were firmly in his grasp. He and Natassja had planned so much together, and Averland looked set to have another Leitdorf at its helm.

He let his gaze drop from the horizon. The memory of Natassja was painful. Like a drug, being away from her was hard. He hadn't realised, perhaps, how much he'd relied on her, how far the preparations for conquest had been hers, and how many of his considerable resources had been diverted into her policies. The joyroot had been her creation. He had no idea where she'd sourced the first samples. Perhaps he should have inquired more carefully.

For all her wisdom and perceptiveness, it hadn't helped them when the hammer blow fell. No doubt Grosslich had tracked her down by now, and she languished in one of the dungeons of the citadel. Somehow he doubted her spirit had been broken, but feared her body might have been.

It was unpleasant to dwell too much on that. He had failed her, and he had failed his family. The experience of the entire Empire turning against him, seemingly on the whim of Schwarzhelm and his damnable spy, had shocked him to his core. He should have paid more attention to his lessons in diplomacy. The old fool Tochfel might have been worth listening to more carefully.

The situation with the Reiksguard was even more puzzling. He could understand well enough Grosslich's desire to have him hunted down and killed, but to extend it to the Emperor's own troops? That was bravery bordering on folly, and in the long run such arrogance would surely cost him dear. He'd never have dared such a thing himself, even if matters in Averheim had gone otherwise.

Leitdorf looked over his shoulder at the carriage, shaking as it was dragged along the uneven tracks towards Drakenmoor. He knew the Marshal was recovering. The knights' morale had lifted as a result, and they now went more proudly than before, as if defying Grosslich's pursuers to find them. It was amazing what the presence of a commander could do for his men.

Leitdorf found himself reflecting on what his own vassals thought of him. The closest to him, soldiers like Klopfer, were surely dead now, caught in the ruin and confusion of Averheim. Even if they hadn't been killed, none of them would have rushed to fight by his side again. He knew his temper had driven half of his allies away. Like his father, his blood ran hot, ever ready to spill out into some petulant tirade. He'd never been forced to confront the consequences of that, to examine himself against the measure of other, better men. Now, when he looked in the mirror of introspection, he saw a petty character, a bully and a tyrant.

A shadow passed across him. Skarr had drawn up alongside, controlling his horse with an enviable ease.

'You look troubled, my lord,' he said, and his severe face twisted awkwardly into something like a smile.

Skarr had become less brooding since Helborg's partial recovery. The preceptor still held him responsible for the events of the Vormeisterplatz, but an uneasy truce had developed between them. At least he was being referred to as 'my lord' again.

'I've only been here twice,' replied Leitdorf. 'And yet it feels like home. I can't tell you why.'

Skarr shrugged. 'I like this place too,' he said. 'The air's healthier. I can see what your father was thinking.'

They rode on in silence for a while. Tangled copses of black-thorned briars passed by as the horses trod the winding path. The calls of birds, or something like birds, echoed in the distance, faint against the vastness of the open sky.

'You know, he wasn't the madman everyone says he was,' said Leitdorf at length. 'He had a temper, but he wasn't mad.'

Skarr said nothing.

'When he came up here, he was more himself.' Leitdorf found himself suddenly wishing to explain everything, to make it clear why things had turned out the way they had. 'Everyone said the same about him. It was Averheim that made him angry.'

'The city?'

'I saw it for myself. He never slept properly. There were bad dreams. It was almost as if...'

Leitdorf trailed off. It was painful to recall those sleepless nights, the screams of his father echoing down the long corridors of the Averburg. Nothing the physicians could do would ease the pain. Though his father had known the courtiers were laughing at him behind his back, Marius never once shirked his duty as a result of the night terrors. Not once, even though it drove his mind to the brink of breaking.

'They say he was a proper swordsman,' acknowledged Skarr, and his voice had a grudging approval in it. 'The Marshal wanted to offer him a duel, but the opportunity never arose.' The grizzled knight smiled again, this time less forced. 'Perhaps, when he's recovered, *you* should take up the challenge.'

Leitdorf felt his pride stung at the mockery, and went red with anger.

He pushed it down. This was his problem. He had no means of coping with the banter of ordinary conversation. That was why he was feared rather than loved, ridiculed rather than respected. Instead, he did his best to return the smile.

'I'd not give him much of a fight.'

Skarr couldn't disagree, and gave an equivocal shrug. Leitdorf winced.

'You don't think much of me, do you, preceptor?' he said.

Skarr looked surprised.

'It's not important what I think. It's about survival now.'

'Perhaps.' Leitdorf looked up ahead. The road was curving round to the right, snaking steadily up a long, shallow incline. Remnants of the mist curled around the hooves of the horses as they laboured up it, ghostly and insubstantial. The Drakenmoor castle was close, staffed by members of his father's most devoted staff and safe – for the moment – from the prying eyes of Grosslich. This had been his decision, perhaps the first he'd ever truly made without his father or his wife peering over his shoulder. That was an odd thought.

'Maybe I don't think that much of myself, either,' he said. 'A man's defined by what's around him. I'm beginning to wonder if the company I've kept has always worked to my advantage.'

'War can change a man, my lord,' said Skarr. 'I've seen it happen. It asks a question of you.'

'We're at war?'

'Assuredly. The Marshal has no thoughts of escaping. He'll take the fight back to Grosslich.'

Leitdorf pondered that. Such a course was hugely dangerous. Grosslich had the resources of the entire province at his disposal. It would be easier for Leitdorf to slip over the mountains into Tilea, to lick his wounds amongst old allies of his father and gather strength slowly. Staying in Averland was the riskiest option of all.

And yet the Marshal had not built his reputation for nothing. Now Leitdorf – chubby, tantrum-ridden Rufus Leitdorf – had the chance to ride alongside the legend.

'So the question will be asked,' he mused. 'Let us hope, when the time comes, I have the right answer.'

The Iron Tower kept growing. Every hour, more metal beams were lowered into place, slotting into a plan of dazzling complexity. Even semi-complete, it had the look of a building that could survive a thousand years. Great spars shot into the air, now reinforced by hundreds of cross-beams. A thick outer shell had begun to creep up in their wake, hard and shiny like the carapace of an insect.

Halfway up the monstrous structure, a chamber had been created. It was small, just a foretaste of the mighty halls which would fill out the shaft in due course. Giant crystal windows covered three of the walls, and in the centre a curved throne had been placed. There was no other decoration, just blank panels of iron. Natassja's aesthetic sense had not yet been brought to bear, for this was Grosslich's commission.

Standing by the windows, nearly a hundred feet above the centre of the circular plain below, the elector gazed down on the majesty of his creation. Natassja preferred to remain below ground. That relieved him. Though she was as addictive as the narcotics she created, her presence was wearing on his nerves. Grosslich had seen what happened to servants who failed her. From time to time, a nagging doubt even entered the back of his own mind.

Will I be next?

No. That wouldn't happen. He was the lord of this realm, and she was his ally. They both needed each other for the fulfilment of the great vision. Though the mask was gradually slipping away, just as it had to, there was still the appearance of normality in Averheim. The ordinary people could grumble about the imposition of rules and military tithes, but none of them suspected the truth behind the manoeuvrings. The knowledge would come later, once all was ready. In the meantime, they had the joyroot again to addle their minds.

Grosslich looked down. The elaborate pattern of stonework on the courtyard below was almost complete. It was dazzlingly beautiful. From three hundred feet up, the eventual height of the Tower, it would be even more impressive. The Mark of Slaanesh, etched in circling rows of obsidian and picked out with silver. At ground level, the shapes were unintelligible, and only here was their true purpose apparent.

He followed the progress of a pack of dog-soldiers as they crept across the open space, far below him. Once he'd have baulked at having such creatures working for him. No longer. He'd seen for himself what the Empire really was: a club for the privileged and the noble-born. It didn't matter that his bloodline had sent its sons to die on the sodden fields of war, had built up a trade in cattle-rearing from nearly nothing and donated vast sums to the Church of Sigmar and the Knights of the Blazing Sun. For the elite in Altdorf, the Grosslichs would always be commoners. The electoral battle had been about nothing more than blood proofs. The fact that Grosslich was twice the warrior Leitdorf would ever be counted, seemingly, for nothing.

All that had changed with Natassja. Until she'd proposed her alliance, he'd been a minor landowner and frustrated powerbroker, nothing more. It was she who'd taught him how to use his money, how to influence the right people, buy the right alliances, smooth over the trifling difficulties of the law, and dispose of those who couldn't be bought.

Heinz-Mark had learned the lessons well. Only later had the joyroot emerged, and then soon after that the knowledge of her corruption. She'd come to his rooms at night, draped in perfume, and the seduction into the dark had begun.

Though he'd not known it at the time, that had been his last chance to turn back. By then, though, he was entangled in a thousand deals and treaties. She showed him visions of such splendour, gave him experiences of such magnificence, that he'd been unable to say no. He denied her nothing after that, trapped in the honeypot she'd so skilfully placed before him, addicted to the pleasures she doled out to him like toys to a child.

Grosslich still liked to tell himself that she needed him, that the plan would have ground to a halt without his efforts. Perhaps that was true in part, but he wasn't deluded enough to put any faith in it. He was the lesser partner, and that made things dangerous for him. When the Tower was completed and his armies mustered, perhaps Grosslich would have to do something to reinforce his position. She was powerful, to be sure, but only a woman. He was a warrior, tempered by combat since childhood and destined for command. Surely the Dark Prince would reward him when the time came. He had, after all, done so much to please him. There would be opportunities. There were always opportunities.

There was a knock from the corridor outside. Grosslich turned, his dark cloak following him like furled wings. He gestured with his finger, and twin doors slid back into the iron walls. Eschenbach and Heidegger came in. Far from the prying eyes of the Averburg, they were free to shed their appearance of normality. Eschenbach had let his eyes resume their pink hue and had donned robes of subtly shifting colour. Heidegger looked perfectly normal, although the mania in his eyes was more pronounced. The poor dupe was working under a heavy burden of interwoven spells, and still believed he was doing Sigmar's holy work. Despite the abundance of evidence of Chaos around him, the part of his mind that could discern the world truly had been drilled out by Natassja. Now he only saw what she wanted him to see.

Grosslich had to hand it to her. Subverting a witch hunter was hard.

'Report,' he ordered, walking over to the throne and taking his seat.

'The executions you ordered have been carried out,' said Heidegger, his eyes flickering back and forth. The man's mind was cracking. 'The objections of Steward Tochfel seem to have been overcome, though I wasn't able to see him personally to confirm this. More heretics have been unearthed and justice handed out according to your instructions.' The old man shook his head. 'So much corruption here,' he mused. 'When will they ever learn?'

'When indeed?' agreed Grosslich. 'Thankfully, your services have been invaluable, Herr Heidegger. Continue the programme. We cannot stop until all faithless have been uncovered, though I assume you have not yet found the spy Verstohlen?'

'Not yet, my lord. We found evidence of him at a boarding-house on the east side of the river. He must still be in the city, since the ordinance on movements prevents any unauthorised departure. The end will come soon for him, you may be sure of it.'

'Good,' said Grosslich. 'Then I will not detain you from your work. Go now, and report to me again in two days.'

The corrupted witch hunter bowed again and shuffled out, the doors sliding open to allow his passage.

Eschenbach watched him go with ill-concealed scorn. 'Do we need his services still? His stench sickens me.'

'You should learn to value him,' warned Grosslich. 'As with everything we've done, appearance is important.'

'Really?' said Eschenbach, his teeth exposed. 'Leitdorf and his men are gone, Schwarzhelm is gone, and the spy will soon be dead. It offends my sense of propriety that we continue to maintain this charade.'

Grosslich frowned. He'd promoted Eschenbach himself, one of the few members of the cabal not to be brought in by Natassja. Could he really be so stupid?

'I don't think you fully appreciate the balance here,' he said. 'The Emperor knows of our allegiance now. Do you think he will hesitate to send an army here? One is already marching, and it will be ten times the force Schwarzhelm had. While we prepare for it, we must maintain the little game, keep the province quiet and give us the space we need.'

Eschenbach shook his head. 'It disgusts me. I have to deal with dullard thugs in the Averburg as if they were equals. I would rather tear their stomachs from their fat bodies and eat them before their own eyes.'

Grosslich listened with some weariness. Eschenbach was proving a disappointment. He didn't need sadists and madmen around him – the dog-soldiers were perfectly capable of dealing out terror. He did need advisers with a clear head and a strategic grasp. He began to suspect that Natassja had let him promote Eschenbach *because* he was a liability.

'There'll be plenty of time for that,' Grosslich said. 'In the meantime, double the supply of root to the markets, and see that the price goes down. And speed up the recruitment drive. We've not got enough men yet, and she's getting impatient.'

'Gold supplies are running low. These troops aren't cheap.'

'Keep spending it. More will come. Don't disappoint me, Steward.'

Eschenbach gave out one of his fat, thick-lipped smiles. 'Of course not,' he replied smoothly.

Something about the man's manner stung Grosslich then. He extended his hand, and a nimbus of lilac quickly formed around Eschenbach's neck. The Steward clutched at it, suddenly panicked.

'What is this, my lord?' he blurted, eyes bulging.

'I'm not sure you're taking my advice seriously enough, Steward,' snarled Grosslich, giving vent to all of his many frustrations. 'Perhaps something of a lesson is in order.'

'No, my lord!' shrieked the Steward, writhing against the nimbus. 'All is perfectly well understood!'

'Even so.'

While Eschenbach writhed in the grip of his luminescent collar, Grosslich flicked out his left hand. An iron wall panel slid open, revealing a new chamber beyond.

'Look at him, Eschenbach.'

The Steward struggled, unwilling to gaze into the chamber. 'It's not necessary, my lord! Really, you've no need to–'

'*Look at him,*' commanded Grosslich, feeding the nimbus energy and twisting the man's neck round to face the revealed chamber.

Eschenbach's eyes widened further, and his pale skin went grey with horror. A figure was suspended in the chamber, seemingly hanging in the air. An angry red glow surrounded him, as if flames licked his body. The man's eyes were even wider than Eschenbach's. If he'd wanted to close them, he would have needed his skin back. The white of bone glistened amongst the glossy red of the exposed muscle. He should have been dead, killed long ago by shock, but through some forbidden power the unfortunate soul was still alive. His face, what was left of it, was fixed in an open-mouthed howl of utter, unending agony. The pupils stared straight at Eschenbach, pleading for help. From his tortured mouth came only a silent, never-ending scream. He couldn't produce anything else. He'd never be able to produce anything else.

'Watch well, Steward,' said Grosslich, ensuring the spectacle had its full effect. 'This man once thought to replace me. His family ruled this province, and saw me as a tool for returning to power. This is what happens to those who seek to use me, Herr Eschenbach. This is what they become.'

The Steward started to whimper, unable to bear looking at the horrific scene before him but prevented from looking away. His smoothness of manner had been torn away. The lesson was having its effect.

'I can see it!' he cried, desperately trying to avert his eyes. 'I understand!'

Grosslich kept him locked in place. The memory of this would keep him loyal, and now more than ever he needed men around him he could trust.

'I hope you do,' said Grosslich, enjoying the power flowing from his fingertips. It was at times like this he didn't regret the choices he'd made. 'Forget it, and you'll end up in an agony chamber. And that's *really* not something you want to happen. Isn't that right, Ferenc?'

The man in the chamber couldn't respond. There was only misery left for him, only sensation, only terror.

In such circumstances, Grosslich could allow his doubts to subside, and to glory in his future power. Averheim was already being moulded to his will. By the time the Empire armies arrived, it would be his own domain, the home of whole legions of terror troops. He would be at the forefront of them, drenched in the gifts of the Dark Prince, ready to meet the weary response of Karl Franz. It would be *his* realm, the mightiest between the mountains and the sea.

He tightened his grip on the nimbus, enjoying Eschenbach's choked crying. The prospect made all the compromises worthwhile. By whatever means, through whatever sacrifice, he would have what he'd been put on the earth for.

Dominion.

CHAPTER SEVEN

The net was closing in on Verstohlen. The harder he tried to get out of the city, the closer his pursuers got to him. Things were getting difficult.

Grosslich's army had swelled to ridiculous proportions, and there were soldiers everywhere. Lines of men waited outside dingy offices in the basement of the old Alptraum residence, desperate to sign up to Grosslich's expanding ranks in return for their pile of cheap coins and promise of glory. The amount of money changing hands was phenomenal. Every hour, another hundred or so infantrymen swaggered out of the burgeoning drafting houses, each dressed in a crimson tunic and carrying a curved scimitar. Soon there would be more soldiers in Averheim than ordinary citizens.

That wasn't the worst of it. There were witch hunters among them, though they weren't like witch hunters Verstohlen had seen anywhere else. They seized people seemingly at random, dragging them off to the Averburg over the screams of their family. Fear had gripped the city again. No one would say it out loud, but it was slowly becoming apparent what kind of a man Grosslich was. Some still welcomed the firm hand of authority, judging it preferable to have a strong elector than none at all. Others kept their mouths shut, eyes sliding from side to side, waiting for the knock at the door to come for them and watching the streets empty with the coming of the dark.

All gates to the city were now watched. Verstohlen had visited every portal, hugging the shadows and assessing the chances of slipping out. Passes were now required, issued only by captains in the elector's direct employ. Only the soldiers seemed to be let in and out at will, plus the carefully scrutinised train of merchants bringing in building materials and weaponry. Some of the traders had strange looks on their faces, and Verstohlen doubted any were Averlanders. Some looked barely human at all.

So it was that he'd been forced to lay low in Averheim for a second day, observing the degeneration around him, seeing all he'd worked to prevent coming to pass. He felt disgusted at himself. Maybe he'd become arrogant, too pleased with his own skills. Whatever the reason, he'd failed. They'd all failed.

As night fell, he made his way back to the richer parts of the city, close to the Averburg and the old cathedral. Some of the richer merchants still had a measure of independence, and the streets were slightly freer of soldiers.

Verstohlen wrapped his coat around him, keeping one hand on his concealed pistol. Ahead of him a broad street ran south, flanked by three-storied townhouses. The buildings were decorated across their gables with scenes of bucolic contentment, all etched in wood by master carpenters, a sign of the wealth of the owners. In the past the windows might have glowed with firelight; now they'd all been shut fast, the doors bolted with many locks.

Verstohlen hesitated. He didn't know what to do. The hostelries were dangerous for him now. He'd not been able to get anywhere near Tochfel. Perhaps the Steward had been taken. If so, it would be another mark of guilt to set against his complacency.

Ahead of him, one of the lanterns flickered and went out. The street slid into darkness. A few still burned further ahead, but they gave off an uncertain light. Mannslieb rode high in a tortured sky, broken by fast-moving clouds from the east.

Verstohlen leaned against the wall of one of the houses, trying to think. He couldn't stay outside all night. Perhaps he could go back to Valgrind's forge, though if Tochfel had been taken that would be as unsafe as anywhere else. His fear was clouding his judgement. Two days without sleep were taking their toll.

Once again, he remembered Schwarzhelm. *There are many ways of attacking a man, subtle ways*. Had he said that? It was hard to remember.

He crept out from under the shadow of the house, determined to keep moving. There might be a safer tavern open in the poor quarter. He needed something to eat and drink, even if it carried a risk with it.

Another lantern flickered out. That was strange. Verstohlen looked back over his shoulder. The street behind was empty and sunk into darkness. He turned back, flicking his collar up against the chill.

Then he saw the figure, hunched and cloaked, standing in the middle of the road, no more than a hundred yards away and coming closer. As it came on, the lantern above it guttered and died. They were all being put out.

'*Verstohlen,*' the shape hissed, and steam curled from its mouth.

Verstohlen felt a cold fist of terror close over his heart. His mind raced back to Natassja's pets, creeping around in their world of blind misery.

The cloaked figure limped towards him. From under its cowl, something clawed and curved emerged.

Verstohlen withdrew his pistol and fired. The crack of the report echoed down the empty streets. The creature staggered, bending low. Verstohlen fired again, and the cloaked shape crouched over, rocking on its feet.

Then, slowly, terribly, it rose again. Under the cowl, two

points of lilac flared into life. Metal flashed in the night. It
was smiling, and its teeth were made of steel.

'*Verstohlen*,' it hissed again, as if by way of confirmation. It
had a scraping, rattling voice that was only barely human,
but nonetheless horribly familiar.

Verstohlen felt his breath quicken. Terror gripped him, held
him tight in place. Then the creature came for him, exposing long talons, curved and gleaming in the moonlight. It
loped towards him in a broken, stumbling run.

'Holy Verena...'

Verstohlen fled. Drawing his dagger as he went, he turned
on his heels and sped down the streets. Behind him, he heard
the horror set off after him. It was faster than the other ones,
and something told him it wouldn't need Natassja nearby
to maintain its strength.

Buildings sped by in the night, blurring like dreams. He
felt his foot skid on a patch of slime, and nearly went down.
Behind him, close on his shoulder, he could hear the clicking, the scuttle of bone against stone.

It was getting nearer. He couldn't turn to check. He couldn't
fight it. He couldn't escape. With the prescience of those
about to die, Verstohlen saw everything clearly. He would
be overtaken. The horror would catch him. In every patch
of shadow, he saw the masks leering at him, laughing at his
failure. The signs had been there. He should have known.
Only his pride had let him think he'd defeated them. Now
it was over.

His heart hammering, his lungs bursting, Pieter Verstohlen
ran for his life.

The candle burned low and its light began to fail. Leitdorf
reached for another, lit it and held it over the flame until
the wax softened, then pressed it into the brass holder. A
warm, golden light flooded back across the desk. It was late.
The journey had been long and he was tired. He knew he
should go to bed. Something, perhaps the sense of familiarity, kept him up.

They'd arrived at the Drakenmoor castle in the late afternoon. The old stone walls had towered over the bleak land, just as he'd remembered them doing. It wasn't a true castle, more a fortified manor house in the heart of the moors. The crumbling battlements were mostly for show, and the walls wouldn't have withstood a determined attack with any kind of artillery. The sheer-sided roofs were missing a few tiles, and broken panes of glass hadn't been repaired. Still, that was hardly the point. It was secret, and it was far from Averheim. The few resident staff had welcomed him back like the forgotten son he was to them. Gerta, the old nursemaid, nearly blind and bent double with age, had kissed him on the forehead and clamped her arms around him for so long it had become embarrassing. Even Skarr had broken into a laugh at that.

Now the old house was quiet again and the hastily lit fires were burning low in the grates. Helborg had been given the old count's master bedroom. The Marshal had been able to hobble up to it unaided, but only just. Even so, it was clear the man's strength was returning.

Skarr had organised a watch. Through the night Reiksguard would patrol the countryside around them. For the first time in days, a semblance of safety had returned. It was possibly illusory, and certainly transitory, but at least it was something.

Leitdorf had taken his father's private study to sleep in. Alongside the huge desk, still stacked with parchment that the servants had been too timid to remove, there was a narrow bed set against the wall. The old man had often slept there after working late, too exhausted to drag himself along the creaking landing to the opulent master suite. Unlike most of Marius's private rooms, the study was sparsely furnished and decorated. Icons of Sigmar and Siggurd hung on the dark green walls, flaking with age.

Unwilling to sleep, Leitdorf had started to leaf through the old papers. It was a sobering business. Most of them were routine orders and reports detailing the dreary minutiae of state. A dispute over land on the Stirland border, a revision of the tax thresholds for smaller farms, a visiting delegation from Wissenland to discuss levies on wine imports. His father's bold hand was on all of them, making notes or issuing orders to his secretary. The signature, written in a heavy, flowing script, was everywhere.

Rufus remembered seeing him work when he'd still been a child. He'd managed to evade his nannies and had stolen down the winding interior of the Averburg, darting from shadow to shadow. At that age he'd imagined his father sitting on a golden throne, dictating matters of war and alliance to a waiting army of knights and battle wizards. Instead, when the young Rufus had found him, Marius had been bent over a desk much like the one he sat at now, scribbling on parchment, hunched over a flickering candle flame.

Rufus remembered the smile creasing the man's weary face, beckoning him over.

'This isn't for you, young one,' he'd said, looking over the piles of parchment with forbearance. 'Be thankful for it. Leopold will inherit this.'

Of course, Rufus hadn't been thankful then. He'd grown resentful, spoiled and fat as the years passed. Getting his father's attention had been difficult. Rufus had tried to get noticed in other ways, throwing wild parties and balls, bedding eligible women and then casting them aside, gorging on food and wine while the peasants in the fields laboured to produce it. Even after Natassja he'd continued to indulge his rampant, clumsy lusts, riding out to isolated villages on his estates and picking a girl for his enjoyment over the protests of the serfs. The last one, a few months ago, had proved hardest to tame. She'd given him a brace of scratches to remember her by. He could still recall the look of defiant hatred in her eyes, glistening with hot, furious tears.

Pathetic. He'd become a laughing stock, a figure of casual hatred, only loved by those so steeped in the Leitdorf blood, like Gerta, that they were blind to the extent of his follies. And in the end, of course, Marius's mind had begun to turn, and it was too late. Everything was then about plots, and war, and screaming in the night. When Ironjaw had taken the old man at last, perhaps it had been a mercy.

Leitdorf pushed the papers to one side. Such was his family's legacy, and such was his inheritance.

As his fingers ran over the surface of the desk, they caught on a small, leather-bound book, buried under the heaps of paperwork. Knowing full well he should retire and keep his strength for the following day, Leitdorf flicked it open. There were handwritten entries on nearly every page, also in Marius's script. Some were written as confidently as the signature on his orders; others looked shakier, as if scribbled down in haste.

He began to read. Some of it was illegible, and other passages didn't make sense at all. Perhaps written when his father's mind was beginning to drift.

And then, as if it had been burned on to the page for that very purpose, there came a sentence that chilled his heart. He dropped the book, hearing it thud on to the desk. It fell open where he'd been reading.

Leitdorf stayed still for a moment, lost in shock. He no longer needed to read the phrase to see it. He couldn't have been mistaken. There it was, scrawled in black ink, as plain as a hawk against the open sky.

Her name is Natassja. And she will kill me.

Verstohlen felt his strength begin to give out as he ran. His coat streamed behind him, more a hindrance than a help. The houses passed by in a haze of half-seeing. The moonlight covered everything with a faint outline of silver, but the pools of shadows were ink-black and deep as souls.

The streets were deserted. He had no idea where he was. Perhaps the terror was driving him somewhere in particular. Perhaps not. There was no time to think. He felt his legs protest, his muscles burn. This would be over soon.

He tore round a corner leading into a small square. Tall buildings on all four sides cut off the light, and it felt like running into a well of shadows. Behind him, the rattling grew even louder. The creature was almost close enough to reach out and touch him.

Verstohlen veered sharply to the left, darting to one side and trying to wrong-foot his pursuer. Something snagged at his coat, tearing the leather. Footfalls echoed around the enclosed space, making it sound like there was more than one of him trying to run. The illusion was cruel, only reinforcing his desperate isolation.

Bone-hard fingers clutched at his coat again, slicing through the expensive leather as if it were the flimsiest of gauze. One more lunge, and the creature would have him.

Verstohlen spun round, bringing the dagger up hard. He had a glimpse of the monster's face. It nearly caused him to miss his aim. A ravaged visage, stripped of skin and eyes, studded with brass spikes and needle-tipped incisors. The blank eyes glowed lilac, shining in the night like corrupted stars. An inhuman shriek echoed round the square as Verstohlen's blade scraped across what remained of the flesh.

Then he was moving again, running as before, heart labouring, sweat streaming from his brow. The creature barely paused. It scuttled after him, wheezing as it came. There was no blood on the dagger, just scraps of dry skin and sinew.

Verstohlen had seen enough. The horror had once been a man he knew. Tochfel's features, or what was left of them, still existed, distorted by pain and artificial hatred.

The talons groped for him. He felt one of them scrape down his back, cutting through his clothes and drawing blood. Verstohlen roared with pain, twisting away from the agonising touch, feeling himself stumble.

Verstohlen rolled as he fell, getting his dagger up just in time to parry a fresh plunge of the talons. The Tochfel-creature's robes fell away and Verstohlen saw the full extent of the man's transformation. He was naked underneath the flimsy draping, though not much of his old human form remained. He was as much bone and iron as flesh, animated by some dread power and kept alive by forbidden sorcery. Spikes studded his ruined flesh, curved and barbed. A chasm had been cut in his chest and the ribs were still visible across the wound. Within that exposed shell beat a heart, though it was no natural organ. It pulsed with a lurid light, strapped in place with iron bands and surrounded by the eight-pointed star. Tochfel's residual flesh curled away from it, as if burned by the terrible energy within. The stink of jasmine was pungent and close, as sweet as death.

The talons raked down, aiming at Verstohlen's eyes. Frantically, driven by nothing more than pure fear, he fended off the blows, his dagger scraping along the scythes.

The end would come quickly now. Tochfel's strength had been augmented three-fold and his sorcery-laced limbs quickly pinned Verstohlen to the ground. Talons scrabbled at his face again and he only just got the dagger up in time to ward them. The blade was knocked away by the force of the strike, sent spinning across the ground. Then he was defenceless.

Verstohlen looked up into the eyes of his killer. There was no humanity left there, just a sickening grin where Natassja had inserted rows of needle teeth. The Tochfel-creature's smile widened, and its cheeks stretched impossibly taut.

'Verstohlen,' it whispered a final time, as if the name somehow gave it the power to kill. It opened its jaws wide and prepared to lunge.

Light exploded, blinding him. There was a heavy blow from somewhere close by, and Verstohlen felt the creature knocked into the air. He scrabbled free, rubbing his eyes. Something huge and heavy strode across his field of vision. Moonlight flashed down the length of a mighty sword, carved with runes and with the sign of the comet etched on its surface.

'You're a hard man to find,' growled Schwarzhelm, before plunging after the wounded Tochfel-creature. His sword flashed again in the night, and battle was joined.

Deep under the Iron Tower, the screams now never ceased. Insulated from the surface by many feet of solid stone, they resounded from the polished walls of the lower dungeon, rising through the snaking vaults and shafts before spilling out across the throne chamber, mixed together in a symphony of suffering. As the catacombs had expanded, hewn from the rock by Natassja's growing army of Stone-slaves, the scope for experiments had only grown. So many of the fine young men who'd volunteered for Grosslich's forces had ended up serving a rather different mistress. No doubt those coins didn't look like such a good deal now.

Natassja knew that Grosslich didn't like her taking a tithe of his warriors for her own purposes, but that really was too bad. She understood, as he could not, what purpose they served. The inflicting of pain was not merely done for her enjoyment – though, to be sure, she did enjoy it. There was method behind it, a necessary accumulation of souls in anguish. The time was coming when the object of her labour would become apparent. Not yet, but soon.

Natassja walked down towards the Chamber of the Stone. She was already far below ground level and the floor was still sloping down. The rock walls of the corridor had been carved recently and she hadn't had time to decorate them yet. Maintaining an appropriate aesthetic was important, and she would have to set her architects to work on the lower levels without much further delay. Grosslich thought such work was a waste of effort, which only went to show how meagre his understanding of the great plan was.

Natassja reached the archway that led to the chamber. From within, she could hear Achendorfer chanting away. He'd been busy, the little lizard. Such diligence really deserved some kind of reward. Perhaps one of the slave girls from the upper pens could be given to him before too much work was done to her.

Natassja entered the domed chamber, feeling the waves of suppressed energy surge towards her, bathing her body in the raw essence of the aethyr. The Stone recognised her.

The chamber was perhaps forty feet in diameter and perfectly circular, though it rose far higher than that and the roof was lost in shadow. At floor level the rock had been ground smooth and reflected the light like a mirror. Torches had been placed high up on the walls, covering the scene in a lurid purple glow. Achendorfer stood to one side, reciting passages from the book he'd taken from the Averburg library. As he read, the flames seemed to wave and flicker in appreciation. Something in the chamber was listening to him.

Natassja looked up at the Stone, the centrepiece and foundation of everything she'd done. Only the merest tip of it had been exposed and even that was massive, thrusting up from the floor like a miniature mountain. It was pure black, shiny and diamond-hard. She didn't know exactly how long it had lain under Averheim, locked deep within the earth, cold and forgotten by men. What she did know was that it was gigantic, a vast fragment of tainted substance, hidden away since the forgotten wars of the great powers at the dawn of the world.

The Stone. Ancient and malignant, locked out of sight for millennia, exposed to human contact again just two days ago. Even now its energies were bleeding upwards, suffusing the structure of the Tower and taking it over. With every cry of agony, the slumbering giant groped more surely to awakening.

Natassja breathed in deeply, feeling the throbbing air fill her lungs, glorying in the latent, thrumming energy around her.

'How long have you been working, Uriens?' she asked, gazing fondly at the little insect.

'Six hours,' he replied, looking exhausted.

'Get some rest,' she said, stroking his bald head absently. 'I'll have something nice sent to your chamber.'

Achendorfer closed the book and bowed, his limbs trembling from fatigue. Dried blood had collected around his cracked lips. He shuffled back into the tunnel, leaving Natassja alone with the Stone.

She walked up to it and ran her fingers down its many-faceted surface. It was warm to the touch. The spirit

had been roused. Her pupils dilated, and a smile of satisfaction spread across her elegant face.

'Not long now, then,' she breathed. 'Not long now.'

Schwarzhelm strode forwards, whirling his sword back into
position, watching as the horror before him gathered itself
to strike. It was like some massive, terrible insect. Its limbs
cradled around itself, stretched and distended.

It looked up and screamed at him. The sound was
unearthly, like a man's and a woman's voices mixed together
and stretched almost beyond recognition. The lilac eyes
flashed, the teeth snapped in the dark.

Then it sprang. The talons extended, slashing at his eyes.

Schwarzhelm brought the sword up sharp, cutting the
blade into the oncoming torso and bending back out of
range of the swiping talons. The creature crumpled around
the sword and a flash of light shot out, just as before. The
horror was sent flying back, its scrawny legs cracking as it
hit the stone. Quick as hate, it was back on its claws, scuttling into the attack.

It leapt at Schwarzhelm. The Champion parried the claws
away, stepped back out of the range of the snapping jaws,
working his blade with phenomenal speed.

The Tochfel-creature dropped low, coiling to pounce at
Schwarzhelm's legs. Its movements were fast but clumsy, like
a spider trying to manage too many limbs. It sprang, both
hands outstretched.

Schwarzhelm darted back again, the Rechtstahl flickering
in a defensive pattern. Next to the ruined amalgam of man,
machine and sorcery, he looked even more solid and immovable than usual, a bulwark of coiled force and endurance.
No emotion crossed his craggy features as he worked, no
fear shone in his eyes. In combat Schwarzhelm was irresistible, as elemental as the storms of nature, as unyielding as
the bones of the hills.

Verstohlen staggered to his feet, dagger poised. He had
no chance of intervening – this fight had been taken from

him. The Tochfel-creature struck again, screaming with frustration as it tried to find a way past Schwarzhelm's wall of steel. Every time it lashed out, a flash of light broke across the square. The Rechtstahl had been forged for monsters such as this. No ordinary blade would have withstood the clattering talons or gnashing incisors, but the Sword of Justice had been wound with spells of warding and drenched in litanies of destruction.

Schwarzhelm waited patiently, watching the horror flail at him, keeping it engaged until the opening emerged. It leapt up again, trying to rake at his eyes with its sweeping claws. He slammed the sword round, connecting solidly with the Tochfel-creature's iron-bound chest and sending it spinning through the air. It hit the stone hard, and there was the sound of something snapping. The lilac light in its eyes flickered for an instant.

Schwarzhelm went after it quickly, rotating the sword in both hands and holding it point down. The horror was almost too quick. As soon as its spine hit the ground it began to gather for another strike. Only for the briefest moment was its ruined torso exposed. Schwarzhelm plunged the Rechtstahl down cleanly, through the flesh and bone. The tip went down into it all, rending as it went, impaling the abomination like a fly on a pin.

The Tochfel-creature screamed, flailing wildly, raking its talons and trying to claw at Schwarzhelm's eyes. The Emperor's Champion held firm, keeping the blade lodged in place, letting the holy steel purge and cleanse.

Slowly, punctuated by shrieks, whines and hisses, the light in the monster's eyes dimmed. Its iron heart lost its lustre and the ravaged limbs fell still. Schwarzhelm kept the sword in place, not daring to withdraw it until the last energy had been bled from the creature of Chaos. It took a long time for the final twitches to subside. Eventually, the fire extinguished, and the talons clanged to the ground, bereft of a guiding will, as inert as an unwielded dagger.

Schwarzhelm pulled the Rechtstahl free, keeping it poised

for a second strike. It wasn't needed. The terror had been extinguished.

He felt Verstohlen limp to his side before he saw him. The man looked terrible. He'd lost weight, and his face had the pallor of one who'd stared at his own death. Blood stained his shirt and coat, and he looked like he was having trouble keeping his feet.

'Where've you *been*?' he demanded.

'We'll talk later,' replied Schwarzhelm, supporting him with his free hand and keeping the Rechtstahl unsheathed. 'For now we need to get out of the city. Come with me.'

He dragged Verstohlen back into the shadows, out of the square and towards the eastern gates. There'd be more fighting before they'd be out, but at least the guards there would be human.

Once they'd gone, the square sank back into silence. No lights shone from the buildings around it. The only signs of the struggle were a couple of long bloodstains on the stone, and the crumpled shape of Dagobert Tochfel, his reign as Steward finally over, his suffering ended at last.

Clearing the orcs' filth from Black Fire Keep had taken long, wearying hours. Fresh from the last of the fighting, soldiers had been forced to douse the floors and scrub them until their fingers were raw. The refuse left behind by the fortress's occupiers defied belief. They'd lived worse than animals, fouling every recess or secluded corner, destroying any furniture not made of solid stone, smearing foul slogans and symbols over every open patch of wall.

The stench remained even after the last of them had been rooted out of the castle and dispatched. In the narrow bunk rooms where the exhausted infantry tried to snatch sleep, the foul reek was indescribably bad, like a mix of all the ill-kept cattle-pens, slaughter-houses and public privies in the seamiest and most dilapidated of Altdorf's slum districts, amplified and concentrated into a heady musk of singular, unforgettable horror.

Such things did little to dent Bloch's pleasure at having achieved what he'd been commanded to do. Once the last of the bitter combat had ended he'd led the victorious human armies under the gates in triumph, casting down the leering symbol of the moon and restoring the Averland coat of arms in its proper place. Now the Solland sun flew again over Black Fire Pass beside the banners of the Empire, Reikland and the bergsjaeger.

The toil hadn't ended with the fighting. Bloch had been determined to order the defence of the Keep personally before the deep of the night fell on them. Only after many hours of labour did he retire at last, retreating to a chamber high up in the Keep as the bulk of his men slept below. Once sleep took him, it took him soundly. He knew that if any orcs remained alive in the mountains, they would be pitifully few in number and unable to do more than squat in the clefts and hollows of the hills, waiting for a warlord to unite their fractious bands again and lead them to more fruitless bloodshed.

Morning broke cold and severe, as it did every day in the high peaks. The sky was low, and dark clouds had passed overhead in the night. The wind remained strong, blasting across the bare peaks and tearing down the glens towards the lowlands to the west. It brought with it rain, which did much to wash the scrawlings from the walls of the castle.

Bloch woke with a start, reaching for his weapon and wiping his eyes. It took a moment for him to remember where he was and what had happened. He'd been dreaming of the wide grasslands again, of Grunwald's last charge in the heart of the horde.

'I avenged you, at least,' muttered Bloch, swinging his legs from the narrow cot and on to the icy stone flags. 'You stupid bastard.'

His cell was narrow. From the curve of the wall it was evident it was on the edge of the fortress's outer wall, high in one of the five towers that rose above the points of the star. There wasn't much in it: just a bunk, a rickety table and a pitcher of frigid water. The sole window was an arrow slit, unglazed. A chill breeze sighed through the gap. He'd not had much more to keep him warm than his cloak and some ragged furs he'd found somewhere or other. If the chamber had once housed the trappings of a commander, the orcs had long since taken them all.

Bloch shivered and pulled his cloak tight around him. He felt as dirty and ragged as a hound. He splashed water from the pitcher across his face and rubbed it into his eyes. His temples were sore and he had bruises all across his body, but he could still walk without a limp, so that was better than usual.

He found Kraus and Drassler already awake and sitting at a long oak table in one of the tower rooms. There were four windows, all narrow but giving a panorama of the mountains in each cardinal direction. The peaks stretched off towards the far horizons, majestic, ice-bound and massive.

'Morning, commander,' said Kraus, rising gingerly. He'd taken a heavy blow to the ribs from a warhammer during the last phases of the castle recovery and only his armour had saved him. Though tough as old bones, he'd not got back on his feet quickly and it had been the Averlanders who'd saved his hide.

'So it is,' replied Bloch, coming to the table. Drassler nodded as he and Kraus sat down, the mountain guard captain looking as rangy and implacable as ever.

'Sweet dreams?' he asked.

'Very sweet,' replied Bloch, seeing a plate of stale bread and grabbing a handful greedily. 'Me and the nice girls of Madame de Guillaume's. Shame to wake up.'

Drassler grinned. Kraus looked disapproving.

'How's the Keep looking?' asked Bloch, speaking through mouthfuls of bread.

'All is in order,' muttered Kraus. In many ways he was a lesser version of Schwarzhelm, though not quite as humorous. 'The artillery and supply wains have been recovered, though we'll need to send for more food soon. The Keep has its own water supply, but ale's running low.'

'Too bad,' said Bloch. 'The men deserve a drink.'

'Watches have been arranged and the company captains given their orders. The place stinks, but it's secure.'

Bloch nodded with satisfaction.

'You've got your castle back, Herr Drassler,' he said.

'That we have. It was a bold plan.'

Bloch shrugged. 'The only plan. Now we have to decide what to do next.'

'You might want to look at these,' said Kraus, handing him some fragments of parchment.

'Have you slept?' asked Bloch, taking them.

'I don't need much.'

Bloch grunted and started to look at the papers. The edges were black and serrated, as if someone had tried to burn them. There were instructions written across them in Reik-spiel. Here and there were seals and official stamps.

'Where did you find these?' he asked.

'The garrison commander's chamber,' said Kraus. 'The orcs had been in there, and not much remained.'

Bloch leafed through the remnants. It was as Drassler had said. Orders for the garrison to disperse and move out to meet several threats. There was correspondence too, from months ago. Reinforcements delayed, supplies refused. Each item, considered alone, was routine enough. Taken together, they amounted to a serious weakening of the pass defences.

'These came by courier from Averheim?' asked Bloch, speaking to Drassler.

'Just as ever.'

Bloch kept reading. It all looked in order. He'd received similar instructions himself while serving in garrisons across the Empire. Whoever had written them knew the ways of the Imperial bureaucracy.

'They're fakes,' he said, letting them fall to the table.

Kraus raised an eyebrow. 'You're sure?'

'Schwarzhelm knew it. He told me we were being used. The orcs crossed the border just when the battle for the new elector took place. This was all part of some move to frustrate him.' He balled his fists and pressed them against his temples, trying to think. 'Have we heard any word from Averheim?'

'None.'

'Grenzstadt?'

'From nowhere, commander. We're on our own.'

It was too convenient. All those troops, drawn east, away from where the real decisions were being made.

'How many men do we have left?'

'A thousand men able to bear arms, plus the mountain guard,' said Kraus. 'Many of the wounded will recover, given time.'

'Not as much as I'd like.'

'So what do you intend?'

Bloch pushed his chair back and sighed heavily.

'Here's how I see it. We know the orcs had gear and money from Altdorf. Plenty of people in the capital have a stake in the new Elector of Averland. Someone in the army could have issued those orders, and you'd never have known. They had to know the codes, sure, but nothing's impossible at the right price. Maybe they wanted to keep us fighting for months, bogged down against the horde. If they did, then Schwarzhelm put paid to that when he broke them open on the plain. So they may not have banked on us recovering the Keep so soon, and that might be a good thing.'

Drassler said nothing. These affairs were beyond his experience, and there was little for him to contribute.

Kraus listened intently, his narrow eyes glittering. 'I was in Averheim with Schwarzhelm,' he said. 'Verstohlen said there'd been letters being sent back and forth from Altdorf, though he didn't know what was in them. He was more worried about the joyroot.'

'The what?'

'Smuggling. He thought it might lead to something bigger.'

'Maybe it has.'

Bloch felt indecision creep across him. Battlefield tactics were one thing, but making the larger choices was still unfamiliar. He'd been told to recover the Keep and wait for orders. After so much labour, so much hardship, that would have been the safest option. It was the one he'd be expected to take. Not so long ago, he'd been a halberdier captain, hardly more senior than Drassler was now. Every once in a while, he still felt like one.

'I'm going back,' he said.

'To Averheim?' asked Kraus.

'Yes, and you're coming with me.' He turned to Drassler. 'We'll take two companies of infantry, the Reiklanders. The rest will stay here. You'll have supplies and artillery, and almost as many men at your command as before.'

Drassler looked unsure. 'There's much to do here.'

Bloch nodded. 'We'll stay to secure the Keep and pass. The way-stations need re-manning, and the damage done here repairing. A few days, but no more.'

'Why Averheim?' asked Kraus, just as warily. 'We could send messengers down to Grenzstadt. If Schwarzhelm needs you, he'll summon you.'

Bloch shook his head. 'Don't you get it, Kraus? Whoever arranged this was arranging things there as well. I want to see what's been happening with my own eyes.'

He looked at the honour guard captain, and his expression was dark.

'There's work to do here, and I won't leave until it's done, but I won't stay on the edges forever. Schwarzhelm knew something was happening in Averheim and he was worried about it. Now that we're finished here, I'm worried too.'

Kraus looked unconvinced, but didn't voice any objection.

'Call it instinct,' said Bloch, feeling only half as confident as he sounded. 'Something's not right down there. It's about time we found out what.'

CHAPTER EIGHT

The sky was chopped up and stormy. Far to the east, heavy clouds had built up on the horizon. A chill wind whipped the grass, tousling it like hair. Stirred by the breeze, the crowns of the trees swayed to and fro, an endless rustling that preyed on the nerves.

Verstohlen woke late. As he moved, he felt a dull pain in his back. Slowly, the memory of the previous night returned to him. He shivered, trying to blot it out.

He pulled himself upright, moving slowly to avoid opening the wounds on either side of his spine. The air smelled of charred meat. Something was cooking.

A few yards away, crouching over a fire, was Schwarzhelm. Two rabbits were roasting, their discarded skins glistening on the grass close by. There were trees all around, and between their slender trunks Verstohlen could see the open, rolling plains of Averland. Not much in the way of cover, but better than nothing.

The big man looked over his shoulder. He didn't smile, and went back to cooking breakfast.

'You slept late,' he grunted. He was right; the sun was high in the sky.

Verstohlen tried to stretch, but the movement sent pangs of pain down his back. He shuffled closer to the fire, limbs stiff and unresponsive.

'How did we get here?' he asked. The events of the previous night were confused. He remembered Tochfel and he remembered a chase through the streets of Averheim. Schwarzhelm had killed men, many of them. Then the gates had slammed open, and there was more running. After that, everything was hazy.

'I brought you here,' he replied. 'When you passed out, I carried you. We're twenty miles east of Averheim. Not far enough. We'll have to move again soon.'

Twenty miles. Schwarzhelm must have walked all night and into the morning. Had he slept at all?

Verstohlen crawled closer to the fire. The rabbit smelled good. He couldn't remember the last time he'd eaten properly.

'I had no idea what happened to you,' he said, staring at the flames, remembering the long days with no communication.

Schwarzhelm didn't reply, and turned the rabbits over on their twig spits.

'I was wrong,' said Verstohlen again. He thought of Natassja, of Grosslich, of Leitdorf. 'I was wrong about everything.'

'We were both wrong,' said Schwarzhelm. 'Blame won't change that.'

He pulled the rabbit meat from the fire and tore it into chunks. He gave Verstohlen half and started munching on the rest. Verstohlen ate quickly, ramming the hot meat down his throat, feeling a bloom of warmth and energy return. Schwarzhelm kicked earth over the fire, killing the smoke. Then he sat back to chew.

'I sent you messages from Altdorf,' he said, his great jaw working steadily. 'You didn't get them?'

Verstohlen shook his head. 'Not much has come and gone out of Averland.'

'So how much do you know about what's happened?'

'Not as much, I guess, as you.'

'You guess right.'

Schwarzhelm sucked at his fingers, leaving flecks of fat in his beard. He looked somehow older than when Verstohlen had last seen him. A cold grief marked his features that hadn't been there before.

'Helborg was no traitor,' said Schwarzhelm. There was no emotion in his voice, no condemnation, just the bald facts. 'But there was corruption. Heinrich Lassus, my old tutor. He was the one who arranged for me to come here. He knew me better than any man alive. He knew what would prey on my mind, and what would cloud my judgement.'

As he spoke, the trees hissed in the wind. Verstohlen kept eating, saying nothing.

'Above all, he knew I'd make the wrong decision. You were allowed to see Natassja Leitdorf, and you were allowed to escape to pass on the tidings. Certain things are now clear to me. She and Grosslich were in league with one another. I don't know whether Rufus, the husband, knew of their plans or not. Is he dead?'

'No one knows.'

'In any case, he's irrelevant. Grosslich has what he wants. The province is his, and there are men streaming to join him every day. Natassja, you may be sure, is by his side. We have delivered Averland to Chaos, you and I. No mean feat.'

Verstohlen let the tidings sink in. With every revelation, his part in things seemed more sordid, more damaging.

'Does the Emperor know?'

'An army is being gathered. I left him in no doubt of the threat.'

'But what's Grosslich's purpose? He must know he can't fight the whole Empire, not once the deception is unravelled. There's something more to this.' He looked up at Schwarzhelm, doubt etched on his face. 'Why was Lassus involved?'

Schwarzhelm swallowed the last of a gristly chunk of meat, wiped his fingers and reached into his jerkin. He withdrew a bundle of letters.

'These are from his private chambers. The answer will be in them.'

'So what do they say?'

'I've no idea.' Schwarzhelm tossed them to Verstohlen. 'They're written in cipher. Not one I recognise.'

Verstohlen unwrapped the bundle and started to look through the leaves. The script was unintelligible. As he scanned the characters, nothing meaningful formed.

'Me neither.'

'Then you should get to work. You're the spy. There'll be plenty of time to look at them as we travel.'

Schwarzhelm hauled himself to his feet and went over to his sword, hung from a nearby branch. Leaning against a tree trunk was another blade. It was naked, and a notch had been taken from it halfway along its length.

'Where are we going?' asked Verstohlen. He knew they needed to move, but his body still ached. He could have slept for another whole day under the shade of the trees.

'East,' replied Schwarzhelm, buckling the Rechtstahl to his swordbelt. He took up the other sword and gazed at the steel blade for a moment. 'This is Helborg's weapon. It needs to be returned.'

'But we don't know if he's still alive,' protested Verstohlen, getting to his feet with effort. 'There's been no news since–'

'He's alive,' snarled Schwarzhelm. For a moment, his eyes flashed with a savage light. 'The spirit of the blade is eager to be made whole. It will lead us to the shard.'

Verstohlen looked doubtful. Averland was a big place, and the mystical power of ancient swords seemed like a poor guide.

Unconcerned, Schwarzhelm hoisted his bag over his shoulder and began to walk. He had the grim, almost cavalier air of a man who had nothing more to lose. It made Verstohlen uneasy. He looked down at the letters, still clenched in his hand. Nothing made sense. Nothing had made sense for a long time.

'If you say so,' he muttered to himself, limping after Schwarzhelm and trying to ignore the pain in his back.

* * *

The parade ground of the Imperial College of Arms was full of men. Regiment after regiment entered the open space, wheeled around, paraded across the gravel and wheeled back again. Sergeants shouted orders and cuffed those who failed to keep up. The pace was relentless. The white and grey of Reikland was predominant, but there were many other state colours on display.

Over eight thousand men, all marching in step. The earth shook under their boots, and this was less than a quarter of the army Volkmar was assembling. When the final host departed for Averheim, it would clog the roads for miles. The baggage train alone was nearly as well-manned as the entire force Schwarzhelm had taken with him to Averland. Chasing greenskins was one thing. Taking back a renegade province was another.

'They look sloppy,' said Gruppen, standing with Volkmar on an observation platform on the south side of the parade ground. The two of them were alone behind the railing. Above them, the sky was a lighter grey than it had been. The rain was clearing, driven west by powerful winds piling in from the far distant mountains.

'What do you expect?' said Volkmar. 'They'll learn discipline on the road.'

'Where do these men come from? I thought the regiments were all in the north.'

'Some were called back. Some are from the reserves. Some are fresh-drafted.'

As Volkmar spoke, one unfortunate infantryman stumbled, bringing three of his comrades down with him. The detachment halted in confusion, earning them a tirade of abuse from the sergeants clustered around them. Gruppen shook his head.

'Little better than murder, sending *them* into battle.'

Volkmar scowled. 'If I had more time, things would be different.' He turned away from the pacing ranks. 'The Emperor wants more speed. The Celestial College has seen portents of a terror growing. We can't afford to linger until they know how to hold a halberd.'

Gruppen narrowed his eyes disapprovingly. 'A shame

they didn't report such portents before,' he said. 'Have they released any magisters?'

'Two. And we have three Bright wizards, and a trio of Light magisters. Not the best, of course – they're in Middenheim still – but powerful, all the same.'

Volkmar had once marched at the head of a host that filled the valleys of Ostland from peak to peak. He'd commanded whole batteries of heavy artillery, capable of razing companies in a single barrage. At the city of the White Wolf he'd stood alongside the defenders while the numberless hordes of Archaon had besieged the walls and the skies had been torn apart by the shadows of madness. Those campaigns had taken weeks to muster. For the retaking of Averheim, Karl Franz had given him days.

And there was still the doubt gnawing at him. He had yet to discover if Archaon had destroyed more than his body in that duel. He suppressed the doubts, pushing them down beneath an external shell of calm.

'I won't lie to you, Gruppen,' he said, his expression like flint. 'We could have a hundred thousand such men, and it wouldn't matter. This battle will be fought by others. The priests. The magisters. The knights. You've faced the great enemy before, so you know what to expect.'

Gruppen nodded bleakly. 'How many of those poor scum do, I wonder?' he said, gesturing to the parading regiments.

'They'll do their duty,' said Volkmar. 'A man should expect nothing more from life.'

More men filed into the parade ground. These were Middenheimers, greatswords by the look of them, and they marched with the confidence of seasoned campaigners. Gruppen broke into a grim smile.

'That's better,' he said. 'They look like they won't run at the first sight of killing.'

Volkmar said nothing. War was always a dirty, terrifying business, but he wasn't worried about that. Even the meanest peasant in the Empire had seen killing, and they could all be taught to hold their ground.

But Chaos was different. He'd seen the reports from the Celestial College, and the looks of fear on the faces of the seers. Something terrifying was growing in Averheim, and if it wasn't staunched at the source, that terror would just keep spreading. The Emperor was right. They had to meet it head-on, and there was no time to waste.

'There's no running from this, Gruppen,' said Volkmar, his voice low. 'Not for any of them. It's stand fast, or die.'

Kurt Helborg limped along the landing of the Drakenmoor castle, his shoulder aflame with pain, sweat beading on his forehead. He leaned on a staff like an old man, wincing with every step. The infirmity made him furious. Every passing hour wasted in the cause of recovery fuelled the smouldering sense of injustice and frustration. He needed to escape, to take up his sword again, to find the ones who'd done this to him.

The wound Schwarzhelm had given him was still weeping blood. He'd seen off the fever, but his sinews needed time to knit together. All he could do was rest and wait. The enforced inaction was far more of a torment than the stabs of pain that still ran across his upper body.

He barely noticed the finery around him. Though the bronze busts of ancient warriors were coated in dust and the woodwork was showing signs of worm, Drakenmoor was still a place of shadowy majesty. The stairways were broad and sweeping, the floor laid with slate tiles, the ceiling plastered and richly decorated. Marius Leitdorf had been wealthy even by the standards of his office, and as Helborg shuffled along he passed priceless urns, irreplaceable statues and portraits by the finest painters in the Empire.

None of it made the slightest impression. He might as well have been limping through a desolate wasteland. As he went, his breath came in ragged gasps and his teeth clenched hard. His waxed moustache, once his pride and joy, had become straggling and wild, and his dark hair hung down to his collar in matted clumps. Only his eyes, the clear blue eyes that had won the hearts of so many women across so many provinces, still flashed with their old icy intensity.

Helborg reached the door to Marius's old study. The old count's feckless son had spent most of his time locked away in there since they'd arrived. That was no longer good enough. If they were going to survive the storm to come, he'd have to make himself more useful.

Without knocking, Helborg kicked the door open. It swung back heavily, banging against the wooden panels of the wall.

Leitdorf was sitting with his back to the door, hunched over his father's old desk, surrounded by papers. The deposed elector spun round, snapping closed the book he'd been reading. His face was pale, as if he'd been reading horror stories. By the redness of his eyes, Helborg guessed he'd been at it for some time.

Helborg shook his head. The boy was no warrior. Never would be.

'Found anything interesting?' the Marshal growled, hobbling over to the single bed against the wall.

Leitdorf pushed the book under a pile of parchment.

'My lord,' he replied, ignoring the question. 'How are you feeling?'

'Like a newborn lamb on a warm spring morning,' Helborg rasped, hoping the sweat on his brow wasn't too obvious. 'Any more stupid questions?'

Leitdorf looked instantly chastened.

'Then I'm glad you're recovering,' he said.

The last time Helborg had spoken to Leitdorf had been in the Vormeisterplatz. After that, there hadn't been the chance. It felt strange to be looking at his face again. Leitdorf had lost some weight. Something of the old arrogance had been knocked out of him too, maybe. If so, that was all to the good. Helborg settled on the bed, feeling his muscles protest as he moved.

'And what are you doing with yourself, Herr Leitdorf?' he said. 'How will you aid our fight for survival?'

'I'm no warrior, Marshal. But if you order me to fight for you, I'll do what I can.'

So meek, so defeated. The old Leitdorf would at least have shown some spirit. Helborg didn't know which incarnation was worse.

'Damn right you'll fight,' he snarled, letting his disdain come to the surface. 'If you hadn't brought this province to the edge of ruin, none of this would have happened. Sigmar's bones, I *still* don't know why we're being chased down by this provincial rabble, nor why that madman Schwarzhelm did what he did.'

'I do,' said Leitdorf quietly. 'I didn't up until now. Truly, I was as deceived as you. But now some things are becoming apparent to me that should have been clear a long time ago.'

Helborg paused.

'Maybe you'd better tell me what you know.'

Leitdorf turned back to the desk and retrieved the book.

'I don't know why I tried to hide it from you,' he said, looking at the cover mournfully. He opened it and began flicking through the pages. 'This is my father's journal. It's nearly full. The last months of his reign are chronicled here, when the madness was at its height. The final entry describes his preparations to face Ironjaw. A few weeks later, he was dead.'

Leitdorf had a crushed expression on his fleshy face. As he spoke, there was little sign of the shrill self-importance that had coloured his speech in Averheim.

'Much of it will be of interest only to me, I suspect. But there's something else. He mentions dreams, terrible dreams in which the great enemy comes to him, tempting him to turn to darkness. He sees war over Averland, vast armies clashing under a tower of iron. Again and again, he mentions a woman, tempting him to join her, offering herself to him if only he will turn. Each time he resists, the madness gets worse. He knows it's killing him. That's why the coming of Ironjaw was, in its own way, a relief. Better to die fighting than lose his mind.'

Helborg listened carefully, resisting the temptation to interrupt.

'She had a name,' said Leitdorf. 'Natassja. Not a common

name in the Empire, as you know. The kind of name you'd remember. He mentions it over and over again. Sometimes he descends into gibberish, but always returns to Natassja. He knows she's trying to turn him to the darkness, and can't do anything about it. He couldn't find her in the real world, just in the dreams, but he knew as surely as anything that she was going to drive him mad.'

'Your wife,' said Helborg, finally remembering the name from the briefing Skarr had given him in Nuln.

Leitdorf nodded bitterly. 'The same.' He looked up at the Marshal, horror in his eyes. 'Even now, even after being driven out of Averheim, I thought she was the one ally I had left. The worst of my many errors. She destroyed my father, and now she's destroyed me.'

Helborg let the information sink in, weighing up the implications. A sorceress, then, working to subvert the ruling line of Averland. If she could turn minds to insanity, then that explained Schwarzhelm's rages. Helborg had always assumed Marius's madness was due to a weakness in the man's blood, just as had the rest of the Empire. Perhaps that explanation had been too simple.

'Your *wife*,' he mused. 'So what are you telling me, that you didn't know she was corrupted?'

Leitdorf shook his head. 'I thought the accusations were lies, spread by Grosslich. By all that's holy, Marshal, by the blood of Sigmar and all the saints, I swear I never knew.' His eyes seemed to lose focus. 'I never knew...'

Helborg pushed himself up from the bed with difficulty and got to his feet.

'Don't you *dare* start whimpering, man,' he growled. 'She was your responsibility, and you let her play you for a cuckold. A sorceress and an elector. Morr's teeth, Leitdorf, can you see what you've done?'

Rufus looked up at him, a flash of the old anger in his eyes.

'Remember who you're talking to!' he snarled. 'I may have lost the city, but I *am* the rightful Elector of Averland.'

Helborg smiled inwardly. This was better.

'So you say. You've nothing to back up that claim but old heirlooms and a crumbling castle. I'm not impressed.'

Leitdorf sprang to his feet. He looked more comical than threatening, clad in his sagging, travel-worn clothes and carrying the vestiges of his pot-belly. The fury on his face was real enough, though, and he drew his ancestral sword, the Wolfsklinge, with a deadly flourish.

'I have this,' he hissed. 'Where is your blade, mighty hero of the Empire?'

They locked eyes. Helborg met his gaze. For a moment, Leitdorf managed to hold it, driven by his anger. Then his face fell. Next to Helborg he was little more than a soft, aristocratic fop, and he knew it.

'I have no sword,' said Helborg. 'You know why that is. But you have an armoury here – I'll take one of yours. And we'll use it to arm the others who will come.'

He leaned forwards and grasped Leitdorf's shoulder. The grip was tight, and his fingers dug into the pudgy flesh unmercifully.

'We've all been betrayed,' he said. His voice was as hard as pack-ice. 'You can sit here and cry about it, or look for a way to strike back. You have natural allies here, men whose allegiance was to your father. We can use that loyalty. Today, we have fifty men under arms. Tomorrow, we'll add another fifty from the villages around. By the time Grosslich gets here, the countryside will be alive with his enemies.'

Leitdorf raised his head again. There was a kind of strangled hope in his face, but also doubt. He'd never been forced to command before. For all his bluster, the man was afraid, deeply afraid.

'They'll follow you,' he said. 'Why would they follow me?'

Helborg maintained the vice-like grip on his shoulder. It burned his wound to hold the position, but he ignored the pain.

'Because you're the *elector*, Herr Leitdorf. It's what you said you wanted. Now it's here, what will you do? Will you keep running? Will you bury yourself in old books, hunting for answers? Or will you turn and fight? This is the test, my friend. Your father faced it. Now you must choose.'

Leitdorf stood still for a moment, his body tense, his face wrought with indecision. He wavered. For a moment, Helborg thought he'd turn away again. Then the torment passed. Leitdorf withdrew from Helborg's grip and sheathed his sword, sliding the steel back into the scabbard clumsily.

'There's more in the notebooks,' he said, his voice calmer than before. 'I'll study them. But when the time comes, I will ride beside you, Marshal. I'll find the one who wounded me, even as you will find the one who wounded you. Averland will be restored, and I will lead it.'

Helborg smiled again, this time with no rancour. There were challenges ahead, but first test had been passed.

'So be it,' he said. 'We'll ride together.'

Gerhard Fulleren locked the doors carefully and headed back to the kitchen. The geese were still hissing in the yard as if the End Times were upon them, but he couldn't see anything out there. A fox, perhaps, prowling round the edge of the farm, sniffing for loose chickens. Wolfen, his old hound, slunk along beside him, eager to get himself in front of the range and warm up. The air had a chill in it which didn't bode well for winter. A cold mist had rolled down from the highlands, out of season and unwelcome.

Gerhard sat down in front of the range, opened the iron door and threw another log on the fire. The still-warm embers flared up. It was late, nearly two hours after dark. The old farmer sat forwards, warming his hands as the timber crackled and spat. He had to get some rest. He'd be up before dawn with the animals. The summer had been a good one, but there were always shortages, always things to buy. The long plough had finally given out, and there was only so long he could rely on the ancient shire horse to keep going.

He was getting too old for this himself. It was about time one of his sons took the business over. They were too fond of ale, and too fond of the women that came with it. The time had long passed for them to take a step forwards and assume a man's proper role.

Wolfen gave a weary snort and lay down in front of the range. The old hound had stopped shivering, which was a relief. Gerhard had never seen him so agitated. The mist had done it to him, probably. Spooked him. Anything out of season would spook a farmer's dog.

There was a noise behind him, and he spun round, heart beating. Rosamunde stood at the foot of the stairs, carrying a candle and looking full of slumber.

'What in Morr're you doing, woman?' he snapped irritably.

'Can't sleep,' she mumbled, coming over to the fire.

She was a big-boned woman, and always had been. When she sat next to him on the bench, the wood flexed under her weight. Gerhard couldn't complain about that. He liked a bit of meat to hold on to in the cold winters, and she'd given him five sons, two daughters and a handsome dowry. At least one of them was bound to turn out for the good. For all her carping, Rosamunde was a fine woman.

'I'll draw you a cup of milk,' said Gerhard, getting up and heading to the corner of the kitchen where a collection of earthenware jugs stood, covered in fabric. Outside, the wind was getting up. The geese kept hissing, and in the far distance he heard a dog barking wildly. Wolfen pricked his ears up.

'That Dieter's hound?' asked Rosamunde, waking up a little.

'Guess so. There's a wind up tonight.'

Rosamunde shook her head to clear it. 'I had bad dreams.'

Gerhard brought a mug of milk over, frothy and pungent from the udder. 'Forget about it. It's a wild night.'

She took the mug and cradled it in her palms. Her normally rosy cheeks were pale.

There was a rattling sound from outside the window. Rosamunde stiffened.

'What's that?' she asked, eyes suddenly wide open.

Gerhard felt his heart start to thump again. He'd heard it in the yard, and it had sent the geese wild. They were still hissing and honking like a crowd of flagellants on a holy day. He was beginning to get unnerved himself. Something was out there.

'Ignore it,' he said, failing to keep the fear from his voice. 'Go to bed. I'll take Wolfen out for a look.'

More rattling. The hound started to whine, and crept under a bench, tail shivering between his legs. Much use he was.

Rosamunde stood up. The mug of milk fell to the ground, and the liquid streaked across the rushes on the floor.

'There's someone in the yard, Gerhard,' she insisted, looking more scared by the moment. What had her dream been about? 'Get the axe.'

'It's in the shed.'

'What's it doing in the shed?'

'I left it there.'

'Morr's bones! Go and get it!'

Panic was rising. Gerhard knew he wasn't going outside, not for all the jewels of Ind. He threw another log on the fire, sending more light across the kitchen. As the wood left his hands, he saw how much they were shaking. He was scared. He hadn't been this scared since his service in the regiment, and that was now years ago.

'What're you going to do?' demanded Rosamunde. Her voice was climbing up the register, getting higher pitched with fear. The clicking got louder.

'Go to bed, woman,' growled Gerhard, picking up a poker from next to the range. Wolfen whimpered and crept further out of harm's way. 'I'll handle this. It'll be lads from the village, playing a prank.'

She stayed where she was, rooted to the spot. She spun round, looking at the window on the far side of the room. It was beginning to open.

'Gerhard!' she screamed, pointing at it and shaking.

Gerhard found that he couldn't move. His limbs seemed welded together, as stiff as beams of iron.

'Do something!' she shrieked, equally unable to move. Something was climbing inside. Bone fingers crept over the sill, scraping against the plaster. A vase was knocked over, sending the cut flowers skittering across the floor.

'Wolfen!' ordered Gerhard, pointing at the window with trembling fingers. 'Get 'im!'

The dog bolted, not for the window but for the stairway leading up to the bedrooms above. He'd never been allowed up there. The terror had overridden any commands Gerhard could have given him.

'Who are you?' Gerhard cried out, feeling himself lose control of his voice. He backed towards Rosamunde, clutching at her instinctively. She clutched back, and the two of them huddled in the middle of the room.

The bone fingers reached down to the floor, followed by a thin arm. A cowled head emerged, pushing the lace curtains aside.

More rattling sounded from the other side of the room. Something was scrabbling at the door. There were more of them.

'Get out!' screamed Rosamunde, tearing at her hair. 'Get out of my house!'

The figure at the window dropped inside, sprawled on the floor like a crushed spider. Its hair hung lank around its slim face, and iron studs gleamed from its limbs. It looked like a girl, near-naked. She must have been perishing cold, and her skin was as white as the moon.

Gerhard wanted to say something, do something heroic, get them out of his farmhouse. The door was now rattling on its hinges. They were going to knock it down.

'What do you *want*?' he pleaded, nearly sobbing with terror. They kept rattling, just like mechanical dolls.

The first one lifted her head. She had no eyes, just blank plates of metal. She grinned wide, exposing drilled-sharp teeth. Her fingers clacked together, dagger-quick blades rubbing against each other like a butcher's sharpening knives.

'*Helborg!*' she hissed, her voice echoing from the walls. '*Helborg!*'

'What?' screamed Gerhard. 'This is Mofligen, by Ruppelstadt! Not Helborg! Leave us!'

The door slammed open, ripped from its hangings. Another horror came in, clad in rags like the first, hissing and wheezing. Its knife-like fingers trailed on the ground, leaving grooves in the hard stone.

'*Helborg!*' it cried.

There was another one behind it, just like the rest. Three of them. They limped towards Gerhard and Rosamunde, their grins impossibly wide, skin stretched tight, teeth snapping as they came.

'*Helborg!*'

Gerhard felt his heart hammer so hard he thought it would explode. Rosamunde snatched at him frantically, pushing him in front of her, anything to get away from the creeping terrors.

He knew he should run. Do something. Try and get away. But there was nothing he could do. His body was drenched with sweat. The terrible maidens closed in on him, raising their fingers high.

'*Helborg!*'

'I can't help you!' cried Gerhard, falling to his knees and bursting into horrified tears. 'Sigmar's *mercy*, I can't help you! Leave us alone!'

Then the first talon fell, slicing down with speed and skill. The others joined in, carving up the huddled pair like raptors on the carcass of a stricken deer. For a few moments, the screams of the victims rose into the windy night, mingling with the cries of the geese and the howling from upstairs. Then all was silent. The kitchen was still, apart from the crackle of the firewood, the distant whimper of the dog and the expanding pools of blood on the floor.

The three handmaidens stepped back, admiring their work. Flesh was strewn all across the rushes, diced into neat segments. For a moment, they paused, each breathing gently, lost in appreciation of their art.

Then one of them looked at the others, and the grin left her face. A signal was given, and they limped back to the door. This quarry hadn't been what they sought, but killing was good. It reminded them of a life before the one they had now, when there was more than simply pain and orders. For some reason, the pleading for mercy, the desperate entreaties to be left alone, appealed to them. Maybe they had done the same thing, a long time ago before their minds had been taken away and all had descended into the long grind of horror. There was no clear memory of it, just a vague sense.

They passed through the door, rattling as they went. Outside, the wind howled around the farmhouse, and a loose shutter banged wildly. A gale was coming, a storm wind from the Grey Mountains to the south.

The maidens departed. They knew they were getting close. They never tired, they never gave in, they never lost hope. All they had was the single word, the reason for their existence.

'*Helborg*,' whispered the last of them, before they stalked off into the night, heading south and east, away from the pastureland and up into the gorse of the high moors. Their prey was drawing closer.

CHAPTER NINE

Verstohlen looked across the scattered fragments of parchment again. The light was beginning to fail. His limbs throbbed from the long march across country, and that affected his mind. Nothing came easily, and the cipher remained firmly locked in place.

Over the past two days Schwarzhelm had driven them hard, striding across the countryside with the iron resolve he'd used in the past to lead armies. He spoke even less than normal. Apart from the Rechtstahl at his side, he'd eschewed his armour, and seemed diminished both physically and mentally. Something had broken within him.

Though Schwarzhelm never explained how, he seemed to know where he was going. Every so often, he'd stop walking for no reason at all. Once he'd drawn Helborg's sword and held it up to the sun, turning the metal and watching the reflection in it. Then he'd set off again, silent and brooding, striding purposefully as if nothing had happened.

They kept clear of the roads, lying low whenever they sighted Grosslich's men on the horizon. Even so far into the wilds there were patrols. They'd seen one column of men, at least five hundred strong, heading east. The new elector's reach was extending.

As the hours of furtive trekking had passed, Verstohlen had watched his master carefully. There was none of the mania that had affected him in Averheim. He now had a cold, calculated fury, directed inwards. The cure to this sickness was obvious. If Helborg were alive, Schwarzhelm would return the sword. Verstohlen didn't like to speculate too much on what Helborg would do when he got it – the Marshal wasn't renowned for his compassion. Still, one way or another it would bring some kind of resolution.

On the rare breaks between the marches, Verstohlen had plenty of time to contemplate the coded messages taken from Lassus's chambers. At first glance, he'd assumed the code would be relatively easy to break. Ciphers used for routine messages were rarely complex – if they were, uncovering the meaning for the recipient would be too arduous and time-consuming to be useful. In the normal run of things, in a world where so few men could read, Imperial codes were generally only used to keep messages secret from opportunistic thieves.

Lassus's code, on the other hand, looked like total gibberish. Verstohlen had started on the assumption that some kind of substitution code was being used, and had drawn out a table of alphabets using a stick of charcoal on parchment Schwarzhelm had brought from Altdorf. After that, he'd worked on a single phrase, the opening words of the final letter. Every variation produced a fresh line of nonsense. If he'd had more leisure to work, Verstohlen might have been able to do things more thoroughly. Even so, after hammering away at the problem, he knew he was missing something.

Schwarzhelm didn't appreciate the difficulties. As they travelled, he'd demanded answers. The man was a near indestructible master of swordcraft, but he had little appreciation of the literary and philosophical arts. He could read, it was true, but his penchant for language games didn't extend far.

Verstohlen found it hard even to explain the nature of the problem. Whenever he had to confess his lack of progress, Schwarzhelm didn't fail to show his frustration.

'This is important, Pieter,' he'd say.

'I know it is.'

'We don't have time to speculate.'

'I know we don't.'

'Then crack it.'

On the second day out from Averheim, they'd come across an abandoned farmhouse on the edge of what looked like fallow fields. There were no settlements within eyesight. The light was beginning to fail, and even Schwarzhelm looked ready to halt the march.

Verstohlen looked at the roofless building before him, watching the way the evening sun struck the stone. Around them, beyond the margins of the ploughed and empty fields, the endless seas of grass whispered. Schwarzhelm looked as if he was remembering something. Whatever it was, the memory wasn't a happy one.

'How close are you?' he asked again.

'Are we stopping here?' replied Verstohlen. 'If so, I might be able to concentrate.'

'I'll gather wood for a fire,' Schwarzhelm said, stalking off. 'Do what you can.'

So it was that Verstohlen found himself huddled in the corner of the ruined farmhouse, surrounded by scraps of yellowing paper. The characters, all written in a small, discursive hand, began to stream in front of his eyes. He ran the substitution tests again, this time isolating a different phrase in the letter, near the end. He worked on the sentences in his head, trying to spot patterns emerging for each shift. Whatever he tried, nonsense emerged. By the time Schwarzhelm came back, Verstohlen was tired and frustrated. Lassus was no fool. Verstohlen needed time, space, the use of a desk, quill and mathematical tables. It was hopeless.

Schwarzhelm crouched down some distance from him and began to pile the wood. A few moments later he'd struck his

flint and the kindling at its base began to burn. It wasn't until
Verstohlen saw the fire flare into life that he realised how
cold he'd been getting. The nights were drawing in across
Averland, turned chill by the gathering storms in the east.

'Progress?' asked Schwarzhelm curtly, sitting down with
his back against the wall. Verstohlen shook his head, knowing the reaction it would provoke.

To his surprise, Schwarzhelm didn't admonish him. The
big man stared into the growing flames moodily, watching
the dry wood catch. All around them, the shadows began to
lengthen. Another day had passed and they were no closer
to their goal.

'We'll have to work without the letters, then,' he said. 'Maybe
things will become clearer when we're back in Averheim.'

Verstohlen raised an eyebrow. Schwarzhelm clearly had
the future all mapped out. Verstohlen almost asked him to
explain what he had in mind, but then decided against it. He
was too tired. As far as he could see, the quest to find Helborg
was doomed to failure, and the march across the countryside
was merely a way for Schwarzhelm to exorcise his inner daemons. He sighed, and began to collect the scraps of paper
together. He could start work on them again in the morning.

'I need to get my bearings,' said Schwarzhelm, looking like
he was speaking half to himself. 'This whole place seems
foreign to me.'

'So it should,' muttered Verstohlen. 'It's changed since you
were a child.'

Schwarzhelm grunted in agreement. Verstohlen returned
to the fire and held his hands against it.

'You never told me much about your time here,' he said.

'What do you want, my life story?'

'Not all of it.' Verstohlen was inured to Schwarzhelm's
prickliness. 'But you're a hard man to understand, my lord.
Is there a man alive who knows anything about you?'

Schwarzhelm remained stony-faced.

'Not alive,' he said.

Verstohlen took the hint and fell quiet. For a while, the

only sound was the crackle of the fire and the sounds of the land. In the distance, a triangle of geese flew low across the setting sun, crying as they went. Below them ran the sound of the grasses, rushing endlessly in the wind. Verstohlen resigned himself to a long, sullen evening, but then Schwarzhelm, against all expectation, spoke.

'I was born a few days' ride from here,' he said. He continued to look into the flames, and they lit his eyes with a dancing light. 'In a village like any across the Empire. Less than a hundred souls, all of them poor. Getting into the army was my dream then, just like any other lad's. I didn't expect much from it, just a schilling in my pocket and the chance to escape the grind. Turned out I was good at killing. My one true talent. I got noticed, then got sent to Altdorf. After I started to train with Lassus, I never came back. Even now, I've never been back. The Empire became my home, and my roots seemed unimportant. Maybe that was a mistake.'

By Schwarzhelm's standards, it was an unprecedented confession. For a man who rarely strung more than a few words together, and those usually curt commands, his answers to Verstohlen's questions were a revelation. Perhaps it was necessary. Maybe the wounds opened up by his failure in Averheim needed some kind of purgation before they were closed. Even the Emperor's Champion could be damaged.

'Close to here, eh?' said Verstohlen. 'So this is your country.'

Schwarzhelm nodded. 'That it is. Wenenlich, the village was called. I don't even know if it still exists.'

At the mention of the village's name, Verstohlen froze.

'What was it called?'

'Wenenlich.'

Verstohlen felt his mind start to race. That wasn't the first time he'd heard that word. Someone had uttered it recently, somewhere important. He sat back, leaning his head against the wall and looking into the darkening sky, trying to think.

'Holy Verena,' he swore, feeling the memory return. 'They used that word.'

'Who?'

'It was the password. To get into Natassja's sanctum. The soldier at the gates required it.'

Verstohlen got to his feet, brushing his clothes down as he rose. Something had occurred to him. Schwarzhelm followed him more slowly, clambering to his feet stiffly.

'What is it?'

'An idea,' said Verstohlen, taking out the letter again.

He scrabbled for the crude table of characters he'd drawn up, talking rapidly as he did so.

'Suppose you create a table of characters, each axis being the alphabet in sequence, and each row starting with the letter in the leftmost column – like this one. This is what Menningen uses, based on a system devised by Vignius. Now suppose you read an "a". Take the first letter of the key, say "w". Find the row starting with the key, and move along to the cell containing the cipher character. The character of the column header will be the one you write.'

As he spoke, Verstohlen turned one of the parchment scraps over and scribbled on it with the blunt charcoal. Schwarzhelm looked completely blank, watching Verstohlen work with little comprehension.

'If you say so.'

Verstohlen kept writing, referring back to the original letter. The stream of letters looked as impenetrable as ever.

jlyvrataakpnwgxmuzwkrpfdmpaoshxusqutwrtvhaxguerb-
wgwipkkryctccpdwpqvrxikuossgbxuuawjsavwtdlsmgllzcu-
vkrpeaywvoapcjrpttlcvrxszzrhnxvrgsqudwwgmzpejljpbzro-
pktwwfsapdgujsjhbyswvadmaojttnininorlaksutesppmfzfs-
lvbzbfpoxeipomrvomgiqdmebniycnwtgsoivrulvfzpmyppl-
cvpkrnkntvuadiyfbcodbpcbyzlsgvsrzmaocrhbxrvzfkjdkv-
xkepmpzgmawepiffpscpnjxcyphrjrykgzsinorymfhjhsya-
oatlyfsoflngsuly

'The important thing is the key. Using the word unlocks the meaning.'

'Why Wenenlich?'

Verstohlen shot Schwarzhelm a wry look. 'Perhaps their idea of a joke. Lassus knew you like no one else.'

His fingers ran across the table, cross-referencing each character in the letter with the one the key pointed to. Letters emerged. As he wrote, Verstohlen could feel his hands begin to shake. It didn't exactly make sense, but it wasn't gibberish. The letters followed one another without a break as Verstohlen decoded them.

ndfundsrecbfksafehl

Verstohlen stopped transcribing and ran the charcoal stub back along the letters.

'It'll still be truncated, and may start mid-word.' He began to draw a line between the likely words, watching for abbreviation and filling out the expansion. 'Some of this is guesswork, but maybe this will make more sense.'

and funds received black fire keep safely hl

Verstohlen stared at his handiwork, his heart thumping. He'd cracked it.

'About time,' said Schwarzhelm gruffly. 'I'll get us some food. You can make a start in the morning.'

Verstohlen smiled to himself. Effusive praise wasn't the big man's style. More importantly, though, the tone of his voice had changed. The cold note of self-judgement was diminished. In its place, and for the first time since he'd returned to Averland, there was hope for some answers.

The muster was complete. Across the plains south of Pohlbad in the lower Reikland, Volkmar's host was ready to march at last. Companies had been moving down the short distance from Altdorf in an incessant stream for days and gathering in the sprawling country estate of Duke Raffenburg Olsehn. With every new arrival, the numbers of men stationed in the huge marshalling yards swelled by another few hundred. Caravans of food and supplies had already set off, heading south under heavy armed guard. Messengers had been sent on fast horses, handing out warrants from the Imperial Palace for more materiel and men. Requisitions had been made of the Gunnery School in Nuln, already working at breakneck pace to supply the war in the north and now expected to arm another whole army with only days' notice. The fabric of the Empire, its finances and its resolve, were being stretched to their very limit.

Volkmar stood on a high stepped platform overlooking the duke's grand parade ground, watching the fruit of his labours stand in row after row, detachment after detachment. The standards of the various companies hung limply from their poles. The morning had dawned overcast and still, turning the stone of the mansion house behind them a dark, dull grey.

'Good enough?' mused Maljdir, watching the final units take their places in the muster. He was standing beside Volkmar, as was Roll. Volkmar was arrayed in the ceremonial robes of his office, and the eagle of Sigmar, cast in steel, adorned his breast. The collar of his cloak, a deep ceremonial red, rose high above his head, making his already massive frame even more imposing. Roll wore the robes of a warrior priest and carried a double-headed axe in his clenched fists. Maljdir wore the plate armour and chainmail of his Middenheim heritage. His cloak was white, trimmed with the dark blue of the northern province.

'We'll see,' said Volkmar, his eyes trained on the host below. 'Give the signal.'

The message was passed down from the platform, and a trumpet blared out from rear of the parade ground, soon repeated across the open space. Men stood to attention, and the sound of their boots snapping together echoed through the air.

'Men of the Empire!' roared Volkmar. His huge voice boomed out, spreading to all corners of the parade ground. Few men would have been able to make themselves heard across such a wide area, but Volkmar's oratory, honed by a lifetime's service to the Cult of Sigmar, was fuelled by his inexhaustible faith. 'You know why you've been summoned here. I'll not weary your ears by talking of Averland and its troubles. You need know only one thing. The great enemy has made Averheim its home, and we march to expunge it from the face of the Empire.'

As he spoke, Volkmar swept his eyes across the ranks. Every man present, nearly thirty thousand infantrymen, remained silent, listening intently to his words. None dared raise so much as a smile in his presence. The Grand Theogonist, master of the arcane mysteries of the Church of Sigmar, was a figure of awe and majesty.

'There will be no deception between us. The task will be arduous. Before the victory, there will be death. Even as we assemble here, they are recruiting men of their own, arming them and readying for the battle to come. By such means do they hope to destroy our resolve, to crush our spirit when the time of testing comes.'

He took a step forwards, gripping the brass railing and leaning out over the masses.

'Do *not* be afraid!' he roared. 'Do *not* give in! We know, as they will never do, of the secret power of mankind, the source of his greatness! Only in purity and steadfastness is there salvation. The mind of the loyal soldier is more terrible to the false gods than anything our weapons of steel and blackpowder can devise. While we profess our faith, they are powerless against us!'

The host remained rapt, hanging on every word. Volkmar knew how important the speech was. There would be few chances to address the entire army again. He had to inspire them while the sun shone and the world seemed hopeful, for he knew how dark the road would be.

'Look around you, my sons,' he said, sweeping his arms in a wide gesture. 'See what the hand of man has built here. Look at the powers ranged in our defence. We have gunnery from Nuln capable of tearing down the walls of any castle standing. We will have magisters of the colleges in our ranks, each of them masters of the winds of magic. I myself will command a full regiment of warrior priests, all sworn enemies of the heretic and the daemon. Alongside them will ride the Knights Panther, deadliest swords of the Empire.'

He pointed out each elite company as he spoke, noting Gruppen's nod of acknowledgement as his finger isolated the proud regiment of knights, standing not more than thirty yards from him.

'And so you do not march alone. For every sword they possess, we possess a sharper. For every fallen sorcerer, we have an exalted master of magic. For every twisted warrior, cursed with the warping gifts of their dark masters, we have armoured knights wearing sanctified armour and carrying the blades of their forebears. So when the moment comes, stride forth with confidence! Let anger be your guide, not fear. Let fury drive you, the fury of the just man at the insolence of those who have taken our lands and despoiled them!'

Volkmar's voice rose, channelling the anger he felt himself. It was always there, just beneath the surface. As he spoke, he remembered Be'lakor's twisted face, the savage leer of the daemon as it turned to horror in the face of his implacable wrath. He had triumphed then, and the taste of victory had never left his lips. He was strong enough for this.

'We will give them no mercy!' he bellowed, and a ripple of agreement passed across the army. 'We will drive them into the ground! We will rip their false idols down, burn their blasphemous temples and tear their souls from their gibbering carcasses! We will sweep through Averland like an avenging storm, with the fire of Holy Sigmar in our hearts and the steel of His Empire in our hands!'

The army pressed forwards. Men raised their fists, stirred by the emotion shaking in Volkmar's words. They were almost ready to be unleashed.

'Remember who you are!' he shouted, his knuckles white as they gripped the railing. 'You are *men*, the rightful masters of the world! None shall stand before us, not the beast of the forest, the orc of the mountain, nor the corruption from within! We shall cleanse Averland just as Middenheim was cleansed, as Praag was cleansed, and as every city will be cleansed that is defiled by those without faith, without honour, and without hope!'

The murmur turned into a swell of acclamation.

'So we ride, men of the Empire! We ride to glory, not for

ourselves, but for the one who leads us. For Karl Franz! For Sigmar! For the Empire!'

The army raised its fist as one, hurling cries of 'For the Empire!' into the air. The noise was deafening, a wall of sound that rose up from the gravel of the parade ground and swelled up to the highest pinnacle of the mansion house beyond. The earth drummed as the stamp of thirty thousand feet hit home. As if a gale had been sent by Sigmar Himself, the standards of the massed regiments suddenly burst into life, streaking out and displaying the proud devices of the myriad companies.

Volkmar felt his heart beat powerfully. On either side of him, Roll and Maljdir had raised their weapons high, and were stirring the host into new heights of fervour. The sea of men, filling the ground before him, had been roused. They would remember this moment on the long march ahead, and when the clash finally came, it would fill their hearts with the courage they would need to weather the storm.

Volkmar raised his arms high in a gesture of defiance, then stepped back from the edge of the platform. The host continued to roar with undiminished enthusiasm. He turned to Maljdir, and his grim face was set.

'Bring my charger,' he growled. 'Now we march.'

High in the Iron Tower, work continued apace. Metal was twisted around metal, ever rising, ever growing. The pinnacle now dominated the city, casting its shadow over the poor quarter and stretching to the river. Nowhere in the city was now free of its gaze, and the skeleton framework of the topmost chambers was already snaking into the sky. A thousand Stone-slaves now toiled on its construction, their spirits crushed by the malevolence of the shard buried beneath them, their eyes glazed and wills destroyed.

Night was falling. Outside the perimeter fence the ceremony was starting up again. Hundreds of soldiers moved through the streets of Averheim, isolating those not performing their duties with sufficient zeal and dragging them to the holding pens. Iron lamps had been lit at every street corner, throwing an angry red glow across the stone. Numbly, the citizens of the city emerged to do obeisance to their new lords and masters. Most had the telltale signs of joyroot addiction around their eyes.

The populace had been told the ceremony was a ritual of praise to Sigmar, held to erase the sins of the citizens during the time without an elector. Many of them believed that, and sang the words with devout fervour. Others, knowing that they weren't Reikspiel and had the ring of some unholy foreign tongue, did so reluctantly. They had little choice but to comply.

Many of the people still supported Grosslich, despite the steel fist that had descended on the city. Money continued to flow, and the food and root were both plentiful. Relaxations on long-standing edicts against drunkenness and fornication were popular in the slums, and the nobles who would normally have opposed such measures were Grosslich's allies, or had been cowed into submission, or were dead.

From his crystal chamber in the Tower, the elector looked out across the city, watching with satisfaction as the points of light spread out from the centre like a spider's web of flame. Far below, he could see shuffling masses in the streets, whipped into a frenzy of chanting by the soldiers around them. Some of them had looks of religious transport on their faces.

Though they were doing his work, he despised them more than he could express. At least those who opposed him had some backbone. Until Natassja got her hands on them, that was.

'Enjoying the view?'

He hadn't heard her enter. No doubt she enjoyed these demonstrations of her superiority, but they were beginning to become trying. He turned slowly, attempting to look as if he'd known she'd been behind him all along.

'The mask has almost slipped now,' he said. 'Few will be fooled for much longer. Is any of this pretence worth keeping up?'

Natassja came over to stand beside him and looked out across the twinkling mass of lights.

'It most certainly is,' she said. The blue tinge in her skin had become more pronounced and the pure black of her eyes glistened. 'Why reveal ourselves before deception becomes impossible?'

Grosslich shook his head. 'I can't understand how they don't see it.'

Natassja shrugged. 'Because they don't want to see it. You were chosen to end the anarchy. Right up until the end, there will be those who fail to see what you've done with your power.'

She turned away from the window. As ever, her manner was cool and controlled. Despite the outlandish nature of her appearance, it was hard to reconcile the grace of her bearing with the terror she was capable of inflicting.

'Maintain the ceremony,' she said. 'The hymns aid the awakening of the Stone, and it gives the rabble something to do.'

Grosslich didn't like the tone of command in her voice. For so long, he'd been willing to let her dominate him, aware he had much to learn, but now his own powers were increasing. The issue of respect was something he'd have to address.

'Is the chamber below complete?' he asked.

Natassja nodded. 'Achendorfer has been busy. The process will quicken soon, and then you'll have tools at your disposal no mortal elector has ever possessed.'

'I'll look forward to it.'

'Enjoy them while you can. The Stone is useful in other ways. I've seen a great army heading south, commanded by the master of the boy-god's church. They're travelling fast.'

'Do they pose a danger?'

'Everything is dangerous.'

'And do you ever give a straight answer?'

Something like a smile played across Natassja's purple lips. With a sudden pang, Grosslich realised how well she was playing him.

'You can handle them, my love,' she said, coming up to

him and placing a slender hand on his chest. Despite everything, Grosslich felt a shudder of desire at her touch. 'With the powers I will give you, no mortal army will be able to stand against us.'

She came closer, her lips parted, her dark eyes shining. Grosslich could feel her breath, laced with lilac perfume. This was her most potent weapon. Herself. He had no means of combating it.

'Have no fear,' she whispered, pressing her body against his. 'The outcome has already been determined. By the time they arrive, this place will be a fragment of the Realm of Pain on earth. We will crush them, my love, just as we have crushed Averland.'

From down in the city, the noise of frenzied revels was growing. Grosslich felt his will sapped, his resolve weaken. Natassja was more beautiful then than she'd ever been. Thoughts of trying to resist her divine mastery seemed not so much foolish as pointless.

'We *have* crushed Averland, have we not?' he murmured, running his fingers up to her hair.

'Oh, we've only just started,' breathed Natassja, and her pupils seemed like chasms to a whole new realm of terrible wonder. 'Believe me, my love, this is only the beginning.'

CHAPTER TEN

Bloch paused for a moment from the march, shading his eyes against the setting sun. The sinking orb was huge and red, and the sky above was angry and inflamed like a giant wound. He stood with Kraus at the head of his small force, less than two hundred men, poised at the mouth of the passes. The Keep was several miles behind, garrisoned and provisioned after two days of hard work. Ahead of him, the land fell sharply, falling in a cascade of cliffs and sharp defiles. The road threaded through the broken land before snaking eventually down through the highlands and towards distant Grenzstadt. On either side, the shoulders of the mountains reared into the evening sky, their snow-streaked flanks rosy from the dying sun.

'You all right?' asked Kraus, looking at him keenly.

'Fine,' said Bloch, starting to walk again. He'd be pleased enough to get down out of the high passes and back into warmer climes. There was still another hour before they'd make the next way-fort, and he'd kept the pace hard.

In truth, though, something about the sunset troubled him.

He remembered Schwarzhelm's face before he'd left. Whatever he was returning to face in Averheim had scared him. And that was where he was headed too.

'We need to pick up the pace,' he muttered, striding down the road with purpose. 'Marching down here in the dark will be dangerous.'

Behind him, the column wearily picked up their weapons, and the trek resumed.

Skarr crouched down low under the cover of the trees. The sky was a light grey, overcast with high cloud and full of the chill of a failing summer. Around him his men did likewise, keeping their blades sheathed and armour covered. There were thirty of the Reiksguard with him, the majority of those who'd escaped Averheim and joined Helborg in the wilderness. He felt his body tense for action, his muscles responding instantly despite the long days in the wilds. His fingers remained tight around the hilt of his sword, still in its scabbard but ready to be drawn.

His eyes narrowed. After a couple of yards the trees gave out, revealing a slope of grassland and gorse. Thirty yards away, down at the base of a shallow depression, was the road, one of the main trade routes running east towards Heideck. On the far side of it the land rose again, enclosing the route on either flank.

The position was far north of Drakenmoor. Word had come to Leitdorf's men that Grosslich was using the road for the transport of arms and supplies. No doubt thinking the province entirely subdued, the guard was light. Such complacence would have to be punished.

Skarr studied the descent carefully, noting the quickest routes down.

'I see them,' hissed Eissen, crouching to Skarr's left.

From the west, to the left of the hidden Reiksguard, a caravan of wagons and carts made its way steadily towards the cleft in the hills. There were about a dozen of them, heavily built and drawn by a team of four horses each. All were covered, and the scarlet boar's head of Grosslich had been painted on their wooden flanks. In front of the wagons was an escort of twelve mounted troops armed with spears and round shields. At the rear were perhaps two dozen more, marching on foot and arranged in a loose column formation.

Skarr watched carefully, judging the character of the guards and their likely responses from the way they moved. Their captain, mounted on a sable charger at the head of the escort, was a burly man with a shaven head and a heavy coat of mail over his broad shoulders. He didn't look like an Averlander. A mercenary, perhaps, brought into the province by Grosslich's famed bottomless coffers.

The trail of wagons crawled closer. As it neared the depression an order was barked out from the head of the escort and the guards drew closer together. There was no real urgency about their movements, just a calm, professional caution. They had no reason to suspect resistance; as far as they knew, Averland was entirely at peace.

The first horsemen came into range. Skarr gestured to Eissen in Reiksguard battle-signals, flickering his fingers to indicate deployment and tactics. He was to take ten men to deal with the rearguard, while Skarr and ten more dealt with the armoured column at the front. The remainder would hang back, mopping up stragglers and ensuring none got back to Averheim to report the ambush.

Wait for my signal, he gestured, then turned back to the road.

The head of the escort passed them and the carriages came into the centre of the view, swaying on their heavy axles under the weight of the cargo.

Now, signalled Skarr, balling his fist and plunging it down.

Silent as ghouls, moving as one, the Reiksguard burst from cover. Skarr tore down the slope, drawing his sword and aiming for the leader.

It took a few moments for them to be noticed. By the time the alarm was raised, the Reiksguard were almost on them.

'Ambush!' came a cry from one of the horsemen, and the

carriages ground to a halt. From the rear of the column the infantry guards reached for their weapons, hurriedly pulling on helmets and buckling up loose breastplates. A second later and Eissen's men tore into them, felling three before the rest began to mount any kind of defence.

Skarr felt his blood pumping fiercely. After so long skulking around like thieves, it was a savage joy to get back to proper fighting.

The escort leader kicked his horse towards him, shouting invective in some foreign tongue and pulling a curve-bladed halberd from his back. Skarr ran straight at him, keeping his sword loose in his hand. On either side his comrades fanned out, running at full tilt into the heart of the cavalry formation. They all knew the effectiveness of cavalry on the charge, but also how vulnerable the animals were once men got among them.

The black charger went for him, hooves kicking up turf as it laboured up the slope. Skarr waited until the last possible moment before swerving sharply to his right, dropping low and ducking under the swing of the rider's halberd.

The horse thundered past him. Skarr spun sharply, stabbing his sword-edge deep into the beast's hamstrings, severing them cleanly. With a scream, the horse tried to rear, buckled, and collapsed onto its side, pinning its rider beneath half a ton of muscle, tack and armour.

Skarr whirled round, hearing a second horse go down as his men carved their way into the panicking squadron. Another halberd blade plunged at him, stabbed down by a rider kicking a chestnut mount straight towards him.

Skarr spun his sword round, switching to a two-handed grip just in time to meet the strike. He parried it away and leapt clear of the charge. As the rider careered past, Skarr pulled a knife from his belt and hurled it at the man's back. He turned away to his next target, hearing with satisfaction his blade thump into its target and unseat the rider.

The Reiksguard were everywhere by then, hacking at the horses to bring them down or pulling the riders from their saddles. Two of the convoy guards, seeing the destruction of their unit, tried to ride off down the road and away from danger. Both were soon toppled from their steeds, clutching at the daggers flung with expert precision at their backs.

As the defence collapsed, a third rider attempted to engage Skarr, spurring his terrified horse at him and working to bring his halberd to bear. Skarr danced away from the challenge, watching with contempt as the panicked swipe missed him by half a yard. The rider's horse stumbled on the uneven terrain, caught up in the confusion of rearing steeds and flashing steel. Skarr powered forwards, leaping up and grabbing the jerkin of the struggling rider with his free hand. He pulled the man from the saddle and the two of them hit the ground hard. In an instant the Reiksguard was on top of the stricken soldier, sword edge at his throat, pressing deep into the skin.

'Mercy!' the man screamed, scrabbling for his own weapon.

'Not for you,' Skarr rasped, and yanked the blade down, severing the man's head cleanly. Then he was up on his feet again, poised for a fresh attack, sword swinging into position.

The skirmish was over. Eissen's men had wiped out the rearguard and were hastening to the head of the column to join him. The convoy's riders lay amongst their dead mounts, slaughtered to a man by the sudden assault. The Reiksguard were the deadliest troops in the Imperial army, and the fighting had been almost embarrassingly one-sided.

'Secure those carts,' spat Skarr to Eissen, wiping the gore from his face and looking round to check for casualties.

On the ground, whimpering from pain, the leader of the escort still lived. Half of him was trapped under the flank of his steed, and his attempts to crawl free were pitiful. Skarr walked up to him and crouched down close, keeping his blade unsheathed. The man's face was pale, and lines of blood ran down from the corners of his mouth. It looked like his ribcage had been driven in, and his breathing was thin and halting.

Skarr grabbed him by his hair and yanked his head back sharply.

'Who sent you?' he hissed. 'You're no Averlander.'

The man's eyes narrowed in pain, but he somehow managed to spit a gobbet of phlegm into the Reiksguard captain's eyes.

Skarr laughed harshly.

'Good man,' he said, wiping his face and letting the man's head fall back against the turf. 'Do it again, though, and I'll cut your balls off.'

He pressed his blade against the man's neck, watching as the honed edge parted the flesh. The rider grimaced, and his defiance ebbed.

'So I say again, who sent you?'

'You no Averlander neither,' the captain panted, his teeth red with blood, his speech slurred and heavy with a north Tilean accent. 'All this for she. You stand no chance of it. Not against she.'

He tried a crooked smile, but the effort was too much. Blood and phlegm rose up his throat, and he began to retch.

Skarr withdrew, watching the man die impassively. Eissen came up to him, wiping his blade down with a handful of grass.

'Get anything from him?'

Skarr shook his head. 'Dogs of war,' he said. 'They know nothing. Let's get the carts open.'

As the Reiksguard dragged the bodies into a pile at the front of the caravan and retrieved the surviving horses, Skarr and Eissen mounted the first of the wagons. The driver shrank back from them as they climbed up, face white with fear. Unlike his escort, he looked like a proper Averland merchant, full-cheeked and running to a comfortable layer of fat. Skarr ignored him. Behind the driver's position there was a locked door. He kicked it heavily and the wood around the lock splintered and broke. Inside the wagon were crates, all of them bound with iron and locked tight. He pulled one out with difficulty. It was heavy, and the clink of metal came from within.

'Money,' said Skarr.

'Lots of it,' agreed Eissen. He turned to the cart's driver. 'Are all the wagons full of this stuff?'

The man nodded emphatically, eager to please. 'And arms. The elector's been recruiting hard.'

Further down the convoy there came the sound of Reiks-guard breaking into more caches. Skarr clapped his hand on the shoulder of the driver, and the man winced under the impact.

'You're a good Averlander,' the preceptor said. 'You don't need to spend your time working for these people.'

The driver looked back at him, still terrified, his fingers clutching the reins of his horses tightly.

'What'll I do? What do you want me to do?'

Skarr smiled, and the lattice of pale lines on his face creased.

'My men'll take these carts south. Take heart, my friend. An army is growing, and you're going to be a part of it.'

The driver didn't seem to know whether to look pleased by that or not.

'Play that part well, and this could be good for you,' continued Skarr. 'Lord Helborg knows how to reward those who serve him.'

'Helborg!' gasped the driver, eyes widening further.

'That's right. Get used it. You're working for the Reiks-marshal now.'

Volkmar pushed his warhorse up the ridge above the road, feeling the cleansing wind ruffle his cloak. Efraim Roll was with him, as was a guard of twenty mounted warrior priests, all clad in heavy plate armour and carrying warhammers inscribed with the livery of the Cult of Sigmar. The The-ogonist himself had donned bronze-lined armour of an ancient lineage, covered in runes of destruction and adorned across the breastplate with a priceless jade griffon, pinions outstretched.

He carried the massive Staff of Command in his hands at all times. A lesser commander would have had it taken up by an underling, but such luxuries were not for Volkmar. Though his palms were already raw from the weight of the iron and ash he kept his grip on the sacred weapon tight.

Below them, his army crawled along the road. In the vanguard came the companies of knights, Gruppen riding at their head. Their squires, spare horses, armour and lances came in a long caravan behind them, such that they almost constituted a small army in their own right. Behind them came the long train of halberdier and spearman regiments, marching in close-knit squares and decked out in their state colours. Drummers kept the pace tight. There was little of the casual joking and bawdiness of a regular campaign. Volkmar drove them hard, and the sergeants had kept the men on a short leash.

It took some time for the long lines of infantry to pass Volkmar's position. He watched them as a hawk watches its prey, scouring the ranks for weakness and insubordination. Some of his own warrior priests were among them, clustered in tight groups of half a dozen. Those fanatics asked for neither rest nor privilege.

Behind them came the artillery train. Huge assault cannons were hauled by teams of horses up to six strong, followed by the infantry-killing pieces, the Helblasters and Helstorms. Handgunners, artillery crew and engineers sat on their carts in their wake, keeping a close eye on the wagons of blackpowder, matchcords, ammunition and spare parts. Volkmar's brow creased with disapproval as he surveyed them. He trusted blackpowder less than he trusted faith and steel. Still, they would be called on, just as every other part of the massive force would be called on.

Behind the artillery caravan came the auxiliary companies, archers and irregular troops who'd been drafted in since the march had begun. There was never a shortage of men willing to fight for a schilling, and much as Volkmar loathed mercenaries too, he had the resources to employ them and turned no man away.

The main baggage train followed, wagon after wagon

loaded with stores. Barrels of ale were piled high on open carts, mixed up with cloth-covered food wains. Armour, cloaks, bundles of arrows, heaps of firewood and fodder for the horses were all stacked closely and guarded watchfully by Roll's own men, as incorruptible as zealots. Dozens of his soldiers, clad in the scarlet colours of Altdorf's Church of Sigmar Risen and Transformed, swarmed around the pay wains, the all-important guardians of the cases of coin that kept the soldiers loyal.

Finally, bringing up the rear, were three companies of greatswords and a unit of pistolier outriders, their steeds stepping impatiently. Every so often a squadron of six of them would kick into action and ride up the flanks of the huge army, peeling off into the terrain on either side of the road to scout ahead before returning to the long slog, their need for adventure satisfied for the moment.

Over thirty thousand regular troops, with maybe five thousand more dogs of war who'd joined on the march from Pohlbad. More would come at the rendezvous south of Nuln. A whole regiment of warrior priests to augment those he already had, plus more artillery and heavy cavalry. It was a formidable force, scarcely less powerful than the massive armies that marched across the north of the Empire against the scattered warbands of Archaon's invasion. If the predictions of the Celestial magisters proved reliable, it would need to be.

'You look displeased,' said Roll, his bald head gleaming in the cold light. The tone was one of mild remonstration. No other man in the Empire would have dared to speak thus to the Theogonist.

'What use are mortal men here?' Volkmar muttered. 'When have they ever been able to stand firm against the great enemy? We're leading them to their deaths.'

Roll spat on the ground.

'It's as you said. They'll do their duty. The enemy will have mortals too.'

Volkmar said nothing. He remembered the ranks of men

marching into ruin in the Troll Country with him at their head. As the daemons had screamed across the sky and the rivers run with blood, mortal faith had done little to stem the tide of insanity and pain. Above all, he remembered Be'lakor, grinning from ear to ear, the daemon's eyes little more than windows on to a world of utter, terrifying horror.

'This will all come down to us, Roll,' he said.

'Don't forget Helborg.'

'Helborg? Even if he lives, what can he do?'

'And Schwarzhelm.'

He looked south. The dark leagues of endless forests were behind them, and the country was now beginning to open up. Far in the distance lay the wide ribbon of the Aver, winding through the grassland ahead.

'Schwarzhelm has done enough. If he attempts to interfere again before this thing is ended, I have the authority to prevent him.'

He turned to Roll, and his gaze was bleak.

'I have *all* authority in this. The Emperor's Champion has served faithfully for a generation of men, but weakness is weakness. I will judge the matter when he's found.'

Roll raised an eyebrow, but said nothing. Volkmar paused for a few more moments on the ridge, before kicking his horse onwards, back down to join the vanguard of the immense host. His guard did likewise, and soon the high place was bare once more, home to nothing more than the sigh of the wind and the rustle of grass.

The Tower was nearly complete, and the last veils over the charade were close to being lifted. Smaller versions of the Tower were being built at six points on the city walls, each also made of iron and given the same spiked profile as the master construction. The vista across Averheim had been marred irrevocably. Ancient halls had been demolished, the stone carted off to bolster the new fortifications springing up across the old walls. Merchants' townhouses had been commandeered for garrisons, while the Averburg was now

nothing more than a vast store of arms. Soldiers were everywhere, thronging the streets, clustering in the squares,
camped out to the north of the city on the flat plains running towards Stirland.

Above it all, the Grosslich banner hung proud. The
six-pronged crown of the Tower had been completed at last,
and long pennants with the crimson boar's head draped
down towards the massive courtyard, three hundred feet
below. Red and gold were ubiquitous, drowning out the
memory of any other allegiance the city may once have had.
Alptraums and Leitdorfs were forgotten. Now only the new
dispensation had any meaning.

As night fell, the new aspect of the city showed itself to
most effect. The Tower was lit along its entire height by a
series of lilac beads, each glowing like stars. At the summit a
pale flame burned incessantly. Lanterns in the streets below
shone with a range of intense shades, banishing shadows
from the night and bathing the city in a mingled fog of colour. Those citizens not steeped in joyroot found their sleep
interrupted and fractious. A certain faded elegance had been
replaced by rampant excess.

Those few clear-sighted citizens who remained now knew
beyond all doubt that Grosslich was a tyrant, and one whose
perversion of the Imperial law had only just started. Insurrec-
tions were ruthlessly put down, and the hated witch hunters
of Odo Heidegger kept the furnaces burning. Any faint flicker
of revolt was overwhelmed by the vast numbers of troops
arriving every day from every corner of the wastelands south
of the Grey Mountains, drawn by the promise of money and
glory. Some were paid in joyroot, and that seemed to satisfy them. Just as it had been in the spring, the roads were
lined with drooling, vacant-eyed figures, slumped against the
stone and lost in dreaming.

All of them, deep in their reverie, whispered the same thing.

*She is coming. She is coming. Blessed be her path, everlast-
ing be her reign. Queen of pleasure, mistress of the world. She is
coming. She is coming.*

Endlessly they mumbled the mantra until their lips were calloused and cracked, and they crawled off to find more root to numb the pain. Whatever debaucheries Averheim had known before, it suffered a hundredfold more then, stepping down a path of ruin as surely as if guided by the Lord of Pain himself.

Elector Grosslich now rarely ventured from the pinnacle of his precious Tower. The topmost chamber had been fitted out in silks and upholstered with fine soft leather. The floor was polished marble, veined like a flayed muscle, shining in the light of a dozen suspended orbs. There were six windows in the iron walls, each overlooking one of the massive suspended spikes.

The view was commanding. Grosslich's armies, so long in the mustering, were now mobilising. The numbers astounded even him. Where there was corruption and power, humans seemed to drawn to it like insects around a candle flame.

Grosslich himself was swathed in crimson robes, beautifully lined with fur and monogrammed with the flowing 'G' motif. A tall crown had been forged for him in the hidden pits of the Tower below, a swirling sculpture in steel which tapered to a point above his forehead and sent tendrils of slender metal curling down across his cheeks. Natassja had designed it herself, but he'd made it his own.

The city was his too, locked in an iron grip of control. More dog-soldiers were being spawned in the basements, all answering to his command. There were other creatures down there too, terrible products of Natassja's imagination, taking shape under her pitiless tutelage. Soon the whole host would be ready, a legion of terror ready to sweep across the river and destroy the army he knew had been sent from Altdorf to rein him in.

A chime sounded from outside the chamber. Grosslich turned from the windows and sat down on his throne, an obsidian block composed of tortured limbs, just like the one Natassja had used to dupe Verstohlen.

'Come,' he said, and marvelled at how his voice had

changed. Gone were the gruff, plain tones that had drawn peasants flocking to his banner in the early days. Now his speech was clipped and refined, almost as smooth as Natassja's own. The Dark Prince had changed him in many ways, not all of them to Grosslich's liking. Still, it was too late for regrets.

A glass door at the far end of the chamber swung open silently and Holymon Eschenbach entered. The man had continued to change. His eyes were now entirely white-less and glowed a subtle pink. His flesh was bleached and his lips stained the colour of old wine. Like Achendorfer, he walked with a pronounced limp, as if some terrible rearrangement had taken place beneath his robes of swirling colour. The old smugness had gone, wiped from his features by Grosslich's merciless drive to bring the city under his control. Eschenbach had assumed all the duties of Stewardship in the wake of Tochfel's unfortunate demise, and the burden had proved heavy.

'You asked to see me, your excellency?' he whispered. He could barely speak above a sibilant hiss these days, another result of the improvements made to his otherwise unremarkable body.

'Steward, perhaps you could tell me the names of the fugitives we have been so assiduously pursuing since our ascension to the electorship.'

Eschenbach looked nervous. He knew what was coming.

'The traitors Leitdorf and Helborg, as well as the spy Verstohlen.'

'Well done. And can you inform me how close we are to tracking them down?'

'Your armies are spreading further east with every day. Courts of inquiry have opened in Heideck, and Grenzstadt will not be far behind. It cannot be–'

Grosslich extended a hand lazily and clenched his fist. Eschenbach gasped and fell to his knees. As he did so, his neck seemed to constrict, veins bulging on his temples. He choked, falling forwards, scrabbling to release the pressure.

'You think I don't *know* this?' Grosslich hissed, watching with only mild pleasure as the fat Steward writhed in agony. 'You have the entire resources of a province at your disposal. Your orders are simple. Find them and kill them.'

Grosslich released the vice around Eschenbach's neck, and the man fell forwards, panting like a dog.

'All Leitdorf's houses have been stormed,' the Steward gasped. 'His estates have been plundered. I have men scouring the countryside. What more could I do?'

'Listen carefully,' snarled Grosslich, leaning forwards in his throne. 'Things are approaching a delicate stage. The mistress's plans are nearing fruition, and the Empire is beginning to wake up. An army will be here within days. It is imperative that this matter is concluded before then.'

Eschenbach nodded miserably.

'There's another aspect to this,' continued Grosslich, choosing his words carefully. 'The mistress has dispatched creatures of her own to dispose of Helborg. It would be... *preferable* for my own troops to find the Marshal first. As for the Leitdorf pup, I want to bring him in myself. This is very important to me. I'm not convinced you're giving your work the attention it deserves.'

Eschenbach began to panic. He'd been on the end of too many punishments from Grosslich already.

'I am, your excellency! A thousand men have been sent east this very day. They have orders to bring in Helborg and the pretender. There have been reports of supply columns being raided in the far south, towards the moors. If he's there, he'll be uncovered.'

'Double the numbers,' he ordered. 'They have licence to burn the countryside to a husk if they have to. Spare no expense, and give them no respite. Helborg must be found.'

Eschenbach nodded. His eyes gave away his misery. Raising that many troops would be difficult, especially given the numbers he'd been instructed to make ready for the defence of Averheim.

'And the ceremony?'

'No delays. It goes ahead as planned. There's no point in further secrecy, whatever the mistress says.'

He narrowed his eyes, thinking of the power on the cusp of grasping. His army was nearly ready, the one that would deliver the dominion he craved.

'Ensure the root supply remains high, and give your orders to the priests,' he said. 'The mask will be removed. It is time to show the people what they've taken on by serving me.'

CHAPTER ELEVEN

Dawn had broken. The moors were still shrouded in a fine mist. Scraps of cloud hurried westwards above the drifting pall, driven by the relentless winds from the mountains. The weather was converging on Averheim, as if the world's winds were being sucked into a vortex above the distant city. Out on the high fells, though, the air was crisp and damp, as cold and clear as a crystal goblet in the Imperial Palace.

Eissen came to a halt. He'd been riding through the night to return to the Drakenmoor, carrying with him welcome tidings for the Marshal. Before Eissen had left, Skarr had captured three supply trains and roused half a dozen villages to the cause. His men under arms now numbered more than a hundred, and more joined them daily. Part of this was due to the plentiful supply of gold and weapons they'd obtained since the capture of the caravans, but there was also no love for Grosslich in this part of the world and recruits were ready converts.

Most of the Reiksguard had remained with Skarr to press home the assault and spread dissent in the lands running towards Heideck. A couple of others had been assigned to the caravans to guard their passage to Drakenmoor. Eissen had gone on ahead to deliver his report to Helborg. He'd covered many leagues in the night, riding his steed hard.

Now he gave it some respite, dismounting and letting it walk through the gorse and heather. The animal went warily, treading inbetween the glistening clumps of dew-bedecked grass, clouds of steam snorting from its nostrils. Eissen led it through the meandering moorland paths carefully, keeping one hand on the reins and the other on his sword. In every direction, the mist curled up about him, grey and thin like gruel. Lone trees, blasted and curled over by the wind, came and went before the gauze-like clouds swallowed them up again. Only the ground beneath his feet was solid, and everything else was as shifting and fickle as a woman's promise.

'Easy, girl,' Eissen whispered, noticing his steed's shivering flanks. She needed to be rubbed down and given a bucket of hot oats. Still, Drakenmoor wasn't far. He'd wait for the mist to lift, get his bearings, and be there before the end of the day.

Then the horse stiffened, tugging back on the reins and stamping. Its eyes began to roll.

'Mist got you spooked?' asked Eissen, looking around. There was no sound except for the faint rustle of the gorse. 'Better get over it.'

The Reiksguard shook his head and smiled to himself.

'Talking to my horse? Time to get–'

He froze. There was something out there. Eissen felt the hairs on the back of his neck stand up stiff. The chill was still acute and he shivered under his leather jerkin.

Ahead of him, the curtain of grey sighed past, driven by the breeze, as cloudy and opaque as milk. Still no sound.

Eissen drew his sword. The steel was dull in the diffuse light. After a night's riding his muscles felt sluggish and stiff.

'Declare yourself!' he cried. His voice was sucked into the fog like water draining from a sink. There was no reply.

Eissen's horse was beginning to panic. It tried to rear away, only held firm by Eissen's tight grip. A line of foam appeared at its mouth.

Eissen pulled it savagely back into line, keeping his blade raised defensively. Despite all his training and experience, his heart was hammering like a maiden's on her wedding night. He felt a line of sweat run down his chest, cold against his flesh. He backed towards his horse, head craning to see anything among the shifting sea of occlusion.

'Helborg.'

The voice was unearthly, a bizarre mix of a young woman's and a boy's, scraped over metal and given the sibilant whisper of a snake. As soon as he heard it, Eissen's resolve was shaken. He gripped his sword, keeping hold of his tugging steed with difficulty.

'Show yourself, ghoul,' he commanded, but his voice sounded reedy and foolish.

Ahead of him, three figures slowly emerged from the clouds. They were hunched like old women, draped in rags, limping uncertainly across the uneven ground. At twenty paces away they were wreathed in a shifting cloak of translucence, as muffled and indistinct as shades. Only their eyes were solid, six points of lilac brilliance, emerging from the obscurity like stars.

Eissen felt the dread grow stronger. His steed reared, snatching the reins from his fingers. He turned quickly, grabbing at the leather straps, but he was too late. It turned and broke into a gallop, bounding back into the gloom and disappearing from view. He was alone. Heart thudding, he turned to face the newcomers.

'Helborg,' they hissed again in perfect unison. The words were taut with malice.

Eissen grabbed the hilt of his sword with both hands. He'd faced the undead before – where was his courage?

'He's not here,' he replied, trying to keep his voice level. 'Who sent you?'

The creatures seemed not to hear, and advanced slowly. One of them extended a hand from under its rags. Eissen stared in horror as the long talons extended. Another reached out, exposing ravaged flesh, white as ice, studded with metal and knots of protruding bone.

'Sigmar preserves!' he roared, trying to summon up some kind of resolve. As the nearest horror drew close, he charged at it, swinging his sword round to decapitate.

Something like laughter burst out. The creature snapped up its talon to block the strike and steel clanged against bone. The horror's movements were staggeringly fast, more like those of an insect than a human. Eissen sprang back, moving his blade warily, watching for the attack.

'*Helborg!*' they hissed, driven into some kind of ecstasy. The lilac glow became piercing, and they lost their stooped hunches. The one in the centre pounced, leaping into the air and spreading its claws wide.

Eissen withdrew, swinging his sword up to block the swipe. Again the metal clanged, and he felt the force of the blow shiver down his arm.

Another sprang at him, screaming with glee. Eissen spun round to deflect, only to feel the burn of a raking claw plunge into his back. He cried aloud, ripping the talons from the wound as he turned, seeing his own blood fly into the faces of the horrors. Another pounced, and something stabbed into his stomach, slicing into the flesh as smoothly as a stick into water.

Eissen lurched back, trying to shake them off him, slashing at their brass-bound hides with his sword. They ignored his blows and dragged him down, tearing at his flesh, pulling the muscles from the bones, cackling with a childish delight.

Eissen lost his sword when he lost his fingers, cleaved from his forearm with a single jab from a barbed set of claws. He heard screaming, lost in the fog, before realising it was his own. Then he was on his knees, and the creatures really got to work. They didn't go for the kill, but for the dissection, taking off chunk after chunk of flesh until what was left of Eissen finally collapsed in a gore-bedraggled mess, bereft of eyes, hoarse from screaming, lost in a world of pain, beyond wishing for death and sucked into a slough of horror.

The final blow was reluctant, a grudging stab to silence his jaw-less mewls of agony, regretfully delivered by the lead ghoul. As before, they stood in silence for a while, admiring what they'd done. One of them raised a taloned hand to its ruined face and licked at the blood-soaked bone with a black tongue. Its eyes glowed brightest then, perhaps blazing in remembrance of what it was like to be hot-blooded and encased in mortal flesh.

When they'd finished they hunched over once more and the light in their eyes faded. In the far distance, a frenzied whinnying could still be heard, growing fainter with every second.

Then, one by one, they turned south, trudging after their real prey again, insatiable until the one whose name they carried was found. If they were capable of feeling any emotion other than malice, they didn't show it. Perhaps, though, there was a faintest trace of excitement in their movements. The journey had been long, but they knew they were getting close. They shuffled into the fog, rags trailing behind them, whispering the name, the one name they still knew how to say.

When they were gone, the moor returned to silence. The mist curled around the long grasses, pale and ephemeral. Down in the mud, the sweet smell of death, mingled with the faint aroma of jasmine, stained the chill air, and the blood sank slowly into the soil.

Schwarzhelm looked up. The moors were high on the southern horizon, still laced with scraps of mist. In the far distance he thought he could hear some strange bird's cry, repeated over and over until it faded away. He listened for a repeat, but none came.

The sky remained grey and the light of the sun was weak. The cold didn't bother him much, but he pulled his cloak tighter across his huge shoulders in any case. As surely as he knew his own name, he knew the Sword of Vengeance had guided him well. Somewhere up on those bleak, wind-tousled moors lay Helborg. The spirit of the blade longed to return to its master.

As the day of their meeting drew ever closer, Schwarzhelm found his iron will begin to waver. His dreams were still haunted by the old warrior's face.

Why are you doing this, Ludwig?

He looked away from the brooding highlands. He'd made up his mind. Justice demanded the return of the sword. Schwarzhelm's entire existence depended on honour, on keeping his word, on being the very embodiment of the law. Without that, he was nothing, just a killer in the service of the Emperor. He didn't know whether he'd ever raise the Imperial standard again on the field of battle, but he was certain that if he didn't carry through this duty then he'd never regain the right to. Redemption was never handed over; it was always earned.

He stamped back up to the treeline he'd come down from, slinging the brace of hares over his shoulder. The forest had sheltered them for the night and had yielded a rich bounty. It was a good thing he knew how to hunt and trap. If he'd been relying on Verstohlen, all they'd have eaten would have been air and fine words.

Once back under the cover of the trees, he found the spy trying to light a fire with trembling fingers. He looked cold, and crouched low over the pile of damp wood, his coat flapping over his slim form as he moved. Verstohlen was as clumsy out in the wilds as he was accomplished in the city. Schwarzhelm almost felt like smiling.

'So you've decoded the letters,' he said, flinging the carcasses on the ground and reaching for his flint.

Verstohlen sat back from his abortive fire, giving up in disgust. 'Indeed. They made for interesting reading.'

Schwarzhelm ignored Verstohlen's tumbled pile of branches and began building a fresh fire from the dry scrub he'd collected at the edge of the forest.

'Tell me.'

Verstohlen pulled a sheaf of notes from his coat pocket,

covered in messy scribblings from the charcoal. He'd been busy in the rare moments Schwarzhelm had halted the march and allowed him to decipher.

'They were mostly replies to messages sent by Lassus,' Verstohlen said. 'I don't know who wrote them. The final one is from Lassus himself. It's unfinished, no doubt because you interrupted him before he could send it.'

Schwarzhelm watched as his kindling took. Gradually, shakily, washed-out flames began to flicker. He fed the nascent blaze with more twigs, trying not to let his feelings about Lassus impair his attention to Verstohlen's findings.

'The conspiracy didn't start with him,' said Verstohlen. 'The power behind it was a woman. There's no name here, but I'd stake my life it's Natassja.'

'So you've always maintained.'

'Whether or not she intended me to see her engaged in those rites, I could not have been mistaken about the fact of her sorcery. From this, it's clear she approached Lassus three years ago, soon after the death of Marius Leitdorf. At that point she wasn't Rufus's wife – they married eighteen months later. The two of them, Lassus and she, evidently found much of mutual interest to discuss.'

The fire grew. Schwarzhelm began to prepare the carcasses, ripping at the skin with expert fingers.

'Lassus had been passed over for promotion,' said Verstohlen. 'He felt wounded by the Imperial establishment. He was also old. He hid it from you, I suspect, but he was a bitter man, bereft of an honourable position in the hierarchy and banished to a retirement in a part of Altdorf he hated.'

Schwarzhelm remembered the old man's words at their first meeting in Altdorf. *There are more ways than one to make a success of one's life. Maybe when you're as old as I am, you'll see that. My battles are over. I've been granted the grace to retire from the field and see out the rest of my days in peace.* At the time, the words had seemed like such calm, resigned wisdom. All of it had been lies, then, just another layer of deception.

'Natassja's powers were strong. She's a beautiful woman, and he was a frustrated failure. I've no idea how she corrupted him, but I'm certain she did so. From then on, he was her tool, using his money and influence in support of her and Grosslich's ends. The letters make it clear that Lassus arranged the weakening of the defences at Black Fire Keep. Gold was found to induce the orcs to invade, and weapons too. It was all timed with impressive precision. By the time he'd seen to it that you would be sent to handle the succession, the passes were already under attack.'

'The greenskins had Imperial weapons.'

'A novelty for them, no doubt. Though I can't imagine what they did with the gold.'

Schwarzhelm tore the skin from the hare carcasses roughly. As he remembered the fighting on the plains of Averland, the memory of Grunwald came unbidden to his mind.

'What did he hope to achieve?'

'He would have joined Natassja and Grosslich in Averheim. The Ruinous Powers offer the foolish an extension of their natural span, and he expected to live for another hundred years. You should reflect on that, my lord. Had you not killed him, the powers in Altdorf would only now be learning of their danger, and Lassus would be safely hidden and growing in strength again.'

Schwarzhelm grunted. Such attempts to placate his sense of guilt were unwelcome.

'And after that?'

'I can't tell what their plans were beyond the coronation of Grosslich, but they weren't stupid. They knew the deception would only last for so long. They needed time to do something else, something involving Averheim. By deflecting accusations of treachery towards Rufus they let the world believe that corruption in Averland had been defeated, and that has given them the space they needed.'

Schwarzhelm let the tidings sink in, dissecting each morsel of information, weighing it up against what he already knew. The process was painful. He himself had been the tool by which Natassja and Grosslich had corrupted the province, and the knowledge weighed heavily on him.

'So Rufus Leitdorf was an innocent in this.'

'He was. A dupe. I was to blame, my lord. When I witnessed his wife, I assumed he was implicated. Grosslich and she played their parts well.'

'That they did.'

Schwarzhelm finished skinning and dressing the hares, and skewered them roughly. The fire was now burning fiercely, and at last the warmth began to cut through the chill of the early morning.

'Anything else?' he asked.

'Not that I can decipher. There's some link with the Leitdorfs that I don't yet understand, and I have no idea why Averheim is so important to them. If you truly want to fight this, then we should go back there.'

'We will,' muttered Schwarzhelm. 'I've thought of little else, besides finding Kurt.'

Verstohlen paused. 'And you're still sure you want to do that? You don't have to. He may be dead, or he may be–'

'He's alive, and he's close,' snapped Schwarzhelm, shoving the skinned hare into the fire. 'Don't try to dissuade me. I know some things about this that you cannot. I had the dreams, sent to me by that witch. They didn't expect Helborg. He's the element in this they couldn't control. That's why Grosslich was so keen to kill him, and that's why we have to find him first. Kurt Helborg with the Sword of Vengeance will be a foe they cannot ignore.'

Verstohlen looked at Schwarzhelm for a long time then, pondering his words.

'He's not a forgiving man.'

Schwarzhelm nodded, watching the flesh of the hares crisp and char in the flames.

'Of course,' he said, and his voice was low and steady. 'So it's always been with him.'

He turned the meat in the fire, roasting it gently.

'Not long now, Pieter,' he said. 'He's nearby. The sword and its master cannot be kept apart.'

* * *

Leitdorf took a deep breath before emerging on to the balcony. He could hear the expectant mutter of the crowd outside, and they were getting impatient.

'How many are there?' he whispered to Helmut Gram, the seasoned Reiksguard who'd been assigned to him as bodyguard.

'Five hundred,' replied the knight, showing no trace of emotion. 'Not many. Better than nothing.'

Leitdorf swallowed. Addressing armed men had always been something he'd dreaded. Not much of a soldier himself, he'd never been able to look them in the eye. He'd made up for his natural reticence with a kind of studied arrogance, but he knew it had fooled few of them. When he remembered his churlish behaviour with Schwarzhelm back in Averheim, he shuddered.

'Should I take the sword?'

Gram's eyebrow rose in surprise. 'The Wolfsklinge? Of course. It is a holy blade.'

All this fuss about swords. That was the one thing that seemed to unite the fighting men of the Empire, a universal reverence for their antique blades. His father's weapon was hardly as prestigious as the runefangs or the Sword of Justice, but it had a long and proud history nonetheless. Like all such blades, there were runes hammered into the steel, augmenting the belligerence of the wielder and guiding the edge to its target. He'd never felt comfortable in its presence, and it hung heavily from his sword-belt.

'Yes, of course,' he mumbled, and stepped closer to the balcony. Outside, clustered in the courtyard of the Drakenmoor castle, were the recruits the Reiksguard had worked so hard to draw together. There were hundreds more, he'd been told, flocking south to be armed and trained to fight for him. As a result of all that activity, Grosslich must surely have discovered where they were by now. The only option left was to take the battle to him.

'They're waiting, my lord.'

Leitdorf swallowed, then pushed aside the doors leading to the balcony and stepped outside.

Below him, rammed tight into the enclosed space, the core of his new army stared up expectantly. Most were well armed, the product of his own armouries as well as Skarr's raids on the supply caravans. Here and there he could see men wearing the blue and burgundy of the Leitdorf house, as well as the black and yellow livery of Averland. Such men were to be the captains and sergeants of the greater host to come, the leaders of the peasants and farmhands who'd flesh out the ranks. Many of them looked experienced and capable. Others looked worryingly callow.

'Men of Averland!' Leitdorf cried. His voice sounded thin, snatched away by the breeze, and he worked to lower it. 'You all know why you've been summoned here. The traitor Grosslich has seized this province and plans to deliver it to the great enemy. This muster marks the very beginning of our struggle. We will fight our way north of here, gathering men as we go, raising the countryside against those who dare to take it from us. I will lead you, Rufus Leitdorf, son of electors and master of this realm!'

There was a sporadic burst of applause, and a few men broke into a cheer. It wasn't convincing. With a sick feeling in his stomach, Leitdorf realised he was losing them. They all knew his reputation. He tried to remember what he'd planned to say, but the words slipped from his grasp.

'So I say, do not fear! The five hundred of you here today will be a thousand by dawn tomorrow. As we march, more will flock to our standard. By the time we reach Averheim, the hills will tremble at our coming.'

The murmurs of approval began to die out.

'I have fought Grosslich before!' shouted Leitdorf, trying to work up some enthusiasm. 'He is nothing but a peasant, a low-born master of horse manure! I, on the other hand, am a noble-born leader of men and hence blessed by Sigmar. March with me, and I will return Averland to the rule of those fitted for it!'

That didn't go down well. Most of the troops were low-born, even those given command roles. Grosslich's popularity had always stemmed from his mastery of the common touch. Leitdorf realised his error too late, and began to lose his thread. The crowd had fallen silent.

Then the doors behind him slammed open. Leitdorf turned to see Helborg striding to stand beside him, though for a moment he hardly recognised the man.

The Marshal was wearing the heavy plate of the Reiksguard once more, cleaned and restored by his knights and shining like polished ithilmar. He'd donned his hawk-winged helmet, and the sun glinted from the steel pins holding the feathers in place. A heavy cloak hung from his shoulders, draped across massive pauldrons. Helborg's visor was lifted, his craggy face exposed. The moustache had been trimmed, waxed and moulded back to its former glory, the envy of men and fascination of women. His skin was no longer grey, but full of a tight, uncompromising vigour. His blue eyes, two points of sapphire set deep in that lean, handsome face, fixed the crowd below with an unwavering gaze. Beside his imposing frame, Leitdorf suddenly felt meagre and superfluous.

Helborg placed his gauntlets on the balcony railing with a heavy clang. The murmuring of the crowd picked up again. All of them knew who he was, though most had only dreamt of seeing him in the flesh. Men shuffled closer, eager to catch a glimpse of the legend.

'Men of the Empire!' roared Helborg, his voice echoing in the narrow courtyard and resounding from the high walls of the Drakenmoor castle. Leitdorf's entreaties were instantly forgotten. Helborg's voice was grinding, rumbling, stone-hard, tempered by years of command on the battlefield and infused with the expectation of obeisance. When the Reiksmarshal spoke, all other voices were stilled.

'You have heard the words of your elector. Listen to them! He is the rightful heir of the realm of Siggurd and the true bearer of the runefang. Averheim is in the hands of a traitor, one who has sold his soul to the great enemy and even now plots to deliver this proud province into ruin.'

His voice softened, but his glare remained fierce. As his

eyes swept the crowd, each man felt his soul being examined, tested on the anvil of Helborg's unyielding conviction.

'Perhaps some of you supported Grosslich in the early days.
Maybe you thought a man of the people would right the
wrongs of the past and give you a life of comfort and justice.'

Helborg's gauntlet balled into a fist and slammed the railing. Fragments of stone showered on to the crowd below.

'Lies!' he bellowed, spittle flying from his mouth. 'The man
is a creeping worm, the most contemptible of animals, the
progeny of traitors and the scion of whores. The least of you
is worth a hundred such crawling beasts, for they have forgotten themselves and become less than the insects of the dung
heap. For as long as he remembers the law and the word of
Sigmar, the lowliest serf towers over such degenerate scum.'

His eyes narrowed, and he pulled himself to his full height.
Sunlight glinted from his helm, and his cloak lifted in the
wind.

'Maybe you joined this army for gold, or for glory, or out
of some long-earned pledge of allegiance. If so, then you
may as well return to your homes now and live the rest of
your life cowering in fear. Gold you will have, and glory
there will be, but it is for *honour* that we are mustered here
today. Your realm has been stolen from you, your heritage
debased and your future ransomed to the fickle will of the
Dark Gods. Have you no shame for that, men of Averland?
Have you no *anger*?'

The crowd started to murmur again. Helborg's words held
them rapt.

'*This* is why we march!' he roared, sweeping out his sword
and holding it aloft. 'To take back our birthright. To hold
our heads high and resist the usurper, the heretic and the
traitor. I will lead you in this, men of Siggurd. I, who have
commanded armies that made the very earth tremble, whose
holy blade has run dark with the blood of the Emperor's
enemies. I, Grand Marshal of the Reiksguard, Hammer of
Chaos, Kreigsmeister, the hand of vengeance!'

His voice rose in fervour. Men below were shouting in

acclamation now, fists clenched, roused to a pitch of emotion. They would do anything for him. Leitdorf watched in awe as Helborg moulded them to his will. So *this* was why he inspired such devotion.

'Go back to your villages!' he roared, sweeping his sword down and pointing the tip at each man in turn. 'Bring your men to me and I will make them killers. With me at your head, no army shall dare oppose our will. We will not relent until we have cleansed the city of the filth that squats in it. They sowed the seeds of this war through treachery, but we will repay them twenty times over in their own blood. March with me, men of Averland, and I will deliver you! For the Empire! For your elector! For the holy blood of Sigmar!'

As one, the men below rose up, shaking their fists and repeating the cry. They were seething, ready to sell their lives for the cause. The army had been born.

As *For the Empire!* rang out across the courtyard, Helborg swept his imperious gaze back to Leitdorf.

'How do you *do* that?' asked Rufus, still watching the frenzied crowd below.

'Learn from it,' snapped Helborg. 'And learn it fast.'

As he pulled back from the balcony, Helborg winced. His wounds had not entirely healed.

'I'll not wait here any longer,' he rasped. 'The time has come to lead these men. War calls, Herr Leitdorf, and I will answer.'

The mayor of Grenzstadt was no fool. Unlike in Heideck, the proximity of the eastern town to the Worlds Edge Mountains had bred a certain toughness in the place. Klaus Meuningen was a lean, angular man, grey-haired and clean-shaven with a warrior's bearing. In his youth he'd commanded a regiment of mountain guard, and knew the ways of a soldier. When Schwarzhelm's commander had passed through the town on the route to Black Fire Pass, he'd spared every man from his garrison that he could. The news that none of them would be coming back was an unwelcome reward for his generosity.

'And what I am supposed to do about the defence of

Meuningen smiled coldly. 'Make the best of it. What else can we do?'

Bloch turned to Kraus. 'How soon can we leave?'

'We could be on the road at dawn. You'll have trouble pulling the men from the taverns until then. They haven't seen a tankard or a woman for a long time.'

Bloch didn't smile. 'Me neither,' he said ruefully.

'Where will you go?' asked Meuningen.

Bloch sighed, and ran his hands through his cropped hair. 'I said to the men we'd go back to Averheim. We'll have to head west for a while, maybe as far as Heideck. We're small enough to keep out of trouble until then, and I'll have a look at things when we get closer. I'll not run across the fields again like a fugitive. There are two hundred of us, all battle-scarred. If Grosslich wants to bring us in, he'll have to work for it.'

Meuningen nodded.

'Very well. The grace of Sigmar be with you. You deserve it.'

'As do you, mayor,' replied Bloch, looking sincere enough. 'So I hope he has grace enough for the both of us.'

The villagers crowded round, suspicion heavy in their dull, stupid faces. The settlement of Urblinken was as unremittingly grim as most of the hamlets on the slopes, untouched by the prosperity of the lower Aver valley and left to scratch a living on the unproductive highlands. In that respect, it resembled many of the grimy places of the northern Empire; beds of poverty, incest, disease and superstition.

Perfect recruiting grounds, mused Skarr, sweeping his gaze across the murmuring throng, gathered in what passed for a marketplace. All around him, low, mean buildings crowded. Their wattle and daub walls were streaked with filth and stained from cooking fires. Chickens pecked through the refuse and children splashed through grimy puddles. An ill-repaired wall ran around the perimeter of the houses, crumbling at the summit and with a flimsy iron gate at the opening.

The Reiksguard, all twenty-seven of them, looked like messengers from some mighty deity compared with the mean folk who'd clustered to hear him speak. Their armour flashed in the afternoon sun and the iron cross of their regiment fluttered proudly from their banner. The villagers had no real idea what *Reiksguard* were, but they knew the power and reputation of knights. If Skarr had told them the Emperor himself had sent them, they would have believed him readily enough.

'How many men can you muster?' he asked the headman, a slack-jawed, unshaven brute with a lazy eye and unspeakably foul breath.

'How much're you paying?' asked the man again, fixated on the idea of gold.

'You needn't worry about that,' said Skarr coldly. 'Have you no idea of honour? Your lands have been usurped. You can be part of the campaign to take them back.'

The man looked blank.

'All recruits will be paid,' Skarr added grudgingly. 'They'll be fed too. If they fight well, the Lord Helborg will find ways to reward them.'

At the mention of the Marshal, a ripple of excitement passed through the crowd.

'Helborg!' gasped several of the men.

Skarr never ceased to be amazed by that. Even in the darkest corner of the Empire, the name was spoken with reverence.

'Is it true he can summon fire from the heavens?' blurted a hulking blacksmith. He wore a fearsome beard and his head was shaven. Piercings glinted from his muscled arms. He looked as belligerent as an orc, but at the mention of Helborg's name his expression had taken on a childlike curiosity.

'Is he really twelve foot tall?'

'Can he level the hills?'

Skarr looked at the throng contemptuously. Just by talking to them he felt sullied, dragged down to their bone-headed level.

'Yes, and more,' he said. 'If you march with him, you'll be able to tell your children's children of it.'

Some of the younger men gained an eager light in their eyes. Getting out of the village always appealed to the young bucks who hadn't yet been crushed by the tedium of rural life. They had aspirations, girls to impress, dreams of riches and adventure to nurture.

Even the headman looked fleetingly interested.

'We've fifty men who can bear arms here. There are more in the valleys to the north.'

Skarr nodded. The forces were coming together. Grosslich hadn't penetrated this far east yet. Until he did, these men were Helborg's.

'Then muster all you can,' he said. 'Every man will need his own boots and must be ready to march at an hour's notice. We'll provide the weapons.'

He let a sliver of threat enter his voice.

'You're under orders now, headman,' he said, holding the fat man's gaze. 'Don't let me down. I'll come through here again in two days. If your men aren't waiting, the vengeance of Helborg will be on your heads.'

The man's eyes widened and a murmur of fear passed through the crowd.

'Don't worry,' said the headman, looking over his shoulder for encouragement. 'We'll be ready.'

Skarr turned away from them, indicating to his men to pass through the crowd and get a closer estimate of numbers. If even half of the villages provided what they said they would then he'd have added over a thousand men to the Marshal's tally. This whole region was ready to march, for gold if for nothing else.

Adro Vorster, his deputy in Eissen's absence, strode up to him.

'Word from Drakenmoor,' he said, clutching a roll of orders in his hand. 'The Marshal's back on his feet. We're to press on south of Heideck and continue the muster, but the march won't be long now.'

'That order can't come soon enough,' grumbled Skarr, brushing some accumulated grime from the edge of his cloak. 'These people sicken me.'

Vorster smiled in sympathy.

'They're scum, sir,' he agreed. 'But they're our scum.'

'And Sigmar be praised for that,' muttered Skarr, shaking his head.

CHAPTER TWELVE

Night in Averheim. Fires burned in the braziers placed across the city. The dull sound of massed chanting resounded along the narrow streets. Broken clouds circled the pinnacle of the Iron Tower, ripping away from it as the arcane energies thrumming along its massive flanks flared and whipped around the six-pronged crown.

The citadel was complete, glinting darkly, a vast spike of curling metal erupting from the very heart of the corrupted city. It dominated the entire valley, thrusting into the tormented air from the great circular courtyard below.

No sane man could possibly have doubted its baleful intent now. Lilac tongues of flame licked at it from pits sunk deep into the heart of the earth. Vast engines had been chanted into life by gangs of shackled supplicants, constructed in secret by scores of mutated workers and branded with smouldering icons of ruin. The machines churned with a deep, pounding murmur, gouts of coal-black smoke rising around them like pillars, billowing up through deep-sunk vents and fouling the air above the ground. Deep vibrations cracked the older buildings of Averheim, shattering walls that had stood since the very foundation of the Empire and jarring the rich merchant townhouses into piles of rubble.

From deep within the dungeons of the Tower, ranks of dog-soldiers emerged. They marched in close formation, wheezing and growling, their humanity now long forgotten behind masks of beaten metal, riveted to their tortured bones and daubed with the blood of their live human prey. They swung crystal-bladed halberds fresh from the underground forges where packs of Stone-slaves toiled without hope of release. The dog-soldiers fanned out from the Tower and into the streets, thousands of them, all once men, now turned into voiceless, inexorable bringers of death.

The populace of Averheim had been addled by joyroot, now billowing in vast columns of lilac smoke from furnaces all across the city. The six lesser towers burned night and day with the narcotic fumes, dousing the houses, garrisons and taverns with the mind-altering cocktail prepared in hulking underground vats. As the twisted warriors marched to their allotted stations, mortal men cheered them wildly, lost in a haze of visions. None slept. None had slept for days. The houses were empty, and the squares were full. Madness had come to Averheim, and the debased populace revelled in it.

At the summit of the Tower, out on the open platform at the very pinnacle of the huge citadel, Grosslich and Natassja stood alone.

Natassja was revealed in all her dark majesty. The wind, whipped up by the latent forces surging beneath Averheim, screamed past her, rippling her black robes and tousling her long raven hair. Her body now glowed a deep, luminous blue, and tattoos as black as night writhed across her exposed skin. Her white-less eyes glittered in the night air and her lips were parted. She gazed on the maelstrom, and the maelstrom gazed back.

'It begins,' she murmured.

Grosslich wore a new suit of armour, blood-red and forged from some unnatural alloy created in Natassja's forges. It shone like an insect's shell, jointed with astonishing precision, encasing his entire body below the neck. In place of a sword he carried a slender wand of bone, carved from skulls and fused into a single channel for his forbidden magicks. He was a sorcerer in his own right now, gifted by the Dark Prince for the damage he'd wrought to the Empire he'd once called his homeland. His expression was eager, though there was a note of uncertainty.

'The lesser towers are lighting,' he said.

One by one, the six smaller spikes of iron protruding from the old city walls burst into sudden flame. Each was a different colour, vivid and searing. As the torches kindled, the florescent hues mingled in the air above the rooftops, turning the deep of the night into a bizarre and perverted copy of the day. Shadows swayed wildly across the city as the illumination switched from one shade to another. All of Averheim was ablaze, drenched in a riot of sorcerous, sickening colour. Only the central Tower, massive and nightshade-black, remained untouched by the luminous blooms. It was waiting, biding its time, holding for the moment.

More mutant soldiers, some bearing bronze studs in their flesh as the handmaidens did, began to file from the gates at the base of the Tower, marching behind the dog-soldiers to take up their places within the city. The ranks of troops emerging from the surgeries and dungeons seemed endless, hundreds upon hundreds of twisted creatures who'd once been men. The mortal inhabitants of Averheim cheered them on, their own senses distorted and insensible to anything but a vague impression of excitement. The madness was now universal, soaked into the walls and stained deep at the roots.

Below it all, the Stone waited. Its spirit was alive, sentient and searching. In its hidden chamber, Achendorfer read the rites endlessly, the blood flowing over his chin and dripping to the polished floor. It remained as black as a corrupted soul. As the chanting continued, it became *more* black, sinking into an utter absence of light impossible to create in the world of untainted matter. As Achendorfer stumbled over his spells, the glossy sheen disappeared, replaced by a purity of darkness he'd never seen before. It deepened, falling away to a shade he could only describe as *oblivion*.

Out on the pinnacle, Natassja sensed it. She sighed, flexing her long, taloned fingers. The aethyric energies surging up the Tower resonated with her body, fuelling the transformations within. She felt subtle harmonics, so long cultivated, shift into alignment.

'Here it comes...' she whispered.

Far above, the clouds broke. High in the sky, the Deathmoon rode, as yellow as a goblin's tooth, full-faced and leering. Morrslieb, bleeding corruption, was abroad. As the final shreds moved away from it, baleful light flooded across blighted Averheim, blending with the fires on the walls and drenching the Aver valley in more layers of diseased virulence.

'*Ah...*' Natassja breathed, feeling the tainted essence of the moon sink over her. The tattoos on her flesh whirled into new shapes, spinning and extending like a nest of snakes.

Below, in the fevered city, the chanting broke out with fresh ardour. The fires on the towers sent plumes high into the sky, tearing up towards the glowing disc, wreathing it in fingers of outstretched witch-lightning.

'Will you say the word?' asked Grosslich, fingering the wand. He looked half-enraptured, half-terrified.

Natassja hardly heard him. She was lost on a higher plane of sensation. Below her, the Stone sang. Above her, the vast ball of warpstone sailed through the heavens. Between them was the Tower, the fulcrum on which everything rested. She could feel massive waves of power run up the spell-infused iron, resonating like the peals of great bronze bells. The earth cried out, though only she could hear its tortured wails. The barriers separating her from the raw essence of Chaos were finger-thin.

Then the moment came, the conjunction of all she'd worked for. After so much suffering, so many years of toil, her vision was realised. The failure with Marius now meant nothing. Lassus's failure meant nothing. She had the tools she needed to complete the great work. The servants now answering her call would be of a different order to any who had come before.

She raised her arms high, and coruscating energy blazed from her palms. The Tower beneath her shuddered, trembling as a vast, uncontainable force suddenly surged along its frame.

'*Now*,' she hissed.

And Averheim exploded.

Verstohlen awoke, covered in sweat. It was still the deep of the night. He rolled over, tangled in his cloak. The wind was rippling across the moors, racing through the tussocks of grass. A storm was brewing.

That wasn't what had woken him.

Schwarzhelm was already standing, arms folded, gazing into the north-west. Overhead, the clouds were racing. Morrslieb had risen, just as it had over the Vormeisterplatz. The heavens were in motion.

'I dreamt of...' Verstohlen started, but his words trailed away. The nightmares had come back. Visions of daemons leaping from roof to roof. An endless cycle of screams, flesh pulled from the bones of living men, soldiers with the faces of dogs. Above it all, a tall, slender tower of dark metal, looming across the carnage, covering the world in a shadow of insanity.

'You weren't dreaming.'

Verstohlen clambered to his feet, shivering against the cold. Far in the west, a tongue of flame burned bright on the horizon. It was like a column of blood, impossibly distant, impossibly tall. It stood sentinel over the land, neither flickering nor weakening, a pillar of fire.

'Holy Verena,' Verstohlen breathed, making the sign of the scales on his chest. 'What *is* that?'

'It is Averheim, Pieter,' said Schwarzhelm, voice grim. 'It is what we've done.'

'That's impossible. Averheim must be over a hundred...'

Verstohlen broke off again. As he watched, he knew the truth of it. The city was burning.

The two men remained silent, watching, unable to move or look away. The column remained still, staining the boiling clouds above it crimson. If there had been any doubt in his mind, it was banished now.

The city was damned. With a terrible insight, Verstohlen knew that no force within the province could hope to counter such terrible sorcery. Whether Helborg received the Sword of Vengeance or not made no difference now.

This was a power no mortal could hope to contest, and it had entered the world of the living.

The wizard screamed. Drool flew from his lips, splattering against the dirt of the camp floor. His fine sky-blue robes ripped as he rolled across the ground in his agony, eyes staring, nostrils flared. Blood ran down from his ears in thin trails and his fingers clutched at the air impotently.

'What is this?' roared Volkmar, lurching to his feet. He'd sensed something too, but Magister Alonysius von Hettram, Celestial Wizard and the Master of the Seers, evidently felt it more keenly.

'*She is coming!*' he shrieked, scrabbling at his eyes feverishly. '*She is coming!*'

Efraim Roll strode forwards, lifting the man from the ground and shaking him like a doll. The other members of Volkmar's command retinue, clustered in his tent overlooking the encampment, hung back in horror. Hettram was now vomiting, his limbs shaking uncontrollably.

'*She... is... coming!*' he blurted between heaves.

'Enough of this,' snapped Volkmar, moving to the tent entrance. He pushed the canvas to one side and strode out into the night.

Below him, the lights of the camp glowed in the darkness. Men slept in their rank order, curled in cloaks and watched over by teams of sentries. Far to the south, a storm had been brewing for days. Now it had broken.

'Sigmar's blood,' murmured Roll, coming to stand beside him.

Many miles away, a column of fire, slim as a plumbline, disfigured the southern horizon. The swirling clouds above it were as red and angry as an open wound.

'How far is–?'

'Averheim,' said Volkmar. He felt a cold fist clench around his heart. It was the Troll Country all over again. Chaos ascendant.

'Are you sure?'

'What else could it be?'

Above the vision of flame, the malignant orb of Morrslieb peered through the tattered streams of cloud. The line of fire rushed to meet it, streaming into the high airs and tainting the very arch of the sky. The pillar was far away, very far away, but even so the stench of dark magic clogged his nostrils. Something of awesome magnitude had been discharged, and the natural world recoiled from it in horror.

Back in the tent, the Celestial wizard was busy raving. All across the camp, men were woken from their slumber, knowing even in their mean, base way that some terrible event had taken place. When they saw the distant column, voices were raised in alarm.

Volkmar felt his resolve waver. Anything capable of rending the heavens in such a way would be untroubled by blackpowder or halberds. What had Schwarzhelm unleashed here? How deep did the corruption run?

'Theogonist?' asked Roll, his voice as flat and savage as ever. 'What are your orders?'

Volkmar said nothing. He could think of nothing to say. The commotion across the camp grew. More of his commanders stumbled from the tent, gaping at the distant glow. Maljdir was among them, for once speechless. Gruppen too. They all looked to him.

He clasped his staff. It gave him no comfort. Placed beside the abomination ahead, all the weapons they had seemed like so many trinkets and charms. He felt despair creep up, just as it had when Archaon had come for him in the north. The great enemy were too strong. They were *too strong*.

'Theogonist?' asked Roll again.

Volkmar looked away from it. That helped. Just gazing on the searing line of flame seemed to bleed the hope from him. He looked down. His palm was raw from clutching the ash shaft of the Staff of Command. He remembered Karl Franz's final words to him in Altdorf. *Can I trust you, Volkmar? Can you succeed where both my generals have failed?*

'Yes, my liege,' he muttered through clenched teeth. 'You can.'

Roll looked confused. 'My lord?'

Volkmar whirled on him.

'Light fires of our own. Banish the dark, and the men will no longer be plagued by it. Get an apothecary for the wizard, and minister to him yourself too. He cannot be allowed to die – we'll need him.'

Then he turned on the rest of his men, his face lit with a dark certainty.

'What did you *expect*?' he snarled, feeling both faith and fury return to him. 'That they'd welcome us with open arms? Know your danger, but do not fear it. That is our destination. That is the crucible upon which your devotion will be tested.'

He turned back to the face the pillar of flame. This time his resolve was solid.

'Search your souls, men. Purge all weakness. The storm is coming. If we fail here, then all the world will know the horror that Averheim knows now.'

Balls of blood-red fire soared high into the sky, racing upwards, coiling round the Tower in a vortex of dizzying speed. Screams from below fractured the very air, ripping it open and exposing the shimmering lattice of emotion beneath, the naked stuff of Chaos.

All along the length of the Tower, iron panels withdrew. The citadel's innards glowed an angry crimson, like hot coals. From the newly-revealed recesses, *things* emerged.

To Natassja, they were objects of transcendent beauty, diaphanous intelligences, winged and noble, possessed of an ineffable wisdom derived from the realm of the infinite. They soared into the fire-flecked air like angels, swimming in the void, drinking in the unleashed power crackling through the air.

To mortal eyes, they were women, lilac-skinned, claw-handed, clad in scraps of leather and iron, lissom and fleshy, screaming from mouths lined with fangs, trailing cloven hooves as they swooped. They were visions of lust and death, fusions of sudden pain and lingering pleasure, the incarnation of the debauchery of their Dark Prince and the fragments of his divine will.

They flew down like harpies, crashing into the roofs of the houses and shattering the tiles, drinking in the sheets of flame lurching up around them, growing larger and more substantial as the aethyr bled into the world of matter, sustaining them and firming up insubstantial sinews.

In Averheim, the sky no longer existed. The air was as red as blood, thundering upwards in a vast column of roaring aethyric essence. In the midst of it all was the Tower, focussing the torrent, keeping it together, directing the inexhaustible will of the Stone.

Natassja laughed out loud, glorying in the rush of the fire as it surged past her, rippling her skirts and tearing at her hair.

'Behold the Stone!' she cried, and from hundreds of feet below a rolling boom echoed across the city.

Grosslich staggered away from her, his face drained. Torrents of aethyr latched on to him, clutching at his armour and then ripping away in shreds. The daemons came soon after, tugging at his hair and laughing.

'Unhand me!' he commanded, brandishing the wand. They laughed all the harder, but none dared harm him. Instead they limited themselves to lascivious gestures, wheeling around the pinnacle like birds flocking to a storm-tossed ship. As they screeched, their voices echoed across registers, at once as flighty as a girl's and as deep as the pits of the abyss.

'What is this, Natassja?' he demanded, turning on her, eyes blazing with fear and anger.

The queen of Averheim gave him a scornful look.

'The allies we seek,' she said. 'What mortal army would dare to venture here now? The Stone sustains a portal, one which can last for centuries if I will it. This is the stuff of Chaos, Heinz-Mark, the raw material of dreams. Daemons will come. While the column of fire lasts they will endure, terrible and deadly. We have created what we wished for, my love! A foothold of the Infinite Realm in the heart of Sigmar's kingdom!'

Grosslich looked as angry as before. His armour made him nearly invulnerable and he'd developed powers of his own – he would be a formidable enemy if she chose to pick a fight with him. Formidable, but not insuperable.

'This is not what I wanted!' he roared over the torrent. 'I wanted dominion over men, not a realm of magic! What good is this to me?'

Natassja's eyes narrowed dangerously. She was flush with power, suffused with all the roaring energy of the Stone. Grosslich had served a useful purpose and at one time she'd been fond of him, but he was playing a perilous game.

'This mortal realm is yours for the taking, my love,' she said, keeping her voice low. 'Only the daemons cannot venture from the column of fire. All my other creations will serve you in the realm of the five senses.'

'But you have destroyed them!'

'Look around you, fool!' she snapped, tested almost beyond endurance by his stupidity. 'Do you see the buildings burning? Do you see your troops withering? This is no earth-bound fire. These flames burn souls, not flesh.'

Grosslich hesitated, then stalked to the edge of the platform. Bracing against a huge buttress of iron and stone, he leaned far out over the void. Natassja came to his side, fearing nothing of the precipitous drop. She was fast becoming impervious to physical harm.

'Watch them, my love,' she purred. She couldn't stay angry

for long, not when so much had been accomplished. 'See how they relish what we have done for them.'

Far down on the streets of Averheim, the dog-soldiers still marched, filing from the gates and assuming defensive positions outside the walls. The citizens of the city had been transformed in their turn, moulded by the power of the Stone and warped into something greater. Where their eyes had been there were now smouldering points of light, blazing in the smog of the furnaces like stars. All their previous cares and infirmities had been shaken off, and they stood tall, glorying in the rush of aethyr around them. Grosslich's army, already huge, had been bolstered by thousands more, their wills bound to the Stone, their bodies hale and ready to bear arms.

'Don't you see it?' murmured Natassja, caressing Grosslich's cheek and speaking softly into his ear. 'The daemons are for me, here in the Tower. Your realm will stretch for many leagues to the north, to the south, to wherever you wish it. Only here will the raw essence of the world of nightmares be permitted to endure.'

Grosslich looked sullen but impressed. Far below, the hordes of Stone-bound slaves had begun to form into crowds and head towards the courtyard below them. Even as they did so, dog-soldiers prepared to hand them weapons. The Everchosen himself could hardly have wished for a more devastating host to command. The joyroot had prepared them, and the Stone had completed the great work.

'I believed we would rule Averland together, you and I,' he muttered, torn between rival lusts. 'I thought that's what you wanted too.'

'I do, my love,' said Natassja, pulling his head round from the scenes below. The furnaces, the screams, the capering daemons, the palls of smoke, all of these were forgotten for a moment.

'This is what we have done, you and I,' she said, pulling him close to her. 'Why can't you be happy with it?'

'I am, my queen,' Grosslich replied, his anger dissipating

as her eyes bored deep into his. Resisting her was never easy, even after he'd been taught so much. 'It's just that... my vision was different.'

'Then revel in *this*. See what glories will be achieved here. Our names will pass into the annals of legend, not in this fading world, but in the libraries of the gods, etched on tablets of marble and placed in halls of perpetual wonder. You have taken a step towards a new world, Heinz-Mark. Do not falter now, for there is no way back.'

He nodded weakly, all resistance crumbling. His will was always so easy to break. Not like Schwarzhelm, and not like Marius – they had been made of more enduring material. As she spoke, she sensed the doubt in his mind. Had it always been there? Perhaps she should have paid more attention.

'Remember my words,' she warned, making sure he'd taken her meaning. 'This is the future for us, the future for mankind. I will say it again, in case you failed to hear me: there is *no* way back.'

Kurt Helborg turned uneasily in his sleep. In the past, his slumber had been that of a warrior, complete and unbroken. Ever since the fires of the Vormeisterplatz, though, the pattern had been broken. He saw visions before waking, faces leering at him in the dark. There was Rufus Leitdorf, fat and pallid, gloating over his failure to secure the city. Skarr was there too, mocking him for the loss of the runefang. And there was Schwarzhelm, his face unlocked by madness, brandishing the Sword of Justice and inviting the duel once again. It was all mockery and scorn, the things he'd never encountered in the world of waking.

At the vision of the Emperor's Champion, Helborg awoke suddenly. The sheets around him were clammy and blood had leaked from his wound again. The pain was ever-present, a dull ache in his side. He could ignore it in battle, just as he'd ignored a thousand lesser wounds before, but the architect of it would not leave him in peace.

Helborg lay still, letting his breathing return to normal.

The room around him was dark and cold. Dawn was some hours away and the shutters had been bolted closed. At the foot of his massive four-poster bed hung the sword he'd been lent by Leitdorf. It was a good blade, well-balanced and forged by master smiths of Nuln. It was nothing compared to the Klingerach.

Helborg swung his legs from the bed and walked over to the window. He unlocked the shutters, letting the moonlight flood into his chamber. Mannslieb was low in the eastern sky, almost invisible. It was Morrslieb, the Cursed Moon, that rode high. Helborg made the sign of the comet across his chest, more out of reflex than anything else. He feared the Chaos moon as little as he feared anything else. Far out in the north-west, he noticed a faint smudge of red against the horizon. Perhaps a fire, lost out on the bleak moorland.

He limped back to the bed and sat heavily on it. Being isolated, cut off from the Imperial chain of command, was an experience he'd not had for over twenty years. Even in the fiercest fighting he'd always had access to some indication of how things stood in Altdorf. Now things were different. For all he knew, Schwarzhelm still hunted him. If so, then the man's soul was surely damned.

Leitdorf had told him of the corruption recorded in Marius's diaries, the sickness at the heart of Averheim. He'd seen it for himself at the Vormeisterplatz. Whatever force had the power to turn Schwarzhelm's mighty hands to the cause of darkness was potent indeed. The old curmudgeon had always been infuriating, stubborn, grim, taciturn, inflexible, proud and prickly, but he'd never shown the slightest lack of faith in the Empire and its masters. Not until now.

Prompted by some random inclination, Helborg took up his borrowed sword and withdrew the blade from the scabbard. He turned it slowly, watching the metal reflect the tainted moonlight. A weak instrument, but it would have to do. Nothing about his current situation was ideal. Leitdorf was a simpering, self-pitying fool, the men at his command were half-trained and liable to bolt at the first sign of trouble, and Helborg had almost no idea what Grosslich's intentions or tactics were.

So be it. He'd never asked for anything other than a life of testing. Being Grand Marshal of the Empire brought with it certain privileges – the loyalty of powerful men and the favours of beautiful women – but these were not the things that drove him onwards. It had always been about faith, an ideal, something to aspire to. He'd come closer than ever to death in Averheim, and no man remained unchanged in the face of his own mortality. Maybe he'd been too flamboyant in the past, too ready to orchestrate the defence of the Empire around his own ambition. Maybe Schwarzhelm had been right to resent his success. Maybe some of this had been his fault, despite the long, painful hours he'd spent blaming his great rival for all that had befallen.

Things would have to change. Whatever the result of the war, he could not go back to Altdorf as if nothing had happened.

He began to re-sheathe the sword when a faint rattling sound caught his attention. He paused, listening carefully. It was coming from outside the window. Helborg's room was on the first storey of the mansion, more than twenty feet up from ground level. Leitdorf's chambers were down the corridor, and the other rooms were empty.

The rattling sounded again. Helborg placed the scabbard on the bed and took the naked sword up in his right hand. For some reason his heart began to beat faster. His armour had been hung in the room below, and he wore nothing more protective than a threadbare nightshirt. There should have been Reiksguard patrolling the grounds. The noise outside was like nothing he'd heard in his life, at once artificial and full of a strange, scuttling kind of life.

He stood up from the bed and edged towards the window. He listened carefully. Nothing, save the faint creak of the floorboards beneath him and the rush of the wind from outside. Helborg stayed perfectly still, blade poised for the strike, watching.

Still nothing. Heartbeats passed, gradually slowing. Perhaps he'd imagined it.

The window shattered with a smash that resounded across the chamber. A bone claw thrust through the jagged panes, scrabbling at the stone sill, hauling something up behind it.

Helborg sprang forwards, bringing the sword down on the talons with a massive, two-handed hammerblow. The stone fractured, sending shards spinning into the air, but the blade rebounded from the claw, jarring his arms and sending him staggering back. There was a thin scream and something crashed back down to earth. Helborg regained his feet. The talons had gone. Whatever had tried to get in had been sent plummeting back to the courtyard.

It had not been alone. With a spider-like pounce, another creature leapt through the shattered glass, crouched on the floor and coiled for another spring.

'Helborg!' it hissed, and there was something like ecstasy in its warped voice.

Helborg stared at it in horror. The stink of Chaos rose from it, pungent and sweet. The body of a young woman, naked and covered in scars, squatted on the floor, draped in the remnants of rags. The flesh was as pale as the Deathmoon and caked with mud and filth from the moors. Old blood had dried on its needle teeth and ribbons of dry skin clung to the talons. Its eyes glinted with the dull sheen of tarnished iron, then blazed into a pale lilac fire.

It pounced. Helborg swung the sword to parry, using all his strength to ward the scything claws. The horror's strength and speed were incredible. It lashed out, striking at his eyes and fingers, following him across the chamber as he withdrew, step by step.

Helborg's sword moved in a blur, countering the strikes and thrusting back. He was the foremost swordsman of the Empire, but this blade was no runefang. The curved talons of the handmaiden scored the edge of it, scraping down its length in a shower of sparks and shivering the metal.

More clambered in, two of them, their eyes lit up with the

same lilac blaze. They rushed into the attack, limbs flailing, trying to break through Helborg's guard.

He pulled back to the door, whirling his blade in tighter and faster arcs. The edge seemed to have no effect on them. Every time his sword connected with flesh, a hidden layer of bone or iron bounced the shaft back. The creatures were like the automata of a crazed surgeon's imagination, pitiless and unstoppable.

One dropped down low and went for his legs. He kicked the creature hard in the face, knocking it on its back, before leaping away to dodge the attack from the others. As he withdrew again he felt hot blood running down his shin. Morr's teeth, the thing had *bitten* him.

The first creature pressed the attack, trying to impale him against the wooden door frame, jabbing its talons in hard and straight. Its face came close, locked in a contortion of pain. Helborg veered his head out of the way and blocked a sideswipe from the second with the flat of his sword. The third got back on its feet and coiled to leap again. They were all over him.

Feeling the door at his back, Helborg kicked it open and retreated out to the landing beyond. It was darker there, and the pursuing horrors' eyes glowed with malice in the gloom. Step by step they pushed him back, slicing at his exposed flesh, pushing for the opening. It was only a matter of time. He couldn't hurt them, and they never tired. Even as he knocked away a lunge, Helborg felt a sharp stab of pain as one of the talons got past his guard.

He broke away, fresh blood dripping from the wound, twisting and blocking to evade the merciless attack. They were going to break through. They'd blooded him, and the taste of it in the air drove them into a fresh mania.

'*Helborg!*' they cried together, gathering themselves for the strike like coiling snakes. Helborg held the sword steady, waiting for them in the dark. His teeth clenched, breath coming in ragged gasps. He tensed, ready for the impact.

'Sigmar!'

He heard the cry, but the voice wasn't his. A dark shape plunged past him, wielding a blade and swinging it with clumsy abandon.

The new sword swung down, connecting with the lead creature as it made to leap. A flash of blinding light broke out across the landing, briefly showing up the scene in stark, dazzling relief.

Leitdorf was there. *Leitdorf*. The fat, slovenly man laid into the horrors with his broadsword, as naked as the day he'd been born, roaring with a kind of blind, panicked fury. Helborg lurched after him, desperate to stop the man being cut to pieces. The elector was no swordsman – he was a fool, a buffoon, a spoiled brat.

The horrors fell back. Incredibly, they shrank away from the heavy swipes of the Wolfsklinge, eyes dull with horror, talons curled up into impotent fists. Leitdorf ploughed into them, jabbing left and right with slow, inexpert strokes. Every step he took, they scrabbled back, screaming at him with an unmistakable expression of terror.

They were *afraid* of him.

There was no time to be astounded. In a heartbeat, Helborg was at his side, matching the elector's clumsy blows with precision strikes. Under the twin assault, the creatures seemed to shrivel into a tortured impotence, holding their tortured hands up in front of their ravaged faces, scuttling to escape, desperate not to face the heavy bite of the Wolfsklinge.

'Follow my lead!' roared Helborg, dazzling one of the creatures with a glittering backhand swipe before bringing the edge back sharply. The horror, so eerily efficient before, clattered backwards. Its guard destroyed, Leitdorf landed the killer blow, his sword cleaving the creature from neck to stomach in a single movement. Old flesh, iron bindings, clockwork bearings and rune-stamped plates scattered across the landing floor, skittering and bouncing as the creature was ripped apart. A cloud of jasmine perfume billowed out, sighing across the darkness of the landing before rippling into nothingness.

CHRIS WRAIGHT

The two remaining handmaidens turned to flee, wailing like lost children in the night. With every blow from Leitdorf's blade a fresh blaze of light seemed to cow them further. Leitdorf and Helborg pushed them back into the bedchamber, steel ringing against bone and exploding in flashes of light and sparks.

One of them coiled for a counter-attack, jaws wide in a scream of fear and hatred, talons extended for a desperate, gouging assault. Helborg was on it in an instant, his blade hurtling round to sever the horror's wrists. As ever, his weapon bounced from the creature without biting, but the impact was enough to knock it off balance.

'Now!' he roared, and Leitdorf was quick enough to obey. The elector jabbed down, his grip two-handed, and the creature was smashed apart by the power of the Wolfsklinge.

One remained. It scrabbled backwards, face contorted in terror. It stared at Leitdorf with anguish, all thoughts of its mission forgotten.

Helborg shot Leitdorf a quick look. The man's face was white with terror and his temples were drenched in sweat. He was panting heavily, mouth open and jaw loose. He looked like he'd stumbled into a nightmare.

'Finish it,' Helborg growled, edging forwards. He had to provide the opening. He let the tip of his sword sway back and forth, distracting the creature as it crouched miserably.

Then he struck, darting forwards, slipping the blade under the horror's outstretched talons, going for the midriff.

It slapped the sword away contemptuously, ignoring his attack, eyes still on Leitdorf. But the distraction had been enough. The elector was on it, hammering down with the Wolfsklinge, shattering iron bonds and ripping dry skin.

The handmaiden, Natassja's killing machine, the perfect assassin, shattered under the flurry of blows, its tortured hide carved open, its spell-locked innards dented and smashed. Helborg staggered out of the way, ducking under a wild swipe from Leitdorf. The man hacked and hammered in a frenzy of rage and fear, obliterating the cowering horror with blow after crushing blow. Even when it was nothing more than a heap of dented iron and twitching sinews he kept going, pounding away until the floorboards beneath were hacked up and in danger of collapsing.

'Leitdorf!' cried Helborg.

The man kept going, eyes wild, hair swinging around his head like flails.

'*Leitdorf!*' roared Helborg, grabbing him by the shoulder and swinging him round. For a moment, he thought Leitdorf was going to attack him. The elector stared at him wide-eyed, his face lost in a mask of terror.

'It's *me*, Rufus,' said Helborg, eyes locked with his, hand clamped on his shoulder.

Leitdorf froze, sword ready to strike. His limbs were shivering. His fat belly was streaked with sweat. Slowly, haltingly, he let the Wolfs-klinge fall from his fingers. It clanged amongst the shattered carcasses of the handmaidens, now lost in the darkness of the chamber.

'What... I...' he mumbled, frenzy giving way to shock. The blood had drained from his face. He looked ready to pass out.

'Get some clothes on,' said Helborg, keeping the grip on his shoulder tight. Already there were sounds of commotion from below. 'I'll get some guards up here. Then we need to talk.'

CHAPTER THIRTEEN

Leitdorf sat in his father's study. His hands still shook each time he raised the glass of wine to his lips. From the landing outside he could hear the guards clearing away the last of the wreckage of the assassin creatures.

Dawn had broken, and a meagre light had slowly crept over the moorland outside. The clouds that had been building up for days continued to mount, blocking the light of the sun and turning the sky as dark and sullen as a musket-barrel.

Leitdorf placed his goblet back on the desk. In front of him, as always, was his father's diary. He'd read it all, some parts several times over. Even the most obscure passages had begun to make some sense. Over the final few weeks' entries, though, Marius's handwriting was near-illegible, and there were still long sections where Rufus could make nothing out. In the centre of the page he was looking it, the old elector seemed to have drifted off into random scrawlings.

...bedarruzibarr'zagarratumnan'akz'akz'berau...

There was more of the same. One page was entirely covered in such nonsense. As he reflected on a proud mind laid low, his spirits sank further. He'd not been close to his father in life, but no son wanted to witness such degeneration. If he'd known at the time, maybe he'd have done something. Or maybe he'd have stayed mired in the excess and privilege he'd always known.

There was a knock at the door.

'Come.'

Helborg pushed the door open. It had been courteous of him to knock. Over the past few days, the Marshal had got into the habit of bursting in uninvited. Helborg walked over to the desk and leaned against the wall beside Leitdorf. He looked untroubled by the events of a few hours ago. No doubt he'd seen worse.

'Feeling better?' asked the Marshal.

'Yes, thank you.' The wine had helped calm his nerves. Leitdorf noticed Helborg had had his wound freshly bound again. He looked a lot more formidable out of his nightshirt and back in his standard military uniform. Not many men would have seen the Master of the Reiksguard fighting in his nightwear. Then again, at least the man had been wearing *some* clothes.

'Interesting reading?'

Leitdorf glanced back down at the page. 'Like looking inside the mind of a dead man.'

He pushed his chair back from the desk and turned to face the Marshal.

'You know what's been bothering me?' Leitdorf said. 'For over a year we lived as a couple in Altdorf. She had access to all of my resources, all of my men. Why didn't she ever try to corrupt me? Why did she use Grosslich?'

Helborg shrugged. 'You're sure she never tried? The ways of the enemy are–'

'Subtle, yes, I know,' muttered Leitdorf. 'And yes, I'm sure. She tried to subvert my father – and failed. How could that be *possible*? She had the power to walk in men's dreams. Just look what she did to Schwarzhelm. Somehow, Marius resisted her for all those years where the Emperor's Champion couldn't. He was untouchable.'

As he spoke, Leitdorf felt a fugitive pride in that.

'Not all men give in to temptation,' said Helborg.

'Of course. But something else is at work here. You saw what happened with those... creatures. It's only confirmed a suspicion I've had for some time, ever since I first read this book.'

Helborg looked doubtful, but said nothing.

'You know as well as I that the bloodlines of the electors are ancient. There have been many ruling families in Averland over the centuries, but the Leitdorfs have always been among them. Ever since the time of Siggurd my people have taken up swords in the defence of this realm. We're bound to Averheim like none of the others. This has always been the root of our hold over the runefang, even during the dark times when it was wielded by others. We were the first ones.'

As he spoke, Leitdorf thought of all the fine words he'd rehearsed for this speech. It sounded ludicrous, contemptible even, in his head. Still, he had to say it.

'My father believed there was a hidden presence in the city. *Under* the city. His dreams were full of it – a source of power, or evil, or knowledge. That's why he hated Averheim, even as he fought to retain it. Men have long joked that the place was cursed, destined forever to be ruled by the insane. My father thought he knew why. There were always clandestine forces at work there, nagging away in the shadows, whispering in the silences.'

Helborg narrowed his eyes, still listening intently.

'And then there was this woman, this Natassja, making all those fears explicit, coming to him in his sleep. Despite everything, she failed to turn him to the enemy. Why? He was too strong, too indomitable. In the end, tiring of her seduction, she let him ride out to face Ironjaw and turned her ambitions away from the Leitdorfs. She had to.'

As he spoke, Rufus held Helborg's gaze, his brown eyes steadier than they'd ever been.

'It's in our blood, Marshal,' he said. 'We can't be turned. I'd always been told it by nursemaids and tutors, but I never

really knew what they meant until now. We have our fail-
ings, to be sure, but one kind of corruption we are free of.
The whispers of the great enemy are useless against us. It's
not just a matter of will. It's in the *blood*.'

Helborg looked sceptical. 'You think that explains what
happened here?'

Leitdorf smiled. 'You know my reputation as a fighter, my
lord. And yet, against her creations, I had the mastery. I will
always have the mastery. She must have known that. So she
needed to find another champion.'

Helborg remained incredulous. Leitdorf couldn't blame
him. The idea sounded preposterous to him too in the cold
light of day. And yet only he – fat, stupid Rufus – had been
able to defeat the creatures. The hero of the Empire, the
Hammer of Chaos, would have been carved apart by them.
There was some link between the Leitdorfs and Natassja,
something that made him powerful.

'I've heard of such things,' said the Marshal at last, evidently unconvinced. 'There are weapons, the Wolfsklinge
maybe, which have power over individuals and their works.
Maybe some long-forgotten father of your line performed
a distant feat of faith which explains your victory. Beyond
that, I would not safely go.'

Leitdorf smiled again, this time with resignation. He
couldn't expect anyone else to understand. This was between
him, his father and Natassja.

'No doubt you're right, my lord,' he said. 'Only consider this.
There is a force for corruption in the city that my family has
resisted for generations, even to the extent of being driven into
madness. Is it not possible that we have developed some counterpart power of our own? And if this were so, would it not be
a matter of great hope for the Empire? For mankind, even?'

Helborg thought for a moment, then gave a noncommittal
gesture. 'There are many strange things in the world. Be careful where your pride takes you, elector. Many have thought
themselves immune to the call of corruption. They have
always been the first to fall.'

Leitdorf bowed his head. 'Of course. These are just speculations.'

Helborg looked at Leitdorf carefully then, like a farmer sizing up an unpromising foal with a view to producing a future prize stallion. Some of the unconscious scorn had left the Marshal's manner, even if his habitual pride still remained sunk deep in his battle-ravaged features.

'In any case,' he said, 'you have my thanks. Whatever the reason, your sword bit into those creatures where mine did not. When the grace of Sigmar descends, it is foolish to ask too closely the reason why.'

The unaccustomed praise made Leitdorf feel awkward. He'd never been complimented on his swordplay before by anyone, let alone by a legend such as Helborg.

'Then maybe you should take the Wolfsklinge, my lord,' he said, although, deep down, he was loath to lose it. 'Your hands will wield it more skilfully than mine.'

Helborg laughed and shook his head. 'A generous offer! Maybe this war will make a man of you yet, Rufus.' He pushed himself away from the wall and made to leave the room. 'I'll not take it up. There's only one sword for me, and I still plan on recovering it. Until then, I'll make do with what weapons I can find.'

He started to walk towards the door.

'We'll both have the opportunity to use our blades again soon. Our army, such as it is, is ready, and I've given Skarr his deadline to make the rendezvous. We march within the hour. Collect yourself, elector. Averheim beckons.'

The town of Streissen lay between Nuln and Averheim, the first of the large market towns that straddled the main trading route into the heart of the Empire. It was the only settlement of any note before the capital and commanded a key crossing point over the river. Like most Imperial towns it was walled and garrisoned. Tiled roofs rose up within the ramparts, close-packed and divided only by narrow, winding streets. In its own way it was an attractive place, a bustling, hard-nosed town made rich through trade and commerce.

In the days between the electors its defences had fallen into disrepair. Grosslich had put that right soon after his coronation. The walls had been strengthened and an extra two thousand men drafted into the garrison. The old icons of the province had been removed and the crimson boar's head now hung from the gatehouse. Streissen had always been home to many Grosslich supporters, and it was far in both distance and sympathy from the lands once controlled by the Leitdorfs. The merchants had welcomed the changes brought in by the new elector, and for a brief time the trade had picked up again.

Now it was paying for its choices. Volkmar had given the burgomeisters almost no time to consider his demands for surrender. Before any reply had come back the walls had been surrounded by his army, nearly forty thousand strong since taking on reinforcements from Nuln and itching for a fight.

The Theogonist stood to the north of the city on a conical hill, his commanders, musicians and messengers around him. The storm in the south had grown fiercer, and black clouds raged on the horizon, flecked with lightning. The column of fire was still visible, though far paler in the daylight. It was ever-present, a reminder to all of the destination that awaited them.

On the plain below, his army was deployed in a wide circle, out of bow-shot and musket-range of the walls but close enough to advance at a moment's notice. Placed in readiness for combat, the volume of men looked fearsome. They covered the undulating land in front of the gates like a vast chequered carpet, over a mile wide from flank to flank. The auxiliaries were desperate to mount an assault; the regular troops less so. Morale had been strangely affected by the apparition in the night sky. Some men had responded with aggression, others with fear, others with fatalism.

'We still haven't heard from the burgomeisters,' said

Maljdir, frowning at the beleaguered town as if it had personally offended him. 'Give them more time?'

Volkmar shook his head.

'They've damned themselves by waiting. Launch the assault.'

Maljdir hesitated, then bowed and gestured to the trumpeter standing to his left. The man blew a series of long notes into the air, which were then taken up by other musicians. The signal passed to the west flank, where the big guns had been placed along the edge of a low ridge.

As soon as the notes reached them the crews sprang into action. Shot was rammed home and fuses lit. With a deafening boom, the great cannons roared out, hurling their shot straight and true. As the smoke rolled across the battlefield, the walls of Streissen cracked and buckled. To the right of the cannons, arranged high on the north flank of the battlefield, men began to shuffle forwards. Cavalry units mounted and adjusted their armour, taking up lances and handguns. The vast bulk of the infantry, the halberdiers, spearmen and swordsmen, held their positions, watching the destruction begin with a mix of relish and anxiety.

The cannons roared out again, a thunderous barrage of stone-cracking power, shaking the earth beneath them and rocking the town to its foundations. A jagged line appeared in the north-west corner of the walls, showering dust and mortar as the blocks were knocked loose.

'There's the breach,' said Volkmar, watching the action unfold through his spyglass. 'Order the Third and Ninth into position. Knights Panther on their left flank, Horstman's cavalry on their right.'

The orders were conveyed and a mass of men crept forwards, still in company order, nearly three thousand halberdiers marching cautiously in offensive formation. Squadrons of armoured horsemen drew alongside them, guarding their flanks from counter-assault. As the infantry pulled itself into position, the first arrows whined down from the walls. Ranged against the might of Volkmar's forces, the defences looked pitiably weak.

The cannons roared a third time, then a fourth. The breach opened further, exposing the masonry within. The halberdiers moved closer, kept in tight ranks by their sergeants, shadowed by the cavalry, waiting for the order to charge.

'Move the auxiliaries to close the leaguer,' said Volkmar, watching the movement of men below him intently. 'Maintain the barrage. Assault on my word.'

'My lord, there are flags on the ramparts,' said Maljdir, pointing at Streissen's turrets, only half-visible through the rolling clouds of blackpowder smoke from the cannon barrels. 'They wish to submit.'

'How is that relevant, Odain?' Volkmar said, observing the fifth barrage as it blasted the breach wider. The gap was now wide enough to drive a carriage through. There were defenders swarming over it like flies round a wound. 'They've had their chance, and we'll show them the price of defiance. Order the advance.'

Maljdir looked hesitant. The huge Nordlander was not a man given to pity, but still he paused.

'They're asking for quarter, my lord. They're men of the Empire.'

Volkmar let the spyglass drop and rounded on the priest, eyes blazing.

'They're *traitors*,' he growled. 'Order the advance.'

Maljdir resisted for a moment longer, eyes locked with Volkmar's. Then they dropped. He turned to the musician and gave him the instruction. Fresh trumpet calls blared out, and a roar of recognition rippled across the army. They knew what was coming.

The final cannon barrage boomed out, shattering the broken section of wall further. The cries of those crushed under the stone rang out, audible even over the roar of the charging halberdiers. Volkmar's vanguard was unleashed and surged forwards en masse, loping over the broken ground, blades kept low in the front rank, raised high in the following. They swarmed across the shattered walls and the sound of killing rose above all others.

'Fourth and Eighth in behind them!' ordered Volkmar, his pulse beginning to race. This was the first action of the campaign, and the men needed a crushing success to bolster their morale. 'Greatswords into reserve!'

His orders were conveyed and the massed companies of men moved to follow them. The halberdiers were still pouring through the walls, storming across the overwhelmed breach and piling into the town, blades flashing in the grey light. There were plumes of smoke as enemy handgunners returned fire, but they were soon extinguished under the weight of the assault. Like a single, massive animal, the invading army began to wheel around the centre of tactical gravity and close in on its prey.

As the last of the cannon smoke lazily drifted across the plain, it was already evident the defence was doomed. Volkmar stowed his spyglass with satisfaction and turned to Maljdir.

'Come with me,' he ordered, his eyes alight with savagery. 'We've cut our way in. Time to follow the halberds.'

With that, the Grand Theogonist strode down the slope of the hill, flanked by plate-armoured warrior priests, to take his prize.

Maljdir watched him go, arms crossed over his massive chest, unmoving, unwilling to be a part of a slaughter with no glory in it. He'd come to hunt Chaos troops, not misguided merchants and farmhands.

The power of command was too strong, though. In the end Maljdir shook his head, took up the vast, gold-studded warhammer Bloodbringer and stalked down after his general. For the first time since leaving Altdorf, the big man found himself eager to get to the real fighting in Averheim. At least there was an enemy there which deserved to be put to the sword.

And they'd be in range soon enough.

Bloch screwed his eyes tight, peering into the distance. The sun had started to lower in the west, obscuring the land ahead in a lowering haze.

'It's a blockade,' he said.

Kraus shook his head. 'More than that. There must be hundreds of them. It's a camp. They're on the march.'

Bloch looked back at the horizon. The road west ran over the grassland before them. They were in the cattle-country south of Heideck, having made good progress on the long journey from Grenzstadt. As they'd neared Averland's second city, Bloch had decided to take a detour to the south. He had no desire to run into Grosslich's men before they drew nearer to Averheim. With only two hundred troops still under his command, he was vulnerable.

For a few days, his strategy seemed to be working. They'd seen merchant convoys on the roads, all heavily guarded by private militia. Apart from them, there had been almost no movement on the highways. Bloch's company had been able to travel quickly and in the open, lodging in or around villages where the people had heard nothing from Averheim in days. The province of Averland seemed to have shut down. That would have been cause for more concern if it hadn't aided their passage so much, and of Grosslich's vaunted armies in particular there had been no sign.

Until now.

Thankfully, Bloch had stumbled across the encampment while his men were still under cover, overshadowed by the crumbling walls of a ruined farmhouse high on the hill. He, Kraus and a handful of men had scouted ahead of the main column of soldiers, planning the remainder of the day's trek and looking for a site to make camp.

It seemed Grosslich's men had had a similar idea. They straddled the road ahead, dozens of soldiers wearing the crimson and gold tunics of the new elector, starting the laborious process of erecting tents and raising an embankment for the night. They clearly expected trouble from someone. Perhaps Meuningen had been wrong about the succession issue being completely resolved.

'Nice colours,' said Bloch.

'Helpfully visible,' agreed Kraus.

'So what are we going to do about them?'

Kraus pursed his cracked lips. The weeks in the wilderness had given him a ragged, almost canine look. Like all of them, he'd lost weight and gained muscle.

'We can't evade Grosslich's forces forever. Perhaps now we'll see what his intentions are.'

Bloch pondered that.

'Too many to fight,' he said.

'What d'you mean? It can't be more than two to one. We'll tear them apart.'

Bloch grinned. 'Don't get cocky. I want to get back to Altdorf in one piece.'

'You're in the wrong trade, then.'

Bloch motioned to one of his men, a sandy-haired halberdier. Like all the troops marching with him still, this one had fought under his command since the death of Grunwald. They were good men, these, the kind you'd trust with your life.

'Bring the lads up here,' he told him. 'We'll form up and march towards them with our heads held high. No reason for us to suspect they'll be hostile.'

But there was. Meuningen's warning still echoed in his thoughts. Everything about Averland since his return had felt deeply, terribly wrong. The further west they went, the stranger it felt.

The halberdier slipped off to muster the rest of the men.

Kraus was satisfied. He'd never been happy with avoiding conflict, and looked eager for another fight. He drew his sword and looked carefully along the edge, searching for defects.

'Keep that sheathed when we get up there,' warned Bloch.

'You really think they'll let us pass?'

Bloch shrugged.

'Your guess is as good as mine. Since Schwarzhelm left, I've got no idea what's been going on here.'

'And if they don't?'

'Same as always,' he said. His voice was flat. 'We'll kill 'em all.'

* * *

Verstohlen shaded his eyes against the grey sky and shivered. Either autumn was approaching very fast or there was
something decidedly strange about the weather. Each day
dawned colder than the last and the rush of clouds from
the mountains continued unabated. The scudding masses
seemed to be drawn north-west like water rushing down a
whirlpool. In the distance, where the column of fire was still
just visible on the edge of sight, a vast maelstrom of circling
storm-bringers had accumulated. Tongues of forked lightning
flickered against the dark shadow of the rolling grassland.

He flipped the collar of his Kartor-Bruessol coat up around
his neck and stuffed his hands in his pockets. The attire he
was so proud of was suffering badly out in the wilds. He
knew that he was worse than useless in such an environment.
The skills he prided himself on were suited to cities and
stately houses, places where information was more deadly
than swords. Since decoding Lassus's missives, he'd not been
able to contribute much more to Schwarzhelm's quest than
the occasional grumble. He was tired, dog-tired, and the pain
of his wounds still throbbed in his back.

Schwarzhelm himself strode on as powerfully as ever,
thrusting aside bushes and clumps of overgrown gorse with
unconscious ease. The trials of the past month had done
little to dent his sheer physical presence. Even out of his
customary plate armour he still exuded a raw, almost bestial
menace. He'd been described as a force of nature, and such
a description served him well. Verstohlen had known him
for years, but only on this journey had he displayed more
than the most fleeting of weaknesses. This journey had been
remarkable in many ways, though, none of which Verstohlen
wanted to see repeated.

'Keep up, man,' Schwarzhelm growled irritably, pushing
through a briar patch and hauling himself on to a shallow
ridge of crumbling clay soil.

Verstohlen sighed, hoisted his bag over his shoulder once
more and followed wearily. They'd been on the highlands
for two days now and there was little enough sign of any

habitation at all, let alone the hiding place of Kurt Helborg. The country had gone from open moor to a twisting landscape of defiles and narrow coombs, all thickly forested or choked with undergrowth. The going had got harder, and tempers had frayed.

'I'm coming, damn you,' muttered Verstohlen, crawling up the ridge with difficulty. When he crested it, Schwarzhelm was waiting for him with a face like thunder. Behind him, a wall of low, wind-blasted trees clustered darkly, cutting off the grey light of the sun.

'Can you go no faster?' he snapped, eyes glittering with impatience.

'*Faster?*' gasped Verstohlen, breathing heavily. His head felt light from the exertions he'd already made. 'Verena's scales, we'd need wings to get across here in less than a week. This is a fool's errand, my lord. We should turn back.'

Schwarzhelm glowered at him. Though the man would never admit it, the fatigue was playing on him too.

'Remember who you're talking to,' he rasped, moving a hand instinctively to the hilt of the Rechtstahl. 'You have your orders.'

Verstohlen's eyes widened. 'What're you going to do? Draw that on *me?*'

Schwarzhelm took a step towards him, his expression one of gathering fury.

'Don't tempt me. I've marched with Tileans with stronger stomachs than–'

He broke off, suddenly tensing. From the treeline, a twig snapped.

Schwarzhelm whirled around, both swords drawn. Verstohlen was at his shoulder in an instant, dagger in hand. They were being watched.

Men broke from the cover of the branches, clad in leather jerkins and open-faced helmets. Their swords were naked and they were ready for a fight. There were six of them, all with the grizzled faces of professional soldiers. With a sudden lurch of remembrance, Verstohlen realised what they were.

Reiksguard.

'Lower your blades!' cried their captain, pointing his sword-tip at Schwarzhelm and advancing menacingly.

Schwarzhelm stood still, slowly letting the Swords of Vengeance and Justice down until the points grazed the ground. He knew what they were as well as Verstohlen did, but for the moment at least the knights didn't recognise him. They'd probably never seen him out of armour before.

'Perhaps you don't remember me,' he said.

As soon as he spoke, a ripple of amazement passed across the faces of the knights.

'Schwarzhelm!' one of them gasped aloud. Another advanced with purpose, looking like he wanted to run his blade through the big man's chest. Schwarzhelm remained motionless, keeping both his swords out of position. Verstohlen clutched his dagger tight, ready to act. This was dangerous.

'Wait!' snapped the leader, holding his fist up. His stubble-lined face was grimy and studded with scabs. He'd been in the wilderness for a long time. He kept his blade raised, watching both of them intently. Schwarzhelm's reputation preceded him, and the knight seemed lost in a mix of awe and hatred.

'Are you alone?' he asked.

Schwarzhelm nodded.

'Why are you here?'

'I seek the Lord Helborg, if he still lives.'

One of the Reiksguard snorted with derision. 'If he lives!'

'Silence!' ordered the captain. 'He's alive, though no thanks to you. Tell me why I shouldn't kill you now myself, traitor?'

Schwarzhelm looked directly at the knight. His gaze was blunt, hard to read. There was defiance there, belligerence too, but also shame.

'Do you really think you could harm me, Reiksguard, if I chose to prevent you?' His voice came in a deep growl. 'I have two swords in my hands, both as ancient as the bones of the earth. You're walking a dangerous path.'

Verstohlen thought he was going to strike then, and sweat broke out across his forehead. He clutched his dagger more tightly. The Reiksguard held their ground. The merest spark would light this fire.

Then Schwarzhelm's massive shoulders slumped.

'I did not come here to spill fresh blood,' he muttered. Sorrow weighed heavily on each word, and the threat drained from his speech. 'Take me to the Lord Helborg, and he shall be the judge of things. There are tidings he must hear.'

The Reiksguard captain made no move.

'Surrender your swords, then,' he said.

'Not to you.'

'How can I take you to him when you will not disarm?'

Schwarzhelm grunted with disdain.

'You forget yourself, Reiksguard. I am the Emperor's Champion. I will come as I am.'

Still the tension remained. The knights looked to their captain. If he ordered it, they would charge. The man frowned, wrestling with the decision. Verstohlen could see the frustration in his eyes, but the Reiksguard's respect for the sanctity of rank was near-absolute.

'I will take you to him,' he said at last, nearly spitting the words out. 'There is an army on these moors, Schwarzhelm, an army raised to right the wrongs you have caused. Think on that, should you choose to wield your swords in anger. Your reputation goes before you, but if you raise them again, you will die before the blade leaves the scabbard. This I swear, as do all the Reiksguard that remain in Averland.'

Schwarzhelm said nothing, but nodded wearily. He sheathed the Rechtstahl and the Klingerach in a single movement. The captain gave a signal to his men and they fanned around the two of them, blades in hand.

Then they started walking. There was no conversation, and the atmosphere was frigid. As they went, the wind howled across the gorse like mocking laughter.

'Merciful Verena,' muttered Verstohlen to himself as he stumbled along behind the implacable form of his master. 'This just gets better.'

* * *

Bloch strode casually at the head of his column, Kraus by his side. Behind him, his men marched in formation, six abreast, a compact column of fighting men. After so long on campaign they looked more than a little shabby, but their manner of quiet, efficient confidence was unfeigned. They were the remnants of an army that had driven the greenskins over the mountains, and they had every reason to walk tall.

As they drew closer to the camp, shouts went up from the sentries and the guards took up their places. By the time Bloch approached the perimeter the detachment commander was waiting at the camp entrance. He was flanked by several dozen men, all heavily armed. More clustered within, protected by the spiked embankment. They were wearing crimson tunics over plate breastplates. Their swords were strangely curved, and some had barbs forged into them. Not very Imperial. Half the troops looked like Averlanders, but the rest had the darker colouring of Tileans, Estalians or even soldiers of Araby. Grosslich must have paid out handsomely to get mercenaries from so far.

Behind the camp commander the earthworks rose up several feet, surmounted by a row of stakes. The deployment looked well organised. Kraus was right; this was a part of an army at war.

'Halt,' ordered the camp commander. 'State your name and business.'

Bloch took a good look at his opposite number. The man had the air of a seasoned warrior. His armour was more elaborate than that of his men, and a golden boar's head had been sewn into the breast of his tunic. He wore a crimson cloak that fell to the ground behind him. Like the rest of his men he wore a close-fitting, open-faced helm. As with all else, it didn't look Imperial. Everything was too bright, too clean. Too beautiful.

'I answer to the Lord Schwarzhelm,' Bloch responded, keeping his voice carefully neutral. 'Who are you?'

'Captain Erasmus Euler of the First Averheim Reavers, and Schwarzhelm has no authority here. You've overstayed your welcome in Averland, Commander Bloch.'

Bloch was instantly irritated by the man's manner. If he'd known who he was, why ask for a name?

'I was warned there was a shortage of gratitude in Averheim,' he replied coolly. 'I can live with that. Let us pass, and we'll be on our way.'

'Your men may pass. You're wanted by the elector.'

'Is that right?' Bloch let his free hand creep an inch closer towards his halberd stave. 'Sadly, that won't be possible. Your elector has no jurisdiction over me. Like I said, I answer to Schwarzhelm.'

Euler withdrew a step and grasped his sword-hilt. His men did likewise.

'Don't push your luck, commander. You're outnumbered two to one.'

Kraus let slip a low, growling laugh. 'I knew it,' he muttered. 'We'll tear 'em apart.'

That settled it.

'As far as I'm concerned, you can bring it on, captain,' said Bloch, sweeping up his halberd in both hands and swinging the blade into position. 'We've been fighting greenskins for weeks. If you reckon you're a match for them, be my guest to prove it.'

Behind him, Bloch's men instantly snapped into position, halberds gripped for the charge, faces set like flint.

For a moment, a ghost of doubt crossed Euler's face. The two forces stood facing one another, both bristling for combat.

Then, from behind the camp, there came sudden cries of alarm. There were horses galloping and metal clashing against metal. A trumpet blared out in warning. A long, strangled scream was followed by a massed roar of aggression. Something was attacking the camp's defences from the far side, and whatever it was had hit it hard.

Euler stared round in confusion, backing away from Bloch's column, clearly unsure how to react.

'Reiksguard!' came a cry from within the encampment. At that, some of Euler's guards started to run back through the entrance, swords drawn. Others stayed with their captain, confusion and apprehension marked on their faces.

'*Reiksguard?*' asked Kraus, incredulous. 'What in the nine hells are they doing here?'

'Morr knows,' said Bloch, picking out Euler with his blade and preparing to charge. 'And I don't care. We've had the luck of Ranald here, so let's use it.'

At that, with the tight-knit, lung-bursting roar they'd perfected out on the grasslands, Bloch's halberdiers surged forwards, blades lowered and murder in their eyes.

Grosslich sat on his throne of obsidian in the pinnacle, watching the clouds churn above him. Lightning streaked down, licking against the Iron Tower and screaming down to the courtyard far below. The aethyric fire still coursed through the air, staining everything a deep, throbbing red. Even the daylight failed to penetrate it. The maelstrom gathering above the Tower made the waking hours almost as dark as night.

The daemons still swam in the shifting winds, endlessly circling the Tower, forever screeching their delight at being embodied in the world of mortals. Every so often they would swoop down to ground level and bring up some unfortunate to be torn to pieces for their pleasure. Not that the denizens of Averheim seemed capable of horror any longer. They'd been transformed into shambling automata, driven by the will of the Stone and blind to all else.

The Stone controlled the slaves, and Natassja controlled the Stone. Now that there was no longer any attempt to hide what they were doing from the Empire, Grosslich's position had become more perilous than ever. He was no fool. He'd known it when Alptraum had tried to manipulate him, and he recognised the signs again. He'd never be as powerful as Natassja in terms of sorcery, and there were few other cards left to play.

As Grosslich brooded on the throne, chin resting on his fist, a daemon slipped through the iron walls of the pinnacle chamber and pirouetted in front of him. He'd tried to place wards to prevent them from doing that, but the whole city was so drenched in dark magic that it had proved impossible. They were deeply irritating, these capricious horrors, and they enjoyed provoking him.

The daemon stopped spinning and blew a kiss towards him. She was impossibly lithe, as they all were, shimmering like a mirage, her flesh taut and rich and tantalisingly exposed. For some reason the fact that her hands were crab-like claws and her feet ended in talons failed to detract from the powerful allure. Even as steeped as he'd become in the arts of magic, it was hard not to rush towards her, arms extended, ready to be lost in the delicious pain of oblivion.

'What d'you want?' Grosslich drawled, at once aroused and put out by her presence.

'To watch you, mortal,' she replied. The voice was like a choir of children, all slightly out of sync with one another. 'It amuses me. Your desire is palpable. Why not give in to me? I might not even kill you afterwards.'

Grosslich sneered. 'And I might not kill you.'

'Kill *me*? Impossible.'

'Maybe. I'm learning new things every day.'

The daemon laughed, revealing her pointed incisors and a long, flickering tongue like a lizard's.

'What a good boy,' she said. 'That'll keep her happy.'

Grosslich scowled. The inane chatter was supremely annoying. Eschenbach would be here soon, and there were important matters to discuss. The Steward was one of the few humans left in the city with a mind of his own. Whatever she'd said about it, Natassja had destroyed his ambitions in that damned rite of hers. He had no wish to rule over a city of psychotic imbeciles.

'I could help you, you know,' said the daemon, sliding up to the throne and draping herself across one of the arms. Her fragrance was powerful, as intoxicating as the root.

'I doubt that,' said Grosslich, ignoring her and hoping she'd go away.

'Don't be so sure. You have no idea what she's going to do.'

'And you do.'

'Of course. I know everything.'

The daemon came close. Her eyes were as yellow as a cat's, blank and pupil-less. Grosslich looked away too late. The orbs were mirrored. He caught himself in them, faint and rippling as if seen from underwater. There were other things in there too, fragments of other men's dreams and nightmares. Terrible things. The stuff of which daemons were made.

'Just what do you think her ambition is in all this?' the daemon murmured. Her choir of voices became ever more seductive, curling around the syllables like the caress of a lover. 'Do you think she'll rest content turning this city into a playground for the likes of us?'

'She has what she wanted,' said Grosslich, trying to avoid the eyes. The daemon's sweet musk was beginning to affect his judgement. 'This is what we planned.'

The daemon laughed again.

'I know you don't really think that. She's given you a fortress of puppets. Of course, *we* love it here. At the end of time the whole world will be like this. In the meantime, I feel sorry for you. We don't like to see a handsome man disappointed.'

'There's no pity in your body,' Grosslich growled. 'You're an *absence* of pity, so don't try to tell me you feel sorry for anything.' He turned to face her. 'Your words don't impress me, for all they impress you. You're *nothing* next to a man, daemon. You're just echoes of our dreams. You talk of the realm of the senses. You cannot know it, not like we can. You exist only in a world of reflections.'

He lashed out and clasped his gauntlet around her neck, squeezing the aethyr-born muscle tight. The daemon's eyes widened in surprise.

'*Feel* it,' he hissed. '*This* is the flesh you can never know. You may mock us, but you envy this.'

The daemon blinked and was suddenly several feet away, eyes shining with delight. Grosslich's armoured fingers snapped closed on thin air.

'Masterful!' she laughed, rubbing her neck lasciviously. 'I knew a man like you once. He said much the same thing. I kept his eyes as baubles.'

'Just say what you came to say or go,' muttered Grosslich. The daemon sickened him. Much of what he'd done had begun to sicken him.

She sidled back close.

'Natassja cares nothing for the realms of men,' she whispered. 'The Stone is just the beginning. This is all about her. You'd better act fast, or you'll be the one with no eyes.'

'And what do you advise?'

The daemon looked suddenly serious. Her pouting lips calmed down.

'You have an army,' she breathed. 'Only a mortal can command it. That's the one thing you still own. Remember that.'

Then she shot up into the air, spinning with the supernatural grace of her sisters, diving and swooping with astonishing suppleness.

'I've enjoyed this chat,' she laughed, winking at him as she circled around the chamber. 'Come outside and see me some time. I'm sure we could have fun.'

Then she was gone, slipping through the window as if the glass wasn't there. Grosslich slumped back on the throne, his mood darkening. He knew better than to trust the words of daemons.

Still, they rankled.

A chime sounded from outside the chamber. Grosslich flicked a finger and the doors slid open. Eschenbach shuffled in. He looked emaciated, his skin drawn tight over his bones and his eyes staring from their sockets. The Dark Prince only knew why – there was plenty of food in the Tower storerooms. Perhaps he'd lost his appetite.

'You asked to see me, your excellency.'

'I did, but I've changed my mind,' said Grosslich. 'I have another task for you. A simple one.'

Eschenbach swallowed.

'Go down to the dungeons,' said Grosslich. 'Enter the

chamber of the Stone. Discover what the mistress intends
for it. Then report back.'

Eschenbach's eyes widened, exposing red threads of veins.
'You cannot mean...' he began. His fingers started to tremble. 'Why do you not–'

He seemed to see the futility of the question, and stopped
talking. Resignation shuddered through his tortured body.
He, like so many others, had found service in the Tower less
fulfilling than he might have hoped.

'I will do it,' he said, and bowed as low as his rearranged
spine would let him. Then he was gone, limping back down
into the central shaft of the Tower, broken in spirit as well
as in body.

Grosslich remained silent. He gestured with another finger, and the braziers in the chamber guttered and went out.
Alone in the dark, surrounded by the whoops of the daemons in the sky outside, the Elector of Averland pondered
his next move.

As things stood, they didn't look good. He was alone, lord
of a realm of nightmares, master of nothing. Something
would have to be done.

Something *would* be done.

CHAPTER FOURTEEN

Skarr kicked his steed forwards, hacking on either side with his broadsword. Grosslich's men scattered before him, running for cover. The rest of the Reiksguard swept along in his wake, cutting down any of the guards too slow or too stupid to get out of the way. Behind the horsemen came the footsoldiers he'd equipped over the past few days. They were a ragged tide of soldiery, wielding their weapons clumsily and clad in a whole range of drab peasant garb, but at least they were enthusiastic. They ransacked the rows of tents, stabbing at any men they found inside or dragging them out to be butchered.

The raid seemed to have taken Grosslich's camp entirely by surprise. Storming the embankment at the west end of the enclosure had taken mere moments, and the defence was cleared out by the first cavalry charge. Once the perimeter had been seized, the interior was theirs and the knights ran amok, slaughtering any who got in their way.

A knot of the elector's men, two dozen strong, some still with helmets or breastplates missing, mustered near the centre of the encampment, swords clutched with both hands, desperate to form some kind of resistance.

Skarr laughed harshly.

'Reiksguard, to me!' he cried, spurring his horse on. The stand was brave but foolish. Few detachments in the Empire could withstand a massed charge from nearly thirty of the Emperor's finest knights, and these startled mercenaries would barely make him miss a stride.

The spearhead of Reiksguard thundered onwards, hooves drumming on the beaten earth. Even before the crash of the impact half the defenders had broken, turning and running wildly towards the east end of the encampment.

Skarr kicked his horse on and the knights crunched into the wavering band of men. Hooves lashed out, cracking ribs, breaking necks and knocking men cold. Behind them came the flickering blades, swooping down to kill like raptors. The few survivors turned tail, fleeing in almost comical terror, their spirits broken by the speed and power of the charge.

Skarr pursued them with cold efficiency, cutting down any he caught up with, maintaining the gallop. The momentum took him to the other end of the camp.

As the far embankment neared he slowed his pace, struck by the sight before him. There was fresh fighting ahead. The captain of Grosslich's troops was surrounded, pushed back into the compound in a concerted assault by a column of halberdiers in Reikland colours. Caught between twin attacks, the elector's troops were being hammered into submission.

The rest of the Reiksguard squadron drew alongside Skarr. Behind them, the camp had been overrun. The preceptor's newly recruited troops were going after the few defenders that remained, killing with a zeal that promised good things for the future.

'Relieve those halberdiers,' Skarr ordered his men, kicking his horse back into a canter. 'Let's finish this.'

The Reiksguard plunged into action again, tearing through the dispirited resistance with disdainful ease. The halberdiers were equally savage. They fought expertly in close formation, supporting one another at the shoulder and wheeling to avoid the flank attack. Their captain, a thick-set man with the look of a brawler about him, was devastating at close range, wielding his heavy halberd as a lesser man might swing a longsword. Even as Skarr watched, he felled Grosslich's commander.

'Here's my name *and* business!' the man cried as he plunged his blade straight through the stricken captain's neck. His comrades laughed coarsely, finishing off the remainder of the defenders with a savage, feral energy.

They were serious fighters, thought Skarr, almost unconsciously hacking down a fleeing soldier as he careered from their assault and into his path. Possibly useful fighters.

The slaughter came to an end. In truth, it had been rank butchery. Several hundred of Grosslich's troops lay dead, strewn across the camp, their broken bodies trampled into the dirt by the rampaging peasant mob.

Skarr dismounted heavily, thumping to the ground in his plate armour. He'd have to impose some discipline on the worst of his troops in time, but for now they could enjoy their victory. Sterner trials lay ahead for them.

He strode over the heaps of crimson-clad corpses towards the halberdier captain. The man was being congratulated by his peers, all of whom were still whooping with the brutal enjoyment of the kill.

'Master halberdier!' cried Skarr, extending his gauntlet in friendship. 'I'd thought there were no foes of Grosslich left in Averland.'

The halberdier turned to face him and returned the handshake. He was grinning from ear to ear, his face splattered with blood and with a purple swelling disfiguring his left eye. He could have stumbled out of a fight in any disreputable tavern of the Empire.

'Nor I,' he said. 'That was good riding.'

The remainder of the Reiksguard dismounted. Most walked over to Skarr, swords in hand; others began to fan back through the camp, hunting for survivors.

'We could use men like yours,' said Skarr, looking over the body of halberdiers with approval. 'You're wearing Reikland colours. Who's your commander?'

'The Lord Schwarzhelm,' replied the halberdier, still smiling.

Skarr moved instantly. His dagger was out of his scabbard before the man could move. He whirled the halberdier round, got his left arm in a lock and hooked the blade up against his neck, pressing hard against the muscle. By the time the man knew what was happening, he was pinned.

'Schwarzhelm?' Skarr hissed, his good mood immediately shifting to a cold, heartfelt hatred. 'Well, this *is* my lucky day. Now tell me how to get to him, or you die where you stand.'

Streissen lay in ruins. The walls to the north of the town were little more than piles of rubble, smoking gently from the cannon barrage. The boar's head of Grosslich had been torn down and replaced with the Imperial griffon and the old colours of Averland. The dead lay in their hundreds on the streets, mostly defenders, too numerous for the priests of Morr to handle. Women wept openly as carts were loaded with cadavers, some of them showing signs of mistreatment after the combat had ended. All had been stripped of their weapons and valuable items. The dogs of war in Volkmar's army had paid scant regard to the conventions of combat and only the strenuous efforts of the warrior priests had prevented a wholesale massacre of innocents.

Resistance had been sporadic during the assault, and most of it had concentrated around the large central square, once enclosed by richly decorated houses and an elegant, tree-lined fountain. Now the fountainhead was smashed and the cobbled space covered in a stinking brown lake. The trees had been felled for firewood and the grandest townhouse taken over by Volkmar's retinue.

As the long, slow task of securing the city began, the Grand Theogonist sat in the uppermost chamber, flanked by his captains of war. He had taken the high seat, a tall-backed chair carved from a single block of oak. The others sat in two long rows on either side, facing inwards. The subject of their interrogation stood alone, dwarfed by the armoured figures bearing down on him.

'That's *all* you know?' Volkmar snarled, leaning forwards, his hands gripping the chair arms tightly. His hard face was twisted with disbelief.

The man standing before him didn't look like he was lying. He hardly looked like he could stammer his name out. Hans von Bohm, mayor of Streissen, had had plenty of time to regret his delay in coming to terms. The stench of smoke and burned flesh was a potent reminder of his failure.

'It is, my lord,' the mayor insisted. 'The elector–'

'The traitor.'

'The *traitor* sent us men from Averheim to bolster the garrison. They were all normal men, good stock from the land around these parts. None of them were tainted. If they had been, we wouldn't have taken them.'

Volkmar grunted with dissatisfaction, turning to Roll.

'Is he telling the truth?' he asked his confessor.

Roll shrugged. 'There's no aura of a lie.'

Volkmar turned back to the mayor.

'If you weren't in league with Grosslich, why did you not submit earlier? There are many deaths on your head.'

The mayor looked dumbfounded. 'We had barely time to read your demands! No war has been declared. What was I supposed to think, when an army suddenly appeared from the north and began to deploy? I was charged with the defence of this place.'

'And the column of fire did not alert you? The lack of contact from the Empire? At no stage did you doubt the loyalty of your new masters?'

'There had been no time!' cried the mayor, his exasperation getting the better of his fear. 'We are loyal subjects of the Empire, and you're asking us to know the impossible!'

Volkmar rose from his seat, glowering like thunder. The mayor shrank back, looking around him for some kind of support. None came.

'There are no excuses for ignorance,' the Theogonist said, looking like he wanted to leap across the floor and tear the man apart. 'You were placed in authority here. You should have acted sooner.'

The mayor said nothing, and hope left his eyes. Like a bewildered child asked to learn some lesson beyond his capability, he froze.

'Go now,' ordered Volkmar, bristling with suppressed anger. 'Gather what remains of your men and see that they're re-ordered into marching companies. They're under my command now. Fail me in this and I'll have you hanged.'

The mayor bowed and scuttled from the chamber, face flushed and sweaty. As he left, Volkmar slowly took his seat again. He sat, brooding, for a few moments. The sound of men working to clear the streets rose up from outside the townhouse, mixed with the sound of weeping and bells tolling.

'How quickly can we move again?' Volkmar asked at last.

'Whenever you order it, my lord,' said Gruppen.

'Then we leave within the hour,' said Volkmar.

'The men need rest,' objected Maljdir.

'They will get none.'

The big Nordlander raised his bearded chin, looking defiant. 'If you expect them to fight when they reach Averheim, they cannot march again.'

Volkmar looked at his priest darkly. It was one thing to have dissension from others of the command council, but to have it from one of his own retinue was intolerable.

'Are you telling me how to conduct this war, priest?' Volkmar asked, and there was a low note of threat in his gravelly voice.

Maljdir held the Theogonist's gaze. 'It is my counsel,' he replied. 'Why have a council of war, if you will not listen to its views?'

There was an intake of breath from one of the more junior captains. Roll, used to the fearless ways of his comrade, made no sign.

Volkmar's face went pale with anger. When he spoke, the muscles in his broad neck tensed.

'In the years we have fought together, you and I, you have never dared to speak thus. Perhaps you have more to say.'

'I do,' replied Maljdir. 'There were deaths here that should never have taken place. You know me well, Theogonist. Never have I hesitated to kill in the name of the law, but we could have taken Streissen without this bloodshed.'

'They were *heretics*,' hissed Volkmar, eyes blazing. 'They deserved nothing better. This will warn the others.'

'Heretics? They were instruments, as blind as moles.'

'So you *are* telling me how to conduct the war.' Volkmar's voice lowered, and the threat remained in it.

'And if I am? You've not commanded an army since your return from the Wastes, my lord. What happened to you would change any man. You never relished slaughter before.'

Volkmar leapt to his feet and grabbed the Staff of Command. The shaft burst into a blazing golden light, cracking and spitting as it channelled his rage.

'You *dare* to accuse me!'

Gruppen and Roll rose from their seats, consternation etched on their faces.

'We don't have time for this,' warned Roll.

'That is right, confessor,' spat Volkmar, staring belligerently at Maljdir. 'Retract your words, priest, or this matter will be taken further.'

For a moment, Maljdir's fingers crept towards the handle of Bloodbringer, still by his side. He remained seated, his vast bulk crammed into a scholar's chair. His broad face was sullen and defiant.

Then, slowly, he withdrew.

'I do not intend disloyalty,' he said, his jaw tight. 'But the men need more time.'

Volkmar remained on his feet. The staff continued to shimmer with angry golden energy. No one spoke. Eventually, grudgingly, Volkmar let the aura fade and flicker out.

'I will consider it. For now, this council is over. We have real work to do.'

He shot a final look of warning at Maljdir, then swept from the chamber, cloak streaming out from behind him, staff thudding on the floor as he went.

Once he'd gone, Gruppen moved his hand discreetly away from the pommel of his sword and relaxed.

'What're you *doing*?' said Roll to Maljdir.

'He's losing it. Surely you can see it.'

'I see nothing but your thick neck.'

'This is personal for him. He wants to make up for Archaon. Tell me truly, does this fury seem *normal* to you?'

Roll shook his head. 'You should have spoken out earlier. Averheim beckons. He will lead us there, whatever qualms you've suddenly developed.'

Maljdir clambered to his feet. 'If he directs it at Grosslich, I'll be right beside him. If he takes it out on our own kind, I'll not stand aside again.'

He hefted Bloodbringer lightly, and his expression was grim.

'You may count on it.'

Bloch froze. The dagger parted his skin, worming through the flesh. The pain was sharp. His day had just gone from surprising to downright insane.

'Get back!' he yelled at his men, some of whom had started to edge forwards. He knew something of Reiksguard from his time in the ranks. They were terrifying bastards and he had no doubt the preceptor would twist home his knife in an instant if he felt the slightest justification for it.

'Time's running out,' the preceptor warned, keeping the metal close.

Bloch felt a line of sweat run down his temple. After all he'd done, this continual ingratitude was getting ridiculous.

'I've no idea where he is,' he said, trying to keep his voice as steady as possible. 'On Sigmar's honour I don't. Now why don't you tell me why you're so happy to kill me to find out?'

The Reiksguard kept his scarred, ugly face close. Bloch could feel the man's breath on his cheek.

'Not good enough,' he snarled. Something had made him very angry indeed. 'One more chance.'

Bloch swallowed. The knife dug a little deeper. A hot trickle of blood slipped down his collar. It would be important to get the next few words right.

'I can't tell you, because I don't know,' he said, speaking slowly and carefully. 'The last time I saw him was weeks ago. He ordered me to retake Black Fire Keep from the orcs. I did that. Now I come back here, and everybody wants to kill me. Perhaps I wouldn't be so angry about that if I had any idea why.'

The Reiksguard paused. Bloch dared to start hoping again. From the corner of his eye he could see Kraus, itching to pile in.

'You weren't in Averheim with him?'

'No, though I was hoping to find him there.'

Another pause.

'You really have no idea why I might want to spill blood to find him?'

'No idea at all. Less than none. Though if you do find a lead, perhaps you'd let me come along with you. There's a lot I'd like to ask him too.'

As suddenly as he'd struck, the preceptor withdrew the knife. Bloch spun out of the armlock and staggered away, feeling his neck gingerly. His men took a menacing pace forwards again.

'Enough!' he rasped, waving them back. Something very strange was going on, and this was his best chance to find out what. 'Morr's balls, that *hurt*.'

The preceptor didn't look obviously sorry. He and his men radiated aggression.

'Be thankful I didn't finish the job. If I hadn't seen you fighting against Grosslich's men, you'd have died a lot sooner.'

Bloch winced. That didn't make him feel a lot better.

'Look, we could put all this behind us if you'd just tell me what in the nine hells is happening here. When I headed east, there was a battle for succession going on. Now it seems like this Grosslich is in charge and he's killing anyone left who isn't him. I'm pretty sure that's not what Schwarzhelm intended.'

The preceptor regarded him suspiciously. His knights stayed poised to attack. It didn't seem to matter to them that it was thirty knights and a rabble of ill-trained peasant filth against two hundred battle-hardened infantry. Reiksguard were crazy like that. They'd take on anyone.

'You haven't heard about Lord Helborg, then?' asked the Reiksguard darkly.

Bloch shook his head. The last he'd heard, Helborg had been in Nuln.

'Then we have much to discuss, you and I,' said the preceptor. 'I will tell you what I know. Perhaps you can explain the rest. Then, once things are a little clearer between us, I'll decide what to do with you.'

Another drear, cold day was drawing to a close. Blankets of cloud obscured the sunset, but the darkness stealing from the east came on quickly enough. Helborg stood on a ridge, his gaze drawn north. He was alone. The rest of the army was busy erecting camp half a mile away. While the light remained, the Marshal surveyed the country ahead, planning the next day's march, weighing up the dangers ahead, choosing where to recover more supplies, horses and fodder to fuel their onward progress.

The army had reached the edge of the highlands. To the north the land fell away sharply, turning from barren scrub into the rich grassland for which Averland was famous. From Helborg's position, right on the summit of a scarp on the borders of the moor-country, he could see for miles. The heart of the province beckoned, its grasses ruffled by the ceaseless wind, its open skies marred by storms.

The column of fire weighed on his mind. Now, just as the army was poised on the cusp of descending into the interior, it was ever-present, visible even during the middle of the day. The broken clouds swirled above it, drawn inwards as if summoned by a Celestial magister of awesome power.

The Marshal gazed at the angry glow for a while, reflecting on the paucity of men he had under arms. Nearly two thousand now marched with him, the gleanings of Leitdorf's ancestral lands. As a result of Skarr's plunder he had money to pay them, supplies to give them and weapons to arm them with. That might well not be enough. The more Leitdorf told him what was in Marius's notebooks, the more he dreaded the encounter to come. Not for his own sake – he was a fighting man, and battle had never held any terrors for him – but for the sake of the Empire. If the corruption was not staunched at its source then it would spread as surely as the pox in a whorehouse. The Empire was already overstretched with the endless war in the north. A drawn-out campaign in Averland would be disastrous. Maybe even fatal.

Two thousand men. On such meagre forces did so much depend.

'My lord.'

Helborg turned to see a group of Reiksguard standing to attention. They were led by Rainer Hausman, the one he'd sent ahead to scout the flanks of the rearguard.

'I gave instructions to be left alone,' he said.

Hausman bowed in apology.

'I know. We have a prisoner.'

As the man spoke, his captive stepped forwards.

It was perfectly clear the man was no prisoner. He stood nearly a head taller than the knights around him and was more powerfully built than them even out of his armour. His beard looked a little greyer, his skin a little tighter, his stance a little less upright, but there could be no mistake about it.

It was him. After so many nights of dreaming of that mighty face, contorted with rage and madness, he was back.

Helborg felt his blood begin to pump. The wound in his shoulder suddenly flared, as if recognising the man that had dealt it. His hand flew for his sword quicker than thought and his fingers curled around the grip. His jaw locked. For once, his fluent speech deserted him. His knuckles went white.

Schwarzhelm stood motionless. His face was as grim as it had ever been. He said nothing. The Reiksguard withdrew, leaving the two peerless warriors alone, exposed on the escarpment, facing one another as the wind whipped about them. From the north-west, a rumble of distant thunder rolled across the plains.

Helborg took a step forwards, face taut with rage. The anger burned him; the deep, smouldering sense of injustice that had burned since the duel in Averheim. For so many nights, drifting on the borders of death, that rage had sustained him. For so long he'd lived for nothing more than the thought of vengeance. Now his fury flared into the real world, animating his sinews, firing his lungs, screaming at him to wield the blade.

It felt unreal, like the lingering memory of a dream. The grip on his sword grew tighter. He couldn't lift his arm.

On the far horizon, the column of fire flared, angry and raw.

Schwarzhelm moved first. Keeping his gestures obvious, unthreatening, he unfastened a naked sword from his belt. The blade was notched halfway along its length. In the low light, the metal looked black with age. There were runes on the steel, obscured in the darkness.

Helborg remained frozen, driven by fury, imprisoned by indecision. This was *wrong*. Schwarzhelm was his brother.

He was a traitor.

The big man edged forwards, carrying the Sword of Vengeance on his upturned palms. As he drew closer, Helborg saw the grief on his face. The man was wracked with it. The last time he'd seen those features, they'd been lit with a fire of madness. Now what was left was grey and empty, like embers that had long since burned into husks.

Schwarzhelm halted less than a yard away. He extended his arms, offering Helborg the Klingerach. With stiff fingers,

Helborg loosed his grip on his borrowed blade, raised his right hand and took it at the hilt.

The weight was familiar, the balance almost the same as before. Helborg bore it up. The spirit of the weapon was coiled within, as ancient and powerful as the lost forges on which it had been made. As Helborg took the grip, he felt death locked into the instrument. It had killed for millennia, this thing, drinking deep of the blood of men and their enemies alike. It thirsted still. It would thirst until the end of time, never satisfied, never at peace.

Only one taint remained on its glinting surface, the shard Schwarzhelm had taken from it. That had still to be healed.

Schwarzhelm sank to one knee then, his limbs moving awkwardly. Only then, kneeling before Helborg, did he speak. When they came, his words were shaky and thick with emotion.

'This is yours, Kurt. Wield it as your heart dictates.'

The tide of rage broke. Schwarzhelm's voice unlocked it.

'Damn you!' Helborg roared, snatching up the blade in two hands and raising it high. 'Damn your arrogance! You should *not* have come.'

Helborg held the Klingerach high over his head, grip tight, poised to strike. He locked it in place, shivering with anger, waiting for the resolve to bring it down. Schwarzhelm bared his neck, looking Helborg in the eye, refusing to flinch. He said nothing more.

I will find the one who did this to me.

Still Helborg hesitated. He felt as if his fury had become so great that it would destroy them both if he moved. The fire within him raged beyond all control, greedy and consuming. His shoulder flared again, sending jets of pain coursing through his body. The wound goaded him, his anger goaded him, the sword goaded him.

My name itself is vengeance.

Still they remained, locked in a grotesque masque of execution. Heartbeats drummed, heavy and lingering. The runefang wavered, eager to plunge.

When it fell at last, toppling from his fingers to land in the grass, he hardly heard it. It rolled away, discarded in the mud like a child's toy.

'Not this way.'

Helborg reached down. Extending a hand, he raised Schwarzhelm to his feet. The big man hauled himself up slowly, unready to face him again.

The anger was still there. The grief was stronger now. Even during the darkest times, it had always been stronger. They were the titans of the Empire, the two of them, the foundations upon which all else was built. That could never be forgotten, not while any shred of forgiveness existed within the world.

Helborg looked into the man's face. There were the familiar features he had fought alongside for so many years, the cracked cheeks, the deep-set eyes, the unsmiling mouth. The madness had gone from them. Schwarzhelm was diminished in some respects, unchanged in others.

Emperor's Champion.

'*Brother*,' said Helborg, gripping him by the shoulders.

Schwarzhelm met his gaze. The old warrior had seen it all. Loss and victory, faith and treachery. He'd witnessed the fires of war tear across the Empire. He'd watched, defiant, as the tides of ruin had swept down from the wastes of the north and the hopes of mankind had dimmed. In all of this he had been unmoving, implacable, emotionless.

Only now did he falter. Only now, as Helborg embraced him at last, did his eyes glisten with tears. Clumsily, he returned the gesture, his mighty arms locked round the shoulders of his rival. There they stood, together once more as brothers in arms, the bitterness purged, the anger drained away.

The Reiksguard watched, silent as tombs, none daring to move. At their side was Verstohlen, lost in contemplation. After so long in the wilderness, the circle had been completed. About this, as with so much else, he had been wrong.

Forgiveness had been sought. Honour had been satisfied. Restitution had been made.

* * *

Achendorfer hurried through the corridors of the under-Tower, clutching the book to his breast as he always did. He had no choice. The leather-bound tome had merged with the fingers of his left hand. The book was one with him now, and he was one with the book. Little by little, the pages of spells and arcane recipes of death within had melted away from the parchment, all except the one he needed, the one he recited every day. The one that coaxed the Stone into life.

All around him, muffled moans and sighs ran down the twisting passages. Every so often a pale hand would reach out from the ornately carved walls, clutching at him desperately. So many slaves had been trapped within the filigree of iron that he'd lost count of them. They couldn't die in there, but neither was their agonised existence truly life. Some brave souls retained enough of a sense of self to implore him to release them, their fingers scrabbling against the cage walls to gain his attention.

Achendorfer ignored them. Where could they go, even if they were set free? All of Averheim was a furnace now, a shrine to the singular lust of one individual. They didn't matter to her, no more than they had in their former miserable lives.

He turned a corner sharply and followed a winding path between high, arching walls of obsidian. He went as surely as a rat in a cellar. He knew all the routes, all the myriad ways of the under-Tower. Another gift from the queen. Even when the walls shifted, as they often did, he could still follow them.

Achendorfer scurried quickly, knowing the penalties for missing an appointment. On his right, the wall suddenly fell away, exposing a huge shaft. Hot air blossomed up from it, flaked with ash. Deep down below, massive engines toiled and churned. Natassja's thousands of minions had been busy. Such infernal devices magnified her power many times over, storing the energies of the Stone in vast crystal cylinders. The machines growled angrily as they turned, fed incessantly by a host of Stone-slaves.

Achendorfer pressed on, feeling the book crackle expect-antly under his touch. How long had it lain, forgotten, in the library of the Averburg? It had been a spoil of war, prob-ably, recovered by an elector count and dumped, unread, in his stash of trophies and trinkets. Now, after so many thou-sands of years, the words were being heard again in the lands of the living. Perhaps the author, if some shred of him still existed, was pleased about that.

Achendorfer left the shaft behind and drew closer to the heart of the under-Tower. The walls began to throb with a suf-fused pink light, bleeding from behind the black iron like the organs of a dissected corpse. Natassja liked those little touches.

He paused for a second, reflecting on how far he'd come. It was five years ago that the dreams had started, leading him to the library under the Averburg and its terrible secret. Back then Natassja had kept her face covered, whispering secrets to him and promising the wealth of Araby if he would inter-pret the scripts for her. And so he had done so, working night and day in the gloomy recesses of the archives, his skin turn-ing grey and his hair falling free in clumps.

It had been worth it. All the pain, all the humiliation. He was now her *true* lieutenant in the Tower, whatever Grosslich thought about such things. Achendorfer had been given gifts beyond measure and had seen things no mortal could dream of. He had a personal guard of fifty augmented dog-soldiers, exclusive chambers near the centre of the under-Tower and a playroom lined with shackled, quiescent pets.

All of that was immaterial, of course, besides the *power*. That was what convinced him he'd been right to turn. For the first time in his life he held the lives of men in his hands. The knowledge of that thrilled him. By the time this was over, she would make him a god. That's what she said. The prospect made him moisten his purple lips with anticipa-tion. She'd promised so much, and always kept her word.

A scream broke out from up ahead, resounding down the curved walls. Achendorfer smiled. So it had started.

He came to a set of double doors, each inscribed with a

glowing lilac sigil of Slaanesh. He gestured with his free hand and they slid open.

The room beyond was circular and lined with marble. There was no furniture or adornment, just perfectly smooth, faintly reflective walls. There was no ceiling either. The polished walls went up, on and on, hundreds of feet, until they emerged near the summit of the Tower, far above the roofs of Averheim. The laughter of daemons could be heard from the distant opening, and fire flickered around the rim.

A single figure crouched on the floor, hands clasped over his ears. Odo Heidegger, Templar of Sigmar.

'So you know the truth,' said Achendorfer, closing the doors behind him.

Heidegger looked at him imploringly. His skin was white with fear and horror. He'd torn his scarlet robes apart. Beneath them Achendorfer could see protruding ribs, stark across the man's wasted torso.

'What is this... *madness*?' he cried, spittle flying from his dribbling mouth, eyes staring.

Achendorfer smiled.

'What you've helped to create. All of this has been built by you, witch hunter.'

Heidegger's horror grew. His mind, for so long on the brink of insanity, was breaking. Natassja had lifted the veil from him, and the pleasure of the moment was exquisite.

'You killed every enemy who could have worked against us,' said Achendorfer. 'You delivered Alptraum to us. You killed Morven and let Tochfel be taken. You burned the rebellious and tortured the questioning. The queen is pleased with your work. She asked me to thank you in person.'

Heidegger looked like he might be sick, but there was nothing to retch up in his ravaged frame. He fell to his knees and wracking sobs shook his body.

'No,' he gasped. 'This is an illusion. I have been working for the Lord Sigmar, who protects and guides. Long may He–'

Achendorfer laughed, and his distended stomach wobbled beneath his white robes.

'Oh, you are subject to an illusion,' he admitted, coming to crouch down beside the distraught Templar. 'All that you did *before* was an illusion. This is real. This is more real than anything you've ever known.'

Heidegger's eyes began to flicker rapidly back and forth. Lines of foamy drool ran down his chin, glistening in the light of the fires above.

'I do not...' he started, then seemed to lose the power of speech. A low howl broke from his bloodstained lips.

'You were a *sadist*, master witch hunter,' whispered Achendorfer, loading his words with malice. 'You broke men for pleasure, whatever stories you told yourself about righteousness and duty. You were no different from us, except perhaps in honesty.'

From far above, the howling was reciprocated. Something was coming down the shaft, travelling fast.

'How many of our kind did you hunt down in your career? Dozens? Not a bad total. Now you have killed *hundreds*. All of them innocent. You are a murderer and a traitor, Herr Heidegger. The blood of Grosslich's treachery is on your hands. When your soul is dragged before the throne of your boy-god, he will not deign to look at it. It's *ours* now.'

The howling grew in volume. It was nearly upon them. Achendorfer got up and withdrew, looking down with satisfaction at the weeping, broken man before him. He backed towards the door, wishing he could stay to see the final act.

'Do not fool yourself that this death will be the last one,' he sneered. 'The Lord of Pain has plans for you. Eternity, in your case, will seem like a very long time.'

Then the daemons landed, slamming down from their screaming descent, eyes lit with infinite joy and malignance. They opened their fanged mouths, and the tongues flickered.

Achendorfer slipped through the doors and closed them just in time. As the barriers fell into place something heavy slammed against them and was taken up the shaft. There was no more screaming from the witch hunter. Heidegger's mortal body had been broken and the daemons had taken it. Unfortunately for him, physical death meant little to a daemon. Their sport was only just beginning.

The camp had settled for the night. Watch fires burned on the edge of it, throwing dancing shadows across the gorse. The guards patrolled the perimeter in detachments of six men, all fully armoured. The rotation was strict. Rumours still ran through the army about creatures made of bone and iron that stalked the moors at night, unstoppable and eager to drink the blood of men. Some said they had talons of wire and eyes that glowed with a pale flame, though the more level-headed troops were quick to disregard such exaggeration. Since leaving Drakenmoor, the columns had encountered nothing more threatening than foxes and kites, though they were all perfectly aware things would change as they neared the city. The watch fires were burned partly for security, but also to blot out the terrible fire on the western horizon, the one that never went out.

Verstohlen sat on the edge of one such camp fire, cradling a cup of beer in his hands and watching the men nearby as they noisily prepared for the night. They slept in their cloaks, huddled around their own small fires, laughing and telling obscene stories. Soldiers were the same across the whole Empire. Verstohlen remembered how they'd been at Turgitz. Then, as now, he was on the outside. Now, as then, men looked at him askance, questioning his presence, unsure of his role.

A dark shape loomed up from the shadows and stood before him. Unlike the rest of the troops, he didn't hurry on by. Verstohlen looked up, and his heart sank.

Rufus Leitdorf stood there, dressed in a breastplate and greaves, a sword at his belt. He'd lost weight, and looked less bloated than he'd done in Averheim. He still had the long hair and ruddy cheeks of old, but there was a residual hollow expression that marred his fleshy face.

'Verstohlen,' he said, and the tone was cold.

Verstohlen sighed. The meeting had to happen sooner or later. Perhaps best to get it over with now.

'My lord elector,' he said, inclining his head but remaining seated. 'Will you join me?'

Leitdorf shook his head.

'No,' he said. 'That might indicate to the world that we were friends. That is not the way of it, nor will it ever be.'

'I see.'

Leitdorf moved to stand in the light of the fire. His features, lit from below, looked distorted.

'I have spoken to the Lord Schwarzhelm,' he said. Verstohlen thought his voice was less haughty than before, and there was a gravity to it that he'd never noticed in Averheim. 'After reconciling with the Marshal, he apologised to me. Profusely. I have accepted it. Do you have anything you wish to add?'

'I'm glad you two made up,' said Verstohlen flatly. 'You don't want to prolong a feud with Schwarzhelm.'

'Is that all you have to say? Gods, your arrogance knows no bounds. Truly, I don't know why you came back. You offer us nothing now.'

Verstohlen swept to his feet in a single, fluid movement. He was taller than Leitdorf and considerably more deadly. Leitdorf, startled, held his ground, and the two of them faced off.

'There were errors,' Verstohlen said coolly. 'For these, I am sorry. But you *lived* with her, Leitdorf. If she could deceive you so completely, then perhaps you will understand why we made the decisions we did.'

'You should have contacted me. The war you started was unnecessary.'

'Don't fool yourself. If it hadn't been me, she'd have found another way to implicate you.' Verstohlen's face edged closer to the elector's, lit with threat. 'It might make you feel better to blame me for what took place, but you'd do well to reflect on your own conduct. If you'd not taken Natassja to your bed, there'd be no joyroot, and no corruption. We have erred, my lord, but you set this thing in motion.'

Leitdorf's hand slipped to his sword-belt.

'Even now, you dare–'

'I dare nothing. I state the facts.' Verstohlen shook his head in disgust. He was too tired for this. 'What do you want from me? Guilt? Oh, I've got plenty of that. We both have. Every night when I close my eyes I see Tochfel's face. He tried to warn me. Do you know what they did to him? They cut out his heart and replaced it with a ball of iron. *Your wife.*'

Verstohlen looked away, filled with revulsion by the memory.

'So don't try to pretend this is something you don't share responsibility for,' he muttered. 'We're all guilty, and we all had choices.'

Leitdorf removed his hand from his sword-belt. Verstohlen expected him to fly off into some tirade. To his surprise, the man remained calm.

'And you don't think much of mine, do you?' he said.

'It hardly matters now.'

'I disagree.' Leitdorf raised his chin defiantly. 'Whether you can stomach it or not, Herr Verstohlen, I am the elector now. Kurt Helborg leads my army, and Ludwig Schwarzhelm stands beside him. Soon my claim will be put to the test, and this time there can be no doubt about its legitimacy. Either we will die in battle, or I will rule Averland. Those are the only outcomes possible. Which one would you prefer?'

Verstohlen smiled grimly.

'I have no wish to see you dead, Leitdorf. Nor, for that matter, myself. But unless you've grown much wiser in a short space of time, I have no wish to see a dissolute count ruling in Averheim either. I do not say this to wound you, but your reputation does you no credit.'

Leitdorf returned the thin smile. 'So others have said.' He looked back over his shoulder. Near the centre of the encampment, Helborg was conversing with Schwarzhelm and the other captains. 'I see the warmth between us has not grown. If you'd spoken to me thus in Averheim, I'd have had you driven from the province in disgrace. Even now, a part of me would not regret to see you leave.'

He took a deep breath. As his chest rose and fell, Verstohlen noticed a book, wrapped in fabric and strapped to his belt. An unusual ornament for the battlefield.

'I've changed, Verstohlen,' he said, 'even if you haven't. Perhaps, when this is over, you'll see the proof of it.'

Verstohlen paused before replying. There *was* something different about the man. Not enough to be sure about, but hardly insignificant either.

'Perhaps I will,' was all he said, and he returned to the fire.

CHAPTER FIFTEEN

Holymon Eschenbach made his way down the spiral stairway in the central shaft of the Tower. As he limped from one step to the next, the dull rumble from below grew louder. The iron around him reverberated with the drumming sound of machines turning in the depths. The lower he climbed, the hotter it became. In every sense, he was coming to the source of things.

The stairs finally came to an end, and he stood at the base of the Tower. A long gallery led away in front of him, shrouded in shadow. There were doorways along either side, each with a different rune inscribed over the lintel. At the far end was an octagonal chamber containing an obsidian throne. There were no dog-soldiers around. The only noise was the muffled growl of the machines and the endless rush of the fire as it swirled in the air outside.

Eschenbach swallowed painfully, feeling his neck muscles constrict around the pitiful trickle of saliva he was capable of generating. His transformations had built up over the past few days. What he'd initially thought of as improvements had turned out to be serious handicaps. For some reason, the Dark Prince seemed displeased with him. Eschenbach knew of no cause for that – he'd faithfully served the elector since his coronation – but that didn't make the pain go away.

He knew his death was close. He could feel it stealing up behind him, padding in the dark like a cat. The only question was when, at whose hand, and how painful they'd make it. Some reward for the service he'd rendered.

Eschenbach shuffled forwards awkwardly, feeling his altered bones grind against one another. The rooms on either side of him were deserted. In the earliest days Natassja had conducted her experiments here, creating the first of the Stone-slaves. Now she had whole levels of the under-Tower devoted to her invasive surgeries, and the screams of the tormented and augmented echoed into the vaults like massed choruses in a cathedral. Dog-soldiers had been born in their thousands there, filled with bestial savagery and strength, utterly loyal and without fear.

Other horrors had been made. He'd seen trios of handmaidens, eyes glowing, scuttling through the lower reaches like a gaggle of bronze-tipped spiders. There were men's heads grafted on to women's bodies, eyeless and earless horrors stumbling around in the dark, lost beyond hope of rescue. They had no conceivable use in the war, just amusement value for the queen.

The earliest augmentation chambers now lay abandoned, the instruments lying where she'd left them, the tables stained with old blood and the stone walls as cold and silent as ice.

'I see you, Steward,' came her voice.

It was as familiar as a recurrent nightmare. Eschenbach shivered to his core. It came from the chamber at the end of the gallery.

There was no choice but to follow it. He limped forwards, trying to ignore the residue of agony in the open doorways as he passed them by.

Natassja was waiting for him. She sat on the throne, painfully elegant, searingly beautiful, radiating an aura of such terrifying power and malice that he nearly broke down in front of her before managing his first bow. Elector Grosslich had his powers, to be sure, but Natassja was something else.

'Why are you here?' she asked. There was little emotion in her voice. No anger, no spite, just a faint trace of boredom. She looked at him with the same casual disinterest a man might use on a particularly nondescript worm.

Eschenbach did his best to look her in the face.

'I was sent by the Lord Grosslich,' he rasped, feeling his jaw nearly seize up with the effort.

'For what purpose?'

'He wished me to check on the progress of the Stone.'

'He is welcome to come himself.'

'Shall I ask him to, my lady?'

Natassja shook her head. The movement was so slight, so perfectly poised. The queen seemed incapable of making a clumsy or ill-considered gesture. She was flawless, the living embodiment of a dark and perfect symmetry.

'No need. You may see for yourself.'

She raised a slender hand. Behind her throne the stone walls shifted. Soundlessly, gliding on rails of polished bronze, two panels slid backwards and out, revealing a roaring, blood-red space beyond. Something astonishing had been exposed out there – even Eschenbach's paltry skills could detect the volume of power being directed from below. He held back, reluctant to venture any closer.

'Take a look,' said Natassja. Her voice sang as softly as it ever did, but the tone of command was absolute. If she'd ordered him to pluck his own eyes out, he would have done it then without question. As he shuffled into place, Natassja rose from the throne, her dress falling about her like wine slipping down a grateful throat, and followed him.

The rear walls of the chamber opened out into the side of a massive shaft. The scale of it took Eschenbach's breath away. Sheer walls were clad in dark iron, moulded into a thousand pillars, arches and buttresses. Sigils of Slaanesh and Chaos had been beaten into the metal and shone an angry crimson. A hundred feet below, the base of the shaft was lost in a ball of slowly rotating fire. Above him, the columns soared into the far distance, lined along their whole length with elaborate sculptures and gothic ornamentation, before being lost in a fog of flame and shadow. Beautiful, terrible figures carved from iron and steel peered out from lofty perches on the high walls, their blank eyes bathed in flames.

Eschenbach knew without having to ask that the shaft went all the way to the summit of the Tower. Whenever he'd had his audiences with Grosslich, he'd been standing on top of it. The elector's chamber was nothing more than the fragile cap on this mighty well of fire. He wondered if Grosslich knew that.

The air inside was a mass of roaring, rushing and booming energy. Aethyric matter surged up the narrow space, pressing against its iron shackles, throbbing and fighting to be released. Now, at last, Eschenbach knew the purpose of the citadel. The whole thing was a device with a single purpose: to conduct the will of the Stone, to magnify and condense it into a point, far above the level of the city. As he watched the titanic levels of arcane puissance balloon along the spine of the Tower, as he heard the roar from below, he began to gain some appreciation of the scale of what had been achieved here.

'What do you think?' asked Natassja, standing by his side on the edge of the precipice. The rush of flames licked against her ankles, curling around her body like whips. The red light lit up her face, and her dark eyes glowed.

'Magnificent,' murmured Eschenbach, for a moment forgetting the pains in his mortal body. Beside this, nothing else seemed significant. 'It's magnificent.'

Natassja looked like she barely heard him. She was gazing into the shaft herself, eyes lost in rapture.

'This is what the suffering has achieved,' she murmured. 'The merest savage can inflict misery. We never act but for a higher purpose. The Stone is roused by agony. It *is* agony.'

Eschenbach listened, rapt. Natassja ignored him, speaking to herself.

'Every spar of this Tower, every stone of it, is in place for a reason. There lies the true beauty of this place. The *necessity* of it. Only that which is necessary is beautiful, and the beautiful is all that is necessary. That shall be my creed, when all is done here.'

She smiled, exposing her impossibly delicate incisors, tapered to a vanishing point of sharpness.

'My *creed*. Ah, the blasphemy of it.'

Natassja turned to Eschenbach.

'Enough of this. Have you seen what you came for?'

'I have, my queen.'

The pain in Eschenbach's body had lessened. His senses were operating at a heightened pitch of awareness. Visions rushed towards him like waking dreams. He saw the numberless host of Grosslich's men, legions of darkness, marching in endless ranks, unstoppable and remorseless. He saw the daemons circling the Tower like crows, ancient and malevolent, glorious and perfect. He saw the full extent of the Stone buried in the earth below, as black as the infinite void, a mere fragment of the future.

Some things began to make sense then. He no longer regretted his choices.

'Will you report back to your master?'

Eschenbach shook his head.

'No, my queen.'

'Good. So you know what will please me.'

'I do.'

'Then please me.'

Eschenbach grinned. The movement ripped his mouth at the edges, the muscles having long wasted into nothingness. He didn't care. Pain was nothing. There would be more pain, but that was nothing too. Only the Stone mattered.

He stepped from the ledge and was swept upwards by the vast power of the shaft. The flames seared him, crackling his flesh and curling it from the bone. He laughed as he was borne aloft, feeling his tortured face fracture. He was rising fast, buoyed up by the column of fire, speeding past the sigils of Slaanesh. They glowed back at him with pleasure. He had finally done well.

His eyes were burned away. He breathed in, and fire tore through his body and into his lungs. At the end, before his charred figure slammed into the roof of the shaft, he felt his soul pulled from his mortal form, immolated by the will of the Stone, sucked into its dark heart and consumed. In a final sliver of awareness, he knew just how much closer his sacrifice had brought forward the great awakening. Before he could be pleased by that, he was gone, the candle-flame of his life extinguished within the inferno of something far, far greater.

On her ledge below, Natassja remained still, watching the flames as they screamed past.

'Now then, Heinz-Mark,' she breathed, stretching out her hand and watching the torrents caress her flesh. 'Your servants are all gone. The time has come, I think, for you to face me.'

Helborg's army had descended from the highlands and made good progress across the rolling fields of Averland. The men had been organised into standard Imperial formations and strode down the wide merchants' roads in squares of halberdier and spearman companies. Their livery was patchy and irregular, but they were well armed and highly motivated. Helborg had made sure they were fed and paid, and they rewarded him by maintaining good discipline. With every mile they travelled, more came to join them. All the villagers in the region had seen the column of fire in the west, and even their simple minds had felt the corruption bleeding from it. Carts and supplies were commandeered and added to the straggling baggage caravan. At the end of the first full day of marching into the interior, his forces had swelled to near three thousand. The few remaining Reiksguard were the only truly deadly troops among them, but the rest at least had blades and some idea of how to use them.

At the end of each day, the army established camp in the

Imperial manner, raising earthworks around a close-packed formation of tents and ramming stakes into the defences. As the army had grown, this task had become more arduous and time-consuming, but it was necessary work. Grosslich's forces had yet to engage them, but the closer they came to the capital the more inevitable an attack became. They were now little more than a day's march away, almost close enough to see the tips of the city's spires on the north-west horizon.

With the raising of the encampment, the men retired to their positions for the night, sitting around fires and speculating about the booty they'd receive for aiding the Reiksmarshal on campaign. They avoided discussion of the forces ranged against them, or the growing presence of the pillar of fire, or the reports from the forward scouts of a strange dark tower thrusting up from the heart of the city.

In the centre of the camp the command group held council, screened from the rank and file by canvas hoardings and sitting around a huge fire. Helborg stood in the place of honour, his breastplate glowing red from the flames. The Sword of Vengeance hung again from his belt, and it had made him complete. His habitual flamboyance seemed to have been replaced with a kind of grim majesty, and in the firelight he resembled nothing so much as the statue of Magnus the Pious in the Chapel of Fallen.

On his left stood Hausman, in Skarr's absence the most senior Reiksguard. On his right was Leitdorf, looking uncomfortable in his armour. There were four other captains drawn from the ranks, all veteran soldiers and Leitdorf loyalists wearing the blue and burgundy.

Opposite Helborg, completing the circle, was Schwarzhelm. The Emperor's Champion looked almost as imposing as Helborg. He was back in armour, and it seemed to have had a restorative effect on his demeanour. Verstohlen stood, as ever, by his side. He remained in the margins, observing the deliberations rather than contributing, just as his long service in the clandestine arts had equipped him to do.

'You have all seen the pillar of fire,' said Helborg. 'You

know the story of treachery we march to avenge. But there are greater forces at work here. Lord Schwarzhelm has more knowledge of the foe we face than any of us, so I have asked him to speak.'

All turned to the big man. The bad blood between him and Helborg seemed purged after the drama of their first meeting, but the atmosphere remained brittle. None of the captains seemed to know how to act around him. Schwarzhelm, as was his manner, gave away nothing.

'We do not march alone,' he said, and his growling voice seemed to reverberate from his newly-donned battle-plate. 'The Emperor has been warned, and we can be sure there will be Imperial forces hastening to counter the threat. How close they are, I do not know. We may encounter them at Averheim, or they may still be weeks away.'

His eyes swept the captains. There was a light kindled in them, one Verstohlen hadn't seen for many days. Not since Schwarzhelm had ridden east from the succession debate to crush the orcs. He lived for this kind of test.

'In either case, we cannot wait. I have been in Averheim. It has been turned into a den of Chaos, and our duty is to purge it. We must do all in our power to weaken the defences, whether or not other Imperial forces are committed. Our survival is unimportant.'

The Averlander captains looked concerned by that. Helborg had promised them victory, not sacrifice.

'How many men does Grosslich have under command?' asked one of them.

'We don't know,' said Helborg. 'Nor does it matter. Schwarzhelm's verdict is the only one – as soon as we're within range, we'll commit to an assault. I've sent messages to my lieutenant to gather all the men he commands. We'll join forces south of the city and make directly for it. The bulk of the troops will engage the enemy while a strike force composed of myself, the Lord Schwarzhelm and the Reiksguard will penetrate the Tower. Grosslich is the heart of this – if we kill him, the edifice around him will crumble.'

Leitdorf shook his head.

'Madness,' he muttered.

All eyes turned to him. The elector looked up guiltily, as if he'd been talking to himself.

'Well, it is,' he said defiantly. 'Even Ironjaw couldn't storm the heart of the city. It's built to withstand a siege from armies five times as big as this.'

Helborg glowered at him. 'You forget who marches with you. The Swords of Vengeance and Justice are not to be taken lightly.'

'No doubt. Neither is Natassja. And perhaps you've noticed the bonfire she's created over there – it'll take more than two pointy sticks to put it out.'

Verstohlen smiled in the dark. Against his better judgement, he was beginning to like the elector.

Helborg showed no such tolerance. 'Then I take it you have a better plan,' he said, and his voice was icy.

Leitdorf shrugged. 'The only hope is to rendezvous with this Empire army. Your swords may be of help against the sorcery within the Tower, but you'll have to get close enough first.'

There was an uncomfortable silence. Helborg was unused to being challenged, but Leitdorf had grown in stature over the past few weeks. He'd also saved the Marshal's life, which gave him something of an edge in the discussion.

'They'll come from the north,' said Leitdorf. 'Invading armies have always taken the high ground above the city before attempting an assault. That's where we should join them. You say that Preceptor Skarr has more men? Good. We can sweep up the eastern side of Averheim, rendezvous with his troops and then march to occupy the Averpeak. From there we'll be able to hold our ground until the Imperial forces arrive. If they're already there, we'll be well placed to reinforce them ourselves. It's the only course of action.'

Leitdorf's voice had grown more confident the more he'd spoken. Unlike at Drakenmoor, his captains actually listened.

Helborg said nothing, pondering the counsel. He still

looked undecided. Leitdorf's manoeuvre would take longer, and they all knew time was running short. Despite that, there was sense to it – this was his country, and the elector knew the way the land was laid.

'We cannot be sure the Empire has responded yet,' said Schwarzhelm.

'Indeed,' said Verstohlen, giving Leitdorf a wry nod of support. The elector had the self-command not to look surprised. 'But they are our best chance of success in this. We should plan our advance around them. If we arrive and they're not there, then we can consider the other options.'

'We'll lose the element of surprise,' muttered Helborg. 'They'll see us come up from the east flank.'

'There *is* no element of surprise,' said Leitdorf grimly. 'They know where we are as surely as they know the positions of the stars. Trust me, I was married to the woman.'

There was another long silence. Helborg shot an enquiring glance at Schwarzhelm, but the big man said nothing. Eventually, the Marshal let slip a scraping laugh.

'So be it!' he said. 'The elector has made his judgement. Skarr will rendezvous with us to the east of Averheim, from where we'll take position in the north. Messengers will ride out tonight, and we break camp at dawn.'

He looked over at Leitdorf, and his expression was a mix of amusement and approval.

'Not many men overrule my judgement in matters of war, Herr Leitdorf. Let us hope your confidence repays us with a victory.'

Leitdorf bowed in return. There was neither diffidence nor arrogance in the gesture.

'This is my realm, Reiksmarshal,' he said. 'It is time I took control of it.'

The plains north of Averheim had once been lush, covered in the thick grass that had made the wealth of the province. The wide river Aver had fed a dozen smaller tributaries, all of which had watered the fertile black soil and nurtured the thick vegetation. Herds of cattle had been driven across the rolling country for centuries, growing fat and sleek on the goodness of the land.

Now all had changed. The city was still consumed by the column of fire. Its streets were havens of horror and madness, its residual inhabitants in hopeless thrall to the Dark Gods. Though the daemons did not venture outside the cordon set by their mistress, others of Natassja's creatures had not been slow to venture beyond the city walls. They marched in file, rank after rank, trampling the grass beneath their iron-shod feet. Great engines of war were hauled up from the depths of the forges, swaying on iron chains the width of a man's waist. Channels of witch-fire were kindled in the six lesser towers. These ran swiftly from their source, burning what little remained of the once healthy country and turning it into a bare, stark wasteland of choking ash. For miles in every direction, the canker spread. Averheim stood alone, a city of twisted iron spires amid a desolate plain of ruin.

Upon that charred and fouled wilderness, the Army of the Stone made its camp. Lines of tents were raised, each surmounted with the skulls of those slain resisting the elector. Braziers were set up, sending clouds of smog rolling over the land and coating it in a cloying pall of soot. Massive spikes were hauled from the forges under the Tower and placed around the edges of the vast encampment. Trenches were dug by a horde of mute slave labour, then filled with quick-kindling oils, roaring with green-tinged flames.

Above it all, the Tower loomed, vast and brooding, isolate and defiant, a shard of night-black metal thrusting up from the tortured land like a blade. The storm circled around it, its clouds drawn to the pinnacle by the rupture in the world's fabric, furious and yet impotent. Lightning danced under the eaves of the piled mass of darkness, flickering along the flanks of the Tower, throwing rare glimpses of light into the perpetual gloom of the lost city. It might have been night, it might have been day – beneath the wings of the storm it was impossible to tell. The aegis of fire remained, boiling and churning as it tore into the heavens, drowning out all other sounds, the terrible mark of the corruption of Averland.

Two miles distant, a high ridge ran around the northern approaches to the city. No trees had grown there even in the days of health and plenty, and from its vantage one could see across the entire Aver floodplain. South of the ridge, the land fell smoothly down to the level of the river, the road looping and circling towards the flat ground before the mighty gates of the city. Men had long called the ridge the Averpeak, and they said it was Siggurd's barrow that caused the earth to rise. At its summit it was broad and smooth, running east to west for several miles before the rolling hills broke its curving outline. In the semi-remembered past, armies had camped on the mighty bulwark, poised like eagles to swoop down on the city below them. Only Ironjaw, the last great besieger of the city, had rejected its advantages, so drunk had he been on the wine of conquest.

Grosslich knew his history, as did the silent commanders who now stalked among his legions. So it was that the camp was set in opposition to the Averpeak, and the trenches cut off the lines of assault from the high places. The old road was dug up and embankments raised across it. As if the embellished walls of Averheim with their six subordinate towers were not deterrent enough, the plains before the gates had been turned into killing fields, laced with instruments of murder and marked with rivers of unholy fire.

All this Volkmar saw as he crested the summit of the Averpeak. He rode at the head of the army, the first to come to the edge of the ridge and gaze down on the plain below. As the view unfolded, he halted, staff in hand, and was silent.

Behind him the rest of the army took up their positions. Maljdir, Roll and the warrior priests lined up in the centre, standing grim and resolute with the light of the fires reflecting from their breastplates. The battle wizards came behind them. There were two Celestial wizards, including the recovered Hettram, their sky-blue robes reflecting the fires like mirrors. Alongside them were three Bright wizards, their staffs already kindling with flame, and a triad of Light magisters clad in bone-white robes and already making preparations for their communal spellcasting.

Once the command retinue was in place, the massed ranks of halberdiers, spearmen and swordsmen spread out across the Averpeak, arranged in assault formation. They too were silent. There were no songs of defiance as they edged towards their positions. They stood in their companies, mutely staring at the horror below, only half-listening to the hymns of hate and defiance droned out by the priests. On the far left flank, to the east of the battlefield, came the light cavalry, pistoliers and handgunners. The horses, even those used to the ways of war, stamped nervously.

Only when the artillery was hauled into position did something of a cheer run through the ranks of men. Mighty iron-belchers were dragged into place by their teams of sweating horses. Piles of cannonballs were unloaded from the heavy carts and made ready. Helblasters, Helstorms and mortars were brought up from the engineers' caravan. There were dozens of them, alongside over thirty cannons of various sizes. The broadside from such a collection would be monstrous indeed.

Volkmar had chosen to place his heavy guns on the right flank of his army, to the west of the city. Here the Averpeak came closest to the city walls, and the cannon had a devastating view over the plains. As soon as they were in position, earthworks were raised around them. Six auxiliary companies fell into place to guard the guns from assault, bolstered by a detachment of greatswords decked in the colours of Altdorf.

Behind the front lines, Volkmar placed nearly five thousand men in reserve. For the time being they were deployed among the baggage train, though no one doubted they would be called into action before long. There were also archer companies, fast-moving and lightly armed, held back behind the front ranks for rapid deployment. These took their allotted places as nervously as the rest of their peers, double-checking their strings and anxiously making sure fresh arrows were close to hand.

Aside from Volkmar and the warrior priests, only one detachment of the entire army truly marched without fear. Gruppen was last into position, his four hundred Knights Panther having held back to allow the rest of the army to spread along the ridge. As he took his station with the artillery on the extreme right flank, the cheers from the men around him took on some real enthusiasm. His men were decked in their full plate armour and exotic pelts, mounted on chargers with broadswords at their sides. Their pennants were raised defiantly against the swirling winds of the storm, a forest of leaping panthers and slender figures of Myrmidia.

Leonidas Gruppen was foremost among the knights, his visor up and his harsh face exposed to the horrors below. He went proudly, his armour draped in the hide of a black panther from furthest Ind, his standard-bearer at his side. The preceptor gave the word and the banner was unfurled, a glorious tapestry to Myrmidia picked out in gold and ivory.

Gruppen turned to Volkmar's position and raised his fist in salute. As he did so, the remaining banners of the army were swung into position. Standards of Reikland, Nuln, Middenheim, Talabecland, city-states of Tilea, Averland and the mercenary companies all flew out, caught by the buffets of the storm and exposed in all their varied splendour.

In the centre of the ridge, Volkmar gave Maljdir a curt nod. The burly Nordlander strode forwards, Bloodbringer swinging from his belt. He carried the Imperial standard in both mighty hands. Planting the shaft firmly in the soil, he let the Theogonist's own banner stream out. The golden fabric rushed into view, exposing the Emperor's own coat of arms: two crimson griffons rampant flanking a sable shield with the initials *KF* emblazoned in dazzling argent. At the sight of the famous colours, the most revered in all the lands of men, the infantry regiments cried out with genuine fervour. If the Emperor had gifted Volkmar his own devices, men reasoned, then all hope had not gone.

With that gesture, the army was in place. Forty thousand

troops deployed along the ridge, all facing south, all armed and ready for combat.

Volkmar looked back over the plain. The enemy army waited silently a mile distant, sprawled before the walls of the city in their sullen magnificence, spread like a vast black contagion over the once pristine plains. No banners flew. No brazen trumpets called them to arms. Instead, the braziers continued to belch smoke, the fires continued to blaze, the engines continued to churn.

Then the sign was given. High up in the Iron Tower, a lilac star blazed out briefly, cutting through the columns of fire for an instant. A sigh seemed to pass through the distant ranks of waiting troops. Drums started to beat across the walls. All over the waiting host, men – or things like men – took up their crystal halberds and locked them into readiness.

Volkmar looked across the enemy formation impassively. The traitor host was larger than the Imperial army, though the smog made it hard to gauge by how much. This Grosslich had been busy. Now his designs would be put to the test.

'So we come to it at last,' he growled to Roll, taking up the Staff of Command. The gold reflected the distant lightning, glowing proudly against the gathering dark.

'Sigmar preserve us,' said Roll grimly, drawing his sword. 'Sigmar preserve us all.'

Natassja waited in the throne room. The doors to the shaft beyond had been closed and the roar of the fires was subdued. She could feel the power beneath her feet growing, though. The time was fast approaching. Both her body and mind were changing. Her awareness, already more acute than the limited senses of mortal women, had magnified a thousandfold. She could feel the heartbeat of every soul within the city, could feel the slow burn of their stunted emotions as they readied themselves for the coming assault. From the augmentation chambers in the pits of the Tower to the daemons circling above, they were all transparent to her.

The transformation had some drawbacks. Her grasp on the

material world was becoming ever more tenuous, and she had to concentrate to ensure that she retained her proper place within it. This was a dangerous time for her. If she lost her grip too soon, before the Stone had reached the appropriate pitch of awareness, the process would never complete and she'd be left torn and rootless.

That would *not* happen. Not after so many decades in the preparation.

Ever since her youth, almost forgotten on the plains of Kislev, she had known she was destined for greater things. The life of a serf had never been enough for her. Even before she'd known of any existence other than the casual brutality of the ice-bound villages, some voice had reassured her that the future held improvements. That voice had never left her, her constant companion as the years had worn on.

It had all changed with the coming of the dark ones. Out of the Wastes they'd ridden, tall and slender and bearing the curved scimitars of raiders. She'd loved them at once, relishing their cruelty and skill. The villagers hadn't stood a chance. The headman had been the last to go, roaring with pointless resistance right up until the lead horseman put a spike through his temple.

Then they'd taken her. She'd been pretty and young enough to be worth corrupting. Ah, that had been a hard time. Even during the worst of her misery, manacled in the hut of the bandit chieftain, subject to the crude tastes of a savage and ignorant man, the voice hadn't gone away. The raiders were His people, and He promised to deliver her from them. If she was just patient for a while and accepted the trials He sent her, then the path would open up to worlds of discovery.

And so it had proved. In the far north, there were wonders fit for a mind of her subtlety. Her knowledge grew, fed by the snatched tutelage of shamans and their slaves. Beauty was an asset amongst such people, and in time she learned to use it. Each night she abased herself before the Dark Prince, and He gifted her luck. When she finally escaped the chieftain and was free to explore the fringes of the realm of madness,

He gave her the Vision. She could remember it as clearly as ever. It had been *so beautiful*. By comparison, the bleak steppes became dreary and tedious to her. So she worked harder as she traversed the hidden realms, studied forbidden books, learned secret rites, delved into the wellspring of dark magic which gushed so fulsomely on the edge of the mortal world of matter.

The years passed. Others aged, and she did not. When after so long in the far north she finally discovered the old bandit chieftain again he was in failing health, ready to put aside the cares of mortal life and join the symphony of souls in the hereafter. Natassja kept him alive for another fifty years, every day of which was a fresh and unique agony. By the time she was ready to let his shrivelled soul slink into oblivion, her powers had become swollen and overripe. The hunt for a greater challenge was on. She needed to find a way to fulfil the Vision.

She never regretted leaving the steppes. The warmer lands were so much more interesting, bursting with opportunity and places to practise the art. Over the long, wearing years she'd lived in many places – Marienburg, Altdorf of course, Talabheim, the heart of the Drakwald, a Lahmian citadel in the Middle Mountains, a hundred other places great and small. The world aged and grew colder while her blood and flesh remained hot and vital. The Vision never left her. She was just waiting for the right moment.

She thought it had come with Marius, but he'd proved impossible to subvert. Then she'd found Lassus, and the possibilities began to coalesce. Four hundred years of searching, and the Vision had been vindicated in Averheim, that most provincial of Imperial cities. Turning the dull, prosperous, strait-laced pile of dung into a cacophonous oratory to the Lord of Pain had been the most pleasurable thing she'd ever done. The men of Averland were no better than the cattle they reared, and their fate was well and truly deserved. It was an appropriate place to begin her new life, and her gratitude to the Dark Prince was profound and sincere. To those that pleased Him, He asked for so little, and gave so much.

Now she'd passed beyond the power of any in the province
to hinder her. Helborg, for so long the one she'd feared, could
do nothing in the time that remained to him. Schwarzhelm
even less so. Volkmar and his little band of sword-wavers
might be an irritation, but her vast legions stood between
her and the Theogonist. All she needed now was a breathing
space, just enough for the harmonies to reach their optimum
pitch. It wouldn't be long.

'Natassja!'

Grosslich's voice was thick with anger. She turned to see
him framed in the doorway to her throne room. He was
still dressed in his ridiculous red armour. The Dark Prince
only knew what had made him design such a thing. He carried his bone wand in one hand and a black-bladed sword
in the other.

He looked hugely annoyed. She didn't blame him for that.
If she'd been him, she'd have been hugely annoyed too.

'My love,' she murmured, walking over to the throne and
taking her place on it. The little gestures were important,
even now. 'What brings you–'

'You know damn well what brings me here,' Grosslich said,
advancing towards her. There was a powerful aura about him.
He'd grown strong. In another place and another time, he'd
have been a mighty warlord. The waste of it saddened her.

'You seek Eschenbach.'

'Seek? No. I know full well what you did to him. Sacrificed
to your power, just as you intend to sacrifice me.'

'And why would I want that?'

'To rule this place alone,' spat Grosslich, eyes blazing.
'That's why you made it a home of capering devils. None of
this is what I wanted.'

Natassja raised an eyebrow. 'Then stay here with me. I'll
show you how to enjoy it. I never lied to you, Heinz-Mark.
Believe me. If you stay in the Tower, there are still many
things we could accomplish together.'

Grosslich laughed harshly. A fey light had kindled across
his features. The power he'd accumulated was already leaking,

spilling out from his fingertips like water. He couldn't handle what he'd been given. Ach, the *waste*.

'Perhaps you'd like that,' he said. 'Perhaps that would give you all you wanted from this arrangement.'

He laughed again, a bitter, choking sound. 'I won't do it, Natassja. There's one role left I know how to play. Your army needs a commander. I'm leaving to take them. I'll destroy the challengers, and then I'll make my next move. Perhaps I'll bring them back here. Perhaps I won't. You've given me the tools to carve out a realm of my own – it doesn't need to be here.'

'I could prevent you,' Natassja said, and the sadness in her voice was unfeigned.

Grosslich shook his head. 'I don't think so. My skills are greater than you think.'

Natassja knew that wasn't so. She could kill him with a word, but to do so would solve nothing. Out of affection, she would give him a final chance, after which he would have to make his own decisions.

'If you leave the Tower, I cannot protect you. If you stay, you will remain safe. You have my word. You will never be the master, but you will be provided for. You may yet become truly mighty, a regent worthy of long service.'

Grosslich smiled to himself, as if a joke he'd heard a lifetime ago had suddenly made sense.

'A *regent*. Tempting. I'll bear it in mind.'

He bowed low.

'Farewell, Natassja. When I return, master of the armies you've created, perhaps our negotiations will go differently.'

He turned on his heel flamboyantly and marched out of the chamber. Natassja watched him go. Despite everything, despite the centuries of malice and intrigue, she was not unmoved. There had been a path for the two of them she'd foreseen, one of discovery, knowledge and enlightenment. The fact that he'd chosen to reject it was regrettable.

'So you let him go,' came a sibilant voice from behind the throne.

A daemon curled up from the floor, her naked flesh snaking lewdly across the obsidian. Natassja ignored the gratuitous attempt at provocation. For beings of infinite intelligence and power, daemons could be tediously infantile.

'Of course,' she replied. 'Maybe it was wrong of me to expect more of him.'

The daemon laughed. 'Or maybe he decided his position was no longer secure. That *is* a mighty army out there. It will make him feel safer.'

Natassja turned to look at the daemon and frowned with disapproval.

'Did you plant that idea in his head? If so, I'll rend you apart.'

The daemon giggled, though the laughter was suffused with a note of fear. She darted away, hovering near the outlet to the shaft.

'That's not in your gift, my queen,' she reminded her.

'Not yet,' said Natassja, rising from the throne. 'But watch yourself.'

She began to walk from the chamber.

'Are you *starting* it, then?' asked the daemon excitedly, following at a safe distance.

'Why not? I have the city to myself now.'

The daemon whooped with pleasure. 'Then you're not worried about their armies? Helborg draws close, and he carries the sword.'

'What can he do now? His time has passed.' Natassja turned to the floating daemon and gave her an affectionate, tolerant smile. 'Return to your sisters, dark one. There'll be more play for you before the day is out.'

Then she turned back, heading down the long gallery and towards the spiral staircase.

'The Chamber of the Stone will be warded until all is complete,' she warned. 'Wait for me outside the Tower. It is, at last, time for my birth.'

CHAPTER SIXTEEN

Out on the plain, something had changed. The legions continued to take up their positions, but a new presence had come among them. Volkmar strode forwards, peering down into the smog-clad gloom of the battlefield.

'My spyglass,' he snapped, and a priest hurried to bring it.

He swept across the ranks of enemy troops. Some were men, clad in Grosslich's colours, their eyes glowing strangely. Others were obscene corruptions of men, their legs twisted backwards and crouching like dogs.

Then he found his quarry. The gates of the city had opened, and a man had emerged, mounted on a coal-black charger. The horse was as corrupt and twisted as everything else in that host. It had clawed pads in place of hooves and a scaled hide in place of skin. Its mane and tail shone like polished onyx and had been plaited and decorated with jewels. Tabards decorated with forbidden sigils hung from its flanks, and its eyes smouldered like hot embers. It was massive, at least a foot taller and broader than a mortal beast, and when it trod on the broken earth the claws sunk deep.

The figure mounted on it was no less impressive. Enclosed
from head to foot in crimson armour, glistening from the
fires around him, the master of Averheim had emerged. He
wore a tall helm crested with a plume of gold, the only opening of which was a narrow slit for his eyes. In his right hand
he carried a black-bladed broadsword with a serrated edge.
It looked as if molten pitch were continually dripping from
the dagger-sharp points, pooling like blood on the earth as
he passed into the heart of his men. In his left hand he bore
a wand of bone.

As he made his way through the ranks of soldiers they
withdrew silently. Perhaps once they had fought under him
as mortal men, hopeful of the new dawn he would bring to
Averland. Now such memories were lost, subsumed beneath
the crushing will of the Stone and its mistress.

With their commander among them, the legions began
to advance.

'So it begins,' said Volkmar, handing the spyglass back. 'The
master has left his lair. Give the signal.'

Trumpets blared out from the command position and
passed down the line. The gunnery crews sprang into action.
Just as they had done at Streissen, they worked quickly and
well. These were crews from Nuln, the best in the Empire,
and they were masters of their deadly trade.

Orders roared out, cannonballs were rammed home and
rags doused in flame. Crews and escorts scrambled to get
out of the way as the iron-belchers were primed and loaded.
Seconds later the thundering boom of ignition shook the
earth and a wall of death screamed out from the Averpeak
on to the plain below. Huge clouds of blackpowder smoke
billowed from the gun-line, swept up into the air by the
swirling storm and dragged across the battlefield.

The enemy vanguard continued to advance into range,
heedless of the power of the artillery. They were cut down
in clumps, blasted apart by the sudden wrath of the heavy
guns. Heedless and undaunted, they came onwards, clambering over their fallen without pause. Like a massive pall of

black fog, the enemy rolled across the plain, marching slowly, claiming more ruined ground with every step.

'Maintain fire!' ordered Volkmar, looking down at the enemy ranks. All along the ridge, men were poised to counter-attack. Soldiers fingered their weapons, sweat on their brows and ice in their heart. Minutes passed while the iron-belchers reloaded. The waiting was the worst part.

The cannons bellowed out again and a fresh cloud of black-powder discharge tumbled down the slope. This time the barrage was laced with the scything fire of the Helblasters, slamming into the front ranks of the Army of the Stone and tearing open whole companies of marching troops. In their wake the fizzing trails of Helstorm rockets screamed, spinning into the sea of men and detonating with devastating effect. Limbs were torn free and armour shattered by the volleys as they thudded home, round after round of murderous power.

But Grosslich was no savage or raving maniac. In his old life he'd been a master tactician, a peerless moulder of men, and he didn't send his vanguard idly into harm's way. After the advance had gone so far, they halted, halberds raised, and began to dig in. Spikes the length of a man were brought up from the heart of the host and rammed into the ground. Earthworks were raised and the ground behind them cleared. Under withering fire from the Imperial guns, the forces of Grosslich toiled with neither fear nor hurry. Whenever an exposed company was torn apart by a well-aimed salvo, another would take its place. The artillery barrage was costing them dear, but it couldn't dislodge them.

Horns blared from the walls of the city, and the reason for their death-clogged advance became apparent. Huge engines of war, each forged in the hells of fire beneath the Tower, were dragged from the open gates by straining teams of mutated horses. Their wide mouths gaped twice as wide as the largest Imperial cannon. Each device was decorated with writhing bands of bronze and encased in a spiked cage of iron. Smoke poured from beneath them where furnaces had been stoked and fuelled to a flesh-blistering heat. Stone-slaves crawled all over them, polishing the bronze and adjusting the spider webs of pistons and valves even as the towering constructs were hauled towards the forward positions. As the line of guns ground on, each monstrous engine was flanked by whole companies of heavily armoured infantry, all covered in thick iron plate, their faces hidden behind masks in the form of leering beasts.

From the angle of those mighty barrels, it looked as if their range was less than the Imperial guns. What they lacked in distance, however, it was clear they made up for in power. As Volkmar gazed at the rumbling tide of death his eyes narrowed, calculating the distances and gauging the outcome of a volley.

'Target those embankments!' he roared, and the order went down through the ranks.

'We have to *advance*,' hissed Maljdir, his hands eager to clasp Bloodbringer. 'Once those things–'

A fresh boom of cannon fire echoed across the battlefield, backed up with a hail of rockets. The gunnery crews weren't fools, and had adjusted their aim to meet the new threat. One of the rumbling war machines was hit by a whole flurry of artillery fire. It cracked open, leaking green-tinged flames. The horrific structure listed for a moment, wracked by internal explosions, then blasted apart, showering the troops around it with white-hot metal shards.

A cheer went up from the watching Imperial forces, but it was short-lived. Other war machines were hit and suffered little, protected by their thick iron plating. More than a dozen still remained, all crawling into position, all aimed up at the ridge. The nearest drew up to the allotted positions, their bronze-lined maws grinning like hungry wolves.

Still Volkmar held back the charge.

'Magisters,' growled Volkmar, determined to delay the engagement until the last possible moment. 'Destroy them.'

The Celestial wizards strode forwards, staffs crackling with sapphire lightning and their robes rippling from winds seen and unseen. Alonysius von Hettram, the senior battle wizard of the entire army, gave the Theogonist a proud look.

'It will be done,' he said, and the winds of magic began to race.

Bloch watched the column of fire grow as he rode west. The sight was enough to render him mute. He'd seen nothing like it in his life, and he'd done a lot of campaigning. The spectacle at Turgitz had been something, but the destruction of Averheim was on a whole different register of impressive.

Kraus was beside him as ever, riding a grey steed and keeping his mouth shut. The honour guard captain hadn't liked what he'd heard about Schwarzhelm any more than Bloch had. The big man inspired near-fanatical loyalty from the fighting men close to him, and hearing of his actions at the Vormeisterplatz had made sobering listening.

Behind the two of them, Skarr's army of infantry streamed out, marching in a semi-organised rabble. A rabble, that was, except for Bloch's own halberdiers, who stuck to the well-drilled squares he'd insisted on. They'd keep their discipline even in the fires of hell.

Ahead of them rode the Reiksguard. Skarr hadn't spoken much to Bloch since they'd exchanged their stories. He was still angry. Bloch couldn't help but think the preceptor would have liked to punish him for Schwarzhelm's alleged crimes just to make himself feel better. Typical high-born.

Despite it all though, he couldn't entirely blame the preceptor. Bloch remembered the strain on Schwarzhelm's face east of Heideck. His words had remained with him. *Since arriving in Averland I've not felt myself. It's been as if some force has turned against me, weighing down on my mind. The city is at the heart of it. It may be that Averheim is perilous for me.*

Perhaps he'd been right about that. There was little else that could explain Skarr's testimony. The few details Bloch had been able to add – Leitdorf's treachery, the long process of legal divination, the Imperial armour on the greenskins – hadn't really helped matters.

Even after the preceptor had allowed Bloch to accompany him to the rendezvous with Helborg, much still remained to be settled. The Reiksguard were suspicious, and their blood-oath against Schwarzhelm remained intact. Bloch found himself confronted with the terrible scenario of marching against his old master. For all he knew, Schwarzhelm *had* turned to darkness. He couldn't quite bring himself to believe that, but the thought wouldn't leave him alone.

'So is this what we drove the orcs out of Averland for?' muttered Kraus, staring sullenly at the distant red clouds.

Skarr's column was little more than a day's march from Averheim, summoned by Helborg's orders of a muster. At the appointed location, Skarr's two thousand troops would join up with Helborg's three thousand. Not much of an army to take on the forces of the great enemy, especially as over three-quarters of them could barely point their sword in the right direction without being shown how.

'I'd rather have one enemy than two.'

Kraus shook his head irritably.

'I don't believe it,' he said. 'He hasn't turned. And I won't believe he made a mistake either.'

'You said yourself he was acting strangely.'

'The man's commanded armies for thirty years. He's no weakling.'

'Skarr never said he was. This is the great enemy.'

Kraus said nothing, and turned his eyes away from the angry sky. On the far horizon there came a low, grinding rumble, as if the earth were as troubled as the heavens above it.

'We should be glad we made it back here, Kraus,' said Bloch. 'We've been part of this from the beginning. It'll all be decided in Averheim, one way or the other. Couldn't miss that.'

Kraus remained stubbornly quiet. Bloch looked up, watching the way the clouds were sucked across the sky into such a massive, slowly rotating spiral. He knew as well as anyone that their army couldn't fight power of that magnitude, whether or not Helborg rode with them. Just more crazy Reiksguard heroism, a final fling of bravado before they all died.

That suited him. Fighting was what he'd been born for. It had to end some time or other, and it might as well be against a decent enemy. All he'd need was a sign that the sacrifices had been worth something and he'd happily march into that storm of fire, halberd in his hand as always, searching for the next victim, doing what he'd been put on the earth to do.

Hettram was first to cast. Raising his hands high, he cried aloud, summoning the storm to his aid. His companion, barely out of his twenties and with a lean face, joined him, adding his raw power to that of his master.

Above the battlefield, the clouds swirled fast. The storm, already raging, accelerated into a frenzy of anger. Lightning slammed down from the boiling tumult above, immolating all it struck and sending fresh fires blazing up from the heart of the beleaguered city.

'Storm, unleash thy wrath!' roared Hettram, summoning fresh power from the elements.

Rain began to hammer down, whipped into flurries by the wind. It bounced from the streaming barrels of the war engines, fizzing and hissing. Bolts of silver fire scored the heavens, streaking and tearing into the lumbering hosts below.

Another of the war engines tilted over, hit by a thunderous blast from the skies and cracked down the length of its gaping muzzle. Still it was dragged on, listing in the mud, gouging a huge furrow as the horses strained against their chains. The beasts had been driven mad by whatever foul experiments had been performed on them, and they foamed against their halters, churning up the mire until it became a blood-coloured soup.

'We're not stopping them,' muttered Maljdir, watching darkly as the rest of the guns were hauled into their firing positions.

The Imperial cannons roared out again, sending blackpowder plumes rolling into the heart of the maelstrom. More
lightning slammed down on to the field, burning brightly
as it plunged into the heart of Grosslich's legions.

Still the engines came on, rolling as the chains pulled tight,
islands of iron amidst a morass of men.

'More power!' snarled Volkmar, seeing the engines settle
into place and chains being run across their armoured backs.

The Bright wizards joined their Celestial counterparts. Their
art was better suited to close-pitched combat, but they raised
their staffs and summoned up the Wind of Aqshy. Chanting
in unison, they called the words of their pyromantic craft
aloud and shook their blazing shafts, eyes wide and riddled
with sparks.

Now the lightning was laced with a consuming fire. The
bolts summoned from the skies smashed into the advancing
horde and burst into waves of hungry flame. The immolation spread quickly, taking the shapes of ravening wolves,
sweeping across the ranks of glow-eyed figures and wrapping
them in an agonising, rolling death. Every artillery impact
exploded in a ball of orange, surging across the blasted land
and leaping up into the braziers and trenches.

Hundreds perished in that onslaught, burned alive
by the sheets of fire-laced lightning, caught up in the
heaven-summoned inferno. Two more engines were consumed, wreathed in leaping tongues of flame before
exploding in a halo of spinning iron and bronze. Horses
screamed and reared against their bonds, tugging the vast
engines out of position. Another toppled over, lost in a wel-
ter of chains, hooves and struggling limbs. Cannons bellowed
again, and the shell was cracked.

Still the rest came on.

Volkmar watched as the first engine was made secure, protected by earthworks, crowned with a bristling cordon of
spikes and surrounded by the massed ranks of Grosslich's
elite guard. Fresh fire was kindled at its base and huge piles
of shot were unloaded behind it, ready to be hoisted into

the unholy mechanism and hurled into the waiting ranks of Empire troops.

Volkmar looked round at the Light wizards. They were still preparing their magic, locked as it was in complex rites and rituals. The Celestial wizards were beginning to tire, and their powers would be needed later. He had no more to give. The advance of the guns had been slowed but not halted. Their deadly power would soon be unleashed.

He turned to Maljdir.

'We've done what we can,' he said. 'Give the order to charge.'

Out on the far west flank, Leonidas Gruppen heard the trumpet blare out and his heart leapt. The moment had come.

'Lances!' he roared, and his squires rushed forwards with the steel-tipped shafts, staggering as they tried to keep their footing on the slippery ground.

All around him his knights formed up into squadrons of twenty, each man with a lance and all prepared for the first, vital charge. Behind them, the second wave waited impatiently. In two sweeping assaults, all four hundred Knights Panther would slam into the enemy lines, clearing a path for the infantry and carving their way towards the war engines. They were the tip of the spear, the sharpest instrument in the armoury of Sigmar's heirs.

More trumpets resounded from the centre of the ridge and the massed host of halberdiers began to run down the shallow slope of the Averpeak, hollering cries to Sigmar and Ranald as they went.

Gruppen looked down at the battlefield below. Less than half a mile distant, the first ranks of the enemy waited. They'd had time to dig in, but not enough. Empire artillery had blasted huge gouges in their lines of trenches and swathes of the vanguard were in disarray from the bombardment.

He picked his target and took up his lance.

'For Myrmidia!' he cried. All around him his brother knights did likewise, and for a brief moment the shout of the Knights Panther drowned out the rest of the Imperial army.

Then he snapped his visor down and kicked his horse down the slope. The squires sprinted clear and the squadrons tore towards the enemy line, picking up speed as they hurtled towards the front ranks.

Gruppen felt his heart thumping within his armoured chest as his steed accelerated into a pounding gallop. The gap between the armies shrank rapidly. As at the Turgitz Cauldron, the knights formed into a wall of steel, their lances swinging down into position as each man picked his enemy.

Gruppen narrowed his eyes. The battlefield was a riot of fire and smoke. Flashes of lightning still arced down, exposing the vast extent of the enemy formations in vivid detail. He saw men lumbering into his path, hauling pikes into place to frustrate the charge.

Too slow. The ride of the Knights Panther was like a sudden deluge from the high peaks. Travelling at speed, their hooves a thudding blur, the squadrons smashed into the lines of defenders.

Gruppen was at the forefront. He aimed for a knot of men trying to erect fresh spikes. They tried to pull back when they saw him bearing down, but they had no chance. He spurred his charger on, sweeping through them and impaling the leader clean through with his lance. On either side of him his knights did likewise, slicing open the defences and scattering the loose formations.

Then they were amongst the press of men and the charge ground into its first resistance. Gruppen dropped his lance and drew his broadsword, whirling it round in the air as it left the scabbard. His men ploughed deep into the enemy ranks, crunching aside any obstacle. At this range, Gruppen's horse was as deadly as he was. His charger's hooves lashed out as it slowed from the gallop, crushing skulls and cracking ribs. His blade followed up, sweeping in mighty wheels to slash out at any infantry foolish enough to get close.

Gruppen spurred his horse on further, maintaining the momentum, carving his way towards his objective. It loomed up in the dark, far larger than he'd guessed from atop the ridge. The war engine towered thirty feet into the air, a heavy muzzle of iron and bronze, studded with rivets and under-pinned with its growling furnace. Iron-masked men milled around it like ants, readying it to fire.

As the knights swept closer the defence became more stubborn. Grosslich's heavy infantry, rendered impervious to glancing blows by their plate armour, formed a defensive line between the knights and the war engine.

'Onwards!' roared Gruppen, kicking his steed back into speed, knowing they had to break them on the charge. The knights swept into range, still in formation, their line intact and deadly. They crashed together, a solid bastion of iron against a thundering curtain of steel.

The assault instantly descended into confusion. Knights were knocked from their steeds, hurled back in the saddle by halberd jabs. Defending infantry were tossed aside, tram-pled into the mud, their armour cracked.

Gruppen felled his target, riding him down and swing-ing heavily with his sword on the follow-through. His right-hand man was not so lucky, steering his horse into a thicket of blades and being dragged from the saddle by a dozen armoured hands.

Gruppen whirled his steed round. He needed to keep mov-ing. A soldier lumbered towards him, halberd stabbing at the flanks of his horse. The charger kicked out at him, shat-tering the staff before Gruppen could bring his sword round in a decapitating arc, aimed precisely for the gap between helm and breastplate.

Gruppen looked up. The knights had carved a trail of death, just as they'd been commanded. Now the melee would undo them. Already four of his men were down, and the rest were struggling.

'Withdraw!' he roared, kicking his steed back into motion.

As one, displaying their peerless horsemanship, the knights pulled their mounts round and fought their way free. Another rider was dragged to earth as they turned, unable to escape the grasping fingers of the defenders, but the rest broke clear.

'To the ridge!' cried Gruppen, urging his horse onwards. The knights swept back, pulling away from the avenue of death they'd created. As they galloped back for fresh lances and fresh steeds, they swept past Imperial infantry heading the other way, swarming along the cleared territory, desperate to engage at last.

Gruppen smiled. His blood was up. Another pass and the engine would be destroyed. The enemy seemed to have no answer to the sudden cavalry charge. Just as the beasts had found at Turgitz, there was little in the Empire that could withstand their driving wedge of steel.

Then the engines fired.

The massed boom of their report made the earth itself reel. All along the enemy lines, the infernal devices detonated their charges and sent their cargo of death sailing into the sky. Vast streaks of blazing red fire scored the storm-wracked heavens, tearing through the bolts of the Celestial magisters. Whips of flame wrapped themselves like serpents around the discharges, flicking and snapping angrily. The massive engines slammed back hard from the recoil, crushing the men behind them before the binding chains went taut with a shower of sparks.

The Averpeak ridge disappeared. As the shot impacted it bloomed into a screaming inferno, hurtling across the exploding earth as if kindled on a lake of oil. Lilac and crimson blasts ripped the skyline apart, flaring up with sudden, eye-watering brilliance. Echoes of the impact resounded across the battlefield, swiftly followed by the anguished cries of men caught in a sudden and terrible wall of fire. It felt as if the world had been shattered, cracked open by the devastating power of the Chaos engines.

As the backwash from the explosions rippled out, the vast plumes of lilac-edged smoke rolled clear. Huge sections of the ridge had been demolished, crushing men beneath the earth, burying them under the bodies of their comrades. Fires kindled on nothing, sweeping through what was left of the defences. Some standards still flew, but whole companies had been destroyed. Gruppen couldn't see Volkmar's position for the smog.

One of his knights rode up alongside him, pulling his steed to a halt. Gruppen did likewise, shaken to the core by what he'd seen. Nothing could resist that degree of firepower. Nothing.

'Orders, sir?' the knight asked. The man's voice was tight.

Gruppen took a deep breath, looking about him for some evidence that his senses had deceived him, that what he'd just seen hadn't been quite as devastating as it looked. None came.

'Send the second wave in,' he growled. 'Then get a fresh horse. We've got to get those engines down, or this'll be over in an hour.'

Volkmar picked himself up from the ground, his robes covered in mud and blood. He tried to stand, and staggered, falling to one knee. His vision was black, picked out with spinning points of light. The roar of the battle rushed back to him slowly, as if coming from far away.

'My lord!' Maljdir was at his elbow, helping him up. The priest was similarly covered with debris. All around them men were regaining their feet. Others didn't get up.

'Unhand me!' growled Volkmar, shaking himself loose. Signs of weakness were the last thing he needed to convey. 'Do we have the musicians?'

'Some.'

'Order the second wave in. We can't survive another barrage – we have to get amongst them.'

Maljdir nodded sharply and rushed off to find a surviving trumpeter. Volkmar looked around him. The dying and wounded stretched along the ridge in both directions. Some companies had been entirely destroyed, others only maimed. Those who'd been quickest on the charge had escaped the volley, though they now grappled with the front ranks of the enemy alone. Those who'd been held back for the second wave had been decimated.

Volkmar retrieved his staff. His men were outnumbered and outgunned. He needed to act fast.

'Where are the wizards?' he demanded. The younger Celestial magister limped forwards, blood running down his face. Two of the Bright wizards had survived the blast, and the Light magisters were untouched, set back as they were further down the far side of the ridge, still working. Hettram was gone, lying face down in the filth and debris, his robes stained dark red.

'Come with me,' Volkmar rasped to the Bright wizards. 'We're going down there. As for the rest of you, I need something big, and I need it soon.'

The Celestial wizard nodded numbly, still in shock. His Light counterparts, lost in their preparations, made no response.

All along the ridge, the army was beginning to recover. Maljdir's orders blared out, and the infantry companies still held in reserve started to stream down the slope. The warrior priests, grim-faced and bearing their warhammers, formed up around Volkmar, ready to take the battle to the enemy. Maljdir was among them, carrying the torn and charred standard in his massive hands. Roll was at his side hefting his broadsword eagerly.

Lightning still lanced down, the residue of the Celestial wizards' casting. The Army of the Stone was advancing again, rank after rank of steadily marching troops, eyes glowing in the dark. All across the battlefield, loyalist and traitor clashed with desperate ferocity. As company after company committed to action, the battlefront unfurled to over a mile long, a seething mass of straining bodies broken only by the avenues carved by the cavalry charges and artillery fire.

Volkmar looked across the plain and cursed under his breath. The bulk of his forces were engaged and the rest were racing to do so. There was no pulling back, and no room to manoeuvre. Those damned engines had turned the pattern of the battle and he was now dancing to the traitor's tune.

The Theogonist felt the rage well up within him, the

desperate mania that had afflicted him since Middenheim. Like a tide pushing against a dam, cracking it and poised to overflow, the currents of his fervour rose to breaking point. Streissen had unlocked it, and Averheim had pushed wide the door.

There was no point in suppressing it now. Frenzy had a purpose, and he had to use it.

'Follow me,' Volkmar growled, planting the Staff of Command firmly in the soil. As he did so it roared into life, blazing with a swirling golden aura. 'We'll find the bastard who caused this. I want his *eyes*.'

Seen from five miles to the east, the column of fire was shrouded in a thick grey pall of smoke. It rose from the base of the city like a rolling sea mist, dousing the angry blood-red of the pillar until the shaft of it pierced the obscurity again a hundred feet up in the air. The very earth vibrated with its muffled roar, thrumming under the hooves of the horses.

Helborg had driven his forces hard. Leitdorf's decision had been vindicated by the obvious signs of battle around Averheim. Judging by the drifting shreds of blackpowder smoke in the air, the Empire had arrived to the north of the city. Despite the presence of the looming Tower, hope had spread across his own men like a fire through dry scrub. Eager to join up with the besieging forces from the north, the infantry columns had speeded up and left the lumbering baggage train far behind.

Helborg rode with his Reiksguard escort at the vanguard, willing the miles to pass quicker, itching to draw the runefang in anger. If they went as quickly as they were able, his men would arrive at Averheim before the day's end and in time to make a difference. All depended on Skarr being at the designated muster, now imminent. Helborg had no doubt he would be.

As the vanguard rounded a long, shallow bend in the road, his expectations of the preceptor were vindicated. Under the lee of a sweeping curve of grassland the reinforcements waited, Skarr at their head, the banners of Leitdorf and the Reiksguard fluttering in the swirling, unnatural winds.

The Marshal kicked his horse on ahead, casting a critical eye over the ranks of soldiers as he approached them. Some looked very useful, standing in ordered ranks and with the proper air of belligerence. Others looked little better than flagellants. Still, that was to be expected. The numbers were impressive, given the time in which they'd had to work. Helborg estimated the combined total under arms at five thousand on foot, plus a hundred or so horse.

'Preceptor,' he said gruffly.

Skarr saluted, fist on breastplate.

'My lord,' he replied. 'The men are ready to be led.'

'Very good. Take up the rearguard and ensure they keep the pace tight. I'll be at the spearhead. We leave at once – I don't want to arrive when this is over.'

Skarr bowed and made ready to take up his place when he suddenly pulled up.

'My lord,' he started hesitantly. 'Is that... but forgive me.'

'Is it what?' snapped Helborg.

'Your sword. It's the...'

As the words left his mouth, Ludwig Schwarzhelm loomed up from amongst the column of men at Helborg's rear. The Emperor's Champion was unmistakable, a massive and brooding presence even among the escorting Reiksguard. Skarr's jaw fell open. For a moment he looked like he might draw his blade and charge. Then he whirled back to the Marshal, confusion etched on his face.

'The runefang, yes,' said Helborg, his expression as hard as ever. 'Much has changed since you rode north. You'll have to learn the rest on the ride.'

As Schwarzhelm drew closer, some of the halberdiers under Skarr's command recognised him and rushed forwards in greeting. In the forefront was a thick-set man with a bruised face and the look of a tavern brawler.

Skarr shook his head in disbelief, hand still on the pommel of his sword.

'I thought...'

'Did you not hear me, Skarr?' asked Helborg. 'Your vengeance can wait.'

The preceptor snapped back into focus.

'Forgive me,' he said again. Then he reached around his neck and unhooked the trophy he'd been wearing ever since the last battle of Averheim. The shard of the runefang, salvaged from the Marshal's own wounded cheek, kept safe even while the blade itself had been taken hundreds of miles away.

'At least let me give you this.'

Helborg extended his gauntlet and took the fragment of steel. He held it up to the glowing red of the sky. It twisted on its cord of leather, winking in the dull light.

'The final piece,' he mused, watching the metal turn.

Then, reverently, he hung the shard around his own neck, threading it under his breastplate for protection. The metal was cold against his skin, a reminder of what had been warded for so long, preserved against the day when the Sword of Vengeance would be united with its wielder.

'You did well, Skarr,' Helborg said, taking up the reins. This time his voice was a little less harsh. 'When this is over, I *will* explain. Until then, trust my judgement. We ride together, Schwarzhelm and I. That very fact should give you hope.'

He looked up then, gazing west across the heads of his men towards the Iron Tower, visible in the distance as a spear of darkness at the foot of the shaft of fire. Clouds of smoke billowed around it, driven into great eddies by the unnatural storm. There were blackpowder plumes among them.

'Enough talk,' he said, and his expression was dark. 'The threads gather on the loom. We've done what we can to prepare. To the city.'

Gruppen wheeled his steed around under the shadow of the Averpeak and prepared for the charge. It would be his third foray into the enemy ranks. Of his original squadron, only six remained. He quickly commandeered more troops from two of the other depleted detachments, making up a restored line of twenty-two knights.

'One more time!' he yelled, his voice cracking. The resistance around the big guns was tough, far tougher than he'd expected. Two more of the bronze-bound monsters had been destroyed by cannon fire but the rest still thundered out, reducing any exposed Imperial positions to scorched earth and scraps of bone.

In order to survive, the bulk of the Empire troops had piled forwards, locked in close melee combat with the enemy infantry. They fought bravely, but they were outmatched by Grosslich's troops. Things had been *done* to the defenders. The Averheim troops fought without fear and their formations never broke, no matter how savagely they were mauled.

That was just the human soldiers. There were others among them, more like beasts than men. Gruppen had nearly been felled by one such creature on the last withdrawal, a vast armoured brute with a face like that of a dog. Rumours ran wild along the ranks that there were worse horrors along the east flanks: scuttling fiends with talons for hands, unstoppable killing machines tearing a swathe through horrified Imperial companies.

Gruppen shook his head. No point in worrying about that. The battle was on a knife edge. The enemy had been hurt by the initial barrage of cannon fire, but now the field was swinging back their way. Above it all, the Tower glowered, dark and forbidding.

'Stay close!' he bellowed at the knights mustering around him. The men were gathered at the base of the ridge where the squires had hurried to avoid the worst of the artillery punishment higher up. 'Tight formation, keep on my shoulder. We strike fast, we strike hard. Remember who you are! For Myrmidia!'

The knights shouted back the name of their goddess, fists clenched, their martial spirits undaunted. The Knights Panther were the finest soldiers in the Imperial ranks and they knew it.

'Come about!' bellowed Gruppen, kicking his charger into position. 'Charge!'

Just as before, the line of riders tore across the battlefield, lances lowering, accelerating towards the enemy lines with a thunderous chorus of hooves.

Those lines were closer than they had been. Gruppen had barely made full gallop before the first defenders came into view. A company of the hideous dog-soldiers was loping up towards a beleaguered regiment of Empire swordsmen, halberds held two-handed and faces hidden behind iron masks.

'Take them!' Gruppen roared, spurring his horse even faster, feeling the beast's muscles strain as it propelled the burden of man, armour and weapon. His men remained at his shoulder, lances down, visors closed, all moving as a single body. As he ever did, Gruppen whispered a prayer to his patron goddess before bracing for impact, teeth clenched, heart pounding.

Impact came. The line of knights slammed into the dog-soldiers, knocking the foremost aside and riding them down. Six of the mutants took lances full in the chest. The wooden shafts shattered as their victims crumpled to the earth. One knight was unhorsed as his lance shattered against a breastplate, spinning through the air before crashing headlong into the ranks of fresh terror troops. The rest tore onwards.

Gruppen speared his victim, feeling the sharp recoil as the lance bit deep. He dropped the shaft and reached for his sword. A dog-soldier, eerily silent as it moved into position, swung at his horse as it charged on. Gruppen leaned out, switched grip on his sword and plunged it into the creature's neck before wheeling away, kicking at his mount's flanks to maintain momentum.

'Onwards!' he roared, pointing his bloodstained blade ahead. 'To the engines!'

His horse bounded forwards, leaping over the grasping hands of another dog-soldier and riding down a second. The surviving knights thundered along beside him. Three more had been felled, but the dog-soldier column had been utterly torn apart. The charge remained strong, sweeping resistance before it as the Knights Panther bore deep into the heart of the defenders.

Gruppen knew the danger. If they plunged in too far, they'd not be able to cut their way back out. Despite all that, he was unwilling to withdraw just yet. The enemy continued to fall back before him, dropping under the advance of the knights' hooves and blades, opening up a road to the towering war engine ahead.

Gruppen surged onwards, slashing left and right, heedless of his personal danger. The engine had to be taken down. He held his speed and the horrific machinery drew nearer. The enemy melted away before him.

They were drawing him in.

The realisation hit him too late. Gruppen pulled his horse up sharply, twisting around in the saddle, trying to gauge his position. Only ten of his squadron had followed him so deep. They formed up around him, facing outwards, swords held ready. On every side, dog-soldiers and mortal troops recovered their structure and began to turn back in. The space around the knights shrank. They'd come too far. The nearest Imperial ranks were distant, kept busy with desperate combat of their own.

'Easy, men,' growled Gruppen, keeping his nervous, bucking steed under control. 'We'll cut our way back. Take the–'

'*Leave him.*'

The new voice came from up ahead. It dominated the sounds of battle, slicing through the bedlam like a knife through cooked flesh. It was thick with a world-weary scorn, echoing into the night and resounding from the iron belly of the war engines close to hand. It was no human tongue that spoke the words, though it belonged to a speaker who had once been a man.

Gruppen wheeled round, feeling a sudden chill strike his breast. The ranks of dog-soldiers parted. In their midst was a figure on a dark horse, clad in crimson armour and carrying a black sword. The rider came forwards slowly, deliberately, singling out Gruppen and lowering his blade towards him.

'You can take the others,' Grosslich snarled to his men. 'This one's mine.'

Volkmar strode down the slope and into the thick of the fighting, his staff burning with a corona of golden flame, his face locked into a mask of mania. The Bright wizards flanked him, pouring bolts of screaming orange brilliance into the ranks before them. Warrior priests came in their wake, deadly and unbreakable, swinging their warhammers to crack the skulls of any who survived the magisters' barrage. Maljdir was among them, holding the standard aloft, bellowing hymns to Sigmar and rousing the troops in earshot. Behind came the columns of regular infantry, pulled along by Volkmar's spearhead, sheltering behind the white-hot path he carved through the sea of enemy blades.

None could stand before the Grand Theogonist. Working from afar, the Light wizards had cast at last, and their protection was on him. He shimmered beneath an aegis of swirling luminescence. Those closest to him in the Imperial ranks could see that he'd lost all semblance of control. His whole being was suffused with the searing drive of faith. His armour blazed like the morning sun, throwing spring-yellow beams of dazzling brilliance into the heart of the horde. Grosslich's troops, immune to fear, blundered into his path only to be blasted apart limb from limb, ripped into flapping shreds of flesh by the power of the staff.

Stride by stride, the golden vanguard ploughed deep into the massed ranks, an isolated pool of streaming light amid the spreading cloud of ash-streaked darkness.

'There!' roared Volkmar, pointing ahead.

A war engine loomed out of the fiery gloom, surrounded by ordered ranks of iron-clad infantry. It was preparing to fire again. Coils of steam rose from the furnace at its base and a dozen Stone-slaves crawled across its surface, adjusting levers and mumbling prayers to the Lord of Pain. The

daemon-bound machine soared into the night, vast and terrible, as large as a siege tower and glowing with the angry
sigils of the Dark Prince.

Undeterred, the Theogonist raised his bare arms into the
air and swung the tip of his staff at the mighty construction.

'Shatter!'

His staff exploded in a nimbus of blinding light. A ball of
golden fire kindled in the heart of the cannon barrel, shining in the well of darkness like the full face of Mannslieb.
The fluorescent sphere grew, rushing outwards, bulging at
the iron flanks of the massive machine and cracking its
metal hide.

The infantry around it surged forwards, crystal-bladed halberds lowered, lumbering towards the bellowing Theogonist.
From within their narrow visors a lilac glow bled out, and a
low canine growl rumbled in their iron-cased chests.

'Forward!' roared Maljdir, rushing into the fray to protect
his master, swinging the standard aloft as he went. Warrior
priests swept around Volkmar and crashed into the advancing ranks of masked dog-soldiers, their warhammers coming
into play with devastating, neck-breaking force.

The Bright wizards stood back and sent a hail of crackling
bolts spinning into the flanks of the war engine. The bolts
caught and kindled on Volkmar's holy fire and exploded in
their turn. The cannon barrel expanded further, stretched
almost to breaking point by the vast forces unfurling within
it. A filigree of cracks, each leaking golden light, rushed across
the beaten iron. The furnace began to stutter, sending rolls
of soot-clogged smoke coughing into the night.

'Shatter!' Volkmar roared again, eliciting a fresh inferno
from the Staff of Command.

Still the war engine resisted, somehow maintaining its
structure in the face of the onslaught. The swirling maelstrom
within it bulged further, bleeding golden incandescence from
the growing web of cracks. Metal, hot as coals, showered
down from the hulking barrel as the iron fractured. Bronze
bindings broke and spun free. The furnace choked out and

flared back up again, knocked out of rhythm by the cease-less, grinding power of the Theogonist.

Then there was a great crack, a rolling boom. The air shud-dered, and the earth rocked. With titanic force, the vast war engine blasted itself apart.

The huge shell of iron flew high into the air, pursued by a deafening explosion of shimmering gold. The carcass of the monster was cloven into pieces, reeling in all directions as the heart of the cannon was torn asunder. Men and beasts alike were blasted from their feet, lost in the whirling storm of consuming power.

Volkmar's fire flared up against the daemonic energies locked in the core of the device, flattening the troops beyond and tearing up the earth on which it rested. Priests were bowled over alongside the creatures they grappled with. The wizards were hurled back and the Imperial standard ripped from Maljdir's desperate grip. A backdraft of green-tinged flame rushed out in a corona of destruction, spiralling into the night and blasting aside all in its path. Men were thrown up like leaves in a gale, their armour shattered, and hurled into the cowering forms of their comrades further back.

Only Volkmar stood firm, his robes rippling against the howling aftershock of the cannon's demise. He kept his arms raised, defiantly screaming his wrath amid the shards of spin-ning iron. The halo of unleashed power expanded further, ripping through the ranks of soldiers, shaking the ground and echoing out across the plain.

As the worst of the backwash passed, Maljdir clambered to his feet and staggered back to Volkmar's position. All was confusion. Bodies, twisted and broken, were heaped up against the steaming hide of the ruined war machine. Dog-soldiers lay amongst warrior priests, steeped in a cock-tail of their own blood. The Empire spearhead was in ruins. The device had been destroyed, but at a massive cost.

'What are you *doing*?' Maljdir roared. This was no strat-egy, no tactical advance, just a headlong charge into the heart of darkness. Already the vast hosts of enemy soldiers were coalescing around Volkmar's position, drawn by the destruction of one of their totems. Elsewhere across the plain the Imperial forces were being driven back. Only Volkmar pressed forwards, carving his way deeper into peril. The unity of the army was fracturing.

The Theogonist looked back at Maljdir, hardly seeming to recognise him. His eyes were wild and staring. His knuckles were white from grasping the Staff of Command and a sheen of glistening sweat covered his exposed flesh. His torso shivered with hatred.

'I will find him, Odain,' Volkmar hissed. 'Do you not see it? *He* is here.'

Maljdir recoiled in horror.

'You do not–' he started.

It was too late. Volkmar brushed past him, striding through the wreckage of the war engine, his staff a golden halo amid the fire-wracked gloom.

'*Everchosen,*' he whispered as he went, and his staff kindled again with snapping, crackling fire.

In his wake came the surviving priests, the limping wizards, the remnants of the halberdier vanguard. Inspired by his rampage, the Empire troops just kept on coming.

'Tears of Sigmar,' cursed Maljdir, ignoring them and stooping to retrieve the charred standard from the blood-soaked earth. Efraim Roll came to his side, emerging from the press of men, his sword running with blood. The confessor had a long weal across his neck and his armour was dented. The man had been busy.

'We've lost him,' reported Maljdir grimly. 'He's gone mad. You should've let me restrain him at Streissen.'

'*Restrain* him?' Roll shook his head in disbelief. All around them the Imperial troops piled forwards, filling in the wounds in the defence rent open by the Theogonist's inexorable advance. 'You're the madman. He's the only hope we have left.'

'But his soul...'

'Damn his soul!' Roll's voice shook with fervour as he

barged past Maljdir in pursuit of Volkmar. 'This is about survival now. Keep waving that damn flag, priest. If we falter now, *all* our souls will be forfeit.'

CHAPTER SEVENTEEN

Grosslich flicked an armoured finger and his dog-soldiers surged forwards. They crashed into the circling Knights Panther, studiously avoiding the one he'd picked out. The preceptor was soon isolated, cut off from the battle raging around and left for Grosslich to deal with. Gruppen remained on his horse, raging pointlessly as his comrades were driven further from him, hacking at the dog-soldiers swarming around them in ever greater numbers.

'You have doomed them, knight,' said Grosslich, waiting patiently.

The preceptor whirled to face him. His visor was still down and his expression hidden, but Grosslich could sense the anger boiling within him. He knew he'd pushed too deep.

'Do not *speak* to me, traitor!' spat Gruppen. 'You *disgust* me. You're filth. Worse than filth. The lowliest serf on my estate–'

Grosslich snapped his fingers again, and the tirade stopped. The preceptor would never speak again. If he'd wanted, Grosslich could have killed him then with a single casting, but he had no intention of doing so. Sorcery was a useful tool, but it was no substitute for proper combat, fighting the way a man should. Despite all Natassja had done to him, Grosslich had still not forgotten his roots.

'Save it,' he said, wearily. 'You're a dead man, so at least try to make this worthy of a song.'

He kicked his steed, and the hell-beast lurched forwards. Gruppen did likewise, sword whirling, and the two men crashed together. The preceptor was quick. He got his blade round sharply against Grosslich's flank before he could respond. The metal bounced from the spell-wound armour and the knight was nearly knocked from his saddle by the recoil.

Then Grosslich brought his own blade to bear, lashing heavily with his broadsword. The edge of it bit hard, carving through the knight's plate and digging into the leather beneath. The preceptor pulled back, somehow managing to haul his steed round in the tight space and drag himself away from the assault. Grosslich pressed the attack, bringing his blade back for a decapitating lunge.

Instead of pulling away, Gruppen darted back towards him, displaying incredible mastery of his steed. He ducked low to evade Grosslich's blow and slashed at his mutant steed instead. The knight aimed truly, slicing into the warped creature's scaly face and pulling the flesh from the bone.

The monster reared, almost throwing Grosslich from the saddle. Its clawed legs kicked out in agony. Grosslich cursed, trying to bring it under control, reeling around and out of position. The knight pursued the advantage, landing a heavy strike on Grosslich's back. Again, the armour was his saviour, though the force of the blow knocked him forwards, further maddening his pain-deranged mount.

Grosslich snaked back round in his saddle just in time to see the knight's blade coming back at him again, aimed for the head and moving with bone-breaking force. Grosslich snatched his gauntlet up. He grabbed the sword-edge and held it tight. Gruppen frantically tried to pull it back, seizing it with both hands and yanking at the hilt.

Smiling beneath his helmet, Grosslich crushed his fingers together, squeezing the metal and bending it out of shape. With a final twist, the sword shattered. Still the knight didn't give up. He continued to attack, jabbing with the broken stump of his weapon, trying to find some way to penetrate the spell-soaked armour.

Grosslich kicked his steed forwards and the pain-maddened beast lurched straight into the knight's skittish mount, knocking it sideways and causing it to stumble. Whip-fast, Grosslich grabbed Gruppen's cloak and hauled him from the saddle, hurling him to the ground with a sickening crack.

Gruppen tried to rise again, dragging himself to one knee and bringing his broken blade up for a new lunge at the mutant's shanks. The beast was now in range, though, and the animal knew the author of its pain. With a throaty scream it reared again, scything its clawed feet before bringing them down on the still-rising preceptor. One taloned hoof slammed against his breastplate, crushing the plate and cracking the man's chest. The other crunched hard against his helmet, breaking the metal open and shattering his skull.

Gruppen fell back, choked on his own blood and bone. Grosslich rode over his body, trampling it into the slick of mud beneath, letting his wounded creature take its revenge. Only when there was nothing left to stamp on did he pull the raging beast away, tugging at the reins hard. The scourge of the Drakwald was gone, his proud career ended at last on the corrupted plains of Averland, alone and surrounded by the enemy.

'Enough,' said Grosslich, calming his snorting mount. 'There'll be more.'

The dog-soldiers had finished off the others. They stood around stupidly, waiting for fresh orders. Beyond them the battle raged, intensifying in scope as more and more troops were committed by their desperate commanders. The Imperials were showing commendable spirit, but there weren't enough of them and they weren't of the same calibre as Natassja's creatures.

Grosslich wished he could take some pleasure in that. Slaughtering such men was nothing to be proud of. Even as victory edged towards his grasp, he felt a deep and stubborn sickness lodge deep within him.

He'd dreamed of *glory*. Of a realm that men would admire and envy. Whatever the result of this battle, he'd never be granted that now.

'Oh, go and find something to kill,' he muttered to his guards, and watched bitterly as they loped back towards the fiercest fighting. They never questioned a thing. They'd never question anything.

With a heavy heart, his armour streaked with blood, the elector withdrew from the frontline, back to the position of command, leaving his slaves to continue the struggle. Above him, the Tower loomed, a roost of daemons and sorcery, the mark of his failure.

Maljdir looked around him, blood and sweat clouding his vision. Volkmar's vanguard had penetrated far across the plains, fighting their way through the maze of trenches and across the ridges of spikes. Even though the Light magisters' spell had waned, Volkmar still blazed a trail. Though the casualties around him grew ever heavier, the Imperial army still clustered to his call. As the day waned and the meagre scraps of shrouded sunlight bled away, his was the only pure fire left on the battlefield. Like moths around a candle-flame they huddled close to its warmth, given heart in the face of the endless hordes raging towards them. The Theogonist was heading to the centre of the defences, and a light of madness was in his eyes.

Maljdir took up the standard in his left hand, hefting the heavy stave against his shoulder. In his right hand he carried Bloodbringer, swinging it with as much vigour as the other warrior priests. The dog-soldiers were everywhere now, snarling and tearing at the Imperial troops, bringing them down through sheer savagery. The armour-plated priests were the only infantry in Volkmar's retinue capable of taking them on one-to-one. The mutants were taller, faster and stronger than the average halberdier and killed two of them for every one of their warped kin that was taken down. Against such losses, Volkmar's surge was doomed. Soon they'd be cut off entirely, their defences whittled away and the spearhead isolated.

A dog-soldier leapt across Maljdir's path, growling as it swept up its halberd, aiming for his chest. Its iron mask had been torn from its head, exposing the distended muzzle and canine teeth. The flesh was human-like, ripped and moulded into its new shape by surgery and sorcery. Maljdir dodged the blow, dropping back with surprising speed before spinning back with a counter-strike. Bloodbringer swung heavily, slamming into the soldier's flank, smashing the breastplate in and cracking the ribs beneath it. The mutant was knocked sideways, stumbling across the ground before recovering and coiling for a second attack.

It never came. Bloodbringer swept back on the reverse angle, catching the horror square in the face. With a rip and a snap the dog-soldier's head came off, dragging the body up after it on a string of sinews before the whole corpse thumped down into the mud, feet away.

Maljdir hardly broke stride, crushing the severed skull under his boots as he ploughed after Volkmar and looked for the next victim. The momentum was relentless, exhausting. The Theogonist seemed to have no tactics other than rampage. The vanguard was moving ever closer to the walls of Averheim, still barred by a sea of foes and clothed in a thundering wall of flame. Dark shapes swam within that blood-red curtain, curling like fish around the column of madness. Maljdir could sense the corruption there, spilling out from the inferno.

Volkmar must have sensed it too. That was where the Theogonist was heading. He cared nothing for the battlefield now, nothing for the lives of the thousands of men who still fought in the trenches and under the shadow of the war machines. He was after Archaon, and the rest of the army was expendable to that delusion.

'He'll damn us all,' growled Maljdir, dispatching another dog-soldier with a crunching blow, hardly pausing in his onward march.

Bloodbringer felt light in his hands. Volkmar was only a few paces ahead, raving and spilling golden light from his fingers. His back was unprotected.

'Sigmar's blood,' he said, judging the path his hammer would have to take to end it. 'He'll damn us all.'

'Reiksguard, to me!'

Helborg crested the final rise before the city, and its damnation was laid out before him. They'd arrived to the east of the battlefield. The fighting was less than a mile away, spread out across the plain below.

All thought of gaining the Averpeak was instantly abandoned. The ridge smouldered away in the north, its flanks broken by the power of Grosslich's war engines. Six infernal devices still survived, their jaws gaping red and angry. Around each of them were thousands of troops, staining the land black with their numbers. At the very foot of the Averpeak, a mile distant from the walls of the city, the line of battle ran in a vast, snaking curve.

Helborg squinted through the drifting smog. There were banners flying. Many infantry companies fought, but they were heavily outnumbered by Grosslich's defenders. There was no *shape* to the Imperial assault, just a straggling melee towards the walls. Only at one point did the Empire army seem to be making headway. A column of soldiers had pierced deep into the enemy lines, moving fast towards the city gates. There was a brilliant golden light at the tip of the column, blazing in the heart of the darkness.

'Volkmar,' said Helborg as his knights clustered around him. Forty-six Reiksguard remained. The swirling clouds reflected from their armour, glowing red from the fires on the plain below. 'I've seen that power wielded before.'

'He's out of position,' said Skarr, frowning. 'His army's coming apart.'

Schwarzhelm came alongside them. The Rechtstahl was naked in his hands, ready for action. There was no time for deliberation. The Empire army was in disarray, outnumbered, out-fought and leaderless.

'Lord Schwarzhelm, lead the infantry to bolster the Imperial lines. Rally the men, and give them some purpose.'

'And the Reiksguard?' asked Schwarzhelm.

Helborg drew the Klingerach. The dark metal glinted, still marred by the notch on the blade.

'We can cut through those troops,' he said, snapping his visor down. All thought of the long days of sickness had left him. His heart pumped powerfully in his chest again, fuelling the arms that carried the runefang. 'We'll fight to Volkmar's position. This field isn't lost yet.'

Last of all, Leitdorf drew up to the height of the rise, his ruddy face aghast at the devastation below.

'My inheritance,' he announced grimly, gazing across the carnage.

'Indeed so, my lord,' said Helborg, readying for the charge down into the inferno. 'You will ride with me. My blade is keener than it was the last time we fought together and my body is restored.'

Unholy winds, laced with ash and throbbing with heat, rushed up from the battlefield. Helborg's cloak billowed out, revealing the splendour of his ancient armour. The hawk-pinions of his helmet seemed to catch an echo of the golden rays streaming from Volkmar's staff, etching the metal with a faint sheen against the shadows.

'If Sigmar wills it,' he said, raising the Sword of Vengeance and pointing it towards the heart of the horde below, 'we will yet bring destruction to those who have turned away from His light. Ride now, and may His protection be with all of you.'

Achendorfer let the last pages of the book crackle and fade away. His long fingers, warped and melded with the leather, curled back round, free from the weight at last. The grimoire had been burned away like so much else.

No matter. Its work had been done.

He gazed up lovingly at the Stone. No light reflected from its sides even though the lamps in the walls of the chamber still burned strongly. It was as black as a pupil, a void at the base of the city. By contrast, everything around it was flickering and ephemeral. The shaft above it soared into the far distance, hundreds of feet of thundering fire. He stood alone at the base. This was the origin, the source of all that was to come. The thought pleased him.

Achendorfer took a deep breath and closed his eyes, feeling the heat of the flames enter his lungs. Down here, the blood-fire was at its thickest. It didn't consume or damage mortal flesh, but it *hurt*. He felt the searing heat of it against his throat, scraping at the flesh, testing him and probing for weakness.

'Is all ready, lizard?'

Achendorfer hadn't heard the queen enter. He snapped back to attention, whipping round to face her.

'Of course. The Stone is waiting.'

Natassja didn't smile. Such mortal gestures were losing their grip on her. Her humanity was now little more than a skein, a fragile barrier between the world of laws and the raging Chaos within her. Achendorfer could see it in her eyes. Those white-less orbs, for so long two cool, tolerant points within that sleek face, had now sunk into darkness, mirroring the Stone. He doubted that she even saw the world of matter truly any more. For such as her, a realm of pure sensation awaited, a flux of emotion and desire. Perhaps the same would come for him one day.

'Then begin again,' she said.

Achendorfer bowed. He no longer needed the book for such work. The words had been burned on to his mind across the many hours of labour. His lips formed around the words unbidden, his muscles fully attuned to the shapes of the forbidden speech.

'*Bedarruzibarr,*' he intoned. The bloodfire in the chamber flared up at the sound. '*Bedarruzibarr'zagarratumnan'akz'akz 'berau.*'

On and on the syllables droned, just as they had for weeks, soaked into the walls of iron and etched in the blazing sigils far up the shaft.

Natassja walked slowly towards the stone, her steps mannered and ceremonial. From far above, beyond the wards, there came the sounds of daemons singing.

'*Akz'akz'berau,*' they chorused, and a feral joy was locked into their fractured, cherubic voices. '*Malamanuar'neramum o'klza'jhehennum.*'

Natassja raised her slender arms in supplication. Her skin darkened to nightshade, glowing darkly like embers. With a faint hiss, her sheer gown slipped from her shoulders and coiled around her feet.

Achendorfer knew he should look away then. He remained rapt, and a thin line of drool ran down his chin.

He kept chanting. The daemons kept chanting. The bloodfire seared the air, pregnant with the coming storm. Natassja's hair began to lift, rippling like wind-lashed silk, exposing the sweeping curves of her flawless outline. Across her flesh, signs of Slaanesh glowed into life, swimming over the skin and moulding into new and wonderful shapes.

She began to grow.

Blood replaced the drool on Achendorfer's skin. A kind of ecstasy gripped him.

'*Abbadonnodo'neherata'gradarruminam!*' he raved, swaying with the movement of the bloodfire.

This was it. This was what the joyroot had been for, the deception, the armies, the torture, the construction, the book, what all of it had been for.

For so long She had been coming. Now, finally, She was here.

Bloch marched at the head of his detachment. His halberdiers went steadily. There was no running or hollering, only a disciplined, well-ordered advance. He'd arranged the men into four companies of forty men, ten across and four deep. A few extra men had been tacked on to his lead group. Not much of a return from the thousands who'd marched under Grunwald.

As he went, he muttered a prayer to Sigmar, to Ranald, to Shallya, and a general benediction to anyone he'd left off the list. The enemy ranks were within sight and the charge would not be long coming. The clash of arms was huge and heavy, echoing across the plains and rebounding from the ruined Averpeak. The nearer they came to it, the darker the skies became.

The rest of Helborg's irregular infantry marched in semi-ordered detachments on either flank of Bloch's troops. They looked scared and uncertain. The prospect of liberating Averland, so attractive under the warm sun, now seemed like a fool's errand. They were heading into the depths of Chaos, and even the simple-minded knew the great enemy when they saw it. Bloch placed little faith in them. At the first sign of serious trouble, they'd break. The only hope was to join up with the larger Imperial forces before that happened.

Ahead of them all rode Schwarzhelm, Kraus and the few cavalry Helborg had given them. The Emperor's Champion looked as stern and unyielding as a mountain. He, and he alone, inspired some faith that this wasn't merely a vainglorious march to death.

'Herr Bloch.'

A forgotten voice rose over the growing clamour. Bloch felt his heart sink.

'Herr Verstohlen,' he replied, looking up to see the familiar figure of the spy riding alongside. Something of the habitual smug expression had been erased from the man's lean face. His eyes were ringed and heavy with fatigue, and his tailored clothes were ripped and stained. 'You're still here, then.'

'Just about.' Schwarzhelm's agent had his pistol in his free hand, loaded and ready to fire. 'I've not seen you for some time.'

'Strange, that.'

'And you've lost your lieutenant.'

'Captain Kraus is back where he belongs.'

Verstohlen smiled. There was little mirth in it, just a wry grin at the foolishness of the world.

'As we all are,' he said. 'Look, I'm not much at home on the battlefield, commander. It disagrees with me. The last time I fought under Schwarzhelm, you were good enough to let me tag along.'

Bloch squinted up at him, wondering, as ever, whether Verstohlen was mocking him.

'We're infantry,' he said. 'Your horse won't fit in.'

Verstohlen swung down from the saddle, landing lightly beside Bloch. He gave his steed a thump on the flanks, and it lurched away from the approaching battlefront, no doubt pleased to be heading away from the horrors ahead.

'Any better?'

Bloch scowled. He'd not known what to make of Verstohlen at Turgitz, and he had little enough idea now. The man was an enigma, and enigmas were no use to him.

'If you want to use that gun, then be my guest. But get in the way, and I'll skewer you myself.'

Verstohlen nodded seriously.

'Quite right, commander,' he said. 'I wouldn't expect anything less.'

Ahead of them, the rearguard of the enemy finally spotted the advancing ranks of Schwarzhelm's troops. Soldiers began to turn to face them, still several hundred yards off.

'To arms!' came the cry from Kraus.

All along the line, steel glittered as it was swung into position. Men made the sign of the comet, adjusted their helmets, pulled breastplates down, mumbled prayers.

Steadily, silently, Grosslich's men broke into a run towards them. The soldiers looked strange, as if their eyes had been replaced with pools of witch-fire.

'On my mark!' roared Kraus.

Schwarzhelm clutched the Rechtstahl with his right hand and bowed his head in a silent dedication. He'd be the first one in.

'I feel that we never had the chance to get to know one

another properly,' said Verstohlen as the pace of the march picked up. Though he tried to hide it with levity, his voice was shot through with fear.

'Some other time, perhaps,' muttered Bloch, waiting for the order to charge.

'I'd like that.'

Then Kraus swung his sword wildly over his head.

'Men of the Empire!' he bellowed. 'Death to the enemy! Charge now, and Sigmar guide your blades!'

With a massed roar of their own, the halberdiers surged forwards. Behind them came the Averlanders, faces pale with terror, hands clasped tight on their weapons, sweat glistening on their brows.

At their head rode Schwarzhelm, sword blazing red against the flames, his throaty cries of defiance and hatred rising above the tumult. In his wake, desperate and valiant, five thousand infantry streamed into the well of fire and death.

Helborg felt the ash-hot air stream past him as he spurred his horse into a gallop. Schwarzhelm had committed his troops, drawing attention away from the Reiksguard and leaving the field clear for the charge. The squadron comprised fewer than fifty horsemen, including himself and Leitdorf – a laughable force with which to threaten a host of thousands.

The wedge of riders around him tightened. Their massed hooves drummed on the packed earth as the knights swept towards their target. Half a mile to their left the walls of Averheim rose up into the storm-raked air, vast and dark. Ahead of them were file upon file of marching infantry, each clad in close-fitting plate armour and bearing a crystal halberd. Somewhere beyond them was Volkmar. The Theogonist's position had been obvious enough from the vantage of the rise, but was now lost in the smoke and confusion of the battlefield.

The success of the charge all depended on speed and power. The first blow would settle things.

'Karl Franz!' roared Helborg as the first lines of the enemy came into view. The dog-soldiers before him turned to face the onslaught. Too slowly. They'd be ripped aside.

'The Emperor!' replied the Reiksguard, crying aloud as one. Skarr was at the forefront of the charge, his ravaged face enclosed in steel and his blade flashing.

Rufus Leitdorf rode on his left shoulder, leaning forwards in the saddle and with the Wolfsklinge unsheathed at his side.

'For my father,' he murmured, too low for the others to hear.

The gap shrank, closed and disappeared. The wedge of cavalry, a steel-tipped spear of white and red, slammed into the defenders. Grosslich's infantry were ridden into the mire or cut down by the precision of the Reiksguard sword-work. Helborg kicked his horse onwards and it leapt into the press of Grosslich's rearguard, lashing out and kicking its hooves as it laboured through the mass of bodies.

Startled by the sudden onslaught, the resistance was weak. A group of heavily-armoured dog-soldiers attempted to form a line against the charge.

'Take them!' cried Helborg, pulling his horse's head round to meet the threat.

The Reiksguard wheeled, every horseman controlling his steed superbly. Without any drop in speed, the knights galloped at the wall of iron and steel. They crashed into the defence again at full tilt, breaking open the nascent line of shields and scattering the mutants. Some knights were knocked from the saddle or raked with a desperate halberd-stab from below, but the wedge remained intact, tearing forwards, heading ever further into the files of the corrupted troops.

'D'you see him?' shouted Skarr, crouching low in the saddle, his helmet drenched in blood and his sword still swinging.

'Not yet,' replied Helborg, impaling a dog-soldier with a downward plunge before bringing the Klingerach smartly back up for another victim.

Helborg felt stronger than he'd done since leaving Nuln. His shoulder spiked with pain, but he ignored it. Like Schwarzhelm, he lived for combat. Creeping around in the hinterland of Averland had been a drain on his soul. Now, surrounded by the filth he'd dedicated his life to eradicating, the tang of blood on his lips and the thunder of hooves in his ears, he was back where he belonged.

'Keep on this course!' he bellowed, directing his galloping steed towards a fresh attempt to halt them. 'Rally to the Theogonist when we see him. Until then, kill all who get in your way.'

With that, Helborg swerved to avoid a looming dog-soldier, carving a deep gash in the mutant's shoulder as he passed, before powering onwards to the line of mustering defenders.

His eyes narrowed under the visor and a warm smile creased his battle-scarred face. The hooves of his horse thudded as he hurtled towards his next target.

'Sigmar preserves those who fight,' he murmured to himself, licking his cracked lips with anticipation. '*Blessed* be the name of Sigmar.'

Schwarzhelm strode forwards and the Rechtstahl trailed a line of ripped-free gore behind it. He'd dismounted once the press around him had got too close and now went on foot amongst his troops, carving his way towards the sundered Imperial lines. Kraus was at his side, hammering away with his blade.

There seemed to be no end to the mutants, horrors and dead-eyed mortals looming up out of the dark, faces blank and blades swinging. The assault on Grosslich's flank had almost stalled. Bloch's men were capable of holding their own but the Averlanders were less accomplished. Schwarzhelm had seen dozens of them running from the field, crying with fear and leaving their weapons in the mud behind them. Those that remained were now surrounded, enveloped in the endless ranks of Grosslich's legions. The mutants exacted a heavy toll for any forward progress. Only Schwarzhelm kept the drive going, hauling his men forwards by the force of example.

'No mercy!' he roared, stabbing the Rechtstahl through the wheezing throat of a mutant and ripping it out. 'Keep your formation! Fear no traitor!'

He knew time was running out. They were too deep in to disengage.

'Where now?' panted Kraus, fresh from felling his man. His armour looked big on him, as if the weeks in the wild had physically shrunk the honour guard captain.

'This is the right course,' said Schwarzhelm, dragging a halberdier back out of harm's way before crushing the skull of his looming assailant. 'Unless the Empire army has fallen back to–'

With a scream, something dark and clawed flung itself from the enemy lines. It was cloaked in rags and had talons for fingers. The halberdiers shrank back, bewildered and terrified.

Schwarzhelm brought the Rechtstahl round quickly. Steel clashed against bone, and a flash of witch-light burst out from the impact. Kraus leapt forwards, blade at the ready.

'Get back!' roared Schwarzhelm, his sword dancing in the firelight, parrying and thrusting at the scuttling creature. 'Your blade will not bite this.'

Kraus fell away, blocking instead the advance of a slavering dog-soldier. Schwarzhelm worked his sword with speed, matching the spider-sharp movements of the horror. Every time the Rechtstahl hit, a blaze of sparks rained to the ground. The creature leapt at him, screaming with frustration, talons lashing.

Schwarzhelm ducked under the scything claws, shouldering his mighty pauldrons to the assault and swinging the blade fast and low across the earth. The horror reacted, spinning back on itself to evade the strike, but too late. The Sword of Justice sliced through sinew and iron, taking off the creature's legs and leaving it writhing in the blood-soaked mud.

Schwarzhelm rose to his full height, spun the sword round and plunged it down, pinning the horror's torso as he'd done with Tochfel in Averheim. It let out a final screech of pain and fury before the light in its eyes went out.

With the destruction of Natassja's pet, the dog-soldiers began to withdraw. None of them could stand against Schwarzhelm. In the shuffling confusion the halberdiers were finally able to push them back.

'Morr's blood,' spat Kraus, looking at the twisted carcass still twitching in the slime of the field. 'What *is* that?'

'Another one I failed to save,' replied Schwarzhelm grimly, stalking back to the front line. At his approach, the dog-soldiers fell back further. Soon his massive shoulders were busy again, hacking and parrying, driving the mutants inwards.

'Reikland!' came a voice then from further down the line of halberdiers. Schwarzhelm recognised it at once. Bloch. The halberdier commander was still unstoppable, as tough and enduring as old leather.

Schwarzhelm whirled round, hope rising in his breast. Drifts of smoke still obscured the battlefield beyond a few paces and the ash-choked darkness did the rest, but he could see the shadows of men running towards them.

'Hold your positions!' he bellowed, his gruff voice cracking under the strain. He couldn't afford for his troops to get strung out.

Then, suddenly, there were halberdiers around him. They weren't Bloch's men, but wore the grey and white of the Reikland. They looked exhausted, their faces streaked with blood and their breastplates dented.

'Against all hope...' one of them stammered, limping towards Schwarzhelm like he was some shade of Morr.

Bloch burst from the right flank after him, grinning like an idiot.

'We've broken through, my lord!' he cried, exposing the bloody hole in his smile where something had knocked half his teeth from his jaw. 'These are our men!'

Even as he announced the news, more Imperial troops emerged from the gloom. There were dozens, possibly hundreds.

'Maintain the assault!' growled Schwarzhelm, glowering at Bloch and pushing his way past the limping Reikland troops. 'You pox-ridden dogs, form up like you're in the army of the Emperor.'

Bloch's men immediately responded, swinging back to face the dog-soldiers and charging the disarrayed lines. Their commander disappeared with them, in the forefront as ever, hefting his halberd with brutal enjoyment.

Schwarzhelm turned on the nearest Empire halberdier. Everything was in flux. They were still heavily outnumbered, and their only hope lay in restoring discipline.

'Who's the senior officer here?' he demanded.

'I don't know, my lord. Kleister is dead, and Bogenhof is–'

'You'll do then. Get these men into detachments. Four deep, ten wide. Do it now. Follow my lead, and we'll clear some space around us. This isn't over yet.'

The halberdier looked back at him, first with surprise, then with a sudden, desperate hope.

'Yes, my lord!' he cried, before rushing to form his men up as ordered.

Schwarzhelm turned back to the fighting. If there were any more of those creatures, he knew he'd be the only one who could take them on.

'What now?' asked Kraus, hurrying back to his side.

'Get in amongst these men,' said Schwarzhelm, striding without break to catch up with Bloch's men. 'Get them organised and follow me. There'll be more of them as we go, and they all need leading.'

'So where are we taking them?'

Schwarzhelm turned back to shoot Kraus a murderous look.

'Grosslich must have seen us by now,' he said, his eyes narrowing under his helmet. 'He's here somewhere, and when I find him, he's my kill.'

Then Schwarzhelm stalked off, massive and threatening, his sword thirsting for the blood that followed it whenever it was drawn.

* * *

The walls of the city soared up into the sky, braced with
iron and crested with thirty-foot-high sigils of Slaanesh. The
curving symbols glowed red, throbbing in the darkness and
spilling their unnatural light across the storm-born shadows.

Volkmar was close enough now. He could taste the tang
of corruption streaming from Averheim, locked in the column of rumbling fire. There were presences in the aethyr,
darting shapes swimming in the currents of translucent crimson. He could see their outlines, a twisted fusion of woman
and Chaos-spawn.

'I am coming for you,' he growled, swinging his staff round
to blast a lumbering mutant from his path.

Volkmar knew neither fatigue nor fear now. As truly as he
knew his own name, he knew the Lord of End Times had
come back to face him again. This time, the result would
be different. He'd seen the other side of reality, had gazed
across the planes of immortal existence and felt their cold
embrace. Now enclosed in the sinews and blood of a man
once more, he would not return there. Not until the Everchosen lay at his feet, drowning in his own betrayer's gore.

Volkmar felt a sudden hand on his shoulder, huge and
heavy. He spun round, the Staff of Command responding
instantly with a blaze of sparkling faith-fire.

'This is *enough.*'

Maljdir stood before him. The huge man was covered in
sweat, blood and grime. The battle standard at his shoulder
was charred and ripped. The warrior priests surged onwards
around the two of them, driving the enemy back further.

'What d'you mean?' hissed Volkmar, eager to return to the
slaughter. 'He's *in* there. We're almost on him.'

Maljdir looked agonised. Perhaps it was fear. The old Ulrican had never displayed fear before. That was disappointing.

'Look around you.' Maljdir forcibly turned the Theogonist
to face the following troops.

It took a moment for his eyes to clear, dazzled as they were
by the splendour of his staff.

'Where are my men?' he asked, suddenly filled with doubt.

There were fewer than three hundred left, all bunched together, fighting to keep up with the charge of their leader. Most of those that remained were warrior priests. The wizards were gone, and there was no sign of Roll. Even as Volkmar watched, a swordsman in the rear of his column was torn apart by a ragged thing with talons for hands, his flesh flung over the heads of his comrades as he screamed.

'They couldn't keep up!' cried Maljdir. 'You've dragged them to their deaths. We must pull back.'

Volkmar hesitated, and the light of his staff guttered like a candle-flame. He couldn't withdraw. Not now, not with the city so close.

'We're almost at the gates,' he insisted, shaking off the priest's hands. 'I can feel his presence in the city...'

'You're deluded!' roared Maljdir. 'Chaos is here, but not the one you seek.'

Even as he spoke, more mutants closed in around them. They sensed the end, and were no longer daunted by the staff.

Volkmar reeled, feeling his visions lift from his eyes. The anger was still there, but the mania had gone, extinguished by revelation.

'We cannot...' he started, and never finished.

A snarling pack of dog-soldiers charged into the line of warrior priests ahead of them, knocking them back and hacking them down. Volkmar's forces had become a beleaguered island amid a swirling maelstrom of enemy troops. It was too late to go back, and hopeless to go on.

'I have doomed us,' said Volkmar, his eyes widening with horror.

Maljdir drew away then, hauled back into the fighting by the approaching mutants.

'You still have the staff!' he roared, wading into action and wielding Bloodbringer like a great bell, swinging back and forth. 'Use it! Get us back!'

Then he was gone, ploughing into the attack, laying into the clutching fingers and stabbing blades of the dog-soldiers around him.

Volkmar looked up. The gates were at hand. They were open still, still choked with Grosslich's troops. Under the massive iron lintel, the fires raged out of control. Averheim was ablaze, and daemonic forces swam in the unlocked power of the aethyr. The scene looked just like another world he'd seen once, back when his soul had been unlocked. Now Averheim was just one of those slivers of eternity, a shard of ruin embedded in the world of men.

'No!' he roared, and his staff rushed back into flame. 'No retreat. We end this here.'

He swung the staff round and sent a snarling bolt of fire at the talon-fingered horror still terrorising his men. The creature blew apart in a deluge of bone and dry flesh. Volkmar felt power well up within him again, fuelled by faith and fury. He span back, sending a flurry of spitting lightning into the pressing ranks of mutants. They fell back in disarray, their ranks broken by a power they had no defence against.

Volkmar himself began to shimmer with a golden corona. No Light magister's spell fuelled him now. A halo crested his brow, blazing into the unnatural night and challenging the fires of Slaanesh for mastery. He was Master of the Church of Sigmar, the mightiest of His servants, the head of His Cult on earth, and no power could stand against that secret knowledge.

He took his stand, cracking the earth as he trod it down, his cloak rippling with gold. The servants of Averheim fell back, daunted by the savage forces he'd unleashed. His surging luminescence rose up into the tortured air, defiant and isolated, a shaft of pure flame to challenge the vast pillar of fire ahead.

'Sigmar!' came a roar from his left, deep in the ranks of the enemy.

It wasn't Maljdir, or Roll, or any of his troops. Something had responded to the line of burning gold.

The press of dog-soldiers on his left flank suddenly broke apart, scattered by a new force emerging from beyond them. Volkmar whirled round, ready to face a new terror. Instead, a phalanx of horsemen burst from their midst, swords flashing, hooves churning. They swept aside all resistance, as powerful and pure as a storm.

As they came on, Volkmar's golden light surged to greet them, bathing the oncoming knights in a cloak of brilliance.

They were the Emperor's own, the Reiksguard, and at their head rode Kurt Helborg. The knights surged towards the surrounded Empire troops, careering around Volkmar's remaining men and enclosing them in a wall of steel. Caught between the onslaught of the Reiksguard and the dazzling power of the Theogonist, Grosslich's twisted soldiers fell back further. For the first time, their eyes wavered with fear. Even the most debased servants of the Dark Gods could recognise a runefang when it came among them.

Helborg thundered towards Volkmar, pulling up at the last minute. His charger reared, kicking its hooves high in the air. Helborg slammed open his visor, revealing the familiar hawk-nose and stiff moustache. He looked more magnificent than Volkmar had ever seen him, like a vision of Magnus the Pious reborn, severe and terrible.

'My lord Volkmar!' he cried, controlling his stamping, shivering mount with unconscious ease. 'I bring the rightful Elector of Averland to his throne. Will you join me in battle?'

Volkmar raised his staff high and the corona blazed ever more furiously, banishing the shadows and blinding the reeling, cowering mutants. No madness remained in him then, just the righteous fury of the battlefield.

'I will, my lord Marshal,' replied Volkmar, seeing the armoured figure of Rufus Leitdorf emerge into the light for the first time. The man looked far more commanding than he'd expected from his reputation. He rode his warhorse without fear, and the faith-fire rushed to greet him, dousing him in a cascade of gold.

Volkmar turned again to face the iron gates, still open, still wreathed in daemonic fire. This was a new task, one for which his burning faith was aptly suited. Even in the midst of ruin, there was always redemption.

'To the city, then,' he said, narrowing his eyes against the roaring flames, 'and judgement.'

CHAPTER EIGHTEEN

The plains were dark with men. Aside from the splinter force that had followed Volkmar towards the walls of the city, the Imperial troops still occupied a long line skirting around the north edge of the plain. They had made negligible progress towards their goal, frustrated by the sheer numbers of Grosslich's slave-army before them.

Losses had been heavy. Of the forty thousand soldiers committed to the field, less than half still stood to bear arms. The enemy had suffered too, though their capacity to absorb casualties was greater. The defenders had maintained their positions, grinding down the advancing Imperial infantry with remorseless efficiency. They never took a step back, never withdrew, just soaked up the increasingly desperate attacks, waiting for the Empire lines to break from exhaustion.

Along much of the Imperial battlefront, discipline had broken down. In the absence of a guiding hand at the centre, lines of communication broke. The system of supporting detachments, the pride of the Empire and its most lethal weapon, was hamstrung. Companies found themselves suddenly isolated, ripe for flank attacks. Others assaulted the same point as their comrades further down the line, leading to confusion and a muddled retreat before priority could be established. Fighting even broke out within companies as the fear and fatigue got to them, divided between those who still had the will to fight and those who only wished to save their hides. Amidst all the uncertainty, demoralisation and misunderstanding, Grosslich's men advanced steadily, destroying those who no longer had the power to resist them and squaring up to those that did.

Only on the eastern flank was resistance still solid. Schwarzhelm's reinforcements had bolstered the line just as it was about to break. The men under his command were not the highest quality, but they were fresh to the field and led by the Emperor's Champion. Slowly, methodically, shattered companies were re-formed and given proper support. Assaults on Grosslich's forces were properly coordinated, and the ranks of the halberdier detachments were rotated in good order. Inspired by sudden hope, demoralised men stood up to be counted, and found their courage stronger than they'd thought.

Such resistance attracted attention. The heavier elements of Grosslich's forces began to shift across to the east of the battlefield, steadily increasing in number as the Imperial ranks staunched their horrific rate of losses.

Embedded in the midst of the renewed surge, Bloch pulled his halberd blade from the chest of a corrupted Averlander, watching with satisfaction as the man's eyes flickered and lost their lilac glow. In death, his victim looked just the same as any other battlefield corpse.

He withdrew from the front rank, letting the men around him take up the strain. Bloch had no idea how long he'd been fighting. An hour? Two? More? His arms throbbed with muscle-ache and his palms, each one as tough as horse-hide, were raw and bleeding.

'Where's Schwarzhelm?' he muttered, cursing the smog that obscured everything further than thirty paces away.

'With the Talabheim spearmen,' replied Verstohlen, emerging from the press of men to stand beside him. 'They're assaulting the trenches.'

Bloch rolled his eyes. Even in the middle of a bloody *battle*, the man was impossible to shake off.

'No damn use to us there,' he spat, getting ready to re-enter the front line. 'We can kill these scum, but if we get another one of those dagger-fingered freaks, we'll be in trouble.'

Verstohlen shuddered. His elegant face was bruised, and a long streak of someone's blood ran across his right cheek. Possibly his own, possibly his victim's. The spy had long since run out of shot and now did what he could with his long knife. He was out of place here, and it looked like he knew it.

'We're going to have to withdraw sooner or later,' Verstohlen said. 'We can't drive them back. Far too many.'

'You can tell the big man that,' said Bloch irritably. For a civilian, Verstohlen certainly liked to give his opinion on tactics. 'I was told to hold this front together, and that's what–'

Without warning, a huge explosion detonated from the press of troops before them. Men, both loyalist and traitor, were hurled into the air, spinning through the clouds of ash and soot like chaff.

Bloch was slammed to the ground, knocked clean off his feet by the blast. When he looked up, his vision shaky and ringed with black, a wide circle of devastation had been opened up. For thirty yards in every direction the earth had been flattened. Men lay across the scoured land, some dead, some moaning weakly in pain.

At the centre of the space stood a figure clad in crimson armour. The lightning from the Tower glinted from its glossy surface. He went on foot and carried a sword that dripped black liquid like an open wound. The man stood calmly, waiting for the battle to recover its shape around him.

A few yards ahead of Bloch, Verstohlen was getting to his feet. Somehow the blast had failed to throw him as far as the others. His weapon had been ripped from his fingers, and the gash on his cheek had opened up.

'Herr Verstohlen,' said Grosslich. The tone was resigned. 'I thought you'd had the sense to leave Averheim.'

Verstohlen stood shakily before the traitor elector, his tattered leather coat fluttering in the ash-heavy wind.

'Coming back wasn't exactly my idea.'

At the edge of the circle, Bloch spat a gobbet of blood onto the ground. He'd lost *another* tooth. That made him angry. He reached for his blade. Every part of him ached.

'Then it seems we're both the victim of the choices of others,' said Grosslich. 'I didn't want this either.'

'So give it up. Leitdorf still lives. He'll happily take the runefang back.'

It wasn't clear if Grosslich smiled at that. His helmet obscured his entire face, and behind the eye-slit there was nothing but darkness.

'Your advice hasn't got any better, counsellor. There are other options for me. Though none left, I'm afraid, for you.'

Bloch staggered to his feet, feeling his boots slip against the mud as he scrabbled for purchase.

'Verstohlen!'

He was too slow. With a sickening inevitability, Grosslich drew his sword back. The counsellor stayed still, rooted to the ground, waiting for the strike. Even as Bloch lurched across the circle of devastation, crying out for Verstohlen to evade the blow, Grosslich swung the blade.

Rufus Leitdorf looked up at the gates. Grosslich had enlarged and changed them, replacing the stone blocks with iron columns and decorating the archway with a huge hammered 'G'. The mighty pillars on either side of them soared up nearly forty feet. Within the gaping chasm Natassja's bloodfire raged, filling the air with a surging, roaring sheet of flame. It looked like they were approaching some gigantic stained glass wall. Beyond the cordon, dark outlines of women flickered from roof to roof, swooping through the air like birds.

The legions still swarmed around them, but none could stand against Volkmar and Helborg together. The two men rode at the head of the vanguard, both wreathed in an aura of blazing gold. Any approaching dog-soldiers were cut down, either by the power of the staff or the harrowing edge of the runefang. They were terrified of the sword. It seemed to have some hold over them, like a totem of their destruction.

Leitdorf took some heart from that, and was happy enough to ride in the lee of its protection. He'd felled a few of Grosslich's minions himself on the charge, but most of the deadly work was done by the Reiksguard. Fewer than thirty of the knights remained after their daring ride through the heart of Grosslich's legions, but they still fought with a zeal and skill that defied belief. They were nearing the site of their master's defeat on the Vormeisterplatz and the mood was one of cold vengeance. They would not leave Averheim again without exacting their toll.

'The blood of Sigmar!' roared Volkmar, riding ahead of Leitdorf, urging his troops on to greater feats. Every pace they took, every blood-drenched step, brought them nearer to the city.

A huge man bearing the Imperial standard marched beside the Theogonist, thundering out hymns of defiance even as he swung his warhammer.

'Despise the mutant!' he bellowed, smashing the skull of a growling dog-soldier with a grim relish. 'Purge the unclean!'

It was a brave show. For the time being, they were making progress. It had been a long time since Leitdorf had last been in Averheim. It looked like the place had changed quite a bit.

'You're troubled, elector.'

Leitdorf turned to see Skarr riding beside him, his visor raised and his broken-toothed mouth twisted in a wolfish grin. The preceptor was breathing heavily and his sword was streaked with gore.

'What are we doing here, preceptor?' replied Leitdorf. 'If we make the gates, then what? We'll never make it out again.'

Skarr shrugged.

'Helborg said he'd take you back to Averheim. He always keeps his word.'

The Reiksguard knight had a fey look about him. Leitdorf had seen it before from men in battle, particularly in the elite ranks of the Imperial army. This was euphoria to them, this killing. Fear meant nothing once that mood descended, just a semi-bestial love of the contest.

'Helborg has no idea of Natassja's power.'

'I'd say he does. You heard Schwarzhelm's testimony. She's at the heart of it.'

Leitdorf shook his head.

'Kill her,' he muttered. 'So simple.'

Skarr laughed, a grating sound like the rattling of old chains.

'I thought you'd be pleased to see her again,' he said, pulling his steed round. 'I've heard she's a beauty.'

And then he was gone, spurring his horse into the attack, his sword plunging into the wavering ranks of defenders.

The gates drew closer. As Helborg and Volkmar forged a path towards them, Grosslich's defenders dwindled. None retreated back through that archway. They seemed more scared of the city than of the attackers before them. Or perhaps there was some other reason why they wouldn't enter.

From within the mighty walls, the throbbing echo of power grew louder. Leitdorf could see the Tower properly now. The iron shell contained a heart of deepest vermillion, pulsing angrily like an artery. The clouds swirled still around its tip, dark and forbidding, and lightning lanced down its flanks.

It was vast.

Leitdorf let his fingers creep to the book at his belt, though its presence gave him little comfort. He mouthed the last words recorded there, the ones he'd committed to memory.

She comes for me in my sleep, walking in my mind like a nightmare. I cannot defeat her. None can defeat her. Even now, my mind breaks. There is nothing. No hope, only madness. Her name is agony. Her name is Natassja, and she will kill me.

After that it was nonsense, a stream of half-syllables. Some poorly-remembered fragment of a dream, the final ravings of a great mind brought low by a woman.

'The gates!' cried Helborg, spurring his horse towards them.

The final push came. Volkmar, Skarr, the Reiksguard and the surviving Imperial troops pressed forwards, cutting their way towards the iron columns. Leitdorf, just as he had been at the Vormeisterplatz, was carried along in the midst of them, surrounded by knights and swept like flotsam on the tide.

The last of the defence fell under the onslaught of the Klingerach and the Staff of Command. Helborg rode under the iron portal, his steed stepping proudly. Volkmar followed him, and the golden aura of his passing lit up the agonised faces locked in the metal.

One by one, the surviving Empire troops stepped over the threshold, passing through the curtain of fire and into Averheim. The sounds of battle receded, replaced with the numb roar of the bloodfire.

Leitdorf took a look around him. The city he knew had gone. In its place was death. Nothing but death.

Verstohlen saw the sword come at him. He couldn't move. His muscles were locked in place, held down by some weight. Even as the blade-edge swung at his neck, dripping with black fluid, his limbs remained frozen. He was going to die.

'Verstohlen!'

Bloch's voice, thick as a bull's, roared out from behind him. He was coming, tearing back into the line of danger, just as he always did.

Suddenly, from somewhere, the force clamping him in place lessened. Verstohlen jerked back. Grosslich adjusted too late and the tip of the blade missed its target, slicing across his chest. Verstohlen cried aloud as the metal cut through his leather jerkin and parted the flesh beneath. He fell to his knees, clutching at the wound. Blood, mingled with ink-black slurry, poured over his grasping fingers.

Then Bloch barrelled into Grosslich, knocking him sidelong with the force of the charge then landing a flurry of crushing blows on the traitor elector. He wielded his stave with a ferocious, controlled skill.

'I've marched halfway across this bloody province for this fight,' Bloch snarled through gritted teeth. 'Now you're getting one, you bastard.'

'Leave him!' cried Verstohlen, feeling his vision fade into dizziness. Something in his wound was poisoning him, rushing into his bloodstream and spreading toxins through his body. He tried to rise, but his legs gave out and he fell back to his knees. 'He's too strong.'

Recovering from his surprise, Grosslich began to meet Bloch's attack. His sword-edge whirled in tight arcs, picking out the weaknesses in the halberdier's technique. The twin blades still clashed together in unison. At the edges of the circle, other soldiers were beginning to find their feet.

'A man with the stomach to face me,' mused Grosslich, hammering Bloch back two paces with a single swipe. 'A soldier after my own heart.'

'I'm nothing like you,' growled Bloch, pivoting the staff round and bringing the heel up for a jab.

'Maybe as I was, then,' said Grosslich, evading the blunt stave and switching his grip for a backhanded thrust. 'I'd have found a place for you here.'

'And I'd have died before taking it.'

Bloch jerked the blade back round and parried Grosslich's strike, giving ground with every exchange. Though his eyes glittered with determination, he was unequal to this foe. The battle had already been long, and Grosslich's muscles were animated with an unnatural strength.

Verstohlen clambered back to his feet, the world swaying around him. Stumbling drunkenly, he went for his dagger, thrown yards clear by Grosslich's theatrical arrival. His movements were clumsy and broken. Something virulent was worming its way within him. He grabbed the knife and whirled round, fighting the growing tide of nausea.

Bloch was fighting like a man possessed. Verstohlen had never seen a halberd wielded with such power and speed. Even the troops shuffling forwards on the far side of the circle seemed daunted by it. A dog-soldier made to leap into the fray, but Grosslich sent it back with a dismissive gesture.

'Get back, filth,' he spat.

'Want me for yourself?' jeered Bloch, seizing advantage of the diversion to launch a flurry of downward plunges.

Grosslich met them easily, adjusting his stance to absorb the blows. Verstohlen felt despair grow within him. Even if Bloch's blade connected, Grosslich's armour looked invulnerable. The counsellor limped back towards the duelling warriors too slowly, his dagger clutched in his clammy hands, sweat streaming from his brow. He felt useless, pathetic, wasted.

'A warrior's right,' replied Grosslich, planting his feet squarely and aiming a two-handed thrust at Bloch's chest.

Bloch swerved to avoid it, but the edge scraped along his breastplate, knocking him off balance. He regained his feet just in time to block the follow-up.

'You have no—'

He never finished. Grosslich's follow-up was a feint. His blade spun round in his hands as it dropped down and plunged deep into the flesh below Bloch's breastplate.

'Markus!' Verstohlen cried out as he struggled, mere feet away, his hand outstretched impotently.

Bloch's face contorted into a mask of agony. His halberd, the weapon that had taken him from Turgitz, to Black Fire Pass, and finally back to Averheim, thumped to the ground. The staff shivered as it rolled across the earth.

Grosslich shoved the blade in further, grasping the stricken halberdier by the shoulder and hauling him up along the impaling sword-edge.

Bloch gasped, choked, and a well of thick blood spilled from his throat. He clutched frantically at Grosslich's armour, scrabbling for some kind of purchase. Verstohlen crawled towards them both, nearly overwhelmed with black sickness.

'Markus...' he choked, watching the man die before him.

It was always the soldiers. First Grunwald, now Bloch. Verstohlen was consumed by a wave of self-loathing. His charmed existence seemed like a curse to him then. This was his fault. Again.

Bloch looked at him. His eyes were glazing over. Blood bubbled from his mouth, running down his chest, streaked with black. From somewhere, he summoned the strength to grasp at Grosslich's armoured bulk. He grabbed the elector in a bear hug. He could no longer speak, could barely stand, but the final look he shot Verstohlen was as clear as glass.

Do it.

Verstohlen's grief transmuted into fury. Thrusting aside his nausea, ignoring the pain streaming through his poisoned limbs, he leapt forwards, dagger in hand.

Grosslich sensed the danger and whirled round, trying to draw his weapon, but Bloch's dying body hampered his movements. His sword remained lodged, and for a second, a mere second, he was unprotected.

Verstohlen raised the dagger high over Grosslich and plunged it down with all his strength and skill. It went in between the rim of his breastplate and helmet, sliding through like a stick in water.

Grosslich screamed. He flung Bloch free. The halberdier's body swung into the air before crashing to the earth with a heavy, final thud.

Verstohlen staggered back, his veins thumping in his temples. His hands were shaking. Grosslich grabbed the dagger and hurled it from his neck. It spun through the air, spraying his own blood. Incredibly, he still stood.

Verstohlen began to back away, his dizziness returning, the blackness around his eyes closing in. Across his chest, the wound still leaked hot, pumping slurry.

'Damn you, counsellor,' Grosslich snarled, twisting his helmet off and letting it fall to the ground. His face was drawn with pain. He strode towards Verstohlen, sword brandished in his hand, the dark light of hatred in his eyes. '*That* was the worst of your many errors.'

Verstohlen gazed up at the man's face in horror. It was a pale white, and the eyes were ringed with purple growths. The flesh was as glossy and rigid as his armour. Blood pumped from the wound at his neck, but it barely seemed to trouble him. It should have killed him.

'You could have *resisted* her,' said Verstohlen, feeling his consciousness weaken. He had no weapon. Even if he had, he was now too weak to use it.

Grosslich's face remained contorted with rage.

'Remember this, as I kill you,' he hissed. 'You were our *instrument*. Whatever choices I made, you made them happen. It's over now. The game is finished. You have no blade left that could hurt me.'

'But I do.'

It wasn't Verstohlen's voice. Both men snapped round.

Schwarzhelm was there, a giant amongst men, his armour encrusted with the patina of war, his eyes dark with betrayal. He raised the Rechtstahl, and the blade was as red as blood.

As Helborg rode through the barrier into Averheim he felt the heat of it crush his lungs. He took shallow breaths, almost choking as the searing air filled his throat. Averheim was a furnace.

No dog-soldiers followed them in. Helborg looked over his shoulder. The clamour of battle came from behind the hindmost Imperial soldier like a muffled echo. The enemy troops beyond the gates had turned away from them, back towards the greater mass of Empire soldiers to the north. It was as if, by passing across the portal, they'd ceased to exist.

His men paused, waiting for the next order. A profound sense of dread had come over all of them. Less than three hundred, mostly halberdiers, warrior priests or knights. They now clustered together, eyes wide, bravado forgotten, faces pale.

The battle-fury had gone. The only sound was the low roar of the bloodfire, lifting their hair and pressing against their armour. It was hot but it did not burn. Its purpose was not to injure, but to preserve. Other things, inhuman things, thrived in such rarefied airs.

Helborg looked about him warily, keeping a tight grip on the Klingerach. Everything was blackened by the fire. The street ahead was charred and ruinous. Nothing living stirred on the stone, and the windows of the houses gaped like mouths. Far ahead, some massive brazier sent billows of lilac smoke into the fervid air. The ground thrummed incessantly, as if machines ground away far beneath their feet.

Above it all, the Tower loomed, dark and terrible, shimmering behind a haze of unrelenting heat. The dread leaking from it was palpable, a tight, horrifying cloud of fear. The structure was an aberration. It didn't belong. No mortal could dwell in such a place. Then, and only then, did Helborg understand its purpose. It was no fortress or citadel. It was an instrument. A device. A means of focussing something within the city.

None of the men spoke. None of them moved. Leitdorf looked like he was trying to remember something by mumbling words under his breath. Volkmar had let his golden fire ebb. The madness had passed from his severe features, replaced by the grim determination that had given him his nickname.

Helborg's steed was skittish under him. All the other horses were the same. One of them kicked out in a panic, infecting the others. They were going mad.

'Dismount,' ordered Helborg, and his voice echoed strangely. 'Horses will be of no use to us in here.'

The knights did as they were bid, and the released horses galloped back through the gates, preferring a death on the plain to one in the city. All men stood shoulder to shoulder on the road, swords and halberds held ready.

'Stay close,' warned Helborg, turning to look each of them in the eye. 'Fear is your enemy. It will kill you if you let it. Trust to faith and to your blades. The Tower is our destination. Stay true, and we will destroy the architect of all this.'

He walked forwards. Even as he did so, there was a howling noise from the far end of the street. As if a mighty wind surged towards them from far away, the fire in the air rushed and swayed.

Helborg tensed. The Klingerach felt suddenly heavy in his hands. All around him, men took up defensive positions.

Something was coming. Something fast.

'Trust to faith,' he growled, standing his ground. Beside him, Volkmar's fire flared up again.

Then they came. From the far end of the street, shapes appeared in the air. They grew quickly, hurtling towards the Empire troops like storm-crows, flapping and shrieking. In their wake was pure terror, dripping from the air and pooling on the blasted stone.

They tore past the rows of houses. Their shapes grew clearer. They were women, or parodies of women, impossibly lovely, impossibly terrible. Their flesh was lilac, and their exposed skin shimmered in the bloodfire. In place of hands they had rending claws and in place of feet they had talons like a bird's. Their bald heads were crowned with forbidden sigils, and their mouths were stretched open wide, lined with incisors and poised to bite.

Some of his troops broke then, dropping their weapons and racing back to face their end on the battlefield beyond the gates. Helborg hardly noticed them go. The remainder braced for the impact, fear marked on their ravaged faces. Even the Marshal, inured to fear by a lifetime of war, felt his heart hammering and sweat bursting out on his palms, slick against the grip of his sword.

'Trust to faith!' cried Helborg again, hefting the runefang and preparing to swing.

Faith seemed like little protection. As swift as death, as terrible as pain, Natassja's daemons screamed down the street towards them, eyes black with delicious fury, faces alive with the joyous malice of those about to feed.

CHAPTER NINETEEN

Verstohlen watched as Schwarzhelm broke into a furious, heavy charge. Kraus was at his right hand, as were a whole company of swordsmen in the colours of Talabheim. Behind the sorcerer, a unit of dog-soldiers had formed up. The opening cleared by Grosslich's sorcery began to close back in on itself.

Verstohlen, his vision still cloudy, the sickness eating at his heart, could only watch as the Emperor's Champion swept across the broken earth, his battle-ravaged features blazing with fury. As Schwarzhelm tore towards Grosslich, Verstohlen saw the same dark expression on his face as when Grunwald had died. Though his grim demeanour didn't always make it obvious, Schwarzhelm cared about his men like few Imperial commanders. When one of them died, he *felt* it.

Grosslich took a step back. His hands kindled lilac energy, snapping and snaking around his gauntlets. Tendrils of oily matter strung out along his sword-blade, catching on the viscous fluid still dripping from the metal. As Schwarzhelm closed him down, Grosslich fired a spitting column of it outwards. The pure stuff of the aethyr surged across the narrow gap between the two men.

Schwarzhelm didn't so much as pause. Still charging, he swept the Sword of Justice into the path of the corrupted essence.

The matter exploded. Shards of it spun into the bodies around, burning through armour and cracking metal. Both men and dog-soldiers shrank back from the swarm of glowing embers. In the centre of it, vast and inexorable, Schwarzhelm ploughed onwards, shrugging slivers of sorcerous discharge from his rune-warded pauldrons.

Grosslich tried to blast at him again, but by then Schwarzhelm was in range. The Rechtstahl came across in a sweep of such staggering force that Verstohlen thought it would cleave the man in two. Somehow, Grosslich got his own twisted blade in the path of it. He was slammed back heavily, his legs bending under the impact. A filigree of cracks ran across the crimson armour.

'Faithless,' hissed Schwarzhelm, swinging his blade back for the next strike.

'You can talk,' gasped Grosslich, giving ground and frantically blocking the rain of blows that followed. His face had twisted into a mask of loathing – for Schwarzhelm, but also for himself. The handsome features that had once awed Averheim had gone forever, scarred by the mutating whim of his new master. 'You *made* me.'

'I'd have killed you for Grunwald's death alone,' Schwarzhelm growled, his blade working faster and heavier with every plunge, knocking Grosslich back steadily, stride by stride. 'You need not give me more reasons.'

Verstohlen found himself held rapt by the exchange, unable to intervene, clamped down by the poisons coursing through his body. Schwarzhelm fought like a warrior-god of old, shrugging off Grosslich's attempts to land a blow and raining strikes of crushing weight on the sorcerer's retreating frame. The traitor's armour, invulnerable to the bite of lesser weapons, began to fracture under the assault. Even Bloch, for all his skill, hadn't as much as dented it.

Bloch.

Verstohlen spun round. Where was he? The rush of bodies began to obscure the open space Grosslich had opened up. Dog-soldiers and swordsmen surged across it, a mass of sweat-draped limbs and blood-streaked faces.

Verstohlen staggered along, pushing his way through a press of straining swordsmen. He was unarmed, vulnerable. He didn't care. The battle roared on around him. The sounds of it were muffled, the stench of it muted. As if drunk, Verstohlen clumsily shoved and ducked his way to where Bloch had fallen.

'Merciful Verena,' he whispered, the words slurring from his sluggish mouth. 'As you have ever guided me...'

He didn't need to finish his prayer. A line of Empire swordsmen swept in front of him, driving a detachment of dog-soldiers back several paces. In their wake, a gap opened up. There, lying on the churned earth, lay the halberdier commander, forgotten by the fury that boiled around him. His blood had stopped flowing and his face was as pale as ivory. Somehow he'd regained hold of his halberd, and it lay across him like a monument of honour.

Verstohlen limped over to him, falling to his knees by Bloch's corpse. The commander had fallen awkwardly, his legs twisted and broken under him. His face was fixed in a snarl of aggression. Belligerent to the end.

The virulence was now deep within Verstohlen's bones. Without treatment he knew he'd be dead soon. Then the two of them, scholar and soldier, would find their end together, as unlikely a pairing as a minstrel and a Slayer.

He looked up. The swordsmen had maintained the assault but the right flank had been left exposed. More dog-soldiers crept forwards. There was nothing between Verstohlen and them. They advanced steadily, eyeing the vulnerable figure crouching down next to the body of their master's last victim.

For a moment, he thought his end had come. He was weak. Far too weak.

'No,' he breathed, gritting his teeth and getting to his feet with effort. 'You shall not despoil this.'

He picked up Bloch's halberd. It was heavy, far heavier than he'd imagined it would be. For the first time, he began to understand the scorn of fighting men for those they protected.

The dog-soldiers kept coming. Verstohlen could see the unnatural light within the helmets of the lead warriors. The stench was just as it had been in Hessler's townhouse so long ago, the first time he'd seen one of the creatures up close.

'Damn you,' he snarled, standing over Bloch's body and lowering the halberd blade awkwardly. 'This is *not* for you.'

If they understood the words, the dog-soldiers made no sign. They came on remorselessly. Empire troops, seeing the gap in the lines, came up to Verstohlen's side. He was not alone. Without speaking, needing no orders, they closed in around the body of the fallen commander.

All knew the score. This was ground that would not be yielded.

As the first of the dog-soldiers came into range, Verstohlen narrowed his eyes, swallowed the bile rising in his gorge, adjusted his grip on the wooden stave and braced to meet the charge.

Helborg swept up the Klingerach, aiming at the screeching face of the nearest daemon. It swooped past him, swerving away from the steel and spinning back into the air. They would not take on a holy blade. He swept round, looking to catch another of them with its edge.

They were too fast. Like hawks above prey, they darted into the crowd of men, picking off the weak and hauling them into the fire-laced sky. Their victims screamed with horror as they were borne aloft. Warrior priest or knight, it made no difference. These were foes beyond all of them.

Volkmar kindled his staff again and lightning spat along its full height. He whirled round, releasing a volley of twisting bolts. They streaked up at the circling daemons. One hit, dousing the creature in a ball of swirling immolation. It screamed in its turn, an echoing mockery of the cries of mortal men. Its companions merely laughed, and the sound was alive with joyous spite.

'The men cannot fight these,' muttered the Theogonist. 'The fire sustains them.'

'We won't go back,' said Helborg, watching as the daemons clustered for a second pass. 'Can you do nothing?'

'Hurt them, yes. Kill them, no.'

The daemons swooped back between the houses, their claws now dripping with blood. As they came, the wind howled around them.

Helborg watched them come again, keeping his sword poised to strike. One of them dropped down low, spinning as it dived towards the earth, its face lit with a malign grin of exuberance. It went for the Reiksguard on his left flank, ignoring the bearer of the runefang. The man stood his ground, his trembling hands holding his broadsword in place to ward the impact.

Fast as a stab, the daemon took him. Helborg sprang. Leaping up at the sinuous figure, he whirled the Klingerach down across its kicking legs. The sacred blade sank deep into the daemonic flesh, sinking deep and severing aethyric sinews.

The daemon wailed, dropping its quarry and twisting away from Helborg. The Marshal pursued it, spinning the sword into a two-handed grip and preparing to plunge. The creature spat at him and disappeared. It re-emerged twelve feet away, cradling its wounds and wailing in agony before kicking back into the air. It soared upwards, leaving a trail of purple blood in its wake.

In the meantime more men had been plucked from the midst of the dwindling band and carried up into the high places to be dismembered. A steady shower of blood and body parts rained down on the survivors, evidence of their comrades' fate.

'No more of this,' snarled Helborg, turning to Skarr.

The preceptor looked scared. He never looked scared.

'What, then?'

'We run.'

'Where to?'

Helborg gestured to the Tower, still distant over the roofs of the houses. Lightning flickered across the devastated cityscape, picking out the ruined frames of the buildings, now squatted on by daemons licking their blood-soaked fingers.

'There.'

Without waiting for a response, Helborg broke into a sprint. Needing no orders, his men did likewise. Leitdorf and Skarr went alongside him. The preceptor loped like a wolf, though no longer grinning. Volkmar took up the rear, keeping his staff kindled and doing what he could to ward the attacks from above.

The ravaged company ran through the streets, assailed at every step. The daemons were in their element, sustained and buoyed by the bloodfire, impervious to mortal weapons. The warrior priests had the most success at fending them off, swinging their icon-studded warhammers and slamming the unwary creatures against the charred walls. The big man with the standard still roared out his hymns and hefted his mighty weapon. Bloodbringer, he called it. It was a good name.

Despite the fragmentary successes, the sprint was a nightmare. Knights and halberdiers, both with little defence against the monsters of the aethyr, were plucked from the midst of them almost at will, destined for an agonising death in the spires of the city. With each corner the company rounded, another dozen were taken, whittling them down further.

Helborg was torn between anger and horror. There was nothing worse than a foe that couldn't be fought. He did his best to interpose himself between the daemons and his men, but they slipped past his guard all too easily. He was forced to listen as dying men's screams rang out across the rooftops, accompanied by the echoing laughs of the killers.

'We'll all be dead before we get there,' panted Leitdorf, his cheeks red with the effort of running. He'd managed to cast off some of his armour, but he was making heavy work of the chase.

'Then go back,' spat Helborg, unwilling to indulge the man's fears. 'I *will* find the one who did this.'

A phalanx of daemons screamed low across the heads of the fleeing band, pursued by Volkmar's inaccurate castings. Three of them had struggling bodies locked in their talons, all enclosed in plate armour. They were picking off the Reiksguard first.

'You think you can kill her, if you can't kill these?'

Helborg ramped up the pace, driving his men harder.

'The runefang will finish her,' he growled, his breath ever more ragged. His shoulder wound had opened again and he could feel the hot stickiness under his jerkin. The Tower was still too far away. 'Count on it.'

As he spoke, a daemon tore into them from the roofs on their left, diving down into the press of bodies and scattering them. It had miscalculated, coming in too fast. It rolled across the cobbles with its prey, unable to leap back into the bloodfire quick enough.

Skarr, further back amid the men, was on her in an instant, hacking at her with his blade to free its prey.

'Skarr, no!' roared Helborg, shoving his way through the jostling bodies to reach him.

The preceptor's blade passed harmlessly through the daemon's flesh, biting into the stone beneath and kicking up sparks. The daemon hissed at him, dropped her intended quarry and coiled to leap.

'Get back!' roared Helborg, almost there, Klingerach in hand.

Then the daemon sprang, catching Skarr full in the chest and hurling them both free of the men around. They crashed into the nearest wall, shattering the stone. Helborg saw Skarr's helmet bounce jarringly from the impact and the knight's limbs go limp.

Helborg burst free and leapt after them. The daemon crouched again, ready to tear up into the skies with her latest morsel. The Klingerach was quicker, tearing deep into the lilac-fleshed back, runes blazing as it bit.

The creature screamed, arching back, limbs flailing, trying to turn round. Skarr fell from her grasp, sliding down the stone and leaving a slick of blood on the wall.

Helborg withdrew the blade and the daemon spun to face him. The Klingerach flashed again, carving through the daemon's neck and severing her head. A powerful snap rippled through the air, radiating out and knocking the airborne daemons back up into the heights. For a moment, the severed head of their fallen sister still breathed. It looked up at Helborg with a mix of fear and amazement, before finally rolling over listlessly, lifeless and empty.

Leitdorf rushed to Helborg's side, his own blade drawn, too late to intervene. The surviving troops gazed at the Marshal in awe.

'Nothing is immune from the Sword of Vengeance,' panted Helborg, gazing at Skarr's unmoving body. His voice shook with emotion. 'You ask me how I'll kill her? *This* is how.'

Then he turned on his heel and motioned for the race to the Tower to resume. Far above, the daemons began to circle again, gauging the moment to strike, wary of the blade that had the power to extinguish them.

Along the twisting streets, the stone blackened with ashes, Helborg's men sprinted into the heart of the city, half their number slain, the Tower still distant, and the scions of the Lord of Pain on their backs.

Volkmar ran. His robes curled tight around his huge frame as he went, slowing him down. His bald head was glossy with sweat, both from the exertion and from the pressing heat. Every muscle in his body screamed at him to stop, to hold his ground, to face the creatures that swooped on them.

Perhaps, if he did, he'd take a couple of them down. Maybe half a dozen. He could flay their unsubstantial flesh from their unholy bones, rip them into their constituent parts.

He knew Helborg was right. They couldn't fight this foe, not for any length of time. The bloodfire sustained the daemons, filled their unholy bodies with energy and power. This was their place, a city of mortal men no longer.

The ragged band of soldiers, whittled down to little more than a hundred, kept going. Laggards had been left behind, easy picking for the rapacious daemons. Those that remained huddled close together, gaining what protection they could from Volkmar and Helborg.

They passed over the river. The water boiled black, choked with ash from the fires. The Averburg, the ancient seat of the electors, was an empty shell. Its stark, flame-blackened walls rose up into the raging maelstrom, broken silhouettes against the burning clouds of crimson.

The daemons came at them again and again, giving no respite. With every pass, another man was taken, swept up into the spires for an agonising end. As the cries rang out across the ruins, Volkmar felt hot tears of anger prick at his eyes.

He wanted to stop. He knew he couldn't.

'My lord,' came Maljdir's voice from his shoulder.

The priest still ran powerfully alongside him, despite carrying the standard in one hand and the warhammer in the other. Though his beard was lank with sweat and his face as red as the fires around them, he hadn't given up yet. Damned Ulrican intransigence.

'So you were right,' snarled Volkmar, hardly breaking stride.

Maljdir shook his head.

'No,' he said, his words coming in snatches between his laboured gasps. 'I was not.'

He looked up at the looming Tower, now dominating the sky above them.

'Your zeal led us here.' Though effort etched his every word, there was a kind of satisfaction in his voice. He looked back at Volkmar. 'I should have trusted you.'

Volkmar just kept going. There were no certainties any more. For a moment back there, he'd been close to losing his mind. Above them, the daemons were gathering for a final pounce. There were dozens of them. The portals of the

Tower were visible, dark and gaping, but they'd be lucky to make the nearest of them.

'Save your energy for the daemons,' rasped Volkmar, watching as the first of them plunged downwards. 'You'll need it.'

The daemon hurtled towards Helborg, only turning out of the path of the Klingerach at the last moment. The Marshal ignored it. Unless they made a mistake, they were too fast to engage with. The curtains of fire in the air buoyed them. This was their element. More screams from behind him told him they'd found another victim.

He turned a final corner and ran down a long, straight street. At the end of it, the rows of shattered houses finally gave out, revealing a pair of enormous iron-rimmed gates. Two pillars flanked them, crowned with fire. Beyond the gates, a wide and featureless courtyard opened up. The Tower stood in the centre. Up close, its scale was even more daunting.

'Volkmar!' he shouted, keeping up the pace. 'The gates!'

The Theogonist responded instantly, summoning bolts of golden flame from his staff and hurling them at the iron. The gates shuddered from the first impact, broke on the second. The metal slammed back hard, bouncing from the stone pillars as the hinges strained. Then they were through, the ever-diminishing company tearing across the open courtyard, harried and pursued at every step.

'I can sense her,' said Leitdorf.

The man was suffering. His red face still carried too much fat, and the sweat was running in rivulets down his cheeks. Just as he'd predicted, though, the daemons ignored him. The Wolfsklinge had a heritage they feared. Or maybe it was something more.

'Then you'll be the guide,' said Helborg, gazing up at the column of ruin looming over him.

The Tower was massive, a soaring dark skeleton of iron over a throbbing core of magma-red. Above the pinnacle, the ring of clouds had broken, exposing Morrslieb again.

The power that had drawn the storm in over Averheim was beginning to dissipate.

Volkmar felt it too.

'Weakness?' he asked.

Leitdorf shook his head.

'No,' he said. 'Its work is done.'

Helborg didn't ask how Leitdorf knew that. He risked a look over his shoulder. A few dozen men were left, all haggard and panting from the sprint across the ruined city. No regular troops had made it. The remainder were warrior priests and a scattering of Reiksguard, the only ones with the stomach to endure the horrors of the air. The Tower would be no kinder to them.

'Once we're in, which way?' he asked Leitdorf, watching as the massive Tower gates loomed up out of the fire-flecked dark.

'Down,' replied the elector tersely. 'She's beneath the earth.'

Volkmar shook his head. 'There's nothing human in there.'

Helborg said nothing, but forced the pace once more. The gates drew close. Pillars of adamant framed the huge curved doors, glinting in the firelight. Sigils of Slaanesh adorned the iron, sunk deep into the metal in a sweeping pattern of silver. The vast bole of the Tower rose up into the night, soaring three hundred feet to the summit. The base of it was mighty, bound by pillars of obsidian and engraved bands of iron. The rumble of machines working in the deeps crept across the stone, and bloodfire rushed up the flanks of the enormous structure, washing over the colonnades and parapets as it raced to the apex.

The daemons came for them again, swooping down the sheer sides of the Tower, arms outstretched and ready for more feeding. There were dozens of them now. They'd been waiting for this, their last chance to pick them off in the open.

'Get those doors open,' snapped Helborg, but Volkmar was already working.

The Theogonist swung his staff round and hurled a

stream of leaping fire at the barred doors. They shivered, but remained closed.

Then the daemons landed, crashing to earth and sinking their talons deep into the unprotected mortals below.

'Sigmar!' roared Helborg, tearing into them with the Sword of Vengeance. They darted away from the blade, cowed by the rune-wound power of the steel.

'Averland!' cried Leitdorf, though his meagre voice was carried away by the roar of the furnaces. He swiped wildly at the spinning creatures, and they evaded his blows easily.

Volkmar unleashed another volley, and the gap between the doors fractured.

The daemons kept coming, sweeping more troops up in their terrible embrace and tearing them apart in mid-air. One of them came for the big warrior priest with the standard. He stood his ground and brought his heavy warhammer round with incredible speed. The faith-strengthened head of it slammed into the oncoming daemon. Bright light blazed from the impact, knocking the creature back yards. It hovered for a moment, dazed.

The priest roared his defiance, keeping the standard aloft, whirling the warhammer over his head in triumph.

'Smite the mutant!' he bellowed. 'Purge the–'

A claw punched through his back and out through his chest. He coughed up blood in gouts as he was lifted from the ground. More daemons flocked to him, snapping at his flailing limbs and biting deep into his flesh. Too quick for Helborg to reach him, they dragged the heavy figure into the air.

'Fight the darkness!' Maljdir roared through his blood-clogged throat, still crying aloud as half a dozen daemons struggled to bear him aloft. He dropped the standard but kept swinging his warhammer, slamming more of them aside even as he was taken beyond the reach of help. 'Dawn will come again! Trust to faith!'

Then he was gone, hauled up the flanks of the Tower, his increasingly weak cries of denunciation and defiance echoing down from above before they were silenced forever.

Volkmar summoned fire a third time and the gates blew inwards, crashing back on their enormous hinges. A sickly jasmine stench rolled out to greet them. Beyond the portal, a corridor stretched away, dark and forbidding.

'Inside!' roared Helborg, pushing his men across the threshold, doing what he could to protect the swooping daemons from their backs. They hurried in, those that were left. Leitdorf was at the rear, followed last of all by Volkmar. As the Theogonist passed under the dark lintel, he turned and smashed his staff on the ground. A ball of force raced outwards, a shimmer in the air like the backwash from a massive explosion. The daemons were hurled away, wheeling into the high airs and screaming with frustration.

'Close the gates!' Helborg shouted, seizing a door and pushing against it.

There were fewer than twenty of them left. The priests and Volkmar took one door, the Reiksguard and Leitdorf joined Helborg. Slowly, agonisingly slowly, the gates began to grind shut. Outside, quickly recovered from Volkmar's casting, the daemons rushed back, screaming for more blood. Helborg saw the foremost tearing towards him, her eyes alive with bloodlust.

'Harder!' he roared, straining every muscle. The gap closed too slowly. The daemons hurtled towards it, reaching for the diminishing space. If they got in, then they were all dead men.

At last, groaning and creaking, the mighty iron doors slammed into place. There were heavy thuds from the outside as the daemons crunched into them, followed by howls of petulant anguish. The iron doors buckled but did not break.

'There are wards here,' panted Volkmar, leaning on his knees.

'That won't hold them,' said Leitdorf, drawing huge, shuddering breaths.

All around, the surviving troops slumped to the polished marble. Helborg felt impatience prick at him. They needed to keep moving.

'How long have we got?'

Leitdorf shrugged, his shoulders shivering with fatigue.

'They know this place better than we do,' he said without conviction. 'Not long.'

Helborg looked over his shoulder. The corridor yawned away into the dark, lit only by faint blushes of lilac. The walls were dark and smooth, polished to a high sheen. The muted thunder of the bloodfire still thrummed throughout the walls. The interior of the Tower was filled with strange, echoing sounds. The immense superstructure of iron creaked. From far below, unearthly noises rose up, warped and distorted by their passage through the catacombs. The stain of corruption was everywhere, thick and cloying.

At the far end of the corridor there was a huge spiral stairway leading both up and down. Flickering light, bright and unnaturally blue, came from below.

'Time to move again,' Helborg said. His voice was harsh, his expression unforgiving. 'And I hate to keep a lady waiting.'

CHAPTER TWENTY

Schwarzhelm kept his weight perfectly balanced, watching for the counter-thrust. The raw power of his anger flowed freely, but it did not master him. The duel was too evenly poised for recklessness, and Grosslich was too strong. His natural skill as a soldier had been magnified by his corruption, and he matched Schwarzhelm's blistering assault stroke for stroke.

All around them, the battle was similarly poised. Schwarzhelm's men, a mix of the many companies Volkmar had brought into battle, were locked in combat with the dog-soldiers. Neither side had the mastery, and the line of grappling men stayed static, locked over the same patch of blood-soaked land.

As for the remainder of the army, Schwarzhelm could only hope they were holding together. He'd worked hard to restore some kind of shape to the Imperial lines, but the numbers were still against them. Killing Grosslich might bring some respite, but it wouldn't win the day. Whatever happened between the two of them, there were long hours of fighting ahead.

Grosslich pressed the attack, his sword crackling with lilac energy. As he did so, the clouds fractured over the summit of the Tower. Starlight shone through the gap, exposing the deep of the night above. Then, slipping into vision as the clouds sheared away, Morrslieb spilled its putrid light across the battlefield. Firelight mingled with the yellowish stain of corruption, making even the Empire troops look as ravaged as corpses.

Grosslich risked a glance upwards before meeting Schwarzhelm's challenge again. The swords crunched together, splattering the viscous slurry from Grosslich's sword in a wide circle.

'The Deathmoon,' he said, dodging a vicious swipe at his flanks and twisting Schwarzhelm's blade back at him. 'Sign of your defeat.'

'*My* defeat?' growled Schwarzhelm, letting his sword come back and seizing the grip with both hands. 'I remember you as you were. There's no victory for you here.'

He flung Grosslich's blade up out of position and stabbed at the traitor's midriff.

'Your death will be victory enough,' hissed Grosslich, sidestepping the strike and getting his sword back down into guard. His voice was ragged with effort.

'Tell yourself that, if you need to.'

Grosslich snarled and surged forwards. His sword spun round, spraying black fluid over Schwarzhelm's armour.

'You know nothing of my choices!' he spat, thrusting at Schwarzhelm's guard with renewed vigour. 'Dominion was denied me, though I was twice the man Leitdorf was.'

Schwarzhelm let the flurry of blows come to him, stepping into them, bringing his enormous strength to bear on the parries, engaging the peerless swordsmanship that had made his reputation on the battlefields of the Empire.

'Maybe once. Now you have diminished, and he has grown.'

'He lives?' Grosslich became agitated, and the disquiet fed itself into his sword-strokes.

'Even now he nears the Tower. Husband and wife are due a reunion.'

Grosslich's eyes filled with a mocking light. His face glowed sickeningly as his misshapen mouth cracked into a warped smile.

'She needs no husband,' he laughed, meeting a power-ful thrust from Schwarzhelm and pushing it back. 'He can't destroy her. You can't. Only I have the power. Kill me, and you doom yourself.'

Schwarzhelm feinted to the left before bringing his edge back sharply, probing for the join in Grosslich's armour below the breastplate.

'You overestimate your power,' he said, his voice steely calm. 'Do you not recognise the Sword of Justice? It is a holy blade. It thirsts for your death, and you have nothing to answer it with.'

Grosslich laughed again. Quick as a snake, he pressed the attack, whirling his sword into Schwarzhelm's face. The strike was blocked, but the power behind it was sudden and massive. The locked blades fell back before Schwarzhelm's mighty arms halted the thrust. For a moment, the edge of the metal was close. Close enough for him to see the runes on Grosslich's sword-edge, half-obscured beneath the ever-flowing corruption across its surface.

'You don't recognise my blade either?' Grosslich crowed. 'You gave it to me. The runefang of Averland. The Sword of Ruin. All of this, you gave to me. I have bent it to my will, just as I have this province. It can hurt you, Schwarzhelm. Oh, this can *hurt* you.'

The two men broke apart again. For a moment, Schwarzhelm's eyes still rested on his enemy's sword. A flicker of doubt passed across his face. Above them, the Deathmoon spread its sickening sheen across the mass of struggling men. In every direction, thousands struggled, all lit by the fires of Averheim. All around him, his troops were pitted against a foe they couldn't hope to best. They would die, one by one, even if he halted Grosslich.

Schwarzhelm brought the Rechtstahl into guard, feeling the solid weight of it in his hands. The light of Morrslieb glinted from the steel, transmuted into pure silver by the holy metal. Grosslich waited for him, gathering his strength.

Doubt drained away. All that remained was combat, the purity of the test. It was one he had never failed, not even against Helborg. He wouldn't do now.

'Pain is fleeting, Grosslich,' he said, poised for the strike. 'Damnation is eternal. Let me show you the difference.'

'I'll go first,' said Helborg. His voice resounded from the marble walls of the Tower. 'Leitdorf behind, Volkmar last.'

The men silently fell into their positions. None of them, even the warrior priests, looked sure of themselves. There was something sickening about the Tower. The long nights of agony had left their imprint in the structure, staining it as surely as a birthmark. A man didn't need Volkmar's skills to detect the perversion humming in the air.

'Remember yourselves,' the Marshal warned, peering ahead to the stairwell. Despite himself, his heart beat faster in his chest. After the terrible sprint to the Tower, the sudden eerie quiet was hard to deal with. Something awful lurked here, something ancient and suffused with malignance. 'Death in His service is glorious. Only the traitor fears destruction.'

He crept forwards, and the spurs on his boots clicked against the marble. The paltry band of men, now just eighteen strong, stayed close, eyes wide, knuckles white on the grips of their weapons. At the rear, Volkmar kindled a warm glow from the tip of his staff. It was scant consolation, and did little more than pick out the horrific images engraved on the walls.

They went down the stairs swiftly, hurrying round the broad sweep of the spiral and avoiding the twisted shapes embedded into the iron banister rail. As they descended, it got hotter. Breathing became more difficult and the growl of the hidden engines echoed more loudly. From far in the deeps, there came the sound of clanging, as if vast chains swung together. A muted howling resonated from far above.

'Daemons,' muttered Leitdorf, clutching at the book at his belt.

'Volkmar can handle them,' said Helborg. Terror seemed to invest the air itself, and he was not immune from it. 'Keep your mind clear. We'll be busy with your Natassja.'

'She was never mine.'

'Enough. We're closing.'

They reached the base of the stairs. A long vaulted passage-way led directly ahead. The walls were richly decorated with sculptures, all carved with assorted scenes of creative agony. Limbs and faces were contorted across stone friezes, locked in impossible positions of excruciation. Helborg let his gaze alight on the face of a young woman. The carving was artful, despite the debauchery. Bathed in the light of Volkmar's staff, the subject still retained a warped kind of beauty.

Her eyes flickered open.

'Help me!' she gasped, muffled by the iron clamping her lips together.

Helborg recoiled in shock, bringing his blade up in a flash. The woman struggled against her sorcerous bonds, weeping with terror and misery. All along the corridor, other eyes opened. There were still people alive in there, locked in agony.

'You can't help them!' cried Volkmar, calling to a priest who had swung his hammer back, ready to smash them free. 'They are one with the Tower. Leave them.'

The band pressed on, walking a little faster, avoiding the piteous wails from the walls, hastening to avoid the fingers that somehow managed to clutch at them as they passed.

It kept getting hotter. The roar of the bloodfire became more complete. A doorway loomed up at them from the shadows, high and ornately carved. The corruption came from within it.

As they approached, a cloaked figure burst through the doors, screaming with fury. It might have been a man once, but it had been terribly transformed. Its spine curved over, forcing it to scuttle like an insect. Its flesh was ivory-white, though the eyes were ringed with black. One hand was chronically distorted, now little more than a collection of flesh-ribbons. The other was curled tight into a fist.

'Blasphemy!' it screamed, hurling itself at Helborg.

The Marshal caught it in mid-air with the edge of the Klingerach, hurling it back against the wall. The creature hit the iron with a crack, and slid down to the floor. For a moment it looked like it might get up again.

'Blasphemy...' it croaked. Its mouth filled with purple blood and its eyes glazed over. 'She will punish...'

Then it locked into a spasm, choking and gagging. Helborg advanced to finish it off, but it expired. It slumped, twisted and broken against the iron wall.

Leitdorf gazed at it with horrified recognition.

'Achendorfer,' he breathed, unable to look away from the man's distorted features.

'Not any more,' said Helborg grimly, resuming the march towards the doorway.

Volkmar and Leitdorf joined him. Together with the warrior priests and Reiksguard, they clustered at the portal to the chamber beyond.

Something vast was in there. The sound of a giant heart beating came from beyond the obsidian doors. The sigil of Slaanesh was engraved on each one, burning with the sweet stench of ruin. As Helborg's eyes swept over them, pain lodged behind his eyes.

'Trust to faith,' he said for a final time.

Then he pushed the doors open, and they swung wide. Beyond was a stone. It was massive, rearing up from the floor like a leviathan emerging from the deeps.

They entered the chamber. Helborg looked up. Natassja was there.

And then, only then, did he truly understand what had happened in Averheim.

Schwarzhelm pressed the attack, whirling the Rechtstahl round hard, knocking Grosslich back with the force of the blow. From the corner of his vision he could see his men locked in battles of their own. They couldn't fight their way through Grosslich's men, but neither were they being driven back in their turn. Everything hinged on the duel.

Grosslich's armour was gouged with many rents, all inflicted by the Sword of Justice. Still he stayed on his feet. The wound in his neck had closed, and a ring of solid black blood formed a torc beneath his chin. His skills were impressive, no doubt augmented by the latent power in his sword.

It would do him no good. Schwarzhelm spun his blade at the traitor, pulling back at the last moment and flickering the tip above Grosslich's guard. The sorcerer switched position, but too clumsily. Schwarzhelm stabbed forwards, aiming for a gaping crack in the breastplate.

The aim was good. Grosslich roared with pain a second time. He punched out with his gauntlet, aiming for Schwarzhelm's head. The big man reared back, keeping the sword in place, then plunged it in deeper.

Grosslich's face bloomed with blood like a translucent sac. He staggered, impaled on the sword edge. Schwarzhelm grabbed the man's pauldron with his free hand and hauled him further up the blade.

The two of them came together, their faces only inches apart. Grosslich's eyes went wide with shock and pain. The mutations on his face began to shrink away. The Dark Prince's gifts were being withdrawn.

'So you have sown,' hissed Schwarzhelm, twisting the blade, feeling the holy metal sear the tainted flesh, 'so shall you reap.'

Blood bubbled up in Grosslich's mouth, hot and black. The Averland runefang fell from his grasp. For a moment, his face looked almost normal. It was the face of a mortal man, the one who had inspired a thousand peasants to march under his banner. Before Natassja had twisted those aims, they had been noble enough.

'Dominion,' he drawled, blood spilling from his lips. '*Dominion...*'

His eyes went glassy, and his body went limp.

Schwarzhelm wrenched the Sword of Justice free and Grosslich fell to his knees. For a heartbeat he stayed there, struggling against the inevitable. He looked up at Schwarzhelm pleadingly. The mutations around his face shrank back into nothing. He was as he had been before, a son of Averland.

There was no hesitation. Schwarzhelm drew the Rechtstahl back and swung heavily. Grosslich's head came off in a single sweeping movement. It spun into the air and rolled across the mud, coming to rest amidst a detachment of halberdiers rushing into assault. The men trampled it into the mire, hardly noticing it amongst the horrors of the war around them. Soon it was lost, the skull cracked and smeared with blood and grime, gone amid the detritus of the battle.

The headless corpse teetered for a moment before thudding to the ground. Heinz-Mark's rule as elector was over, ended by the man who had crowned him.

Schwarzhelm bent down and retrieved the runefang from the mire. The black slurry had stopped dripping from the blade and the steel glinted from under the crust of corruption. He wiped it clean on his cloak, then took it up in his left hand. Just as he had done on the journey from Altdorf, Schwarzhelm carried two swords, one the Sword of Justice, the other a runefang.

He turned to face the dog-soldiers already clustering around him. They weren't daunted by the death of their commander, and the battle still surged unabated. Grosslich had never truly commanded them. He'd been a puppet to the last, a tool for the use of subtler powers.

Schwarzhelm narrowed his eyes. He could see Kraus leading the charge on his left flank. There were Imperial troops everywhere, all lost in close-packed fighting. The situation was still desperate, and Grosslich's death hadn't changed it.

He was about to plunge into the ranks of dog-soldiers ahead when he caught a glimpse of something out of the corner of his eye. A long, leather coat, flapping in the ash-flecked wind, worn by a man who had no business being on a battlefield at all.

'The last of the family,' said Schwarzhelm to himself, filled with renewed purpose and hefting his twin blades. 'I swear it now. Death will not find *you* this day.'

Natassja had grown. The last elements of her humanity had been shed, and she now towered ten feet above a mortal span. Her flesh was as black as jet, tinged with a faint outline of blue fire. Her eyes, still pupil-less, blazed an icy sapphire.

Her human raiment was gone. Her flesh was clad in shifting strips of blackened silk, rippling around her and curling over the onyx skin. Her hair raged around her face like a furnace, caught up in the throbbing bloodfire as it whipped across her naked shoulders. The tattoos that had scored her skin for so long were gone, replaced by a single burning mark of Slaanesh at her breast.

Though still achingly beautiful, her features had already been twisted with mutation. Her feet were gone, replaced with cloven hooves. Her fingers ended in talons such as her handmaidens wore. They were sheer points of ebony, slender and curved. She moved impossibly quickly, as if there were no intermediate stage between her being in one location and at the next. Even when her mouth moved to speak, the pattern of her lips was eerie and unsettling. A long, lizard-like tongue flickered between glittering fangs.

Natassja now resembled the daemons that had served her, though it was she who was the greater and more steeped in corruption. For Natassja was no true-born denizen of the aethyr, but that most terrible and despised of creations, a daemon prince, a mortal ascended to the level of a demigod. She had exchanged a finite soul for an infinity of damnation, and the terms of the bargain were daunting. Her power was near-limitless, her invulnerability near-complete, her malice absolute. In exchange for that, thousands had died in terror.

Mortal weapons now had no purchase on her, death little meaning. The world of the five senses, so long her prison, was now fleshed out with a thousand shades of emotion. Her eyes were no longer bound by the trammels of matter but by the possibilities of a profound and piercing sentience. Where a mortal saw appearances, she saw realities, stretching away over a whole range of future states towards an impossible horizon. Men appeared before her as burning souls wrapped in a frail gauze, ready to be plucked out and consumed as a lesser being might select sweetmeats from a tray.

For so long, the Vision had been so beautiful. It did not compare to the reality.

Behind her, the Stone still throbbed with energy. It had been enough to complete her transformation, magnified by the Tower, called into being by the sacrifices of the humans who had died. Averheim was her altar, the stone across which the lambs had been slaughtered. Slaanesh was pleased. The Lord of Pain smiled on her now, gifting her with the merest sliver of His own consciousness. Though her flesh was real, rooted in the world like that of the lowliest creature of the earth, her soul was an inferno, a blaze of coruscation beside which those of mortals were mere candles.

'The Sword of Vengeance,' she said, recognising its pattern within the world.

Her voice was astonishing, even to her. All those who had died to bring her into being shared a part of it. Just as with the true daemons, many tongues echoed throughout her speech. Men, women and children all spoke through her, and the sound echoed from the walls like a massed chorus. As sharp as a scream, as deep and resounding as a sob, Natassja let her new vocal cords play across their full range. It delighted her. Everything delighted her.

From down below, the one called Helborg still stood defiant. He raised the blade she'd named, as if that little spike could hurt her now. Beside him, the worm who had once been her husband did likewise. There was a third man with them who mattered, a disciple of the boy-god. She could see his soul hammering at the bonds of flesh that enclosed it. He was no stranger to the Realm of Chaos, that one. He'd been into it once, and come back out again. Intriguing. That shouldn't have been possible.

'The Staff of Command,' she said, recognising its name from the profile in the aethyr. It was ancient by the standards of the Empire, paltry by the standards of her master. It was capable of causing her some pain, but little more. 'You are the Grand Theogonist of the boy-god.'

She expected the man to rave at her then, to scream some screed about her being corrupted filth that would be driven from the face of the world by the righteous hosts of Sigmar.

He didn't. He stood his ground, and a grey, stinking cloud of dirty smog flared up at the end of his miserable staff. To him, no doubt, it was as beautiful as the rising sun.

'We recognise each other, then,' Volkmar replied. His voice came from far away. Natassja had to concentrate to hear it properly over the choir of psychic voices blaring at her. The world of the daemon was strange, far richer than that of a mortal, but confusing and hard to make sense of. It would take some time to get used to. 'If you claim to know me, then you know that you will not be suffered to live.'

Natassja didn't laugh at that brand of folly. The effrontery insulted her. She knew more about him than he could have guessed. Just by watching his soul writhe in its temporal bonds, she could feel his anguish. This one knew, deep down, the futility of what he did. He'd *seen* the end of the world. He'd been *shown* it. And still he failed to seize the truth in both hands. What the mortals called faith she knew as fear. An inability to see the full picture, a reluctance to receive what was out there to be given. There was nothing laudable in that. It was pathetic. Small-minded. Timorous.

As he spoke, the images swirling across her field of vision began to make more sense. She saw the origin of the materials that surrounded her, the age of the metals and the stories behind them. Such stories were imprinted into the matter of them, scored across the face of the world and stained in time.

The iron in the shaft above her had come from a mine deep under the Worlds Edge Mountains. Even now, it screamed at the perversion around it. The world itself resisted her, knowing her for what she was. The world, however, was old and tired, and she was as young and vital as a flame.

Everything had a story imprinted on it. That was the ultimate truth. There was nothing in the cosmos *but* stories, some given form, some just fleeting shadows. The men before her were stories, unfolding through time, weaving in and out of possibilities like carp amongst weeds.

She gazed down at Helborg again. He'd had many choices. He could have killed Schwarzhelm. She saw that possibility twisting away into a distant future. If he had done, the Empire would have split, wracked by civil war for a generation of men until the hurt could be undone. Helborg had no idea of that. He'd been motivated by pity. So touchingly weak, so endearingly stupid.

'Nothing you can do or know can harm me, priest,' she said coolly, feeling the pangs of her birth still resonating throughout her pristine body. 'Coming here only hastens your second death.'

'So thought Be'lakor,' said Volkmar, his voice holding steady. His staff was beginning to bleed its dark grey sludge profusely, polluting the symphony of colours before her and ruining the glorious harmonics of the Stone. 'So thought many of your kind. You don't know as much as you think you do. I have the power to harm you.'

This was getting tedious. Concentrating on the mortals for long enough to hear their words was frustrating. There were more important, more uplifting things to devote herself to. As a mortal she'd only been able to experience sensation across four dimensions. Now there were twelve to wallow in, and wasting time in chatter was a poor way to begin her new life of wonder.

'Then put it to the test, little man,' said Natassja, looking directly at the shifting figures below her and preparing to use the powers that were curled tight within her. 'Do your best to wound me. Then, when all is done, I shall introduce you to pain of such perfection that the gods themselves will weep to hear you scream.'

CHAPTER TWENTY-ONE

Volkmar fed power to his staff and the tip burst into golden illumination. The nimbus filled the chamber, reflecting back from the utter dark of the Stone and banishing the shadows around the sculpted iron walls. The fury of the bloodfire roared back, swirling around the Staff of Command like a swarm of enraged hornets.

On either side of him, warrior priests surged forwards, all eager to land the first blow on the towering figure before them. With a pang of regret, Volkmar watched as the foremost were reduced to weeping, shuddering wrecks.

The daemon's power was a subtle one. Natassja had been elegant as a mortal and daemonhood had not changed her. There were no sudden bursts of flame or crackling discharges of aethyr-spawned lightning. Her powers were those of the mind, of sensation, of fear and pain.

The first warrior priest to get near her exploded into a ball of blood at a flick from her shapely finger. The Reiksguard at his side was next. She shot a cool glance from her smooth eyes and his armour shattered. Beneath it, his body was transmuted into a writhing, hermaphroditic mess. Fleshy growths wrapped themselves around what was left of his throat and strangled the life out of him.

With every fresh death an echoing boom rushed up the shaft of the Stone. Volkmar could sense the enormous power contained there. It had been enough to grant Natassja her elevation into immortality and it had still been hardly tapped. With a dreadful realisation, he knew that there was nothing he could do to dent it. He might have had a thousand warrior priests with him and the result would have been the same. There was no hope left, not for them, not for Averheim.

'The blood of Sigmar!' he bellowed, defiant to the end.

He whirled the staff around and sent a stream of blazing fire at the daemon. It impacted directly on the sigil of Slaanesh at her breast and exploded, showering the chamber with spinning points of light.

Natassja took a step back, entirely unharmed. She bared her fangs and fixed Volkmar with a withering look of contempt.

He screamed, and staggered to his knees. Something vast and malice-drenched entered his soul. He could feel his essence being ripped away from within, dragged from his mortal frame on barbs of steel. She was destroying him.

His staff fell to the floor as he withdrew his power from it. Resisting the crushing influence of the daemon took all his residual art. He screwed his eyes closed, grimacing with pain. He was being dragged back to the hells he had escaped before. There, in the darkness, he could see the androgynous form of his nemesis. The Dark Prince had been waiting there since his last death, happy to welcome him back.

'Not...' he gasped, digging deep, drawing on every last shred of strength left in his battered body. 'Not *now*...'

Dimly, he was aware of more men rushing past him. There was a flash of light, and the crushing sensation eased.

Volkmar edged his eyes open, gasping for breath. Helborg had engaged the daemon. The notched runefang danced as the Marshal pressed towards the abomination.

Natassja evaded his blows easily. She shifted with incredible speed, darting from one place to another as if the steps inbetween positions had become completely unnecessary. Helborg's attack had at least diverted the terrifying power of her will, and Volkmar climbed back to his feet, picking up the staff again and preparing himself to use it.

'This is hopeless,' came a voice from his right.

Leitdorf was standing there, sword trembling in his hands, staring at the abomination with horror. His face was grey with fear.

'Stand your ground!' snarled Volkmar. 'Damn you, Rufus, stand your ground!'

Even as he spoke, another warrior priest was ripped apart by Natassja's malign will. She nodded curtly and the man's flesh was turned inside out, spilling his entrails across the Stone in glistening rings. Six men had already died without so much as making contact with her. Helborg fought on, roaring with defiance and frustration as she evaded his attacks.

'What good will it do?' Leitdorf wailed. All trace of his self-assurance on the battlefield had drained away, and he looked half-mad with fear. 'She's untouchable.'

Volkmar knew he was right. That didn't change a thing.

'This is your city,' he growled, preparing to kindle the staff again. 'Stand up for it.'

Then he strode back towards the daemon, and golden flame flared up along the shaft of his weapon.

'Scion of darkness!' he roared, sending a spitting column of lightning screaming towards the abomination. 'You will *not* prevail here!'

Helborg leapt forwards, trying to find purchase with the Klingerach. He knew the runefang would bite deep if it connected, but making contact with the flesh of the daemon was impossible. With a twist of his stomach, he saw more of his men being cut down, one by one. Natassja seemed to be picking off the lesser warriors first, toying with them all like a cat with its prey.

He stabbed at her massive thigh, whirling the blade around with blistering speed and force. At the very last moment, she shifted position, appearing a yard away, still in the same pose. She winked at him, flicked her fingers, and the last Reiksguard standing lost his skin. The man collapsed in a screaming, writhing pool of blood, held together by his armour and nothing else.

'Damned witch!' Helborg hissed, keeping his sword in guard and searching for some kind of opening.

Volkmar had got back to his feet by then, and sent a fresh stream of spitting golden fire straight at the daemon. His staff was the only weapon that seemed able to harm her daemonic flesh. Irritated by the interruption in her killing, she turned her attention back to the raging cleric.

Helborg tensed, ready to plunge back into the attack, but then caught sight of Leitdorf. The man had frozen. The Wolfsklinge was in his hands, but only just.

'Your blade, Leitdorf!' bellowed Helborg, rushing to the elector's side. As he did so, he saw Volkmar being beaten back, just as before. 'Remember Drakenmoor!'

Leitdorf shot him a panic-stricken look.

'I *can't*...' he began, but then Helborg was dragging him to face Natassja.

'We attack together!' he cried, pushing him forwards. 'Just as before!'

The Marshal hurled himself at the daemon. Somehow Leitdorf summoned the courage to join him, and the two men charged the monstrous figure.

Then, and for the first time, Helborg almost wounded her. Distracted by Volkmar's attack and faced with the onslaught of two ancient blades, Natassja faltered for just an instant. She pulled back from Helborg's blow, but failed to withdraw from Leitdorf's attack. The Wolfsklinge passed through her flesh without biting and came clean out the other side.

Off-balance, Leitdorf stumbled to his knees. As quick as a whip, Natassja kicked out with a hoof and sent him flying across the chamber floor. He hit the far wall hard. His sword

spun from his grasp, coming to rest by the eviscerated body
of a fallen Reiksguard knight.

Isolated and unable to land a blow, Helborg fell back.

Two of the surviving warrior priests charged at the daemon
then, their warhammers swinging heavily. Natassja turned
to face them and bared her fangs again. One priest simply
exploded, his breastplate spinning across the floor and spraying blood. The other seized up, his face marked with agony.
He shuddered, and his bones burst out through his flesh,
lengthening with frightening speed, tearing the muscles as
they came. The priest collapsed to the ground and dissolved
into a mess of ripped flesh and still-extending skeleton.

By then there were only six priests left, all cowed by the
daemon's contemptuous response to their attacks. Helborg
looked over at Volkmar. The Theogonist was preparing for a
third attack, but Natassja had badly hurt him. Leitdorf lived
too, but he looked dazed and shaky on his feet.

'We can't do this,' breathed Helborg, aghast at the sudden awareness of his weakness. He took up the Klingerach
again and prepared for another charge. Duty demanded no
less, but he held no hope for it. 'We have come too late. The
bitch will kill us all.'

Leitdorf gasped for breath. The merest touch of Natassja's
flesh had been enough to send a searing chill through his
body. He'd felt the vast power coiled up within her then,
and it dwarfed anything he'd ever felt before.

He gazed up at her, watching as she pulled the limbs from
another warrior priest. Natassja looked almost bored, as if
this were a mild distraction before the real entertainment
began. Next to her, Helborg and Volkmar, two of the mightiest warriors in the Empire, looked more ineffectual than
children playing at combat.

Determined as ever, Helborg charged back into contact,
spinning the Sword of Vengeance around him, trying to land
a blow on Natassja's shifting, ephemeral body.

As he did so, Volkmar sent a third barrage of faith-fire at

her. The Theogonist aimed at her face and the swirling column of lightning impacted directly. She was knocked back against the Stone. The impact didn't do any real damage, but the interruption seemed to infuriate her.

She extended her palm and Helborg was flung back through the air, his limbs flailing as the unseen thrust slammed him aside. Then she clenched her fist and Volkmar doubled over. The light streaming from his staff dimmed, and he fell to his knees in pain.

Ignoring his own wounds, Leitdorf limped to Volkmar's side. He clutched at the Theogonist's shoulders as the man toppled to one side. The remaining warrior priests charged heroically at the daemon, drawing her attention away from Volkmar. Their six lives bought nothing but a few moments of respite.

'My lord!' Leitdorf cried, helping the man to the floor.

The Theogonist's eyes were filmy. It looked like he wasn't seeing very much.

'Too... *powerful*...' he gasped, and his fingers clutched at his staff feebly.

Leitdorf felt his despair turn to a desperate, frustrated anger. He looked up. The roof of the chamber was open, and a vast shaft of fire soared away into the distance. This had been Natassja's birth-chamber. The entire structure above was nothing more than an amplifier for the energies needed to bring her into being. That was why she'd needed Averheim. It was nothing to do with temporal power or riches. For her, the city had been a *machine*.

He looked at Natassja. She killed two more men then, flaying them alive with a twist of her fingers. The remaining quartet still came on, still trying to find a way to harm her. Helborg too had staggered back into range. Their bravery was phenomenal, but it would do little to save them.

'Can you ignite the staff again?' asked Leitdorf, a note of desperation in his voice.

Volkmar shook his head.

'Look around you,' he panted. 'This has been centuries in the making. We cannot hurt her.'

Leitdorf slammed his fist against the marble floor. He was no longer afraid, just furious. After all the pain, all the bloodshed, it had come to this at last. His inheritance, turned to ashes before his eyes, destroyed in order to bring a new horror into the world.

'There must be *something.*'

Volkmar shook his head. 'Her daemonhood is complete. Without knowledge of her true name, she is invulnerable to us.'

The last of the warrior priests was riven where he stood, his body torn into ribbons. Only Helborg, Volkmar and Leitdorf remained. The last ones to die, locked beneath the earth under a tower of iron.

From above, the distant howling grew louder. The lesser daemons were still looking for a way in. The bloodfire bloomed anew, roaring and thundering against the iron. The Stone could sense victory, and gloried in it.

'Her *name*?' asked Leitdorf, suddenly feeling a sliver of hope. 'What power would that give you?'

Volkmar looked up at him. There was a grim smile on his face, the resigned look of a man who knows death is upon him.

'I could hurt her then,' he growled. 'By Sigmar, I would *hurt* her.'

Leitdorf began to fumble at his belt.

'Find the power,' he ordered, his voice suddenly resonant again. 'Find it from somewhere. This isn't over yet.'

Helborg pulled the body of the warrior priest back, but too late. The man's skin hung in strips from his frame. For a last few agonised moments, the priest still lived. He fixed Helborg with piteous eyes, blood and tears mingling across his destroyed face. Then he collapsed, just another corpse on the floor of the chamber.

Helborg withdrew a pace, keeping his blue eyes locked on the figure looming over him. Natassja smiled at him and flexed her talons.

'Shall I preserve you?' she mused, looking at the Marshal as if he were a morsel of food at the end of a banquet. 'These ones have died in an instant. Your death will last for an eternity.'

Helborg smiled wolfishly, keeping the runefang between him and the daemon.

'I am sustained by faith,' he said.

Natassja raised an amused eyebrow.

'You believe that *still*? Do you not think these priests had faith?'

'Their deaths were glorious. Their souls are with Sigmar.'

Natassja shook her head with disbelief.

'You mystify me, human,' she said. 'You all mystify me. You are shown the illusion, and still you refuse to see through it.'

Helborg circled round the daemon carefully, looking for any sign of weakness.

'I see enough.'

'Evidently not.'

She moved, quicker than thought, reaching out with a taloned hand to grab him by the throat. At the same time, Volkmar roared into life for a final time. A beam of gold lanced out from his staff and slammed Natassja backwards, dousing her in a cascade of golden shards.

She spun to face the Theogonist. The cool irritation had vanished from her features to be replaced by exasperation.

'Still not dead?' she spat. 'You're beginning to annoy me, disciple.'

She coiled to strike, curling her talons into a fist. Volkmar shrank back, his bloodied figure standing defiant against the coming onslaught.

'*Bedarruzibarr!*' came a voice from the edge of the chamber.

Natassja whirled round, amazement and horror suddenly rippling across her features.

Leitdorf stood before her. He held the book in his trembling hands. He kept reading. Just as it had done for her birth, the bloodfire in the chamber flared up at the sound. '*Bedarruzibarr'zagarratumnan'akz'akz'berau!*'

'Cease speaking, worm!' screamed Natassja, and her hands burst into blue flame.

'*Bedarruzibarr!*' thundered Volkmar, echoing Leitdorf's cry.

The Theogonist raised his staff and sent a flurry of crackling bolts into Natassja's torso. They impacted heavily. This time they seemed to damage her, and she staggered back towards the Stone.

'Cease!' she cried, still wreathed in bands of shimmering golden flame. 'This is forbidden knowledge!'

'*Abbadonnodo'neherata'gradarruminam!*' shouted Leitdorf, his voice growing in confidence, tracing the words from the pages of his father's diary. With every syllable, Natassja seemed to recoil further.

Volkmar sent fresh volleys of faith-fire at her, his face alight with furious relish.

'Hear your name, spawn of Slaanesh!' he roared in triumph. 'Feel the powers at your command unravel!'

Buffeted by a wall of spitting fire, Natassja rocked back. The calm assurance of her superiority was gone. The syllables of her true name echoed around the chamber, fuelling Volkmar's torrent of righteous fire. She reeled under the onslaught, screaming as the fire tore at her.

Then Helborg was on her too, no longer seeming so diminutive. He hauled his blade round in a mighty arc, scything at Natassja's legs. The runefang connected, and a blaze of pure white light leapt up. Blood sprayed through the air, as black as the Stone behind it, sparkling like beads of onyx.

Natassja screamed again, her voice now filled with pain and frustration. She lashed out with her left fist, catching Helborg on his breastplate and sending him lurching backwards. She opened her other hand and let loose the full power within her.

The chamber shuddered, rocked to its foundations by the blast. The bloodfire blazed purple, roaring into a frenzy. Volkmar was knocked from his feet, and the staff spun from his grasp. Cracks ran up the walls and the iron bands around them broke open. Wards were shattered, and the howling of the lesser daemons boomed down the shaft.

Leitdorf jumped aside just as the floor disintegrated under him. The marble rippled like a wave and cracked open. From below, the thunderous roar of the deep engines rolled upwards.

Natassja staggered towards Leitdorf, the last of Volkmar's golden fire streaming from her shoulders. She was badly wounded, and great gashes had opened on her flanks. They wept black essence, as dark and pure as jet.

'Worm!' she rasped, and her voice was fractured with hatred. The choir within her had begun to come apart. 'Utter not words beyond your comprehension.'

Leitdorf scrambled away from her, stumbling around the edge of chamber.

'*Malamanuar'neramumo'klza'jhehennum!*' he shouted, keeping up the recital even as he fled from Natassja's wrath. The very sound of it seemed to wound her.

He couldn't escape forever. The chamber held no hiding places, and Natassja still had the power to move quickly. She stood over the elector, towering above his paltry frame, poised to silence the words that cut through her power so completely.

Leitdorf kept shouting the words out, right until the end. Natassja pulled her hand back, wailing in agony as each syllable resounded around the chamber. A curved dagger unrolled into existence, extending from her flesh like smoke and firming into a wicked, twin-bladed instrument.

Helborg clambered to his feet and charged towards her. Volkmar hauled the staff back into position. It was far too late. The dagger plunged down, seeming to cleave the very air around it. It lodged deep in Leitdorf's chest, pinning him to the stone beneath.

The elector screamed, and his body arched in agony. The book fell from his hands. As it hit the ground, Natassja glared at it and the parchment burst into green-tinged flame, shrivelling and curling into nothing.

But then Helborg was close enough. With the last echoes of the daemon's name still lingering in the shaft above them, he raised the Sword of Vengeance high above his head. The runes blazed in the bloodfire, reflecting the fury of the Stone, bending the rays of contamination back at it.

Natassja whirled to face the new threat, but her aura of invincibility had gone. She bared her fangs again, fixing Helborg with a look of such malice and terror that a lesser man would have crumbled under it.

Helborg's shoulder wound burst open, drenching his chest with blood. For a moment, Natassja's face rippled into Schwarzhelm's, and a bizarre mix of daemon and man screamed its hatred at him.

He didn't flinch. The blade came down in a mighty, crushing sweep. The edge bit true, carving through aethyr-wound sinews as readily as real flesh. A ball of brilliant light radiated from the impact, rushing across the chamber and swirling into the heights of the shaft. The bloodfire guttered in its wake. Fresh cracks radiated from the Stone, rippling across the floor and releasing gouts of smog from the furnaces below.

Natassja cried out with agony, and her many voices rebounded from the iron walls around her. Her face returned to its normal shape, transfixed in pain and fury. She twisted away from the runefang, exposing the huge, jagged wound in her torso. It gushed a torrent of bile, foaming and fizzing as it poured out into the world.

Helborg ducked under a vicious swipe from her dagger hand and swung the Klingerach back at her. The blade sunk deep, cleaving Natassja's stomach open and jarring on the bones beyond.

The daemon fell to her knees, weeping blood. The bloodfire shuddered and veered away from her, suddenly averse to the failing presence in its midst. She dropped down further, bracing herself with a blood-streaked arm.

Natassja looked at Helborg, her face now level with his. Her expression was a mix of scorn, fury and astonishment.

'You have no idea what you've done, mortal,' she rasped, her voices jarring as they overlapped. 'You have *no idea*...'

Helborg didn't listen. The Sword of Vengeance rose high, glimmering in the firelight.

'I see enough,' he snarled, and brought the blade down.

For a moment, nothing happened. Natassja's severed head rolled from her body, coming to rest close to the stricken form of Leitdorf. The bloodfire continued to roar, the engines continued to grind, the wind continued to howl.

Then the daemons came, tearing down the shaft, screaming like vengeful harpies. Helborg stood up to them, and the runefang blazed with a holy fire. All weariness had fallen from his shoulders. Just as before, he looked like one of the heroes of old, clad in sacred armour and wearing the hawk-wing helm of the Reiksmarshal. He waited for them to come to him, his cloak rippling in the bloodfire, still bearing the Sword of Vengeance in both hands.

The first of them hurtled down from the pinnacle, teeth bared, arms outstretched. A second later, she lay on the floor next to her mistress, her body broken by Helborg. Another fell to the same blade, carved in two by the holy metal. The rest of them halted in their onslaught, suddenly looking with horrified eyes at the ruined body of their mistress. They hovered in the air above the Stone, frozen in terrible doubt.

As they surveyed the scene, Volkmar recovered his footing.

'The tide has turned, whores of Slaanesh,' he cried, reaching for his staff and fixing them with a vengeful glare. 'Leave while you can, or the Sword of Vengeance will tear every one of you apart.'

They looked at him, then at Helborg. The Reiksmarshal stared back, grim-faced and resolute. The blade in his hands glowed with residual energy, and the runes resonated. The sword was back with its master, and its thirst for killing was not yet sated.

Then they fled, screeching as they went, buoyed aloft by the surging bloodfire. The shaft echoed from their screeches, dying into nothing as they spiralled towards the distant pinnacle.

The Tower creaked ominously. Pieces of iron and stone detached from the walls and trails of dust ran down from the high places.

Helborg watched the daemons go, then stumbled across to Leitdorf. Volkmar joined him, limping heavily. As they went, the floor cracked further. Great booms rang out from far below, muffled by the layers of rock beneath them.

Leitdorf's face was pale. Natassja's dagger had dissolved into nothingness with the demise of its mistress, but the wound was ugly and hadn't closed. There was no blood, just a dark-edged hole. Leitdorf struggled to breathe. As Helborg approached, he tried to push himself up on to his elbows.

'Remain still,' said Helborg, coming to his side and looking anxiously at his wound. 'Can you do anything, Theogonist?'

Volkmar crouched down next to the Marshal. He placed his calloused hands on the incision, and Leitdorf recoiled in pain. The Theogonist closed his eyes, probing for aethyric residue. When he opened them again, his expression was grave.

'No lies between us, Rufus Leitdorf,' he said. 'This wound is mortal.'

Leitdorf smiled thinly.

'How stupid do you think I am?' Then he broke into coughing. There was blood in his throat, flecked on his armour.

'You have triumphed, elector,' said Helborg, his severe face drawn with pain. 'Do you remember your words in Drakenmoor? You have proved the bane of her.'

Leitdorf cast his weakening gaze over to the broken body of the daemon prince. It lay just a few feet away, huge, ravaged, and yet for all that still perversely alluring.

'I truly believed that I loved her,' he croaked. His face went from grey to white, and a slick of sweat broke out over his forehead. 'Can you believe that?'

Helborg and Volkmar said nothing. The sound of stone and iron grinding against each other grew from below. More debris showered down from the shaft and the roar of the bloodfire became intermittent. The Tower, bereft of its guiding will, was cracking.

'I thought she would deliver more than Averland to me,' said Leitdorf, his breath ragged, still gazing at Natassja. 'I thought she would give me what I wanted. A *son*, Lord Helborg. Blame that desire, if you still need blame. My line dies with me here. I am the last.'

Helborg grasped the dying man's hand.

'You have saved the city,' he said. 'Your deeds will be remembered.'

'No,' Leitdorf replied, and blood ran from his cracked lips. His voice shrank to barely a whisper. 'Tell them what my father did. He discovered her name. Tell them—'

Leitdorf broke into coughing again, and black fluid bubbled up his throat. His hand clenched Helborg's tightly as he recovered himself. In his last moments alive, his face was a mask of pure determination.

'Tell them he wasn't mad,' he said.

Then Leitdorf's eyes went blank. He stiffened, and the fingers of his free hand clutched at the air wildly. He took one last shuddering breath, and then fell still. His pudgy face, speckled with blood and ash, relaxed. In the shifting firelight, the resemblance to Marius was striking.

More debris began to fall from above. A great iron spar tumbled down the shaft, clanging from the walls as it spiralled before crashing to the earth on the far side of the chamber. Flames, real flames, began to lick up from the cracks in the floor.

'We need to go,' said Volkmar.

'I will take the body,' said Helborg, reaching for Leitdorf's prone corpse.

'Leave it.' Volkmar stood up. 'It will slow you. This is his victory, and his realm. No tomb in Altdorf would be finer.'

Helborg hesitated, then ran a hand up to his bleeding shoulder. More cracks ran up the walls, lifting the plates of iron and exposing raw, pulsing aethyric matter beneath. The Tower was suffused with it, a conduit of baleful energies.

He rose, stooping only to retrieve Leitdorf's sword from where it had fallen.

'A pup no longer,' he said, looking bitterly at Leitdorf's body. 'You should have lived to wield this.'

Then Helborg and Volkmar left the chamber, hurrying under the doorway as the Tower began to fall apart. Behind them, the room was marked only by the corpses on the floor and the sinister presence of the Stone in their midst. It glowed in the darkness for a while, as if revelling in one last lingering expression of power.

Then it died, failing back to dull grey. The bloodfire flared around it, swirling in one last angry eddy, and went out.

The bodies were slumped on the earth as if sleep had stolen upon them all. Bloch was dead, and his muscles had grown cold. Verstohlen still lived, but his pulse was shallow and his flesh pale. He lay next to his comrade, insensible to the thunder of battle around him, lost in a private struggle against the poison within.

Standing over them, holding the line against the ravening horde beyond, Schwarzhelm heaved his sword back, dismembering a dog-soldier with the trailing edge of the Rechtstahl. All around him, his men fought on. The line was intact but thinning. Any pretence at an advance had long been given up. The Imperial forces were exhausted, driven to the utter reaches of fatigue by the unending masses of enemy troops before them. The walls of the city were no closer than they had been hours earlier, and the plain still swarmed with lilac-eyed soldiers. Averheim would not be taken by force. The best they could hope for was to hold for the dawn and organise some kind of withdrawal. In the face of the surviving war engines, the retreat would be ruinously blood-soaked.

'We're losing this fight!' came a familiar voice.

Kraus fought his way to Schwarzhelm's side. He'd lost his helmet in the melee and his forehead was shiny with blood. A hasty battlefield tourniquet had been wrapped around it, but it didn't do much to staunch the bleeding.

'You forget Helborg.'

Kraus snorted, and launched into the enemy troops before him. The wound didn't seem to have slowed him down much.

'He's one more sword,' he spat, his arms working hard. 'Just one more sword.'

Even as he finished speaking, though, something changed. A vast, rumbling boom resounded from the city, still half a mile distant and shrouded in smoke.

All felt it. Some stumbled as the earth reeled, their tired limbs no longer able to absorb the shock. The dog-soldiers halted in their tracks. The cultists around them went limp. Weapons fell from their slack hands.

Another boom. The bloodfire, that vast column of thundering, writhing flame, shuddered. The massive pillar of aethyric matter wavered like a waterfall cut off at its source. More crashes resounded out from the city walls. Above them all, the Tower loomed darkly, still wreathed in its corona of fire.

'Stand fast, men of the Empire!' roared Schwarzhelm, raising both swords above his head.

All down the exhausted lines, halberdiers and swordsmen looked up in sudden amazement. The enemy had stopped attacking. Grosslich's mortal troops stood immobile and listless. In the heavens, the circles of cloud broke open, exposing the dark blue of the sky beyond.

There were more distant rumbles, and a cloud of ash and dust rose up from beyond the city walls. The lesser towers crumbled, one by one, falling back in on themselves with stately majesty.

'What is this?' asked Kraus. His face betrayed his hope. Before them, the dog-soldiers fell to their knees and began to claw at their faces. The dread power that had animated them had been withdrawn, and the agony of their twisted bodies now flooded into them. All across the plain, the Army of the Stone descended into a frenzy of pain and self-destruction.

Schwarzhelm didn't smile. He spun round, looking east. The night sky was stained with a faint blush of grey.

'This is the dawn,' he said. His raised blades caught the first glimmers of light.

The Iron Tower, huge and dominating, began to shed its high spars. Cracks ran up its massive flanks, stained red like the wounds of a living thing. Plumes of black soot rolled up from its foundations, effluent from the mighty machines still turning in the deep catacombs. As vast as it was, the withdrawal of the malign intelligence that had built it was too great a strain to bear. It was falling apart.

Men, freed from the incessant fight for survival, gaped up at the sight, their jaws hanging open. Some wept with relief, falling to their knees and crying praises to Sigmar and Ulric. Others vented their pent-up rage, wading into the supine rows of the enemy, laying waste to the defenceless thousands who still stood on the plain.

Kraus sheathed his sword, watching with dismay as the dog-soldiers in front of him clutched at their ruined bodies. Some ripped off their iron masks, revealing their horribly stretched faces. The Empire soldiers around him looked up at him uncertainly, caught between their hatred and confusion.

'What are your orders, my lord?' asked Kraus, looking as torn between instincts as they were.

Schwarzhelm sheathed the Averland runefang, keeping the Rechtstahl naked in his right hand.

'Keep the men together,' he said. 'The bodies of Verstohlen and Bloch are to be taken from here and preserved. If any apothecaries still live, tell them to minister to the counsellor. I would not see him die. Not now, not after all has been accomplished.'

'And what of you?'

Schwarzhelm began to stride through the writhing mass of dog-soldiers towards the city. None hindered his passage.

'The field is yours, captain,' he said, and his voice was free of the anguish that had marked it since the Vormeisterplatz. 'My brother-in-arms has been victorious, and homage is due.'

Ahead of him, the titanic pillar of flame faded and flickered out. The thrum of its burning died away, exposing the charred and crumbling spires of Averheim beneath. Free of the crushing, oppressive weight in the air, a cleansing wind tore across the battlefield. Tattered standards rippled back into life. Shattered detachments of soldiers regained their feet.

With an ominous creak, the Tower listed to one side. More spars fell from it, raining down on the shattered cityscape below. More cracks raced up its sides, breaking open the sigils of Chaos and cracking their symmetry. Real fire flared up from the dungeons beneath the base of the mighty columns, licking at the buckling iron, replacing the sorcerous flames that had wreathed the metal for so long.

There was a final rolling clap of thunder, born deep in the heart of ravaged Averheim and sweeping up into the soot-clogged air. The Tower reeled, shedding spiked buttresses and crossbeams. Its jagged crown tumbled, disintegrating as it spun from the pinnacle, and crashed to earth in a surging cloud of ash and fire.

With terrible slowness, the gigantic framework of Natassja's citadel crumbled in on itself. Iron ground against iron, throwing sparks high into the air. Like a landslip of the high peaks, the abomination slid gracefully into ruin.

A vast cloud of smoke and smog rose up in its wake, huge and threatening. Then it too was borne away by the wind from the east, ripped into nothingness and dispersed as the dreams of those that had made it had been dispersed.

The Tower was gone. The battle for Averheim was over.

CHAPTER
TWENTY-TWO

In the annals of Imperial history, the victory at Averheim would be recorded as a triumph for the Grand Theogonist Volkmar. Honourable mentions would be given to the Lords Helborg and Schwarzhelm, as well as glowing tributes to the heroism of the martyred Rufus Leitdorf. The loremasters would record in exhaustive detail the tactical genius of the Empire commanders and the craven collapse of the forces of the great enemy. As ever, they would use the example of Grosslich's defeat as evidence of the futility of opposing the all-conquering Empire of mankind.

The archivists would not mention the destruction of the city. They would remain silent on the deaths of Averheim's entire population, either killed in battle or during the construction of the Tower. None of them would mention that, out of Volkmar's army of forty thousand, less than a quarter survived to return to Altdorf. Nor would they see fit to record the litany of mistakes and treachery that had led Grosslich to be crowned elector instead of Leitdorf. Confident in the faulty memories of those they wrote for, they knew the passing of time would erase such inconveniences. The important thing was that the enemy had been defeated and the rule of Karl Franz reimposed.

The physical devastation, however, could not be hidden. Averheim was in ruins, scorched by fire and reeking with the residue of corrosion. The river was clogged with ash and the streets wine-red with bloodstains. Though the daemons had disappeared with the passing of the bloodfire, their spoor of madness still hung in the shadows.

It took months to cleanse the place. Hundreds of witch hunters were summoned from surrounding cities. Volkmar himself presided over the ritual exorcism and stayed in the heart of the shattered city for several weeks. His army remained too, though their swords were swiftly replaced with picks and shovels. The task of demolishing the remains of the Tower and restoring what was left of old Averheim was long and arduous.

In the days after the battle ended, there were many, Helborg among them, who counselled that Averheim should be abandoned. The stain of Chaos ran too deep, and the losses had been too grievous. It was Volkmar who overruled them. The greater war still ground on in the north, soaking up resources and manpower, sapping the will of the Empire. The populace needed a sign of victory. They needed to be shown that the lost ground could be recovered.

So he ordered the city to be reclaimed. Broken houses and streets were repaired with the labour of his men. Merchants, soldiers and families were enticed from the nearby towns with the promise of property and wealth. Grosslich's treasuries were discovered and the gold used for the work of reconstruction. Only the iron of the Tower was not reused. The ruins were cordoned off for weeks as a phalanx of priests ritually destroyed the foundations. The reek of molten metal hung over the city in a pall of bitterness long after the last of the iron had been turned into ingots and shipped away.

Beneath it all was the Stone. Only Volkmar descended back down to the hidden chamber during the long months of recovery, and he never said what work was done there. As the autumn faded into winter, the wide courtyard of the Tower was finally paved over again, and the last of Grosslich's gold used to sponsor the construction of a cathedral on the site. In later years, the Church of Sigmar the Destroyer of Heresy rose up in place of the Tower, vast and opulent, a counterpart to the restored Averburg across the river. It would become a centre of pilgrimage as the years wore on, drawing suppli-cants from across the southern provinces of the Empire. Few priests wished to serve in its incense-soaked naves, however. It swiftly developed an evil reputation for ill-luck, and the clerics were prone to bad dreams.

Though it took many more years, Averland recovered much of its prosperity. The people of the province were fertile, the land was still good, and memories were quick to dim. The destruction of Averheim was the making of some families, just as it was the doom of others. Trade resumed along the Aver, and the last of Grosslich's edicts were repealed.

A new Steward was appointed. Klaus Meuningen was a surprise choice, taken from provincial obscurity in Gren-zstadt and given command of the capital. He proved capable enough, however, and loyal to the Emperor in most things. Under his rule, the clamour for a new elector faded again. Whenever the issue was raised, some excuse was found to shelve it. All knew that the matter would have to be returned to at some point in the future, but all also knew that it would be long before Averland was ready again.

In the immediate aftermath of the great battle, none of these things were obvious. Volkmar's troops were mostly just glad to be alive. Under Kraus's leadership, they gradu-ally went about the grim business of finishing off Grosslich's will-bereft forces. When Volkmar returned from the city to resume command, huge pyres were constructed for the dead. As at Turgitz, one was raised for the corrupted, another for the uncorrupted. The latter burned with a pure, angry flame. The former would smoulder for weeks, tinged with lilac.

All knew that the vista would never be the same again. The

old fertile soil had been ruined by Natassja's poisons, and the Averpeak now slumped into ruin where the war engines had demolished it.

Even there, though, the grass would grow again. It just took time, the great healer of all wounds.

Verstohlen lay on a pallet and gazed at the roof of his tent. Despite the blankets and cloak that covered him, he shivered. The wind from the east was bitter, and the last shreds of summer had been driven away. Four days since the battle, and he had barely slept. Worse than that, the poisons still worked within him. Thanks to the expert attentions of one of Volkmar's apothecaries, he had survived the worst of it. He was enough of an alchemist to know that the damage done to him was severe, though. He still couldn't walk, and his vision was cloudy. Perhaps that would improve in time. Perhaps it wouldn't.

The flaps of the tent entrance opened, and Schwarzhelm ducked down through the gap. He was ludicrously outsized for the cramped space, and stooped within like a giant trying to squeeze into the hovel of a peasant.

'How do you feel?' he asked.

'Better,' he lied.

'There are rooms being made ready in the city. You should move to them.'

'I don't think so,' said Verstohlen, shuddering under his blankets. 'Here is fine. I never want to see Averheim again.'

Schwarzhelm shrugged.

'So be it, but I'll be gone soon. The Emperor has demanded my presence.'

'I'm glad of it. He's forgiven you?'

'I doubt it. There'll be penance for this. The north.'

'More fighting? How dreadful for you.'

Schwarzhelm didn't smile, but nor did he scowl. A cloud of bitterness seemed to have lifted from him.

'I could use a spy up there,' he said.

Verstohlen shook his head.

'I think my prowess on a battlefield has been demonstrated,' he said. 'In any case, the days of the family are over.'

He looked up at Schwarzhelm.

'I'm sorry, my lord,' he said. 'There'll be no more of this for me.'

Schwarzhelm raised an eyebrow.

'You're ill, Pieter. Make no hasty choices.'

Verstohlen smiled sadly.

'When Leonora died, all I wanted was a way to fight the enemy. You gave me that. We've done much good together, and I'm proud of it.'

He shook his head, thinking back over the past months.

'Not now. My usefulness is over. Perhaps there'll be some other way to continue in service. Or maybe my time has ended.'

Schwarzhelm pursed his lips thoughtfully. He gave Verstohlen a long, searching look.

'We'll speak on this again,' he said at last. 'There are many ways a man can serve the Emperor, and your gifts are unique. Think on it anew when your wounds are recovered.'

Verstohlen winced at the mention of his wounds. He knew that some of them would never be made whole.

'As you wish,' he said, suddenly wanting to change the subject. 'And what of you, my lord? This has been a trial for all of us.'

'So it has,' said the Emperor's Champion. 'And there will be more trials to come. But we have prevailed here, and that is all that matters.'

He rose awkwardly, hampered by the canvas above him.

'I'm glad to see you recovering,' he said gruffly. 'Remember what I said – make no hasty choices. Inform me of your progress when you can. I've lost many friends here, Pieter. I do not wish to lose another.'

Friends. That was not a word he'd heard Schwarzhelm use before.

'I will,' was all he said.

Schwarzhelm nodded, then turned clumsily and pushed his way from the tent.

Verstohlen lay back on his pallet, worn out by the exertion of conversation. Already he could feel the poisons within him boiling for a fresh assault. There would be no easy recovery from this, no simple road back to redemption.

'Leonora...' he breathed, and closed his eyes.

At the least, some good had been achieved. He saw her face clearly now. There were no more masks looming up in his dreams. The pain would endure, he knew, but the nightmares were over.

On the ruined slopes of the Averpeak, Helborg and Volkmar surveyed the work below. Two miles distant, the ruins of Averheim smouldered. The day had dawned cold, and the smoke of many fires drifted across the wide plain. The stench of burning flesh and molten metal hung heavy in the air despite the sharp breeze still coming from the east.

'You've had word from the Emperor?' asked the Reiksmarshal, gazing over the scene of destruction impassively. His wound had been re-stitched, and he looked fully restored to health. His armour glinted in the pale daylight, and his heavy cloak lifted in the breeze.

Volkmar nodded.

'He's summoned Schwarzhelm back to Altdorf. I'm to remain until the city is secure.'

'Anything else?'

Volkmar smiled grimly.

'He sent his congratulations. I think he wants you back in the north soon.'

Helborg nodded curtly. That was to be expected. He was already itching to leave, eager to find the next battlefield. He'd return to Nuln, then to Altdorf, then onwards to wherever Karl Franz deployed him. Such was his life in the service of the Empire, and he'd have it no other way.

'This was too close, Theogonist,' he mused, looking over at the remains of the Tower. The shards of iron stuck up into the air like bones. 'If Leitdorf hadn't had the name of–'

'He did,' said Volkmar sharply. 'Providence willed it, and faith was repaid.'

Helborg nodded slowly.

'So it was,' he said. 'All the same.'

He turned away from the scene.

'Will there be a cenotaph for Leitdorf?'

'In time. He'll be remembered as a hero.'

'And his last wish?'

'History will not be rewritten. The cause of Marius's madness will not be disclosed.'

Helborg nodded again. He regretted that, but knew the reasons for it.

'Leitdorf thought he was immune to Chaos,' he said. 'I didn't believe it when he told me. Tell me Volkmar, are there bloodlines where corruption cannot hold?'

Volkmar shrugged.

'Perhaps,' he said. 'It matters not. His line is ended, and speculation wins no wars.'

'His words still trouble me. We could have learned much, had he lived.'

'Do not delve too deeply. The ways of the enemy are subtle. Only faith and steel endure.'

'For how long, Theogonist?' asked Helborg, looking at him bleakly. Both men knew what he meant. The war in the north would churn onwards indefinitely. With every victory there came ruinous cost. Averheim was just the latest in the litany of wounds suffered by the Empire. It couldn't last forever.

'Until the last of us falls,' replied Volkmar, and there was no comfort in his voice.

They were interrupted then. A heavy figure clambered up the slope towards them, sinking deep into the churned-up soil in his plate armour. A longsword hung by his side, and a pendant in the form of Ghal Maraz swung from his neck.

Volkmar bowed to Helborg.

'I have much to detain me,' he said, preparing to head back to the city. 'We'll speak again this evening. The dawn may bring fresh counsel.'

'Sigmar be with you, Theogonist.'

'Oh, I'm sure He will be.'

The man limped down the slope, nodding in greeting to Schwarzhelm as the men passed one another.

Then there were only two of them on the ridge, Helborg and Schwarzhelm, the masters of the Emperor's armies.

They both stood in silence, looking back over the city. A fresh column of troops from Streissen had arrived and was making its way across the pitted, trench-laced battlefield. Even from such a distance, both Helborg and Schwarzhelm could see the amazement and horror on the men's faces.

'I hear you're being taken from us,' said the Marshal at last, keeping his eyes fixed on Averheim.

'Soon,' replied Schwarzhelm, his voice rumbling from deep within his barrel chest. 'Karl Franz wishes to hear my penance.'

'Then be sure to tell him everything,' said Helborg.

'I will.'

More silence. Even after the reconciliation on the moors, there had been few enough occasions for the two old warriors to converse. In the aftermath of the battle, they'd found ways of avoiding one another, dancing around the issue between them like old lovers reunited by chance. They were death-dealers, not wordsmiths, and expression did not come easily to either.

'I'm glad you came back, Ludwig,' said Helborg at last. The words were clipped and awkward.

'Duty demanded it.'

'Even so. A lesser man would have kept his distance.' He turned to Schwarzhelm, and a wry smile broke across his face. 'I was ready to kill you.'

'You'd have been within your rights.'

Helborg waved his hand dismissively.

'The great enemy was at work. We both know that.'

'They played on my resentment, Kurt. That was real enough.'

Helborg looked at Schwarzhelm carefully.

'Then maybe you were within your rights too.'

Schwarzhelm said nothing. Helborg turned back to the vista below and drew in a long, cleansing breath. High up the Averpeak, the air was less caustic than on the plain.

'This must never happen again,' he said. 'We will always be rivals, you and I, but we must never be enemies.'

'Never,' agreed Schwarzhelm.

'Will you swear it?' asked Helborg. 'The swords are holy enough. They will witness an oath.'

He drew the Klingerach, and the blade glistened in the cold light. The notch was still present, halfway along the length of the blade. It would be forged anew when time allowed.

'I will swear it,' said Schwarzhelm, and drew the Rechtstahl. The blades crossed, meeting at the hilt. Both men faced one another, divided by the locked steel.

'For the Empire,' said the Emperor's Champion, gripping the Sword of Justice tightly. 'No division between us.'

'For the Empire,' replied the Reiksmarshal, holding the Sword of Vengeance two-handed. 'No division.'

They stood in that position for many heartbeats, letting the spirits of their weapons hear the words, keeping the blades in place while the oath still echoed. Below them, the fields of death stretched away, a monument to the folly and avarice of treachery. The blackened stones still smoked from the fires of war, and the river remained clogged and choking.

Beyond them, though, on the horizon, fields of grass remained as lush as before. Mankind remained the master of Averland. In the distance, the cloud cover broke, exposing shafts of sunlight on the far hills. There was still beauty in the world, still riches worth fighting for.

At length, the swords were unlocked and sheathed. The two men said nothing more, but turned to walk down the slope of the Averpeak and back to the city. Behind them, the wind moaned across the grasses of the ridge, tousling the tufts and running down the far side to where the honoured dead had been buried.

There lay Skarr, and Bloch, and Gruppen, and others who had perished in the final battle for Averheim. No headstone marked their resting places, nor monument recorded their endeavours. Their deeds had been enough, and they were heroes just as much as those that still lived, a part of the tapestry of actions that had shaped the Empire since the days of Sigmar, a fleeting echo amid the clamour of the war that would never end, the war that would give birth to fresh heroes with every sword-thrust and spear-plunge, that would spawn treachery and deceit anew from the halls of madness at the roof of the world, and that would drench the lands of men in blood and valour until the End Times came and the long-honed mettle of humanity was put to the ultimate test at last.

Until then, their trials were over.

EPILOGUE

It was far into the east of Averland, far from the worst of the fighting. A mean place, just a few houses clustered inside a low stone wall. Chickens rooted through the straw and rubble of the only street, and old puddles of grimy water sat under the eaves of the dwellings.

So small it barely merited a name, the settlement had played no part in any of the great events of the province. It sat on the very edge of Marius Leitdorf's old domains, forgotten by all, cherished by none. In the five months since the recovery of Averheim, the new owners hadn't even bothered to organise a tax collection, and it remained as isolated as it had ever been.

At the far end of the village, one house maintained a burning hearth even in the middle of the day. Dirty smoke poured from the unseasoned wood, rolling into the grey sky. There were screams from the house within. Women came and went, some carrying pails of water, others with blood-soaked rags.

There was a girl inside. Maybe seventeen summers. Her cheeks were red with pain and effort, and her skin was glossy with sweat.

'Shallya,' cursed the wisewoman, throwing down another drenched rag and reaching for another. 'We'll lose both of them.'

The mother of the girl, cradling her head in her lap, stroked her daughter's hair.

'Strength to you, my child,' she whispered. Her anxiety made her words tremble.

The girl gritted her teeth for another contraction. Her screams echoed all round the village, shaming the men who stood at the filthy tavern bar. None of them was the father. They all knew who the father had been. They ground their teeth and knocked back the ale, trying to forget the ignominy. They'd done nothing to prevent it.

When the child was born at last, all three women were at the end of their strength. Against all predictions, the girl survived it, though her cheeks were rosy with fever and her eyes strayed out of focus.

The wisewoman wrapped up the baby in a dirty bundle of rags and made the sign of the comet over it. It was bawling with confused rage, fists clenched tight, eyes screwed closed.

'What is it?' demanded the girl's mother, peering at the wisewoman's bundle.

'A man-child,' said the wisewoman, handing the baby to its mother.

The girl took it and looked into the bawling infant's face. It had pudgy features. Not attractive, but redolent enough of the father.

'You must name him,' urged the mother. The anxiety in her voice had been replaced by excitement.

'He will take his father's name,' she murmured, lost in awe at the screaming ball of life in her arms.

'Insolence!' hissed the wisewoman. 'Choose another.'

The girl glared defiantly at her.

'I will name him as I please,' she said.

The wisewoman glared back.

'Choose carefully, girl,' she warned. 'You are favoured, but do not anger the gods. This is a child of the wyrdblood.'

She reached over to the baby and pulled the rags away from its face. It stopped crying and returned her glance. It shouldn't have been able to focus at all.

'Blessed Sigmar,' she whispered, taken aback. 'Keep him hidden, and guard him well. There is a destiny on this one. Just as there was on the father.'

The girl looked down at her child. Her defiance faded as the baby looked back at her. Its brown eyes were steady, and there was no fear in them.

'Siggurd, I will call you,' she said. 'Siggurd, son of Rufus, son of Marius.'

She smiled, and the pain of labour seemed to fall from her features.

'You will be mighty,' she cooed. 'Mightiest of them all. And when the time is ripe, the runefang will be yours.'

The wisewoman looked at her carefully. The girl was already feverish. Her eyes were lit with a strange light. She'd be lucky to survive the night.

'Siggurd, my son,' she whispered, falling into an exhausted slumber even as she held him tight to her breast. 'The rune-fang *will* be yours.'

APPENDIX

My dear Erich,

As requested, please find enclosed the documents pertaining to the Averheim affair for deposit in the Palace Archives. Regrettably, the journals of the late Elector Marius Leitdorf did not survive the destruction of the city, though I have succeeded in retrieving some related papers from His Lordship's retreat at Drakenmoor. These will prove of limited interest, being mostly routine matters of state, but are included for completeness.

The correspondence between Heinrich Lassus and Natassja Heiss-Leitdorf is of more enduring importance. Though much of the communication between the pair will now never be found, the letters the Lord Schwarzhelm recovered from Lassus's office comprise a reasonably thorough account of their intentions.

Regrettably, my somewhat hasty deciphers did not survive the unpleasantness at Averheim, and in any case I would not wish to vouch for their total reliability – you'll understand that I was working under rather unusual circumstances. Since I have now left my previous employment, I judged that the best course of action would be to send you the originals, together with a summary of the means to their deciphering. It is simple enough – surprisingly so, perhaps, given the nature of what was discussed: an orthodox implementation of a Vignius pol-yalphabetic cipher with a substitution key of 'Wenenlich'. For convenience, I have reproduced the table here:

```
  A B C D E F G H I J K L M N O P Q R S T U V W X Y Z
A A B C D E F G H I J K L M N O P Q R S T U V W X Y Z
B B C D E F G H I J K L M N O P Q R S T U V W X Y Z A
C C D E F G H I J K L M N O P Q R S T U V W X Y Z A B
D D E F G H I J K L M N O P Q R S T U V W X Y Z A B C
E E F G H I J K L M N O P Q R S T U V W X Y Z A B C D
F F G H I J K L M N O P Q R S T U V W X Y Z A B C D E
G G H I J K L M N O P Q R S T U V W X Y Z A B C D E F
H H I J K L M N O P Q R S T U V W X Y Z A B C D E F G
I I J K L M N O P Q R S T U V W X Y Z A B C D E F G H
J J K L M N O P Q R S T U V W X Y Z A B C D E F G H I
K K L M N O P Q R S T U V W X Y Z A B C D E F G H I J
L L M N O P Q R S T U V W X Y Z A B C D E F G H I J K
M M N O P Q R S T U V W X Y Z A B C D E F G H I J K L
N N O P Q R S T U V W X Y Z A B C D E F G H I J K L M
O O P Q R S T U V W X Y Z A B C D E F G H I J K L M N
P P Q R S T U V W X Y Z A B C D E F G H I J K L M N O
Q Q R S T U V W X Y Z A B C D E F G H I J K L M N O P
R R S T U V W X Y Z A B C D E F G H I J K L M N O P Q
S S T U V W X Y Z A B C D E F G H I J K L M N O P Q R
T T U V W X Y Z A B C D E F G H I J K L M N O P Q R S
U U V W X Y Z A B C D E F G H I J K L M N O P Q R S T
V V W X Y Z A B C D E F G H I J K L M N O P Q R S T U
W W X Y Z A B C D E F G H I J K L M N O P Q R S T U V
X X Y Z A B C D E F G H I J K L M N O P Q R S T U V W
Y Y Z A B C D E F G H I J K L M N O P Q R S T U V W X
Z Z A B C D E F G H I J K L M N O P Q R S T U V W X Y
```

To decipher the texts in your possession, move to the row indicated by the first letter of the key, then along to the cell containing the corresponding letter in the ciphered text. The character at the head of the column will yield the deciphered character. Then move to the next letter of the key and ciphered text, and repeat. Be aware that the original text has been highly truncated, and that even after decoding it will require further work to render fully legible.

I need not remind you of the sensitive nature of the material, and recommend complete discretion in its handling. The Palace Archivists will be able to advise further, though be sure to seek guidance from one of the more enlightened, and one you can trust. Sadly, one can never be too careful in these straitened times.

I trust this finds you well, and please send my best regards to Alicia and the boys. I had no idea Rikard was in the pistolier corps – how time flies! Before long we will be old men, and such things as these will be long forgotten. As for me, I am uncertain where life will lead me next. I will depart Altdorf soon, perhaps for a long time. If you have some pressing need to contact me, the Shrine of Verena behind the courtrooms on the Salzenstadt may be able to assist, though I place no assurance on it.

I hope we may meet again at some point to discuss these and other matters. Until then, may all harm be warded from you, now and forever.

P. E. Verstohlen
Altdorf, Kaldezeit 2523.

FEAST OF HORRORS

Helmut Detlef drew his steed to a halt. The sun was low behind him. The shadows in the forest were long, and the tortured branches beckoned the onset of a bitter night. If he'd been alone, Detlef might have felt anxiety. The deep woods were no place for a young, inexperienced squire to be after dark.

But he wasn't alone. The figure next to him sat astride a massive warhorse. He was decked in full plate armour and carried a long, rune-carved sword. A thick beard spilled over his chest, falling over the Imperial crest embossed on the metal. His cloak hung down from gold-rimmed pauldrons and the open-faced helm was crowned with a laurel wreath. Only one man was permitted to don such ancient armour – the Emperor's Champion, Ludwig Schwarzhelm, dispenser of Imperial law and wielder of the dread Sword of Justice.

By comparison, Detlef's titles – squire, errand runner, occasional herald – were pretty unimpressive. Still, just to serve under such a man was an honour almost beyond reckoning. Detlef was barely out of the village and less than two years' service into the Reikland halberdiers. In the months since joining Schwarzhelm he'd already seen things men twice his age would hardly dream of.

'That's it?' he said, pointing ahead.

'That's it,' replied Schwarzhelm. His voice was iron-hard, tinged with a faint Averland accent. Schwarzhelm spoke rarely. When he did, it was wise to take note.

The trees clustered near the road on either side of them, overhanging as close as they dared as if eager to snatch the unwary traveller and pull him into the dark heart of the forest. So it had been for the many days since they'd ridden from the battlefront in Ostland. The Forest of Shadows had been true to its name every step of the way.

A few yards ahead, the wood gave way to a clearing. In the failing light it looked drab and sodden, though the bastion rising from it was anything but. Here, miles from the nearest town and isolated within the cloying bosom of the forest, a sprawling manor house stood sentinel. The walls were built from stone framed with age-blackened oak. Elaborate gables decorated the steep-sided roofs rising sharply against the sky. The seal of Ostland, a bull's head, had been engraved ostentatiously over the vast main doorway, and statues in the shape of griffons, wyverns and other beasts stared out across the bleak vista. Warm firelight shone from the narrow mullioned windows and columns of thick smoke rose from the many chimneys.

'How should I address him?' asked Detlef, feeling his ignorance. The task of learning his duties had been steep, and Schwarzhelm was intolerant of mistakes.

'He's a baron. Use "my lord".'

Or, more completely, Baron Helvon Drakenmeister Egbert von Rauken, liege lord of an estate that covered hundreds of square miles. Detlef might once have found that intimidating, but after serving with Schwarzhelm, very little compared.

'I'll ride ahead to announce you.'

Schwarzhelm nodded. His grey eyes glittered, in his craggy, unsmiling face.

'You do that.'

* * *

Their arrival had been unexpected. Despite that, the baron's household managed to put on a good show. Servants preparing to turn in for the night were dragged from their chambers and put to work in the kitchens. The household was roused and told to put on its finery. By the time the sun had finally dipped below the western horizon, a banquet fit for their visitor had been thrown together. Detlef found the process intensely amusing. The combination of irritation and fear on the faces of the mansion staff was worth the long trek on its own.

Rauken's banqueting hall, like all the rooms in the house, was a study in baroque excess. The high-beamed roof was decorated with tasteless frescos of Imperial myths, all lit by an oversized fire roaring in the marble-framed hearth. The floor was also marble, black and white chequers like the nave of an Imperial chapel. The table looked as if it had been carved from a single slab of wood, even though it was over thirty feet long. Its surface had been polished to a glassy sheen, reflecting the light of the dozens of candelabras and sending it winking and flashing from the crystal goblets and silver plates.

The guests, a dozen of them, were no less opulent. All looked well-fed and comfortably padded. The ladies were decked in frocks of wildly varied shades, draped with tassels, bows and lines of pearls. Even at such short notice they'd managed to arrange their greying hair in heaps of tottering grandeur, laced with lines of gold wire and emerald studs. Their sagging faces were plastered with lead whitener, their lips and cheeks heavily rouged. Their male companions were also finely turned out, replete with sashes, medals, powdered wigs and jewel-encrusted codpieces. They strutted to their places, jowls wobbling with anticipation as the food arrived.

From his seat on the edge of the chamber, Detlef watched them intently, trying to pick out the ones Schwarzhelm had told him about. Most of the party were Rauken's blood-kin, but some of his more senior aides had been invited. Among them was Osbert Hulptraum, Rauken's personal physician, a fat waddling grey-faced man with a balding pate and bags under his eyes. Next to him sat Julius Adenauer, the chancellor, all thin lips, clawed fingers and sidelong glances. His scraggy beard looked wispy even in the low light, and he minced around like a parody of a woman.

At the head of the table sat Rauken himself. He was massively corpulent, red-cheeked, with a bulbous nose laced with broken veins. He'd chosen to cover himself in robes of velvet, not that they did much to hide his generous belly. As he beckoned the guests to take their seats, his many chins shivered like jelly.

'We are honoured,' he said, his voice surprisingly high. 'Truly honoured. It's not every day this house hosts one of the finest heroes of the Empire.'

A murmur of appreciation ran across the throng. Schwarzhelm, sitting at Rauken's right hand – the place of honour – remained impassive. He'd heard it all before. He'd exchanged his armour for simple robes in the red and white of the Imperial Palace, but still looked by far the most regal presence in the room.

'So let us eat,' Rauken said, 'and celebrate this happy occasion.'

The guests needed no encouragement. Soon they were shovelling heaps of food on to their plates – lambs' livers, roast pigeon, jugged hare, moist sweetbreads, slabs of pheasant pie, slops of something dark brown with quail's eggs floating in it, pig's cheeks in jelly, all washed down with generous slugs of a dark red wine brought all the way, Detlef had learned, from the vines of the Duc d'Alembourg-Rauken in Guillet Marchand on the banks of the Brienne.

Like all the servants present, Detlef had been seated behind his master in case he was needed during the meal. His stomach growled as he watched the guests begin to cram the fine food into their mouths. At least his position let him hear the conversation.

'So to what do we owe this honour, my lord?' asked Rauken, munching delicately on a fig stuffed with mincemeat.

'The Emperor likes me to meet all his subjects,' said Schwarzhelm. He'd not touched the food, and had taken strips of dried meat from a pouch at his belt.

'Well then, I hope we've not been amiss with the tithes. Adenauer, are we up to date?'

'We are, my lord,' replied the chancellor, dabbing grease from his chin. 'The records are available for scrutiny.'

'Very good,' said Rauken, looking at Schwarzhelm nervously. 'You're not eating, my lord?'

'Not muck like this. I prefer my own.'

Schwarzhelm's flat refusal cut through the conversation like a blunt axe-blade. There was a nervous laugh from one of the women, soon cut off when she realised he wasn't joking.

Detlef smiled to himself. The dinner promised to be an amusing one. It was only then that he caught the eye of the serving girl sitting beside him. She was as fleshy and rosy-cheeked as the rest of them, but much younger. He found his eyes drawn to her chest, appealingly exposed by a low-cut, tight-laced bodice.

She smiled at him, and her eyes shone in the candlelight.

'Have you eaten?' she whispered.

'No,' he hissed back. 'I'm starving.'

'Come and find me when this is over. We'll see what we can do about that.'

Detlef grinned. This evening was getting better all the time.

By midnight, the chairs had been kicked back and the guests had tottered back to their rooms, belching and wiping their mouths. Baron von Rauken had taken his leave last of all, having heroically demolished a four-tier suet pudding arranged in a pretty good approximation of the Grand Bell-tower in Talabheim.

Soon the room was empty apart from Schwarzhelm and Detlef. The candles had burned low and the polished tabletop was slick with grease. Detlef found himself gazing at the extensive remains on the salvers, his stomach rumbling.

'Avoid it,' said Schwarzhelm. 'This is no food for a soldier.'

'Yes, my lord,' said Detlef, privately hoping he'd go away so he could attack the pickled pig-shins.

'Get some sleep.'

'Yes, my lord.'

'After you've cleaned my armour.'

'Yes, my lord.'

Schwarzhelm looked at him carefully. As ever, his expression was inscrutable. It was like trying to read the granite cliffs of the Worlds Edge Mountains.

'Where are your quarters?'

'Above the kitchen.'

'Stay in them tonight. And keep your sword by your bed.'

Detlef felt a sudden qualm. 'Do you expect trouble?'

'I don't call on these fat wastrels for enjoyment,' Schwarzhelm said, not hiding the contempt in his voice. 'The Emperor's worried about this one.'

'Is he behind on his taxes?' asked Detlef.

'On the contrary. He's paid them all.'

Detlef shook his head. The ways of the aristocracy were a mystery to him.

'I'll keep an eye out, then.'

Schwarzhelm grunted in what might have been approval.

'Maybe I'll take one of these for later,' said the knight, pulling a juicy chunk of bull's stomach from the table. Without a further look at his squire, he stalked off to his room, slamming the door behind him.

Detlef waited for the heavy footfalls to recede, then started to help himself. Knowing what was to come, his stomach gurgled with anticipation.

'Take it easy,' Detlef said to himself. 'Just a few of the good bits to keep my strength up. Then I have an appointment to keep.'

An hour later, and the house was still and silent. High up in the west tower, the physician Hulptraum paced up and down inside his bedchamber. He was still dressed in the black robes of his office. His bed was untouched, and a large goblet of wine stood drained on his desk. He looked agitated, and his fingers twitched. Next to the goblet was a long, curved dagger. It was hard to see the hilt in the meagre candlelight, but the blade had some script engraved on it. The language wasn't Reikspiel.

'Tonight,' he hissed. 'Of all nights...'

There was a knock at the door. Hulptraum started, his eyes bulging. 'Who is it?'

'Adenauer. Can I come in?'

Hulptraum put the knife into the top drawer of the desk and slid it shut. 'Of course.'

Adenauer entered, looking terrible. His skin, pale before, was now deathly white. His wispy beard seemed to have become little more than a curling fuzz and his eyes were rheumy and staring.

'Osbert, you've got to help me,' he said, through gritted teeth. One hand was clutching his distended stomach, the other was clasped against his temple.

'You're still here?' asked the physician, not obviously evincing sympathy.

'What do you mean? I'm ill, man. Surely you can see that?'

Hulptraum smiled coldly. 'I'm a doctor. And yes, you're ill. You should be down in the kitchen with the others.'

Adenauer looked bewildered. 'Can't you give me something? I... Oh, gods below...'

He started to belch loudly. A thin line of sputum ran down his chin and his body bent double.

Hulptraum remained supremely indifferent. 'I don't have time for this, Julius. Nothing I could give you now would help. The fact is, this has been prepared for months. All for this night. This one night. The night *he* turned up.'

Adenauer was now on his knees. The sputum became a watery trail of blood. His stomach was writhing under his robes, as if an animal were trying to get out of it.

'Sigmar!' he cried, spasming in agony. 'Help me!'

Hulptraum crouched down beside him, ignoring the increasingly putrid stench coming from the chancellor. 'He can't help you now, old friend. You'd better get down to the kitchen. You'll find the others there too.'

Adenauer's eyes didn't look as if they were seeing very much. Sores had begun to pulse on his face, spreading with terrifying speed. His tongue flickered out, black as ink, leaving loops of saliva trailing down to his chest. He collapsed on the floor, clenched with pain.

Hulptraum got up and returned to the desk. He retrieved the dagger, ignoring the thrashing of the transforming chancellor.

'You will *not* prevent this,' he hissed, no longer talking to Adenauer. 'I don't care who you are. You will *not* prevent this.'

With that, he left the room, padding out into the corridor beyond. Behind him, Adenauer retched piteously. Caked lumps of bile slapped to the floor, steaming gently. He remained stricken for a few moments longer, heaving and weeping, streaming from every orifice.

Then something seemed to change. He lifted his thin face. It ran with mucus like tears. The eyes, or what was left of them, shone a pale marsh-gas green.

'The kitchen!' Adenauer gurgled, though the voice was more like that of an animal. It looked as if he'd finally understood something. 'The kitchen!'

Then he too was gone, dragging himself across the floor leaving a trail of slime behind him. The door closed, and the candle shuddered out.

No candles burned in Schwarzhelm's chamber. The shutters were locked tight and the darkness was absolute. Nothing moved. Deep down in the house, there was a distant creak, then silence again.

Heartbeats passed in the dark.

Slowly, silently, the door handle began to turn. The door swung open on oiled hinges. It was just as dark outside as within. Something entered. Quietly, slowly, it made its way to the bed. A blade was raised over the mattress.

It hung there, invisible, unmoving, for a terrible moment.

Then it plunged down, once, twice, three times, stabbing into the soft flesh beneath. Still no noise. The knife was an artful weapon. It had killed many times before over many thousands of years and knew how to find the right spot.

Hulptraum stood, shaking, lost in the dark. He could feel the warm blood on the knife trickle over his fingers. It was done. Thank the Father, the feast was safe.

Moving carefully, he went over to a table on the far wall. He had to make sure.

He struck the flint and a flame sparked into life. He lit the candle's wick and light spread across his hand. The shaking was subsiding. He'd done it. He'd saved it all. He turned around.

Schwarzhelm smashed him hard in the face, snapping his neck and sending him spinning across the table and slamming against the wall. Hulptraum slid to the floor. Blood foamed from his open mouth, locked in a final expression of shock. The dagger clanged to the stone floor.

'Pathetic,' Schwarzhelm muttered.

He walked over to where he'd hung his sword. The bull's stomach was still leaking fluid across the bed. He took the holy blade and unsheathed it. Still dressed in his robes, he made for the door.

Rauken did have something to hide then. Time to uncover it.

Detlef belched loudly. Perhaps he'd overindulged. Still, at least he'd taken the edge off his hunger. Now he had an appointment to attend to. A final look around his bedchamber revealed Schwarzhelm's armour lying in pieces in the corner, still mottled with grime from the journey. He could polish it all before dawn – the old curmudgeon wouldn't need the suit before then.

Then he caught sight of his short sword lying by the bed, just where Schwarzhelm had warned him to keep it. Perhaps he ought to take that with him. He still wasn't convinced there was anything much to worry about, but it might impress... what *was* her name? He'd have to remember before he found her. In his experience, women – even as willing and fruity as this one – liked to have the little things observed.

Gretta? Hildegard? Brunnhilde?

He grabbed the sword and crept out of the chamber. It would come back to him.

The corridor was drenched in shadow. It seemed almost preternaturally dark, as if the natural light had been sucked from the air and somehow disposed of. He held his candle ahead of him with one hand and kept a tight grip on the sword hilt with the other. There were no sounds, no signs of anyone else about. Now all he had to do was remember the way to her room.

Past the scullery and the game-hanging room, then down towards the kitchen. Should be easy enough.

Detlef shuffled along, feeling the old wooden floor flex under him. He passed a series of doors in the gloom, all closed. The house gently creaked and snapped around him. Dimly, he could hear the scratching of trees outside as the night winds ran through their emaciated branches.

At the end of the corridor, a staircase led directly downwards. From where he stood, it seemed like there was a little more light coming from the bottom of it. Detlef picked up the pace. Perhaps Gertrude had left a candle lit for him.

He reached the base of the stairs. Another corridor yawned away with fresh doors leading from it on either side. One of them was open. He thrust the candle through the door frame. The light reflected from the corpses hanging there, eyes glinting like mirrors.

Pheasants, rabbits, hares, all strung out in bunches on iron hooks. The game-hanging room. He was close. Detlef pressed on, heading further down the corridor. There was a light at the end of it, leaking around the edges of a closed wooden door. Excitement began to build within him. Brigitta had been as good as her word.

He reached the door, making sure his sword was properly visible. All the nice girls liked a soldier. Then, with as much of a flourish as he could muster with both hands full, he pushed against the wood.

The door swung open easily. Marsh-green light flooded out from the space beyond, throwing Detlef's shadow back down the corridor. What lay beyond wasn't Gertrude, Brigitta or Brunnhilde.

Detlef found that, despite all his anticipation, he wasn't really disappointed. He was too busy screaming.

Schwarzhelm hurried down the corridors, lantern in hand. There was no one about on the upper levels. The whole place was deserted. That in itself was cause for worry. He'd slammed open a dozen doors, uncaring whom he disturbed, and the chambers had all been empty.

He barged into Detlef's room, keeping the light high. He saw his own armour, untouched, heaped in the corner. There was a tin plate on the bed with a few crumbs on it and nothing else. There was no sword, and no squire.

'Damned idiot,' he muttered, heading back out. At the end of the corridor, a staircase led down. Very faintly, he could see a greenish glow. His heart went cold. He drew his sword, and the steel hummed gently as it left the scabbard. The Sword of Justice was ancient, and the spirit of the weapon knew when it would taste battle. Schwarzhelm could feel it thirsting already. There were unholy things close by.

He broke into a run, thudding down the stairs and past the empty, gaping doorways. He saw the open portal at the end of the corridor, glowing a pale green like phosphor. Shapes loomed beyond, hazy in a mist of swirling, stinking vapour.

'Grace of Sigmar,' Schwarzhelm whispered, maintaining his stride and letting the lantern smash to the floor – it would be no further use.

He charged through the doorway. Green light was everywhere, a sickly, cloying illumination that seemed to writhe in the air of its own accord. The walls dripped with slops of bile-yellow sludge that ran into the mortar and slithered over the stones. The stench was astonishing – a mix of rotting flesh, vomit, dung, sewage and bilge-water. He felt spores latch on him as he plunged in, popping and splattering as his powerful limbs worked.

Once this must have been the bakery. There was something that might have been an oven, now lost under polyps of mouldy dough-like growths. There were flies everywhere, buzzing and swarming over the slime-soaked surfaces. They were vast, shiny horrors, less like insects and more like pustules with wings.

'Detlef!' roared Schwarzhelm trying to spot the exit through the swirling miasma.

His call was answered, but not by his squire. The guests from the meal dragged themselves towards him, hauling their burst stomachs behind them. What was left of their skin hung like rags from glistening sinew, flapping against the tendons and their crumbling, yellow teeth.

'Hail, Lord Schwarzhelm!' they mocked, reaching for him with pudgy, blotched fingers. 'Welcome to the Feast!'

Schwarzhelm ploughed straight into them, hacking and heaving with his blade. The steel sliced through the carrion-flesh, sending gobbets of viscera sailing through the foetid air. There were a dozen of them, just as before, and they dragged at his robes, hands clawing. He battered them aside, hammering with the edge of his sword before plunging the tip deep into their ragged innards. They were carved apart like mutton, feeling no pain, only clutching at him, scrabbling at his flesh, trying to latch their slack, dangling jaws on to his arm.

Schwarzhelm didn't have time for this. He kicked out at them, shaking one from his boot before crunching his foot through a sore-riddled scalp, crushing the skull like an egg. They kept coming even when their limbs had been severed and their spines cracked. Only decapitation seemed to finish them. Twelve times the Sword of Justice flashed in the gloom, and twelve times a severed head thumped against the stone and rolled through the glowing slurry of body parts.

He pushed the remaining skittering, twitching torsos aside

and pressed on, racing through the bakery and into the corridor beyond. So this was the horror Rauken had been cradling.

The further he went, the worse it got. The walls of the corridor were covered in a flesh-coloured sheen, run through with pulsing arteries of black fluid. There were faces trapped within, raving with horror. Some had managed to claw a hand out, scrabbling against the suffocating film. Others hung still, the black fluid pumping into them, turning them into some fresh new recipe.

Schwarzhelm killed as many as he could, delivering mercy to those who still breathed and death to those who'd passed beyond humanity. The steel sliced through the tight-stretched hide, tearing the veils of flesh and spilling the noxious liquid across the floor. As he splashed through it, a thin screaming broke out from further ahead. He was coming to the heart of it.

The next room was vast and boiling hot, full of massive copper kettles and iron cauldrons, all simmering with foul soups and monstrous stews. Lumps of human gristle flopped from their sides, sliding to the gore-soaked floor and sizzling of their own accord. Thick-bodied, spiked-legged spiders scuttled through the mire, scampering between the bursting egg-sacs of flies and long, white-fleshed worms. Vials of translucent plasma bubbled furiously, spilling their contents over piled slabs of rancid, crawling meat. Everything was in motion, a grotesque parody of a wholesome kitchen.

At the centre was Rauken. His body had grown to obscene proportions, bursting from the clothes that once covered it. His flesh, glistening with sweat and patterned with veins, spilled out like a vast unlocked tumour. Dark shapes scurried about under the skin, and a long purple tongue lolled down to his flab-folded chest, draping ropes of lumpy saliva behind it. When he saw Schwarzhelm, he grinned, exposing rows of black, blunt teeth.

'Welcome, honoured guest!' he cried, voice thick with phlegm. 'A good night to visit us!'

Schwarzhelm said nothing. He tore into the monster, hacking at the yielding flesh. It carved away easily, exposing rotten innards infested with burrowing grubs. Rauken scarcely seemed to feel it. He opened his swollen jaws and launched a column of vomit straight at the warrior. Schwarzhelm ducked under the worst of it, the stomach acid eating through his robes and burning his flesh. He ploughed on, cleaving away the rolls of stinking flab, getting closer to the head with every stroke.

'You can't spoil this party!' raved the baron, gathering itself for another monstrous chunder. 'We've only just got started!'

More vomit exploded out. Schwarzhelm felt a sharp pain as the bile slammed into his chest, sheering the cloth away and burrowing into his skin. Flies blundered into his eyes, spiders ran across his arms, leeches crawled around his ankles. He was being dragged down into the filth.

With a massive effort, Schwarzhelm wrenched free of the clutching horrors and whirled his blade round in a back-handed arc. The steel severed Rauken's bloated head clean free, lopping it from the shoulders and sending it squelching and bouncing into a vat of steaming effluvium. The vast bag of flesh shuddered and subsided, leaking an acrid soup of blood and sputum. Ripples of fatty essence sagged, shrank and then lay still.

Schwarzhelm struggled free of it, slapping the creeping horrors from his limbs and tearing the vomit-drenched rags from his chest. There was a movement behind him and he spun around, blade at the ready.

He turned it aside. It was Detlef.

The boy looked ready to die from fear. His face was as pale as milk and tears of horror ran down his cheeks.

'What *is* this?' he shrieked, eyes staring.

Schwarzhelm clamped a hand on his shoulder, holding him firmly in place.

'Be strong,' he commanded. 'Get out – the way up is clear. Summon help, then wait for me at the gates.'

'You're not coming with me?'

Schwarzhelm shook his head. 'I've only killed the diners,' he growled. 'I haven't yet found the cook.'

* * *

The haze grew thicker. It was like wading through a fog of green motes. Schwarzhelm went carefully, feeling the viscous floor suck at his boots. Beyond the kitchen there was a little door, half-hidden behind the collection of bubbling vats. The flies buzzed furiously, clustering at his eyes and mouth. He breathed through his nose and ploughed on.

The room opened out before him. It was small, maybe twenty feet square and low-ceilinged. Perhaps some storechamber in the past. Now the jars and earthenware pots overflowed with mould, the contents long given over to decay. The air was barely breathable, heavy with spores and damp. Strings of fungus ran like spiders' webs from floor to roof, some glowing with a faint phosphorescence, obscuring what was in the centre.

'You're not the one I was expecting,' came a woman's voice. Schwarzhelm sliced his way through the ropes of corruption, feeling the burn as they slithered down his exposed flesh. 'Where's the boy? His flesh was ripe for feeding up.'

The last of the strings fell away. In the centre of the floor squatted a horribly overweight woman. She was surrounded by rolls of flaking parchment, all covered in endless lists of ingredients. Sores clustered at her thick lips, weeping a constant stream of dirt-brown fluid. She was dressed in what had once been a tight-laced corset, but the fabric had burst and her distended body flopped across it. The skin was addled with plague. Some parts of her had been eaten away entirely, exposing slick white fat or wasted muscle. Others glowed an angry red, with shiny skin pulled tight over some raging infestation. Boils jostled for prominence with warts, virulent rashes encircled pulsing nodules ready to burst. Her exposed thighs were like long-rotten sides of pork, and her eyes were filmy and rimed with blood.

'He's gone,' said Schwarzhelm. 'I'm not so easily wooed.'

The woman laughed, and a thin gruel-like liquid cascaded down her multiple chins. 'A shame,' she gurgled. 'I don't think you've had many women in your life. Karl Franz's loyal monk, eh? That's not what they say about Helborg. Now *there's* a man I could cook for.'

Schwarzhelm remained unmoved. 'What are you?'

'Oh, just the kitchen maid. I get around. When I came here, the food was terrible. Now, as you can see, it's much improved.' She frowned. 'This was to have been our party night. I think you've rather spoiled it. How did you know?'

'I didn't,' said Schwarzhelm, preparing to strike. 'The Emperor's instincts are normally good.'

He charged towards her, swinging the sword in a glittering arc. The monstrous woman opened her jaws. They stretched open far beyond the tolerance of mortal tendons. Rows of needle-teeth glimmered, licked by a blood-red tongue covered in suckers. Her fingers reached up to block the swipe, nails long and curled.

Schwarzhelm worked quickly, drawing on his peerless skill with the blade. The fingernails flashed past him as he weaved past her defences, chunks of blubber carved off with precise, perfectly aimed stabs.

Her neck shot out, extending like a snake's. Her teeth snapped as she went for his jugular. He pulled back and she chomped off a mouthful of beard, spitting the hairs out in disgust. Then he was back in close, jabbing at her pendulous torso, trying to get the opening he needed.

They swung and parried, teeth and nails against the flickering steel of the Sword of Justice. The blade bit deep, throwing up fountains of pus and cloying, sticky essence. The woman struck back, raking her fingernails across Schwarzhelm's chest, digging the points into his flesh.

He roared with pain, spittle flying from his mouth. He tore away from her, blood pouring down his robes. The neck snapped out again, aiming for his eyes. He pulled away at the last moment, slipping in a puddle of slop at his feet and dropping one hand down.

'Ha!' she spat, and launched herself at him.

Schwarzhelm's instinct was to pull back, to scrabble away, anything to avoid being enveloped in that horrific tide of disease and putrescence.

But instinct could be trumped by experience. He had his

opening. As fast as thought, he lunged forward under the shadow of the looming horror, pointing the Sword of Justice upwards and grasping the hilt with both hands. There was a sudden flash of realisation in her eyes, but the momentum was irresistible. The steel passed through her neck, driven deep through the morass of twisted tubes and nodules.

She screamed, teeth still snapping at Schwarzhelm's face, flailing as the rune-bound metal seared at her rancid innards.

This time Schwarzhelm didn't retreat. He kept his face near hers. He didn't smile even then, but a dark look of triumph lit in his eyes. He twisted the blade in deeper, feeling it do its work.

'Dinner's over,' he said.

Dawn broke, grey and cold. His legs aching, his chest tight, Schwarzhelm pushed open the great doors to the castle, letting the dank air of the forest stream in. It was thick with the mulch of the woods, but compared to the filth of the kitchens below it was like a blast of fresh mountain breeze. He limped out, cradling his bleeding chest with his free hand. The cult had been purged. All were dead. All that remained was to burn the castle, and others would see to that. Once again he had done his duty. The law had been dispensed and the task was complete. Almost.

Just beyond the gates, a lone figure shivered, hunched on the ground and clutching his ankles. Schwarzhelm went over to him. Detlef didn't seem to hear him approach. His eyes were glassy and his lower lip trembled.

'Did you find anyone up here?' Schwarzhelm asked. Though it didn't come naturally, he tried to keep his voice gentle.

Detlef nodded. 'A boy from the village. He's gone to get the priest. There are men coming.'

The squire's voice shook as he spoke. He looked terrible. He had every right to. No mortal man should have had to witness such things.

'Good work, lad.'

Schwarzhelm looked down at his blade, still naked in his

hands. Diseased viscera had lodged in the runes. It would take an age to purify.

He turned his gaze to Detlef. It was a pity. The boy was young. His appetites were hot, and he must have been hungry. There were so many excuses, even though he'd warned him not to eat the food. This final blow was the worst of them all. He'd shown promise. Schwarzhelm had liked him.

Detlef looked up, eyes imploring. Even now, the sores had started to emerge around his mouth.

'Is it over?' he asked piteously, the tears of horror still glistening on his cheek.

Schwarzhelm raised his blade, aiming carefully. It would at least be quick.

'Yes,' he said, grief heavy within him. 'Yes, it is.'

DUTY AND
HONOUR

Kurt Helborg, Reiksmarshal, master of the Emperor's armies, wrinkled his nose, drawing briny air into his nostrils, barely hearing the cacophony of shouts, thuds and screams that rose up in a massed brawl of noise from a few hundred yards away. As his face moved, his waxed moustache flexed.

He watched his men die with the blank, severe expression he'd learned to adopt over the course of his long career. His horse twitched beneath him and he adjusted position in the saddle. Beside him, Skarr's Reiksguard squadron waited patiently for their orders.

They would have to keep waiting. All the while, Helborg watched, observed, weighed, judged.

His men fought before him across an empty, forgotten land. Ruined towers broke the horizon, tall and eldritch but blackened by ancient fires. A pearl-grey sky descended to meet the grimy earth, pregnant with unshed rain and darkening quickly towards the dusk. Megaliths stood eerily among rustling tussocks, crusted with lichen and as old as the bones of the world. They loomed mournfully above a formless terrain, mile upon mile of wide, marshy wasteland, barred with glistening channels of slow-moving water.

Below Helborg's position, down a long shallow incline and out on to the wide marram grass plains, two armies of several thousand – one Imperial, one Bretonnian – were entangled in bloody combat. It was a messy engagement, a straggling scrum of thousands of grappling infantry troops, extended far in either direction under the fading light.

Over it all the ravens hung, wheeling and mobbing in the frigid sky. They stared down over a nothing-place, a buffer between realms. When the gods had finished creating the world they had left many such places behind them – unfinished stretches of void, home only to beasts, squalls, and the ghosts of elder races.

To fight over it was beneath him. The dispute with the viscount was a minor one, a sordid exchange of border raids and burned fortresses, petulant threats of war and pillage. Resolving the matter was imperative – the pride of the Empire was at stake – but there was no glory in it, no glory at all.

Helborg watched his men die for a little longer, his expression unchanging.

'We can't win this,' he said at last.

He beckoned, and a squire standing by his horse handed him an open-faced, hawk-winged helmet. Helborg hoisted it over his head and fixed it in place, drawing the straps tight around his clean-shaven chin.

'But we can blood them.'

Skarr, happy to see some signs of movement, made a gesture to the squadron of mounted Reiksguard waiting patiently alongside him. It was a simple thing – a tilting of his gauntlet, a touching of fingers – but the effect was immediate. More squires rushed forward with lances, all of which were taken up.

'Who would choose to own this?' demanded Helborg acidly, seizing his lance and holding it one-handed, tip extended vertically. 'Who would fight for it?'

'They seem to like it,' said Skarr, nodding into the distance.

Helborg followed his gaze.

'Aye,' he said, narrowing his eyes. 'They must do.'

Out in the dusky haze, beyond the struggling lines of infantry, waited the enemy's heavy cavalry. Just as the Reiksguard had, they stood out the day's exchanges, letting the foot soldiers test themselves against one another in a cagey series of half-committed advances. Only now, as the light of the sun dipped towards the west and the blood began to clot in the sand, were they making ready for the charge.

Helborg could make out the pennants of the d'Alembençons hanging limp in the static air. He saw the glimmer of bull's head and fleur de lys devices, set in sable on fields of argent. He saw peasantry scurry around their mounted masters like rats at the foot of old monuments.

He didn't know which one of the dozens of plate-armoured giants was the viscount. The knights all looked much the same to him – heavily armed, gilded, decked out in layers of steel that an Empire warhorse would have struggled to carry, let alone charge with.

Formidable. Not for nothing did men across the Old World fear the onslaught of the knights of Bretonnia.

Helborg spat on the ground and tightened his grip on his lance.

'Ready, preceptor?' he asked calmly, as if he were inviting one of his many consorts out for a stroll along the banks of the Reik by starlight.

'Very much so,' said Skarr, snapping the visor of his helm into place.

'Then give the order, if you please.'

Skarr rose up in the saddle.

'Reiksguard, on my command!' he roared.

The line of knights instantly tensed, adjusting the grip on their long lances. They looked lean, sharp and hungry, like wolves coming down from the treeline in winter. Hooves stamped, horses snorted impatiently, and the red and white banner of the Empire's elite swung heavily up into place.

Helborg felt a sudden burst of adrenaline, just as he always did before action. He felt his thigh muscles tense. His gauntlets curled around the reins.

Then Skarr roared out again, his rasping voice ringing out despite the jaw of his helm muffling it.

'Charge!'

Hooves kicked out in a flurry of mud, sending the squires scattering back out of the way. With a steady, accelerating drum and clatter, the line of Reiksguard swept down the incline and broke into the charge. Helborg drove them hard, watching the enemy ranks draw closer with every buck and stretch of his steed's churning limbs. The grey air whistled past him, sending his cloak streaming out behind. As he had done a hundred times before, he crouched in the saddle, feeling the dead weight of his lance come to bear as the metal tip lowered to its killing angle.

Mercy of Sigmar, but he loved this.

It never got wearisome; it never got stale. He saw the faces of the Bretonnian peasants sweep into focus, blotched with pox and white with fear.

Too ugly to mourn.

He grinned, and picked out his first victim.

You first.

Captain Axel von Bachmeier hauled himself back up the slope, feeling his boots sink into the mud. The ground beneath him was as shifting as the weather, home to a thousand tiny runnels of brackish water. It was a poor place to fight in – the men got bogged down, manoeuvring was difficult, bringing detachments into play was cumbersome.

His retinue laboured alongside him, happy enough to get out of combat for just a few moments. The going had been heavy and arduous, and there was little glory in such work even with the presence of the Reiksmarshal on the field to inspire them.

Bachmeier's breathing became thick. He stopped trudging and turned around, trying to get some sense of the battle's shape. From his vantage, less than a hundred yards back from the heaviest fighting, he could see all across the battlefield. What he saw didn't improve his spirits.

Ten thousand men were locked together, stretched out in two long, broken formations. The Empire troops fought in their squares, maintaining formation, holding ground with typical tenacity. The Bretonnians were less disciplined but there were more of them.

Bachmeier didn't think much of the quality of the enemy foot soldiers. The front-rank fighters were little more than villagers, sent into combat bearing farm implements and kitchen knives. Those in the second wave were tougher, but still no match for a well-trained pikeman or halberdier.

For all those mismatches, the engagement was grinding slowly to a stalemate. Daylight was failing fast, running quickly from a pale to a dark grey – it was only a matter of time before the signals for withdrawal would ring out.

The Bretonnians hadn't committed their full strength yet. Their plate-armoured knights waited out on the flanks, ready to sweep along the full width of the battlefield when required. They were the reason Helborg hadn't been able to deploy his artillery, probably the only thing on the field capable of making a decisive breakthrough. The Reiksmarshal knew perfectly well how devastating Bretonnian cavalry was on the charge – in such empty terrain, he had no chance of deploying guns without risk of them being destroyed before they were ready.

So there it was. The guns would not be deployed for fear of the knights, and the knights would not engage in case the guns deployed while they were wrapped up in fighting. Stalemate.

Only as the sunlight dribbled away toward the tower-studded western horizon were the cavalry units riding out at last – a show of strength, a final attempt to break the deadlock before nightfall forced an end to the day's curtailed brutality.

Bachmeier, with his three decades of service and experience, knew the attempt would fail. Too many infantry formations were still intact and the essential core of each army was solid. The charges would be a chance for the horsemen to get their swords bloody, but that was all.

He leaned on his sword, letting the tip of it puncture the earth at his feet. The spectacle would give him something to watch before duty called him away again.

The Reiksguard moved first, far out along the rear-west flank of the battlefield. They charged down a long, shallow slope, churning up the sodden earth as they came. Their banner streamed out as they rumbled into contact. Helborg was at the forefront, a yard ahead of his nearest supporting warrior and with his cloak snapping and whipping about his broad shoulders.

The knights' armour was pristine in the dull light, and the gaudy feathers atop their helms caught the last of the sun's rays. They wheeled around a beleaguered unit of Empire halberdiers, riding hard and fast, before careering straight into a thick knot of Bretonnian peasant soldiers beyond.

The infantry stood no chance. Bachmeier watched them scatter, breaking from the front and fleeing headlong for the rear of their army's formation. The Reiksguard rode among them at will, first using their long lances, then switching to broadswords as the long shafts splintered.

Bachmeier turned away from the carnage, sweeping his gaze across the enemy lines towards the opposite, eastern flank. The Bretonnians had already responded. Their knights were more heavily armoured and their steeds were huge, shaggy-fetlocked beasts that looked more like carthorses than destriers. They took longer to build up speed, but when they did the momentum was huge. Bachmeier could feel the heavy beat of their hooves thrum along the earth as they galloped down the opposing slope towards a long front of Empire pikemen. Ramshackle masses of Bretonnian peasantry before them scurried to get out of the way. Some of them didn't make it in time, and were ridden down by the remorseless wall of steel and muscle bearing down the incline.

Bachmeier felt his heart stir. He knew he was supposed

to loathe them – they were, after all, the enemy – but he couldn't bring himself to do so. Their armour was spectacularly ornate, their colours dazzling, their horsemanship superb. They rode with a pounding, full-blooded commitment that even the Reiksguard couldn't match.

The pikemen responded well. They dug their long pikes into the yielding earth and a forest of staves sprung up, angled to punch into the warhorses' chests or take the riders out of the saddle. They braced themselves, gripping the shafts of their pikes and planting their boots into the earth.

Bachmeier watched, transfixed.

Hold fast, lads, he breathed to himself.

The knights hit the line, and it dissolved into a storm of screams, snaps, thuds and whinnies. The first row of pikes did some damage, unhorsing knights and sending their steeds crashing back to earth. Behind them, though, the force of the charge was unhindered. Knights broke through the reeling resistance like a storm-tide sweeping aside crumbling sea walls, hammering down the fragile resistance and going after the survivors.

Bachmeier saw the Empire men fall back, reeling from the impact of the charge. They didn't run witlessly – a few of them kept their cohesion, evading the worst of the charge and waiting for the horsemen to lose momentum.

With their lances broken, the knights cast them aside and reached for longswords. They swung their horses round, surging back into the Empire lines and causing more havoc. They lashed out on either side of them, crashing through the mass of broken defenders like galleons bucking through slate-grey swells.

For a moment, Bachmeier saw the potential for the two cavalry forces to come together. Just fleetingly, he wondered if he had been wrong. If the mounted Reiksguard fought their way into contact with the Bretonnian cavalry then the encounter could yet have some kind of resolution.

He pulled his sword from the ground, feeling his heart begin to pump heavily. Perhaps the action was not yet over.

All around him, his retinue hoisted their weapons back into position.

Then the trumpets rang out. The cavalry – Reiksguard and Bretonnian – drew up in their saddles, pulled hard on the reins, and began to withdraw. All along the battlefront, weary troops disengaged or were dragged back from combat by their sergeants.

The light was fading fast. Bachmeier's first judgement had been right. No result could be forced that day, and neither general wished to provoke a slaughter of valuable warriors. No commander, not even one with Helborg's reputation for risk-taking, would countenance throwing away an army for such a miserable tract of worthless border country.

Bachmeier began to move again, heading back to where the units under his command still laboured. They'd need his guidance to achieve an orderly withdrawal, and he had no intention of letting his sections of the line break into disarray.

As he did so, he caught sight of one of the Bretonnian knights, already in the distance and riding hard back to his lines. The warrior's armour glinted warmly in the last of the sun, as if lined with silver. His charger, its caparisons still vivid despite the splatters of grime, powered up the slope with a ponderous, weighty grace. Before quitting the field, the knight brandished his sword with a final flourish – a gesture of arrogance, of self-assurance, of superiority.

Magnificent, thought Bachmeier.

The fire crackled in its pit, sending oily smoke snaking around the tent's central pole and out through vents in the canvas above. From outside, the noises of the camp settling down for the night were clearly audible: cooking pots being swilled out, soldiers singing, the rattle and chink of dice being thrown against pewter.

Within, the mood was colder. Helborg sat in a wooden chair near the fire, slumped like a warrior chief of old. He'd taken his helm off but otherwise wore his full plate armour.

His body ached from riding, but at least the exercise had driven some of the frustration out of him.

'We cannot do this again,' he said, staring into the fire as he spoke.

His captains sat in a circle before him, each of them similarly attired. Most had dents in their armour or bloodstains on their jerkins. One man had a stained bandage across one eye and others displayed hastily stitched wounds across their exposed flesh.

Skarr nodded, gnawing at a stringy piece of chicken.

'We could take them,' he said. 'We'd need to move fast – get in among the knights before they were ready, bring the guns up.'

Helborg sympathised. He'd toyed with ordering the same thing after the midday skirmishes. It had been too risky then, and it would be again. Things were evenly balanced, and losing the Reiksguard on a reckless charge against equally skilled cavalry, all for the sake of a few blackpowder pieces, would be a disaster. If the enemy had been different – if it had been the Great Enemy hammering at the gates of Nuln or the hated greenskins threatening to overrun Averland – then he might have taken the risk. As it was, for a piece of land worth nothing and for the sake of men he'd once fought beside as allies, the waste was unconscionable.

'We can't break them quick enough,' said one of his captains.

Helborg flicked his gaze over to the man who'd spoken – a minor infantry commander. For a moment, he struggled to remember the man's name.

Bachmeier. That was the one.

'What did you say?' asked Helborg, surprised that he'd spoken out.

'I don't think, sir, that we can break them quick enough,' said Bachmeier. 'They know what we need to do to beat them.'

Helborg looked at the man carefully. He knew the type – solid enough, probably passed over for promotion, not the bravest or the most diligent, possibly nearing the end of his career. No doubt that was why he dared to speak so freely.

'And what would your counsel be then, captain?' asked Helborg, humouring him.

Bachmeier shrugged.

'I have none,' he said. 'This terrain gives us nothing. We could dance around the edges of a fight, hoping that they lose their minds and break formation, or we could meet them head on, nothing held back, no sweet manoeuvres. We can win that way, but it'll cost us.'

Helborg nodded, agreeing with the man's assessment even as he found it depressing. He had come to the same conclusion two days previously; perhaps it had been foolish to think that any of his officers was likely to find a better way to win.

He sat back in his seat and placed his fingers before him in a loose pyramid. He'd hoped that a quick, clean punitive raid into the Bretonnian marches in response to repeated skirmishing along the Empire borders east of Marienburg would have been an end to the matter. He'd not wanted to get drawn into a protracted campaign while far more serious threats waited along the Empire's northern borders, but that was precisely what was now at risk. Retreat would be a serious embarrassment and would weaken the hand of the border commanders; staying put risked sucking precious resources into a petty and pointless war.

The whole thing had begun to make his head ache.

'Very well,' he said at last, snapping his fingers closed. 'Here's what we're going to do.'

Before he could go further, the entrance flaps to the tent were pulled aside. A grey-faced sentry entered, bowed, and stood awkwardly before the council.

'Your pardon, lord,' he said, looking at Helborg nervously. 'I did not think this could wait.'

Helborg looked at him sharply.

'What couldn't?' he asked.

'I couldn't,' came a third voice.

Its owner stepped out of the sentry's shadow. He was tall, fair-skinned and with a sharply cut thatch of blond hair. He wore fine robes cut in the archaic Couronne style, lined with gold thread and held at the waist by a thin belt of leather knots. His features were clean, his manner assured and his bearing formal.

He bowed low, finishing the gesture with a flourish of his slender hand.

'Gascard d'Alembençon, lord,' he announced. 'The viscount, may the Lady preserve him, sends me as embassy, with all rights of safe passage under the conventions of ordered nations.'

Helborg's brow furrowed. The man's Reikspiel was fluent but his manner was off-putting. He knew from experience that noble-born Bretonnians were fearsome warriors – as brave as any he'd known and often more skilful than their Imperial counterparts – but that didn't stop them coming over as… *fey*.

'Your brother is a bandit,' said Helborg. 'His men have raided our settlements, causing loss of both life and property. I've come to punish him, and that's an end to it – there's nothing to discuss.'

Gascard smiled coolly.

'Then we clearly have different interpretations of what has been happening here, my lord,' he said. 'The viscount protects his own. If there has been raiding, then it has come from one side of the border only.'

Helborg rolled his eyes, in no mood to debate the history of the whole miserable affair again.

'You wish to make restitution?' he asked. 'That can be arranged.'

The ambassador lost his smile.

'Not quite,' he said. 'The viscount has a proposal. If you will hear it, then I will convey your answer.'

Helborg observed the man carefully. Such gestures were typical of the Bretonnian high classes. They revelled in the theatrical display, the courtly dance of promise and counter-promise. The code they lived by had long since died out in the Empire, a code that placed personal conduct above political consideration and made everything of a man's word, his bloodline and his honour.

Helborg had always found it a tedious philosophy. The world was a harsh place, beset by beasts of darkness and hordes of ruin; there was scarce enough room in it for survival, let alone politesse.

'Speak, then,' said Helborg, jadedly.

'The viscount has no wish to see noble men of the Empire lose their lives,' said Gascard. 'He supposes that you, being a just lord in your part, have no wish to see the flower of the Marches wasted. We both know the truth. Our armies are matched – even the victor cannot leave the field without grievous loss. So the viscount proposes a solution. He offers you the honour of single combat. On foot, longswords, to the death. He who stands at the end shall be declared victorious. The opposing army shall withdraw, ceding right of lawful conquest over all lands under dispute.'

As soon as the ambassador mentioned the words 'single combat', Helborg felt his heart respond. In an instant, the dreary prospect of days of brutal, undistinguished fighting through the marshy hinterlands of a backwards realm was replaced with the chance of a clean, dignified result.

Gascard waited. The assembled captains said nothing. Even the noises outside the tent were stilled – the men had seen the ambassador enter, and they waited to see him leave.

Helborg found himself tempted, sorely tempted. He'd seen the skill at arms of the viscount's men and the duellist within him relished the chance to test his swordsmanship against their master. Absently, his fingers strayed to the hilt of his runefang, resting lightly on the jewelled pommel.

'Go,' he said. 'Wait outside while I confer. You shall have your answer shortly.'

Gascard bowed, and withdrew. As soon as he was gone, Helborg turned to Skarr.

'Can they be trusted?' he asked. 'Will they honour the terms?'

Skarr nodded.

'Honour is everything to them. If the viscount swears an oath, he'll die to uphold it.'

Helborg smiled. A sudden eagerness ran through his tired muscles. He sat up in his chair, flexing his arms.

'So I have always heard,' he said. 'Then I am minded to do it. It's been too long since I took on a worthy opponent. Schwarzhelm has a certain dogged ability, of course, but no finesse. This will be different.'

He swept his gaze across the assorted captains, daring them to object. He felt reckless, and knew it was a failing, but he also knew what talent he possessed and what record he had.

'Cheer up, my lords,' said Helborg, grinning wolfishly and gesturing for the ambassador to be summoned back in. 'This viscount will be coughing on his own blood before noon tomorrow – and we'll be on the march home before dusk.'

The morning brought fresh wind from the north, gusting clear of the megaliths and racing across the dreary plains.

Just as they had done the previous day, the two armies lined up, facing each other across a quarter of a mile of sodden, ripped-up grassland. They remained apart, two rangy formations of brawl-battered soldiers, their weapons sheathed, their banners drifting aimlessly in the swirling breeze.

Helborg moved into the open first, striding confidently from cover, resplendent in full battle regalia. His sword, the Klingerach runefang, clattered at his side as he walked. His gait was heavy under his armour and the soles of his boots sucked at the marshy soil.

He wore an open-faced helm, as he always did in single combat. He liked to look his enemy in the eyes as he killed them, enjoying the knowledge that his frost-hard expression would be the last thing they would see before being ushered into Morr's cold embrace. He'd waxed his moustache until it was almost as stiff as the leather jerkin under his breastplate, and he'd ensured the emblem of Karl Franz was as highly polished as the Imperial dining service.

●

When he reached halfway, Helborg planted his feet firmly, drew his shoulders back, and waited.

A hundred yards in front of him, the Bretonnian lines parted. Between them walked a giant of a man, similarly clad in a knight's full plate. His armour was thicker-set than Helborg's and looked very old. A long crimson cloak hung down from his shoulders, lined with ermine and decorated with lozenges of black and gold.

He strode up to Helborg, coming to a standstill just a few paces away. Helborg scrutinised him carefully. The outline of a goblet had been graven into the knight's breastplate, decorated with fine golden tracery and surrounded by an elaborate, oak-leafed halo. For all its age, the armour had obviously been reverently treated – delicate flutes of beaten metal winked in the morning sun, lending the curved steel an almost palpable glow. The warrior wore a close-faced helm, giving nothing of his features away.

Helborg drew his sword. It left the scabbard with a whisper, and the blade shone coldly in the pale light of morning.

'Viscount d'Alembençon,' said Helborg, inclining his head a fraction.

The viscount drew his own sword. As it emerged into the air, a faint golden sheen spilled from the mouth of the scabbard.

'Reiksmarshal,' replied d'Alembençon.

The man's voice was unearthly, as if subtly altered by something. Even in those few syllables, the resonance was far deeper, far richer than any mortal man's had a right to be.

Helborg's eyes flickered across to the Bretonnian's ornate livery. He remembered something about their legends – stories of a grail, quests and blessings of the deity they called the Lady.

For the first time, he wondered if he should have paid more attention.

'You're bound by your word of honour,' said Helborg, gripping the hilt of his own blade. 'To the death, and the army of the vanquished quits the field. You accept those terms?'

D'Alembençon nodded. Even that slight gesture was suffused with some strange, indefinable quality. It was as if the man were animated by subtle witchery, making his every movement smoother and more decisive than it should have been.

'I do,' said d'Alembençon, and brought his blade into guard.

For a moment longer, Helborg waited. His practised eyes scanned his opponent, looking for weak points in the armour, searching out flaws in his stance.

None were obvious.

'Then let Sigmar be the judge of it,' said Helborg.

'He cannot judge anything,' said d'Alembençon. 'Not here.'

The two weapons moved at the same time, blurring through the air before clashing together with an echoing, biting clang. Helborg applied more force, pressing the metal home, testing out the knight's strength.

It was formidable. D'Alembençon matched Helborg's pressure, then added more of his own. The two warriors maintained the position for several heartbeats before finally spinning apart.

Helborg moved his blade round quickly and pressed in close again, sliding it fast and low. D'Alembençon parried, taking a step back before pulling his sword up and hammering it down two-handed. Then it was Helborg's turn to block. He took the impact above his chest. The shock of the blow sent him into a half-stagger, which he corrected instantly. D'Alembençon pressed the advantage, recovering ground and forcing Helborg back further.

The strikes got heavier after that. The two duellists rocked back and forth, probing each other's defences, teasing, feinting, looking for the way in. Helborg quickly assessed the calibre of his adversary: d'Alembençon knew how to hit hard, but also kept his defence intact. His long blade moved quickly and smoothly, carving through the air like a rapier.

'Not bad,' said Helborg, feeling sweat trickle down the inside of his helm. 'For a master of peasants, not bad.'

D'Alembençon never said a word. The unbroken silence of his fighting quickly became eerie. Helborg found himself wondering if some awful deception had taken place; that perhaps his foe was something more or less than human under all that glittering armour.

You will still die, he thought, handling his blade with assured deftness, stepping back out of a furious challenge before committing to one of his own. *You all die, in the end.*

Throughout all of that, Helborg was only vaguely aware of the presence of the two armies standing around them. He got a blurred impression of them as his body twisted: rows of men, static and impotent, all held rapt by the contest before them, watching for the result that would determine their next move.

D'Alembençon's technique was formal, as Helborg would have expected of a Bretonnian. Helborg tried to undermine that with improvisation – darting stabs launched from nowhere, sudden reversals, sham errors.

Nothing succeeded. Helborg heard his own breathing grow ragged. Handling a longsword in full plate armour was exhausting, and he felt the first stirrings of muscle pain in his arms.

'So you know how to use a sword,' he rasped, turning out of a challenge before planting his trailing foot and pushing back into the attack.

'I do,' said d'Alembençon, speaking at last. His voice was the same as it had been before – calm, resonant, otherwordly.

Helborg stepped up the ferocity of his attacks, discarding finesse for brute force. The blades clashed again, sending showers of sparks spiralling out into the frigid air, making the shafts shiver. He stayed on the front foot, whirling the steel edge ever faster, bringing it down in tight, whistling arcs.

Nothing had any impact. The viscount kept on fighting, doggedly resisting every attempt to knock him out of his stride. As Helborg's attacks got nowhere, d'Alembençon launched into some of his own, driving forward, keeping up the pressure, restricting the scope for movement and withdrawal.

Helborg felt his armour weighing him down, slowing his movements by precious fractions. He pulled back, step by step, blunting the force of the incoming strikes, searching for a way to turn the tide of precise, controlled aggression.

When the first wound came he barely felt it. The attack slipped under his guard, striking him above the waist. Helborg snatched himself away, immediately correcting his stance, before realising he'd been hit expertly – the shell of his armour had been driven in, pinching the flesh and grinding up against his ribcage.

He limped away, parrying the flurry of blows that followed with difficulty.

Now this gets interesting, he thought.

Ignoring the pain, he pressed home the attack. Head down, legs bent, Helborg swung the runefang hard. For just a moment, driven by little more than cussedness, he gained the ascendancy. He thrust his blade with pace and flair, loading power into every blow. He felt the familiar rush of superiority; the knowledge he was seizing mastery of his opponent. D'Alembençon stumbled before the frenzied attack, nearly losing his footing, and Helborg pounced.

Just as before, he never saw the wound coming. One moment, he was racing to finish the task, the next he was staggering away, frantically defending himself against a hail of withering strokes.

It had been a feint, a beautiful, subtle feint of the highest order. Had he seen it done on the parade grounds of the Imperial Palace, Helborg would have smiled knowingly and with pleasure. As it was, he barely prevented the manoeuvre from costing him his life.

He retreated, feeling the pain from newly broken ribs throb through his torso. His breastplate had been cracked, making it hard to breathe. For a few more moments he held off the assault, but then the inevitable came. More thrusts hit their target. He missed his footing, feeling the earth rush up to meet him, and fell heavily on to his back.

As he scrambled to lift the Klingerach into guard,

d'Alembençon loomed over him and pressed the point of his sword to his neck.

'So now you die, Reiksmarshal,' said the viscount, sounding as impassive and ethereal as ever. 'You should not have fought me.'

Helborg stared up at him. He felt neither fear nor anger, only astonishment; astonishment that someone had beaten him at last.

'What... *are* you?' he asked.

D'Alembençon reached up to his helm, and pulled it free.

The man's face was human enough – lean, taut features, a ruddy complexion, sea-green eyes, thick hair the colour of sand. He looked the very image of a Bretonnian lord, save for one thing.

Everything shone. His skin shimmered like ivory in moonlight. The effect was subtle, just on the edge of perception, but impossible to ignore. When he spoke, opalescent light spilled from between his lips.

'I am blessed by the Lady, Reiksmarshal,' he said. 'I have supped from the Grail and taken on its power. Did you not recognise my devices?'

Helborg's eyes slipped down to the image of the goblet on the viscount's armour.

'A warning,' he muttered. 'How admirable.'

D'Alembençon drew the tip of his sword up, ready to plunge it into Helborg's exposed throat.

'I regret killing you,' he said mournfully. 'You fought–'

His words were obscured by the sudden crack and boom of artillery fire ringing out across the empty plain. From the north, out on the far left flank of the Bretonnian lines, plumes of rolling smoke began to boil up into the sky. A whole barrage thundered out, sending mortar shells whistling into the close-packed ranks of infantry.

The effect was immediate – peasant soldiers broke into a stampede, clambering over one another to escape the bombardment. Helborg heard the frantic neighing of horses, followed by the horrific screams of men being ridden down.

D'Alembençon's head snapped round, his mouth open. His sword wavered, just for a moment.

'How is this–?' he started, his voice weak with disbelief.

Helborg knew he only had seconds to act. With an almighty heave, he smashed the viscount's sword aside and hauled himself back to his feet. The runefang felt light in his hands, as if the spirit of the weapon knew what deceit had been practised and approved of it.

Helborg swung two heavy blows into the knight's torso, sending him staggering back. D'Alembençon's poise had been completely undone. He parried hurriedly, but his blade was smashed out of his hands. It flew away, end over end, before landing in the mud and lodging fast. Before d'Alembençon could go after it, Helborg jabbed his sword up, pinning the viscount by the neck.

The roles were reversed. As the two men stood facing one another, the roar of more artillery filled the skies. Helborg heard the sound of his own men breaking into the charge, ready to exploit the disarray in the Bretonnians and turn confusion into slaughter.

'*Faithless!*' hissed d'Alembençon, his face scarlet with rage and disbelief.

Helborg pressed the edge of the runefang's blade into the viscount's neck, parting the flesh.

'You don't have to die,' he said. 'Call the surrender, and lives will be spared.'

For a moment, d'Alembençon hesitated. The noise of his men dying punctuated the ongoing rumble of the guns going off. He looked agonised, rocked to his core by the deception.

It was then that Helborg knew Skarr had been right. The Bretonnians had planned to keep their word. The notion that anyone might behave differently hadn't occurred to them. The idea that Helborg might use the distraction of the duel to bring his artillery into position and shatter the balance of power hadn't occurred to them. The full measure of Helborg's determination, his obsession, his utterly unswerving devotion to the prestige of the Empire – none of it had occurred to them.

D'Alembençon moved. He lunged for his sword.

Helborg had known that he would. He thrust out with the runefang, aiming the blade perfectly. The ancient sword severed d'Alembençon's head and the man's decapitated corpse thumped to the ground, just inches from where his own weapon had lodged.

Helborg looked down at him, breathing heavily.

Even in death, the man's profile was magnificent. His armour was far finer than any he'd seen in the Empire; beside it, his own felt gaudy and overblown. The strange moonlit lustre lingered for a while on his skin, glimmering like silver fire, before finally flickering out.

Helborg bowed his head. He felt drained. His whole body ached. He'd been taken to the limit.

'Lord!'

Skarr's voice roared out from close by. Helborg snapped out of his reverie and looked up.

Skarr's squadron had ridden up across the no-man's-land between the main ranks, eager to press on into the enemy.

'I have your horse, my lord,' said Skarr, gesturing to a riderless charger that had been led behind his own. His eyes were alive with the pleasure of the coming fight. 'They're falling back – we'll tear them apart!'

Helborg grabbed the horse's saddle and dragged himself up into it. He kept the runefang in hand, blood darkening the metal. Once mounted, he could see the truth of the preceptor's words: the Bretonnians were retreating across the whole length of the field. The artillery brought up stealthily along their left flank had caused havoc, breaking their unity and causing widespread panic. All around him, Empire troops were advancing in formation, moving in for the kill with commendable discipline.

Helborg was about to kick his horse into a canter when he caught sight of the infantry captain who'd spoken out at the council. Bachmeier was marching at the head of a unit of pikemen. Unlike Skarr, he looked far from eager about the killing to come.

'So what say you now, captain?' shouted Helborg. 'You still believe we won't break them?'

Bachmeier looked up at him. The expression on his lined face was ambiguous. Helborg thought he caught something like disgust written there.

'Not by honourable means,' Bachmeier said.

Helborg kicked his horse over towards him, riding so close that he nearly forced the man to slip backward into the mud.

'Honour's for pig-herders and virgins,' Helborg snarled, fixing Bachmeier with a stony gaze. 'This is war.'

Bachmeier returned the glare. For a moment, he remained defiant, as if he were tempted to protest further.

Then, something stopped him. Perhaps he finally understood the necessity of what had happened, or perhaps he simply realised how dangerous it would be to bandy words with the Reiksmarshal.

Bachmeier bowed stiffly in submission. When his head rose again, there was a measure of reluctant respect in his expression, an acknowledgement, maybe, of the choices made by those in command.

'There is still duty, though,' he said. 'Mine is with my men.'

Helborg watch him trudge away, back to where his soldiers waited for him.

For a brief moment, he almost envied the man's certainties. Perhaps, once, he too would have balked at using such tactics to destroy his enemies. If he had ever felt that way, though, the habit had been beaten out of him long ago. Now only the cold purity of success remained with him – the will to conquer, to endure, to achieve victory by whatever means proved possible.

That was the difference between men like Bachmeier and him, the reason that Helborg had risen to the pinnacle of command and Bachmeier hadn't.

There were times when Helborg wasn't proud of what a career of constant battle had made him into. There were times when he reflected on another life, one in which the finer instincts of mankind were preserved, not suppressed.

But such thoughts seldom detained him long. The need for violence was ever close at hand, dragging him back to the front, demanding the use of his peerless capacity to rally his men, to drive them onward, to make them lethal.

Honour was optional; duty never slept.

Helborg turned away from Bachmeier, pointing his charger back toward the enemy. What remorse he felt for d'Alembençon's death was already draining away. In its place came resolve – the iron-hard resolve that had carried him to a hundred victories and by which the writ of the Emperor was maintained across a world of endless war.

That was what sustained him, what defined him, what made survival possible; anything else was a luxury he could never indulge.

'For the Empire,' Helborg whispered, lowering the runefang and preparing to charge. 'For there is nothing else.'

ABOUT THE AUTHOR

Chris Wraight is the author of the Horus Heresy novel *Scars*, the novella *Brotherhood of the Storm* and the audio drama *The Sigillite*. For Warhammer 40,000 he has written the Space Wolves novels *Blood of Asaheim* and *Stormcaller*, and the short story collection *Wolves of Fenris*, as well as the Space Marine Battles novels *Wrath of Iron* and *Battle of the Fang*. Additionally, he has many Warhammer novels to his name, including the Age of Sigmar novella *The Gates of Azyr* and the Time of Legends novel *Master of Dragons*, which forms part of the War of Vengeance series. Chris lives and works near Bristol, in south-west England.

LORD OF
CHAOS

Rob Sanders

An extract from

LORD OF CHAOS
by Rob Sanders

Leading the way with the faintly glowing blade, Archaon moved through the rib-lined chambers and rachidian passageways of the palace. He was focused. He was ready. Should any daemon servant proceed from the darkness or rush him from the strange architecture, the dark templar would cleave them in two. There was nothing, however. No horrors haunted the palace. No things waited for him in the shadow. The Forsaken Fortress seemed empty. Yet Archaon felt like he was being watched. The darkness that afflicted the lengths of bone-lined corridors was a mirror through which he could not see but could be seen.

You are far from home…

The voice was everywhere. The boom was bottomless, like the abyss, and the words seethed like hellish flame. It was a voice he had known his whole life yet had never heard… until now.

The Chaos warrior moved across a large chamber, looking about him. He slowly turned and swished *Terminus* all around. He peered into the dark recesses of alcoves. He crooked his neck to look back the way he had come, the path now lost to shadow. As he moved through the nightmarish interior of the palace, the murk receded to reveal a large figure in the centre of the chamber. Like the Forsaken Fortress, it was horned, cloven-clawed and broad of wing. To Archaon, it appeared to be a replica of the fortress in miniature.

At first, he took it for the daemon overlord of the palace itself, but as his shuffled steps and defensive turns took him closer, he saw the infernal figure for what it was. A throne. Crafted from the same rough stone as the palace in which it sat. The daemon prince's crouching legs formed the seat, its star-scarred chest the back and its clasped talons the arms. The horned horror that was the daemon's grotesque head formed a kind of crafted crown, while the leathery, outstretched wings, hewn from volcanic rock, gave the throne a hellish grandeur. For all its imposing abomination, the throne was empty, like the palace.

'I am where I need to be, daemon,' Archaon answered back finally. His words returned to him with a strange quality, echoing through the torturous skeletal structure of the daemon palace.

That is more true than you can ever know. Though not many who have sought out the Forsaken Fortress have found it.

'I am Archaon,' the Chaos warrior spat, angling his helm about the dark entrances to the chamber. 'I am the chosen of the Dark Gods and the end to the entire world. Nothing is beyond me.'

I am beyond you, chosen one.

'And yet here I stand, *Be'lakor*,' Archaon spat. 'I have your name, daemon. I have all your names. Shadowlord. Dark Master. Cursed of the Ruinous Gods. You, who have watched me from oblivion, like the craven being you are. I stare back, abyssal thing. I see you now, daemon prince, though there be little or nothing to see. And here I stand, before your cursed throne within your cursed castle.' Archaon waved *Terminus* at the darkness in invitation. The blade smouldered with expectation. 'Time for us both to take a closer look, don't you think? If I'm lucky, as with your palace, I might get to see inside.'

As Archaon turned, his weapon ready, his good eye and the darksight of his ruined socket everywhere, he set his afflicted gaze once more on the mighty throne. In it, crafted in his own image, sat the insanity that was the daemon Be'lakor within a rocky palace that was the same.

'Daemon,' Archaon told it. 'You have an undue fascination with yourself.'

The beast laughed. It was horrible to hear. Like the deep torment of rock and earth, as the land quakes and continents heave.

And with you…

As the creature spoke, the blue inferno burning within him escaped his ugly maw.

'I'm here to put an end to that, creature,' the dark templar told it, moving slowly and steadily in on the thing in the throne. A great infernal blade of jagged black steel stood upright before the throne, held in place by the loosely clasped talon of the stone arm. The daemon prince's own claw rested on the pommel spike of the weapon.

Oh, you are, are you?

'But first you will give me the satisfaction of all that is unknown to me, but known to you,' the Chaos warrior threatened.

You want secrets…

'I want truths,' he told it. 'And I'll have them, even if I have to cut them out of you, dread thing.'

The living truth that is Archaon, chosen of the Chaos gods.

'Aye.'

Archaon moved in. The daemon prince reared from his throne of stone, dragging his colossal blade with him. The beast's wings spread and he thrust his ferocious daemon head forward, shaking the crown of horns as he spoke.

Well you can't have it, mortal, Be'lakor roared at him, his words searing with hellfire. *You impudent worm – bold of word but feeble of flesh.*

'I thought you might say that,' Archaon returned. As Be'lakor dragged the tip of his infernal blade across the floor of the throne room and turned it upright in his claws, the Chaos warrior did the opposite. Turning *Terminus* about in his gauntlets, he aimed the point of the crusader blade at the floor. 'See, you can't give what you don't have, daemon.'

Archaon stabbed his Sigmarite sword straight down into the floor of the throne room. Instead of turning the blade tip aside like the smooth rock it appeared to be, the material admitted its length with a shower of sparks. The blade steamed with the honour of its past deeds in the name of the God-King. The stone about it began to bubble and churn. Be'lakor let out a roar that descended into a hideous shriek. The palace trembled about Archaon and the daemon. It shuddered. It quaked. The daemon prince clutched his chest and crashed to his knees. The Ruinous Star scarred into his flesh steamed also. The infernal blade tumbled from his grip, falling straight through the floor with a splatter of stone, as though it had been dropped into a lake.

Archaon turned his greatsword in the broiling stone of the wound. Be'lakor screeched. His wings flapped and his spine arched. His knees sank into the floor and his claws trailed stringy stone where he had splashed the morphing material in his infernal agonies.

'Now we're talking,' Archaon told the daemon. 'This is a language that both of us can understand.'